Books by the author

Plus: A Fantasy

Viral

Running

www.jtcooperauthor.com

NIGHTBLOOMING

a novel by

J. T. Cooper

Nightblooming
©2021 J.T. Cooper

ISBN 978-0-578-97358-6 PRINT

September 2021

Published and Distributed by
IngramSpark

http://www.ingramspark.com

This is a work of fiction, a product of the author's imagination.
FICTION / General / 2. /Kentucky. / 3. Family Saga. / 4. Historical.

For Jane Cooper, the best mother-in-law, friend and

encourager ever.

With love

NIGHTBLOOMING

J. T. Cooper

PART ONE

August 1902

Chapter One

Garnet felt sweat trickle from her precise center part to her tight copper braid. Her little brother trotted beside her, and she slowed her steps to let him catch up. He hummed a little tune, happy for the trip to the store and figuring he'd get something from Mrs. Lawrence's candy case. A buzzard floated in the white sky. Baked dust squished between her toes. She hadn't wanted Lowell to tag along because she wanted to buy him a birthday present. Mama had said not to bother, that Lowell wouldn't know it was his birthday unless someone told him, but Garnet was determined and sneaked upstairs to get two quarters from her pipe tobacco can before they left. As they walked she asked, "Lowell, when's your birthday?"

He scrunched his freckled nose. "August the two, three, four, five!"

She laughed. "Well, not exactly. It's August the twenty-fifth." Maybe Mama was right. "That's tomorrow."

His eyes widened. On Saturday, Papa had cut his hair, and a wide band of untanned skin marked his forehead. "Will I get a dollar from Grandpa?"

"I reckon."

"And a spanking?" He didn't look as happy about this.

"Yes, five licks. One for every year."

Lowell's mouth turned up into a quirky smile. "You get lots, don't you?"

"Mm, twelve come October, but I'm getting too old to spank."

They passed Grandpa's little bridge, which crossed the shallow and, now, dried creek bed bordering the road. At Garnet's house a narrow swinging bridge did the same duty. And then they walked by the school. Papa would be buying tablets and pencils for Franklin and Lowell when they went to town this Saturday. But not for her. She'd be glad to get shoes, though, and Lowell's clothes were shabby. He mostly used what Franklin outgrew, and those were little more than rags. Right this minute, with her bare feet and Lowell's stained shirt, Mama'd say the two of them looked as common as Deer Creek trash.

Up ahead Mattie Lawrence's store shimmered in the sunlight. It was nothing more than a house with the front room serving as a business but Garnet loved it. She smelled store scents the minute she walked in: root vegetables, hams, and a briny whiff of dill from the pickle barrel. At the counter, Mrs. Lawrence was serving a tall woman Garnet didn't recognize. She had dark hair scraped into a tight knot, and her pale shirtwaist fitted smoothly into a dark skirt. Everything about the woman was trim and neat, and her quiet way seemed to hush Mrs. Lawrence's normal chatter.

Lowell pressed his nose against the candy case, leaving a smudge wherever he moved while Garnet scanned the shelves laden with boxes and cans. Not an inch of space went unused; even the ends of shelves had nails for fly swatters and feather dusters. She'd like to own a store someday.

"Will that be all now?" Mrs. Lawrence asked, wrapping up the strange woman's order in brown paper.

She murmured a reply and paid. As soon as the woman moved toward the door, the storekeeper reverted to her louder, friendlier self. "Well, howdy Garnet! How's your mother and that new baby?"

The dark-haired woman stopped at the doorway, stared at Garnet, and left.

"Right well, Mrs. Lawrence." Garnet tipped her head toward the door. "Who was that?"

"Oh, Lorena McDaniel. She used to be Lorena Colson before she married. Her man died back in April."

"Colson." The Colsons lived down in Deer Creek. "Why'd she come all the way up here to shop?"

Mrs. Lawrence ignored Garnet's question. "So the new baby is a girl?"

Garnet nodded, glancing at Lowell. Leaning close to Mrs. Lawrence, she whispered, "Can you get him out of here? Birthday."

Mrs. Lawrence grinned. "Lowell, honey, I need your help."

Lowell left his vision of heaven, only brightening when Mrs. Lawrence said that if he'd get her a basket from the back porch there might be a piece of candy in it for him. "Oh, and Lowell?" she said. "There's some kittens out there you might like to see. Look around and find them." He sped out the door.

Mrs. Lawrence didn't have much in the way of toys, but finally they decided on a carved wooden wagon. It was big enough to load with a rock or two or maybe some twigs, and, best of all, Garnet had enough money to buy it. Mrs. Lawrence said, "A carpenter down the road peddles these. He makes them through the winter when he don't have much trade." She wrapped the wagon before Lowell could return. "So what did your mother name her baby girl?"

"She's Violet. And I need a pound of sugar to make jam."

Lowell burst through the door with a disintegrating basket. "The black kitten tried to bite my finger, Nettie!"

"Aw, she's just teething, honey," Mrs. Lawrence explained. "Now what kind of candy does this boy want?"

While Lowell agonized over his decision, Garnet wandered to the front window where Mrs. Lawrence kept her houseplants on an old table covered with oilcloth. She liked plants as much as Lowell loved candy. One plant was tall and spiky, "mother-in-law's tongue," Mrs. Lawrence called it, and there were flowering ones as well as ivy crawling between the pots.

"There you go," Mrs. Lawrence said, getting the sugar. Lowell popped a lemon stick in his mouth. "Let's see," she said, tapping her lips. "I want to send something to your mother to celebrate the baby." She gazed around the store. "Violet, you said? Why, I know just the thing." She marched to the plant table, sunlight glinting off her round spectacles. "Louise should have a violet for Violet." She plucked a small pot from the table. Fragile purple flowers rose up from mounds of furry leaves.

Garnet loved it. "Look at how sweet the flowers are," she said. Mrs. Lawrence told her how to care for the plant and tucked it into the basket beside the sugar and wagon. The basket grew heavier on the way home, and Lowell complained about the long walk, but Garnet was so pleased with Lowell's gift, she paid no attention.

That evening, after a full day of making jam, fixing supper, doing the dishes, and rinsing out Violet's diapers, Garnet ducked behind the green curtain that partitioned off her end of the attic and took out Lowell's gift. The brown paper and twine seemed so plain. Digging around in her chifferobe she unearthed a bedraggled blue hair ribbon to replace the twine, and then, suddenly inspired, padded downstairs to find a red pencil on Papa's desk and drew stars on the paper. They didn't show up very well, but it was better than nothing.

Through the window she heard frogs singing, and a moth wandered into her room to flutter around the lamp. As she drew stars, she listened to her parents' voices floating up from the front porch. Mama's was as insubstantial as the fireflies drifting around the garden. "Say it to me, John. You know," she murmured. And then Garnet heard Papa recite Mama's favorite poem, the one that began "Come live with me and be my love . . ." in his soft, deep voice.

Garnet wondered if anybody'd ever call her "my love." Mama never talked about it much, but Grandpa'd told her that her parents' courting was the romance of Evans County. He'd said that for years droves of boys, all cleaned-up and red-faced, used to sit on the porch at the farm and compete to be Miss Louise King's beau. But Mama hadn't given any of them the time of day until Papa arrived from far away to teach at the Bethel School in Kentucky. Garnet had said it was like a fairy tale, and Grandpa'd laughed, saying she was just like her mother.

Garnet finished the stars and wriggled out of her tight dress. Mama said that she should wear her school dresses, that her everyday ones were too tight and too short, but she hadn't been able to make herself wear them yet. It wasn't that she still had hopes of returning to school. When Papa first told her that she would begin staying home and helping Mama, she couldn't believe it. He was a schoolteacher and education always mattered more than anything. At nearly aged twelve, she would've been in his class of older students. She'd looked forward to that. And she always did well in school; he couldn't be ashamed of her, could he?

But then she had overheard her parents talking, Papa saying that pulling Garnet out of school was the hardest thing he'd ever done and Mama insisting that she needed her daughter home. The baby was coming. She didn't want to lose another one from exhaustion. There'd been two babies between Lowell and Violet. Both of them were weak, sickly little things. The little boy lived three weeks and the girl two months. Garnet had stiffened her spine and vowed she would not be the cause of another lost baby even she did mourn leaving school.

She scooted around the curtain to where the boys slept. Franklin lay sprawled on his back, his sheet wadded beneath his feet. Beside him, Lowell curled up, knees nearly to his chest, with his thumb in his mouth. He wasn't much more than a baby himself, she thought, laying the gift by his bed.

***

Lowell woke the whole house with his whoop of joy the next morning.

"Happy birthday," Garnet said.

"It's my birthday?"

"Yes," said Franklin. "Do you need help opening that?"

Lowell shook his head but handed his brother the package. "And this is for me?"

"Well, silly, who else?" Franklin removed the aggravating ribbon, and Lowell ripped into the star-studded paper.

"Oh my, oh jiminy!"

Franklin beamed at Garnet; he was glad she'd done it. "Get your clothes on, baby brother, and we'll go up to Grandpa's. I'll give you a ride on one of the mules."

Garnet nodded at Franklin. He was doing his part too.

Later that morning, still feeling pleased with herself, Garnet attacked the breakfast dishes and figured that wagon was already worth every penny. And Mama hadn't said anything. But five minutes later, Mama lit into her with a voice as sharp as a hatchet. "I told you not to make a fuss of his birthday."

She'd pretty much expected this. She turned from the dishpan. "Yes, ma'am."

Mama sighed as if Garnet's behavior was a tremendous burden. "I can't tolerate this kind of foolishness so soon after the baby." She gazed out the window at the sun creeping up through tired trees. "Finish those diapers, and I've told you twice that I want you to brush the sofa." Mama breezed across the kitchen toward her bedroom.

Garnet felt hot and tight all the way down her spine. It was her money and her brother, and she didn't see how she'd committed such a terrible crime. Feeling mean and unsettled, Garnet called, "Oh, Mama, I wanted to ask you something."

Mama stopped at the doorway. "What?" Aggravation dripped from her voice.

"There was a woman I'd never seen before at the store yesterday. Mrs. Lawrence said she was Lorena McDaniel, but she used

5

to be a Colson before she married. Is she one of the Colsons you're always talking about?" Mama hated the Colsons.

Mama wiped her hand down her skirt. "She was at Mattie Lawrence's store?"

Garnet nodded.

"Why would Lorena Colson trade at Mattie's store?"

"That's what I wondered, but her name's McDaniel. Mrs. Lawrence said she's a widow. Her husband died back in April."

Gripping the door facing until her knuckles whitened, Mama breathed, "McDaniel died? You're sure, Garnet?"

She didn't understand why this was important but nodded.

Her mother made a low noise and whispered, "That son of a bitch."

Garnet's mouth flew open. Uttered in Mama's honeyed voice, these words were as shocking as a rat in her underwear drawer, but there was no opportunity to question her further because Mama went into the bedroom and closed the door. Who was Mama cursing? Garnet grimaced at the greasy dishwater. She reckoned she could add upsetting her mother to her sin of disobedience, but she didn't care as much as she should. All day Garnet received frozen, tight-lipped orders from her mother. The next day was no different. Every morning she woke up hoping her mother would thaw, but Garnet guessed she'd have to pay for her sins all week.

Chapter Two

Early Saturday morning Garnet tiptoed downstairs, still buttoning her brown school dress. After gobbling the breakfast Papa had left her, she piled her dirty dishes by the sink with Papa's and Franklin's. Mama wouldn't like that, but Garnet didn't have time to wash them, and besides, she was going to town and didn't have to worry about Mama the entire day. She sped out the back door. Rolled up in her hand she carried a pair of stockings she'd need as soon as she had her new shoes. As much as she loved the feeling of being barefooted, she was mortified about going to town that way.

Rounding the house, she flew across the swinging bridge, setting it swaying. They were waiting for her with Papa sitting on the wagon seat holding the mules' reins and Franklin kneeling on feed sacks in the back. As she climbed up to sit by Papa, she saw that Lowell, nightshirt trailing in the dust, had followed her. He was too afraid of the swinging bridge to venture onto it alone, but he stood near it, tears on his cheeks.

"Oh, hell," Franklin swore. "Get back in the house you little pest."

"Franklin," Papa said. "Improper and unacceptable language." But even he sighed as he climbed down from the wagon and knelt by Lowell.

Franklin punched her arm. "You woke him up."

"Don't hit me. I was quiet."

Papa and Lowell disappeared inside the house. Although the sky was just then lightening to a rosy gray, it was already hot and airless. Thick dew drenched the grass, and the air smelled stale.

"Just watch. He'll bring the brat. Anything to keep things peaceful for Mama and the baby," Franklin sneered. His brow furrowed into a stormy line. "If she'd get out of bed we wouldn't have to wait."

When Papa came back with Lowell, washed and dressed, Franklin muttered a forbidden oath and flounced down on the wagon bed, turning his back to them. But Lowell stayed on the other side of the bridge as his father crossed it. The little boy looked solemn, but there were no tears. She wondered how her father had managed it.

The Grants traveled to town only a few times a year, but Garnet knew the way. First they drove for well over a mile before they passed all of Grandpa's acres. Although Deke King was just Grandpa to Garnet, people said he was one of the largest landowners in the county. Next they came to the school. Franklin twisted around to glare at it. "You're so lucky, Garnet. Wish I didn't have to go back."

When she thought about how she'd never again walk to and from school with Papa or see Millie and her friends or get smiles from Miss Alice Carter for her work, Garnet didn't feel one bit lucky. "I think *you're* lucky since you get to go to school," she declared. Too late she wondered if she might be hurting Papa's feelings, but she still blamed him, at least a little, for ending her school days so early. But then, she knew very well what came from opposing Mama.

Papa responded to neither of their comments. Most of the time it was hard for her to read what her father was thinking. Mama called him "still water," and even though Garnet wasn't quite sure what that meant, she assumed it had to do with his quiet ways and closed face.

Franklin turned his back on the school building, saying, "I just wish me and you could trade places."

"That would suit me better than it would you."

Papa slid his eyes sidewise at her, amused.

"You see, Franklin, I would be delighted," she took her time over the word, "absolutely delighted to be in the schoolroom while you look after Mama and Violet and Lowell and cook and clean and do the wash and even learn how to do dreadful old embroidery. Yes," she nodded at the road ahead, "I would love to trade places with you." She turned and gave him a cool stare.

"Ah, well, I didn't mean I'd do all that girl work. I want to trade places so you could go to school, and I'd work all the time for Grandpa."

Papa smiled at the mule's tail. "But that wouldn't be trading places, would it?"

Franklin shut his mouth. They'd seen no one on the road until, just past Mrs. Lawrence's store, a narrow track curled to the right. Heavily rutted with chunks of limestone, it was flanked by stands of locust trees and wild honeysuckle. Here they saw a tall man walking, and from the sweat on the back of his shirt, he'd been at it a while. Papa nodded at the man who returned the greeting. He was thin with crow-black hair under his battered hat. Garnet thought he looked familiar, but Franklin called him by name, hollering, "Luther! We're going to town."

The man paused, smiled, and wiped his face with a blue bandana. Then he strode off toward Grandpa's. "Who's that?" Garnet asked.

Franklin answered first. "That's Luther Colson."

"Oh." The name Colson always seemed to have a significance she didn't understand. "Wait!" she blurted out. "He looks like that woman I saw at the store the other day. Mrs. Lawrence said she was Lorena McDaniel, but she used to be a Colson. They look alike."

Papa said, "And well they should; they're twins."

"Mama had a fit when I told her I ran into that woman at the store." She looked over her shoulder. The tall man was no longer visible, but she remembered the road that wound off to the right. "That road back there goes to Deer Creek, doesn't it?"

"Yep," Franklin said. "Grandpa and me took Luther and Lorena home once."

Garnet turned to Franklin. "So Lorena works for Grandpa too?"

Papa held up his hand. "Talk about the Colson family upsets your mother. Yes, Garnet, Mrs. McDaniel, and, by the way, it's not your place to call her by her first name, Mrs. McDaniel does some work for your grandfather. Franklin and I are aware of this; however, since it upsets your mother, we don't speak of it. I'd appreciate your discretion as well."

She frowned and played with the end of her braid. "I don't understand what Mama has against Colson people."

Giving her the full force of his serious, dark blue eyes, Papa repeated, "Nothing more needs to be said now or to your mother. Do you understand, Garnet?"

She nodded, chastened but puzzled. When she glanced back at Franklin, he shrugged. Maybe he knew more, and maybe she'd ask him when she got the chance. For the time being, though, she tried to keep her balance on the wagon seat. They moved from countryside to occasional houses to dwellings one upon another. Some looked much like their little house, but as they neared the center of Ashton, she saw brick and stone houses with wide porches resting under shade trees. None of these resembled the mansions Grandpa described from his Lexington trips, but they were far finer than the Grants' shabby house or even Grandpa's place. Soon the main business district of Ashton crowded upon them, and the jumble of horses, mules, carts, and people made her feel shy.

Papa stopped the team in front of Trosper's Emporium and told Garnet to get down. He and Franklin would be taking the mule to the blacksmith, and she was to wait in front of the store. Garnet looked up at the bench on the porch and noticed a bent old man sitting at one end and wearing some sort of faded gray uniform. Propped against his knee was a twisted cane that looked like a gigantic snake. She shrank back. "I can go with you and Franklin."

"No. Sit up there and wait in the shade. We'll be back soon."

She went to the porch and sat, stretching her skirt over her legs, as white and skinny as the chalk in Papa's schoolroom, and hiding her bare feet as far back as she could. The old man glanced at her and then stared straight ahead into the street. Up close she could see that he had on ordinary clothes, not a uniform, but he'd attached insignia to his shirt and wore a grimy old soldier's cap decorated with blue braid. He spat a stream of tobacco juice into a jar and turned to fix his blurry eyes on her.

"What's your name, gal?" he shouted, making her jump.

His face was crazed with wrinkles and dotted with white stubble. "Garnet Grant," she whispered.

"Hey? Speak up, little sister."

She raised her pointed chin. "Garnet Grant."

"Grant? You say, Grant? That's an unholy name. Where's your people from?" He gripped his cane so fiercely she wondered if he was going to use it on her.

"We live out at Bethel," she replied.

"Bethel? Don't know any Grants from Bethel. Where's your daddy's people from, then?" His voice was like shards of glass.

"My father's people come from Tennessee." She wondered if she could find her brother and father.

"Tennessee? So I don't guess he's kin to old You-Lysses S. Grant then." This seemed to satisfy the old man. "So what's your daddy do in Bethel?"

"He's schoolteacher at the Bethel School."

The old man snorted. "Schoolteacher? A man? That's work for prissy old maids." Garnet bristled. "Was his kin in the army?"

"His papa was in the Confederate army, and he died."

The old man softened. One gnarled and spotted hand reached over and patted hers. "A hero, I'm sure. Sorry for the loss, little girl."

She'd never considered it a loss since that grandfather died way before she was born, actually when her own father was only a few years old. But, in a way, she supposed it was. She'd never been able to love him the way she loved her other grandfather.

She squared her shoulders. "He really was a hero, as a matter of fact."

Ready for a story, the old man rested his weight on the snaky walking stick and leaned toward Garnet. She said, "My papa's father was a preacher, and he didn't hold with going to war, but he was the best sharpshooter in the county so he felt it was his duty to help the Cause. He died at Shiloh."

The old man shook his head. "It was a terrible time, little sister. A terrible time."

Garnet decided she was having a fairly terrible time herself just then. If Papa and Franklin didn't appear soon, this old man was going to drive her crazy. He asked, "And what about your ma's people? Are they from the county?" He seemed to have a deep need to establish her pedigree, but then everybody she met had the same compulsion. "My mother's from Evans County, and her father is Deacon King." She reckoned everybody knew Grandpa.

She was right. Startling her again, the old man let out a whoop and slapped his leg. She wasn't sure at first if he was joyful or angry, but then she saw his foggy black eyes crinkling with merriment. He shook his head, he sighed, he snorted, he almost giggled. "So you're Rooster King's little chick? I'll be durned. Bless us, Deke King. Good Jesus, what a rascal that Rooster was."

He went on and on. Garnet knew her grandfather was a colorful character; he always seemed bigger and more exciting than anyone else. Still, the old man's outburst amazed her. "No disrespect, little sister, but he was a son of a gun during the war. Joined neither side but made money off the both of 'em selling 'baccy and beef."

Garnet stiffened but kept silent.

"Now I'm not saying he weren't smart; oh, no, little sister, he was a smart 'un all right. He made lots of money, and I'll say this for him: he was as fair to one side as the other. But he should've been fighting for Jeff Davis."

The old man sighed. Then he brightened again, smiling to himself. "When you think about it, Deke was cunning and sly, more of a fox than a rooster. Nobody was his boss." He chuckled. "But I reckon he deserved the name with that bright, carroty hair." He stopped and looked at Garnet's head. "And the ladies! All the little hens loved Rooster." He cackled at his joke.

Garnet pulled her braid over her shoulder. Her hair was not the shade of carrots, nor was her mother's. Their hair was amber, Mama said, their crowning glory.

With another sudden mood change, the man sobered. "I guess you never knew Caroline, your grandmother. Now, there was a lady. She come from a fine family in Lexington, and her daddy owned a bunch of burley warehouses. Caroline was pretty as a spring morning. Don't know what she seen in a hustler like Rooster, but she loved him fierce, I hear."

Although Garnet had heard tales about her grandparents' romance, how they'd met in Lexington when Grandpa took his crop to her father's tobacco warehouse, how Grandma defied her family to marry him; she was still intrigued. "So how do you know my grandfather, sir?"

He shrugged. "My name's Combs, lived in the county all my life. Couldn't grow up around here without knowing Deke King. And one of my younger brothers used to run with the Rooster when they was bucks. Can't remember whether it was Thomas or Horace," he mused. "Well, whichever, they'd get liquored up and chase the girls down at Deer Creek and over in the next county. Old Rooster knowed all the willing girls for miles around."

As Garnet gazed down the street for perhaps the tenth time, she saw her father's dark head. She prompted the old man. "Colsons?"

"Yep, Colson girls. Especially one Colson girl. But I reckon you know about her."

Garnet nodded. She didn't, but figured the old codger wouldn't tell her a thing if she let on to ignorance. Her father was nearing the store. "Lorena?"

The old man spit again. "Yes, and sweet Caroline not dead yet."

Franklin yelled, "Hey, Garnet. We're going to another store first."

Mr. Combs waved her by and said, "Tell Rooster hello, little sister." He was still muttering and cackling as she left the porch. "He'll remember me."

"Who was that?" Franklin asked.

"Oh, some old man who knows Grandpa." She wasn't supposed to talk about the Colsons, so she said no more. Besides, the sun was high now, and the street was scalding her feet.

Papa noticed the way she was hopping. "I thought we'd try the new dry goods store first to get your shoes."

Franklin teased, "That's so we don't have to be seen with a poor, trashy barefoot girl anymore."

She drew back her fist to give him a punch in return for the one he'd given her in the wagon but stopped, too happy with the day to mind his pestering. She'd also try to ignore what the old man had told her even though it sounded as if her grandpa might be a terrible sinner. She wasn't quite sure, but she thought old Mr. Combs was talking about adultery, which preachers were better at condemning than explaining.

Inside the store she smelled new fabric and leather. A plump lady in a bright purple dress brought the shoes: shiny, smooth, and black as licorice. Garnet loved them. Grabbing her bunched up stockings from her pocket, she started to pull these on before trying the shoes. "Oh, they're so rumpled. Don't you need a new pair, little girl?" the woman asked.

Garnet looked up at Papa. The woman was being polite. Not only were the stockings wrinkled and damp from being clutched in her pocket, they showed numerous frays and holes, both darned and undarned. Papa nodded. "Better make that three pair." Garnet grinned.

They went on to buy collars for Papa and fabric for shirts. They purchased socks and handkerchiefs and then came to long counters containing bolts and bolts of dress goods. "Choose something for yourself, and then see if you can find something for your mother," Papa said. "She didn't ask for anything, but I'm sure she'd like a new dress."

At first Garnet was leery about pleasing Mama, but she soon spotted a bolt of dark, green wool, lightweight and soft. Mama liked green. And Garnet settled on a clear blue fabric sprigged with darker blue leaves for herself. She thought it looked more grown up than her usual calico or gingham.

The clerk was helping Franklin find some britches, so Garnet wandered to the front of the store. She could've spent hours roaming around. On a small counter sat the fancy goods: jewelry boxes, a few brooches and other baubles. In a lovely box decorated with gilt and tied with pink ribbon were four heart-shaped bars of soap tinted palest pink and smelling faintly of roses. They were the prettiest things she'd ever seen, and a gold sticker said they'd been made in France.

"Papa, come look," she called, holding up the box. "Wouldn't this make a nice gift for Mama?" Her mother loved pretty things but never asked for them. Everybody said Grandpa owned more land than anybody in the county, except maybe the Clarks. Papa accepted their house and wages from Grandpa, along with occasional gifts of food, but he was too proud to take money without working for it. They did fine, her parents declared, but she wondered if her mother might miss such stuff.

"Oh, I thought I'd get her more of that Cashmere Bouquet powder. The tin I bought her for Christmas is gone," Papa said.

"Is the soap more expensive?" she asked.

Papa read the tag. "It's not so bad. Sure, Garnet," he said with a smile. "It's kind of you to think of her."

They stowed their purchases in the wagon, walking down a little alleyway to get to it. From there Garnet could see the backyards of some houses. She peered over a whitewashed fence, nearly as high as her chin, at a yard more beautiful than anything she'd ever imagined. Beyond the fence was a profusion of flowers, with lovingly tended grass and shrubs. At one corner rambling roses climbed the fence, and in another black-eyed susans drank in the noontime sun. Little gravel paths ran from one group of plantings to another. Garnet stared and stared, catching sight of lantanas and cleomes, flowers she'd glimpsed only in seed catalogs. Forgetting her father and her brother, she burned a picture of the garden into her memory, knowing she'd think back to it.

"Would you come on, Garnet?" Franklin grumped. "I'm starving."

She asked, "Who lives there, Papa?"

"Someone who loves flowers as much as you do."

After they ate sandwiches from Trosper's, Papa led them to the bank, and Garnet was glad for her shoes, even if they were starting to rub blisters. The building felt as sanctified as church, and it would've been terrible to enter such a place in bare feet. They didn't actually go into the bank but went up steps bound by an ornate wooden banister to offices for the Evans County newspaper, a dentist, and George A. Pierce, attorney at law. This was the door Papa chose.

Inside, a plain woman with a toothy smile greeted them. "Well hello, Mr. Grant. These must be your children."

"Two of them, Mrs. Pierce. How are you?"

Garnet and Franklin stood behind their father. A solemn picture of George Washington hung over a cracked leather sofa. Mrs. Pierce's large mahogany desk was covered with papers and stacks of heavy, important-looking books. .

"Could Mr. Pierce spare me a minute?" Papa asked.

The woman bobbed her head. "He doesn't have another appointment right now. If you'll just let me tell him you're here," she trailed off, hopping up and motioning for him to follow her.

Papa pointed at the sofa. "Sit quietly. This won't take long."

They sat, enjoying the cool smoothness of the leather beneath them. Mrs. Pierce scurried back to her desk and smiled, crinkling up her nose. Garnet decided that with her dark eyes magnified by tiny spectacles, short nose, and protruding teeth, the lady looked like a squirrel.

Franklin sighed. He didn't suffer waiting well. Garnet gave him a stern look but then exhaled quietly herself. The sofa was far too big to be comfortable; neither her feet nor Franklin's came anywhere near the floor. This made her think of her shoes, and she lifted her legs, sticking them straight out so she could admire their shiny newness. As she did, her body slid on the slippery leather. Using her arms, she pushed herself back up. Franklin watched her and a flicker of a smile crossed his face. He held his legs out, relaxed his upper body, and slid down several inches.

Garnet grinned and glanced over at Mrs. Pierce who was writing in a ledger and didn't seem to be paying any attention. So, Garnet tried it again, giving a little push downward with her hands. Soon they became flushed with silent laughter as they attempted to slip farther and farther off the sofa. Finally Franklin succeeded in propelling himself all the way off and his rear end landed on the floor with a soft thud. Both of them looked at Mrs. Pierce. She continued working, scratching away with a pen. Without looking up she said, "Slippery stuff, isn't it?"

It was as bad as getting tickled in church. The more they tried to stifle their giggles, the worse it got. Hearing footsteps behind the office door sobered them, though, and they were sitting like angels by the time their father and Mr. Pierce came into the outer office. Unlike his tiny wife, the lawyer was a big, stout man, his square head covered with thick, light brown hair he wore rather long and combed straight back. His voice was pitched for reaching the farthest corners of any courtroom. "So, John, you'll take this paperwork to Alice Carter? The Board is very pleased with the job you two are doing at the Bethel School."

Papa replied, "I appreciate that, sir. Alice and I are also grateful for the new maps the Board has seen fit to purchase."

"Not at all. We may be a rural backwater here, but we do try to educate our children." He peered at Garnet and Franklin. "These two are yours, I take it."

"Yes, sir. Garnet and Franklin. I have a five year old son and a new baby daughter at home."

"Well, well. Keeping the school full of good students, aren't you?" Mr. Pierce laughed and shook their hands.

As they exited the airless shade of the bank building, Garnet said to Papa, "Have you ever thought that some people look like animals?"

He chuckled. "And what animals do you make out of the Pierces?"

"I think he looks like the lion in your geography book."

"He roars too!" Franklin giggled.

"And she looks and acts like a squirrel," Garnet added.

Papa laughed and put a hand on each of their heads. "I can't fault your comparisons. And just imagine a lion and a squirrel married to each other."

As the mid-afternoon heat thickened, the Grants loaded the last of their purchases: beans, cornmeal, flour, lard, brined bacon. It would be a celebration when they arrived with gifts to share with Mama and Lowell. In Trosper's they'd found wooden horses to go with the wagon she had bought Lowell. Franklin had new pants and red suspenders. And she had her shoes, stockings, and material for a new dress.

The mule plodded down the winding road that wavered with heat. Except for the goldenrod, bright as the sun, the grass and weeds looked as tired and hot as Garnet felt. No one was talking. She thought about that cool and pleasant garden and imagined what it would be like to have such wonderful flowers. Franklin had made a soft pile of feed sacks and was sleeping, cheeks flushed and hot. Yawning, Garnet glanced at her father. She'd like to ask him about what Mr. Combs had said. Still, thinking about what Mama's comments about the Colsons, she asked, "Papa, what does it mean to be common? Is it being poor or going barefooted or saying ain't? Are we common or uncommon?"

His dark moustache rose. "I suppose you could say we're uncommon, but that doesn't mean quite the same thing."

She used the tail of her skirt to wipe dust from her shoes. "Grandpa says *ain't*, and Millie's house isn't very tidy. Are they common?"

Papa turned serious. "It's a judgmental word, Garnet, a pronouncement upon people, and to call someone common implies you think you're better than he is."

Feeling feisty, she said, "Mama says it all the time."

A full smile creased Papa's face. "Maybe your mama *is* better than everybody else." She laughed, mostly because she'd made him smile, but the thought of Mama and her recent disapproval dropped Garnet back into silence.

When they arrived home, Mama held the door open. She looked serene and pretty with her bright hair twisted neatly up the back of her head. As Papa lugged sacks through the doorway, he stopped to kiss her nose. "Let's wait to put everything away," she murmured. "I have supper ready."

The kitchen looked tidy and welcoming. Garnet smelled cornbread and baked beans, and Mama had sliced tomatoes and cucumbers onto a pretty glass plate. It was the most she'd done since Violet's birth. She asked, "Is Violet's colic better?"

"Yes, we've had a good day."

Mama's voice was pleasant, raising Garnet's hopes, but when she went to wash, she noticed that the breakfast dishes she'd left were still sitting by the sink. Mama wasn't quite done with her yet.

After supper, Garnet cleared the table, and Papa fished around in the packages. Lowell had figured out there might be another present for him and was hopping with impatience. He crowed over his wooden horses and was through the door like a rabbit to unite them with the wagon. Mama exclaimed over her new dress fabric and approved Garnet's as well as her cherished shoes. As Franklin and Papa gathered up the items that needed to go to the cellar, Garnet frowned. "Papa, what about that other thing?"

"I'll take care of that in a bit, Garnet."

So she washed the supper dishes as well as the breakfast ones, debating whether she should tell Franklin what old Mr. Combs had said about the Colsons. He must see those Colson people on a regular basis and not pay them any mind, regardless of Mama's judgments. She'd best keep her mysteries to herself.

When she joined her family on the front porch, Mama and Papa were rocking quietly with Violet sprawled on Mama's shoulder, and Franklin was watching Lowell navigate trails under the rose of sharon bush with his wagon. Papa reached down for the one remaining parcel. "About to forget this," he said, although Garnet knew he'd been waiting for her.

Slowly and deliberately he reached in his pocket for his knife and cut the twine. First he took out a stack of tablets and two bouquets of unsharpened pencils, dividing both between Franklin and Garnet. She shook her head. "I said that we'd continue your schooling here at home," Papa explained. "I know you've been hankering for more mathematics." It was true. She yearned for the mysteries of algebra like some folks might dream of the ocean.

Then Papa took a book from the parcel and gave it to Garnet. "Much as you'd prefer it, education isn't all about numbers. "This is Little Women; most girls like it."

Garnet's mouth flew open. She'd never owned a book. Touching the binding with one finger, she decided she'd put it on the rickety table in her room, next to the old vase for flowers she picked and the little pot of violets her mother hadn't wanted.

He then gave the delicate gilt box to Mama. "Whatever is this?" she asked.

Papa just smiled, but he was smiling at her, not Mama.

As Mama lifted the lid, the soft scent of roses floated across the porch. "Aren't these the prettiest soaps?"

"Your daughter thought you might like them," Papa said.

Wary, Garnet glanced at her mother, but Mama's smile was as warm as the evening air. "You have excellent taste, Garnet."

She exhaled slowly and supposed she was forgiven. Maybe it would be a while until the next storm.

Chapter Three

October brought rain, days of it. It drizzled, it showered, it peppered down until the ground became bruised and saturated with water. Garnet's twelfth birthday came and went without a glimpse of sun. And the mud! It seemed like all she did was mop the kitchen floor. Although the sky boiled with clouds, the temperature was warm, making the house damp and close. Papa said Grandpa was fretting that the tobacco in the barn would be ruined, but not even Deke King could control the weather.

Garnet felt as dull as the sky. Up to her wrists in sticky, floury bread dough, she kneaded the shapeless mass, sprinkling a bit more flour as she attacked it. "Gently, now, Garnet," Mama warned from the kitchen table. Most everybody Garnet knew considered cornbread and biscuits their daily bread, but Grandma Caroline had favored light bread, passing the ability to bake it to her daughter Louise. Once she'd taught Garnet how, Mama could sit back and rest easy.

It was quiet, like most every other morning. Mama was mending. Although no one could call her much of a housekeeper, she was skilled at sewing. She preferred creating new garments, but Franklin's clothes always needed patching, and Lowell worried the buttons off his shirts like a game. Garnet was just glad her mother didn't make her do it. Violet lay on her stomach on the floor grunting at the colors of the quilt underneath her. Sometimes Mama would look over at the baby and give her the sweetest smile. Garnet wondered if Mama had ever smiled at her that way.

She had tried hard not to mourn school. She'd canned about a million jars of tomatoes and pole beans and apples, and, when she could snatch a moment, she read Louisa May Alcott's book, identifying with Jo and crying over Beth. It irritated her, though, that Jo turned Laurie down, and she thought Amy was a precious little brat even though she did seem to change by the end. Anyway, she was keeping up her education, Papa said, as he gave her arithmetic problems most nights.

Garnet watched her mother's needle pierce Franklin's worn shirt, back and forth. The rain, the kneading, the needle— the whole world was a rhythmic and deadly bore. Interrupting the dull cadence, she asked, "Is this ready to divide into loaves?"

"Yes. Get your pans ready."

She was greasing the pans with creamy, white lard when there was a knock and a holler at the kitchen door. "Ain't fit for nothing but ducks out there, Louise," called Grandpa, as he came in. He stomped and blew and big patches of dirty water from his boots spread over the wooden floor. More mud.

"What brings you over here?" Mama asked, frowning. Grandpa rarely stopped by and was even more rarely invited.

"Well, I got to thinking that you need your mother's sewing machine. Especially with the little 'un." He leaned down to grin at Violet and touch her spiderweb hair.

Garnet had dusted that machine every Saturday when she worked for Grandpa and earned her quarter, wondering why it sat unused when they needed it. Mama never walked up to the big house and did every bit of her sewing by hand. It took ages.

When the only replies he received were Violet's gurgles, he went on. "Anyway, I took a notion to bring it down here today. Where do you want it?"

Mama's brow creased. Grandpa pulled out a huge handkerchief, removed his hat, and dried his shiny head. Mama said, "I don't know where we'll put it."

He marched toward the bedroom, hat back on his head.

"Papa!" Mama shouted. "Your boots!"

He halted. "Sorry."

Mama gave him a narrow look and went to her bedroom door, shaking her head. Then she walked into the front room, eyes darting. And finally she sprinted up the steps to the second floor. The whole time Grandpa stood dripping where she'd stopped him. When Mama came downstairs, it was at a slower pace. "There isn't enough light up there. I suppose it'll have to fit in the kitchen."

She grabbed Violet, bunching the quilt around her while Garnet and Grandpa shifted the table. Still frowning, Louise swayed back and forth with the baby. "It'll work, Mama," said Garnet, "even if it is crowded. And you'll enjoy having it."

"I suppose we could cut out fabric on the kitchen table," Mama thought aloud. Garnet remembered the huge cutting table at

Grandpa's house in what Mama called the sewing room. Imagine having a whole room for one purpose.

"That's the ticket!" Grandpa exclaimed as he made for the back door, and in a minute he returned, carrying one side of the tarp-covered machine. Lifting the other was Luther Colson wearing a wet hat that hid his eyes. When she saw him, Mama made a noise low in her throat and squeezed Violet so firmly the baby complained. Neither man looked at Mama. Luther Colson hurried out the back door with the tarpaulin. He hadn't spoken a word.

Grandpa kept nodding at Mama. "Well, there you are." He backed toward the door, looking uneasy. "I guess I'll be seeing you." He continued to nod and then noticed Garnet. "Gal, I need you to scald out all your sorghum pails, and we'll go up to the Clark's tomorrow, if that's all right, Louise."

Garnet glanced at Mama.

"I need you early, now, you hear?" he said to Garnet. "And John and Franklin too, if you can spare them. When I was at the bank Clifford Clark offered me some hardwood him and his sisters don't want. I'll need some help."

Grandpa left, and Mama narrowed her eyes at the Singer.

***

By the next morning the rain had stopped almost like Grandpa had commanded it, and they set off as a cool, watery sun was starting to rise. Sorghum pails clanked in the wagon bed where she and Franklin sat. The mules made slow progress on the muddy road, but Garnet didn't care if it took hours. The sky continued to clear until the light became crystalline and the sky was the color of cornflowers. A mile or so before the outskirts of Ashton, Grandpa turned the mules down a narrow track. Sitting well back from the road was a big frame farmhouse, larger than Grandpa's but plainer.

He stopped the wagon close to the house and got down. Wiping her hands on a vast flowered apron, a huge woman stepped onto the porch. "Law, Deke, did you finally stop that rain?" she asked.

He grinned and gave a half-bow. "I sure did, Fanny."

Franklin elbowed Garnet and winked. Last night he'd told Lowell that the Clark sisters were giants that ate children, mostly to keep his brother from wanting to go with them. Fanny Clark wasn't exactly a giant, but everything about her was oversized. Her head looked as big as a pumpkin with dark brown hair pulled into a tight braid and wound into a knot. Her shoulders were as broad as Grandpa's, and she topped him by at least four inches. She rested big, fleshy hands on her wide hips and peered at the wagon. "And who'd you bring with you, Deke?"

Papa jumped down and shook hands with her. "John Grant. How do, Miss Clark."

She nodded and then pinned Garnet and Franklin with her dark eyes. "These your grandbabies, Deke?"

Franklin squirmed until Garnet elbowed him back. "Yes, ma'am," she said. "This is Franklin, and I'm Garnet."

"Well, might as well stay put. Gert's waiting for you down at the press. I'm baking just now," she stated, heading off any visiting.

Tipping their hats, Grandpa and Papa climbed back onto the wagon seat. Before he clucked to the mules, Grandpa asked, "Fanny, you sure about that walnut tree? From what Clifford said, it's a mighty nice one."

She shook her head, jowls. "I got no use for it, and it doesn't look like Clifford's ever going to set up housekeeping. I hate to see pretty wood go to waste. You going to have something made?"

"Maybe. The tree's down yonder?"

She nodded, pointing with one hand and holding the other against the massive bosom of her dark gray dress. "Gert'll show you, but, yes, you just head on down the track past the mill. We had some clearing done down there, but we wouldn't let the men touch that walnut."

She waved them on their way. Franklin tried not to giggle until they got out of earshot, and Garnet fussed, "Your manners, Franklin! Sitting here like you don't have a voice and then getting a fit of the giggles!"

Papa smiled. "She is a fairly humorous character."

Grandpa grinned too. "And you ain't even seen Gert yet, boy."

Franklin burst into full laughter. "I think Miss Clark likes you, Grandpa. Maybe she wants to be your sweetheart!"

"There was a time, boy. Yes, there was a time."

The track headed down a hill where a boy half-heartedly prodded a mule moving in a circle around the press, and Garnet smelled the burnt caramel of molasses. It smelled like autumn. Off to the side was a shed about twice the size of an outhouse, and near it was an open shelter with a long, shallow pan sitting on an old stove. Wreathed in steam, a huge woman stood near the stove, wearing what looked like a man's white shirt, an immense black skirt, and a bright red scarf wrapped around her head. She shaded her eyes.

"Hey, Deke King!" Garnet was surprised at how sweet her voice was.

Grandpa maneuvered the mules toward the shed and raised his hand. "Good morning, Gert. How you doing?"

She seemed friendlier than her sister. Waving the large dipper she'd been using to skim the syrup, she said, "Can't complain. Wouldn't do any good if I did."

Carrying pails, all of them clambered out of the wagon. From a huge kettle of cooled molasses, Gert ladled the viscous syrup into the pails with big rough hands. Then Papa took a mallet and tapped lids on them. He told Franklin to arrange the pails along the side of the wagon bed so there'd be room enough for the logs. Garnet's job was to carry the pails to Franklin.

She heard Grandpa ask, "Is Clifford at the bank today?"

"Yes, but he'll be home soon. Works half days on Saturdays."

Garnet remembered the bank, cool and dim, and imagined working in Ashton, all dressed up in town clothes and talking to important people all day. She thought she might like it. Her eyes stung from the smoke and the constant motion from shade to sun, but as she brought out the last pair of pails, she noticed a man on horseback coming down the track. Maybe he was the mysterious Clifford. Franklin heard him too, and as the rider neared, the boy shouted, "It's Luther!"

Grandpa said, "I expect he's bringing our dinner. And I figured we'd need his help loading those logs."

Garnet's heart raced. A Colson.

Grandpa delved into his pocket to pay Gert. "I sure appreciate you letting me have the walnut tree. I'm going to get that carpenter from over at Bethel to make me something. He's a dab hand at making furniture."

"I've heard that," Gert replied. "What're you going to get made?"

"Not sure, but maybe you ought to have something pretty made up for yourself."

She waved her ladle. "Get on with you, Deke. We wouldn't have room in the house to put another piece of furniture if the carpenter was Jesus Himself!"

Grandpa laughed, but Garnet wondered if the big woman's words were sacrilegious. Papa smiled, though, so she supposed it wasn't too bad. They rode on down the rough track with Luther following them. Garnet wondered who'd fixed the food. She heard Franklin's stomach growl, and he muttered, "I'm hungry enough . . ."

"To eat a horse?"

He chuckled. "I could never in a million years eat a horse; I love 'em way too much. But I'm about to starve, and that's a fact."

Grandpa stopped the mules, and Garnet saw the cleared area ahead of them, the ground bright with fallen leaves, leathery from the rain. Several stumps dotted the land close by a stream that most times would've been lazy and insignificant but was burbling just inside its shallow banks from all the recent showers. Grandpa strode over to the one standing tree. "By gum, Fanny was telling me true. This is a prince of a tree. Look, Franklin, how straight and fat it is. That's the way of a good furniture tree." Franklin glanced at the walnut, more interested in Luther who had dismounted and was opening a large saddlebag.

Grandpa gazed at all the stumps. "Don't know why Gert was trying to clear this land. The Clarks don't need much pasture. They have hogs; that's where I get my hams. And they keep a few cows for milk, but they mostly raise corn and sorghum cane. And, Clifford has his horses."

Franklin turned away from Luther's preparations. "Who's Clifford?"

"Gert and Fanny's much younger brother. Them big old gals have doted on him to where he's almost spoiled beyond redemption, but he's a likeable fellow. And he's a good judge of horseflesh."

Garnet hung back near the wagon where Papa was unloading the tools they'd need. She was half-scared of Luther Colson even though she knew this was silly. When he announced that the food was ready, both Franklin and Grandpa headed right for the stump where Colson had laid out their meal. Papa dusted off his hands and said, "Let's eat, Garnet." She followed behind him, thinking that if Papa didn't mind a Colson, maybe she shouldn't either. She didn't know what to think.

She picked up a tin plate. Neatly laid out were packets of biscuits, ham, and fried apple pies. Still, she hesitated. "There's plenty, Miss Garnet," Colson murmured. "Franklin didn't take quite all of it."

She was surprised he knew her name. She sat by Papa, as far away as she could get from Luther Colson, and ate, admiring the perfect biscuits and wishing she could bake ones like that. Franklin said hers were like rocks. Even better was the flaky, sweet fried apple pie, seasoned with cinnamon and plump with dried apples. "These are really good," she commented.

"Yes. Be sure to thank Lorena for fixing it," Papa said to Luther.

So that's who'd made dinner, Garnet thought, wondering if she'd sicken from eating it. But again, Papa didn't seem to care. Mama would be having a fit.

***

Until the end of November, Franklin and Papa labored late at the farm every evening, coming home with raw, cracked hands smelling of spicy tobacco. Although Grandpa hired extra men to tie the tobacco into hands, he needed all the help he could get. In the evenings Papa marked his students' papers with shaky fingers, and Franklin sometimes fell asleep over his books.

But once Grandpa left to take his crop to the Lexington market, Papa had a break from the second job he kept from early spring until nearly winter. He whistled as he repaired fencing around the chicken coop and painted the worn back door. He spent hours cutting and stacking wood for the stove. And, to Garnet's delight, her lessons resumed. She filled her tablet with algebra and geometry problems.

But she was nearly as excited about the sewing machine. Mama showed her how to fill bobbins and thread the machine. She learned to work the treadle and soon was searching for any scraps of fabric so she could make things. Mama had always despaired over Garnet's scratchy sewing skills, but learning to operate the sewing machine was another matter.

"I think we can solve Christmas presents with the Singer," Mama said one day in early December. "If Mrs. Lawrence has any nice yard goods, we could make shirts for the boys and your father."

Garnet agreed. She'd been plotting how she could secretly make her mother a new nightgown for Christmas. Although she was uncertain how she'd sew it without her mother's knowledge, she planned to use a piece of soft, pink flannel she'd seen folded up at Grandpa's. With Christmas generosity in mind, the next morning Garnet, Lowell, Mama, and Violet walked to Mattie Lawrence's store. Violet was bundled so carefully that only her tidbit of a nose was exposed. Mrs. Lawrence was friendly but jumpy. Her eyes darted from Mama to Garnet as she showed them her yard goods. Oblivious to

25

this, Mama shifted Violet farther back on her hip to free her hand for touching the fabric. "What do you think of this blue piece for Franklin, Garnet?"

"It's pretty."

Mama set that piece aside. "Oh, I can't do this with Violet stuck to me," she complained. "Here, Garnet, take her out on the porch and keep her amused."

Most of the time Mama allowed no one to touch the baby except maybe Papa. Pleased, Garnet gave Violet a little squeeze and sat down in the sun on the porch step. Before long, Lowell came out and begged to see the cats so they walked to the back of the store. Garnet smiled to herself. Maybe Mama was choosing something for her and didn't want her to see it. Garnet had some secret Christmas business of her own.

When Mama called them, Garnet handed Violet to her mother and said, "I need to see Mrs. Lawrence a minute. I'll carry the fabric and catch up with you."

Mama smiled. "Another Christmas secret?"

Garnet grinned and rushed back to see what colors of ribbon Mrs. Lawrence stocked. She planned to make the neck of Mama's nightgown close with a ribbon tie. Mattie Lawrence pulled out several spools. "You'll want grosgrain; it won't fray out."

"I didn't bring any money today. Could you save some of that pale blue for me?"

"Of course, child. How much will you need?"

Garnet had no idea.

"Have you ever made anything like this?"

"No, ma'am."

"Well, let's see. You'll need it at the neck, and then you might want to trim the cuffs with a little more. Tell you what, I'll cut off a length and put your name on it. Then you can run up here when it's convenient and pick it up. And Garnet, honey, if you'd like me to help, come up on Sunday and I'll get you started."

Garnet replied that she'd be glad of the help. As she turned to leave, Mrs. Lawrence asked, "From the way she's acting, your mama don't know about your grandpa and Lorena, does she?"

Bewildered, Garnet shook her head. Mrs. Lawrence clapped her hand over her mouth. "And I guess you don't either. Aw, I've gone and said too much. Ignore me, girl."

Garnet walked out of the store, puzzling over what she'd heard. Whatever it was, Mama wouldn't like it, and she couldn't ask Papa. Well, if Mama had a hissy, at least this time it wasn't her fault.

***

Grandpa was still in Lexington at the tobacco market so there was no need for Garnet to clean his house the next Saturday. But she wanted to get that flannel, so she lied to her mother and said Grandpa had specifically asked her to come. She didn't figure Christmas lies really counted.

Mama, still happy and peaceful as she'd been the last few weeks, didn't pay much attention, but she did say that Garnet had to take Lowell with her. Garnet didn't mind; Lowell trailed after her like a puppy most of the time anyway. Franklin actually had chores at the farm, so the next morning, the three of them walked up the path to Grandpa's just as the morning sun was making diamonds on the frosted grass.

The farm seemed empty without Grandpa. The house was tidy; Garnet raced around dusting furniture that didn't need it and sweeping up miniscule amounts of dirt, and Lowell amused himself by looking around at the strange decorations Grandpa had bought over the years. He gazed at a dark old painting of an Arabian bazaar until she had to nudge him and tell him to come upstairs with her.

Garnet was very aware of the creaks in the stairs. She worried that Luther might show up in his quiet, almost spooky way and startle her any minute. Passing Grandpa's room she noticed a familiar flowery scent of Carnation Bouquet powder, like Mama's. Things were getting more obvious by the minute. She told Lowell, "Let's go in the sewing room. I'll find buttons for you to play with."

The room looked different. Of course the sewing machine was gone, but the cutting table had disappeared too. In its place was a single bed, made up with a Dresden Plate quilt. Garnet went to the cupboard where her grandmother's tin of buttons and fabric were normally kept but found men's shirts and pants instead. Confused, she whirled around and heard a quiet voice from downstairs, "Hello?"

"I'm up here," she called, her voice shaking. It was Luther, and this had to be his bedroom. He would think she was snooping, but she'd had no idea he'd moved into Grandpa's house. She'd only missed one Saturday of coming up here, but things had changed dramatically.

Before she could grab Lowell and leave the room, Luther stood in the doorway. She clasped her hands behind her back.

He didn't look upset. "Can I help you?"

Garnet stammered, "I, I was looking for the button tin. And some material I remembered being here."

Lowell popped his thumb in his mouth.

"Well, most of the stuff in here got moved to the spare room," he said. "But I couldn't tell you where Lorena put things."

Lorena. Dear Lord. Hardly able to breathe, Garnet followed Luther to the other bedroom, which now held the cutting table and a shiny, brand new sewing machine. Garnet stopped dead when she saw it. Luther looked sideways at her but didn't comment. Opening the chifferobe, he asked, "Maybe in here?"

Garnet pulled open one of the drawers. There was the battered tin of buttons. "Here, Lowell, play with these, but don't you dare put any in your mouth." Her brother had big eyes.

Luther let her look. At the back of a shelf she found the fabric. Grandpa would never care, but she felt like a thief in front of Luther Colson. "I plan on making my mama a nightgown out of this."

"That'll be right nice," he replied.

She grabbed the fabric, closed up the chifferobe, and called, "Lowell, let's clean Grandpa's room."

Thoughts bumped around her in head like bees in a jar. Luther had a room in the house and was all settled in. More amazing, though, was the new sewing machine. Unless Grandpa had taken up sewing, the machine must be for Lorena. Mrs. McDaniel, she corrected herself. She wouldn't even let herself think why the woman would need a brand new machine at Grandpa's.

"Can I get on the bed, Garnet?" Lowell pleaded, bored with buttons and enchanted by the sinuous, carved bedposts that he declared were snakes.

"Take your shoes off."

She eyed Grandpa's large bureau and wondered how guilty she'd feel for opening the drawers. She'd had an excuse when she was searching for the fabric, but this was outright spying. Shrugging, she opened drawers that held Grandpa's underwear and nightshirts. Lowell was occupied tracing the bedpost carvings as high as he could reach. And then she tried another drawer and saw corsets and nightgowns trimmed with lace, finer than what Mama could crochet. She slammed it shut. That woman was living here, not in the guest bedroom, but in Grandpa's very room.

It was just as well Lowell was happy on his own because Garnet ignored him all morning. When she heard two sets of footsteps downstairs in the kitchen, she hesitated. The scent of bacon floated up the steps, and finally Franklin called her. "Come on, Sis, I'm starved."

Luther was cooking. "Could we have some fruit?" Franklin asked, and she nodded, happy to trade the cellar for the kitchen. Even though the cellar was dim, her mouth dropped open when she saw the quantity of canned goods, far more jars than she'd accumulated from her own canning. Jewel-like in the grayish light, rows and rows, several deep, stood on the shelves. She grabbed a quart jar of applesauce.

She could hardly eat, but Luther's presence didn't bother her brothers. Franklin, trying as usual to scare his little brother to death, was relating Grandpa's old story about the black racer that'd chased him down a hill when he was young. Franklin told Lowell that even though they weren't poisonous, black racers could charm a body and squeeze you to death. Lowell's eyes got wider and wider, and Garnet figured there'd be nightmares come evening. Smiling at the nonsense, Luther ate without speaking but handed Lowell the sorghum pitcher when he asked for it.

Lowell had a tendency to pour syrup over everything, and after he'd drenched his bread, Garnet rescued his egg. "Enough," she whispered. The older man looked at her and smiled. His teeth were straight and white against skin still tanned even in December. He had a lean face with furrows down his cheeks. When their eyes happened to meet, she saw no ill feeling or malice. She was having trouble disliking him.

Later, as they walked home in an early twilight. Garnet murmured to Franklin, "You knew that Luther was living at Grandpa's house?"

Franklin nodded. "It was stupid for Luther to walk from Deer Creek every day."

Their house was nearly in sight. "And her? She lives there too?" Garnet asked.

"Not my business. That's what Papa says."

"Mama'll be furious."

"Yep."

What Mama didn't know wouldn't hurt her, she reckoned, and the rest of them were better off for it. Mama's Christmas gaiety lasted all week. She rose early in the morning and cooked breakfast, ordinarily Papa's job. Lowell begged for gingerbread, and Mama made it. One afternoon when the kitchen was warm and steamy from simmering soup beans, Mama stood and flourished the shirt she'd made for Papa, beautifully stitched and sparkling white.

"It's lovely, Mama. It couldn't be better if it'd been made by the finest shirtmaker in the city," Garnet declared.

"Do you think so?" Mama held the shirt by its shoulders and danced a step or two around the crowded kitchen. Lowell clapped his hands and Violet giggled.

"Now," she said, "that nearly finishes your father's shirt, and someone else's is completely done." This was said with a big wink.

"And you have Franklin's cut out, don't you?" Garnet asked.

"Yes, indeed." Mama smiled. "Could you get me the button box?"

When Garnet went into her mother's room, she remembered the other button box at Grandpa's and dread fell over her despite her mother's good humor. Garnet felt like she should grab hold of a strong tree to brace herself from the storm that would break when Mama discovered that both Colsons were living with Grandpa. And she would find out, somehow. She couldn't help but hope it would wait until after Christmas.

Chapter Four

The storm struck only a week later, but later she remembered it as more of an earthquake, tearing big chasms in her world. It was Sunday, and the entire Grant family had attended church, unusual since Mama usually found some excuse to stay home with the baby. After their chilly walk home, Garnet rushed upstairs to change out of her new blue church dress. And that was when she heard knocking at the front door. Nobody ever came to their front door. Franklin was already changed and flew down the steps with her right behind him. With a flourish, he opened it to see his grandfather, dressed in church clothes himself. Behind him, looking smart in a dove gray suit and burgundy hat, was Lorena. Rounding the corner from the staircase, Lowell shouted, "Grandpa, you're home!"

Grandpa held out a hand to the boy but didn't pick him up. "Franklin, fetch your folks." His voice was somber.

Franklin obeyed and returned scowling. No one spoke. Grabbing Lowell's hand, Franklin pulled him onto the floor under the window. Grandpa glanced around the room, and when his eyes landed on the old sepia-tinted photograph of himself, Caroline, and Mama, his mouth tightened. Lorena neither smiled nor frowned.

Papa ushered Mama into the room, his hand on her arm. Her face was a thunderstorm. They'd left Violet in the crib, and she was putting up a fuss about it. Mama's chin was aimed at the dingy ceiling, and in her old housedress, she was the one who looked common.

Grandpa broke the silence. "John, I brought your share of the tobacco money. It was a good crop and a lively market. We did well." He handed Papa an envelope. Mama's hands were clenched.

Grandpa faced her. "I know this won't suit you, Louise, but I can't live my whole life pleasing a grown daughter. Lorena and I married a week ago in Lexington. I reckon I owe you the respect of telling you in person."

He turned as if he'd had his say, putting a shaking hand on Lorena's taut sleeve. Mama stood as still as a statue. Papa glanced at her, and the children all watched to see what she'd do. Lowell had his thumb in his mouth. Grandpa acted like he was itching to leave, but Lorena remained as still as Mama. They reminded Garnet of two cats bushing up their tails.

Mama hissed, "May you burn in hell, you rotten bastard!"

Franklin half-rose at this, but Papa stretched out a halting hand toward him. He said, "It's their business, Louise."

She ignored him. Grandpa's face reddened but he said nothing and moved one step closer to the door. Lorena gazed steadily at Mama.

"Bringing this piece of trash, this whoring common trash into my mother's house." Loud now, Mama pointed a finger at Lorena and took a step toward her.

Garnet trembled. She heard Violet getting really worked up. Lowell had big tears running down his face, and Franklin was ready to punch something.

"Just what I expected," Grandpa muttered and gripped Lorena's arm, insistently this time. She consented but kept her eyes fixed on Mama even as she turned to go. Grandpa closed the door behind them, and all was silent except for Violet's squalling.

Papa placed his hand on Mama's shoulder, but she shook it off, her eyes glittering. "None of you, and I mean none of you is ever going to set foot in that man's house again. You'll not work for him, you'll not visit him, you'll never see him again."

Franklin scrambled to his feet, but Papa shook his head. Then Mama spun around, bumped roughly into Garnet in the doorway, and went into her room, slamming the door. The rest of them stood motionless . Finally Papa walked into the kitchen and they all followed him, Lowell sniffing and hiccupping. Pulling a handkerchief from his pocket, Papa wiped the boy's face and looked first at the closed bedroom door and then out the window. His eyes took on the hue of the colorless winter day. No one spoke for a moment, but then Franklin burst out in a loud whisper, "But never, ever to go to the farm? Never, ever to see Grandpa?"

Giving himself a little shake, Papa said to Garnet, "Feed your brothers."

She nodded and pulled out a bowl for cornbread, mixing the batter and heating the skillet for hoe cakes. All the while her father stared out the window. Eventually he seemed to gather himself and went into the bedroom, shutting the door.

Lowell started sniffling again. Both he and Franklin were sitting at their usual places at the kitchen table. She dropped her spoon and ran over to Lowell, hugging him. "Oh, honey, don't worry. Everything will be fine."

Franklin looked up with dreadful eyes. "Sure, Garnet. And what are we going to do for money? And milk?" He dropped his head and mumbled, "And my horse. What about my horse? Grandpa promised me a horse when I'm fourteen." Any minute he'd be crying like Lowell, and she knew it would shame him. From the bedroom came the staccato sound of Mama's angry voice and the constant drone of Violet's crying. Garnet thought she'd burst into a thousand pieces. She took baked beans from the oven and stacked the hoe cakes on a plate.

"Franklin, go to the cellar and bring up a jar of pickles." When he didn't move, she begged, "Please, Franklin."

Her broken voice made him move. The three of them tried to eat. Both boys helped her clean up and fix plates for her parents, placed on the back of the stove. Lowell pressed close against first Garnet and then Franklin. Out of nowhere she remembered she was supposed to go to Mrs. Lawrence's house to sew that afternoon. Her parents' voices continued sporadically from the bedroom, but Violet no longer cried. Garnet pulled the two boys to her. "I promised Mrs. Lawrence I would go to her house this afternoon. She's helping me make a Christmas present for Mama."

Franklin's face creased into a sneer. "Can I go?" Lowell asked.

"No. It's sewing, Lowell. And I'm visiting; her store isn't open on Sundays. Anyway, I don't think Papa will even realize I'm gone." She looked hard at the boys. "Could you two play for an hour or two and let me do this?"

It was Franklin's decision and Garnet knew it. He rarely fooled with Lowell, preferring to run to the farm at every opportunity, but things were going to be different now. She felt as if she'd fly apart if she didn't get out of the house. He must've seen this in her eyes. "I can't answer for what they'll say if they find out you're gone."

"Tell them it's for Christmas."

He turned to Lowell. "You want to play with my marbles?"

She faltered a minute at the door, clutching the folded fabric under her shawl, but Franklin waved her on. "You'd best go."

She scampered across the swinging bridge. She ran until the cold air made her throat hurt. Everything along the road looked just as it had when they'd returned from church, but nothing was the same. She thought of the changes, big and small, that Grandpa's marriage and Mama's pronouncement would make. How could Grandpa have done such a thing? But then, why should Mama care so much? If Mama would relent, things could go on normally. It's not like they'd have that Colson woman at their house. At least Grandpa and Lorena were married, not living in sin. Then her mind flew back in the other direction. Grandpa knew this would hurt his daughter. Her thoughts twisted and turned like a mountain path, first blaming Grandpa, then Mama, then Lorena McDaniel or Colson or, and this made her stop in the road for a moment, King.

She ran around the side of the store to the back where Mrs. Lawrence lived.   While she caught her breath, Mrs. Lawrence emptied a pan of dishwater out the back door and caught sight of her.

"Land, Garnet, you startled me. Come in out of the cold."

She unwrapped her old gray shawl and looked around. She'd never seen Mrs. Lawrence's house. Every inch of space was filled with furniture or items either decorative or useful. Calendars, religious pictures, photographs, and a match holder were crammed together on the wall behind the kitchen table which was loaded down with catalogs, a Bible, and newspapers along with the sugar bowl and salt cellar. She wondered how the woman ate there.

Mrs. Lawrence noticed Garnet looking and chuckled. "Well, I'm a packrat, girl, can't throw nothing away. But I'm real organized in the store," she said. "Plus, I may be making excuses for myself, but I don't have a minute to tidy things up. I'm on my feet all day long, and in the evenings I just want to set a spell. Only chance I get to work on the house is on Sundays, and that's a sin."

Realizing she was being rude, Garnet said, "Oh, no, ma'am. I just think it's real interesting, lots of things to look at."

"You got that right. Did you bring the fabric?"

"Yes, but do you need to do something else? If this is the only time you can get anything done . . ." Garnet's voice trailed off. She dreaded returning home.

"Heavens, no. The work will wait. Goodness, child, your hands are like ice." Then she frowned. "Are you feeling poorly?"

"No, ma'am. I ran most of the way."

"I think we need a cup of tea before we start. Let me put the kettle on, and then we'll spread out that material. Your mama and I are about the same size so I have a pattern we can use. I don't have a sewing machine, but we can start the hand work."

At the mention of a sewing machine, Garnet shut her eyes. The woman was bustling around, filling a kettle and pulling a teapot from the jumbled-up kitchen cabinet. When Mrs. Lawrence led her into the room directly behind the store, she emptied platters of papers, a couple of vases, a toy train, and an umbrella off the dining room table. "My daughter despairs of me," she said. "Now, let's spread that out."

They unfolded the fabric and pressed it straight with their hands. Mrs. Lawrence went to a dark buffet where she pulled out a packet of folded up dress patterns. It amazed Garnet that she seemed to know where everything was. Rooting around in a large ironstone bowl on top of the buffet, she found a pincushion. "Here we are. Oh, there's the kettle screaming. Try to find the pattern for a sacque dress in that bundle."

Garnet tried, but she couldn't tell one from another and her fingers felt numb and stupid. She said, "I'm sorry, Mrs. Lawrence, but I don't know what I'm doing."

"Don't worry about it. I made sassafras; that'll warm you."

Garnet felt awkward; visiting for tea and conversation was what adults did, and she certainly wasn't adult. It didn't seem to bother Mattie Lawrence.

The first earthy, fragrant sip burned Garnet's tongue, and she set the cup down with a clatter. Mrs. Lawrence eyed her again. "All right. I've known you since you was barely walking, Garnet, and I've never seen you this upset. Is the cat out of the bag?"

She knew she shouldn't be talking about kin with an outsider, but, oh, it was a relief to talk. She told about the scene in the front room, and once she'd exhausted that tale, revealed what she'd discovered at Grandpa's house. And then she talked about how worried she was about her family's welfare without Grandpa's help. In between gulps of story, she took gulps of tea, which Mrs. Lawrence kept replenishing.

Not once did the older woman interrupt. She nodded, shook her head, made comforting little sounds, but said nothing. Then when Garnet had no more to tell and sat twisting her hands in her lap, Mrs. Lawrence cleared her throat. "You know I almost spilled the beans to you in the store the other day. I knew your Grandpa took Lorena with him to Lexington, and I reckoned he was aiming to marry her. It didn't come as much of a surprise after Mr. McDaniel died. But now, you're a good Christian girl; isn't it better for them to be married than living in sin? She was staying up there most of the time except for weekends when he knew you'd be around. Obviously it shamed him enough that he didn't want his grand-daughter to know what he was doing."

Garnet swallowed the last of the tea, cold but very sweet. She focused on the crazed enamel-topped table. "I guess so, but Mama's hates that a Colson is living in my grandmother's house."

"Louise King's always been a proud woman."

"Why does Mama hate the Colsons so much? What did they do?"

Mrs. Lawrence scraped her chair back and took their cups. "I don't think it'd be much different if old Deke had married me, Garnet. In Louise's mind, nobody's supposed to take her mother's place."

"But my grandmother's been dead for years."

"Since your mother was sixteen, as I recall."

Garnet repeated, "Why does she hate the Colsons?"

Mrs. Lawrence fiddled with the patterns. "I just realized what I said: imagine Deke King marrying the likes of me. Better get working on this gown or your trip will've been wasted."

After finding the right pattern, they pinned it to the flannel. Garnet was afraid to cut it, but the older woman forged ahead. They worked until they lost what little light the afternoon offered. Mrs. Lawrence said, "Honey, you'd better be getting home. You don't want to cause more trouble."

Garnet obeyed. Although Mrs. Lawrence offered to let Garnet do her sewing there, she decided she'd work on it in her room. "If I run into trouble, may I come back next Sunday?"

"Sure," Mrs. Lawrence said.

The wind had picked up, blowing stray leaves across the road and whipping the bare trees. At the house, the dark kitchen showed no evidence of supper preparations The food she'd left for her parents had been eaten, dirty plates set by the sink. Under the bedroom door, there was a sliver of light, but her brothers were huddled in the dark front room, waiting for her.

"Don't you two want a light?"

Franklin shrugged. "You've been gone a long time. We're hungry."

Except for the eggs she'd gathered that morning, she didn't know what she could cook for supper. Normally either Franklin or Papa would've been up at the farm today and brought home ham or bacon.

Franklin said, "I thought maybe you'd get something at the store."

"She doesn't trade on Sundays." Garnet's voice was sharper than she intended.

Both boys looked at their feet.

"Oh, never mind. I'll manage something." She brought potatoes up from the cellar and noticed a few flakes of snow sticking to the window.

She set potatoes to fry while the boys waited. "See if there's some bread in the cabinet, Franklin."

"Lowell and me ate it this afternoon."

Franklin's voice dragged with despair and Lowell kept glancing at the closed bedroom door. Determined to cheer them up, Garnet said, "No matter. I'll make biscuits. Oh, and boys, it's started to snow."

Lowell ran to the window. "Please, Garnet, can I go outside and see it?"

"There's nothing much to see yet. It's not even on the ground."

"Please, please?"

"Wrap up and don't go far. We're nearly ready to eat."

He hurried into his jacket, still in a heap by the door where he'd left it after church. After covering the potatoes, Garnet grabbed a bowl and went to the cabinet where she worked lard into flour and baking powder. Then she carried the bowl to the kitchen table and slammed it down. Franklin's eyes widened when she collapsed into a chair and started crying, laying her head on her folded arms.

"What, Garnet?" Franklin's voice was thin and high.

When she could speak, she mumbled into the table, "How am I supposed to make biscuits? We don't have any milk. I used it all in the cornbread at dinner."

"Could you ask Papa to get you some?"

She shook her head. "Has Papa come out all afternoon?"

Franklin whispered, "Lowell and me stayed upstairs most of the time. He came and got their dinners, but that's all."

Garnet sat up and glared at the bowl of unfinished biscuit dough.

"Can you use water?"

"Don't know, but I guess I could try. They may be terrible, but mine aren't much punkin anyway, are they?" She gave him a watery smile.

They were nearly inedible, but the fried potatoes and eggs were hot and filling. Lowell was rosy from running around the yard catching snowflakes, and Franklin, bless him, tried to help by praising the biscuits and forcing several down. Garnet left Lowell in charge of the sorghum pitcher, so he hardly noticed how bad they were. But the closed bedroom door hung over them like doom. The boys had eaten what food there was, leaving nothing for her parents, but Garnet didn't care.

After the boys went to bed, she huddled on her own, wrapped in her shawl, and took the tiniest stitches she could to start the gown. She heard Papa's footsteps downstairs and knew he'd waited until they'd gone to bed to come out. Funny, she'd never realized a person could feel bruised without falling down or bumping into something. But that's the way she felt. She blew out the lamp and, twisting the shawl more tightly around her shoulders, knelt by the window to watch the snow.

A year later on Christmas night Garnet was doing the dishes from their holiday meal and thinking about how much had changed in the year since Grandpa had married Lorena. The Grants had survived. Last Christmas, only a week after their world collapsed, had been more like a funeral than a celebration, although Christmas could never, she thought, be totally without joy. Last year Lowell was a shepherd in the Christmas play at church, and she remembered her pride when he'd gripped his crook and said his lines in a strong, proud voice. She also remembered last year when her father and brothers had exclaimed over their beautiful new shirts. All Mama had cared about was her bitterness, so Garnet had finished them, clipping threads, pressing carefully, and wrapping them in soft tissue paper. And Garnet had received a lovely gift too. Before all the troubles, Mama had secretly made over her old, brown coat into a new one for Garnet. She remembered how Mama had smiled for the first time in a week when she unwrapped the nightgown Garnet had stitched by lamplight with a few frantic visits to Mrs. Lawrence for guidance.

This Christmas night, she could hear her father teaching the boys to play checkers in the front room. The wooden discs clacked against the board, and Franklin bellowed, "King me!" She smiled. This year had been poorer but happier. Mama had birthed another baby, Henry, four weeks ago, and, like always, the business of having a baby improved Mama's mood. This year she glowed over baby Henry who was wiry but strong, and if the presents were fewer, at least Mama was happy.

Just then Mama strolled into the kitchen, holding Henry, and looked over at Garnet. "Almost done?"

"No."

"Shall I send Franklin in to help you?"

"No, ma'am. He's having a big time."

Cooing at the baby, Mama disappeared into her bedroom, and Garnet thought, poor Franklin; she was glad he was having fun. Separation from Grandpa had hit him the hardest. All last winter, he'd moped and mourned, prowling around the yard and over to the dead garden, throwing sticks, kicking clods of frozen dirt, and staring at the path to Grandpa's house. Once, in early spring he'd simply burst free and run down the path. It'd been a Saturday, and she and Papa had been outside turning over dirt in the garden. Evidently Grandpa hadn't turned Franklin away; it was two hours before he returned. Garnet and her father had been prepared to ignore it, but Mama'd noticed, and she'd been waiting for Franklin in the kitchen. Cheeks pink from the chilly air, he'd come inside, more cheerful than he'd been in weeks. But before he could remove his jacket, Mama had smacked him hard, first on one cheek and then on the other, making them redder than ever. Garnet remembered pressing against the sink, hurting for her brother. Mama'd said, "You'll not disobey me."

Papa had been sitting at the kitchen table, marking papers, and he'd scraped back his chair when Mama'd hit Franklin. But he never stood up, and he never said a word. Ignoring Lowell whose mouth hung open, Mama had laid her hand on Papa's shoulder. Leaning into him, she'd murmured, "I must make sure he understands."

Papa'd looked up at her, his eyes dark and miserable, but she'd smiled at him and run her other hand down his jaw. "He'll obey now."

And Franklin had obeyed, for the most part. During the long, summer evenings, Garnet noticed that Franklin sometimes disappeared. He'd been careful, though, and she'd rarely had to search for him. Lucky for him, Mama had been too absorbed with the life growing inside her to pay attention.

They'd all, except Mama, been busier than ever. Last summer Papa'd extended the garden, and, although he and Franklin helped, the plot was Garnet's domain. Her mind ran away from her family when she was tending the garden. She'd put up more produce than they ever had and done it alone, since Mama was always reciting dire warnings about weak and dying babies. Then there'd been Violet. Once Mama had discovered she was pregnant, Violet was left to shift for herself. The little girl was a charmer but had a fierce temper. Mama'd weaned her, but Violet made hard work of it, screaming and shaking her auburn curls. Once she'd learned to crawl and then walk, she'd turned every corner of the house upside down. Franklin never had any patience with her, but Lowell had been good, spending hours holding her dimpled hand as she'd learned to walk around the yard. He'd kept her from eating dirt and rocks and made sure she didn't venture too close to the creek bank.

She finished the dishes. Balancing the dishpan on her hip, she dumped the water off the porch. Outside it was bitterly cold; stars and a nearly full moon glittered on the frosty yard. Christmas, she mused, and what would another year bring? In October she'd be fourteen, nearly an adult. She shivered. From the noises in the front room, it sounded as though one checkers match had ended and another begun.

It had been some kind of divine inspiration when Papa decided to buy the game at Mrs. Lawrence's store. Again she sold a small selection of hand-made toys, carved by Mr. Foster, the carpenter. She wondered what he'd made for Grandpa out of that walnut tree. Garnet dried a plate and settled it carefully in the kitchen cabinet. She'd seen Lorena once or twice at Mrs. Lawrence's store. The woman was polite, almost shy around her. But, whenever she happened to see Grandpa's wife, Garnet lifted her nose and either ignored Lorena or gave her the tiniest of nods. Mattie Lawrence fussed at her, calling her proud like her mother. "She's not the cause of your problems, Miss Garnet," Mrs. Lawrence scolded. "If you want to blame someone, blame your grandaddy or mother."

She wanted to blame someone. Papa'd said nothing about the shortage of money, but all of them had come up with ways to help. Garnet glanced at the table where an ironstone platter held four fat oranges, glowing in the lamplight and smelling of sunshine. Originally there'd been six, one for each family member except the baby, sent as a Christmas gift from Mrs. Lawrence. Since fall, Garnet had worked for her every Saturday, trying to force order into the woman's chaotic house. She wasn't sure she was succeeding, but Mrs. Lawrence was pleased. Garnet would've preferred working in the store but hadn't been able to convince Mrs. Lawrence to allow it. Although the storekeeper never paid her money, every Saturday she sent Garnet home with a bag of potatoes or cornmeal or sometimes a pound of bacon. Papa had declared this a real help, but Garnet itched to do more. Without the tobacco money or meat from Deke's smokehouse and milk from his cows, they needed more than the bits and pieces Garnet brought home.

Papa'd nearly worked himself to death. Over the last year she'd noticed new white streaks in his dark hair and moustache and his hands trembled when he shuffled his school papers. Although he still taught and the Board had raised his salary this past autumn, it wasn't enough. Last summer Papa had gone to see if the Clark sisters could use some help on the farm or at the sorghum mill, and they'd been glad to hire him, but it was such a distance to the Clark's farm that Papa hadn't been able to walk it every day. He'd tried it the first week and nearly passed out one evening, frightening them to death with his gray face and fluttering eyes. Fanny'd found out about the episode and declared he could board in with them, and she wouldn't reduce his salary by a penny.

Garnet dried the cracked teacup and smiled. That plan hadn't worked too well. After three weeks of it, Mama had announced that she wouldn't allow it, even though Papa always walked home on Saturday afternoons and stayed until after dinner on Sundays. Mama had sobbed and screamed that those women were trying to get their hands on Papa. Franklin had run out into the yard to hide his giggles at the thought of Papa being tempted by either Fanny or Gert, and Garnet had to press her face into Violet's tummy to stifle her smiles. Papa protested, but Mama had been deadly serious.

Papa had said he'd quit the job but wearily asked Mama what else he could do. Even if he could find temporary work in Ashton, it was a longer walk than to the Clark farm. Mama had just shrugged, and finally Papa had lost his temper, an event so rare that it scared Garnet. He'd marched out of the house and across the bridge, moving fast and fierce. Mama'd watched him and then announced that she was going too. It had been nearly dark before they'd returned, pink-faced and perspiring.

Garnet remembered that night and how, when they came home, she'd been sitting at the kitchen table snapping beans. Papa had gone directly to his chair at the table. His hair was every which way, and he smelled of sweat. Mama'd brought him a dipper of water, and he'd taken it, his eyes fastened on her face. When a drop dribbled down his chin, she'd used a long white finger to catch it. She acted like Garnet wasn't even there. Then Mama'd moistened a cloth and wiped her face, squeezing the cloth to drip water onto her bodice. Papa never took his eyes off her. The only sound in the kitchen had been the juicy, rhythmic snapping of the beans. Mama had wet a comb and stood by Papa's leg, her arms raised close to his face as she'd combed back his dark hair. Papa'd gazed at the pale oval of Mama's face as she'd combed and combed, leaning closer until his chin nearly touched her bosom.

Garnet shook her head as she draped her dishtowel over the sink. Papa had given in about the job after that strange afternoon but insisted he must walk to the Clark farm on Monday morning to tell them he was quitting. Two days later, Gert Clark had arrived with a mule she said her brother Clifford wanted to sell. She'd told Papa he could work off the money, if only he'd ride it to their farm and continue helping them. Mama'd allowed that this was all right. So, before dawn all last summer, Papa had ridden Caesar to the Clark farm and worked for the two eccentric sisters. He'd remarked once that it embarrassed him that they practically gave him the mule. Garnet remembered that he'd gazed out the window, his mouth set in a straight line, and said he didn't like being beholden. Mama had sniffed and replied that this was the least the Clarks could do in return for his hard work

Franklin had been ecstatic, even if Caesar was a mule rather than a horse. He'd worked like a demon to build a little shed, which he called a stable, for the old beast. Luckily, Caesar was docile enough to allow Franklin to treat him like a pet.

Once school started, Papa had still ridden to the Clark's to work the sorghum mill on Saturdays or make deliveries for Gert and Fanny. Sometimes he and the mysterious Clifford Clark made these rounds together, and Papa often talked about the man, praising his intellect and kindness. But all the work had taken the starch out of Papa. Since fall he'd been so tired that Garnet had helped him mark his papers. There'd been no lessons for her, and she guessed she knew enough. Papa rarely fussed any more when Franklin ignored his books but took pleasure in Lowell's eagerness at school. All Papa's lectures about education being their most valuable tool for success seemed to have run dry. They were too tired to look that far ahead.

Garnet heard Franklin crowing about another victory from the front room. Even he'd found a way to help the family finances. Way behind their little house, but still on Grandpa's land, he'd discovered a grove of walnut trees and gathered the big green globes, harvesting, husking, and later, shelling the nuts. His hands had turned so black that Violet screamed when he came near her. For hours out in the shed, he'd talk to Caesar and use a small hammer against an old flatiron held between his knees to crack the walnuts. He'd slowly filled a sack and taken them to Mrs. Lawrence who'd given him a good price. Papa'd shaken his hand like a grown man and praised his contributions.

Just then Franklin interrupted her thoughts and walked into the kitchen. "When are we going to peel that orange? You said we'd have one tonight."

Garnet had been doling them out, peeling an orange every few nights. "Pick one, and I'll rinse it. I want to save the peeling to bake a cake for New Year's Day."

The burst of citrusy scent drew Papa, Lowell, and Violet from the front room, and Garnet gave each of them a section, like a mother bird sharing out bits to her hatchlings. Mama emerged from the bedroom, claiming two sections, remarking that fruit was good for the baby's milk.

"Merry Christmas," Mama declared, raising her orange section like a toast.

"And may it be a healthy and fortunate New Year," Papa said.

***

A night or two later the full moon spilled ghostly, blue light into Garnet's room. She lay shivering and waiting for her body to generate a puddle of warmth so she could sleep. Crammed next to her was a low trundle bed where Violet had slept since Henry's arrival. Sometimes the little girl made fussy, rooting sounds that reminded Garnet of baby pigs. Tonight, though, Violet slept quietly on her stomach with her legs drawn up. Her round bottom looked like a tiny hill.

As the bed warmed, Garnet relaxed her muscles. Papa, Franklin, and Lowell would return to school tomorrow after the Christmas holiday. She no longer even thought about attending school. A few days ago, she'd seen Millie at church, but they had so few experiences in common now that Garnet felt like a stranger. Even if she couldn't go to school, Garnet wished she could visit her friend. Millie had whispered that she was interested in some boy. Garnet sighed. Her days overflowed with running after Violet, doing things for Mama, and trying to keep the small house tidy. Sometimes Mama worked a little, but most days she sat idle, either nursing Henry, doing fancy needlework, or staring out the window.

Garnet settled into one of her fantasies that usually made her drowsy. Imagining she owned Mrs. Lawrence's store, she rearranged furniture and cleared the clutter from the woman's house. In a crisp apron, she stood behind the counter and greeted customers, sliced bacon, and wrote prices on cans with a grease pen. It was the best dream she could think of.

Several hours later, Garnet heard a small sound, almost a groan, and without fully waking, rolled to the edge of her narrow bed so she could pat Violet. She was nearly asleep when she heard the noise again, and it wasn't coming from Violet. A minute later, Franklin poked his head around the green curtain. "Garnet."

She grunted.

"Lowell's dreadful sick."

44

The floor was icy under her feet. Although the moon's angle had changed, there was still enough cold light to see Lowell lying on his side, moaning and shivering even though his quilts were pulled up to his ears. Garnet sat on the edge of the bed and touched his cheek. His skin was fiery.

"What hurts, honey?"

His eyelids fluttered, and she noticed dark circles under his eyes, made even darker by the odd light. He whimpered. "Grandpa shot the bear."

Garnet looked at Franklin, who shrugged. "Is it your stomach, Lowell?"

His eyes opened for a moment and he mumbled hoarsely, "Hurts, Garnet."

She reached under the quilts and touched his hot, dry hand. He cried out as if she'd pinched him. "I'm getting Mama," she said.

The stairs were dark, but she knew them by heart. Downstairs, the kitchen was flooded with moonlight, casting weird shadows on the floor. Mama and Papa's door was open to capture some of the heat from the kitchen stove. It was noticeably warmer than the attic. "Mama," she whispered.

Papa heard her first. "What is it?"

She took one step into the room. Her feet were freezing. "Lowell's awful sick and talking nonsense about bears."

Mama jerked and sat straight up. "Fever?" Her voice was high and panicked, and she held her hand against her mouth as if she were warding off disease.

"He's real hot and dry and keeps saying things that don't make sense."

Papa swung his legs out from under the covers. "I'll check on him."

Mama grabbed his arm. "No. You'll bring the sickness down here."

Papa hesitated, and Garnet stood on one leg, trying to warm the raised foot against her calf. She could see the whites of Mama's eyes as they jumped around the room. "Don't come any closer. You might be taking the fever too." Her voice was shrill. "You take Lowell and Franklin up to Grandpa's. Stay there until everyone is well."

Garnet stared in disbelief, and Papa jerked around to look at Mama. She said, "I know, I told you never to set foot up there, but I have to protect the baby."

"It's the middle of the night, Louise."

"I want them out now."

"What about Violet?" Garnet asked. She had no idea how she'd manage, but if Mama insisted, she'd have to.

"No, leave her here. She's not much more than a baby herself. Hurry."

Garnet felt befuddled and stupid. She wasn't even sure Lowell could walk.

Papa misread her hesitation. "I'll see to Violet."

Mama's voice rose in panic. "Not until they're out of here. Leave. Now. And shut the door."

Garnet trudged up the steps. She shook her head at Franklin. "She wants us to take Lowell to Grandpa's and stay there until everybody's well."

"Now?"

She nodded, peering at Lowell shivering under the quilts. "I don't know how we're going to get him there."

"I can carry him."

She frowned. "Get your clothes on. I'll dress and then wrap Lowell up."

Franklin was already searching for his clothes before Garnet turned her back. She slipped behind the curtain and checked on Violet, feeling the little girl's cheek. It was cool. Garnet dressed, wrapping the old shawl around her head and then putting on her coat. She touched Franklin's face too. "I'm all right," he said.

"I was thinking. What about the wheelbarrow? Could we pile up blankets in there and wheel him up the path?"

"I know I could carry him, Garnet."

She patted his arm. He had grown into a sturdy boy, but Lowell was dead weight. "I think it would hurt him. Get out the wheelbarrow and fill it with your quilts. I'll wrap him in his covers, bundle him up, and bring him down."

Franklin looked doubtful. "Quilts're gonna get awful dirty."

"Oh, who cares about that? Our little brother's sick to death, Mama won't take care of him, and she's sending us to her worst enemy."

Franklin ducked his head and scooped up his quilts. Lowell kept whimpering, but she yanked the covers from his bed and wrapped him as best she could. Gathering him up, she staggered under his weight. She took the steps, one at a time. Her parents' door stayed shut. Outside, Franklin stood by the small wheelbarrow, and as gently as she could, Garnet placed Lowell on the nest of quilts, tucking the covers around him. She straightened and caught her breath.

The frozen ground made the path rougher than usual. At first Franklin pushed but the jerky movement jarred moans from Lowell. Each took a handle and worked together, their breath making smoky clouds. "What if she won't let us in?"

"Oh, Lorena's not so bad," he said.

"So you still go up there."

"Sometimes."

"Does Papa know?"

"Maybe. He's never said anything."

Lowell whimpered at the rough ride. At one point he mumbled, "Sick." They halted the wheelbarrow, and Garnet held him while he vomited onto the grass. Steam rose from his sickness. They passed the tobacco barn. Not much farther.

"Why did she send us over here?"

Garnet fought to push the wheelbarrow up the slight rise that led to the front porch. "She's scared for the babies. Reckon that's more important than holding a grudge right now." Her heart was pounding as they neared the big house, looming white and silent in the dark.

Chapter Six

She held the wheelbarrow steady while Franklin climbed the steps, his footsteps hollow and loud in the silent night. He hammered on the door until a glow of yellow light appeared. Luther opened the door.

As soon as the door was open a crack, Franklin began babbling. "Lowell's terrible sick, and Mama said Garnet and me had to bring him over here. And we rode him in the barrow 'cause we couldn't carry him, and he's crying now with fever and cold."

Without saying a word, Luther lifted Lowell from the wheelbarrow. And then Lorena appeared in the doorway, tying the belt of her dressing gown. Franklin repeated his story, and she told Luther to put Lowell in the spare room and build a fire. Garnet was gathering up the covers they'd used to cushion Lowell's ride, but Lorena said, "Child, we'll get those later. Come in and get warm."

Garnet had never heard her speak. Every time she'd seen Lorena, the woman appeared trim, neat, and more polished than Mama, but the difference was the voice. When Mama spoke it was as smooth and rich as honey. Lorena's voice recalled the rough hills where she was raised. Common, Mama would've said.

Franklin and Garnet were taking off their coats when Grandpa came downstairs. He still looked healthy and hearty, but more age spots freckled his bald head, and he seemed a little plumper. When he smiled at Garnet, she couldn't help but smile back whether he was to blame for their troubles or not. Then his expression turned anxious. "I heard the little fella is sick. Should I fetch the doctor?"

Lorena said, "It's not but four in the morning, and you wouldn't get him to come any time soon. It'll keep another couple of hours." She went to the kitchen.

Garnet itched to get upstairs to Lowell, but she waited. This wasn't just Grandpa's house any more. In a moment, Lorena came back with a pan of water and a cloth. "You'll want to cool his face and arms to get that fever down. Do you know what he's taken?"

Garnet had never spoken to this woman. She'd ignored her, turned her face, and walked away from her. "No, ma'am," she said. "He's talking out of his head. And he vomited on the way over here."

"Go up and get him settled. I'll have something hot for you to drink in a spell."

In the spare room Luther knelt by the fireplace grate, coaxing the coal fire. He had lit a small lamp and set it on the mantel. Pulling the sewing machine chair to the bed, Garnet wrung out the cloth and dabbed it on Lowell's cheeks. His breathing was shallow and fast, and chills sent tremors down his body. Franklin stood in the doorway with his hands in his pockets. He yawned.

"Bet you could use another hour or so of shut-eye," Luther murmured.

Franklin glanced at Garnet, but she concentrated on Lowell. When she bathed his arm, his teeth chattered. The next time she looked up, Franklin and Luther were gone. The room was warm, and the small lamp gave a cozy glow. She'd always liked this room and had slept here a few times when she was little. The walls were covered with faded, flowery wallpaper, mostly blue with green leaves and occasional spots of yellow goldfinches. Luther had settled Lowell in a hurry, leaving the crocheted bedspread drooping onto the floor. She straightened it.

"Don't mind about that," Lorena said from the doorway. She placed a tray on the cutting table. Garnet saw a teapot, cups, saucers, and a sugar bowl.

"I made you some tea. Thought you might be chilled through." Placing a hand on Lowell's cheek, Lorena frowned.

Garnet smelled the bright scent and poured a steaming cup, adding a lot of sugar and blowing on it. There was a rocking chair close to the fireplace, and she sat there, watching the smoldering coals and waiting for Lorena to tell her what to do. She didn't know anything about caring for sick people. But the woman just kept staring at Lowell. After a pause Garnet spoke, "Where's Grandpa?"

"I sent him back to bed."

Garnet sipped, unsure of what to say. "Mama made us come, but it's not right sending sickness to you. What if you all take it?" It wasn't exactly what she meant.

Lorena fiddled with the teapot. Her dark hair hung in a long plait down her back. "I don't reckon we will. Don't be fretting about that."

Lowell thrashed, mumbling nonsense, and Lorena murmured to him, adjusting his covers. Garnet couldn't recollect when she'd ever felt more awkward. She said, "You can go back to bed too. I guess Franklin went somewhere to sleep. I'll watch."

"Oh, I'm usually up by five or five-thirty anyway, me and Luther." A hint of a smile crossed her face. "We let Deke sleep a little."

Garnet figured it was probably getting close to five o'clock. Grandpa's clock in the dining room marked the hours with a wheezy gong, but she couldn't remember whether she could hear it upstairs. "What should I do?"

"Pour out a little of that tea and put a lot of sugar in it. See if you can get him to take a few drops from a spoon."

Garnet jumped up, glad for a task. She was also relieved when Lorena left, saying something about breakfast. Lowell drank little of the tea she offered him, and Garnet regretted the dribbles that trickled down his chin, staining the pristine pillowcase. She sat by his bed and rested her head against the soft feather mattress, listening to the fire burn and dozing until she smelled bacon and coffee.

That day was a blur. Lorena came up and told Garnet to go down and eat her breakfast. Shortly after sunup, Luther rode off to Ashton to fetch the doctor. At some point, Papa must've come by the house to dump a bundle of his children's clothes on the porch. He never knocked or called out. Lorena set her mouth in a tight line when Grandpa found the clothes. But most of Garnet's attention was focused on the little boy in the big bed. He looked tiny, not much bigger than Violet, and was deathly pale, his hair limp and dark against his hot, white skin. She fought his fever, bathing him even when he whimpered and shivered, and forced tiny bits of water or tea down his throat.

Luther returned saying the doctor would be there before supper, and Garnet fretted silently at this, wanting immediate attention for her brother. Grandpa and Franklin took the wagon to Mrs. Lawrence's store and returned in a burst of frigid air. Lorena chopped up canned beef and started simmering broth. The woman had it all under control, Garnet thought, unlike her breezy, blowsy mother who expected everyone to do everything for her.

Shortly after midday, Lowell opened his eyes, dark as raisins in his pallid face. "Mama," he whispered.

"It's Garnet, honey. I'm here." His hand seemed a little cooler.

Dazed, the boy looked around, and she said, "We moved you up to Grandpa's."

He threw an arm out from under the covers. "Hot."

She folded down the blanket so his upper body was exposed and ran her hand down his arm. It felt like sandpaper with tiny red bumps covering his skin. "You need to drink," she said, pressing a spoonful of water to his chapped lips.

He grimaced. "Throat hurts."

Later, when she went downstairs to get yet another pan of tepid water, she told Lorena about the rash. The woman looked up quickly. "Did you see his tongue?"

Garnet shook her head. Lorena dried her hands and went upstairs with Garnet trailing behind her. "Lowell," Lorena said. He opened his bleary eyes, confused by her presence. "Honey, open your mouth a little bit for me. Can you stick out your tongue?"

He did, and his tongue looked like a strawberry, bright red and dappled with tiny bumps. Lorena nodded, patted him, and said, "That's right. Go back to sleep."

Lorena drew her out into the hall. "I'm no doctor, but I seen this before. It's scarlet fever."

The words sounded grave to Garnet. "Is that bad?"

"It can be, but we ain't going to let nothing happen to your brother."

The endless day went on and on. Franklin stopped by the door occasionally, looking worried and restless. Grandpa seemed to feel the same way. And Luther, as quiet and efficient as his sister, kept the fire burning in the bedroom. Garnet's mind traveled down to her house, wondering if Violet was sick or if baby Henry had come down with it.

Around four o'clock the sunlight faded to gold. Lowell was quiet but felt hotter than ever. She heard a knock at the front door and hoped it was the doctor, but when Luther answered it, she heard her father's voice. She ran to the top of the steps, but he stayed outside. "I don't want to let in the cold, and Louise would have my hide if I came in, but I have to know how Lowell's doing."

Luther said something Garnet couldn't hear. From the top of the steps she called, "He's bad sick, Papa. Lorena thinks it's scarlet fever." She knew her voice was shrill.

Luther murmured something about the doctor coming any minute, and then Garnet hunkered down so she could see Papa. "Are the babies healthy?"

"They were fine this morning. Take good care of that boy, you hear?" he said.

She nodded.

"Best go. Louise'll need me." Luther shut the door.

She wanted Papa to come back, to stay, to tell her what to do. She didn't know how to take good care of Lowell.

She turned back toward the sickroom and was greeted by the sour smell of vomit. Lowell was raised up on his elbows, shaking and looking ashamed of the mess on his blanket. "Sorry, Nettie."

"It's all right."

Tears stung her eyes as she tried to keep the sickness from spilling onto the other blankets. Quiet as ever, Luther was there. He took the edges of the blanket and folded them together. "I'll fetch him another one," he said.

Lowell lay back down and she wiped his mouth, saying what she hoped were soothing things to him. His body was rigid and shivering again. She didn't know how to make him better, and the doctor would never come, and she despaired that her brother could live through this. Luther reappeared and laid an old quilt on top of the other covers. "He can't hurt this'n," he said, smoothing it over the boy and then tucking it in at the foot of the bed. She wiped the back of her hand against the tear tracks on her cheeks, but Luther noticed.

"Why don't you go downstairs and sit a spell in the kitchen? I expect the doctor'll be here any time, and you can talk to him. I'll stay here."

Lifting her skirt tail to do a better job at wiping her face, Garnet went in the kitchen. Lorena pulled out a chair. "You're wore out, girl. Set down."

Garnet obeyed and watched the woman work. Over in the corner she was filling a washtub with soap and steaming water to soak the soiled blanket. "I should do that," Garnet said.

"No. You haven't eaten a bite since breakfast, and you ain't had no rest. What will we do if you get the scarlet fever?" Lorena started scrubbing.

***

Dr. Thomas had great tufting white eyebrows and a booming voice that about half scared Garnet. He'd gone straight upstairs and stayed there a long time. Lorena stirred a pot of stew and slipped a pan of biscuits in the oven while Garnet pleated the edge of her skirt with shaky fingers. Finally the doctor lumbered into the kitchen and cleared his throat. "The boy has scarlet fever, no doubt about it," he said, more loudly than was necessary. He said to Lorena, "Are you his mother?"

She shook her head.

"I'm taking care of my brother, sir," Garnet murmured.

"Oh well, yes." He seemed uncertain.

Lorena said, "We're all taking care of him."

"Very well. You must control the fever. Pack wet towels around him two or three times a day. Persuade him to sip liquids." Lorena and Garnet nodded.

"Open the window in his room one inch but keep him warm. He must have fresh air but mustn't get chilled," Dr. Thomas pronounced. They nodded like puppets.

"Offer him light food: broth, custard, coddled eggs."

Again they nodded

"In a few days that rash will start itching like fire. Grease him down with lard or bacon grease to help the itching. That also keeps the scales from flying around." He raised his dramatic eyebrows and focused on Garnet and Franklin. "If you two aren't careful, you'll catch it from him. It's spread by those scales." Then he turned back to Lorena. "Everything that touches the boy must be boiled or burned, his clothes, bedding, everything."

He closed his bag with a loud snap. "Sir?" Garnet said in a high, shaky voice.

"Yes?"

"We moved him over here because there are two babies at home along with our mama and papa. The babies are a year and a half and just newborn. Will they take the scarlet fever?"

"No, you catch it from the scales. And I never see it in really young children nor in adults. You," and he pointed his thick finger, "are the one at risk."

He lifted his bag, and Grandpa stood up, reaching in his pocket for the doctor's payment. "You're welcome to stay and join us for supper, Doctor," Grandpa said, flashing a pale replica of his normal grin.

"No, no. I must get home. Mrs. Thomas will be worrying."

Garnet had risen from the table and stood by the big man as Grandpa put coins in his hand. "Will he die?" she whispered.

The doctor's face softened, and he leaned down. "I'm an honest man, little girl, and I have to tell you he's a very sick boy." He laid a heavy hand on her shoulder. "Children can die of scarlet fever when they have it bad, and your brother has a severe case. And if they don't die, it sometimes takes weeks and weeks for them to feel stout and healthy again. It all depends on nursing and God's will. You fight hard for your brother, and mayhap all will be well."

He turned abruptly and said over his shoulder, "I'll be back tomorrow."

So, another long night began. They packed Lowell in wet towels, regretting his whimpers and shivers. They tried to coax him to drink. As the night wore on, Garnet heard Luther and Franklin go to their beds. Then Grandpa poked his head in and asked if he could do anything before he turned in for the night. Then Lorena came through the door, burdened with a thick feather bed she dumped on the floor. "I reckon you'll have to sleep with either your head or your feet under the cutting table, but it'll do," she said as she smoothed linens into a neat pallet. Her face was flushed. She gave Garnet a stern glance. "I know you want to watch over him, but you'd best sleep."

Garnet squeezed the cloth she was using to bathe Lowell's face. The rash had spread until his face had a rosy glow instead of its earlier pallor. If she hadn't known better she would've guessed his color was improving. "But what if he needs me, and I don't hear him?"

"You'll hear him. You'll wake up every little bit and check on him without even trying. Give him some water every time, you hear?" She thrust a nightgown at Garnet. "And get out of your dress; you'll rest better. The gown's mine and it'll be a mile too long, but it'll do."

The pallet in front of the fire looked delicious. Her eyes were sandy from tears and lack of sleep. She guessed the woman knew what she was talking about and had to admit she desperately wanted to lie down. Lorena went to Lowell's side and pressed a hand against his cheek. "Poor baby," she murmured and smoothed his rumpled hair. She turned back to Garnet. "I'll check on you two ever now and again." She looked at the pallet and a tiny smile flickered across her face. "Between you, Lowell, and Franklin, I believe we've about used up all the blankets, quilts, and feather beds in the house." Lorena passed her hand over Garnet's arm. "Get some sleep."

Garnet slipped off the clothes she'd worn for what seemed like days. The faded gown smelled sweet and spicy like Cashmere Bouquet powder, and its well-washed softness was a comfort. One more time she went to Lowell and held a teaspoon of water to his dry and cracked lips. He protested with a soft groan, but she persisted and saw his swollen throat work to swallow it. "One more, baby," she murmured and slipped the shiny spoon between his lips. Only a few drops went in this time. Then she turned down the lamp, trying not to get tangled in Lorena's long gown. She supposed it would be saving to extinguish the lamp, but its glow was a comfort. With a sigh, she dropped down on the featherbed. Her hand touched something hard and found a

hairbrush Lorena had left by her pillow. She unbraided her hair and
brushed until sparks of electricity crackled around her head. Then she
plaited it into one long braid. That's the last thing she remembered.

True to her word, Lorena came into the room at least twice. The first time Garnet was already up, bathing Lowell's fiery face and dribbling water between his lips. When she came the second time, Garnet was asleep but Lorena's light step woke her. The woman whispered, "Stay put. I'll give him a drink this time."

Toward morning the boy rested better, and so did Garnet, coming out of a deep sleep to see Luther standing near her pillow. Her eyes shot open, but Luther murmured, "Just seeing to the fire." He gave her a sweet smile and told her he'd sit with Lowell so she could eat breakfast.

"Has the boy eaten anything?" Grandpa asked, cutting his bacon.

"We can barely get him to drink," Garnet said.

"Lorena made him some broth yesterday, didn't she?"

"Yes," she replied, reaching for a biscuit. "But he wouldn't take it."

With his mouth half full, Franklin said, "Too bad we can't give him candy. That's what he loves better than anything."

Garnet gave him a withering look. "He can't eat candy while he's sick."

"But I bought him some yesterday. I always think of Lowell when I see the candy counter," Grandpa said.

Lorena patted his gnarled hand. "And that was mighty kind of you, but I fear he might choke on it."

Garnet gobbled down her food, feeling guilty about having an appetite. Lorena surely could make biscuits. All of them ate quietly as if making noise would disturb little Lowell. Out the window the sky was gray and gloomy with clouds that had gathered through the night.

"It's going to snow," Franklin murmured.

"Doubtful." Grandpa said. "It warmed up through the night."

Lorena stared into space so long that Garnet and Grandpa stopped eating. Suddenly she turned to Grandpa. "What kind did you get?"

"What kind of what did I get?"

"Candy."

"Oh, I got his favorite, lemon sticks. He says they're like that lemonade I made when Violet was born." He shook his head. "I bet he'd drink lemonade if we could get it. But they ain't a lemon to be found at this time of year."

"How many did you get?" Lorena narrowed her dark eyes.

"Why, I don't know, Lorena. Maybe two or three .You said he can't eat candy anyway."

She pushed away her plate. "How do you two feel about going to the store again?"

It suited Franklin who was delighted that he didn't have to go to school. Grandpa bobbed his head. "We can go to the store. What do you need?"

Lorena smiled at Garnet. "We're going to make that boy some lemonade. Buy all the lemon sticks Mrs. Lawrence has, Deke. We'll melt them down."

Cheered by the hope of making something her brother would drink, Garnet nearly skipped out of the kitchen to relieve Luther. But Lowell was no better. The fragile skin under his eyes had a grayish cast, and she could've sworn his poor, rosy cheeks looked thinner. He woke up for a minute and whispered again that his throat hurt. She promised him a nice treat that might make it feel better.

Rolling up her makeshift bed, Garnet tidied the room. She tried to brush Lowell's hair, but he protested so pitifully that she gave up. There was nothing to do but sit and look out the window at the clouds coagulating on the horizon. She gazed at the path that led to her little house and wondered what was happening at home, feeling guilty even though her mother had forced her to leave.

Before Franklin and Grandpa returned from the store, Doctor Thomas arrived. Setting his bag on the cutting table, he shooed her out and started talking to Lowell in his loud voice. Garnet wondered if he frightened the child, but there was no help for it. She waited in the kitchen where steam billowed from kettles on the stove. Lorena was dumping soap into two huge washtubs on the kitchen floor. Beside them were piles of bed linens and clothes.

Garnet offered to help, but the woman refused it. "You can work with that pretend lemonade when they get back."

The doctor's expression dashed their fragile optimism. "There's no improvement at all, ma'am," he said, directing his comments to Lorena. "The child cannot take much more of this fever. It's still well over 104 degrees, and his throat is nearly swollen shut."

Lorena clutched a blanket to her chest.

"If the fever doesn't improve by tomorrow morning, you'll be burying him."

Garnet's head seemed too heavy for her neck. The room darkened and spun and before she knew it the doctor had grabbed her shoulders in his raw-knuckled hands and was setting her in a chair.

"Hey, now. Are you coming down with it too?" he asked, searching her face. His big eyebrows came and went down a dark tunnel. "Stick your tongue out."

Lorena held Garnet's arm while the doctor peered at her mouth and throat. "No, she looks all right," he said, straightening up and sighing. "I'll give you some drops to put in water or anything you can get down the child. They might help. Put two drops in a small teacup and fill it with liquid. Give it to him every couple of hours. Keep bathing him, packing him in wet cloths."

"We've been doing that."

"I know," he said, his voice gentler. "By no means am I faulting your nursing."

Her head finally cleared, and Garnet was able to focus on him as he fumbled in his black bag for a small vial. Luther came through the back door from the barn and stood silently while the doctor pulled on his coat.

"Deke ain't here at the moment, sir," Lorena said. Garnet didn't understand why she said that, but Luther stepped forward, digging into his pants pocket and placing money in the doctor's hand. This was all expensive, she thought miserably: the special food, the candy, the doctor, the medicine, and these people shouldn't have to suffer the costs. Papa always said they shouldn't be beholden to anyone, even kin.

Shortly after the doctor left, Grandpa and Franklin returned. They said they met him on the road after buying every lemon stick, twenty-two of them, that Mrs. Lawrence had. Garnet didn't know whether Dr. Thomas had cautioned them how sick Lowell was, but despite the candy, both picked up the dark mood in the kitchen. Grandpa said he reckoned he'd take a turn with Lowell, and Luther and Franklin escaped to the barn.

Garnet melted the candy in hot water. As it cooled, she tasted it for flavor and added a bit more water. Then she filled a teacup and stirred in two drops of the medicine. "Wish me luck," she said as she took it upstairs.

"You know I do."

Grandpa was pacing the floor in Lowell's room, going from the window to the doorway to the fire. He seemed relieved to see Garnet. "I ain't much good with sick people, gal. I hate feeling helpless." He left.

So did she. Talking to Lowell, she tried to raise his head, first with her hand and then with a pillow, but he didn't respond. The boy did seem worse. His poor lips were purple and blistered, but she tried to part them with the spoon and dribble a little of the sweetened liquid between them. Most of it went down his chin. "It's good, Lowell. It's like lemonade. You love lemonade."

His eyelids fluttered but stayed shut. He swallowed what probably amounted to two spoonsful of the liquid before he turned his head. For what seemed like the hundredth time, she bathed his limp body. He didn't even whimper. I'll try the lemonade again in fifteen minutes, Garnet thought. All along she'd prayed for her little brother, making crazy bargains with God, promising all kinds of wild things. This time she just shut her eyes and said, please.

Whenever she heard the clock chime downstairs, she forced some of the liquid down Lowell. Sometimes he gagged, and she feared he'd vomit, negating all she had achieved. People came and went. Lorena helped her pack him in wet cloths sometime before dinner. Shortly after that, Luther came and picked Lowell up, holding him while Garnet swiftly changed his bedding, sodden from the wet towels. Once they settled him back in the dry, clean bed, she noticed how shallow his breathing was. Luther must've noted it too and held a finger to Lowell's neck.

"What?"

"His heart's pumping awful fast."

She didn't think her spirits could sink any lower. Luther fussed about her not eating any dinner and sent her to the kitchen, steamy both from Lorena's laundering and a mess of beans, seething in a big kettle on the back of the stove. "You need more of that lemon candy water?" Lorena asked.

Garnet shook her head. "He isn't taking much." She stared out the window. Sheets and blankets hung stiffly from the clothesline behind the house. "I was wondering if we should fetch Papa."

Lorena grabbed her hand and squeezed it. "Oh, girl, I don't know. We can still work with the boy. He ain't gone yet."

Garnet stood silently.

"Come on and rest yourself. There's still cornbread from dinner. You eat something while Luther's up there with him."

Garnet shook her head and went back upstairs. Luther sat by Lowell, murmuring to him. The boy lay like he was already dead except for the quick, shallow movement of his chest under the quilt. "I tried to get a little bit of that down him, but I was afraid he'd choke," Luther said, rising from the chair.

"I've been afraid of the same thing."

Late in the afternoon, Franklin crept into the sickroom. Mostly he'd stayed away. He whispered, "He's going to die, ain't he?"

She shrugged, exhausted.

"I was always mean to him."

"Oh, not always, Franklin. That's just brothers." She motioned for him to come to her and wound her arm around his sturdy waist. He leaned against her.

"Grandpa's gone up to the school to tell Papa how bad Lowell is," Franklin said.

"You think he'll come?"

"Don't know."

Downstairs they heard the back door slam shut. Otherwise the house was quiet while the dull afternoon slid into twilight.

"Garnet," Franklin said, stepping away from her. "I think I've taken it. My throat's all sore, and I ache and feel hot."

Garnet looked up at the ceiling, noticing a brownish patch over in the corner. She must not cry.

"Well, let's get you to bed then," she said but didn't know whether to put him in the room with Lowell or send him to Luther's room where he'd been sleeping. Paralyzed, she sat, twisting her fingers together.

"Ask Lorena."

Lorena was ironing sheets. Strange stacks of half-frozen linens lay in odd angles in her laundry basket. The woman set down her iron when she saw Garnet's face.

"It's Franklin. He's sick now too."

Luther was sitting at the kitchen table, quiet as ever. Garnet hadn't even noticed him. The man rose and looked at his sister.

"Put him in your room, Luther. It might be easier to nurse them together, but they'll rest better if we separate them."

Luther nodded. "I'll put the boy in my bed. I don't mind a pallet."

Lorena squinted at Garnet. "I'll get Franklin settled and then make you something hot to drink. You're about to fall over, girl."

Garnet was too exhausted to argue, but as soon as Lorena left, she picked up the iron and began smoothing the sheets. There was something comforting about the rhythmic movement. As she folded them, Grandpa came in, bringing chilled air.

"Did you see Papa?"

He didn't answer. Hanging his coat and hat on a peg behind the door, he let out his breath, full and noisy like he'd been holding it for a long time, and walked to the stove to get warm. He looked old.

"I'll never figure it out in a million years, gal. Your daddy is a good man, the best, and I've always respected him. And I know my daughter loved each one of you children like life itself when you was born. But I just can't figure it out," he said, more to the stove than to Garnet.

She pulled out another sheet. "But he isn't coming up here even if Lowell is about to die. Because Mama said he can't, and he does what Mama says no matter what."

He didn't contradict her.

Garnet positioned the damp fabric on the ironing board. Bitterness rose up in her throat, and her movements became jerky. "And now Franklin's sick too, and they might lose their two boys, but it doesn't matter because it's just the babies that count."

Grandpa's head snapped up. "Franklin's took it too?"

"Lorena and Luther are getting him to bed. He doesn't seem too bad yet."

He sank into a chair. "I wish there was something I could do."

Garnet smoothed the sheet, smelling hot cotton and moving the hissing iron in slow circles. It wasn't right; none of it was right. Grandpa and Lorena and Luther shouldn't have to deal with this, but what would she have done if she'd had to care for Lowell at home? Guarding Henry and Violet, Mama wouldn't have left her room, and Papa would've been teaching. All the laundry and food would have been hers to do, with her poor brothers lying in a cold attic room. Suddenly she set down the iron and flew to her grandfather, burying her face in his shirt.

"Thank you, Grandpa, for letting us come here."

He patted her head. "Oh, Garnet, you know you're welcome. You all are my grandbabies."

She cried then, letting out big sobs she'd bottled up for days, wetting his shirt and snuffling.

Lorena walked in and saw them, noticed the ironing, but said nothing. Garnet raised her head and tried to stop her great gulping sobs. "And thank you, too, Lorena."

Lorena shook her head. "No thanks necessary. Now, get a piece of that cornbread and butter it while I pour you some tea."

Later, after dark, Garnet sank into the chair by Lowell's bed. She dreaded the night, sure it would snatch her brother away. Next door she could hear Luther talking to Franklin. When it was nearly bedtime, the man came in to check on the fire.

"How's Franklin?"

Luther smiled. "He was complaining for a while, but he's getting sleepy now. He don't seem near as sick as the little one." The man's smile evaporated when he looked over at Lowell, pale and still.

"He won't make it till morning, will he?" Garnet whispered.

Luther poked at the fire. "Miracles happen. And my sister ain't done fighting."

Not an hour later, Lorena walked briskly into the room. She touched Lowell's head, face, hands, and then stared at him. Garnet waited, expecting miracles to fly from the woman's hands. Abruptly she left, stopping in the hall to speak to Luther.

The next thing Garnet knew, Luther was gently undressing Lowell, wrapping him in a quilt, and carrying him down the steps. She followed, too tired to question. In the kitchen, Lorena was filling the big, oblong bath tub with first a kettle of hot water and then a bucket of cold. She tested the water and nodded at Luther who lowered Lowell into it. The boy flinched and trembled, his eyes fluttering.

Lorena nodded at Garnet. "I know the doctor said he shouldn't be chilled, but he's still burning with fever, and I reckoned that if I put him in a cool tub, it might bring it down." She took a dipper and sluiced water over Lowell's matted hair, dribbling it down his face. Luther crouched behind the child, bracing him so he wouldn't drown.

Lowell shivered, weakly thrashing his arms and legs and splashing small puddles around the tub. Distorted by the water, his pale body looked like some kind of odd river creature, caught in a huge bucket. The boy made mewling sounds that made Garnet want to rescue him, but Lorena and Luther trapped him in the tub, pouring water over him again and again. The woman rose with a grunt and held up the quilt. Luther lifted Lowell from the water, and together they wrapped him in it.

When Lowell was dry and dressed in a fresh nightshirt, Garnet tucked covers around his shivering body. Lorena sat by the fire, fanning out her skirt to dry it. "Bring your chair over. You can watch him just fine from here."

They both stared at the flames, occasionally glancing at the motionless boy. It was as if the world was holding its breath. Garnet was almost too worn to feel sleepy even though the room was quiet and warm. She felt as though she was dreaming with her eyes open, mesmerized by the licking flames and the lamplight and Lorena's rocking.

Without intending to say it, Garnet murmured, "Why does my mama hate you?"

Lorena sighed. "That's a long story and one you might not like to hear."

Garnet gestured toward Lowell's bed. "If you're meaning to stay up and watch with me, we have plenty of time."

Touching the toe of her neat, black shoe to Garnet's pallet Lorena said, "You'd best sleep some."

Garnet shook her head.

Sighing again, Lorena shifted in her chair. "I reckon it all started a long time ago. You never knowed your grandmother, Miss Caroline, but she was a fine lady from the city, raised to have the best. But when she fell in love with your grandpa, she was glad to move here and be his wife. For many years they was fine, but then Miss Caroline started feeling poorly and nobody knew what ailed her."

She nodded at the fire. "There was always some of my kin working here, either in the fields or the house. Your grandpa run around with Colsons when he and my uncles was wild, young bucks. Deke give us work when nobody else would. My cousin Ethel worked here at the house after your mother was born, and she'd go on about Deke's little red-haired gal, what a pretty little princess she was."

Lorena snorted gently. "There weren't no princesses down at Deer Creek, and I was right jealous of this little girl named Louise who was two years younger than me. Yet in another way I felt sorry for her because Ethel talked about how weak her mother was and how sad the house seemed. By the time I was fifteen and Luther was working up here, Ethel said Miss Caroline pretty much kept to her bed but was cheerful and good-natured with it. Then my cousin met a man and married him all sudden-like, and Deke come down to the house to ask my pa if I could work up here. I was happy to do it because Ethel said the work wasn't too hard, and I wanted to see the fancy house.

She paused and tilted her head at Garnet. "Actually I lived in a little cabin where your house sits now. Luther and I stayed there along with a couple of my boy cousins who worked Deke's fields, because it was too far to walk every day from Deer Creek. I did the cooking and pretty much all the work for your mother and grandparents up here at the house. Louise was still in school then."

Garnet imagined Lorena walking the path through the trees and past the barn just as she had done so many times. The woman must've worked long hours to do all of those chores, and she'd only been two years older than Garnet.

"Ethel was right; your mama was the prettiest little thing I ever seen. I starched and ironed her flouncy dresses and watched her embroider with the finest stitches you've ever seen. Louise and I, well, we sort of became friends. She didn't help me much," Lorena smiled, "but we'd talk while I was working. Her mama was too weak and sick to do much visiting, and I always thought Louise must be lonesome with no brothers and sisters. Luther and me had each other, and practically knew what each other was thinking without talking. And I had my sister and cousins in and out of the place all the time when I was growing up. Louise didn't have nobody.

Garnet watched Lorena's face, turned aside as she told her story. Emotions flickered across it with the telling, but mostly she had herself under tight control. Garnet figured the woman usually had most things under control. She went over to check on her brother. After the bath, his arms had felt cool and clammy, but now his skin was heating up again. For undoubtedly the hundredth time, she wiped his face with a wet cloth, taking care around his burnt lips and sunken eyes. The bath hadn't helped; Lorena had worked no miracles.

When Garnet returned to her chair, Lorena raised her eyebrows, but Garnet shook her head. Then the woman took a deep breath and told about her early life at the King house, how Louise would chatter about school and boys and girlfriends while Lorena ironed or canned or cooked. "She was always talking about these girls who was her best friends, but they never come out to the house, except for Alice Carter ever now and then. I felt sorry for Louise, but she would've died if she'd known that. There was always that pride, and she thought I was common."

Garnet looked down at her lap. Lorena turned from the fire and willed Garnet's eyes to meet hers. "And she still does, don't she?"

Garnet shrugged self-consciously. Things were different now. Downstairs the clock cleared its throat and chimed twelve times.

Midnight. There were so many dark hours left until morning. She glanced at Lowell who had sighed and then at Lorena whose dark head rested against the high back of the rocking chair. Her eyes were closed, but she continued speaking. "And then Miss Caroline took a turn for the worse. She never come downstairs, and she was in terrible pain. Deke moved me into the house to sleep in her room so's I could give her medicine in the night if she needed it. Poor Miss Caroline tried to be strong, but she'd cry out. I know Louise could hear her.

"It was a pity, having to see her mother suffer like that. Miss Caroline got so tiny that the bed near swallowed her. Louise would come visit her mother of a morning before she went to school and of an evening when she come home, and Miss Caroline took a little medicine before each visit so she could talk to her daughter."

"This was when my mother was sixteen?"

"Almost sixteen. And Deke was beside himself. One minute he was full of grief and guilt, just eat up with it. And then another minute he almost acted like he was mad at Miss Caroline for being sick. I swear sometimes he was ready to shake his big old fist at God and challenge him to a fight. Mostly he stayed busy in the barn or out in the fields. He never did know what to do with hisself when someone was sick." She glanced at Lowell and then moved swiftly to his bed, touching his cheek and then his hands.

"Come on, little angel, get well," she crooned. "Your sister's so worried about you."

The woman's tenderness made Garnet wonder if Lorena'd ever had children. She'd never heard of any. Lorena patted on Lowell and said meaningless, loving things to him, and then she raised his head off the pillow and coaxed a spoonful of lemon water between his lips. After slipping silently into the hall to peek into the room next door, she returned to the rocking chair saying that Franklin was asleep. Then she started talking again, rocking faster than before. "Deke brought up another one of my kinfolk to do housework and some of the cooking. I was busy most all the time with Miss Caroline. I didn't see Louise much then because, except for her two short visits a day, she wasn't in her mother's room very often. Louise didn't like watching her mother die, and I can't say I blamed her, but seemed to me like she thought I was the cause of all the misery."

She paused, and Garnet knew the hard part was coming. "Where's that hairbrush?" Lorena asked. "Set your pillow here in the floor, and I'll brush your hair."

Garnet obeyed, laying her pillow in front of Lorena's feet. She felt the woman untwist her braids and start brushing her long thick hair.

"But that's not the whole story of what was going on. The truth is that Deke King's wife had been sickly for years, and he wasn't used to doing without a woman. I had growed up, fairly pretty from what the farmhands told me, and he noticed me." The brush paused. "And I noticed him too. I liked his ways, his laugh; I still do."

Almost roughly, she turned Garnet's head until she could meet her eyes. "I swear to you on everything that's holy that we never did nothing until your grandmother died," she declared. "Never, never would I have betrayed that sweet woman even though your mother thinks I did."

She pushed Garnet's head forward, gently this time and resumed the lovely brushing. "But there was looks, and we'd stand closer than we should've. The sparks was flying out of control, ready every minute to make a fire big enough to destroy the county. And even though I thought we was being secret, I'm sure Louise noticed.

"Anyway, we was nearly eat up with it, him needing a woman because he was used to it and me needing a man because I'd never had one. You may think we was wicked, child, and maybe we was, watching Miss Caroline die and at the same time thinking about what each other's kisses would taste like. Yes, it was wrong, but we controlled it as much as we could."

Garnet didn't know what to think. Shadowy images of her parents' hunger for each other, which she half-noticed and consciously ignored, overlaid the absurd picture of her grandfather ever participating in such acts. She had no other reference for what Lorena was telling her. The clock chimed once. Was that for a quarter hour, a half hour, or was it one o'clock? Lorena divided Garnet's hair and started braiding it.

"You're too young to understand all this, ain't you?" Lorena asked gently. "You probably haven't had such feelings and urges yet. And those of us who do look wild and sloppy to you."

Yes, thought Garnet.

"But I'll guarantee you that at sixteen, Louise King knew exactly what we was feeling. She was no hussy, but she was a flirt, and a little bit of kiss and tickle wasn't foreign to her." Garnet strained to turn around, but the woman was twisting her hair too tightly.

"I'll not get into that; it has nothing to do with you or me, but I know what I know, and Louise understood exactly what kind of flame was burning between her daddy and me."

Lorena pulled a few pins from her coil of dark hair and held them between her teeth. Twisting Garnet's braids into a mass, she fastened them up with a few well-placed pins. Chuckling, she said, "I know you're too young to wear your hair up, but it sure does look pretty."

Released, Garnet rose and went to the mottled mirror over the dresser. She couldn't see well in the dim room, but an elegant, adult shadow appeared in front of her. In spite of herself she smiled and turned her head, first one way and then the other. "You look an awful lot like your mama," Lorena said, lifting her dark brows. "You got the same complexion, fair but not that milky white some redheads have." Lorena smiled. "I guess I'd better take it down."

She removed the pins and let the heavy braids thud against Garnet's back. "Of course the hair's the same; she used to have as much gold in hers as you do." The woman ran a finger down Garnet's cheek. "And the same fine bones and big blue eyes. Lord, they'll be flocking to you in a year or two just like they did to your mama." She scrutinized Garnet's body. "You'll have her figure too, all round and womanly, once you start eating again. I was always straight as a stick, no bosoms at all."

Garnet was glad the dim light hid her blushes. The last thing she wanted was to be examined by a bunch of old boys. From the next room they could hear Luther's slow step replying to Franklin's request for water. "Should I check on Franklin?"

"Luther's tending him. Rest yourself."
The quiet settled in again around them. Both of them checked on Lowell, noticing no change in his light breathing or feverish skin. The clock struck two, and Lorena rocked. She looked tired, her pale skin drawn around her mouth.

Suddenly she started talking again, anxious to finish the story. "Miss Caroline died in June. It was almost a relief to bury her after all that pain and suffering. We'd already cried ourselves dry. Louise said she wasn't going back to school no more, that she was going to be mistress of her daddy's house. I couldn't help but wonder if she was going to be doing all the cleaning and cooking for him when she hadn't never lifted more than a finger in the past. But Deke and I was free then, and, I hate to admit it, we didn't pay much attention to Princess Louise.

"I moved back to the cabin. Deke let my cousin go, and despite Louise waving a feather duster around and maybe sewing on a button, they still needed me."

Agitated by guilt, Garnet interrupted, "But Mama does lots of work now!" It wasn't the truth.

Lorena bowed her head. "I'm sure she does. But she was only sixteen, and, after all, I was hired help and there'd always been hired help at the King house. It was what she was used to."

The woman went on, "Only a fool wouldn't have seen what was going on between Deke and me, and your mother's no fool. Lord, we didn't care. In the barn, in the cabin, in the fields, we took every opportunity we could catch. And Louise, doing her crocheting in the front room, cool and dainty, couldn't help but notice. She quit talking to me but kept sidling up to her daddy, asking him for favors, for new dresses, for advice. He ate it up because he loves your mama. The fact that she won't have nothing to do with him any more breaks his heart. At the time she acted like the way we was carrying on had nothing to do with him. Back then, it was all my doing, but now she's punishing him too."

Most of Lorena's story had been calmly told, but here there was anger. "Of course I was bound to get in the family way. Fool that I was, I expected he'd marry me. Why, I'd been keeping his house for years; it only seemed natural that a widower would marry me. But my plan didn't take Louise into account.

"I swear Deke wanted to marry me. He got all excited about the baby, hoping for a whole passel of kids. Then his daughter got a hold of him. She didn't want nobody common like me being her step-mother, she didn't want nobody influencing her daddy, and she didn't want nobody's children taking her daddy's attention off her. Deke must've told her about the baby; I didn't. Ever since her mother's funeral, she only talked to me to boss me around, never friendly like we used to be. As soon as she found out about the baby, she didn't talk to me at all. Oh, she's called me names, but we've not spoken for all these years.

"So quick as a minute, Deke started talking about how Tom McDaniel had his eye on me and wanted to court me. I cried and cried thinking Deke didn't love me and wondering why he was passing me along like used goods. He told me Louise made him do it, that Louise had lost her mother and didn't want to lose him too. I could tell it grieved him near as much as me, and somehow I got used to the idea."

She stopped, the emotion nearly as raw as it'd been more than twenty years ago. "What would it have hurt?" Garnet whispered.

"What do you mean?"

"What would it have hurt for you to marry Grandpa? You were in love. You were carrying his baby. There wasn't anything wrong with you marrying."

Lorena's eyes traveled to the dim ceiling and then landed squarely on Garnet's face. "Louise disapproved, and that was that. I married Tom McDaniel, never knowing whether he believed the child I was carrying was his or not. I had to leave Deke's arms and go directly to Tom for him to have a chance at believing the baby was his. He was a quiet, easy man, and although we never had two dimes to rub together, we got along all right. I cheated him because I never loved him, and I cheated him because sometimes I'd go to Deke. Tom knew, but he never let on, and I'm ashamed of that.

"So that's the story," Lorena said with a sigh. "I ain't sure if it answers the question of why your mama hates me, but I know she never wanted me to marry her father and it about killed her when I did."

"And he's happy now."

"I do believe he is."

"Was it your Cashmere Bouquet I used to smell here on Saturdays?"

Lorena chuckled. "Yes, honey. Deke always buys it for me as a treat. I made sure I was never here on Saturdays when you came to clean, but I reckon the scent lingered." Her smile faded. "I hated being a sneak, but I love my man. I'll allow that I'm common, but I know how to be true in my heart Now, lay yourself down. I'll watch the boy."

Garnet shook her head. Leaning against the woman's legs she asked, "What happened to the baby?"

When Lorena didn't answer, Garnet glanced back to see her staring at the fire. "The baby died when I was about six months along. I was terrible, dreadful sick, so sick they thought I was going to die too. They said Deke come down to Deer Creek and set on a stump the other side of the road for two days. They said he had big tears running down his face. I lived. But I never could have another baby."

Garnet couldn't figure out what had awakened her. She sat straight up, bumping her head on the cutting table. Lorena must have eased her down onto the pallet. With the fire no more than ruddy embers, the room was darker than ever. Lorena slept in the rocking chair with her head resting against its back and a shawl wrapped around her shoulders. Then she heard a definite noise: Lowell was thrashing around in the bed.

She hurried to him, fearing the worst. Twisting from one side to the other, he threw an arm out over the blankets and then pulled his knees toward his chest. Garnet touched his forehead, his cheeks, his neck. He was drenched in sweat, slimy with it. She shouted, "Lorena, I think he's dying!"

The woman leapt up as if she'd never been asleep. She patted on Lowell, feeling his head and arms, and then a sweet smile transformed her grim face. "The fever's broke. That's why he's sweating."

Lowell grunted and wriggled, calling out, "Mama!"

"It's Garnet, honey. I'm here."

"Nettie?"

"Yes, it's your Nettie."

He looked around the room as if he'd never seen it before, giving Lorena a deep but friendly gaze. He stared past them to the doorway where Deke stood, awakened by Garnet's shout and standing with his fists clenched at his side, ready to wrestle with the Angel of Death. Peering over Deke's bald head was Luther.

Then Lowell said plaintively, "I'm nearly itching to death, Nettie."

Lorena chuckled low in her throat, and the joy spread to Garnet, to Grandpa, and to Luther like a ripple in a river. "That means you're healing, angel," Lorena said. "Luther? Dip out a dab of lard and bring it up here, would you? We'll grease this boy down like a piglet ready for the oven."

Grandpa tiptoed from the doorway until he was close to the bed. "Grandpa," Lowell said on a sigh. He was pitifully weak, but he was Lowell again. Grandpa grabbed his hand.

"You were killing a bear."

"Just a dream." There was a catch in his voice.

Garnet was busy wiping the clammy sweat from the boy's neck and chest. He shut his eyes for a moment. "Nettie, I'm mighty thirsty."

Thrilled to hear those words, they propped him in their arms and the child swallowed big gulps of water. Then Lorena pulled Garnet into the hall and marched her into the big bedroom. Grandpa had dressed and gone downstairs, declaring that five-thirty in the morning was an excellent time to be starting the day. Lorena poked the nightgown she'd loaned Garnet into her chest and said, "Put this on and climb into bed. You need more than three hours of sleep."

"And I don't reckon you need more than that?"

"Feisty, ain't you? I'll catch a nap later."

The woman was turning to go when Garnet called, "Lorena? Thank you."

Lorena ducked her head, again ready to leave, but Garnet spoke up once more. "Lorena?" The woman waited. "Would you teach me how to make biscuits?"

Lorena's laugh came from her belly and blossomed into a broad smile that crinkled her nose and showed gaps in the back of her mouth. "Sure. I'll teach you how to make biscuits."

***

She had no idea how long she'd slept. Outside the clouds lay heavy and low, and occasional flakes of snow drifted lazily, catching on the yew where a brilliant male cardinal perched in a tiny cavern of needles. She stretched, catching scent of Grandpa's bay rum and Lorena's Cashmere Bouquet from the pillows. Both made her smile. Before she went downstairs she peeked in to see Lowell accepting spoonsful of broth from Luther and poked her head into the other bedroom where Franklin slept quietly. The kitchen was warm and smelled eggy and rich from the custard Lorena stirred at the stove. She said that Dr. Thomas had been and gone, proclaiming that Lowell was on the mend but still mighty weak. Franklin, he stated, appeared to have a milder case.

Lorena handed her a plate of breakfast she'd kept warm, and Garnet ate ravenously, wondering if she'd get a taste of the custard later. Grandpa came in the back door, shaking off snow and stomping his feet. He put a cold hand on her head. "I see sleepyhead has finally joined us."

She grinned at him

He asked Lorena for a cup of coffee. "I'll get warm, maybe sit with the boys, and then I'd best see John and tell him his sons are doing better." Catching Garnet's eye, he went on. "Dr. Thomas says Lowell needs six or eight weeks of quiet, warmth, and care before he's out of danger. So I reckon I'll tell your papa that the three of you have to stay eight more weeks. No sense rushing things."

Garnet twisted the end of her braid. "I should go home. I don't reckon I'd bring the sickness to them, and Mama probably needs me."

Grandpa and Lorena looked at each other across Garnet. "Well," he said, "I think Lorena might need you here to help take care of the boys. It's an awful lot of work for her."

"Deke King!" Lorena exclaimed. "You know I can handle the work." Then she smiled at Garnet. "But I'd love to have your company, and we've got us some cooking lessons to take care of. I reckon the boys would feel more comfortable with you here."

"Then I guess I'd better stay with the boys, Grandpa."

"Good! Then it's settled."

So, for eight weeks, Garnet and her brothers lived in the warm cocoon of Grandpa's house. Everyone was busy and happy to help with whatever needed doing. As the doctor predicted, Franklin was up and strong weeks before Lowell fully recovered. Wrapped snugly, Franklin went to the barn to see his beloved mules and horses. His perpetual scowl softened as he followed Grandpa like a fond puppy. Occasionally he'd exult in the fact that he wasn't attending school, but his grandfather always called him down on that and reminded him that he must go back soon.

At first Lowell was content to lie in bed and doze between everyone's visits, but eventually he became bored, demanding checker games and attention. Unlike his brother, he yearned for school. Garnet quizzed him to see how far he'd progressed and started working with him on his writing, numbers, and reading. His quickness amazed her. As he became stronger, Lowell tagged along after anyone who would tolerate him, especially Luther, who, Garnet suspected, could tolerate most anything.

"He's peaceful, isn't he?" Garnet observed, biting off a thread. She was in the kitchen, hemming the dress that Lorena had helped her make.

"Who, Luther? Well, he's always helpful, and you don't have to tell him what to do. I reckon that's peaceful," Lorena replied as she stopped her mopping for a moment. With all the traffic in and out of the kitchen, there were always muddy patches.

"He never married?"

"No, he was always shy. Can't do much courting if you won't open your mouth."

Those cozy afternoons in the kitchen stretched on for weeks. January brought a bit of snow from time to time, but a storm in early February blanketed the farm, making it into a winter fairyland. At night the sky was pink, and they made popcorn and sang. Even Luther chimed in on the old hymns.

Once the snow cleared enough for Grandpa to get out, he visited Mattie Lawrence to get supplies. He brought greetings from the storekeeper who said she was missing Garnet's help. "I reckon you can go tomorrow if you want." Grandpa said. "I told her you'd probably like to get out of the house."

"I'd like that, Grandpa, but if I can work there, shouldn't I be working at home?"

He lifted the lid on a pot of soup and sniffed. "I don't think it matters much. I'm not sure your folks would even know unless they happened to go to the store."

It didn't seem quite honest to Garnet, but she was happy to walk to the little store the next morning in the bright, cold air. Mrs. Lawrence remarked that she was a sight for sore eyes, inquired about her brothers, and put a feather duster in her hands. The house, never tidy under the best of conditions, had suffered in Garnet's absence. Garnet straightened and stacked, swept and dusted, all the while listening to chatter from the store. When there was a lull, Mrs. Lawrence sat with a noisy sigh. "I should've expected all this trade today after the snow, but my feet aren't one bit happy about it." She motioned to Garnet. "Set a spell, and tell me how everything's going up at Deke's."

"Grandpa seems tickled to have us." She didn't mention how she and Franklin dreaded going home.

Mrs. Lawrence nodded, the light glinting off her spectacles. "And Lorena? Did you two make up?"

Garnet looked down at her hands. "I'm ashamed of how I talked about her. She's been nothing but kindness, and I'm convinced she saved Lowell from the scarlet fever. And," Garnet looked up with a sheepish grin, "she's so much fun! Why, she helped me make a dress, and she jokes and sings. I like her."

The older woman kept nodding. "It's not hard to figure out what Deke sees in her, is it? Even though folks say harsh things, and I'm not denying some of them's true, she holds herself well."

The door's bell tinkled, and Mrs. Lawrence hoisted herself out of the chair. Garnet glanced into the store and saw a short, red-faced man standing at the counter. She'd never seen him before, which was an oddity in itself. He shook Mrs. Lawrence's hand, all the time joking and laughing. From her cash register, Mrs. Lawrence handed him an envelope, and he nearly bounced up and down with good humor and quick talk. More customers came in, and it was after Garnet had eaten her quick noontime meal that she had a chance to ask Mrs. Lawrence who the man was.

"Oh, that's Walter Foster, the carpenter, and ain't he a character through and through? Why, I've never seen a man with so many jokes and such a ready smile." She chuckled. "He's the one who makes the little wooden toys. He was picking up the money for the ones I sold through Christmas."

"Is that the same man who made the walnut cabinet for Grandpa?"

"The very same. He's quite a craftsman, but he'll do most anything: carve toys, build houses, anything in the carpentry line. Did you see that cabinet? Is it pretty?"

Garnet nodded. "It's beautiful with cunning little doors and carved trim on the outside. Grandpa gave it to Lorena as a wedding present."

"Walter and his boy live down the road a piece, toward Deer Creek. He has him an acre or so up there with his workshop and a little house. Let's see, his boy, I forget his name, is about your age, and he helps his daddy with the work. They come from further north in the state, moved around a lot after Walter's wife died, he says. I don't know how they ended up in Evans County." The man obviously intrigued Mrs. Lawrence. "They say he drinks," she said. "And that's a terrible sin, but I don't know if it's true. My daughter in Ashton said she'd heard that, but I don't like to gossip."

Garnet bit her lip and asked if Mrs. Lawrence if she'd seen her mother or father and how things were at home. "No, honey, I ain't seen your mama since way before the baby was born, but your papa's been in a time or two. He told me when you all went to Deke's and how bad Lowell was. He seemed kind of embarrassed that Louise sent you all off, but I can't blame her for worrying about the babies. It's just odd that she won't speak to her daddy or his wife, but then she sends her children to them."

And then it seemed like no time when one morning at breakfast Grandpa sighed mightily and declared that all good things must come to an end. The weeks had sped by, and it was time for Franklin and Lowell to go to back to school and the Grants to return home. Lorena announced that she'd prepare a huge dinner for them on Sunday and they could leave on Monday morning. Garnet and Lorena baked a blackberry jam cake and polished the grand dining room table, setting out Miss Caroline's good dishes. Precisely at one o'clock on Sunday, Lorena called them to a full table. Both boys had regained their appetites although Lowell was more interested in jam cake than mashed potatoes. Garnet could hardly chew for smiling. Grandpa teased Franklin about school, saying he'd probably forgotten how to read and write. The boys wriggled and ate, supremely happy, and Garnet gave silent thanks. And Luther was, well, just Luther, she thought. His lean dark face creased into a quiet smile from time to time as he enjoyed both the food and the company. Garnet laughed and chattered too, feeling elegant in her new dress, russet like the prettiest fall leaves. Just for today, Lorena had let her put her hair up in a crown of braids like she'd done the night Lowell's fever broke.

She noticed that the chatter stopped and had to ask Lowell to repeat his question. "What I asked, Garnet, was when are we coming back to visit Grandpa and Lorena and Luther?" he repeated, irritated that she hadn't paid attention.

"I don't know." What difference would these last weeks have made to Mama?

Lorena paused then spoke, focusing on arranging her silverware. "As I see it, your mother sent you children to us because she needed a place for you all to get well. Now, she may not like it, but how can she forbid you from coming when she was the one who sent you here?"

"That's true! That's my wise wife!" Grandpa bellowed.

Garnet considered this. "Seems to me that lots of people go visiting on Sunday afternoons. Why couldn't we?"

"Yes, yes, yes!" Lowell exclaimed, clapping his hands.

"Now, I'd have to see to dinner at home and all that," Garnet warned. "But then we could come visit. It would be best, though, if we just did it like it was normal."

"I always say it's better to ask forgiveness than permission," Grandpa declared. Garnet smiled. She just bet this had been his way.

Franklin had been quiet. He scooted back his chair and announced, "I've got something to say."

Grandpa glanced away.

"Grandpa and I have talked, and I've decided I'm going to live up here instead of at the house," Franklin said.

Lorena shook her head.

"I'll still go to school and see Papa there. If he needs me for something I'll help out. But there's a lot more work for me here than at the house. Grandpa needs me."

Lowell frowned. "We'd only see you on Sundays?"

"And at school, silly brother."

Lowell didn't like it. "But what about Caesar? You love old Caesar."

They all laughed. Franklin said, "I reckon Papa's been taking care of him these last several weeks when I couldn't. But I'll tell you what, on Sundays I'll teach you how to do it. That would be a big help to Papa."

This pleased Lowell, but Garnet saw trouble. "She will have an absolute fit."

Franklin shrugged and suddenly looked so grown up that Garnet hardly knew him. "So she'll have a fit. I'm sorry if it comes down on you, Garnet, but what can she really do? Do you think for a minute she'll come up here and snatch me away?"

"No, she'll make Papa do that."

"Maybe. But as long as I'm in school, I don't think Papa can force me home."

Lorena tapped her lips with her fingers. "It's asking for trouble."

Grandpa spoke up. "And how can it be any worse than it already is? My own daughter won't speak to me. I've never seen my new grandson. Violet wouldn't know me. If Louise begrudges Franklin and me the joy of each other she'll just have to get over it. She can't control her children's actions forever. Besides, I've always said this here boy is a natural born farmer, especially with animals. He should be able to choose what he's good at."

There was nothing more to say since both Franklin and Grandpa were determined. Garnet would miss him; she relied on Franklin. There'd be some kind of outburst, but she'd lived through those before too. Mostly she was envious. After the boys were past the danger from scarlet fever, the days at Grandpa's had been heaven. She'd miss the friendliness, the laughter, but she stiffened her back and reminded herself that she missed her parents and the babies too. If Grandpa needed Franklin, which she doubted, her parents needed her.

On Monday morning Garnet walked home. The sky was a chilly, milky blue, but somewhere deep in her nose, she smelled the fresh, damp smell that forecast spring. Before long she'd be turning over the clotted soil and planting her garden. She spied crocus tips emerging from the ground, and soon the lilies she'd planted around the house would be sending up fragile sprouts.

Garnet wore the russet dress Lorena had made her, figuring she'd get all the uproar over at once. The dress would be the least of it when Mama heard about Franklin. She debated whether it would be better to tell her mother or let the news emerge when Papa came home after school. It was all she could do not to slow her pace when she saw the house.

As soon as she walked in the kitchen her nose was confronted by ugly odors. Violet sat on the kitchen floor playing with an amber onion skin. The condition of her diaper explained one scent. The little girl looked up from under her rampant curls and stared at Garnet, grinning and showing an additional tooth that she started using on the onion skin. "No, no, Violet," Garnet said. Violet clouded up and glared.

The onion skin wasn't the only debris on the floor. And grease-encrusted dishes sat by the sink. She'd have a busy morning.

Then Mama sailed into the room. "I thought I heard you," she said. Garnet and her mother steadily appraised each other without speaking. Mama noted the new dress, and Garnet saw her mother's frowsy hair, thickened waist, and milk-stained bodice. The silence was increasingly uncomfortable until Garnet couldn't stand it. "Where's Henry?"

"Sleeping."

Mama raised her hand to indicate the kitchen. "You'd better change your dress."

PART TWO

February 1907

Chapter One

Grandpa died the summer before Garnet turned sixteen. She remembered exactly when she'd heard the news. That morning had been miserably hot and muggy, and heavy dew blotched her faded dress. She'd been picking tomatoes. Lowell was gathering the last of the cucumbers.

She hadn't noticed Franklin tearing around the side of the house until she heard his ragged panting. Franklin rarely came home. She saw him only on Sundays when she and Lowell visited the farm. It took him a minute to catch his breath, but even before he said anything, Garnet knew something was wrong. She'd straightened and waited for him to speak in his strange new voice. The cracking stage had embarrassed him, but Grandpa had found it so funny that even Franklin couldn't take it too seriously.

After breakfast, Franklin said, Grandpa had been sitting on the front porch when Lorena heard a crash and found him lying on the floor. She'd thought that he'd fainted, but he was dead, just like that. She'd run up to the tobacco field and waved her apron, screaming herself hoarse until Luther and Franklin came to help, but there was nothing to be done.

Lowell, nearly invisible on the other side of the pole beans, heard and rushed to them with tears overflowing. She put her arms around him and asked Franklin if he'd told their mother. He scowled and said he reckoned Garnet could do that.

That day had been a bad dream that wouldn't fade. Mama had been skinning tomatoes, and Violet and Henry had been squabbling. Garnet told her mother about Grandpa and said she reckoned she'd go up to the farm. Mama had answered that she would not; there was canning to finish. Mama never betrayed so much as an ounce of emotion about her father's death as the two of them worked through the day.

78

When Papa'd come home, limp and exhausted by his long ride from Gert and Fanny's farm, Mama had told him tersely that Grandpa was dead. Papa had been washing up at the sink, and his shoulders slumped when he heard the news. He'd said he was sorry to hear it. And that was that. Papa rarely talked much anymore.

After supper Garnet had washed her face, put up her hair, and walked to Grandpa's house. Mama made no comment. Garnet reckoned her mother had an uncanny way of knowing just how far she could control her children without causing total rebellion. Not three paces down the path, Lowell joined Garnet, and both of them gazed at Grandpa's empty chair on the porch. They'd gone to the kitchen where Lorena, idle for once, slumped at the table and stared at the floor. Garnet and Lowell had gone to her, each taking a hand, and the three of them cried together.

Sitting in church months later, Garnet remembered all this, remembered the funeral where they'd gathered in their suffocating best clothes and listened to the preacher drone on about the promise of heaven. The service had drawn a large crowd since Deke King had been a popular man and a scandalous one, at least in his youth, and Papa said that folks seem to revere rascals more than saints. Lorena had sat straight and rigid, ignoring those who whispered about her. Luther and Franklin had flanked her, daring the world to say a word. Mama hadn't attended, and this was cause for gossip too. Papa had come with Garnet and Lowell, and she'd wondered how he'd dared to defy Mama. She had mentioned her father's death only once when she'd announced at supper that she guessed old Deke was in hell now. Violet's and Henry's eyes had widened more at her word than her meaning. Those two had no memory of their grandfather. And that was a shame.

Others would miss him too, she guessed. Gert and Fanny Clark had attended with their very dignified, handsome brother Clifford, and Mattie Lawrence had closed her store to walk to church. From Deer Creek, a flock of assorted Colsons stood apart from the main crowd at the gravesite.

And so, on an unusually mild day in January, Garnet sat in the fusty little Bethel church in the very same pew as she had for Grandpa's funeral. These weren't happy memories, but important ones, and sometimes she picked at them like uneven stitches she must unravel just to feel the emotions again. Lowell was getting impatient for the service to begin and craned his head around to see who was there. Once he waved at someone, and Garnet elbowed him. "Why, I was just saying hello to Mrs. Lawrence. You don't want me to be unfriendly, do you?"

Garnet had always gone to church, first because she was made to and then because it was a comforting habit. These days Lowell came with her. Papa rarely attended any more. He seemed too tired to do much of anything on Sundays. Mama hadn't set foot in church since long before Grandpa's funeral in August. And now she had an excuse because she was expecting again. Garnet sighed. It seemed like the more Papa shrank, the more Mama blossomed. After all the babies, it was hard to find a waistline on Mama, but Papa just wasted away no matter how much he ate. His eyes glittered feverishly sometimes, and he never seemed to get rid of his cough. But he didn't complain.

At least the house was in better shape now. Grandpa had left Mama five-hundred dollars, which seemed like a fortune to Garnet, but she knew that if he hadn't married Lorena, the entire farm would've come to his daughter. It probably made Mama resent that marriage even more, but Mama never said anything. They had used the money to hire Walter Foster and his son to work on their house. The Fosters built walls upstairs so Garnet and Violet had a room with a door, like Lowell and Henry. And they painted inside and out, making the poor old place look a little better. Mr. Foster was bluff and cheery, always joking and whistling. And his son David seemed to need to smile at Garnet any time she came close. She talked to him a little, learning he was her age and that he had eyes that nearly crinkled shut when he smiled.

"David Foster is waving at you," Lowell said. She hissed at him to sit still.

Two weeks in a row now he'd attended Bethel Baptist Church, and last Sunday he'd fallen all over himself to speak to her after the service. Lowell grinned. "He must think you're pretty."

Garnet glared at Lowell but couldn't control her blushes, which made Lowell grin even more. The last three Saturdays, David Foster had managed to visit Mattie Lawrence's store while Garnet was working. Swearing that her feet were killing her, Mrs. Lawrence had finally allowed Garnet to serve customers on Saturday afternoons after cleaning and straightening in the mornings. David always came in the afternoons and never bought much, just a box of matches or a few potatoes. After he'd leave, Mrs. Lawrence, who sat in the room adjacent to the store with her shoes unbuttoned, would say, "That boy's sweet on you, Garnet Grant. He only comes in here on Saturdays."

Garnet wasn't so sure she wanted anybody sweet on her. David seemed nice enough, pleasant and clean, but she had too much to do at home to be bothered with such nonsense, she told Mattie Lawrence. The woman raised her eyebrows and cackled like an old hen.
Where was that preacher? Lowell was getting restless, and the service hadn't even started yet. Restless, she thought. She was restless too. The monotonous days tumbled over each other, full of housework and tedious chores. Her only respites were working at the store on Saturdays and going to church and the farm on Sundays. Although she'd figured Mama would put an end to the Sunday visits once Grandpa died, Lowell and Garnet continued to escape for an hour or two every week. It was Garnet's only chance to see Franklin, and this was the case for Lowell now too since Franklin had quit school last fall. Papa had just sighed at that and put a hand on Lowell's shoulder. Her bright little brother had become the scholar of the family.

Brother Bledsoe appeared with a big smile and a hearty voice. They sang a hymn, accompanied by his wife on the tinny, old piano. It was a singing church, and Garnet enjoyed the music. She and Lowell had most of the old hymns memorized, which was a good thing because there were only a few battered songbooks and most of those were missing chunks of pages. Although she loved the singing and considered herself a Christian, a good Baptist, Garnet rarely thought about religion. As she'd grown older, part of the pleasure of going was in fixing her hair or cajoling Mama into letting her wear her gold bar pin. When Brother Bledsoe finished his sermon and the congregation stood to sing the last hymn, Garnet half-turned to catch a glimpse of David Foster, three rows back. He was watching her and smiled when he caught her eye. She wondered if he'd want to walk her home.

He did, and she let him since Lowell was with her. She was thankful for the Foster boy's steady, easy chatter because she didn't know what to say. David then spoke about the new office building he and his father were finishing in Ashton. Glad to have a topic, Garnet asked how many rooms there were, what paint colors they were using, who'd be moving into it, and soon they were at the swinging bridge. If he thinks I'm inviting him in, she vowed, he's going to be disappointed. She smiled at David and said good-bye, but her smile had more to do with the thought of him sitting in the front room with Henry and Violet crawling all over him and her pregnant mother playing the grand lady in a frayed old dress. She crossed the bridge behind Lowell and felt flushed and odd when she realized that David lingered on the other side, watching her walk.

That night, though, as she snuggled under a thick layer of quilts, she thought about David, how he was only a few inches taller than she but had strong, wide shoulders. She liked his crinkly eyes which, she'd discovered months ago, were a clear, distant gray, like the sky in March. He seemed to like her, but she really didn't know why. He didn't know her well enough to have much of an opinion. Maybe Lowell was right about him thinking she was pretty. Huh, with those dressed up girls in Ashton, surely he'd seen prettier girls, but it was comforting to think someone liked her looks.

Stretching until her feet hit the iron bars at the foot of the bed, Garnet wondered what it would be like to kiss a boy. She'd practiced on her own hand, scrunching her thumb and forefinger together to imitate another set of lips, but she still regarded anything to do with that sort of nonsense as disgusting. It was difficult, however, to ignore the sensual currents in her house. She thought of how Mama sometimes swayed toward Papa or rested her long-fingered hand on his pants' leg. How Papa's voice became hoarse when Mama pressed her breasts against his arm. She knew what it meant, or, rather, she didn't, but she didn't really want to and besides, they were married. Was that what walking home from church with a boy could lead to? Couples courted, married, coupled. Was he imagining similar scenes with her? She shivered, even though the heavy quilts made a warm cave of her bed, and forced herself to think about other things: gardens, stores, pretty dresses. But these days her old fantasies were harder to find.

Chapter Two

After supper Garnet hurried with her work, taking special care to wipe the kitchen table and replace the stained tablecloth. Henry was playing with Lowell's old wooden cart, driving it around chair legs and making horse noises. He was an odd child, saying little and looking unreasonably adult for having just turned three. Glancing up at Garnet, he gave her his heart-breakingly sweet smile, and she bent to give him a hug. Violet tyrannized him at every opportunity, and Garnet wasn't always able to rescue him. "We'll be reading soon, Henry, and you can fight with swords or dance between the scenes."

He nodded, his blue eyes serious and wide. Like a sudden gust of wind, Violet blew into the kitchen saying it was time to dance, dance, dance. The opposite of her little brother, she was robust, nearly chubby, with equally plump, glossy curls all over her head. She had a liking for ribbons and often insisted upon several at a time, in all colors, being tied around her curls.

Violet whirled around and around, singing in a loud tuneless voice. "You'll get dizzy, Violet," Garnet warned and tried to stop her spinning.

"No!" she exclaimed and slapped at Garnet's hand, but she did stop spinning. She gave her sister a shrewd glance and lifted the lid on the lard can. Scooping out a dollop with a finger, she slid it into her mouth, watching Garnet the entire time.

Garnet shuddered. "You shouldn't do that, Violet. Lard's nasty just to eat, and it's dirty to put your finger in it."

Her head flounced up, sending a banner of curls flying, but Violet could hear her parents coming from the front room so she replaced the lid. Thank God she'd be going to school in the fall, Garnet thought. Violet wouldn't behave for her at all, and if scolded, would run to Mama for comfort..

Papa settled at the kitchen table and opened a thick, blue book. Close behind him came Mama, graceful despite her girth. After Christmas, Papa'd announced that in the New Year they would read all of Shakespeare's plays together as a family. So they'd started on New Year's Day and read two or three scenes each night. Passing the book around, Papa and Lowell read the men's parts, Garnet and Mama read the women's parts, and Henry and Violet would either dance, sing, or enact sword fights between the scenes. Sometimes they had a hard time waiting for the breaks.

"Where's Lowell?" Papa asked.

"I'll get him." Garnet called up the steps. More and more Lowell retreated to his room to read. He'd devoured the few books in the house as well as those from Grandpa's until Papa had arranged for him to borrow from the elementary teacher, Miss Carter, who had a fine collection. He was still a sweet boy, and Garnet didn't know what she'd do without him, but when he could, he sneaked away to read, all bundled up in quilts in his cold room, and it frustrated her to be rousting him out all the time.

Papa had started them on A Midsummer Night's Dream, which they'd enjoyed, and now they were finishing Othello. Mama's voice, golden and cultured, read the part of Desdemona, but in tonight's scene, Desdemona died and they listened with grave faces as Papa intoned Othello's tragic grief. Lowell relished Iago's evil ambitions, making dire faces when he spoke. Although there wasn't much for Garnet to read, she envisioned the vivid action and the homely kitchen became a glamorous and dreamy place. When they finished, Henry still wanted to fight with his cardboard sword, but Violet stamped her foot and said they must dance. "It should be a sad dance, Violet," Mama murmured.

This didn't matter to Violet who repeated her earlier whirling spins until she fell into Papa's lap. He said, "Tomorrow we'll start another play."

"Which one, Papa?" Lowell asked. Although he loved their family readings, the pace was too slow for someone who gulped books like water.

Papa considered for a moment. "I think we'll do another sad one, Romeo and Juliet, the star-crossed lovers."

Lowell wrinkled his nose, but Mama placed her beautiful, white hand on top of Papa's darker one. "Are there swords?" Henry asked. He whipped his around so fast the cardboard bent.

"Oh yes, there are swords, Henry. And love and death and suspense."

"Now bedtime," Garnet announced. Henry reluctantly placed his limp sword by the cabinet. Violet, however, stamped her foot and said she wasn't going to bed, she wasn't tired, but she was hungry.

Papa, who did look tired, said nothing but patted both younger children on their heads and went into the front room to replace the book on his desk. Mama floated behind him, nodding at Garnet to handle it. As soon as they were out of the room, Violet sidled over to the lard can.

"Violet!"

"I'm hungry."

"Then I'll fix you a piece of bread and jam. You mustn't eat lard," Garnet said. She sliced two pieces of bread, one for Violet and one for Henry who hadn't asked but looked as if he needed it more than Violet. Garnet raised an eyebrow to Lowell, but he shook his head.

Violet was stormy. "Don't want no nasty bread and jam."

"Talk about nasty," Garnet muttered, spreading blackberry jam.

Lowell caught Violet's hand. "You know, I can understand why you eat lard. It's creamy and smooth, like the ice cream we had in Ashton last summer, isn't it?"

She nodded warily.

"The trouble is, lard is pure fat. It comes from pigs, and you know how fat pigs are. So if you eat lard, you'll soon be fat like a pig, and you don't want that, do you?"

She shook her head. Garnet turned her head to hide a smile.

"Because, Violet, do you know what'll happen if you get too fat?" He paused, giving her time to imagine all kinds of consequences. She nodded her head, yes.

"That's right," he agreed as if she'd spoken. And in a loud whisper he said, "If you eat lard and get very, very fat, then you won't be pretty."

Her eyes were huge. Garnet was shaking, but she managed to set the bread and jam on the table and get the two younger children settled. They ate, she supervised their washing up, and she sent them, unusually subdued, upstairs to bed. Finally Garnet collapsed at the table and laughed long and hard. "I swear I don't know how you do it, but you always find a way to make her behave."

Lowell shrugged, but there was a proud gleam in his eyes. "You try too hard to make sense with her, Garnet. What you have to do is make everything affect her. All she cares about is herself."

The next evening they did start Romeo and Juliet, and Garnet loved it. She would've preferred reading the part of Juliet, who her father said was even younger than Garnet, not that she should get any ideas. Mama read Juliet, however, and Garnet took the parts of Lady Capulet and the Nurse. She knew she'd be missing a few nights of reading soon, and, although she regretted this, she was far too excited about her plans to give much thought to Shakespeare.

On Saturday, Mrs. Lawrence had asked Garnet if she'd mind the store, by herself, the next Friday and Saturday, and stay until Sunday afternoon, even though the store was, of course, never open on Sundays. Toothache had plagued the woman for weeks, and her daughter had arranged to take her mother to Ashton to have her teeth pulled.

Garnet had said that she must ask her father but that she'd like to help Mrs. Lawrence, who yammered on about everything Garnet would need to know from where to hide the money to how to deal with her chickens and cats. Papa had given permission, but only if Franklin agreed to stay in the house at night. Her brother swaggered a bit when she'd asked him and announced that she'd better have a nice supper waiting for him both evenings. Garnet had rolled her eyes at him.

So Friday morning, long before dawn, Garnet dressed and snatched Mama's satchel that she'd packed the night before. Downstairs only Papa stirred, making coffee and preparing to shave. His eyebrows raised as she pulled on her coat. "No breakfast?"

"I can get something at the store, and besides, Mrs. Lawrence was absolutely frantic that I get there by six-thirty."

Papa whipped his mug of shaving soap into lather. "You know everything you're supposed to do?"

"I've been tending the store on Saturdays for months now."

Holding the foamy brush close to his face, he smiled at her. "So grown up." She bowed her head. "Remember, if anything goes wrong or Franklin doesn't show up, lock the store and come get me."

She nodded and bolted for the door, so joyful in her freedom that it was all she could do to keep from running. Running, she thought, would be inappropriate for a great big girl of sixteen with her hair up and a job. It seemed like hours before she could close the door on Mrs. Lawrence and her daughter. The woman kept thinking of things to tell Garnet who tried to look responsible and trustworthy. Finally, they left. She tied on a fresh apron, swept the floor, and searched the cluttered kitchen until she found a cold biscuit. Wrinkling her nose at the difference between these and Lorena's, or even her own now, Garnet swallowed the dry crumbs and faced the day as a working girl.

Every few minutes the little bell tinkled and people came to buy. As Mrs. Lawrence had warned her, one supplier came and unloaded several boxes of canned goods. The storekeeper had told Garnet to leave these stacked, and she obeyed even though she was itching to unpack and mark them with the grease pencil. Business was brisk right up until dinnertime, so brisk that Garnet's dinner consisted of two slices of cheese and a handful of crackers from the barrel, but then there was a lull when she was able to dust, straighten, and pretend the store was hers. After school, a few children strolled in with pennies to make slow, agonized decisions at the candy counter, and following close behind them were Lowell and Papa. Her father looked pale.

Lowell went directly to the candy counter. He'd grown up a great deal, but he had a difficult time staying away from sweets even at the advanced age of nine.

Papa asked if she needed any help, and she remembered the chickens. "I haven't gathered the eggs! But how am I supposed to do that when someone might come in any minute?"

"I imagine Mattie locks up for a few minutes, but I suppose I could gather the eggs for you."

Lowell was bored and no one seemed to be buying any candy for him, so he said he'd do it and marched through the house, picking up a basket as he went.

Papa turned to the candy counter where he bought treats for Lowell, Violet, and Henry. "And give me a packet of headache powders."

"I could tell you didn't feel good."

"It's just a headache."

Garnet tried to joke. "And you're going home to Violet?"

He gave her a wan smile. "Could I get some water?"

After they left, there was another little flurry of business, and then the sun lowered, casting gold stripes across the worn linoleum. Promptly at six, she locked the front door and emptied the cash drawer, dumping the money into a greasy cloth bag that said "Evans County Bank" in faded letters. Oh, she'd love to sit down, but Franklin would be starving when he arrived. She grabbed a can of salmon, washed her hands, and got to work.

By the time she had potatoes frying and the salmon made into a loaf and baking, Franklin was tapping on the back door. "Smells good," he said.

"I'll have it ready soon."

He nodded. They were both tired. He'd spent the day shifting things in the barn, and she'd been on her feet all day, but they both felt terribly adult. Garnet made a pot of tea and gave him a piece of pie from the store. Franklin sighed. "This is all right, you know. I'd like to live like this."

"Huh! You have someone cooking for you every night as it is."

He screwed up his face. "That's not what I mean. I'm talking about being on our own. You don't have the little ones pulling on you or Mama to please. I don't have people telling me what do or giving me another chore. We can just do what we want."

"Is it bad living at the farm without Grandpa?"

Franklin stretched his legs until they touched the base of the stove. He'd grown. "No, not really. It's just that before he died I was the grandson living with his kin. Now I feel like I'm a worker living in." He spoke quickly. "Not that Lorena and Luther aren't good to me. But they aren't family."

Garnet blew over the edge of the cup to cool her tea. "If you wanted kin you could've stayed home, gone to school . . . ."

He interrupted her. "No, I couldn't have. You know I never had much liking for school and wanted to get out the first chance I could. Yeah, maybe I used Grandpa's dying as an excuse to quit, but mostly I felt like I needed to work full-time at the farm to justify them keeping me."

"I'm surprised Mama and Papa let you stay."

"Oh, Papa came up and asked me to come home. But he didn't push it. I don't reckon Mama cared one way or another. And you know me and her would just get into it all the time. It's best that I stay with Luther and Lorena."

He slurped the remaining tea in his cup and poured more from the stained pot. "And they pay me good. I've got a nice little bit of money saved up, and there's always the hundred dollars."

Grandpa had written in his will that each of his grandchildren should have a hundred dollars when they turned eighteen. Lorena had told them about this the Sunday after his funeral, and she'd also stated that Louise could have anything she wanted from the house, any of Miss Caroline's beautiful things. Although Garnet gave her mother this message, Mama's only reply had been a haughty sniff.

"So what will you do with the money? You already have your horse."

He smiled, looking into the distance. "I'm not sure. I'd like to go to Lexington and work with race horses."

"You can't run off on your own at fourteen, Franklin. And you can't have the hundred dollars for four more years."

He sipped. "I know, but I have a feeling a time'll come when I don't feel right living with Lorena and Luther. Maybe she'll get married again or maybe she'll sell up or something. I'm not coming back home." His tone was as firm as Mama's.

"Do you really think Lorena will remarry?"

"I don't know. Widows do, you know, and she's only forty-three. That's a big farm for her to run, and Luther might want to do something else. It's hard for a woman to get on without a man."

Garnet couldn't deny this. "I can't see Luther leaving."

"Well, no, but some man might think getting a rich widow with a big farm would be a pretty good deal. I don't know how I'd feel about living there with her and a new man."

Garnet started washing dishes. "Is anybody courting her?"

"No," said Franklin. Garnet was surprised when he rose to help. "But that don't mean it won't happen."

She handed him a tea towel.

"You remember when I went with Luther to take the tobacco crop to Lexington?"

She nodded.

"It's a fine town, full of huge warehouses for the tobacco and big old houses, but, best of all, there's horse farms all around the city. Those farms are so beautiful, the horses must think they're in heaven. The barns look better than where most people in this county live. I want to work with those thoroughbreds." His eyes were dreamy, and Garnet had to push a plate at his hands to get him to start drying.

She thought about Lexington and giggled. "We always wondered what kind of trouble Grandpa got into in Lexington. Did Luther get into mischief?" She raised her eyebrows. "Did you?"

His cheeks reddened. "Naw. Luther's not one for fooling around. He stayed in the boarding house every night and complained that the food wasn't good."

Garnet waited. Franklin, intent upon drying the teapot, said, "I didn't do much of anything, but one night I walked into one of the saloons down by the warehouses. I thought I might taste me a beer."

Garnet whirled around. "Franklin Grant! You're a terrible sinner."

He grinned. "Well, no, I ain't. The place was dark, and I thought they'd take me for older, but they just laughed at me and told me to come back in a few years."

"Hmm. But you wanted to drink even though you didn't."

"So? I ain't going to be a drunkard or nothing. I just wanted to taste it. Actually, I tried whiskey once," he said.

She flicked dishwater on him. "You weren't brought up to drink liquor."

"No, but Grandpa always had a bottle in the cabinet. You know that. You saw it when you cleaned because you always acted like it was going to jump out and bite you."

"Did you sneak it?"

"Lordy, you must think I'm awful! No, one night Grandpa had a bad cold and he asked Lorena to make him a toddy. She mixed stuff together; oh, I don't know, I think there was some sugar and maybe some lemon, and then she poured whiskey in his cup. Before he drank it, he gave me a sip and winked. Said a man needed to know what whiskey tasted like."

Garnet went to the stove to get the frying pan. "Did you like it?"

"No, it tasted like coal oil. That's why I wanted to try beer. Thought I might like it better, and according to Grandpa, a man needs to drink a little."

"Papa doesn't."

"True, but we don't know nothing about what he did when he was young. Oh, it don't matter, Garnet. I didn't do nothing wrong. Quit fussing."

She shut her mouth. There was no point in arguing with Franklin, never had been. Franklin swatted her with the wet tea towel and said, "And you can't tell me, Miss Prissy, that there aren't some grown up things you're curious about."

She colored and grabbed the towel from him. "Sure there are." But no matter how much he teased, she wouldn't say anything more.

A man with a wagon full of deliveries from Ashton arrived shortly after Franklin left the next morning. Canned goods like milk and soup, twenty pounds of potatoes, pies and little cakes a woman in town made to sell. The day promised to be one of those unexpectedly warm ones February sometimes offers like a gift. Since it was Saturday and a fair day, trade was brisk, but she felt like an old hand after Friday. By afternoon, she was able to do some straightening and water the plants in the front window. There was a new one that Mrs. Lawrence had been bragging about. She'd said a friend had brought it when she heard Mattie was having her teeth out.

The unimpressive plant looked like some variety of cactus crossed with a snake, but Mrs. Lawrence had raved about it having an impressive bloom that lasted only one night and smelled wonderful. She'd said, "It's called a night blooming cereus, and I'll let you know when it's about to bloom."

When the bell tinkled and Lowell, Violet, and Henry trailed into the store, Garnet thought irritably that her family was checking up on her, but Lowell said, "Mama sent me to get more headache powders for Papa. He's feeling poorly and has a fever." Violet poked around in a bushel basket of potatoes.

"Get out of those, Violet; you'll get dirty. Is it a cold or what?"

"He's pretty sick. She made me bring the little ones so he could rest."

Violet sashayed around until she spotted ribbons in the dry goods case. "Oh, look at that pretty blue. I want a ribbon, Garnet. I do."

Henry stood in the middle of the store gazing up and down at the shelves. Just the view was enough for him.

When Garnet didn't reply, Violet repeated herself. "I do want a ribbon! I do!"

"You just got new ribbons at Christmas."

"Oh, and I'm supposed to get a box of tea, too," Lowell said.

Violet began to cry, and Henry wiped his runny nose on his sleeve. Garnet sighed as she set the tea on the counter. "Papa said to charge it." He tried distracting Violet by showing her Foster's carved toys, but then she wanted a locomotive, a cow. Shaking his head, Lowell stuffed the tea and headache powders in his pocket, corralled the two children near the door, and said over his shoulder, "I hope you don't need my help with the eggs."

"I don't, but thanks."

"I'm going to walk them up toward Grandpa's and then down the path. Maybe they'll be quiet after all that."

"I hope Papa isn't too sick," Garnet called as they straggled out.

By four o'clock, trade had dwindled to a trickle, and she started sweeping the kitchen. She'd only done half of it when the bell sounded. Wiping her hands on her apron, she hurried into the store. It was Walter Foster. She smiled in anticipation of his friendliness.

He jammed his hands in his pockets, swayed a bit and boomed, "Well, how do! Miss Prim and Proper is the new storekeeper!"

His words seemed harsh, but he was smiling so she ignored them. He looked jolly enough with his wide if somewhat toothless grin and comfortable paunch. She asked how she could help him. "Aw, I just came for a plug of tobacco and a chat with Mrs. Mattie. Good Christian, Mrs. Mattie. Never fails to point out the error of my ways."

Without commenting, Garnet laid a twist of tobacco on the counter. He raised his chin. "Reckon you are a mighty fetchin' girl, just like my boy says."

She kept her head down to hide the fiery blush crawling up her cheeks and told him what he owed. He made no move to pay and continued to stare and grin at the same time. "You 'bout got him tore up with lust, young lady. And that ain't Christian at all. What would Mrs. Mattie say about you tempting my poor boy?"

Garnet didn't know how to reply. She felt sure she'd never encouraged David Foster, but embarrassment burned her face.

"Temptation, yes, indeed. Temptation and the wages of sin. And you standing there like butter wouldn't melt in your prissy little mouth." The words were bitter, ugly, and didn't make much sense, but the man kept smiling and swaying as he said them. She inched away from the counter.

He threw down coins that rolled nearly to the edge. Leaning over the worn wood, he spat, "You act like such a godly little miss, but you're like most women. Hussies and harlots, all of them." His breath reeked of whiskey, which, although she hadn't admitted it to Franklin, she'd opened once at Grandpa's and sniffed.

Oh, she wanted Franklin. Then Foster leaned back and shook his finger at her, laughing and bobbing his head. He staggered to the door, muttering about bad women. Stubbing his toe on the threshold, he finally exited, leaving Garnet gripping the edge of the counter so tightly her fingers turned white. She let out a ragged breath. Never had she heard such venom. Squeezing her eyes closed, she tried to remember every encounter she'd ever had with David Foster to judge if she'd behaved inappropriately. Most times she'd been cool to him because she wasn't sure she liked him that much. She had been surprised that he hadn't come to the store today. What had she done?

When the bell on the door rang, she jumped, her hands leaping to her throat. It was Franklin. "Did you think I was a ghost?" he asked, then frowned. "What's wrong?"

She told him, and he glowered, muttering that he wished he'd been there, that Walter Foster wouldn't have said those things if he had. Garnet wasn't so sure. Then Franklin calmed down, trying to get her to do the same.

"Well, he was drunk. You said he smelled like a saloon. And people say stupid things when they're drunk. It sounds to me like he wanted to pick a fight. Don't pay attention to a drunk, Garnet."

Franklin went outside to see to the chickens, and while he was gone, Garnet stayed in the kitchen, wanting to be within shouting range of her brother. The store remained empty, and, because she could, she grabbed a can of cream of tomato soup, two fistfuls of crackers, and sliced some cheese to fix for supper. There was still pie, as well. Franklin returned to lock the doors.

"Say, could we have tea again tonight? I liked that."

Through supper, Franklin chatted away, but Garnet ate and said little. Only the tea tasted good to her. She poured herself another cup, and stared at Franklin for a good minute before she spoke. "What could David have said for his father to think such things?" Surely Franklin heard talk about girls from the male community up at the farm. Also, he was a boy, well, almost a man; maybe he understood all this better than she did.

He frowned and fidgeted before he spoke. "Well, Walter Foster has a terrible reputation for drinking. Luther says they talk about him in Deer Creek where he usually goes if he's tying one on. What did Luther call it? A binge." Franklin looked her straight in the eye, dead serious. "Luther's cousins say Foster's a nasty drunk, mean and hateful, and always picking fights. Anyway, he was probably going to jump the first person he saw."

Garnet rotated her cup a quarter turn, a half. This made sense but didn't answer her question. Laying her hands flat on the chipped enamel table, she looked at the faint reflections of last summer's freckles on her fingers. "I swear to you, Franklin, I've never encouraged or flirted with David."

Her brother gave a humorless, one-syllable laugh. "That's probably what it's all about. I expect David complained that you won't give him the time of day. It's pretty obvious he likes you, ain't it?"

"I reckon."

"Well, he's probably said he thinks you're pretty and likes you and you won't have nothing to do with him. That's all."

This made sense too but still didn't quite satisfy her. "But he said I was tormenting David." She stood up. "He said that his son was burning with lust because of me, but I didn't do anything!"

Her eyes blazed until Franklin had to meet them; then his slid away. "Well, I don't know as how you would have to do anything to make David feel that way. I hear the men talk. Seems like they're burning with lust no matter what a girl does or doesn't do."

"You mean they just see a girl, and that's what they're thinking about?"

Head down, Franklin nodded.

"We can just be hanging out the wash or minding our own business?"

He nodded again.

She touched his shoulder, making him look at her. "Do you think that way?"

He grabbed his teacup, but it was empty. "I'm still sort of young."

She laughed, not happily at first, and then it struck her as funnier and funnier. She started carrying dishes to the sink. "Men are strange creatures."

"So are girls! And they've got no idea how miserable they make us."

From the sink she turned around, raising an eyebrow. "I think some know it." She thought about her mother and her little ways.

Like the night before, Franklin helped clean up, and, as they finished, he said that Lorena had asked him to look in the store for thread to match fabric she was working with. He pulled a tiny swatch from his pocket. Garnet peered at it. "I think there's something nearly that color in there. Take a lamp; I'll be in to help you as soon as I dump the dishwater."

She opened the back door. After sunset, the mild day had become a chilly, blue evening. Taking a deep breath, she balanced the empty dishpan on the porch railing and looked to her left, across the road at the church and its graveyard, ghostly in the frosty light. Garnet shivered. It was cold, but she hadn't been outside since sweeping the porch that morning. It felt good to get some air.

"Garnet!" a voice hissed to her right. She swiveled, nearly dropping the dishpan. It was David Foster. She almost ran, she almost hollered for Franklin, but she stayed, gripping the dishpan with her right hand and the porch railing with her left.

"Please don't run! I come to apologize for my pa," he said. Normally his face was so smiley she couldn't see his eyes, but in the blue light, she saw little crescent moons of white around them.

"He told me what he said to you." David dropped his head. "He's mean when he's drinking and you just have to ignore him. Or at least, that's what I do."

She wasn't afraid. He seemed harmless enough, not much different from her brothers. "Evans County is dry. How does he get whiskey?"

"Oh, there's always a way to get whiskey. Pa usually knows somebody who's got it." He looked up at her earnestly. "I try to stay out of his way when he's on a drunk so most of the afternoon I was doing some sanding out in the workshop. I guess that's when he come down here and bothered you. I'm so sorry."

He kept talking. "And when he told me what he said to you, you know, about me, and about you being a . . . well, you know, I couldn't believe it. I ain't never said nothing like that about you. I ain't never," he declared.

Franklin came to the door, saw David, and was ready to charge through it. Garnet stopped him. "I'm fine. I'll be in to help you in a minute." He turned away but went no farther than the kitchen.

David reached up to hold onto the railing, close to where her hand gripped the blistered wood. "I know you're a lady, a proper lady. Why, you're the schoolteacher's daughter and Mr. King's kin. I don't know where my pa got those ideas except that he don't think much of women. My ma ran off, you know. She left one day while he was working, and we never saw her again. So he thinks all women are wicked."

"But Mrs. Lawrence said your mother died."

"Sometimes he gives that out as the story. Guess the truth hurts his pride."

She supposed so too but didn't say anything. David didn't seem likely to say much more about it either. He paused for a moment and then started again, "But, I never . . ."

"Shh." She stopped him, like she would've stopped Henry or Lowell from talking too much. "I believe you."

Then he smiled, his eyes crinkling until they disappeared. "He won't remember none of it once he sobers up."

"Fine for him," Garnet replied. "But how do you forget what he's said?"

"He's my pa. Don't have nobody else."

She didn't know what to say to that.

"Well, It's cold, and you ain't got a coat on. I better walk home and make sure he ain't set the place on fire."

She nodded at him, not wanting to go in until he left. So briefly that she might have imagined it, he brushed her hand, still tightly gripping the railing, and then he was gone. Again she shivered, realizing how cold she was and went in, locking the door behind her.

"What did he want?"

"To apologize for his father."

Franklin made a disgusted noise, but she ignored it, saying, "Did you have any luck finding that thread?"

By midafternoon on Sunday, Mrs. Lawrence returned with a swollen face and false teeth that glinted almost as cheerfully as her spectacles. She wasn't talking very well but managed to thank Garnet, giving her a packet of beefsteak and two dollars. Garnet walked home feeling much older than the girl who'd run towards the store two days ago.

***

The house was as quiet as midnight. "Mama?" she called, but there was no answer.

Setting down her things, Garnet tiptoed to the bedroom and tapped on the door.

Mama opened it, pressing her finger to her lips. "He just went to sleep."

"Who? Papa?"

Mama closed the door and sank into a kitchen chair. "He's very poorly. I can't get him to eat or drink or do anything. I sent Lowell up to the farm with Henry and Violet. I don't want those children around that wicked woman, but your father couldn't get a bit of rest with the little ones running around."

For a moment Garnet said nothing. She chopped off a portion of the beef and set it to simmer into a nice broth for Papa. But she couldn't keep quiet any longer. "She's not a wicked woman. She saved Lowell's life for sure, and she's been good to Franklin and me."

"You don't know the whole story, nor will you ever."

Garnet reckoned she probably did, but it was neither the time nor place for this to be sorted out. Mama stared at the stove and rubbed her swollen belly. "I wonder if we should get the doctor."

"Is he that sick?"

"He's been feverish for three days now. But how am I going to send for the doctor?"

Mama looked so distraught that Garnet laid a hand on her arm. "That's easy. I'll fetch Franklin. He has a horse and could get there in no time. Do you want me to?"

Mama gazed at her pitifully, eyes enormous and shoulders drooping as if the weight of her belly was pulling them down. She nodded. Garnet grabbed her coat and told her mother to add vegetables to the broth.

It was influenza that had gone into pneumonia, said Dr. Thomas. And he didn't encourage their hopes. Poor constitution, he said. Overworked, he said. Perhaps tubercular. For eight nightmarish days, Garnet was too busy to worry about anything but the next doctor's visit, the next dose of medicine, the next meal. She sent Lowell to school, she cared for the children, she cooked and cleaned and washed. Mostly she tiptoed around her mother whose grief and helplessness made the agony of waiting that much more scalding.

Even while it was unfolding, Garnet saw Papa's illness and eventual death as a disjointed series of scenes through which she sleepwalked, unable to give vent to her own grief. The day after he died she suddenly was aware that she was standing by the stove stirring the one decent dress her pregnant mother was able to wear in a pot of wicked black dye. It seemed like such an odd, foreign thing to do. One after another, visitors came to the front door, sat in the front room by the casket looking uncomfortable, and exited quickly after leaving a cake, a slab of bacon, a loaf of bread. The Bledsoes brought prayers, and the lawyer and school superintendent, Mr. Pierce, brought Papa's last paycheck. Throughout these visits, Mama reclined in her dreadful black dress on the bristly sofa, dabbing her eyes with a damp handkerchief, and calling for Garnet to bring coffee or tea.

As Garnet would've expected, attendance at John Grant's funeral was even larger than at Grandpa's. With his current students and the many he'd taught in the past, the Bethel Baptist Church overflowed with solemn-faced mourners. At the gravesite Garnet stood staunchly by her mother, waiting for Mama to faint or falter, but she didn't. Standing on Mama's other side was Franklin, looking fierce and angry in his attempt to stave off tears, holding Violet's and Henry's hands. But Lowell was the lost lamb, leaning into Garnet's skirt. She thought about how he and Papa had shared the same reverence for learning; no one else in the family would ever understand. More than any of them, he'd lost a kindred soul.

People said lovely things for most everyone had admired John Grant. Garnet found that they bled together into a droning hum of sympathy and sentiment. She feared that if she dwelt on her own emotions, observed Lowell's grief too closely, or immersed herself in the sympathy of well-meaning mourners, she would break into a thousand pieces like a cup hurled against a wall. So she kept moving, doing, taking care of everyone else, and falling exhausted into her bed each night, thankful that she was too tired to think.

Gradually, the week after the funeral, other pictures slid into her consciousness. She remembered her father, painfully thin and blue around the lips, looking up at her as she brought him a drink or his medicine. His dark blue eyes looked nearly black but lit up, just for a second, when he saw her. Late one night when the younger children were in bed, and Garnet was sitting at the kitchen table, mending one of Henry's shirts, she heard her father's breathless voice recite to her mother, "Come live with me and be my love . . . ."   But the memory that burned brightest and most painfully came from the night he died when Garnet and her mother had sat by his bed. Mama was slumped in her rocking chair, sleeping awkwardly, and Garnet's head had dropped to her chest. Hearing a small sound, she jerked awake to hear her father saying, "Forgive me." Sensing this was a prayer, she said nothing, but Papa groped for her hand. He had barely moved for hours. She clasped his fingers, wax-colored and chilly, and he gripped her own with surprising strength. "Garnet. Forgive me."

The tears had come then and whenever she remembered it. She'd assured him there was no need for forgiveness, she loved him, and he was the best father. He'd said no more, and within a few hours, his breaths, already brief, wispy things, became even more shallow and infrequent and he'd died, trying to cause as little trouble as possible.

Eventually she left the fog behind. She saw her mother's helplessness, Lowell's sorrow, and the little ones' confusion. Reality and grief collided, sparking a clear awareness of their situation. What were they going to do? How would they live? She would have to hold them together. So, she did the only things she knew how to do: work hard, try harder, and pray.

Several Saturdays came and went, but, even though the family could've used anything Mrs. Lawrence might've given Garnet as compensation, she stayed home. She had visited the store a few times, usually with Henry and Violet tagging along, but those trips had been to purchase groceries. Mrs. Lawrence knew Louise Grant was far advanced in her pregnancy but made no secret of wishing Garnet back at work. On her most recent trip Garnet had bought seeds for her garden, and the packets lay scattered on the kitchen table. They brought bittersweet memories of her father who'd always helped, turning over the dirt and preparing the soil for her. This year would be different, just as her Saturdays were different. She certainly couldn't take the children with her to the store, and it was too much to expect Lowell to care for them the entire day. Lorena had said to send them up to her, but Garnet hated to impose, especially since Lowell, Henry, and Violet marched up there every Sunday to be entertained and fed. Besides, Garnet didn't like leaving Mama alone.

Garnet gathered up the packets, placing them high on the kitchen cabinet. Henry thought they were fun to play with, and she didn't have money to buy more. She had hardly any money at all and must ask her mother for some to buy food. Finding something for supper was going to be a challenge. At least tomorrow Lorena would feed the children, and she usually sent food home with Lowell. Garnet set a kettle of salted water on the stove for boiling macaroni and went to the cellar for a jar of tomatoes.

Outside the air was fresh and windy, spurring her desire to get seeds in the ground. The March breeze whistled around the old shed, empty now, for Lorena and Luther were better able to feed the mule than she. After the funeral Garnet had offered him back to Gert and Fanny Clark, but they told her to sell him. She was fairly certain Luther had given her too much money for poor old Caesar, but she could ill-afford pride when the money paid the doctor and part of Papa's funeral costs. Soft clucking came from the chicken yard, but there were only a few birds making noise. They'd killed two to make broth for Papa and meals for the rest of them, and then a few more had gone to feed them recently. It seemed wasteful to kill a chicken for one or two meals when eggs might keep them eating longer, but Garnet didn't know what else to do. Papa's salary was long gone.

Garnet called everyone for supper. She'd baked macaroni and canned tomatoes into a casserole and doled out the last of the canned peaches for a treat. Mama came from the front room where she'd been crocheting. For weeks now she just crocheted, and the long, narrow band of white lace would probably stretch to Ashton. When Garnet asked what she was going to do with the lace, Mama had smiled and said it would come in handy sometime. Ponderous and awkward, she settled herself at the table, her dress stretched in a curve from her neck to her belly. Sometimes her manner was somber or tearful, but she also could force a gaiety that was nearly as hard to bear. Tonight her mood was petulant. Mama picked at the glutinous mass of noodle and tomato like it was something fit for hogs. She separated a piece of macaroni and poked at it. "I would like something nice to eat. This isn't at all nice."

Garnet had slipped into her chair after laying a slice of bread on each plate. There was no butter. Lowell looked up. He'd been shoveling in the food without paying much attention. Henry, too, was eating hungrily. Violet took a cue from her mother. "This is nasty, Garnet. I won't eat it."

"It's all we have."

Mama looked dreamily at her plate. "Now a little poached egg, all round and white and perfectly formed. That would be very nice." She pinched a bit of bread from her slice and looked up with wide, round eyes. "Couldn't I have a poached egg?"

Garnet swallowed. "I have four eggs, Mama, and I was saving them for breakfast."

"Eggs! I want eggs!" Violet announced. Lowell reached over and played like he was going to eat her macaroni. She protested and he shrugged, saying he thought she didn't want it. Violet might be willful, but she wasn't stupid. She took a bite.

Mama ate her peaches and bread and took a few bites of the macaroni, shaking her head with each mouthful. When she finished, she murmured that the baby needed better sustenance than this. Making sure Henry's mouth was wiped, Garnet shooed the children from the kitchen and sat down next to her mother.

"Mama, I need to talk to you."

Louise looked up with eyes clear as the spring day outside.

"We need food. Everything's gone except a few jars in the cellar and the chickens we still have. Do you understand?" Garnet realized that she was speaking to her mother as she would've to Henry or Violet.

Something broke behind Mama's eyes, and she glanced around the kitchen. "Of course we are. All the food gifts have been eaten, haven't they?" She looked concerned for a moment and then said, almost merrily, "I shouldn't expect you to feed us on air, should I?"

Garnet shook her head, hopeful that her mother was grasping their situation.

"What happened to Papa's last pay?"

Garnet dropped her eyes to the oilcloth covering the table. "Some of it went for coal, and I bought a few groceries last week, but most of it paid for his funeral."

Her mother pressed her lips together. "Fetch my purse."

She went into her mother's room and brought out a worn velvet bag and handed it to her mother. All of them had been threatened with dire circumstances if they ever so much as touched their mother's purse without permission. Garnet still felt odd handling it.

Mama opened the bag and brought out a black silk coin purse. "I've probably had this all along, and here you were worrying," she said. She dumped out several coins that thudded on the table. They probably added up to three dollars.

"Thank you, Mama," Garnet said. "But you know this won't last very long. What are we going to do?"

Her mother frowned, a furrow cutting deeply between her brows. "Well, I suppose you'll have to go to the bank. I'm sure John had money there from my father."

Garnet jumped on this. "The bank? In Ashton?"

Her mother nodded. "You must go to the bank, and have them give you the money in your father's account." She rose awkwardly and walked to the front room, returning with a piece of paper. "I can't find the bank book, but here's your father's account number. Just give them this, and they'll give you money."

Garnet folded it into her pocket. "They'll let me have it?"

Mama waved her hand as she walked back toward her endless coil of lace. "I'm certain they will." She stopped at the doorway. "I'll write down a list of things for you to buy in Ashton .I must get items made for the baby, and time is getting short."

"Aren't there things left over from Henry or Violet?"

"Oh, but they're rather shabby. A new baby needs a fresh layette."

Garnet bit off her tart reply. She should feel relieved that she had a plan, an option, although she wasn't quite sure how she'd get to

Ashton. Mama hadn't addressed that. She supposed she could get Franklin to take her, but that left no one with Mama and the little ones. She heated water. Maybe she could walk; it wasn't exactly a journey to the moon, but she'd never be able to lug home sacks of beans and flour. When she'd finished drying the dishes, she told her mother that she needed to see Franklin about going to town.

Her mother sniffed. Since Papa's death, Garnet never knew how much Mama understood, but invariably talk about the farm and the people who lived there brought her displeasure. She'd just have to get used to it. Times had changed.

Outside cold stars glittered against the dark. The wind was so blustery she half-expected it to propel the stars around the sky. Afraid to be gone long, she ran up the path, and then settled herself, taking a deep breath before she walked in.

Luther, Lorena, and Franklin were sitting in the front room. Draped over Lorena's lap was a shirt she was mending. She looked up quickly as a gust blew Garnet through the door. "Goodness, girl, it's a wonder you didn't blow away coming up here." Lorena said. "Is everything all right? The baby?"

Garnet shook her head, still trying to catch her breath. "I just need to talk to Franklin. Alone, if you don't mind." She stood just inside the door with her arms crossed tightly over her chest.

Immediately Luther and Lorena went to the kitchen. Garnet sat next to Franklin and got right to the point. "We don't have much of anything to eat at the house, and there's no money left. I asked Mama, and she said there's some in the bank so I need to go to town."

Franklin's eyes were wary.

"I reckon I'll walk to Ashton on Monday, but I need you to stay at the house with Mama and the little ones. Lowell will be in school, and I'd be afraid for him to stay by himself with them even if he wasn't," she told him. Not for the first time, she realized how dependent she'd become upon a nine-year old.

"Oh, no," Franklin said, shaking his head. "I'm not going over there to stay. Besides, how would you get stuff home?"

"I have to, Franklin. Did you hear me? We don't have any food. It won't be so bad. You can take Violet and Henry outside, but be sure you don't go too far so Mama can call if she needs you."

He stood and hovered over her. "I said no. I won't do it. She can take care of her own children for once." His voice became louder with each word.

"What am I supposed to do?" she asked, getting louder herself. "I can't go to Ashton and stay at home at the same time."

He yelled back, "Then send the little ones over here, and I'll drive you."

She was near tears and spoke softly to cover the sound of them. "But that would still leave Mama alone, and I can't do that." She stopped and looked up at him, her eyes brimming. "You don't know how she is now."

"Half-crazy, the way she always was and no fit mother," he growled. He paced around the room and stopped by the front window, peering into the dark.

"Franklin, we have nothing to eat, the baby's due in a couple of weeks, and Mama's not herself. I need you."

"And I said I would help you!" he roared. "But I ain't going to be in the same house with that woman."

Lorena stepped from the kitchen. "You'll do what your sister asks. Those are your brothers and sisters at that house whether you have feelings for your mother or not."

He whipped around, startled and not one bit pleased. She continued, "Oh, I know I'm not blood kin, but this is your sister asking for help, and you'll do it."

His face twisted into ugly lumps and crevices. "And about half the problem was caused by you." He threw the words like a hatchet.

Garnet rose and turned away. Shadowy in the light spilling from the kitchen, Luther walked to his sister's side, cleared his throat, and started to speak in his low, calm voice. "This ain't much of a puzzle. Lorena needs some goods from town anyway so I'll just drive Miss Garnet to the bank."

This only solved part of the problem, but Garnet nodded her thanks, afraid to say anything more. Beside her Franklin stood rigid. Luther continued, nodding his head at Franklin. "And, as I see it, Monday's a regular work day for you, and I set your jobs. On Monday you'll go over to the house and see what needs doing. And at the same time you can take care of your little brother and sister."

Luther left no room for questioning. Franklin looked hard at the older man and then let out his breath. There was no apology for Lorena, nor for Garnet, but he gave a brusque nod and sat back down. Taking his time, Luther reclaimed his spot on the sofa. He said, "Likely this weather'll hold and you can till your sister's garden on Monday. That'll keep you and the young'uns out of the house."

Garnet glanced at Lorena, at Luther, and lastly at Franklin, who again nodded curtly. "I guess it's settled then." Her voice shook. "Shall I come over here Monday at sunup?"

"That'll be fine," said Luther.

***

Mama was less than pleased with the arrangements but didn't protest. She'd mumbled something about the unsuitability of her daughter riding to town with "Colson trash" but excused it with the statement that she supposed a hired man should be expected to do this sort of work. About Franklin's presence she made no comment.

Garnet wore her best dress, made with Lorena's help before Christmas and worn for Papa's funeral, which erased most of the joy out of the garment. It was dark blue and fitted snugly with tiny buttons marching up the bodice to a high lace-trimmed collar. She thought the dress made her look adult. Buffing her shoes with a corner of her bedsheet, she heard a hairpin fall to the floor. She still didn't quite have the knack of putting her hair up and did it only for special occasions. She started again, coiling the copper braids around her head and pinning them snugly in place. If the day was windy, she was doomed.

But it was a still day. As she walked toward the farm, the sky glowed like dull pewter, the sun a blurred disc on the horizon. Franklin would have a good day for tilling. By the time she reached the tobacco barn, she met her brother who carried a packet and wore work clothes.

"Lorena sent ham for our dinner," he said.

"They'll enjoy that," she replied, not quite friendly.

"I hope there's money."

"I do too," she answered, ready to continue up the path.

He lingered. "You understand how I feel, Garnet."

In her womanly clothes and upswept hair, she was definitely his older sister, knew it, and acted that way. She appraised him coolly. "Yes, but I can't run away from it, Franklin. And you always have."

She turned to leave again when she heard him say, "I'll make your garden real nice."

Luther was, as usual, quiet company, but Garnet welcomed his silence. Except for a few comments about the weather or the state of the road, they'd traveled halfway to Ashton before either of them said much. More anxious with every mile, she asked, "Will they let me have that money? I don't know anything about banks."

He kept his eyes straight ahead. "Oh, I expect so. It ain't like your mama's able to get to town right now."

She watched the road too, as it wound around the hills. "It's just that I always feel shy in town, and I've never had to do any business there."

She glanced at the man's bony profile. He was smoothly shaven, looking presentable for town in a clean shirt and jacket. For just an instant he looked at her, his nearly black eyes kind and warm. "I feel shy in town too. It was even worse taking the tobacco to Lexington without your grandpa, but you live through it."

They said little more until they reached the outskirts of Ashton. When Luther stopped the wagon, he asked if she wanted him to go into the bank with her, but she decided she must do this by herself. "No. Should I meet you at Trosper's?"

He nodded and gave her a slow, sweet smile. "Lorena's thought up a bunch of things for me to buy."

Garnet jumped down, trying to appear lady-like. He spoke once more. "If you have any trouble, you come fetch me. Or talk to Clifford Clark, Gert and Fanny's brother. He knowed your pa."

Garnet headed toward the bank, clutching the paper Mama had given her and moving it from one hand to the other. She saw the steps they'd climbed when Papa brought her and Franklin to town and visited the lawyer, Mr. Pierce, but she'd never entered the bank itself. It smelled like paper and dust. In front of her, two cages were outfitted with tarnished brass bars, and on the other wall two wide, mahogany desks sat like sentinels on either side of a steel door. She assumed this protected the bank's safe, something she knew about only from tales of bank robberies. Not sure where to turn, she noted that both cages contained whiskery old men dressed in suits. An ancient man with a cascading mane of white hair stood talking to one of the clerks. He was telling a tale, punctuated occasionally by a stream of tobacco aimed at a brass cuspidor in the corner. She was the only woman there.

Although she hesitated, she crept up to the other cage and tried to attract the man's attention. Fingers flying, he was counting coins into little stacks and seemed to want no interruption. She waited, and at last he looked up and said, "Yes?"

It came out in a breathless rush. "I'm Garnet Grant and my mother is unable to come to town. My father is . . ., was, John Grant; he died a month ago, and I've come to collect his money."

The man frowned, his bushy white brows drawn into a straight line. He said, "What money? Did he have an account here? Do you have his bank book?"

"No, Mama couldn't find the bank book, but this is my papa's writing with his name and bank number." She pushed the paper under the cage.

"Bank number?" The teller's voice rose. "I suppose you're trying to say that this is his account number?"

Garnet nodded miserably, her eyes darting around like a trapped animal's. She noticed two men talking at one of the mammoth desks. One was chuckling, putting on his hat and taking his leave. The other sat with one hip on the desk, making light conversation in an easy and jovial way. Suddenly remembering him from the throng at her father's funeral, Garnet knew he was Clifford Clark.

"Young lady! I must have some authorization for this. I don't know you, nor do I know whether your father is actually deceased."

She twisted her hands against her skirt. She could fetch Luther but was too proud to admit defeat. She shook her head and tried again. "My father died a month ago, sir. John Grant. He was teacher at the Bethel School."

Officious as before, the man pushed the scrap of paper back at her. "Perhaps your mother could come to town and verify this."

"No," she said, realizing her voice was becoming thin and shrill. "The baby's due before long, and she's grieving over Papa. She sent me to do this."

"What's the problem here?" asked a deep voice behind her, well above her head. It was Mr. Clark, and if he didn't match his Amazonian sisters in girth, he undoubtedly exceeded them in height.

The teller sniffed and shook the paper. "This girl says she wants her father's money but has no bank book, no authorization, probably no identification." He peered at her with small, pale eyes. "*Do* you have identification, Miss?"

Totally bewildered, Garnet glanced first at the teller and then tilted her head to look at Mr. Clark. He must be well over six feet tall, she thought. Clark shook his head. "I know her. This is my friend John Grant's oldest girl. What's your name?"

"Garnet, sir."

"Yes, Garnet Grant, and I attended her father's funeral last month. By all means, give her what's remaining in her father's account."

The teller twitched, sniffed, but went to a shelf against the back wall and started leafing through a ledger. Garnet whispered a thank you to Mr. Clark, who shrugged. "There are rules, but there's a time for them to be broken." Then he frowned. "I'm deeply grieved by your father's passing. He was a fine man and a true friend."

She thanked him. Glancing up at him again, she noticed his warm, brown eyes, nearly the color of sorghum, and this made her think of his sisters. She asked about them.

"Oh, they're keeping well, both of them too feisty to be sick. He had a lean face with strong bones. "And there's a baby due soon?"

Garnet nodded. "That's why Mama can't come to town. We think it'll be another two weeks or so."

Mr. Clark peered over the brass cage at the clerk. "How many Grants are there?"

She told him, along with ages, and then the teller returned, clearing his throat importantly. "I assume we're closing out this account, Mr. Clark?"

Clark looked at Garnet. "Do you want to take all the money out of your father's account?"

"That's what Mama sent me to do." She thought for a second. "Unless it's a great sum."

The crotchety clerk made a low noise.

Clark said, "Would you please tell Miss Grant the balance?"

The old man threw up his bristly chin and said, more loudly than he needed to, "Eighteen dollars and sixty five cents."

At first Garnet reddened, embarrassed that the amount had been announced so loudly, and then she paled. She'd hoped there would be more, much more. Certainly it would help, but they couldn't live long on that. Both men were waiting and Clifford Clark said, very quietly, "Do you want to draw all of that out, Miss Grant?"

"Yes, please," she whispered.

The teller counted out the cash and handed it to her. Her mind racing with how she could best stretch the funds, she hardly noticed Clifford Clark telling her good-bye and exited the bank in a wave of anxiety, her heart banging against her chest. She talked strongly to herself. There were ways, she thought. The garden could be enlarged. Franklin could come home and bring his pay to the family. Maybe she could work somewhere else. This she dismissed immediately. How could she go out to work every day with a new baby in the house? She hadn't even been able to work for Mrs. Lawrence since Papa died. She took a deep breath. Luther would worry, and there was no point in lingering.

As Garnet walked toward Trosper's, she read through her mother's long list of fabric, notions, and other frivolous items for the baby. This would have to be reduced, and she wondered how her mother, never particularly practical in the best of times, would react. Mama would just have to get used to it: they were desperately poor now. Luther was outside the store, ready to load the wagon but told her to take her time. Garnet spent judiciously, comparing Trosper's prices with those she knew by heart from Mrs. Lawrence's store. For the most part Trosper's was cheaper, so she spent nearly all the money on food, adding a few yards of outing cloth for baby clothes. It would have to do. She'd planned to buy ribbons for Violet, a toy for Henry, a tablet for Lowell, but she couldn't.

Luther was always kind but seemed gentler than usual and insisted she share the lunch he'd bought. He waited until the loaded wagon was lumbering back to Bethel before he said, "I'm thinking there wasn't as much as you'd hoped."

"No, there wasn't. But it'll last for a while."

He said nothing more.

When Luther stopped the wagon at the swinging bridge, Franklin was finishing up in the garden. He wiped his face on his sleeve and helped unload Garnet's purchases. Lowell was home from school and sat on the front porch with Henry and Violet who seemed happy enough if grubby. They waved expectantly; trips to town meant treats.

"I'm nearly done," Franklin announced as he picked up a sack of beans.

"I can see. It looks good. Thank you."

He went to the house with his load. Luther placed her remaining purchases by the side of the wagon and said, "I reckon you all can get these in the house."

He probably didn't want to risk the kind of reception he might get from Mama. "Sure. And thank you, Luther."

She lugged a flour sack and the package of outing cloth to the kitchen, passing Franklin on the way. He raised his eyebrows and she shook her head. "Not much. I spent almost all of it."

The other three crowded into the kitchen and surveyed the pile of purchases with great curiosity. Mama strolled in from the bedroom. "Look at all that food!" she exclaimed.

Garnet didn't want to share bad news more than once so she waited for Franklin to bring in the last of the parcels and then announced, "I was able to get the money from Papa's account, but there wasn't much so I didn't buy treats and surprises. We have food to eat, and I guess that'll be treat enough for all of us." She addressed her mother. "I bought outing cloth for the baby, but I couldn't buy the rest of your list."

Her mother tilted her head and said in her most polite and formal voice, "I'm sure it will be fine, Garnet. We must live simply for a while, that's all."

At Trosper's Garnet had knotted up the remaining money into her handkerchief. She gave this to her mother. "That's all that's left."

Mama took it and smiled. "We'll have to come up with some strategies, children, but nothing can be decided until this precious baby arrives." She stood tall, almost regally for a short woman burdened with a massive belly and pulled Henry and Violet to her. "While Lowell helps your sister put away her purchases, why don't we look over what baby things we have? Time is getting short and we must prepare for the new arrival." She shooed them off to her room, saying cheerful, silly things about Henry who had last used the baby items.

Garnet, dazed by this performance, looked at the pile on the table. She had to admit she was happy her mother had taken the bad news so well but couldn't help but wonder if Mama truly understood the seriousness of their situation. "She's right, you know," Franklin remarked. "There's not a lot anyone can do until she has this baby and can take on what you're doing. Then maybe you can get a job somewhere."

Garnet narrowed her eyes. "Any ideas where?"

Lowell's eyes widened. "Do you want me to put these sacks in the cellar?"

She nodded, still focusing her attention on Franklin who escaped from the kitchen right behind his younger brother. She put away a few things and then followed him to the garden where he was stacking tools in the wheelbarrow. The ground smelled fresh and fertile, and robins explored the upturned soil.

"So you're saying I need to find work to support the family?" she asked in a voice sharp enough to scrape paint.

He seemed surprised that she was so upset. "Well, what else can you all do? Do you think Mama's going to take in washing or something? There's Papa's sister in Tennessee, but I can't see you all moving down there. Mama doesn't have any close kin left in Lexington, does she?"

Garnet shook her head in amazement. "No, Franklin, there's no kin we can go to, nor will Mama be doing any kind of work. But I think you're leaving somebody out of the picture. You know I do most everything around here as it is."

He picked a clod of dirt out of the crevice in his shovel and frowned. "Course I know that. Don't see how you stand it. That's what I mean: after the baby comes, Mama's going to have to take care of the children and the house so you can work every day. Maybe for Mrs. Lawrence."

"And just how likely is that?"

"Mrs. Lawrence is getting awful crippled up with her arthritis, and she likes you."

Garnet had to restrain herself from stomping on the loosened soil. "And she pays me with a pound of cheese or a toy for Henry. How are we going to live on that?"

"Talk to her maybe?"

"Franklin Grant, are you thinking at all?"

He raised vaguely hurt eyes.

"Why aren't you moving home, pitching in around here, and bringing your pay to our house?"

He moved an earthworm with the toe of his muddy shoe. "Did you notice how she just ignored me? And I made the young'uns their dinner, got them washed up. I tilled the garden and kept them outside, and she pretended I wasn't even here."

"Of course she ignores you! You ran off to the farm and have a great time without ever thinking of anything or anyone here." When he met her eyes she realized again that she was an adult to him.

He stared at his feet. "I been thinking about what you said about me always running away."

She waited.

"And I reckon you're right. But I'm not sure things aren't so broken they can't never be mended." He took a deep breath and stretched his body as tall as he could. "I won't come live at home, Garnet. I just won't. I'd be another mouth to feed, and there would be no peace between her and me."

Then he faced her squarely, trying to look as adult as she did. "But I'll come when you need me to do heavy work." He gestured at the garden. "And I'll bring you most of my pay. I have to keep a little of it for clothes and extras."

She wasn't ready to release him yet. "You say you'd be another mouth to feed, but what do you pay Lorena and Luther for your bed and board?"

"Nothing, Garnet. They don't ask for a cent. So I get a day hand's full pay without having much in the way of expenses. You can have it. Or most of it."

Grudgingly she nodded. That was the most she could expect, she supposed. More than likely he was right; moving back home would cause all kinds of upsets. Franklin would never put up with Mama's constant picking and criticizing. He put the shovel in the wheelbarrow and started pushing it toward the pump.

"I'll get these cleaned up and be on my way. Luther pays me on Saturdays so I'll give you my wages on Sundays when you all visit."

Chapter Five

Working in the garden had always comforted Garnet, but even as she dug and planted and sifted the soil between her fingers, she couldn't let go of her worries. Sometimes she had crazy notions like telling Mr. Pierce that she could teach and take Papa's job. Or she envisioned truly terrible things like Mrs. Lawrence dying and leaving the store to her rather than to her daughter. She couldn't think up any way she could help her family besides growing lots of vegetables.

Henry loved playing in the dirt, and she had to watch that he didn't disturb her planting. Sometimes Violet played on the porch with the ratty, old doll that had once been Garnet's, oh, maybe a lifetime ago. Knowing the new baby would arrive soon, Mama sewed like a woman possessed, using every scrap in the house. She set Violet to embroidering simple designs on some tiny gowns, and the girl seemed to have more aptitude for fancy sewing than Garnet ever had. Mama was cheerful, excited about the baby, and remarked that she was glad she had so much lace to trim the little garments. Garnet smiled along with her; things were easier when Mama was happy, but it was a feverish happiness that never quite acknowledged Papa's death or their poverty.

One morning it was windy, the western sky an ominous purple. She'd intended to wash that morning but decided to give the kitchen a good cleaning instead. Mama was in her bedroom, washing down the crib and fitting it with the freshly aired little mattress and blankets. Garnet heard Henry swearing he could still fit in the crib.

Garnet removed every item from the kitchen cabinet and stacked them on the table. Back in the corner she unearthed a small jar of black walnuts left over from the fall. She tasted a piece; they were a little strong but still good. Added to a simple cake batter, that would make a treat for her family. Treats were rare. They weren't hungry, but they'd have nothing truly fresh or good until the garden started producing.

At first she mistook the knock on the back door for the wind that had whipped around the house all morning, but she looked up and saw Luther Colson.

"I brought you a load of coal and a few other things," he said. His hat was pulled low on his forehead.

"You didn't need to do that, but I thank you."

He shrugged, the wind pulling at his shirt. She'd never thought to see Luther Colson anywhere near their house. Curious, Mama lumbered into the kitchen, and Garnet held up both hands. "It's Luther Colson, Mama, with a load of coal."

Louise raised an eyebrow and went back to the bedroom. By the time Garnet had replaced the cabinet items, Luther returned with a huge box, telling her that he'd put a can of coal oil down in the cellar.

As swiftly as her bulk would allow, Mama reemerged from the bedroom, catching Luther before he could escape. Uh oh, Garnet thought. But her mother's face was pleasant and gracious.

"Why, Mr. Colson, what fine gifts!" She gestured at the box that overflowed with lovely things: tea, butter, a huge slab of bacon.

Luther twitched and fidgeted like a boy about to get a whipping, and this would've amused Garnet if she hadn't felt so sorry for him. She couldn't remember Mama ever speaking to Luther Colson. "Just a few things, "he mumbled.

As usual, there was no usual behavior for Mama. She smiled, cocked her head, and glowed at him. Another time, Garnet thought, he would've been treated with the contempt people gave cockroaches. Mama uttered a charming little laugh and said, "How very considerate of you especially with the baby due so soon."

Luther had been focusing on the box, but then raised his head. So low that Garnet could barely hear him, he said, "Don't want Mr. King's folks to be doing without."

That'll kill it, thought Garnet, but Mama continued to smile prettily and held the man's eyes. "These are hard times for us, you know."

He didn't reply but locked his eyes on her. She lifted her graceful hand to the buttons straining across her swollen chest and played with each one, fiddling with them almost like she was going to unbutton them. Garnet hardly dared to exhale, and she was pretty sure Luther wasn't breathing at all. Slowly Mama's hand worked its way up to the neck of her dress where she gently pulled the collar away from her neck. "The children will be delighted," she said.

Luther nodded, his face reddening painfully. If he'd been watching a cobra, he couldn't have been more entranced. Henry and Violet came from the bedroom, quarreling about an old baby blanket, and the spell was broken. Luther lowered his head, and Garnet started sorting through the box. Mama, however, stood still and, when Luther glanced up at her again, used that languid, ivory hand to tuck a stray hair up from the back of her neck. He mumbled something unintelligible and made for the back door like demons were chasing him. And maybe they were.

After he left, Mama said in her usual voice, "So what do we have here?"

Luther must've noticed what Garnet bought in town so there was no duplication, but Lorena had a hand in the gifts too. In the bottom were shiny jars of Lorena's apple butter and green beans. "All kinds of nice food," Garnet said reverently.

Mama had to know the canned items were from Lorena, but she made no comment and turned to settle the fussing between Henry and Violet. The storm broke leaving the air chilly with rain, and Garnet spent the afternoon finishing her cleaning and planning an unusually nice meal.

Five days later, not long after noon, Mama came into the kitchen looking pinched around her mouth and told Garnet to send for the midwife. Garnet was grateful it wasn't midnight. She flew up the path to tell Franklin. About the time the woman arrived, Lowell came home from school and she pointed him, along with Henry and Violet, toward the farm. Feeling like she knew the routine by this time, Garnet boiled water, endured her mother's cries, and cooked enough to keep the midwife happy. Once or twice Mama called out for Papa, making Garnet feel her grief like it was fresh. It was a terrible thing for her mother to go through this ordeal without a husband, and she mourned that John Grant's last daughter would never see her father. Mama named her Desdemona in honor of Papa's beloved Shakespeare, but when the younger children returned home, Lowell commented that Desdemona's name was bigger than she was, and it was only a matter of days before she became Dessie.

Late one evening after the others had gone to bed, Garnet finished her chores and went into Mama's room to ask if she needed anything. The lamp on the dresser cast a honeyed glow upon Mama and Dessie. The baby was two weeks old and had lost her angry, newborn redness. .Mama's face looked tired and thin. She asked Garnet to put Dessie in her cradle, and Garnet sniffed her milky newness. Giving her little sister a kiss on her velvet cheek, she settled her in the tiny bed.

Mama patted the bed beside her and Garnet sat. "I'm feeling much stronger now. "I'll be able to get up tomorrow."

"Good."

Mama smiled at her.

"What?" Garnet asked.

"I was thinking how some might take us for sisters if they saw us by lamplight. You look remarkably like I did at your age."

"Really?"

Mama nodded and smoothed Garnet's cheek. "I never had freckles because I was careful to stay out of the sun. But I know you get those from working in the garden, trying hard to feed us."

"You know I've always liked being outside more than working in the house. Should've been a boy, I reckon."

"And what would I have done if you'd been a boy?" Mama asked. This was as close as she'd ever come to acknowledging Garnet's contributions.

"I bet Mattie Lawrence is missing you."

"She says I'm to come back as soon as you can do without me."

Mama gazed at the ceiling. "Well, today is Wednesday. I think you can go back this Saturday. Lowell will be home from school to help with the two wild ones."

Garnet grinned, then sobered. "I'm going to ask Mrs. Lawrence to give me real pay for my work, not just a token. Do you think that'll make her angry?"

"No. I imagine Mattie's been expecting this. You're not just a little girl helping out any more. But, knowing Mattie, I don't imagine she'll pay you very much."

"I wish I could do more. Franklin's pay helps, and I'm sure I can get a little from Mrs. Lawrence, but one day's pay won't be much." After a pause she voiced the anxious thoughts that shadowed every hour of her day. "Mama, I know how we're going to make it."

Her mother's brow remained smooth and calm. "It's twice now that Luther Colson has brought us food and supplies. That helps."

"Oh, yes. It helps a great plenty. It's kind of him to bring all that over to us."

Mama's eyes turned flinty. "Oh, yes, since they have my father's house and my father's land and my father's money. Quite generous."

"Well, he wouldn't have to do it, considering."

"Perhaps not, considering."

Neither of them spoke for a moment. The house was silent, but it wasn't peaceful. Garnet said, "And, besides, he may not keep doing it."

Mama nodded her agreement. "Nonetheless, I don't think you need to worry about us starving. Things will work out."

Mostly to keep peace, Garnet agreed, but she didn't see how they could. Perhaps Mama didn't realize how tenuous their hold was on Franklin's money. Garnet expected him to bolt or forfeit the agreement any day, and it wasn't enough for them to live on anyway. Mama's optimism mystified Garnet, but the last thing she wanted was to upset her. She rose to go to her own bed, but her mother caught her hand and pulled her down to kiss her cheek. She hadn't done that in years. "Don't worry," she repeated.

***

Feeling like a bird out of its cage, Garnet arrived early on Saturday morning and spent the day serving customers rather than cleaning. Mrs. Lawrence's house was even more chaotic than ever, but she insisted that her feet and knees were more in need of help than the house. The woman sat upright in a rocking chair on just the other side of the doorway and called out greetings to customers as they came in. Her behavior probably had to do more with nosiness than supervision, and Garnet was too happy to be annoyed by it. She straightened cans and polished the counter.

Mrs. Lawrence chattered about this person and that, but mostly she talked about the Tent Meeting scheduled for mid-June, only two weeks away. "Did you see the flyer I put up by the front door?" she asked. "I'm hoping we'll have a good crowd. Brother Bledsoe is posting notices all over the county, including Ashton."

Garnet had never been to a Tent Meeting, although the church had hosted a small revival a few summers back. After giving a small boy change and sending him out with a pound of cornmeal, she asked Mrs. Lawrence what Tent Meetings were like.

"Oh, it's a fine way to win souls for the Lord. The preacher is Horace Vance from Virginia. He and Brother Bledsoe have known each other for years, and it's as a favor that he's coming to such a speck on the map as Bethel. Why, Brother Vance has preached all over the country."

Her impassioned speech was punctuated every now and then by strange little clicks from the new false teeth, and Garnet suppressed a giggle. If Franklin had been there, she never would've been able to keep from laughing. Mrs. Lawrence didn't notice and explained how the Tent Meeting would last for a week and there'd be good gospel singing and hours of inspired preaching and the Lord would bless Bethel.

117

Although Garnet was less than enthusiastic about long hours of preaching, the event did sound exciting, at least by Bethel standards. She wondered if she could escape the house, even for a few evenings. Surely her mother would have no objection to her attending a religious event, and Garnet felt a deep restlessness that occasional days at Mrs. Lawrence's store couldn't satisfy.

In the afternoon when business slowed and Mrs. Lawrence left her post by the door, David Foster came in. He lit up with his huge, crinkle-eyed grin. "I haven't seen you in weeks!"

She allowed that it'd been a while. Between her father's death and the birth of the new baby, she'd been busy at home. His smile fading, he said, "I been thinking about how rough things must be for you."

As she wrapped his order he told her that his father and he were still working most of the time in Ashton, but he'd also been doing some painting down in Deer Creek. "So you'll be here again on Saturdays, Garnet?"

She liked it when he said her name. "Yes, and Mrs. Lawrence was just saying that she'd like to have me on Fridays too, if my mama will let me."

"I reckon the money will come in handy."

"Yes, except we haven't talked money yet."

He grinned. Everybody knew that Mattie Lawrence probably had the first dollar she'd ever made. "Good luck with it," he said, cocking his head toward the house. "She ought to be glad to have you, all smart and business-like."

She liked it when he said things like that too. Giving him her biggest smile, she told him she hoped to see him soon, and that seemed to please him. He strode out the door with a swagger and winked as he left.

Mrs. Lawrence came into the store just as David was leaving and pointed at his back. "There's one who could benefit from the Tent Meeting; his soul is nigh on to starving for the Lord." She appraised Garnet for a moment. "Seems to me that Foster boy is sweet on you. Why don't you convince him to go to the Meeting?"

Garnet felt a flush climbing her cheeks. She hated that red-headed people blushed so easily. "Why, I could never ask him to go to the Tent Meeting."

"Well, it's not exactly like asking him to a party. You'd just be expressing concern about his spiritual life."

When it was time to leave, Mrs. Lawrence surprised her and started talking about wages, which she was willing to pay as long as Garnet spent them in the store. This was fair, Garnet thought, although it meant the money from Franklin would have to pay for everything else. Between Luther's generosity and her store wages, they should be in good shape for food but strapped for other items. And Lowell needed shoes. Promising to ask her mother about Fridays, Garnet walked home, full of news. Papa had always called Mattie Lawrence "the town crier" even though the woman said she deplored gossip. The news would make for a lively dinner at the Grant house.

Mama had made a simple supper and looked flushed and happy to be out of bed. If Lowell was disgruntled after a day of watching Henry and Violet, he didn't show it, although it was rare when anybody could tell what was going on in Lowell's head.

"So, Mrs. Lawrence wants me to work Fridays too," Garnet told her mother.

Mama ate two forkfuls of food before she replied. "If Mattie will wait another week, until Lowell is out of school for the summer, then it would be all right."

Garnet glanced at Lowell, but he had no reaction. He seemed to have some kind of news himself.

Doing a fair imitation of the storekeeper, Garnet told them about the Tent Meeting. "I wish I knew how to make the noise she does with her false teeth," Garnet said, as her family laughed.

"That's not respectful," Mama said, but she was smiling.

"You're right. And you know I think the world of Mrs. Lawrence. Anyway, I wondered if I could go to a few of the services."

Mama crinkled her nose up as if she'd smelled something foul. "I suppose. I'm not partial to these big shouting and preaching events, but there's no reason why you can't see one for yourself."

"I don't want to sit through hours of preaching," Lowell declared.

"And nobody said you had to," Garnet retorted as she rose to clear the table. "I may not like it either, but Mrs. Lawrence said it would be good for me."

"I imagine she did," Mama replied. "You're such a terrible sinner, Garnet."

Violet and Lowell cackled at this, and Garnet joined in. Sometimes she thought they would be just fine. Somehow Mama would manage to hold them together, and Garnet would do everything she could.

At twilight Garnet visited her garden. It was as quiet as it ever got on a summer evening, but the patch never seemed still. She sensed the growth, the energy coming from the soil to the roots and on to the stems and leaves. She didn't notice that Lowell had come up beside her.

"I was going to pull those weeds today, but I didn't get a chance," he said.

"I'll get them tomorrow."

"Why don't you come with us up to the farm tomorrow? Mama'll do fine here with the baby. You haven't come with us since .."

She squeezed his arm. "Since Papa died. I know, and I miss it. Lorena and Luther are good to us, and I hardly ever see Franklin."

"Luther was up here again today. That's why I didn't get the weeding done. I helped him shore up the shed. We're going to move the chickens in there."

"Luther came here?"

"That's what I said."

"Was Mama nice to him?"

"I reckon. He was in the house for a while and then worked on the shed. He asked me to fetch things for him."

Garnet frowned. "He went in the house?"

"Well yes, but he just brought boards and tools today. No food."

She walked to the side of the house where her lilies stood like fragile wands. Lowell followed her, running his fingers along a blade-like leaf. He said, "Miss Carter kept me after school this afternoon."

Garnet straightened from pulling vines trying to choke her flowers.

He took a deep breath. "She wants me to go into Papa's class next year." Garnet waited for him to go on. "I mean the older class. She says I've completed all the work two years early and should go on over with the bigger children."

"Why, that's wonderful. Did you tell Mama?"

He shook his head. Reaching down, he plucked a large pebble from the ground and flung it away from the house, the stone arcing through the dusk like a shooting star. "Naw. I didn't figure she'd care much one way or the other. It's Papa who always wanted us to do good in school. Anyway, do you think I'm too little to go across the hall? Do you think they'll make fun of me?"

His face was earnest. None of the Grants were very large. She was sturdy enough, round-cheeked and full-bosomed for a sixteen year old, but she wasn't very tall. And even though farm work had broadened Franklin's back and thickened his shoulders, he was short, much shorter than Lorena and Luther. Lowell was stick-thin and pale; long dark hair, so much like Papa's, framed his triangular face. All of them, except Violet, were skinnier than they should be, but Lowell looked like a waif and reminded her of the boys in that Dickens book Papa had read them years ago. She could see how he might be the target of bullying and hated the thought. Lowell was such a good boy, rarely complaining, never causing trouble.

She spoke carefully. "They'll be getting someone to replace Papa for good by fall, won't they?" Since his death a series of inadequate, untried teachers had attempted to fill John Grant's place.

"Miss Carter says they've found a man from the teacher's college at Richmond."

"Well, he'll certainly know how to run a classroom and won't let those older children tease you. It might seem strange at first, but you can't turn down an opportunity like this."

He looked at the ground. "There's a girl, your friend Millie's little sister, who's a year older than me, and she's going to move up too."

"See, then there'll be somebody else in nearly your same situation. It'll all work out." As they went into the house, Garnet considered how often she'd been saying or hearing those same words. She just wondered how it could.

Chapter Six

On Sunday Garnet awoke feeling stormy and out of sorts. Everything irritated her. She thought she'd never get Violet's hair brushed for church, and Lowell flatly refused to go. Although Henry was cheerful enough, he squirmed and giggled as she helped him dress. Mama was oblivious to all these minor irritations, and that annoyed Garnet as much as anything. Throughout church she fidgeted as much as Henry and Violet, wishing Brother Bledsoe would finish so she could get up and move. She twisted and turned in the pew, looking for David Foster, but he wasn't in the congregation. This irritated her too. Why did she look for him when she wasn't sure she wanted to see him? She had no patience with the hairpin sticking into her scalp nor with the stays suffocating her midsection. Everything was just wrong.

Once she herded Henry and Violet home from church, she found herself making irritable silent comments about everything her family did or said. At least she kept them to herself. After dinner, Lowell, Violet, and Henry marched down the path to the farm. Mama sat placidly in the front room, nursing Dessie, and suddenly Garnet couldn't stand it any longer. She announced that she was going to visit Franklin and didn't wait long enough for Mama to comment. Tearing up the path, she thought she might fly to pieces any minute. Her life was as flat as the dull, pewter sky.

At Grandpa's house Lorena and Luther greeted her enthusiastically from the porch. The children had scattered to the orchard where Franklin was teaching them the fine art of apple picking. After a while, Luther disappeared, and when Lorena asked if Garnet would like to see the quilt she'd been working on, she jumped up, glad for the diversion.

In the sewing room, Lorena spread the unfinished quilt on the bed. "I finished piecing it through the winter, but I'm not done quilting it yet," the woman said. The quilt was lovely, a star pattern, pieced in mostly pastel calico.

"What fine stitches, Lorena! Oh, I'd never have the patience to quilt."

Lorena shrugged off the compliment and folded the quilt. "When you get older, you don't have much else to do."

"You'll have plenty to do soon with feeding the hands and canning."

"That's true. I may not get this one finished until cold weather." Her sharp eyes scrutinized Garnet. "How're you keeping? I ask the little ones about you, but they don't tell me much. I reckon it's been a bad time with the new baby. I been wanting to see you." They both knew that Garnet had to visit the farm for them to see each other.

"We're getting along. I started back working for Mrs. Lawrence yesterday, and I'm going to work for her on Fridays too once Lowell gets out of school. The garden looks good. I guess we're managing."

Lorena smoothed her skirt over her slender hips. Although she never went to church, Lorena dressed up every Sunday. "And is Louise a help or a burden?"

Garnet grimaced. "I never know. Until Dessie came, she didn't seem to understand what was going on. Now she acts like she has a plan for taking care of us, but I can't figure out what it would be. I never know what's she's thinking."

Lorena's angular face softened. "Well, it's her job to make sure her family's all right. You shouldn't have to take that on, Garnet."

"But I have to. Some days she lies in the bed with Dessie, and some days she cooks dinner. Sometimes she reads to us, and sometimes she doesn't seem to know we're there. If I hadn't brought it up, she wouldn't have realized we were out of food."

"*Do* you all have enough to eat?"

"Oh yes. With Franklin's money and my pay from Mrs. Lawrence, we're eating just fine. And Luther and you have brought us so much. I can't thank you enough."

Lorena shrugged and stepped out into the hall. "We're glad to do it. We have plenty, and if things hadn't gotten so ugly, all this would belong to Louise. It probably still should. But this is the way Deke wanted it. I can't move out and let her have it." Once again her eyes pierced Garnet's. "I reckon you think Luther and I should hand the farm over to you all."

Garnet hesitated. "No, not if it went against Grandpa's wishes. There were too many hurt feelings, and how would Mama manage running a farm?"

They descended the creaking stairs. "True. Anyways, Luther and I aren't about to let you children starve, and I figured Louise would accept food better than money even if she does hate where it comes from."

Garnet said, "I think she feels like she deserves it."

Lorena snorted in a most unladylike way. In spite of her trim figure and plain but impeccable clothes, Lorena really wasn't a lady, Garnet thought. And then she wondered about the importance of her mother's endless chiding about being one. Not sure that goal had much meaning in her life, she stared out the window toward the horizon where the colorless sky hovered over the hills.

Franklin came into the kitchen, trailed by his brothers and sister. They carried baskets and pails of varying sizes, mostly full of hard, green June apples. His eyes lit up when he saw his sister. "I was hoping you'd be coming back soon."

She grinned at him. He could annoy her to death, especially today when she felt like her skin was too tight for her body, but she loved Franklin for being even the fragile support he was.

"Here's a few million apples, Lorena. I tried to keep this crew from eating too many of them," he said, thumping his buckets on the table.

"Oh no, you young'uns don't want to eat too many green apples!" Lorena exclaimed. "But some nice fried apples for supper might be good, right, Violet?"

The little girl brightened, pleased by Lorena's attention. "Yes, yes!" She clapped her hands. "And biscuits too?"

Lorena told her she might manage that, and Henry crowed that he wanted to "cut out, cut out." Garnet remembered that Lorena allowed the little ones to cut out biscuit dough with cookie cutters. In the middle of Henry's repetitious chatter, Franklin picked the child up and bounced him, making the little fellow giggle. It might only be Sundays, and Franklin might be as stubborn as his mules or his mother, but he was trying, Garnet thought.

Still throwing Henry around, Franklin asked, "Where's Luther?"

"I don't know," Lorena replied, sorting apples. "He just disappeared."

"I'll go look for him," Lowell offered.

"Oh, no need." Franklin turned to Lorena. "It's not time for these two to cut out biscuits just yet, is it?"

"No, no. You all go outside and enjoy yourselves."

Franklin was following the children out the door when Garnet stopped him and murmured, "I think I'll be getting back home. I'd better check on Mama."

He frowned. "You're not staying for supper?"

Hands flying as she peeled the gnarled apples, Lorena looked up at this.

"I have to feed Mama, and I worry when she's alone."

"I'm sure she's all right," Franklin said, but he could see that Garnet was determined and told her to wait while he fetched the money. Usually he sent it home with Lowell.

Garnet waited, pleating the seam of her skirt with fluttery fingers. Lorena's paring knife flashed steadily, but Garnet knew the woman wanted an explanation. She blurted out, "It's not that I don't want your food. And it's not even that I have to go see to Mama."

"You just don't know what to do with yourself. All restless and antsy, ain't you?"

Garnet nodded miserably.

Franklin returned and she stuffed the money in her pocket. "You don't have to be good all the time, Garnet."

She gave him half a nod and sped out the door. The afternoon air had thickened, and clouds seemed to press down upon the earth, the valley, the top of her head. She wasn't trying to be good; she just couldn't settle anywhere. Shaking herself like a wet dog, she resolved to control this silly moodiness. When she got home, she'd weed the garden and pull all the vines choking out the flowers around the house. Maybe if she got very busy and worked very hard, she'd feel better.

As she emerged from the trees, she saw her mother sitting on the front porch, her hair neatly twisted up the back of her head and glowing in the cloudy light. With another few steps Garnet noticed her mother wasn't alone; Luther sat across from her, matching her gentle rocking. This almost halted Garnet, but the man had seen her, and it would be rude for her to turn. She approached the porch where Mama, serene and unperturbed, rocked with Dessie lying limply across her lap. "Did you leave the others behind?" Mama asked.

Garnet nodded, glancing at Luther who kept his eyes on his knees. "They're all staying for supper, but I wanted to do some work in the garden."

"On a Sunday!" Mama trilled, her voice full of mock censure. "What a sinful little girl I have! Going to church in the morning and then working on the Sabbath." She beamed brilliant smiles at both Luther and Garnet.

Garnet muttered something about changing her dress. She didn't understand, would never understand, and shook her head as she stomped upstairs. She ripped off her Sunday dress and grabbed one suitable for the garden, wondering why she felt so angry. Why should she care if Luther and her mother were getting along well enough to visit on a Sunday? Wasn't he being as kind as could be to their entire family? And then as she finished buttoning her dress, she realized that she was more afraid than angry. All rules had gone by the wayside; this was a new game.

By the time Garnet returned to the front porch, Luther had left. Mama continued to rock, gently smoothing Dessie's dark, silky hair and humming. Mama was wearing her best dress. Pinning her mother with a hard, straight look, she said, "So what was that all about?"

Mama looked up with an expression bland as milk. "Well, he's useful." And then she looked away, the shutters closing completely on that topic. "So you're going to do some weeding?"

"Yes, and I guess I'll try to chop that high grass by the creek. I thought maybe Franklin would come over and do it, but he hasn't."

"There's no need for that. Mr. Colson noticed, and he's sending one of his hands over tomorrow. That work is too rough for a young lady anyway."

"I guess I do what needs to be done, lady or not."

Mama wouldn't be ruffled. "It will be done."

Not lady-like in the least, Garnet tromped off to the shed and found her hoe. She attacked the weeds, hacking and chopping with a vengeance. Sure, she was glad for help with the chores. She had enough to do, and two days a week at Mrs. Lawrence's store, welcome as they were, would only add to her responsibilities. She was just angry: at her mother's schemes, at Luther Colson's gullibility, at her father's death; just bubbling over with hot, simmering anger. Clods of dirt flew as she wielded the hoe like a weapon.

The sullen sky offered not even a whisper of a breeze and soon sweat soaked her dress and trickled between her breasts. Physical labor was doing nothing to take the edge off her fury. She remembered her brother's comment about her always being so good. Leaning over to throw an uprooted dandelion into the pile of weeds, she decided being virtuous hadn't done her much good and then considered Mama's joke about her being a "little sinner." It seemed to Garnet that everybody thought she was stupid for being good, for minding her responsibilities. Her hair was as wet as when she washed it, and she flicked away a drip from her neck as she glared around the garden for any lurking weeds.

Gathering up the pile, she dumped them by the creek bank. Nobody else seemed to care about being good. Franklin had escaped to the farm years ago, and Mama, oh, there was hypocrisy! She'd never said the name Colson without disparaging it and now she was wearing her newest dress and visiting on the front porch with Luther just so he'd keep bringing them charity. Garnet rubbed her hands together, ridding them of dirt, and marched back to the shed to replace the hoe. She wondered darkly what Papa would think about that, his wife beholden to people she professed to hate. It wasn't right. Papa had always insisted on working hard for Grandpa in return for his pay or any favors old Deke sent them. Papa would be rolling over in his grave. And this brought her nearly to tears, thinking about that thin, stone lozenge carved with her father's name and dates. Oh, she missed him. How proud he would be of Lowell's achievements and pretty little Dessie! And, she thought sourly, how ashamed of what we've become.

Grabbing an old brush, she filled a bucket with water and went to the front porch, lifting the chairs off the porch with more strength than she needed and scrubbing the wooden floor. Soon her knees and skirt were as wet with dirty water as her bodice was with sweat, and muddy drops splattered up her arms. Maybe she'd act like Franklin and run away, someplace farther than the farm. Maybe she'd take off to Lexington or even Louisville and work in a store. The family would do just fine; Mama could keep cozying up to Luther until he and Lorena were supporting them. When a long splinter pierced the heel of her hand, she used her teeth to pull it out, disregarding the grit that stuck to her lips. She'd wear pretty clothes every day, and a dozen young men would beg to take her out on Sunday afternoons.

Breathless, she stood up and sluiced the porch with the remaining water. For a moment she couldn't figure out what to do next, and then she thought of the old chicken coop. No one had cleaned it out since the hens had been moved to the shed. She couldn't bear the thought of stopping and pushed on to the dirtiest of jobs. She hated all this, hated being good and motherly and careful when that was what Mama should be doing. If she ran off, why then her mother would have to do what Garnet did. She laughed bitterly at that picture, thinking about Lowell and Henry and Violet. What would happen to them? Mama loved babies, so Dessie would be fine, but the others would run as wild as wolves.

Getting dirtier and sweatier by the minute, Garnet made a pile of dirty straw and droppings and piled the muck into the wheelbarrow to take to the refuse pile, far from the house. By now her hands were stinging with blisters, but she grasped the pitchfork and tossed the smelly straw into the pile. She couldn't run off and leave the young ones. Piecing together charity and hard work, the Grant family would manage until they were raised up. She could storm around and act half-crazy all she wanted, but she was trapped. Rhythmically lifting and tossing, she could see no hope for changing her life, but that didn't mean she wouldn't keep looking. She was sick to death of being a good girl.

The dull day grew dimmer, her strength fading with it, and her stomach was so empty it seemed to be sticking to itself. Wearily she replaced her tools. Sweat stung her eyes, and she was completely filthy. Trudging to the back porch, she lowered herself onto a step to pull off her dirty shoes. Pulling out what hairpins were left in her hair, she stuffed them in her pocket and walked barefoot through the soft, cool grass to the pump. Using one hand to raise and lower the handle, she ducked and let icy water run over her head and neck. She felt the cold like a toothache. Water tightened her skin and dress, making it a heavy tent that stuck to her legs and weighed her down from neck to hem. Still she pumped. Out of the corner of her eye she caught movement and stopped, sliding the sodden mass of hair out of her face.

Bunched together as if they were posing for a photograph were Lowell, Violet, and Henry, all of them with their mouths open, staring in disbelief at their crazy sister soaking herself, dress and all, at the pump. Lowell murmured, "Good Lord."

"Did you bring food?" Her voice felt rough and hoarse.

They all nodded and Violet and Lowell held out pails to show her.

"Well, take it in the kitchen. Mama and I haven't eaten."

She followed them, squeezing water from her hair and dress as she went. They think I'm as queer-headed as Mama, she said to herself, and they were probably right. Mama waltzed into the room and began poking around in the pails. She glanced at Garnet who stood by the sink looking bedraggled as a wet dog but made no comment. Mama fetched a plate and daintily set out a slice of ham, a small hill of glistening fried apples, and a biscuit, but Garnet took the pails to the sink and ate over it, ignoring the crumbs and apple juice dribbling down her chin. The three children stared at her, but she simply stuffed the food in, dusted off her hands and turned to go upstairs.

***

Garnet's mood continued until she wondered if her head and heart would feel this way forever. Her brothers and sister didn't see it, and Mama never seemed to notice anything she didn't want to notice. She was happier than ever, sailing around the house with Dessie cradled to her chest, and intent on repairing, or cutting down clothes to bolster their shabby wardrobes. She called each of them to her and measured, frowning as she wrote numbers in a little notebook. "The problem is Lowell since we don't have Franklin's clothes anymore," she told Garnet. "I may be able to do something with Papa's, but it will be difficult.

Garnet honestly didn't care. Her restlessness was mirrored by a growing buzz of anticipation throughout the community. Everybody saw the upcoming Tent Meeting in a different way. Mrs. Lawrence swore the Holy Spirit was preparing their hearts for the word of God. Stopping at the store to shop for cousins coming to the event, Miss Carter said that she did declare, it seemed like the air was building up to something. One morning Lowell asked Garnet very seriously if she ever had a feeling that something was going to happen. Nothing specific, he said when she questioned him, just something. To Garnet it was as if a huge hive of bees had settled in Bethel and was swarming around the little town.

On Saturday before the event, she arrived at the store filled with the same nervous energy. Between customers, she flew around the store, unpacking candy and arranging items. They were unusually busy, and Mrs. Lawrence had a hard time staying off her feet because everyone wanted to chat about the Tent Meeting, starting the next day. One customer reported that Mrs. Bledsoe had made chicken and dumplings for Brother Vance who'd arrived on Friday with a big wagon holding the very tent he'd be using. Minnie, Garnet's school friend, was buying more food for visiting aunts and uncles who were eating them out of the house, she said.

Mrs. Lawrence bustled between the store and the kitchen where she was cooking for her daughter and two grandchildren who were visiting for the week. On one trip into the store, Mrs. Lawrence asked, "Now you'll be there every night, won't you?"

Garnet wiped flour off the counter. "Like I told you, I'll be there both services tomorrow, and for certain I'll come next Friday and Saturday nights, but I'm not sure if I can be there every night. Mama may need me."

"Well, I suppose folks do what they have to do, but it would be good if you were there each and every night. It's not often we get to hear the likes of Brother Vance." By mid-afternoon, her family arrived and Mrs. Lawrence shut the door between her sitting room and the store.

Garnet took a deep breath. Then David Foster came in, looking like a thundercloud. She was surprised, not to see him, because he managed to stop by most Saturday afternoons, but by his unusually sour mood.

Before she could speak, he leaned against the counter and asked, "What were you doing smiling at Willie Martin?"

She was speechless. His eyes were nearly as hidden by his frown as they were by his brilliant smiles. Who was Willie Martin? Someone who had come in the store?

"Don't have nothing to say about it, do you? He's off telling everybody about how that red-headed gal up at the schoolteacher's house smiled at him when he was mowing," David growled.

Then she vaguely remembered a lanky boy with a thatch of ragged, corn-colored hair whom Luther had sent to clean up the tall grass by the creek. She supposed he was one of Luther's hands. Before she could speak, David leaned toward her, gripping the counter with tight knuckles. "I told him to keep his eyes off'n you, that you're my girl, and that he shouldn't even be looking at you. And then, as big as anything, he grins at me and says you smiled at him all pretty and sweet."

Garnet tossed her head. This was sort of flattering and exciting, but she knew she had to act affronted. "I don't reckon I'm anybody's girl."

David backed down a fraction. "Well, you're more my girl than you are his. What was you doing flirting with him?"

She widened her eyes in mock horror. This was really getting to be fun. "I wasn't flirting with anybody," she declared and looked straight in his belligerent eyes. "Luther sent him up to our house to do some mowing. I went outside to the garden and smiled at him, because he was doing us a favor and I was raised up to be polite, unlike some people I know." She turned her back to him, making sure her skirts flounced.

"Aww, Garnet," he started, a wheedling tone in his voice. "It just made me crazy thinking you were smiling at some other boy. I don't like you flirting with nobody else."

She turned back to face him, eyes sparkling and cheeks flushed. Let him think it's anger, she thought, but she knew she was having the best time ever. "I don't flirt," she said, knowing that was exactly what she was doing. "Are you here to buy something?"

He stuffed his hands in his pockets and looked down. "Yeah, I need a pound of coffee and a half dozen eggs."

She set the coffee on the counter. "I smile at lots of people."

Thoroughly miserable now, he mumbled, "It just set me off when Willie was doing that bragging. For the longest time, well, ever since I seen you when you was thirteen, I've wanted you to be my girl." This wasn't exactly news to her, but it made her feel good.

He paid for his groceries, and she handed him change, not rescuing him at all. Then she said, "Are you going to the Tent Meeting?"

This surprised him. "Ain't thought about it. It's not exactly what I like to do." He watched her carefully. "But I reckon it wouldn't do me no harm."

"I'm going tomorrow, and then I'm not sure which nights I can get away from home. But I know I'm going on Friday and Saturday evenings. I thought maybe you'd like to go with me." She was amazed at her nerve, but it was, after all, church, and she'd quit caring so much about being a good girl.

He brightened, those eyes crinkling in earnest. "Say, that might be all right. We're just working down the road so I'll be around all week."

She nodded at him, watching him stand taller. "How about we meet at the school on Friday night? They start at seven."

He grinned and then darkened suddenly. "You didn't ask Willie Martin to go with you them other nights, did you?"

She shoved the eggs at his chest. "Who's Willie Martin?"

Chapter Seven

On Sunday morning Garnet walked alone to the schoolyard where the giant tent waited for the grand event. Folks were dressed in their best, and the air smelled of powders, hair oil, and bay rum like Grandpa used to wear. It was a clear, breezy day, and occasionally the wind sneaked under the tent to billow its sand-colored sides, but these puffs brought little relief to the throngs sitting hip to hip. Garnet squeezed in next to Mrs. Lawrence.

The crowd was buzzing but quieted when two little girls and their father came to the front. He played a guitar and the girls sang about Jesus in high, plaintive voices. "From Deer Creek," Mrs. Lawrence whispered. "They normally sing at the Holiness church."

There were hymns and long, beseeching prayers that sounded more like sermons than messages to God, and after a lengthy recounting of their long and blessed friendship, Brother Bledsoe introduced Horace Vance. The congregation sat up a little straighter, craning their necks to see around wide hats or puffy chignons. The great man himself stepped upon the raised platform and raised his hands toward heaven. "God be praised that the souls of Bethel are eager for His word!"

He was impressive, Garnet admitted; coal-black hair covered his large, domed head and a luxuriant silver and black moustache decorated his face. His suit was creamy white, and he carried a worn, oversized Bible. But, by far the most imposing thing about Vance was his voice. It was loud; no doubt even the most ancient and deaf in the tent could hear every word he said. More than loud, though, his voice dipped and swooped, giving meaning and music to every vowel. His Virginia accent trickled over his words like honey from a biscuit.

He didn't shout very often; although when he did, Garnet jumped. Mostly he pled with them, begging them to repent and come to Jesus. But after a while, even his elaborate voice became monotonous, and Garnet paid more attention to her surroundings than his message. Mrs. Lawrence was intent, leaning forward and whispering, "Yes, Jesus" every few minutes. The grandchildren between her and her daughter became more restless as time passed, and every now and then Mrs. Lawrence's daughter glared at them. Garnet wondered how they'd cope with a week's worth of preaching.

The light through the canvas jaundiced peoples' faces, giving them an intent, sickly look. As Brother Vance built the momentum of the service, a woman in the back started sobbing and calling out to God. Punctuated by occasional "amens" and "yea, Lords" and then by outright hollering and sobs, the crowd swayed and bounced, raising their arms along with their voices. Garnet was sweating, and peoples' powders and pomades were giving way to stronger scents. "You must be washed in the blood of the Savior," Vance pleaded. "You must come home to the flock of the Lord."

This acted as a signal for many people to move forward and kneel at Vance's feet. As people moved forward, he started lining "The Ninety and Nine" in a rich, mellow voice. Garnet knew the words.

> There were ninety and nine that safely lay
> In the shelter of the fold
> But one was out on the hills away
> Far off from the gates of gold

By the second verse Mrs. Lawrence wiped her eyes and picked her way over tidy shoes and heavy boots until she could walk up the central aisle and kneel. Garnet wasn't sure what she should do. Brother Vance touched the bowed heads of the people praying, and Brother Bledsoe knelt with some of them. It looked as though this was appropriate behavior for a Tent Meeting, but Garnet felt no spiritual pull.

After all the verses and a long congregational prayer, they were released and urged to come back at seven o'clock that evening. Suddenly faces lost their tension and people greeted each other with relaxed and friendly smiles. A large crowd surrounded Vance, hoping for a handshake from the great evangelist himself. Mrs. Lawrence grabbed Garnet's arm. "Maybe the Lord will work in your heart tonight," she urged, and Garnet took that to mean she should go up front and pray at her soonest opportunity.

That evening, when Garnet returned to the tent, the atmosphere was even more expectant. Again she squished in next to Mrs. Lawrence who handed her a paper fan depicting Jesus and a bunch of lambs. It was even hotter as the tent accumulated the evening sun. Every bench was full and people stood around the perimeter. Before the service started, Garnet twisted around to see who was there and caught the eye of Willie Martin who turned crimson and ducked his head. Even though she knew better and she was, essentially, in church, Garnet kept staring at him until he raised his head and then smiled at him, holding it for a moment before she turned around.

As dusk deepened, men hung lanterns from hooks on the tent poles. The stinging odor of coal oil added to the other hot smells inside the tent, and Garnet fanned herself. When Brother Vance made the altar call, she slipped out and prayed that God would help her give up her wayward moodiness and turn her into a patient, good girl again. But she didn't cry, nor did she swoon like Millie did, right up at the altar.

It was a relief to leave the tent and step into the dramatically cooler night air. Rejuvenated, people lingered and talked outside the festive orange tent, but Garnet headed for home. There was something exciting about walking home alone in the dark, summer night. She'd nearly reached the road when she heard someone say her name. It was David.

"I didn't see you in there," she said.

"Oh, I wasn't. I just come up half hour ago to walk you home."

"I guess I know my way home."

He rubbed the side of his tanned face. "Lots of strangers are coming to this revival. I thought it'd be a good idea."

They set off walking. Few people were going in their direction, and quickly the noise from around the Tent Meeting grounds dulled to a low hum. She heard frogs, insects, and the faraway rumble of a dog barking. It was a beautiful, clear night with a velvet sky and a thorough sprinkling of stars.

"You could've come to the service," she murmured. There was no one near them, but she felt like she should whisper.

"I could've. But today's my only day off, and I had some trim to carve. I'll be there with you on Friday and Saturday, and I reckon that's enough preaching for me."

She took a deep breath. "Smells a lot better out here than in that tent."

He laughed. "I reckon."

She grinned back at him. "Willie Martin was there. If I was scared to walk home alone, I could've asked him to come with me."

He took it well, flashing his eyes in the same way hers were probably glinting. "And you say you don't flirt."

She chuckled but then was surprised, although she shouldn't have been, when he took her hand. She was unsure whether she should squeeze or let hers go limp. She even wondered if she should pull her hand away. His felt warm and calloused.

To cover her confusion, she asked, "What are you carving?"

David seemed easy with the situation, striding along with steps that matched hers He held her hand firmly, like she remembered her father doing many years ago. "Oh, it's a piece of trim for a china cupboard Pa's making. It's oak, which is hard as a rock and mean to carve. I'm making a long decoration that has acorns and leaves on it. Pa says I'm doing fine, but I'm not too pleased with it yet. Maybe it'll turn out."

They passed the road up to the farm and would be nearing her house soon. She felt more breathless than the walk warranted. What if he tried to kiss her? Then his thumb started rubbing her palm, ever so gently, almost like a feather. She felt a strange sensation, sort of a catch, in her belly and her heart thudded so loudly she thought he might hear it. Even though they walked more and more slowly, she could see the gray shadow of her house from the road. She whispered, "My mama might be sitting out."

He stopped and turned to face her, his teeth shining in the dim light. "Then maybe I'll stop here," he said. He clasped her hand more tightly and raised it to his mouth, brushing her knuckles with his lips. She was surprised how warm and soft they were, and again that strange, flickering tightness jumped in her belly.

Releasing her hand, he whispered good night, and she scurried across the swinging bridge. The porch was empty, and she was grateful since it gave her another moment to collect herself. Mama was in her bedroom, brushing her hair, and simply asked if the evening had gone well. Intent upon her reflection in the mirror, she hardly noticed Garnet who was thankful for that too. If she'd been paying attention, Mama would surely have known that she'd walked home with a boy who'd held and kissed her hand. Garnet floated up the steps to her room where Violet dozed in the dark, but it was a long time before she slept. She examined each moment of that walk home like jewels taken from a case.

By morning, though, the evening had little more substance than a dream. Franklin arrived with a wheelbarrow full of apples, so she spent what the morning scalding canning jars and making applesauce. She peeled and cored apples until she had to stop to make dinner, but it seemed as though the mound of apples was still as large as when she'd started.

After she'd started another kettle, Mama appeared holding her old, wide-brimmed straw hat and announced, "I've just fed Dessie, and she's asleep. I'm walking up to the post office and might stop to speak to Miss Carter's kinfolk."

Mama hadn't left the house since Papa's funeral. She'd never been one for visiting, but Garnet understood restlessness, especially these days. What struck her as odd was that Mama wore one of her oldest dresses, cut full to allow for pregnancy and faded from green to nearly gray with years of washing. She couldn't imagine Mama paying calls dressed like that. And Mama hadn't even bothered to put her hair up. A long auburn rope hung down her back, tied with a wide white ribbon. But the strangest thing was that Mama chose to walk down toward the farm. Certainly you could go to both the post office and Miss Carter's house by walking that way, but it meant passing the house where Lorena and Luther lived and then turning down their lane.

Garnet stirred the apples and shook her head. It'd been years since Mama had seen her old home, and maybe she just wanted to look at the house, and, besides, who could ever figure out Mama? Thinking about romantic, moonlit walks with a young man was a whole lot more interesting.

Hours later Violet and Henry clattered into the kitchen talking about the new chicks Luther had brought the day before, and Violet wanted to know if all those apples meant a pie was forthcoming. Over their chatter Garnet heard a thin cry from the bedroom and rushed to get Dessie. The baby was happy enough once Garnet picked her up and settled her on her shoulder, but before long Dessie would want to eat.

Garnet kept glancing out the window to watch for her mother. And sure enough, it wasn't long before Dessie started little whimpers that indicated a full-blown cry was on the way. Garnet swayed through the house, half-rocking the child, then carried her outside. She quit crying, but her gulps and hiccups indicated this was a temporary lull.

Garnet figured Mama had probably been gone three hours at this point, and it was yet another half-hour before she appeared, from the road rather than the path. She was red-faced and hot with half-moons of sweat under her arms. When she heard Dessie's whimpers, wet patches appeared on the front of her dress as well. Mama threw her hat on the sofa, and Garnet saw that her mother's hair hung in a loose tangle down her back. "Did you lose your ribbon, Mama?"

"I must've."

On Tuesday, Garnet washed all morning, and in the late afternoon, she unpegged the clothes and started sprinkling them down, smelling the sunshine and grass in the cloth. Maybe she'd iron after supper. Knowing that the Tent Meeting was going on just up the road made her itchy to go, but she'd stay home another evening. David wouldn't be there, and she didn't exactly love the preaching. The singing was another matter, and she was humming a hymn when her mother called her.

Mama stood by the bed with an expectant smile on her face. "This needs ironing, so I thought I'd give it to you before you finish sprinkling everything down."

She pointed to the bed at a lovely white blouse with a high collar. It was made of batiste, thin and gauzy as tissue. "It's lovely, Mama. You made it for me?" She'd never owned anything so fine.

Mama beamed. "Well, I re-made it. It was mine, years ago, but I haven't been able to wear it since Franklin was a baby. You don't remember it, I'm sure."

Garnet shook her head and touched the finely sewn tucks and tiny pearl buttons. "Of course I had to cut it down. You're as slim in the waist as I once was. Babies do put weight on a woman."

"It's so thin and delicate."

"Oh, that reminds me." Mama turned to the chest behind her. "I made this for you too. You need something pretty underneath to show through." She handed Garnet a camisole made of smooth, snow-white cotton and trimmed with some of the mile-long lace. A thin, satiny ribbon in the palest blue ran through the lace around the neck.

"This is beautiful. When on earth did you do all this?"

"When you work on Fridays and Saturdays."

Garnet looked up to see if this was a reproof, but Mama's face was clear and composed. "Anyway, a young lady needs a few pretty things, and I thought you might want to wear the blouse when you go to the Tent Meeting. You might meet a handsome young man, mightn't you?"

She didn't look so bland when she said this, and Garnet wondered if Mama knew David Foster had been pursuing her. So what? It seemed like they both had secrets.

The pretty things thrilled Garnet, but she couldn't help but wonder what her mother thought she'd wear with the gauzy blouse. She didn't own a skirt. Then Mama touched her arm. "You really are a strange girl, Garnet. So good, so polite."

Puzzled and a little hurt even though the words seemed to be compliments, she looked up. Mama was shaking her head. "Have a little spirit, girl. You should be saying, 'Mama, what do you expect me to wear with this blouse, a petticoat?'"

"Well, I did wonder."

Mama turned again to the chest of drawers and unfolded a soft, dove-gray skirt from a swath of tissue paper. "Ask for what you need. People don't know unless you tell them."

The skirt nearly took Garnet's breath away. "Is it silk?"

Mama shook her head. "It's the finest, thinnest wool crepe. Should last for years."

Garnet smoothed the fabric cautiously, afraid she would snag it with her rough hands. "Was this yours?"

Dessie was cooing in the cradle on the other side of the bed, and Mama went over to pick her up. "No, I made it new for you. The material came from Ashton, just in at Trosper's."

Propped against her mother's shoulder, Dessie fixed her eyes on her sister, and Garnet touched her soft cheek. She didn't bother to ask how her mother had come by the fabric or, for that matter, paid for it. The secrets kept on buzzing. "Thank you, Mama. It's all lovely."

With one thing and another, she didn't iron and woke up early Wednesday morning determined to do so. The sky was ruddy with sunrise, but there was no sun to see. Big, pillowy clouds filled the sky, and when she went to the pump she could smell rain. By mid-morning she was heating the irons, but it was one of those awkward days when she couldn't seem to get anything done. Henry stepped on a wasp and came howling into the kitchen. Lowell disappeared when he was supposed to be feeding the chickens. Mama was remaking one of Garnet's old dresses for Violet who wasn't helping by hovering over the sewing machine and continually asking if it was done yet.

Everyone seemed to settle down, and Garnet started her ironing, doing the lovely blouse first. With a quick gust or two of wind, the rain that had been threatening all morning started in earnest. It was almost a relief. She moved the iron over shirts and petticoats with a hypnotized rhythm. She debated whether she would go to the Tent Meeting that night. She'd skipped two nights in a row and felt like she was missing something. David had waited for her on Sunday. She'd been very specific in telling him she wouldn't be there Monday, but what if he'd watched for her last night? She supposed it wouldn't hurt him to be disappointed, but maybe he would wait again tonight. She left it to fate and decided she'd go if the rain stopped.

Suddenly there was a loud banging at the door, and Luther let himself in. He was carrying the large wooden box as well as a bundle covered in paper. Mama jumped up and tucked her hair behind her ears. As usual, Luther said little, just mumbling something about the rain. He was soaked, and rivulets from his hat made half-dollar wet spots on the floor. Both Violet and Henry ran to him. Garnet continued ironing, but Mama stood staring at him, rather than the box, which the children were trying to peer into. And Luther watched Mama, his eyes glittering like they too were wet from the rain. They just stared at each other without saying a word, and Garnet wondered if Mama was going to stop her sweet as pie ways all of a sudden. Maybe he would be "Colson trash" again this morning.

In a low voice Mama announced, "I need to speak to Mr. Colson privately, children. We'll be on the porch."

She turned, sending her skirts swaying, and Luther untangled himself from Henry to follow her. Violet started after them, but Garnet stopped her. "Mama said she needed to speak to Luther privately. That means with no one else around."

"Is she fussing at him?"

"I don't know," Garnet replied. "And it's none of our business."

Lowell looked up from his geometry problems. She shrugged and folded a pillowcase. The little ones fussed until Lowell said, "Come here, Violet. Let's draw a plan for the most beautiful house you can think up." She sidled over to him, and he warned her, "Now we're not going to draw the outside. We're going to do a plan, like builders do, and show the rooms and doors and windows."

He opened the tablet to a fresh sheet and asked her, "Let's say here's the front door. What room would you walk into next?"

She replied that it would be the front room, silly, and it took him a while to convince her to imagine something different. Very seriously he drew a plan which ended up looking much like Grandpa's house. He added furniture and shaded in some rugs, and then gave Violet the paper, which she studied intently.

"Now I'll do one for Garnet. You describe your perfect house, and I'll draw it."

She switched irons and plucked one of Dessie's gowns from the pile. The perfect house would be one of her own: quiet, clean, and simple, but she said, "Oh, I don't know what I'd want. Do one for Franklin. Let's see," she mused. "I think he'd want to walk in and see a front room too."

Violet caught the amusement in her sister's voice and returned to Lowell's elbow. He drew a porch, an opening for the front door, and then a rectangle.

"And then," Garnet said, pressing a tiny sleeve, "he'd want stables right there in the front room. Make the door really big so the horses and mules could get in."

Violet and Lowell went off into spasms of giggles, and Henry joined in whether he knew what he was laughing at or not. They went on with it and devised a "hay room" and more silly ideas for a quite a while, only stopping when they heard the front door open. Mama came back saying, "What do we have in the box this time, children?"

By late afternoon the rain had stopped and watery sunshine turned the droplets to diamonds. Mama said she had no objection to Garnet's going to the Tent Meeting so after supper she washed her face, wound her braids into a crown around her head, and dressed. Afraid of muddying the new skirt, she wore her dark blue dress again. After all, she might not even see David. It was a beautiful evening, fresh and fragrant after the rain. She reached the tent in good time, and sat, once again, by Mrs. Lawrence.

"Where's your family?" she asked the woman.

"Oh, my daughter's got a headache, and the children have had about as much sitting still as they can stand," Mrs. Lawrence replied. She blinked a time or two, her eyes huge and owlish behind her spectacles. "And to tell you God's truth, I've had about as much of them as I can take."

Garnet laughed. "But you have several days to go."

"No. They're going home Friday. Her man's got people coming this weekend."

Garnet was a little early and didn't feel it was rude to twist around and see who was coming in the tent. Millie had cut a fringe of bangs and was simpering and smiling at a young man sitting next to her. Garnet thought she recognized the boy from years ago at school. "Some courting going on there."

"Courting? Well, I reckon so. There ain't too many opportunities better than a Tent Meeting for that. Sometimes there's as many weddings as baptisms by the end of one." Mrs. Lawrence looked at Garnet. "You'll be doing some courting too, won't you?"

She blushed. "David Foster's coming on Friday and Saturday."

"Mm, hmm. And that's a good thing. Growing up with that heathen daddy of his couldn't have been a godly experience. That man can be as friendly as anything and then turn mean in a minute when the drink's in him. Oh, look! Lord be praised, it's the Clarks! I reckon Fanny's come to play. Some folks say there should never be a fiddle in church, but I don't see the harm in it."

Sure enough, stately as queens, Gert and Fanny walked down the center aisle of the tent. Behind them, just as tall, was their brother Clifford. Garnet remembered him from the bank, and he acted much as he had there, smiling, chatting, and shaking hands with people on both sides of the aisle. You would've thought the Clarks were royalty. The two towering sisters made their way to the front, lowering themselves onto the bench.

"Do you reckon it'll collapse?" Mrs. Lawrence whispered.

"Mrs. Lawrence!"

The older woman grinned and clicked her teeth. Clifford Clark caught up with his sisters and sat next to Gert. His dark hair glowed in the dull light of the tent. Once again Garnet thought about how handsome he was and wondered why he'd never married. She asked Mrs. Lawrence.

"Don't know. Plenty of gals have set their caps for him, but he never married none of them. He could charm the birds right out of the trees, that Clifford. I think he's probably just sort of ornery. His sisters have always taken care of every little thing for him, and he likes it that way. A wife might not be so accommodating," she replied.

The service began, and Fanny Clark played her fiddle. She accompanied the hymns and played a solo. Brother Vance delivered a subdued and sorrowful sermon about those who locked their hearts against Jesus. Garnet was more touched by his grief for unsaved souls than she was by his loud exhortations for salvation. When the altar call came, Fanny stood again and raised her gleaming fiddle. Tucking it under her chin, she closed her eyes, and the big woman looked almost beautiful in the golden light from the kerosene lanterns. She played "Why Not Tonight?" through once, and then the congregation sang:

> Oh! Do not let the Word depart,
> And close thine eyes against the light;
> Poor sinner, harden not thy heart;
> Thou would'st be saved— Why not tonight?

Garnet joined in and prayed as she sang. She felt light and unburdened as she offered her soul to Jesus. She forgot about troubles at home, strange secrets brewing, and David Foster, so that when she left the tent, speaking to people and complimenting Millie on her hair, she didn't think to look for David and started slowly walking home. Then she remembered and stopped, glancing around for him. It would've been silly for him to come every night on the off chance that she'd be there. Friday and Saturday would be soon enough, but she couldn't help feeling disappointed. She'd turned back to the road when she heard him call her.

"You're out early tonight," he exclaimed as he rushed to join her.

"Really? I don't have a watch."

They started walking, and she was thinking that it was too short a walk for the time they wanted together. He reached for her hand, and tonight it felt comfortable rather than frightening.

"Did you wait for me last night?" she asked.

"You don't think I'd miss a chance to see you, do you?"

This made her glad, and she squeezed his warm hand. "I'm sorry you wasted your time."

Garnet thought he seemed unusually quiet. She warned, "Now, I know I won't be here tomorrow night."

"All right." The silence between them lengthened until he murmured, "I reckon I'm not much company tonight."

"What's wrong?"

"Oh, it's been a funny day. We was supposed to do some roofing, but the rain cancelled that. So, Pa and I spent the day putting together some cabinets. It was all right, but he started talking all restless, and it come out that he wants to move."

"Where to?"

"The northern part of the state, Covington. He knows people up there, and they wrote him saying there was plenty of work for a finish carpenter, lots of building going on. We've been up there before. He likes the city, and he likes doing skilled carpentry. Shoot, around here we're doing anything we can pick up: painting, roofing, any odd jobs. Up there he can do what he's good at."

In the dark, on that deserted road, she felt like they were the only people in the world. Occasionally their shoulders bumped as they navigated the furrowed road, and his felt solid and sturdy. "Would you go with him?"

"I don't know. He's talking like I would except the last time I went I hated it. There's a woman he likes up there, and I feel like I'm in the way. And it's easy for him to go to taverns, so the drinking is worse. Then again, sometimes it's better because he's happy with his work and this woman. But I don't know nobody and it's lonesome."

She didn't know what to say, but the thought of him leaving saddened her. Realizing how much she looked forward to his stopping into the store or walking her home, she wondered if she was in love with him. Was that what she was feeling? He stopped and turned to face her. "I don't really care what kind of work I do. I'm not skilled like Pa although he swears I will be if I keep after it and mind what he teaches me. But I like this county; we've been here a while, and I have some friends. As much as we've traveled around, this is the closest thing to home I've had."

He reminded her of her brothers, and she touched his cheek. His response was not at all brotherly. With a little gust of a sigh, he pulled her to him and kissed her. It happened so fast she didn't have time to worry about where her nose went or what to do with her lips. It felt soft and sort of friendly the way his lips met hers and moved against them. He continued to hold her hand, squeezing it tighter, and placed his other hand against her neck. It only lasted a few seconds, but she was breathless when he pulled away. With a shadow of his old spunk he said, "Guess you won't tell me if that was your first kiss or not."

A smile twitched at her mouth. "No."

"No, it wasn't your first kiss, or no, you won't tell me?"

"Just no." She started walking again.

He laughed. "Anyway," he continued as if nothing had happened, "I don't want to go. He has his woman in Covington, and I have mine here."

Garnet hadn't thought of herself as a woman, let alone allowed that she was his. His statement seemed more like a question, but she wasn't able to answer it. "We're almost to my house."

"I know."

"I don't suppose my mother knows exactly when the service gets out, and you said we were early tonight. We could walk on past for a while."

He brightened and then pulled his eyebrows together. "What if she's sitting on the porch and sees us go by?"

Garnet lifted a shoulder. "Then she'll see us."

Chapter Eight

Garnet spent most of Thursday in the garden. Mama had finished Violet's dress and was feverishly sewing on one for herself. It would be fancy, made of buttercup silk. Garnet had so gotten in the habit of ignoring Mama's little ways that she didn't even question why her mother was making such a splendid dress or where the expensive fabric had come from. Besides, she had other things on her mind.

That night she could hardly sleep for thinking about an entire evening with David, even if it would be spent in church. She'd wear her beautiful new clothes, and he might think she was pretty. She imagined herself as Juliet and pictured David shimmying up the tin roof to climb into her bedroom. It would be dark and romantic, just like Mr. Shakespeare's play. And then Garnet had to stifle her chuckles in her pillow. Three feet away lay Violet who'd just moaned in her sleep. The tin roof would crackle and complain about every movement and might even fall in. And, although David was attractive in a charming, boyish way, he wasn't exactly Romeo. Ah, and she wasn't Juliet either, she thought. Her hands were roughened by hours of work, and she had freckles, not a milky, aristocratic complexion. We're just a couple of country people, she decided, and maybe we're fairly well suited.

By the time Garnet reached the store Friday morning, Mrs. Lawrence's kin had already left. "Don't get me wrong, I love my daughter, and those children are my only grandbabies, but, my stars, am I glad to have the place back to myself!"

"Well, I'm here to mind the store, so why don't you rest so you can enjoy the service tonight?"

"I'm going to do just that as soon as I water my flowers. I was so busy I forgot them, and they're probably dying of thirst." She went to her table of plants. "Oh, Garnet, I meant to tell you. The night-blooming cereus has a bud on it. It's still tight, but I bet it won't be long before it blooms. You need to come down and see that."

"I'd like that." The odd, ugly plant fascinated her. She peered over Mrs. Lawrence's shoulder, and there was a large, tightly furled bud hanging from one of its flat, fleshy leaves. It was hard to imagine such a homely plant producing the exquisite flower Mrs. Lawrence described.

About an hour earlier than usual, Mrs. Lawrence insisted that Garnet go on home. "I'm not going to cut your pay, girl. You need to go and get all gussied up for little Mr. Foster, don't you?" Although the reference to David made her blush, Garnet was grateful.

She buttoned the filmy blouse with shaky fingers. Feeling a little breathless, she wasn't sure if this was from excitement or that she'd laced her corset more tightly than usual. All of her family were in the kitchen and made appreciative noises when she came in. Mama was attaching lace to her elegant dress and nodded approvingly. Garnet escaped before there were more questions or, God forbid, grubby little hands clutching at the cloud-soft skirt.

At first she started up the road at her usual fast clip, but the evening was steamy and she was afraid she'd perspire and ruin her blouse. Anyway, her usual stride didn't take into consideration an unusually tight corset. Just as she passed the road up to Grandpa's, she saw David walking toward her. She waved, amused that he should be so eager to see her. He looked nice in a pale, neatly pressed blue shirt and dark gray pants, but she thought his face looked awfully red, and as he neared her she realized he was deeply sunburned. He stopped a pace ahead of her and gave a low whistle. "You look just fine, Garnet."

She smiled. "You look a little overcooked."

He shrugged as if he was trying to keep his shirt from touching his shoulders. "I've been roofing."

They crowded onto a nearly full bench at the back and sat very close together, so close it made Garnet a little uncomfortable. David chatted away about his day on the roof and about this person and that. Millie came in with her young man, and her eyes widened when she saw Garnet with David. Before long the service started, and it seemed more frenzied than ever. A quartet of men led the hymn singing. David stood but didn't sing. Tonight Brother Vance used every one of his thespian skills from emotional whispers to thundering pleas. He was preaching on the Book of Revelations, and the scenes of doom and devastation were terrifying.

By the time the men lit the lanterns, it was breathlessly hot. Even though the flaps were raised, not a whisper of a breeze found its way into the tent. Garnet had forgotten her fan in her rush to get ready. Pulling a little lace hanky from her sleeve she dabbed daintily at her upper lip, which was growing an appalling moustache of sweat. She felt her lovely blouse wilting and wondered how badly the skirt was wrinkling under her bottom. While Brother Vance's voice swooped and soared about the Apocalypse, a woman fell right off the end of a bench and fainted. Shouted hallelujahs and amens greeted her fall, but David whispered, "She probably keeled over from the heat."

His sunburn glowed in the sulfurous light. Taking a big white handkerchief from his pocket, he rubbed it over his face and grinned at her. She loved the way his eyes crinkled up. He whispered, "Do you reckon hell's any hotter than this?"

She giggled and realized she was happy, truly happy for the first time in forever. It was nearly as good as when Papa praised her or when Lowell got well or when she and Lorena were laughing in the kitchen. Brother Vance had the congregation trembling in fear of eternal damnation, and all Garnet Grant could do was smile.

They stood, glad to move, when the hymn-singing and altar calls started, and she tried to smooth her skirt. People were pouring to the altar, hands outstretched and tears flowing down their faces. David touched her arm and murmured, "I'm parched to death. Could we leave and get a drink of water?"

She didn't mind. Most people were focused on the dramatic activity at the front anyway, and the loud singing and shouting helped to cover their exit. After they'd walked a few paces from the tent, David said, "I'm not sorry I went, Garnet, but I don't think it was any hotter up on that roof this afternoon."

"I know. Let's see, where can we find some water?" She thought a minute. "Let's use Mrs. Lawrence's pump."

Taking deep breaths of fresher, cooler air, they circled around the back of Mrs. Lawrence's house. Garnet led David to the pump.

"There's no cup. I'll pump and you get a drink," she said. He did so and saturated his handkerchief to wash his face. Then he did the same for her, and, of course, she splashed water on that blessed blouse, making her wonder if fine clothes were really quite the thing for a girl like her.

Refreshed, they laughed and both of them jumped when one of the cats flew across their path. Neither of them wanted to go back to the tent or to Garnet's house. Without really making a decision, they wandered across Deer Creek Road to the deserted churchyard.

"Did your father say anything more about leaving?" she asked.

"Oh, that's all he's talking about. He swears that when we finish this roofing job and then the painting in Ashton we're leaving."

"How soon would that be?"

"Maybe two weeks. We'll be done with the roof tomorrow. And I reckon that painting job might take us a week and a half, maybe two."

They were walking the perimeter of the graveyard along a heavy hedge of honeysuckle. Its sweet aroma washed over them.

"I'll hate to see you go."

He stopped and looked at her intently, his gray eyes light and silvery in the dark. "Do you mean that? Really?"

She started moving again, edging closer to the tangled vines. "Of course I will."

He buried his face in the rampant hedge, sniffing deeply. "Oh, that smells good."

She chuckled. "You wouldn't be doing that during the day unless you wanted your nose stung to pieces."

He straightened up, his expression quizzical. "You're a funny girl, you know. Most girls are all into flowers and sighs and other girly things. Not Garnet Grant. She's always practical and thinking about bee stings."

She wasn't sure how he meant this. "I guess I am practical," she said slowly. "But I do love flowers and pretty things. I reckon I'm just me, good or bad."

"Oh, it's good; believe me, it's good." His eyes glittered like stars.

She placed her hand on his shoulder. Under the cotton his skin felt like an oven. "I guess the heat in that tent was even worse with a sunburn."

His response was to pull her violently toward him, crushing her body against his. He kissed her, but it was nothing like their first kiss. She felt teeth grazing hers and his mouth was fierce and demanding. All at once she felt her breasts smashed into his chest, the roughness of his chin, and the shocking sensation of his tongue against her own. At first he frightened her, but then she felt a melting that made her lean into his embrace. He responded by holding her even tighter and kissing her as if he were going to eat her up. Crushed so closely she sensed something else, and again she had that fluttering sensation just there, where she felt him, and it terrified her. She twisted her head away and pushed as hard as she could against his shoulders. He stepped back, panting, his eyes slitted shut. He walked a few steps away, laying his hand on a crooked gravestone with his back to her.

Patches of sweat darkened his shirt, and she wondered if they were from the heat of the tent or from what had just happened. She smelled the honeysuckle and thought that it did, indeed, smell a little like honey. She'd never realized that before.

"David," she said. He didn't move. "I'm sorry if I hurt your feelings."

She stepped closer, but she was afraid to touch him. It seemed like every time she touched him, even in a friendly way, he grabbed her. But she didn't want him angry with her either. "I like you. I like you a lot, and I'm glad to spend time with you."

He straightened but didn't turn around.

"I just, well, I just got scared. This is all new to me, and it's fast and---."

He turned with an odd smile on his face. "It's my fault. I couldn't control myself with you standing there looking so pretty in the dark."

She blinked.

"It's all right," he said and traced her jawbone with his finger. She fought the urge to flinch. "You was right to stop me. I'd better be walking you home."

Nodding, she started toward the road, leaving the heady honeysuckle behind. He said, "Can I hold your hand?"

She smiled and offered it to him. There was lamplight in Mrs. Lawrence's window so they speeded up, knowing they'd lingered too long. When they reached the school, the tent was deserted, but the lamps were still lit, and their orange glow accompanied them a ways down the road. Garnet felt awkward. She wished that she had that knack of careless conversation which came so easy to other people, but she had important things to say to David, things he needed to understand. She finally said, "I have responsibilities, you see. I can't just go and get serious about a boy. Things are not so good at home."

He slowed his pace. "What do you mean?"

So she told him about how life had been since Papa's death, how she had to work for Mrs. Lawrence, and how her mother depended upon her.

"I would've thought you'd move up to the big house when your father died."

"Well, that's a long story, but there's sort of a feud. It's Lorena's house now. I think she and Luther feel guilty about it and that's why they're always sending food and things over to us."

"I hear he's a good man."

"He is. They're both good, and yet there are things in the past— " her voice trailed off. "My mother holds grudges, and well-- let's just say that judging who's right and who's wrong isn't easy."

She took a deep breath and looked down the dark road. "And right now I have to hold us all together, David. They have to come first."

He didn't say anything. Off to the left, fireflies flickered through the night. They approached the road up to Grandpa's, the tobacco plants ghostly in the dark. "Do you all have enough to eat and everything?" he whispered.

"Oh, yes. My brother Franklin's helping, and we have everything we need," she replied. "I'm just not sure we have everything we want."

He stopped her then, pulling on her hand. "I don't understand."

She felt an intense need to make him comprehend. "Everything might be going along fine today, but I never know about tomorrow. What if Franklin leaves? What if Mrs. Lawrence packs up and moves in with her daughter? What if Luther and Lorena quit being so generous? I don't like living this way. I want to feel safe." She said the last in a whisper and ducked her head. She'd never expressed those thoughts to anyone.

She guessed he was probably wondering if he was supposed to hold her but was afraid she might think he was repeating what happened in the graveyard. She shrugged and lifted her head. "We'll survive, and I didn't tell you this to get your sympathy. I just wanted you to understand why I can't get all involved in courting and having fun. I'm not just flirting with you."

She glanced at him in time to see a shadow dance across his face. For a second she thought it was nearly a sneer, but it fled, and she decided she was wrong. He said, "It's not like there are all kinds of opportunities for having fun around here anyway. But I bet you could come walking with me every now and then. If you wanted to?"

She felt her apprehensions melt; he was trying to understand. "Sure I could. On Sundays I go up to the farm to see my brother sometimes, but I don't do anything of an evening. We could walk after supper on Sundays."

"Well, that's what we'll do. The next week or two I'll be in Ashton all day, and we'll probably stay there nights too. So Sundays would be the only chance I'd get to see you anyway." They were nearly to her house.

"And then you may be going far away."

At the bridge they stopped, and he took both her hands. "Maybe. We'll see. Until then we have another night in hell talking about heaven, don't we?"

She laughed. "Are you sure you can stand it?"

"Of course I can." He leaned forward, carefully keeping his body away from hers, and kissed her on the cheek. Then he stepped back, and she turned to the little house where a lamp burned in the kitchen. Walking across the bridge, she waved at him. She did like him. She liked him a lot.

***

Mama was sitting at the kitchen table with the silk dress spilling over her lap. She was hemming, her needle flashing in the lamplight.

"How was the Tent Meeting?" she asked.

"It was fine. Hot. One woman fainted, but I think it might've been from heat rather than the Holy Spirit," Garnet replied. She walked over to the water pail.

"And did your young man like your new clothes?"

Garnet didn't turn around. "Yes, he did."

"That Foster boy, isn't it?"

Garnet didn't even wonder how Mama knew.

"Yes."

"I suppose he's suitable for practicing on, but you know you can do better." She looked up until Garnet met her eyes.

"Do you need help with the hemming?" Garnet didn't care for where the conversation was heading.

"It's a little difficult for two to hem at once, but I do want to get this dress finished tonight."

Garnet started unbuttoning her blouse. "I'll be right down to help you."

So the two of them worked on the exquisite dress. Garnet sat in her nightgown, relieved to be rid of her blasted corset, with her mother right next to her. Their needles and thimbles moved in unison as they sewed.

"So, has he kissed you yet?" Mama reached for the spool of pale yellow thread.

Garnet concentrated on her stitches. "Yes."

"Hmm. And did you like it?"

150

"Not particularly." It was so quiet she could hear the tiny pops of their needles piercing the fabric.

"Oh, to be so young and pretty and have such power. You don't even appreciate it, do you?"

Puzzled, Garnet met her mother's sparkling eyes.

"Most girls waste their power. They don't even know they have it until they've squandered it. You can get anything you want right now, girl."

Garnet shifted the dress. "I don't know that there's anything I want."

Mama made an odd noise.

"We're about done."

"It's a good thing. Dessie will be wanting to eat again soon."

"What's the hurry on this dress, Mama?" She had another eight inches of hemming to do to meet the portion Mama had completed.

"I just want it done."

"It's beautiful. Awful fancy, though." Garnet was thinking about how her mother rarely left the house, not even for church.

"I wanted a pretty dress. It's been years since I had a silk dress."

"Some people would say it should be black."

"Everybody in this county knows how I loved your father. The color of my clothes is no indication of my feelings."

Garnet stayed silent. They sewed awkwardly, trying to meet each other's finished work. From the bedroom there was a scuffling sound and a tiny protest. "My little one needs me," Mama said. "There's just this little bit. Can you finish that?"

Garnet nodded. When she finished, she lifted the dress and admired the pointed, hand-made lace at the cuffs. It was like some kind of creamy dessert. Holding it by the shoulders she carried it to her mother's room where a tiny lamp burned on the chest. Mama was sitting on the bed nursing Dessie. "Where shall I put this?"

"Just lay it across the bottom of the bed," Mama said. "All I have left to do tomorrow is finish the trim work."

Garnet did so, straightening and smoothing the dress. "We didn't wrinkle it much, did we?"

"No, and you were good to help me. I would've been up much later to get it done."

"It's late enough."

"I bet you're tired from all that praying and courting."

Garnet took the teasing with a smile and was turning to go when her mother said, "Oh, Garnet, wouldn't it be easier if you took your clothes in the morning and dressed at Mattie's? All that rushing around is senseless. Mattie won't care."

Garnet was pleasantly surprised. "That makes sense. You sure you don't mind?"

"Not at all. Sweet dreams."

***

Mrs. Lawrence agreed with the sense of it but said, "Will your beau know to pick you up here, though?"

Garnet blushed at David's new title and said they were planning to meet at the tent. Then, however, she remembered how he'd walked toward her house the night before and hoped he'd make his usual Saturday visit to the store so she could tell him.

It was a pleasant day. Mrs. Lawrence mostly bustled around the house but couldn't resist coming into the store to chat with Garnet every so often. She said the woman who'd fainted had been overcome with the spirit of the Lord and had risen from her swoon to beg forgiveness for her sins.

"There are rumors about her. She lives close to the Clarks, almost to Ashton, and some folks say she entertains men when her husband's away."

"That's terrible gossip, Mrs. Lawrence."

"Well, I didn't say it was true, did I? Don't know the woman. Anyway, she and probably thirty others are going to be baptized down at Deer Creek tomorrow morning. You ought to come."

"Aren't they having regular church tomorrow?"

"No, Brother Vance is doing a big baptizing ceremony, and then he has to get back to Virginia. It'd be your last chance to see him."

"I don't think I can go that far," Garnet said, flicking a feather duster at the shelves.

"Oh, they're getting several wagons together at the church and going to take big bunches down. Making more than one trip if they have to. You ought to come along,"

"No, I don't think I will, Mrs. Lawrence, but thank you for telling me. I would've showed up at an empty church."

Mrs. Lawrence pointed to the night-blooming cereus. "Look at this bud! I bet it blooms by Monday. How am I going to let you know when it's ready?"

"I guess I could run down here on Monday or send Lowell. I don't want to miss it," Garnet replied, and she meant it.

Late in the afternoon David did come in, looking redder than ever. Mrs. Lawrence laughed at him. "You probably glow in the dark, boy. Land, what a sunburn!"

"Yes, ma'am, and it don't feel too good either." He turned to Garnet and gave her one of his deep smiles that made his eyes disappear. Then he glanced back at Mrs. Lawrence. "Ma'am, do you have anything to make it quit burning?"

She scurried behind the counter, lifting first one and then another of her tubes and bottles of patent medicine. While the woman searched, Garnet told him she'd be leaving for the Tent Meeting directly from the store.

"Here!" Mrs. Lawrence crowed. "This'll take the sting out."

"I wonder what this smells like," he said, looking at the little jar. "I may run people out of the tent if it's too bad."

He left, promising to see her in a little while. Mrs. Lawrence insisted on closing the store early and handed Garnet a little pink box. "I know this ain't as fancy as the stuff they sell in Ashton, but a young lady out courting needs some special things."

The box said "French Violets." Garnet lifted the lid to find a pink puff decorated with a ribbon, and then she sniffed. The powder had a clean, light smell. "Oh, thank you, Mrs. Lawrence! This is just lovely. With the heat and everything— ."

"That's what I was thinking."

So Garnet felt as special with her new powder as she had with her new clothes the night before. When she saw David turning the corner from Deer Creek Road, happiness rushed over her like a wave. The sun glinted off his hair, turning the curls golden, but his bright, white shirt made his face look redder than ever. She called out a hello and asked if the salve made him feel any better. "Not really," he said, grinning at her. "But at least it don't have much scent." He leaned toward her. "Mmm. But somebody smells good."

She thanked him. In the back of her mind she worried that he'd leave and never come back. There would be girls in the city: pretty, fashionable girls who were wise and skilled at attracting boys. She could never hope to best them with homemade clothes and country store bath powder.

He was chattering away about finishing the roofing job and seeing his friend Hayse Simpson that afternoon. "Who is Hayse Simpson?" she asked.

David pointed his thumb back toward the store. "He lives down in Deer Creek. He's got a small farm, mostly planted in corn. Actually it's his pa's farm, but the old man's not able to do much anymore. Hayse and his sister Flora live there."

The road grew crowded with others walking to the tent. Garnet had just nodded to Miss Carter and her elderly cousins when David continued. "I thought you might know Hayse and Flora. Lorena and Luther Colson are their kin, and she's helped out up at the farm a few times."

Garnet couldn't recollect having met her. "How old is she?"

David shrugged. "I couldn't say for sure, but I think she's about our age, maybe seventeen or eighteen."

"I'm still sixteen."

"Well, I turned seventeen in February. I know Hayse is twenty or thereabouts, and she's younger. They said they might be coming tonight."

Excitement was building as much as the heat in the tent. This was, after all, the culminating night of the Tent Meeting. Once again they had to crowd in near the back, but this time Garnet felt less shy about sitting hip to hip. Her blue dress didn't tend to show wrinkles, and she'd brought her fan. She waved a little gust of air at David.

He chuckled. "That don't help much, but I guess it's better than nothing."

The service opened with announcements, and Brother Bledsoe went to great lengths about the baptizing down at Deer Creek. David whispered, "Are you going?"

She shook her head. "Too far. And I want to see Franklin tomorrow."

He moved his mouth close to her ear. "And tomorrow night we'll go walking."

She nodded, facing straight ahead. She mustn't let him know how much she liked feeling his breath on her skin. Suddenly she turned and whispered, "Maybe you ought to go and get baptized."

"Been baptized. When I was nine."

This surprised her. Sometime she must get him to tell her about his complicated life. Maybe they could talk about it when they walked. If she thought up some questions and subjects ahead of time, she might not feel so shy. Through the singing and Horace Vance's histrionic preaching, she envisioned it. They'd have a couple of hours instead of these bits and pieces of time. She almost wished she were bold enough to leave the service and have the next hour and a half with him.

But she knew they had to stay; people would talk something awful if they left that early. She tried to concentrate on the sermon but found her mind wandering. She watched the people become flushed with heat and emotion, and, truly, by the time folks were shouting and crowding to the front, she felt disgusted by it. How many of them would return to their old ways once the Tent Meeting was over? How many of them were simply caught up in the heat and emotion? It was just as hot as the night before, and she felt nearly sick from it. She waved her little fan, but it didn't help, and she was sure the sweet, dry powder she'd dusted all over her body had turned to paste. When the service was over, dozens of people still knelt, but Brother Vance gave the benediction, and those who were sitting in the airless oven of the tent rose gratefully.

As David and Garnet made their way out into the schoolyard, he touched her arm and guided her to a young man and woman who were standing over to the side. "This here's Hayse and his sister Flora, like I was telling you about. This is Garnet."

They looked like Colsons. Both of them were tall, slim, and dark. The girl was very pretty even though her clothes were a little too bright, and she wore her hair down, not quite respectable in a girl her age. Garnet didn't much blame her, though. Flora's hair was a mass of dark, shining ringlets, and she swung it around every chance she got. Hayse gave Garnet a longer and more probing look than she liked and grinned at her. "So this is the beautiful Garnet I hear about all the time."

She didn't know what to say to such a comment, but that didn't seem to bother Hayse. "I can see what this rascal is talking about now. Mm, hmm, yes, I can. Have you ever seen such red hair, Flora?"

Flora didn't seem particularly interested. She turned her attention to David, slanting her dark eyes at him. "You was already gone by the time we passed your house so I left that shirt I mended with your Pa." She smiled at him and lowered lashes thicker than any Garnet had ever seen.

"Thank you, Flora," David replied, and he offered her his brightest smile, the very same one he gave to Garnet. Flora tilted her head, looking for all the world like she was waiting to be kissed.

Hayse was watching all this like it was excellent entertainment. "Yep, my little sis is a demon with a needle, ain't you, Flora? A demon, anyway."

David laughed, and Flora glanced down with a strange little half-smile. Garnet tried to look pleasant, but she was steaming inside. After a bit more silly chat, the Simpsons walked off. Garnet didn't say anything for a minute, but when he reached for her hand she jerked it away and declared, "I guess *I* can mend your shirts!"

David laughed. "Oh, that's just Flora. She was born flirting with the men. She don't mean nothing by it."

Garnet doubted this but didn't want to look like a fool. "No, I mean it. I'll do any mending you need done."

"I'll remember that." He didn't seem to want to discuss Flora. "Lord, I'm as thirsty as last night. Do you want to go back to the store to get your things and a drink?"

"I'll get them some other time. You can get a drink at my house."

The crowd thinned until they were by themselves, and she couldn't think of anything to say that could compete with Flora's eyelashes and curls. She might not be wise in the ways of courting, but she'd bet money that Flora was after David.

David noticed her silence. "Hey, cut it out, Garnet. This is as silly as me being jealous of Willie Martin." He looked straight into her eyes. "There ain't nothing going on with me and Flora Simpson. I'm down there a lot to see Hayse, and we tease and joke around sometimes. That's all."

"If you say so. Have you kissed her?"

He looked away, and she knew the answer before he gave it. She just wondered if he'd be honest. "Well, yes. I've kissed her. I've kissed a few girls along the way. But it was a long time ago, I swear. Last summer when we got back from Covington I kissed her maybe once or twice, but not since then."

"Really?"

"I swear it, Garnet."

She decided to believe him. After all, she thought, he was older and had lived in the city. And boys got around more. "I don't think she liked me much."

"Flora don't much like other girls. Guess she sees them all as competition."

Feeling obstinate and contrary, she pulled on his hand to stop him. They were by Grandpa's lane. "Kiss me," she demanded.

He hesitated, and she knew she'd confused him, but she didn't care. He pulled her to him and kissed her, chastely this time, but it lasted a while, and she liked it. It was a victory, and she remembered what her mother had said about power. He touched her cheek and said in a low voice, "I know things are kind of uncertain with my pa and everything at your place, but I want you to be my girl, Garnet."

A little burst of breeze floated over them, and the trees across the road sighed with it. "I am your girl, David Foster," she whispered. "Even though I don't quite know how things are going to turn out, I'm your girl."

He shrugged into that puppy-like wriggle he did when he was happy and grabbed her hand again. "I'll treat you right. I promise," he vowed, and she had to laugh.

They made plans for meeting the next evening. He would come to her house and call for her properly since her mother knew about him anyway. He would try to convince her mother that he was a fine, upstanding young man, worthy of calling on her daughter. For practice, Garnet thought, hoping her mother would change her mind about him. They were at the swinging bridge when she realized there was no light coming from the house.

"Is it so very late?" she asked David.

He pulled his watch from his pocket and tilted it to pick up light from the moon. "No, it's nine-forty, about the same time we got here last night."

"I can't imagine that Mama would already be in bed."

"Do you reckon everything's all right?"

"I don't know." She started across the bridge with David following her.

"I'll just make sure, and then I'll go home," he said.

She nodded, walking fast. She went into the front room, lit only by moonlight. "Mama?"

There was no answer. "Could we have missed them at the Tent Meeting?"

Garnet shook her head. Sweeping past him, she went to the kitchen to light a lamp. Light poured over the silent, tidy kitchen. There were no dishes in the sink, and the stove was cold. Nearly frantic now, she exclaimed, "Where could they have gone?"

"Look upstairs," he said. "Maybe the little ones are up there."

She raised her skirt and tore up the steps with David following more slowly. A quick glance showed that the both rooms were empty.

"Look," David said, pointing at her bed. There was a note written in Mama's florid hand.

Garnet, Mama wrote, *Mr. Colson has taken Dessie and me to town. I sent the others up to Franklin for the day. We should be home around dark. Mama.*

"Well, there you go," David said cheerfully. "Do you want to go to the farm to get the others?"

"No, it's too late. Lorena's probably put them to bed." They went downstairs and she dropped the note on the kitchen table. "This is very strange."

"It ain't strange to go to town of a Saturday, and I don't guess she'd have any other way to get there."

"But she'd never be seen in town with Luther," Garnet explained, and then added to herself, *or at least that's the way things used to be.*

David got a dipperful of water. "Have a drink."

"And it's so late."

He squeezed her shoulder, and she realized he had no idea how strange this was. He must think she was behaving like a hysterical girl.

"Let's go sit out on the porch and watch for your mother," he said. "It's best we wait out here. It wouldn't look good for the two of us to be in the house by ourselves."

The last thing on her mind was the sterling quality of her reputation, but she nodded. Her heart was thumping like she'd been running. "You can go on home if you want. I'll be all right by myself."

"No, I don't think I'll do that."

She rocked furiously, tapping her feet against the wooden boards and glancing up at the road every few minutes. David tried to talk about one subject or another, but she refused to be distracted. Once she said, "Maybe there was an accident."

"Well, I suppose the wagon might've lost a wheel, but it's unlikely."

She clenched her arms against her chest. "Maybe the baby got sick."

"Calm down. I'm sure everything's just fine."

She didn't reply, but in a few moments asked him again what time it was. Twenty minutes had passed. The breeze was picking up and sent a pleasant coolness over them. Otherwise the night was quiet.

Then David looked past her head and said, "Here they come."

Garnet twisted around toward the path from the farm. She hadn't expected Mama to come from that direction, but there she was in her creamy dress with Luther following, Dessie sprawled as limp as rags against his shoulder.

David called out a greeting to let them know he was there and stood up. Mama glided across the yard, Luther a dark shadow behind her. She said, "Hello, Mr. Foster. I see you kept Garnet company while she was waiting for us."

He nodded, but Garnet blurted out, "Where have you been, Mama? I've been worried to death."

Mama stepped past them and opened the door. "I left you a note. There was no need to worry." Then she looked back at David. "All is well here; you can go on home."

Garnet looked wildly first toward her mother and Luther entering the house and then at David stepping into the yard to leave. She didn't want him to go and stretched her hand out to him. David squeezed it. "I'll come for you at seven tomorrow evening."

She let him go, watching until he disappeared in the dark. She heard Mama cooing to Dessie and Luther's heavy steps. Surely he'd be going back to the farm any minute, but he didn't, although she waited on the porch for a good while. She went in the house and saw the two of them sitting at the kitchen table and, God help her, holding hands.

"Come in, Garnet," Mama said. "We have something to tell you."

She knew. Now that she thought about it, it wasn't even a surprise. Somehow her legs moved and she sat, glancing at Mama's flushed and happy face. She couldn't look at Luther.

"Luther and I got married today. We wanted it to be a surprise and didn't want any kind of fuss, so we just eloped!" Mama's laugh tinkled around the kitchen.

Garnet couldn't speak. She wanted to run after David, but he wouldn't understand. More than David, she wanted Franklin, who would.

"I'm sorry we worried you. We had dinner in town to celebrate and then went for a long drive. We stopped up at the farm to tell the others, but the little ones were already in bed," Mama chattered. She looked at Luther with soft eyes.

Garnet's voice felt rusty. "Did you tell Franklin?"

"Well, yes," Mama said. She used her little finger to caress the back of Luther's brown hand and move the dark hairs back and forth. "Unfortunately he was a bit shocked at first, but I'm sure he wishes us well. You're happy for us, aren't you Garnet? Won't it be lovely to have a man taking care of us again?"

Garnet rose from her chair and made herself nod at her mother and glance at Luther, uncomfortable and odd in his formal clothes. She thought it was more than clothes that made him look miserable. Garnet kept nodding, feeling like a doll with a wobbly neck, and then she muttered something about being tired and backed toward the steps. Mama smiled. "Sweet dreams. You'll be able to spend more time dreaming now that Luther is your step-father."

Step-father! She whirled around and fled up the steps. She stood in the middle of her room with her fists clenched. What on earth would Lorena think? She sank to the bed. Would Luther still work the farm with his sister? Would she let him? Garnet's thoughts jumbled and bumped against each other like pigs in a chute. She couldn't decide which she detested more: her mother's hypocrisy and disloyalty to Papa or Luther's weakness and gullibility. She wanted to run: to David, to Franklin, to Lorena.

But she could do nothing. She couldn't even talk to anyone this late. Her room was shadowy and still, and she missed Violet's tousled curls lying on the bed beside hers. She could see a thin stripe of light from the kitchen under her door and hear her mother's chatter. Once she heard Luther's quiet voice. She undressed and pulled a nightgown over her head. Stretching out on top of her quilt she watched wispy clouds blow across the window. Dessie cried briefly, ready to be fed. It was about midnight, the same time Dessie had awakened last night when they'd been hemming the dress .Her mother's wedding dress. She clenched her fists so tightly the skin beneath her nails tingled.

She tried to relax, to sleep, but it was no use. Glancing toward the door, she noticed that the light in the kitchen had been extinguished. Maybe they were asleep now or in bed anyway, she thought and shuddered. Again she watched the sky and told herself to think about David, to imagine how pleasant it would be to go walking with him the next evening, but it was no good. She'd thought she'd never sleep, but she did.

Not sure what awakened her, she tiptoed to the window where she could see the sky lightening. She threw on an old housedress, and, not bothering with shoes, crept through the kitchen. As late as they'd been up, surely the newlyweds would be sleeping sound, she thought. In the colorless yard, she felt dew against her feet as she ran, as fast as she had when she was a young girl, up to Grandpa's.

Chapter Nine

She had a stitch in her side and her feet were stinging, but only when she saw the big house looming in the half-light did Garnet slow her pace. She could make out Lorena on the porch, sitting with her hands dangling off the arms of the rocking chair. She didn't seem surprised to see Garnet.

After trudging slowly up the steps, Garnet sat. She was breathless but could've spoken if she'd known what to say.

"I didn't think the dawn would ever come," Lorena said in a rough, tired voice.

"You haven't been to bed?"

Lorena shook her head.

"I don't guess Franklin's up yet."

Lorena raised her eyes slowly, as if they were sore. "Franklin's gone. Left about midnight and said he was going to get work in Lexington."

All night Garnet had been waiting to talk to her brother.

"He wrote letters for you and me." Lorena waved her hand in front of her face as if she was shooing away a mosquito. "Silly boy forgot I can't read. Get yourself some tea and bring the notes out here."

By the time Garnet returned the sky was stained pink. She unfolded Franklin's notes, written on tablet paper with a soft pencil. Folding the paper had smudged his writing. She took a sip of scalding tea and said, "I'll read yours first:

Dear Lorena, I'm sorry to leave you like this but you know I always wanted to try my hand with the horses in Lexington. I reckon Luther will still work here now that he has a family to support so you will not be left with no help at all. I wouldn't want that. I can't stand the thought of living so close to a woman who didn't respect her father or my father or us children. She uses people and now she's getting back at you at the same time. I hope my brothers and sisters will still come see you because you been good to all of us. I thank you for all you done and even if Luther is a fool I thank him too. Respectfully, Franklin Grant

Garnet folded it back up. "Did you talk to him before he left?"

"A little. But you know Franklin; he wouldn't listen."

"Did you see this coming?"

Lorena gazed toward the barn. The birds' twittering had grown from an occasional trill to a full chorus. "You know how you get a feeling about something and when it happens you realize you should've known all along?"

Garnet knew.

"The last few weeks, Luther would be gone, and I wouldn't know where he was. It's a big farm, and I didn't always know what he was working at. I seen something was up, though. We're twins, and I usually know when something's fretting him. Oh, something was fretting him for sure this time," she said. "Anyway, he said he was going to town on Saturday, and I didn't know what he was going after, but he'd been making regular trips to town, mostly for you all. One time he said Miss Garnet needed material for clothes, and one time he went after coal oil. I reckoned you all was asking him to fetch stuff, but I never minded because we decided we was going to do what we could for Deke's family."

Garnet interrupted. "I never asked for that skirt, Lorena."

Lorena lifted a shoulder. "Like I said, we never minded. But yesterday he didn't say nothing about what he was going after. He just appeared in his funeral suit, and said he'd be gone most of the day. I thought it was queer, but I had things to do and didn't pay him no mind. But then, not a half hour after he left the house, here come Lowell and the little ones saying their mama's told them to stay with Franklin. Lowell looked sort of funny."

"He doesn't miss much," Garnet murmured. The tea was soaking into her body and slowly unclenching her taut muscles.

"No, he don't. He's a smart little rascal," Lorena replied, a faint smile playing around her thin lips. "So, I come to the conclusion that Louise must've decided to go to town with Luther, and they was both trying to keep it a secret. Didn't make no sense considering how Louise feels about us, but who can tell with her? I was busy with my work and the children. I fed them, and then it was coming on to dark and still there was no sign of Luther or your mother. I sent Lowell down to your house, but he said no one was there. I knew you was working for Mattie, and Lowell said you was going straight to the Tent Meeting."

"I did. Mama suggested it."

Lorena narrowed her eyes. "She's a dab hand at conniving, ain't she? Henry fell asleep on the sofa, and I put them all to bed. So, Franklin and I sat out here and waited. Every few minutes he'd get up and go toward the road and walk back. Finally one time he looked me right in the eye and said, 'You know what they're up to, don't you?'

And I said that yes, I did, but I hadn't knowed it before. By the time they pulled up in the wagon, he was hissing like a cat."

She stopped and rubbed her hands over her face. "It was real ugly. Luther went to unhitch the wagon, and Franklin called your mother every nasty name in the book. She just stood there, holding that little baby against her shoulder. She told him she didn't need him anymore because she'd found a way to provide for the family. He could just live over here with, and, well, I'll not say what she said he could live with. I stayed on the porch and didn't open my mouth, but I was hoping the little ones were good and asleep. Luther didn't say one word to me and walked off with her. As soon as they went down the path Franklin sat in that chair and cried his eyes out. There's nothing as heart-breaking as hearing a man cry, and, even though he's not but fifteen, Franklin's a man."

Garnet's throat was sore with unshed tears, and she gulped the rest of her tea to ease it. With a grunt Lorena stood up and walked to the edge of the porch, her back to Garnet. "When he quit crying, Franklin said he was leaving which didn't surprise me none. She all but told him to leave. I guess he left you all a while back, but he still thought of himself as part of your family." She twisted her head back and forth to stretch her neck. "He asked me for paper and set in the kitchen writing for a while, and then he stuffed his things in an old sack, saddled up his horse, and left. I asked where he'd sleep along the way, and he said it was warm enough to sleep rough if he had to. And that's all I can tell you."

Garnet was in no hurry to read her note; she could guess what was in it. "He's right, you know," Lorena said. "About her getting back at me. She took my brother just like she thinks I took her daddy."

"I guess she'd see it that way."

"For damn sure, she'd see it that way. Miss Louise cooked up a pretty smart plan. Who could blame the poor widow for providing for her children? A little quick, some might say, since the grass ain't even growed over her husband's grave, but still, a woman's got to do things like that."

"And there's truth to it."

"I reckon. But I remember when she was your age, how she'd go out to the barn or the fields in her big straw hats with satin ribbons hanging off them and laugh and tease those boys working out there. After dark, she'd look for them, and there'd be the touching and the sighing and the rubbing. Luther was plumb crazy about her. Oh, yes, she did it to him too, tormenting and teasing, and her hating every drop of Colson blood in both of us. Why, there's a whole box of cheap trinkets upstairs them boys give her. This ain't no different except she's getting more than trinkets now."

From the barn, a cow lowed mournfully. Lorena softened her voice. "I know she's the only mother you've got, girl, and I reckon I shouldn't be saying these things. But my brother was ripe for picking, and I just hate to see her use him. And I hate that I have to see him and depend upon him every damned day to run this farm. How could he marry a woman who treated me and Deke so terrible?" The words trembled.

"I'm sure he married her thinking he'd be helping us out." Lorena's words hurt, but they were only what she'd started to piece together herself. She wondered if loyalty could run dry in the end.

Lorena snorted. "He's probably making excuses like that, but we was already helping out, both of us, and gladly. That's not the only reason he married Louise."

She stepped off the porch and said over her shoulder, "Read your note, drink your tea. Since the bride and groom are honeymooning, I have to see to the milking. When I get back, we'll feed these children and send them home. You know I love all of you, but I'm not going to make things easy for Louise no longer."

She strode toward the barn, and Garnet read Franklin's scribbled note.

Dear Sis, I guess you'll say I'm running away again but you probably knew this was coming and it won't be no surprise to you. Luther makes plenty of money more than Papa did and besides he's saved every dollar he's ever made so you won't miss my pay. You and the little ones should have it pretty good and I hope you do. I don't know how you'll stand living with her and seeing her use him up like she did Papa and knowing she don't care nothing for him except for money and maybe something else you know what I mean. If she truly loved Papa how could she marry again so quick? I feel sorry for Lorena. Mama said terrible things about her and I don't see how Luther can stand hearing that about his own sister. I'll write when I have an address and let you know what I'm doing. Wish me luck Garnet and you know I wish it to you too. Your brother, Franklin.

She refolded the letter and let it lay in her lap as she stared at the puffy clouds over the barn. She supposed they'd all survive and even get used to the situation. At least Luther was a good man. She wondered if he'd find happiness, if having a wife would be worth enduring his sister's bitterness. She doubted her mother would stay sweet and starry-eyed forever. She went into the house and rinsed her cup.

When Lorena came in with the milk, they made breakfast. She could tell Lowell was waiting for an explanation. As she flipped pancakes, Garnet whispered to Lorena, "Should I tell them?"

"I reckon. Otherwise they're going to get a mighty big surprise."

So, once they were settled and sorghum had been dribbled over their pancakes, Garnet told them that Luther and Mama had married, and he would be living with them from now on. Both Violet and Henry crowed with laughter and clapped their hands. They loved Luther and were probably greedy enough to think the treats that arrived in the big wooden box would continue coming. Lowell stared at his plate. His hair needed trimming and a good wash, for that matter. While the others dug into their breakfasts he hesitated. "He won't be happy," he said.

Lorena and Garnet both looked up. "What do you mean?" Garnet asked.

He shrugged. "I just don't think he'll be happy. He's used to things being quiet and calm, and they're not that way at our house."

He took a bite. "Besides," he said with his mouth full, "he's used to Lorena's cooking, and he won't like the food if Mama fixes it."

They had to laugh. After breakfast, Garnet made sure that at least the sticky hands and mouths were wiped and sent them home, threatening a major scrubbing later in the day, and then, after she'd helped Lorena with the dishes, said she was going home too. "You can stay," Lorena said. "You look as tired as I feel, and there won't be no rest at home."

"I know, but there's no point in putting this off. I have to get used to it."

"I do too, but I'm glad I don't have to face Luther until tomorrow."

Garnet had said she was leaving, but she found a towel to fold and a chair to push in. She looked up to see Lorena smiling at her. "I hear you're walking out with David Foster. I forgot to ask you about him with all this other confusion."

"Where'd you hear that?"

"Oh, Lowell tells everything he knows. Is he a nice boy?"

"Yes."

Lorena put a strong, sinewy arm around her. "He's not the only nice boy out there."

The embrace was so sweet that she almost let go of the tears hovering behind her eyelids. "I know. Besides, he may be moving up north."

And then there was nothing to do but walk down the path. She had no idea of what to expect, but she reckoned she'd cope with it. Mama sat on the porch with embroidery in her lap. They must've bought thread while they were in Ashton because the brilliant silks were wound on new spools. Mama was watching Luther use a scythe to clear out weeds by the creek. Garnet sat opposite her mother and searched for something to say. Then she mentioned that David was coming for her at seven, and she thought she'd have a bath. Mama nodded and started making French knots with bright blue thread.

"Where are the children?" Garnet asked.

Mama shrugged. The skin around her mouth was mottled with pink, and she looked tired. "Dessie's asleep."

Garnet yawned. "I wouldn't mind a nap myself."

Mama frowned. "Violet said you were going to give them baths."

Garnet stood up and stretched. "And I guess I will." From the corner of her eye she noticed her mother's left hand where she wore a new diamond ring in place of her old wedding band from Papa. She must make an effort. "That's a pretty ring, Mama."

"Yes, it is. Real diamonds too. My other one was just plain gold."

Then she lowered her hand to the embroidery hoop and continued stitching. Garnet felt her face reddening but told herself to hush. She went to look for her brothers and sister.

Later Garnet cooked their supper, and the newlyweds came to the table holding hands. Lowell whispered, "It's a good thing you cooked or he'd leave tonight."

She acted like she was going to swat him and he scurried away, his clean hair nearly as shiny as the mischief in his eyes. Bless Lowell. Mama sat very close to Luther, and watching the two of them made Garnet feel sick. She slid her food onto Lowell's plate without anyone noticing.

When David crossed the bridge, she was waiting on the porch. He grinned as soon as he saw her although he looked a little nervous. Her face felt tight, and when she smiled, she knew it was a stingy one. "Is everything all right?" he asked.

"I'm not sure, but I'll tell you about it later."

"Where's your mother?"

"In the kitchen. Why?"

He opened the screen door and said, "Because I'm going to say good evening to her and tell her I'm walking with her daughter. I don't want to be sneaky about this."

"I don't think that's such a good idea."

He whipped his head around. "Why? Are you ashamed of me?"

"No, no. It isn't that at all. It's just that things are a little odd around here." He looked confused and a little annoyed, so she relented. "Go on. We'll speak to them."

They walked to the kitchen where Mama had pulled her chair close to Luther's. They were looking at each other as if they'd like to crawl into each other's skins, but Mama gazed up when David asked if he could walk with Garnet. She gave him a dazzling smile and turned it on Luther who couldn't take his eyes off her long enough to give David a glance. "Isn't this sweet, Luther? Little Garnet has a beau."

Neither David nor Garnet knew how to reply to that, but they both blushed which made Mama chuckle. "Go enjoy your walk and be good children," she said and turned back to Luther to whisper something in his ear.

As they left the porch, Garnet exhaled noisily and kept shaking her head. She was walking so fast that David grabbed her elbow to slow her down. "Hold on, and tell me what the hell is going on. What's Luther Colson doing at your house?"

She looked at his silvery eyes, round with concern, and the string that had stretched all day snapped and flapped like a broken harness. Sobbing, she dove into his shoulder. With the tiny portion of rational sense she had left, she thought how bad it looked to be weeping into a boy's arms in the middle of the road and was glad no one was there to see.

David patted her back and murmured comforting words. She was starting to get the sobs under control when he said, "Come on. Let's walk and you can tell me what's troubling you, honey."

That did it. When he called her honey, she lost herself all over again. "They married," she cried. "Mama's gone and married her worst enemy!" She shook her head so furiously that crystalline tears flew from her face, and hairpins fell into the dusty road. David stooped to pick them up and slipped them into his pocket; then he took her hand and propelled her down the road. By the time they could see the school, she was nearly done crying and used David's huge handkerchief to blow her nose.

"I'm sorry," she whispered. She must look blotchy and ugly.

He squeezed her hand. "There's nothing to be sorry for, but I'm mystified. I thought you liked Luther Colson."

She nodded and gulped another time or two. "I do."

They were near the store by then, and he asked if she wanted to get a drink. She shook her head. Mrs. Lawrence would be there and she couldn't face seeing anyone. They kept walking, and she realized that he'd turned her down Deer Creek Road. For a while they went downhill, but then they climbed a sharply curving rise that took her breath. She felt wobbly and odd and still didn't want to talk, glad to use the steep climb as an excuse. David didn't push her, and she wondered if he thought she was crazy. He kept glancing at her.

"I know I look dreadful."

"Well, yes, you do," he said. "But not how you mean. Your face was all red from crying, but now you're going sort of gray, and I was wondering if you were going to faint right here in the road."

She did feel bad, floaty and strange. "I'd love to sit down a minute."

"Can you hold out until we get past the top of this rise? Our house is there."

She felt a clutch of fear. The last thing she wanted was a confrontation with Walter Foster, especially if he'd been drinking. David seemed to read her mind. "Pa's not there. He's already gone to Ashton for that painting job."

By the top of the hill she was panting and cold sweat bubbled up on her face, dribbling down her neck. She looked down; it was more than she could do to keep her head up, and she saw the dusty road become thick, tussocky grass in front of her feet. It was a good thing David had hold of her arm and was steering her because she couldn't see right. Then the light turned funny, eclipsed by a darkness that made the grass change color. She reached a flailing hand toward David, and the eclipse was total.

When she came to, she kept blinking and seeing jerky pictures of David's face, all crumpled with concern. He called her name over and over, and she fluttered her fingers to let him know she heard him. Her mouth felt sticky, and she had a difficult time finding her voice. "I fainted," she said in a faraway tone she didn't recognize.

"You sure did. I grabbed a hold of you, but you just went down in a pile." He massaged her hand with warm, rough fingers.

She opened her eyes completely and saw she was lying in deep grass. Behind David's head was a white frame house. "Is this yours?"

"Yes. If you think you can walk, I'll get you in the house."

She sat up, and the world spun, but it didn't turn dark. Clutching his hands, she let him pull her up and then leaned against him. Inside, he lowered her into a brown armchair. She shut her eyes, and he leaned over her. "Are you going to make it?"

She nodded. "Could I have some water?"

He darted off toward what she imagined was the kitchen and was back immediately with a large coffee cup full of water. After her first cautious sip, she took a larger one and felt better even though there was still a strangeness in her, like her skin was only barely holding her body together. David dashed off again in another direction and came back with one of his big, snowy handkerchiefs. He dipped an end of it in the water and started wiping her face. This was bliss. She shut her eyes. "I think . . ."

"You think what?" He took the dry end of the hankie and blotted her face.

"I think I love you," she said, opening her eyes.

He leaned back on his heels and stared at her, serious at first, and then he grinned his widest, most eye-crinkling smile. "Now I know you've lost your senses."

Her mouth seemed too tired to smile, but she did, and she raised her hand to touch his cheek. The faint burr of whiskers running down his jawbone felt novel. "You're being so good to me."

"Do you want more water?"

She nodded and he went back to the kitchen. Turning her head to look around the plain, neat room, her hair flopped against her neck and she realized it had come mostly undone. So much for trying to wear it fashionably pouffed rather than sensibly plaited, she thought, and raised her arms to remove the remaining hairpins. When David returned, her hair had fallen in a wave of copper around her shoulders and down to her waist. He stopped dead and stared at her, holding out the cup. "My Lord, you're beautiful." He sounded like he was praying.

She smiled up at him. "No, I'm a complete mess with my hair falling down, and fainting in your front yard, and crying like a child in the road. I'm ashamed of myself. Thank you." She took the water, which she downed thirstily this time.

After she drank she combed through her hair with her fingers and started braiding it. He watched her, and she watched him watching her, their eyes locked. Garnet felt stronger, but her pulse raced with the realization that they were alone in his house, a forbidden thing, and she'd told him she loved him, something she'd never meant to say. She broke away from his winter sky eyes and quickly coiled her braid. "Do you still have those hairpins I lost in the road?"

He gave a little shake and pulled them from his pocket. "Are you better now?"

"Yes."

"You ain't getting sick, are you?"

"No, I don't think so. But I didn't get much sleep last night."

"Did you eat any supper?"

She had to think. "No, I couldn't eat. And I didn't eat dinner either." She smiled apologetically. "See, it's my fault."

In an instant, he'd pulled her out of the chair and guided her into the dim kitchen. Gently pushing her into a chair, he announced, "There's not much here, but maybe I can find you something." He looked around and thought for a minute. "Would you like a cup of coffee or tea?"

He wanted so to please her that it warmed her heart. "I don't drink coffee, but I'd love some tea if it's not a bother."

His teeth flashed. "There's something we have in common; I love tea even though my pa says it's girlish."

After he raised the blind she could see the kitchen better. The stove took up one end of it, and the small table where she was sitting filled the other. There was a sink under the window with pails of water waiting to be used. On the other wall stood a beautifully crafted kitchen cabinet. Any she'd ever seen had been painted white, but this one showed the natural wood; oak, she thought, and gave off a warm glow. She pointed to it. "That's pretty."

David looked up from the stove. "Oh, ain't it? Pa made that several years ago, and we've toted it around everywhere we've gone."

He brought out a teapot, a box of tea, and a dingy sugar bowl. She kept silent, but he chattered about one thing and another, a comforting sound. Then he cut a thick wedge of cold cornbread and spread it with butter. Taking a plate from the back of the stove, he said, "There's only one piece of chicken left, but maybe this'll do for you."

"It's lovely," she said and bit into the cold chicken, tender and still moist even though it'd probably been fried hours before. "It's good," she said, and realized she wasn't being polite. She was hungry.

When he'd made the tea and brought it to steep, he asked, "Did you mean it?" His face had gone a dull red.

She used her finger to wipe around her mouth. Then she motioned for him to sit down, giving her a minute to swallow. He sat and watched her. She knew what he was talking about. "Yes. I meant it."

He grabbed her hand, greasy with chicken, and pulled it to his lips. "I was afraid to say it. I was afraid I'd chase you off; you seem so prickly and shy and scared of everybody. But I've been wanting and wanting to say it to you." His eyes were silver then like Miss Caroline's pewter cups or moonlight on the creek. "I love you too, Garnet. I've been wanting you for years."

She reclaimed her hand and broke off more of the cornbread. His declaration made her shy. "I'm glad, David. It's just a shame that you have to move. You'll come back to see me, won't you? After a while?"

"You know I will. I'll find a way."

He found cups and poured out the tea while Garnet finished eating. Food helped but the happiness she felt had little to do with cold chicken. Then, in an unpleasant wave, she remembered her family and she sighed. "I have a long story to tell, don't I?" She stirred sugar into her tea and asked if they could take it outside. Somehow the telling might be easier under the lowering sun.

He said they didn't have a porch; his pa had been intending to build one and even had the lumber. But, he added, there was a sort of stoop out the back door, and they could go out there if she didn't mind sitting on the steps. So she followed him through a doorway and a tiny room that was a sort of closet and pantry combined. She sat on the top step and he sat one down from her. "I have to start the story way back when my mother was my age. But these are private things, family things, David, and it's hard for me to tell them."

He nodded and blew on his tea. "I understand. You can trust me."

She smiled. "Do you realize just how much I've trusted you already?"

He twisted around at this. "I know I never should've brought you into my house alone. People would talk something awful, but I didn't know what else to do with you. I intended for us to walk up here because I wanted to show you my place, but I never intended to take you inside."

She clutched the cup with both hands. "I don't care. We know we're not doing anything wrong."

And then she told him about Grandpa and her grandmother's sickness and Lorena. The evening light faded, becoming pink then blue. She told him how much she missed her father and how much it hurt for Franklin to leave and how bitter Lorena was. She had nothing more to say. The tea was gone and the sky fully dark. He made few comments, only patting her a time or two when tears threatened again. With a shuddering sigh, she stopped her story. "I'd better not cry or I'll have to use another one of your handkerchiefs."

He chuckled. "Oh, I've got a ton of 'em. Aunt Martha sends me a dozen every Christmas."

"And they're all ironed up so pretty. I suppose you do the ironing? Or is it your father?"

He shifted uncomfortably, stood up, and stretched; they'd been sitting on the steps for quite a while. "If you must know, Flora does our ironing along with our mending. Pa made an arrangement with her."

"I sort of figured that."

"Sometimes you're just plumb evil," he said, realizing she was teasing him.

Then he was serious. "As hard as all this is, Garnet, there's some good to it."

There was hardly enough light to read his face.

"No matter what you think of your mother for marrying him or him for betraying his sister, Luther's a good man, and you all will be taken care of."

She nodded.

"And," he went on, "it sort of frees you up, don't it? You don't have to feel like it's your responsibility to keep everything together. You said Franklin would've left before long anyways, and you'd still be depending upon the Colsons."

She picked up their cups. "I suppose you're right, but I still have to watch her use Luther and act like Papa never existed. And I think it's terrible how sneaky she was."

"Here," he said, it's pitch dark in there." He took her hand and led her back into the kitchen. "Oh, I'm not saying it'll be easy getting used to what she's done, and I know you'll miss your brother."

He gathered her to him and held her. It was hard for her to believe this was the same David who'd crushed her in the graveyard only a few days ago. He whispered, "Try not to care so much about them. You have your own life now." Then he kissed her, this time making her feel precious and cared for, and she wanted it to last even though they were alone in the dark house inviting scandal, but David broke away and said they must be walking back.

He said his father had taken off that afternoon for Ashton to start painting but had left David behind to finish attaching doors to some cabinets. The man was coming after them Monday afternoon, David said. And his father had told him to cut the grass since he was trying to find someone to rent the house.

"So, I'll be here until Tuesday morning," David said.

They turned the corner at Mrs. Lawrence's store where all was dark and locked up for the night.

"I don't guess you'll have to work at the store no more," David ventured.

"But I hope Mama'll let me. I enjoy it, and it gets me out of the house. Marrying Luther won't change Mama's housekeeping."

Her thoughts flew on down the road. Living with all the changes would be difficult enough, but it was nearly unthinkable to contemplate doing it now without David.

"Will you leave for Covington straight from Ashton?"

"I doubt it. We'll move all our tools up north, and he'll not want to take them to Ashton to sit in the cart or stuff into a boarding house."

"Then I'll see you again before you go."

"Oh, sure," he said. "You can see me tomorrow night if you want to."

She told him about Mrs. Lawrence's flower. "I don't know if it'll be tomorrow or not, but I do want to see it."

"Well, when will it bloom?"

She chuckled and punched his arm. "I'm sure I don't know. I figure it's like babies; you can't exactly set a time when they're going to arrive."

He reacted to this with a smile, but she could tell it irritated him that she'd spend their last evening watching a flower bloom. "From what Mrs. Lawrence said, it blooms after dark, so you could come by the house early and we could walk a while before you drop me at the store."

He immediately cheered and she marveled at how easy it was to keep him happy, remarkably like Franklin when she had to jolly him out of his dark moods. The thought of her brother passed like a shadow, especially since they were nearing the farm. "I wonder where my brother is tonight."

"There's no telling, but I bet he'll find a place on one of those big horse farms in no time. Before you know it, he'll be sending you a letter."

He walked her all the way to her door, saying he didn't want to be accused of doing any sneaking around himself and, besides, he didn't want her toppling off the bridge into the little creek. She laughed at him, declaring she was fine and let him kiss her once more as they stood on the porch. Inside the silent house everyone was in bed, but there was a lamp burning in the kitchen. She could hardly imagine Mama remembering to do it for her.

Chapter Ten

As tired as she was, Garnet rose at her usual early hour. No one else was stirring, and she wasn't sure whether Luther still slept behind the bedroom door. If he'd already left for the farm, he'd done it without breakfast for the stove was cold. She went through her usual morning chores clutching memories of the previous evening with a strange, giddy joy. David had been wise to tell her not to care so much. Maybe pride and honor simply didn't hold up under the strain of everyday life. She wondered how Lorena would cope when she saw her brother; she wasn't one for dismissing pride or honor.

Well up into the morning, Mama finally appeared in the kitchen, yawning and complaining about her back. Obviously Luther had left, and Mama said, "You'll need to be getting up earlier. Luther needs a good breakfast before he goes to work."

"I'm supposed to make his breakfast?" Garnet's voice rose with each word. She'd rarely made her own dear Papa's breakfast, and Mama certainly hadn't.

"Certainly. He's your stepfather and will be providing for us."

Garnet clenched her teeth and went into the yard to stifle some retort sure to cause trouble. She hollered for Lowell and found him on the other side of the garden, poking a small snake with a stick. "What're you doing?"

"I'm observing this snake. It's scientific."

"It just looks like you're tormenting it to me," she said. "Listen, I need you to run to the store. Mrs. Lawrence has the clothes I wore on Saturday and my hairbrush, and I need them. Also, ask her if the flower is going to bloom tonight."

"What?"

"Oh, it's scientific," she said. "Just go and take the little ones while you're at it."

"Do I have to take them?"

"Yes. Just like I always had to take you."

By afternoon the euphoria from David's sweet words had thinned, and she was mourning his departure. What did it matter if they loved each other if he was miles away? She'd be at home working, making Luther's breakfast, and pining away. Likely he'd find a girl in Covington who was twice as pretty and he'd settle up there. She washed out the dress Lowell brought her and hung it on the clothesline. She hoped to wear it that evening.

Although he shook his head at the absurdity of the message, Lowell said Mrs. Lawrence was sure the flower would bloom that evening. Thinking she'd better tell her mother about her plans, she went into the bedroom where Mama sat on the bed fooling with her hair. Garnet described the flower and its exotic blooming patterns. "It's called a night-blooming cereus, and Mrs. Lawrence says it'll be something to see. But before I go there, David and I are walking . He leaves tomorrow to work in Ashton."

Mama studied her reflection in the mirror. "Do you think I should go back to parting my hair in the middle?"

Determined to be patient, Garnet said, "Oh, I don't know. That's sort of old-fashioned, isn't it? You never see it in the catalogs."

Mama brushed through her hair, once nearly as amber as Garnet's but now dulled by silver strands. She parted it on the side, as usual, and then tried knotting it low on her neck. "Maybe it looks better this way."

Garnet tried again. "So if I watch this plant bloom, it may be very late when I come home. I have no idea how long it'll take."

"Most stylish women are wearing it sort of puffed out like you do sometimes. I saw that in a book in Ashton."

Ready to give up, Garnet said, "Then that's where I'll be. David and I are going to walk for a while, and then he'll leave me at Mrs. Lawrence's store."

Narrowing her eyes, Mama said, "I don't believe you'll need to work for her now. Luther can take care of us."

"But I love working in the store, and Mrs. Lawrence needs me. Her feet hurt, and it rests her to have me a couple of days a week." She couldn't believe her mother was taking this from her.

"You've been faithful and generous, Garnet, and I appreciate it. Nonetheless, it's time for you to enjoy your girlhood. We'll get you some fine clothes; that skirt and blouse were just the beginning, and maybe some handsome young men will come courting. You deserve some fun." Mama beamed at her.

"I have a young man courting me, Mama. Besides, who else even knows me?"

"Oh, word will get around, and gentlemen from all over the county will come calling. That carpenter boy is not suitable for you, and it's unfair to encourage his attentions." She rose and patted Garnet's cheek. "You're far above that boy, just like you're far above working in a store." She paused for a moment, looking thoughtful. "The Pierces have girls, but I think Mr. Mitchell has a son. Seems like I heard he'd married though." She pursed her lips, unaware that Garnet was glaring at her. "There's Clifford Clark, odd family, but money."

Garnet screeched, "But he's *old*, Mama! He's way older than I am."

"Not so very old," Mama replied, calm as a pond. "I remember what a sweet, funny little boy he was. But," she sighed, "there are those sisters of his."

Garnet thought she'd scream with frustration but tried to keep her voice under control. "I did promise to see David tonight, and I promised I'd watch the flower bloom. I don't see how I can go back on my word."

Mama swept by her. "Oh, all right. Go watch your flower and walk with your little friend if he amuses you, but you must let him know you'll be seeing other young men, fine, *suitable* young men in the future. He's simply not marriage material."

Mama stopped by the window and peered out at the cloudless, late June sky. "Is that your dress on the line?"

"Yes."

"Why didn't you do all the wash? I don't understand why you think only your clothes are important." She sailed back through the kitchen and went to the front room to work on her embroidery.

And exactly how, Garnet thought bitterly, am I supposed to sit on the porch in fine dresses and wait for gentleman callers when I'm also supposed to do all the work? She would've slammed something on the table or thrown something against the wall except she knew her mother would deny her permission for the evening if she had a tantrum. Instead, she shut her eyes against hot, angry tears.

Throughout the afternoon she worked hard, having unspoken conversations with her mother about David and the store. She put dinner on the table when Luther walked in, spent from both his work and, more than likely, harsh words from his sister. Mama was animated and lively as they ate, making references to the "carpenter boy" and the nonsense of going to watch a flower bloom, but Garnet kept silent except to murmur once that his name was David.

Luther glanced up from his plate and said that he'd heard David Foster was a good boy, a hard worker, despite his father's reputation.

Mama sniffed. "Well, blood will tell, they always say."

Luther turned his hot, dark eyes on her then, and she had the sense to look down. Asking for more green beans, she patted Luther's hand and said that sayings weren't always true.

By seven, Garnet was pacing the front room. She would've waited on the porch, but Mama and Luther were out there, and Mama'd have a fit if she hiked down the road to meet David. As usual, he was prompt and spoke politely to both Mama and Luther. It was strange to hear her mother addressed as Mrs. Colson, and she wondered if it bothered her. When they said their goodbyes, Garnet reminded her mother that she might be very late, but Mama was whispering to Luther and simply waved her sparkling hand. Garnet exhaled mightily.

"Why is it you always seem relieved when you leave your house?" David's eyes glinted with humor.

"It's because I *am* relieved to leave my house, today more than ever."

She told him about her mother's announcement that Garnet could no longer help Mrs. Lawrence. "She says I'm too much of a lady to work at the store, but then she says I have to get up earlier so I can make breakfast for Luther," she said.

"Why can't she make his breakfast?"

Garnet rolled her eyes. "And it gets worse. She's planning on decking me out and inviting every eligible boy in the county to come courting. She says I must see other fellows, that you aren't good enough for me."

She didn't think how this might hurt him. For a minute all she heard was a mourning dove cooing from a pine tree and their shoes crunching the rocks in the road. Then he asked, "Is that what you think?"

"No, no, no!" She stopped and spun around in front of him. "I don't think that at all, but what if she won't let me see you? Luther took up for you and said nice things, but Mama's stubborn."

She had felt his mouth on her hands and lips, but she'd never looked at it with any particular interest. It was wide but thin, and just then it stretched into a taut line. His eyes were slitted nearly shut.

"I guess that was good of him."

"Oh, David," she said, touching his arm, "I never should've told you that. She just infuriates me with her notions."

Hunching up his broad shoulders, he muttered, "Some folks would agree with her." He took her hand and gave it a gentle squeeze, but she could tell he was still hurt and angry.

"And they'd be wrong, wouldn't they? Please, don't let her ruin our walk. We have so little time left."

His mouth relaxed. "Agreed. Where shall we walk?"

She was ready for this. "I want to go back to your house and see your workshop and your hammers and tools and all that. Then when you're gone I can imagine you working and you won't be so far away in my mind."

He closed his eyes for a second and smiled. "If any of those gentlemen come to your porch, they'll fall for you in a second." This confused her. "Sure, we can do that. Maybe you won't keel over this time."

As they neared his property she smelled the fresh tang of newly mown grass and remembered he'd said he'd be cutting it today. It was a hot, bright evening, and the clear light illuminated the little white house. He steered her over to the right where there were two outbuildings. "That," he said pointing to the farther one, "is where we keep the mule and the cart. Pa has them in Ashton, of course. And this here's our workshop."

He opened the door, and a shaft of sunlight exposed floating dust motes and flecks of sawdust. Garnet smelled the warm, sweet aroma of wood and the sharp scent of varnish. While David pointed out the workbench and stacks of lumber waiting to be used, she handled the tools. She lifted one and raised an eyebrow. "That's a sanding block," he said. "Try it," and he handed her a scrap of wood.

When she announced that she wanted to see the house again, he shrugged. "Sure. I reckon we already broke all the rules last night so you might as well come in when you're able to look around."

She grabbed his hand to pull him along. She felt giddy, almost childish in her desire to wring every bit of enjoyment out of this last evening.

The front room was much as she remembered it: the ugly brown chair, the unadorned walls, and the coal stove in the corner. She noticed a cane-seated rocking chair on the other side of a window covered by shabby white curtains.

"And I do remember the kitchen." The shade was up and the light lent a golden glow to the beautiful kitchen cabinet. "This is so pretty," she murmured, touching the smooth wood. He nodded at her and waited; he was humoring her, she knew, but she wanted to dream.

And it must've felt the same way for him. "I reckon it's foolish, but sometimes when the evenings get long I go from room to room and imagine what it'd be like for you to live here with me. I think about you working at the sink or sitting in the front room when it's winter and the stove makes it cozy. And then I think about how fine it would be for you to come out to the workshop of an evening to call me for supper when the sun's like fire in that hair of yours."

He was leaning against the door, looking down at his hands, but then he raised his head and met her eyes. "That's what I'm doing too," she replied.

Neither of them moved. "So I guess we're dreaming about the same thing." It was a question.

She swallowed and nodded.

He filled a dipper with water, offering it to her. She drank and gave it back. Those eyes of his never seemed to blink. "And I reckon the dream has to be here, in this house or thereabouts."

She drew up her face into a little frown.

"What I mean is, you wouldn't consider going to Covington with me, would you?" he asked this and then shook his head briefly. "That didn't come out right. I mean, would you consider marrying me and moving to Covington? Or is it too soon for that?" He turned as red as last week's sunburn. "I know we ain't been seeing each other long, and I'm probably being a fool for talking like this, and you're going to go and get all shy on me again, and . . ."

She put her hand on his mouth to interrupt him. He'd said it: marrying, and even though she knew that's what they'd both been talking about, the word itself took her voice. She could tell he was waiting on her reply, standing there breathing like he was afraid to take in much air, but she needed a moment to say it right. Reaching for the dipper, she took another drink.

"No, I wouldn't consider moving to Covington. I'm not a city girl, and, to be honest, I'm not sure how comfortable I'd feel being around your father." She faltered and looked up at his face; it was blank and tense with the mouth gone all thin and tight again. She could've gone on to say that even though Luther was providing for her family, she didn't feel right about leaving Lowell and the little ones. Mama was unpredictable at best. But she knew this would hurt him even more than the comment about his father. "But," she said, "I'd like very much to marry you and live here."

His mouth relaxed into a gigantic, genuine grin, one of those irresistible smiles he did so well. "You mean it? You want to marry me?"

She smiled back at him. "I do." And they laughed at her choice of words.

Punctuating his words with quick touches of her cheek or her hand, he spoke rapidly. "Then I'll work very hard up in Covington and save all my money, and when the work slacks off, maybe around Christmas time, I'll come back and we can get married. And maybe I can persuade my pa to let us have this place, and maybe he'll be so happy up in Covington, he'll stay up there, and we can have it to ourselves."

She nodded. There was nothing more to say. The plans were so full of maybes she could hardly comment. "Christmas," she murmured. It sounded like an eternity, but it was a promise.

He squeezed her awkwardly and mumbled, "I never in a million years thought you'd say yes to me."

"Why ever not?"

He just shrugged and pointed at the window. "Don't you have to be at the store by dark for your silly flower?"

The shadows were lengthening, and she nodded.

"Well, you've seen the pantry, haven't you?"

She walked over toward it and gave it a glance. Then she followed him back through the front room into the bedroom. He said, "This is Pa's room."

Suddenly she felt awkward and shy at the thought of being in a bedroom with him. He seemed to sense it. "Look at this bed, Garnet. It's solid cherry. And see how Pa made these posters."

The bed was made up with a bright nine-patch quilt. Glancing around she saw a dresser, store-bought, she thought, and pointed at the walls. "Kind of an odd paint choice, isn't it?"

The walls were a deep mauve, too elegant for the simple bed and cheerful quilt. "We used up leftover paint," David explained. "Don't the kitchen look familiar?"

She thought for a minute. "Oh, it's the green paint from my house!"

He grinned. "That's right. We were finishing up this house about the same time we were working for your father."

Then he led her through another door into a dark box of a room painted the color of milky coffee. Against the back sat a small iron bed, not so different from the one she slept in, and opposite it was a scarred chifferobe.

"This is my room, just a cubby-hole. When Pa's away I sleep in his room because it's cooler in the summer and warmer in the winter. When I'm dreaming," he said, his face coloring, "I imagine the front bedroom is ours." Garnet ducked her head.

They left the house, but he turned and pointed at it. "Before we get married I'll put a porch on the front and paint the front bedroom if you don't like the color."

Relieved that he'd quit talking about shared bedrooms, she said, "I don't guess we'll care much about a porch in December." He laughed. "And I'll want a garden." She surveyed the land quickly. "Over there, I think, although I'd need to give the dirt a good look."

"I don't think you'll care much about a garden in December neither," he joked.

So they left laughing and hurrying down the road to get to the store before dark. Once he stopped and asked if he could kiss her because he didn't want to do it in front of the store. She let him and tried to ignore how fierce he was again, breathing hard and pressing against her like that night in the graveyard. After all, she'd agreed to marry him; she should allow more now, and it shouldn't frighten her. By the time they reached the store, the sun was completely down although the sky held a milky blueness.

"I'll see if I can get back next Sunday. Pa'll have me working way up in the day on Saturday, but even if I have to walk the whole way, I'll come."

"I'd like that. And then the next week?"

"Then we'll probably come home for a day or two before we leave for Covington. This isn't goodbye yet."

"Good." She noticed that the door to the store was open, and, knowing where the night-blooming cereus sat, Garnet was sure Mrs. Lawrence could hear everything they said. "Until then," she whispered.

"Until then," he repeated, also in a whisper. "I love you, Garnet."

"And you."

He started to walk away but whispered again, roughly this time, "And no gentleman callers!"

She chuckled but felt empty as his footsteps faded. Sure enough, Mrs. Lawrence sat right between the door and the table that held the plant. She'd squeezed two kitchen chairs next to each other for them to watch the bloom.

"I was afraid you'd not get here in time. Look!" The woman pointed.

The long bud curved down, and at the tip lacy bits were unfurling into delicate spikes. Garnet sat. "I don't think I've missed too much."

She knew what was coming: Mrs. Lawrence started firing a barrage of questions about Mama and Luther. She'd learned about it when Lowell came that morning for Garnet's things. Only two days ago Garnet would've welcomed someone to talk to, but by now she was weary of it.

There was just enough light from the kitchen lamp to make Mrs. Lawrence's spectacles glint. She said, "I can't believe Louise would change her tune like that. She must be shrinking up every time someone calls her by her new name."

"I've wondered about that."

"But you never could tell what Louise King was going to do. She sets her own rules, and she's as likely to change 'em as keep 'em. About the only thing she never varied on was her opinion of the Colsons, and now she's up and married one." Mrs. Lawrence peered at the bud. "It's not going anywhere right this minute. I have sassafras tea; would you like some?"

"Sure. Do you want me to get it?"

"No, sit still, girl." Glad to rest, Garnet melted into the chair. She'd worked hard but no harder than she always did. It must be, she thought, all the emotion and the upsets. Years ago, Grandpa had made a swing for his grandchildren and attached it to a big maple tree. She remembered the dizzy feeling of flying high and the corresponding low when she neared the ground. Her life seemed a lot like that swing these days. She wondered why she wasn't jumping around and shouting; after all, weren't girls supposed to get all excited about a marriage proposal? And she *was* happy. It was just all the uncertainty that worried her. Walter Foster could demand that his son stay with him or rent out the house so they'd have no place to live. Or David could change his mind. He said that he'd admired her for years, but that hadn't stopped him from kissing Flora Simpson. Or Mama might force her into a different marriage. She put nothing past her mother.

Holding two teacups, Mrs. Lawrence peeked at the bud and said, "I bet Lorena's taking it bad."

"She thinks Mama did it to spite her for marrying Grandpa."

Mrs. Lawrence sipped. "Louise might be surprised at Luther Colson. Oh, right now, I suppose he's feeling like the lord of the county, wedding and bedding Miss Louise King. But when he gets past that he might not be as biddable as she thinks. Luther's got eyes in his head."

Garnet decided she might as well say it and get it over with. "Mama says I can't work here anymore."

The woman jerked up her head. "She did? Now why's that?"

Looking down at her lap Garnet said, "She says I'm above working in a store, that I should be thinking about pretty clothes and lots of beaus coming to call."

"Hmph. I don't think there's nothing common about working in a store."

Again Garnet regretted that her mother's words had hurt someone, but she wouldn't lie to make her mother look better. "I don't either, Mrs. Lawrence. I *want* to work for you, but I don't know how I can if she won't let me."

"Are you pining away for them pretty frocks and boys?"

"No." She felt an urge to pace the length of the store, but she was too tightly wedged between the table and the wall to move. She squirmed. "Who's going to come see me? I don't know where she got such an idea."

Mrs. Lawrence pointed at the bud. "Look, the petals are loosening now." The woman thought for a moment. "Louise is trying to get you to live the life she did. Deke was sociable. He had fellers coming and going all the time, trading horses or making deals, and when Louise became a beauty, the boys came flocking. Luther ain't so sociable, and likely the only men coming to your house would be hands from the farm to ask him about their chores. Unless she's planning to put up signs in Ashton, I don't reckon anybody'd know you were out here." She laughed and her eyes encouraged Garnet to do the same, but she could only manage a wan smile.

"Even if she made this happen, and even if I wanted it to happen, how am I supposed to tend the garden, mind the children, do the cooking, and, Lord knows, everything else, and sit on the porch all dolled up like the belle of the county?"

Mrs. Lawrence shook her head. "Well, regarding the store, I guess I can make it without you although I'll allow I'll miss you. We'll give it a week or so. Maybe she'll change her mind, get another scheme in her brain."

They watched the plant. The hairy, twisted leaves reminded Garnet of an unlikely cross between a snake and a spider, but there was no denying that the bud's beauty compensated for the bizarre nature of the plant. She thought she detected a slight vibration as the petals struggled to open.

"And Franklin's gone, Lowell said." Whether it was sitting in the dark or some strange desire not to disturb the blooming, they both spoke quietly. Garnet twisted her hands together. Mrs. Lawrence patted them. "He's a restless boy, Garnet, always has been. He never wanted to stay in school or even in one place. About the only people he ever took up with much were your grandaddy and you. He would've gone anyway."

"He could annoy the spit out of me, but I always counted on him."

"Well, it appears to me you've got somebody else wanting you to count on him now," Mrs. Lawrence said, her eyebrows rising above her glasses. She yawned and shook her head. "Land, it's late."

"What time is it?"

The woman pulled a silver watch from her pocket and squinted. "It's just past ten. I ain't stayed up this late in years."

The bloom was unfurling before their eyes, but the motion was so slow it reminded Garnet of a clock, always moving, but so gradually that you could hardly tell. She sniffed and caught a luscious perfume, both sweet and sharp.

"I smell it too." Mrs. Lawrence inhaled deeply.

They smiled at each other. The rest of the world might be in bed, but they were watching this rare flower open and spread a glorious scent around them.

"I don't want those boys coming to my porch," Garnet said. "He's asked me to marry him."

Mrs. Lawrence tweaked her chin. "And why ain't I surprised? Honey, the boy's been mooning over you for months. So what did you tell him?"

"Oh, Mrs. Lawrence, everything is so confused. I want to marry him, but Mama says he isn't good enough for me. And he wanted me to go off to Covington to marry him, but I can't go that far from the little ones. Besides, I don't want to be anywhere near his father. And then he said he'd come back at Christmas, and we'd marry. But so much could go wrong between now and then."

"Not good enough for you? Well, I think he's a likeable little fellow, and I don't know how any boy could be more besotted with you. I reckon you love him too?"

Garnet watched the flower. The center was opening into soft-edged, creamy petals with the spiky sepals spread around them. In the middle were silky strands that reached out into the darkness. "Yes, he's kind to me, and I think he has a good heart."

"There've been marriages made for worse reasons." Mrs. Lawrence half-rose and buried her face in the bloom, saying reverently, "Thank you, Lord, for letting me see this beautiful flower."

"Do they bloom just once a year?"

"If you're lucky. They might behave different where they live natural. But when people keep them as houseplants you have to wait and wait for your chance to see a bloom. Ain't that a sight? Why, it's near as big as a saucer."

No flower Garnet had ever seen had smelled so heavenly. It was late, she'd seen the bloom, and she probably should walk home. But she made no move to leave. She touched the delicate, creamy petals. "Will it be wilted by tomorrow?"

"As soon as the light hits it."

Garnet felt a thrill of determination course through her. "I have to go."

With a little groan Mrs. Lawrence stood. "God bless you, child."

Garnet took off at a near run up Deer Creek Road, not bothering to conceal her destination. With the sweet, musky scent of the flower still in her nose, she walked as fast as she could without stumbling on the jutting rocks. A half-moon cast deep shadows from the trees along the way and offered her just enough light to see. Thoughts tumbled in her mind, and she chose from these, expanding them into arguments for marrying sooner than Christmas. She wasn't sure whether David was simply being patient or unwilling to create trouble. Maybe he hadn't thought of alternatives. Maybe he needed a little push. Maybe she was being foolish. A rustle in the tall grass by the road made her shiver, and she pushed on faster even though the road was starting its slow rise.

As she crested the hill she saw his white house glowing in the distance. With the back of her hand she wiped perspiration from her upper lip. Should she knock or call him at the window?

He'd be asleep. Would her visit annoy him? She brushed aside a wave of fear and tried to feel strong; this was what she wanted. Mama said she should ask for what she wanted. Mama said she had powers she wasn't even aware of.

She could still smell a faint scent of cut grass as she walked across the yard she'd visited three hours ago. The house was dark and silent. All she heard were night sounds, insects and birds. Peering into the front bedroom window, she was unable to see anything at first, even though the shade was partially raised. Then her eyes adjusted, and she could make out a white lump on the bed and his arm, dark against the sheet. There was no one around to hear her, but she called to him in a low voice.

He shifted a bit, unwilling to wake, and then she called his name again. Like a bird startled from its hiding place he sat straight up and said, "Garnet? What's wrong?"

Despite the moonlight, she couldn't make out the expression on his face. "Nothing's wrong, but I have to talk to you."

Still fuzzy with sleep, he started to lift the sheet. "Go to the front door," he mumbled. "I have to put on some clothes."

She did as he said and waited. The world was colorless and strange. In a minute he was opening the door and trying to button his shirt at the same time. When he moved to light a lamp, she stopped him. "We don't need a light. I've been sitting in the dark for hours."

"What is it?" Sleep had left his voice, but he seemed wary. Maybe he thought she'd reconsidered.

"I've been thinking," she said and then realized these words wouldn't reassure him. She went on. "I've been thinking about us getting married and how much I want that."

He stood with his arms rigid at his sides as if he were preparing for a blow. Those words hadn't been enough. She stepped closer to him, close enough that she smelled the bed-scent of him. Boy-smell, she used to call it when she changed her brothers' sheets. David's eyes caught enough of the moonlight coming through the front door to appear almost white. Inching forward until her chest was nearly touching his, she murmured, "I don't want to move to Covington, but I don't want to wait until Christmas either."

He didn't move or speak. Laying her hand on his chest, she felt the warmth of it through his shirt. "I want to get married right away before my mother makes any silly plans for me or you find someone else in Covington."

He almost spoke at this, but she insinuated a finger between the shirt buttons and moved it against his warm skin, feeling the roughness of the curly hair on his chest. "Don't you want it to happen right away?"

She waited and watched him, all the while moving her finger slowly, caressing him like a snake moves when it's not in a hurry. He shut his eyes and made a small, agonized sound in his throat. They both were breathing quickly, and he hardly had enough air to gasp, "You know I want it."

"Well, then," she said, removing her hand from his chest, "suppose you talk to your father and tell him we want to marry right away. He was going to rent this house anyway, so why couldn't he rent it to us?"

His eyes were open again and glittering in the moonlight. Liquid silver, she thought. She reached down for his hand and lifted it to rub along her cheek. "I bet he turned down jobs around here when he decided to go to Covington, didn't he?"

In a soft, strangled voice, he said, "Yeah, there were some jobs."

He let her move his hand wherever she wanted. Clutching it gently she ran the back of it down her neck and moved it to her mouth where she touched it with quick, airy kisses. "Were any of the jobs ones you could do on your own?" She struggled to remember the arguments she'd mustered.

Touching his knuckles with her tongue, once, twice, she tasted him, salty and pleasant, and she almost missed seeing him nod. His eyes were closed again. "Then we'd have something to live on, wouldn't we?" She didn't recognize her voice.

"God almighty," he whispered, but he stood completely still.

"We could live here," she went on, "and I could work at the sink and call you for dinner, just like you dreamed about."

She slid his hand down her throat and then rested it against the top of her breast, which was heaving like she'd been running. "And we could sleep in that beautiful bed," she whispered.

With a noise almost like a sob he moved then, crushing her into his body until what little breath she had was nearly cut off. She opened her mouth to him and breathed through him, wondering at this strangeness, and willingly pressed against him, flattening her breasts against his chest and straining her belly against his. There it was, oh, indeed, there it was.

She pulled her mouth away from his and put her lips against his ear. "I don't want to wait until Christmas. Do you?"

He shuddered in her arms and eased his hold just a fraction. His mouth was at her ear, pulling at her earlobe with his teeth. "I can't wait until Christmas."

"So you'll talk to your father this week?"

"I will. Don't know why I didn't think of it."

"Do you think he'll agree?"

He ran his hand down her spine and she shivered. "Probably. Maybe. God, Garnet."

He slid his hand to where her rear end swelled and then back up again. Oh, but she felt strange and trembly.

"What about that mother of yours?"

She wasn't sure she could speak. "I'll manage it somehow."

Then he kissed her again, mumbling into her mouth, "Come on, Garnet. We can do it now. Please, I'm dying."

She shook her head, but he followed her mouth, holding it with his. With the greatest effort she made herself duck her head, interrupting the kiss. Panting hard, she gasped, "I can't. I won't."

He let her step back then, and she said, "We can wait that long, can't we?"

He ran his hand through his crinkled hair and then rubbed his nose. He released a deep breath. "I reckon we can."

"Maybe two weeks or so?"

He nodded. "After the job in Ashton."

"I'd better go."

"Not much time to plan a wedding."

"I don't want a big wedding."

He frowned. "I should talk to your mother and Luther."

"You can, if you come home next weekend." She felt timid again. "You'll come home next weekend, won't you?"

He nodded like it was a silly question. "You're not going to tell them?"

She shook her head. "What if it doesn't work out with your father?"

"Oh, it'll work out. We're marrying in two weeks, and my father'll just have to get used to the idea."

She glanced down at his naked feet; he had high, delicate arches, almost like a girl's. "I was afraid," she murmured. "I kept thinking something would come along to ruin it between now and December."

"Won't nothing ruin it." He turned toward the bedroom. "Just let me find my shoes, and I'll walk you home."

"No. Stay here. I'll be fine walking home. There's nobody out."

"Except that wild Garnet Grant," he replied, trying for humor. His eyes raked her body, and suddenly she felt shy again. He looked solid and fierce despite his joking.

"Yes, except that wild girl," she agreed.

"I'm dying to kiss you again, but I'm not sure I could stop another time."

"Sleep, David. I'll see you next weekend."

He chuckled harshly. "You think I'll sleep after that?"

She made no reply and walked rapidly through the silvery grass to the road. Knowing he was following her with his eyes, she pivoted once and walked backwards a step or two to wave at him and then flew down the road, picking up speed downhill. Nothing frightened her now, and her feet barely seemed to touch the road.

That week stretched as long as the taffy Mama once let her and Franklin make. Mama accused Garnet of pouting, but she wasn't; she was simply keeping her mouth shut because if she didn't, everything would come spilling out.

By Friday she thought she'd go crazy. The whole time she was ironing or cleaning she conjured up every difficulty their parents could cause. One afternoon she nearly invented an excuse to run to the store since Mattie Lawrence was the only person who knew what was going on, but she didn't. Instead, she canned beans and watched her mother pore through a catalog, commenting upon which dresses would suit Garnet.

By noon Saturday she started watching the road. She'd taken extra care with her hair and stayed out of the garden to keep her fingernails clean. When she cooked the evening meal, she added a little extra to everything in case David came. By suppertime, though, he hadn't arrived, and she took her place at the table in a state of despair. Maybe he wouldn't come until tomorrow. Maybe he wouldn't come at all. Her mind was splitting like a melon.

She was clearing the table when she heard a tapping at the front door. Violet raced to the front room and came back with David who smiled at all of them but locked eyes with Garnet. She hadn't realized that she'd been holding her breath, but exhaling felt good. "Have you eaten?"

"No, but I don't want to put you all to any trouble."

Luther scooped Henry onto his knee and gestured for David to sit. When she handed David his plate, Garnet touched his shoulder, and he looked up and gave her such a sweet smile that her fears disappeared. All of them watched him eat. She'd have been uncomfortable, but he ate as if he was at home and talked to Luther and Lowell about news from Ashton. Violet hung on his chair until Garnet told her to sit down. Mama said little. She murmured a few short answers to David's questions about her health and the baby but offered nothing else. She knew.

When David finished, Garnet whisked away his plate and sat beside him. Lowell gave her a long, strange look. He knew too. David gathered himself and started. "I reckon I should get to the point, Mr. and Mrs. Colson. The fact is that Garnet and I love each other and want to marry." His face was bright red, but he spoke calmly.

Other than a quick giggle from Violet, there was no response. Garnet's heart thudded so hard she thought David might hear it. She watched Mama, not David, who didn't realize the danger in her pale, serene face.

"Now I know some folks would say we're mighty young, but I think both of us know our minds about this. We thought about waiting, but we just don't want to. I guess you all understand about being in love," David said, turning his gaze from Luther to Mama. A nice touch, Garnet thought.

Luther cleared his throat and grabbed Mama's hand, placing it on the table under his. "I heard your pa was going to leave the county."

"Yes sir, he is. He's got work in Covington and plans on moving soon, but when he made his decision he turned down several jobs around here. All week I been going around to see if folks would hire me instead, and every one of them agreed. People is used to hiring us, and I think if I do good work, they'll continue."

This was good news, but Garnet's throat was so dry she couldn't have spoken. Mama's face was blank, and she still hadn't said a word. Violet danced around the kitchen singing about weddings and love, but Lowell seemed anxious. He asked, "Where will you all live?"

David turned to him with a smile as sweet as the one he'd given her. "The same house where my pa and I've been living; he's going to let us rent it. You can come visit your sis anytime."

Lowell nodded and then all of them, except Luther, looked at Mama, waiting for some kind of comment or question. Under Luther's grip, the tips of Mama's fingers were turning white. She asked, "When?"

"Well, as I said, we don't want to wait, but we ain't really talked this through." He glanced at Garnet. "Pa and I reckon this job'll be done about Friday, and then we're both coming home. With him packing up to leave and me trying to get the house in shape for a wife, I reckon we could be ready for a wedding in two or three weeks."

Mama's eyes narrowed and focused on Garnet's mid-section. David caught the glance too, and his face colored. He faltered, "It's not like there's any need for hurry, but neither of us wants a fancy wedding."

Mama made a slight noise in her throat. Lifting her chin, she said, "We had hoped Garnet would reach a little higher."

Luther whipped his head around to look at her, but before he could say anything, David met her icy eyes. Garnet was agonizing for him, but at this point it was best if she said nothing. Biting at his lower lip, he said, "I understand, Mrs. Colson, 'cause she's a beautiful, wonderful girl, and I know I ain't much, just a carpenter, but it's honest work, and I'll do everything on earth to make your daughter safe and happy."

His eyes were the clearest gray then, and Garnet thought of heroes: princes rescuing damsels in distress, knights riding off to noble causes. She'd never loved him more. Luther slid Henry off his knee, released Mama's hand, and stood. "Don't reckon we can ask for fairer than that." He stuck out his hand.

"Thank you, sir." David stood to return the handshake.

Mama toyed with the salt cellar, turning it one way and then another. Keeping her eyes down, she drawled, "I don't suppose you're in a position to give permission or not, Luther."

Garnet had been rising from her chair but collapsed back into it. Beside her, Lowell gasped. Luther looked at Mama for a long minute, but she continued to regard the salt cellar as if it were the most fascinating thing on earth. "Well, Louise," he said. "Garnet eats the food I bring to this table and wears the clothes I willingly provide for her, so I reckon I can give her permission to marry." He looked at Garnet. "Does he make you happy, girl?"

"Yes," she whispered.

"Then that's all you and I should care about, Louise." He placed a heavy hand on Mama's hair. "How can we refuse anybody who wants to marry?"

Mouth tight, Mama nodded once at David and then Garnet. She wasn't one bit happy about it, but was beaten for the moment. Then all of them were standing and talking, except for Mama who retreated to the front room. Violet had hold of David's hand and was chattering, flouncing her gorgeous hair back and forth. Garnet dodged all of them, trying to start the dishes, and then Lowell was at her side, announcing that he and Violet would do them. Garnet kissed his thin cheek.

Luther was talking to David but stopped when she approached. "Guess you two have plenty to talk about." He smiled.

David agreed and asked Garnet if she wanted to walk. Her answer was to untie her apron and hold out her hand. He grinned, and they strolled out the back door. She led him to the path toward the farm, and a few yards along the way they sighed simultaneously, bringing on a burst of hysterical laughter.

"Now I know why you sigh when you leave that house." He shook his head. "She's a rare bird."

"Don't think she's done, either. There'll be hell to pay until I leave."

"Does she really disapprove of me so much? I may not be much, but she don't know me well enough to hate me." Anger crept into his voice.

Garnet squeezed his arm. "It's not you. She just doesn't want her little plans upset, and," she added, "she wants me here to do the work. What did your father say?"

"Oh, he wasn't happy about it either. He complained and argued for a while. But he then came around, and I think he's relieved we'll be looking after his place. I don't think he cares much one way or the other."

"I care."

"I know, and that's why we're going to be so happy." He threw his arm around her shoulders and hugged her to him. "Where're we going anyway?"

"To the farm. I want to tell Lorena."

"Well, if she's anything like her brother, she's a fine person, no matter what folks says about her."

She let this pass. Of course he'd heard talk about Lorena. "I never expected him to take up for me against my mother." She frowned. "He'll suffer."

"I'm not so sure. I think your mother might've met her match."

Garnet gave a bitter laugh. "Then it'll be a long and ugly war. She never gives in. The only time you get any relief is when she changes her mind."

David squeezed her shoulder. "Do you know what Luther said? He asked if Pa was going to take the mule and cart to Covington, and when I told him yes, he said he has an old cart that just needs a little repair. He's planning on giving it to us."

"Why, that's wonderful!"

Somewhere above their heads, a mockingbird rehearsed its entire repertoire, and the air was warm and fragrant. She was having a hard time walking sedately as a nearly married woman should. Finally she just had to skip a few steps, passing David along the path and stopping to grin back at him.

"You're that happy?"

He seemed to need reassurance, and after what he'd been through she was glad to give it. "I'm that happy." She reached up to hold his face between her hands and kiss him. He pressed her against him, fumbling for her breasts, but she laughed and wriggled free, running ahead of him.

As soon as Lorena opened the door they told her, and she beamed at them. It looked like the first smile she'd tried on in days, but she shook David's hand and hugged Garnet, whispering in her ear, "I reckon you do love him. You sure look happy."

Lorena asked if David wanted coffee. He hesitated, and Garnet said, "We both like tea, Lorena, if that's all right."

She chuckled, said this was handy, and narrowed her eyes at Garnet. "Did Louise give you a bad time?"

"She was awful and would've been worse if Luther hadn't managed her. And David handled it all beautifully."

Heart bursting, she glowed at him. When she looked back at Lorena, the woman's eyes were warm and sweet as fresh bread. "Well, I'm glad that sorry brother of mine was good for something. I figured Louise might be surprised at what she got. We're stubborn as mules, the both of us."

She served them tea and applesauce cake, which David attacked with gusto. Garnet noted this and wondered what other foods he especially liked. There were so many things to learn about him. All of them chatted about plans, and Garnet said she intended to talk to Brother Bledsoe about the wedding after church the next day.

"I can go with you," David offered, between bites. He was on his second piece of cake. "Are we going to invite anybody or make anything of this?"

"I don't know. I've thought of a million things this week, but the actual wedding wasn't one of them. I'd like my family to be there, although I doubt Mama will go. What about your father?"

"No, he'll be long gone by then. I expect we'll get back here on Friday, and I wouldn't be a bit surprised if he leaves the next day. What about you, Mrs. King? We'd love to have you at the wedding."

Lorena gave him a gracious nod. "I thank you, David, but I don't think that would be smart, especially if Louise comes. She likes to pretend I don't exist and ain't happy when she's reminded that I do." She thought for a moment. "When do you think you'll have the wedding?"

Garnet and David looked at each other. "I don't know," she replied. "I suppose it depends upon Brother Bledsoe, but I was thinking two weeks from today."

David agreed.

"Surely to goodness Luther and the children will go even if Louise stubs up about it. And I bet Mrs. Lawrence would close the store to go to your wedding, Garnet. Maybe Miss Carter? She's always thought a lot of you. What about you, David? Do you have any kin or friends who would be there?"

"Well, I reckon Hayse might come. I don't have any kin around here."

"Hayse Simpson? That ornery nephew of mine?"

"He's my friend."

"Hmm. He's not worth a nickel." Lorena laughed. "You're keeping bad company."

"Oh, he's all right even if he does get into trouble now and then. He takes good care of his father."

"That's true, and Albert hasn't been much force since my sister died." Lorena gave herself a little shake. "So Hayse might be there, and Flora, would Flora come?"

David dropped his eyes. "No, I don't reckon Flora would come."

Lorena leaned back in her chair, gazing at the ceiling. "I wish Flora would settle down and marry. My sister's dying left that girl afloat."

Garnet stared hard at David, but he didn't say anything. Lorena kept her eyes on the ceiling and then looked back at them. "Well, here's what I was thinking. Louise, if she's any kind of mother at all, will go to the wedding and maybe have people back at the house for cake or something afterwards. So you two will spend the afternoon smiling and socializing and wishing you could escape."

She grinned knowingly at them, and they both blushed. "Now that's all fine," she continued," but the last thing a bride should have to do is fix supper on her wedding night. So, after all the hullabaloo, why don't you two come up here and eat, and I won't say a word about you all rushing off as soon as you're finished."

Garnet giggled, and David offered one of his eye-crinkling smiles. "I can't think of nothing any nicer, Mrs. King. Thank you."

She frowned at him. "Now, look here, boy, I'm damned proud to have been Deke King's wife, but I won't have you calling me Mrs. King. I'm Lorena for now and evermore, you hear?"

He ducked his head. "All right, Lorena."

"I know everything that's going on, and you two need some time to make plans. Why don't you show him around the farm, Garnet? You still have time before dark. Oh, and Garnet, tell the children they're still welcome on Sundays even if Franklin ain't here. That is, if Louise don't have a fit over it."

Garnet showed him all her favorite places: the orchard, the maple tree where the swing once hung, the tobacco barn. As they meandered he told her he had to leave right after they talked to Brother Bledsoe. She said she wanted to make curtains for the house, and he declared that the week before the wedding he was going to build a front porch.

On Sunday he met her at church and afterwards, spoke with Brother Bledsoe who agreed with the date and suggested 2:00. Mrs. Lawrence was still lingering in the churchyard, and they told her their news. Later Garnet said, "Now anybody who might want to come will know about it."

David smiled. "I guess telling Mrs. Lawrence is better than advertising in the paper."

And then they parted. He went to get his things, and she walked to her house alone, surprised at how suddenly she'd adjusted to having him near. At home she told them about the time and date of the wedding, but Mama said nothing.

That afternoon Garnet was working in the garden when Luther joined her. "Looks like you're getting a good crop of pole beans," he said.

"Yes, but we need rain." She wanted to thank him for his support the previous night but thought this might embarrass both of them.

He kept standing there with his hands in his pockets while she pinched beans off the vines. Then he said, "I reckon you'll want a new dress for the wedding." He pulled his hand out and handed her a roll of bills. "I can't get away this week, but maybe you and Lorena could go. I ain't asked her, but I bet she'd take you."

"Oh, Luther, I don't need a new dress," Garnet protested.

"Yes, you do. Your mother had a new dress for our wedding, and you should have one too. I'll ask Lorena."

"Thank you. You've been so good to us."

He shrugged as he walked off, a solitary man, and she thought that he would take good care of her brothers and sisters. Everything would work out.

***

It didn't take Garnet long to turn her thoughts from a wedding dress to the general condition of her wardrobe. The shabbiness of her underclothes and nightgowns made her squirm. Someone else would be seeing those holes, rips, and frays, so that night after supper she bundled up the dilapidated items and sat on the porch with her needle and thread, trying to make them presentable. She hadn't been sewing long before Mama came out with her arms full of quilt, embroidery, and Dessie. After settling the baby, she started stitching too. It should've been a peaceful, companionable scene.

Squinting as she threaded her needle, Mama said, "I suppose you have no idea how much better you could've done."

The unspoken agreement among all of them, except Franklin, had always been to humor Mama, to avoid confrontation, but perhaps it was David's courage that gave Garnet some asperity. "I don't think I could've done better at all."

Mama was too lady-like to snort, but the sound she made was similar.

"Mama, you and Papa brought me up to live simply and work hard. You were reared to be beautiful and pampered and admired. We just want different things, and neither of them is wrong or right."

Her mother's needle made a popping sound as it passed through the fabric stretched taut on the embroidery hoop. "But he's just a boy, Garnet. And he's just a carpenter; look at his father."

"There's no reason to think he'll be like his father. He is young, but he's been working for years and seems awfully responsible for his age." Garnet's needle trembled.

"I don't know how I'll get everything done without you."

Ah, thought Garnet, there's the real problem. She measured out her words. "Well, come September, both Lowell and Violet will be in school, so you'll just have Henry and Dessie at home during the day. And Lowell's smart and good with the little ones. He's a willing little fellow if you keep his nose out of a book, and I can help you with some things. It's not like I'm moving to the moon." She used her best ammunition. "David wanted me to move to Covington, but I wouldn't because I wanted to be around here where I could help you."

"My stars, Covington?" Garnet knew she'd scored points. Her mother looked at Garnet's lap. "What're you mending?"

"Oh, this sorry-looking nightgown and some underthings. I never paid any attention before, but I'm sort of ashamed to have David see how shabby they are."

Mama lifted an eyebrow. "You're looking forward to that part, aren't you?"

Garnet mumbled, "I don't know."

"Hmm. Let me see that nightgown."

Mama held it up, clucking her disapproval. "This is nothing but a rag. Surely your others are in better condition."

"I only have one other, and it's worse."

Mama shook her head. "You must have something pretty for your wedding night and some new petticoats and knickers too."

Trying to head off talk about wedding nights, Garnet said, "Luther gave me money to get a dress for the wedding."

"Did he?" Evidently this was news to her, and it didn't please her. But she focused on the shabby things in Garnet's lap. "So I guess you'll be going to town. Maybe that money would stretch to buying fabric for other garments. What kind of dress are you thinking about?"

And suddenly they were like any normal mother and daughter, planning the wedding and moaning that there was so little time to get everything done. Mama said she'd make a list and went into the house to fetch paper and pencil. Garnet smiled to herself: as she'd told David, Mama never gave up but did occasionally change her targets. By the time Mama returned she was saying how there might not be time, but Violet really needed something new for the wedding, and she was so glad she had her own lovely dress to wear. And before long she was wondering if a little party, something simple like cake and lemonade, might be nice after the ceremony. In the midst of all this planning Luther walked up to the porch and asked Mama if she'd like to take a walk.

She raised her chin. "No, we're busy. You can just walk by yourself."

He did so, not showing any hurt or disappointment, but that didn't mean he didn't feel it. Loping along in his slow, steady stride, he crossed the bridge, heading away from Bethel. Garnet eyed her mother's pursed lips. Maybe she was being a little too brave, Garnet thought, but she spoke anyway. "You know, one by one, we're all going to leave. Franklin's already gone, and I'm about to marry. Oh, the little ones have a ways to go, but that means you have quite a while to provide for them too. I believe I'd keep Luther sweet."

Startled, Mama opened her mouth and then frowned at her list. "Put this on the kitchen table where I can add things if I think of them. I must look up that recipe for a Lady Baltimore Cake, but I'll do that tomorrow. Watch Dessie."

And she stood, twitched her skirt, and took off down the road in the same direction as Luther. Garnet leaned over and smiled at Dessie lying on the quilt. "Life is full of surprises, baby sister. It really is."

Chapter Twelve

A few years back, Papa had brought home a newspaper featuring articles about the death of Queen Victoria. He spoke at length about the historical significance of the British monarch's long reign, but Garnet paid little attention. What drew her was the picture of the queen, a stout little woman whose expression reminded Garnet of someone who'd been too close to a poorly kept outhouse. And she was fascinated with details about the royal family and their privileged lives. She imagined having maids and ladies-in-waiting just to fasten fabulous jewels around her neck. During the days before her wedding, she decided she'd caught a glimpse of what it might be like to be royalty. For once in her life, she was the center of attention.

Oh, she didn't recline on the sofa; she worked harder than ever, waking before dawn and staying up until her eyes blurred and her back creaked. Mostly she sewed. And Mama sewed. All day long the Singer whirred. They made underclothes and nightgowns, they stitched camisoles and another blouse for her gray skirt, and they created two lovely dresses. One was for Violet, and, appropriately, it was dark lavender and trimmed with so many ribbons and bows that Violet stood in the middle of the kitchen floor and clapped her hands when she saw it. And then there was Garnet's wedding dress.

Mama was probably perturbed that Lorena accompanied Garnet to choose the materials for the dress, but she refrained from saying anything. And truly, Garnet had done all the choosing. She told Lorena she didn't want anything too fussy because the dress must see regular use for church or special events, but both of them made a beeline for a bolt of sage green silk. Made plainly, Lorena said, it would serve all sorts of needs. Lorena went on to purchase gloves, lacy hankies, and a gorgeous confection of a hat with real ostrich feathers. It was then that Garnet, despite being embarrassed by Lorena's generosity, started feeling like a princess. The woman brushed it off, saying she didn't have anything else to spend her money on, and they'd laughed like girlfriends all the way to Ashton and back.

Late one night Garnet finished hemming her wedding dress but refused to go to bed until she trimmed her glorious hat with fancy ribbon. Other nights she attached Mama's crocheted lace to petticoats or camisoles or whatever was next in the stack. As Mama'd said, all those yards and yards of lace did come in handy.

When she wasn't sewing, Garnet worked in the garden. Lowell pitched in even though he was more inclined to talk about the parts of plants than to hoe weeds. His most recent career aspiration was to become a scientist, and he related everything he was learning from Miss Carter's biology book until Garnet had to remember how helpful he was to refrain from gagging him. Even Violet, who was enthralled by the concept of a wedding and well on her way to becoming a minor princess herself, helped by embroidering pillow cases.

Mama was worried about the cake. "It must be a Lady Baltimore Cake. Hand me the recipe again." She sighed and furrowed her brow every time she read the recipe, which was about three times a day as the wedding neared.

"Have you ever made one, Mama?"

"No, but my mother used to."

Sighing, Garnet gestured for her mother to hand her the recipe, which she read with increasing dismay. A Lady Baltimore Cake involved four layers with a filling of nuts, raisins, coconut, and boiled icing. When Garnet asked if they couldn't do something simpler, her mother's face fell.

"I reckon I can try to bake it," Garnet said.

"The children and I will do the cleaning".

Where, thought Garnet, were the maids and the cooks and the ladies-in-waiting?

The prince was working hard too. Garnet hardly saw David who was painting during the day and building their porch in the evenings. But one day he surprised her as she was sewing some of Mama's never-ending lace on knickers. She stuffed the embarrassing garment into her sewing basket. "Come here, Garnet, and see the wedding present Pa gave us!" he shouted, looking proud and happy. He pointed across the swinging bridge.

She obliged, walked across the bridge, but saw nothing but a placid mare. He couldn't stand it. "The horse, Garnet! Her name is Maggie, and now I'll have her to pull that cart Luther's giving us."

He petted on the mare and whispered sweet things to her, and Garnet managed to do some patting as well. Luckily, Luther came out the back door about that time, and David hollered at him. The two of them examined the animal and went off to the farm to examine the cart. Certainly she was grateful that Walter Foster and Luther were providing the means for David to do his work, but it was difficult to get excited about a gift that would eat oats and produce manure.

Finally the day arrived, and Garnet was relieved that it was sunny. Nerves and excitement woke her early. A quick trip to the cellar told her the cake was holding up well, all trimmed out with nuts on top. She strolled to the garden, her garden, and felt a wave of nostalgia. She wondered if Papa would've approved of David. She clenched her toes around the warm dirt. Would he have been like Mama and wanted her to aim higher? Papa'd never cared much about wealth, so higher wouldn't have meant more social standing or money to him, although he might've preferred someone more educated.

And she wished Franklin could be there. Yesterday while she was baking, Lowell had run into the kitchen and flourished a grubby envelope bearing Franklin's scrawl. He was fine, he wrote, and had a job on a big horse farm outside Lexington. It didn't pay much, but he was learning and loving the horses. She wasn't to worry about him, and she should give his best regards to his brothers and sisters and Lorena. She had smiled and told Lowell to run to the farm and read the letter to Lorena. Garnet would write him next week about her wedding.

She stood quietly as the sun rose, burning off the dew and heating the rich dirt. Bright, fat tomatoes, almost too heavy for their vines, dotted the garden like rubies. She was happy; this day was what she wanted, but she wondered if it was always hard to go ahead without looking back. Hearing a step, she saw Luther coming toward her from the path. "You're up early," she said.

"You too."

"I didn't think you were working today."

"I'm not, but I didn't want to leave the milking for Lorena. I hear she has a special supper to fix." A smile brightened his dark eyes.

"Oh, yes, but I haven't said— "

He interrupted her. "And it won't be said. No sense stirring things up."

They both gazed at the plants. Her bare feet enjoyed the dewy grass. Soon enough she'd be encased in yards and yards of fabric and new, probably uncomfortable shoes. Luther said, "The garden looks mighty pretty. That rain yesterday helped."

"I'm going to miss it."

"Oh, you'll have your own soon enough. I'll tend this one for you."

She turned toward the house. "I reckon I should be getting breakfast."

"Seems like you might be spared making breakfast on your wedding day," he said. "I think I still know how to fry an egg if there are any."

She rolled her eyes. "I don't know. That blessed cake took six."

"I can rustle up something. By the way, I put the trunk upstairs so you can pack your things in it."

And so the day both crept and flew by. After her bath, she was folding clothes, new and old, into the musty trunk, when she had a moment of panic. She remembered drying the body that had belonged only to her thus far; she'd have to share it soon. At dinner she felt a rolling wave of nausea when she tried to eat, and another of resentment when Mama insisted she must choke down at least a piece of bread and butter. She heard Henry's reluctance at wearing church clothes and Violet's delight in her new dress. As Mama brushed her coppery hair, she felt tears of nostalgia.

Then she was trying, with shaking hands, to arrange her hair, sure she'd be late and heard Mama reply that she didn't think they'd start the wedding without her. In a final blur of activity she viewed her pale reflection in the mirror and almost didn't recognize herself as Mama poked a hatpin through the gorgeous new hat and told her she looked lovely. Somehow she fitted her hands into ivory gloves and slid a lacy hankie into her sleeve, and before she quite knew how it happened, she was in the wagon with Luther, Mama, and Dessie, slowly following the others walking ahead of them. She heard Mama tell her she was too pale and should pinch her cheeks, and she saw Luther gaze at her with pride and anxiety at the same time. Mostly she remembered thinking that she must not sweat and she must not faint.

When they arrived at the church, Mama insisted that Garnet hesitate at the door and walk in well behind them. With a nervous glance around the room, she obeyed and saw people turning their heads to get a glimpse of her. David was up front smiling, his eyes crinkled so tightly they disappeared. Above his snowy high collar, his face was flushed, rose on tan, and the sight of it comforted her. With a deep breath, she walked down the aisle toward him, brave enough now to return his smile.

He leaned close enough to whisper, "You ain't going to faint, are you?"

She couldn't help but giggle and reached to hold his hand. It was impossible to tell who was gripping more tightly. Brother Bledsoe said the words, they spoke their vows, and when the time came, David slipped a ring on her finger. She'd forgotten that he would give her a ring. It didn't seem right to look closely at it just then, but she saw gleaming gold and a dark red stone, garnet, she thought, and this pleased her. Then David kissed her, and Mrs. Bledsoe played the tinkly, old piano. They turned and faced the smiling faces, and Garnet noticed Mrs. Lawrence wiping her eyes.

Most people were coming to the house, and Garnet's family disappeared to prepare for the little party. She wondered if she and David would have to walk to her house, but as the final well-wishers departed, David led her to the side of the church where his sturdy cart and the mare were tied up. Acting like she was made of glass, he helped her up. "You're the most beautiful thing I've ever seen."

She touched his face with a gloved hand. "And you're the most wonderful thing I've ever seen."

He cleared his throat and urged Maggie to walk. "Do you like your ring?"

"I've hardly looked at it." She pulled off her glove. The ring was plain with an oval garnet set deeply into a gold band. "I love it."

"I bought it in Ashton while Pa and me was doing that painting job. I knew I had to have a garnet." He turned and grinned at her. "And now I do."

The women's dresses looked like flowers scattered on the grass in front of Garnet's house. Luther and Lowell had moved the kitchen table onto the yard and covered it with a long white cloth. Pitchers of lemonade stood on the table along with mismatched glasses and cups. When Mama promenaded around the corner of the house bearing the big cake, people exclaimed over it, and Mama accepted all their compliments.

Luther brought out kitchen chairs and found level places for them. Garnet longed to sit, but, like David, she must circulate among their guests. She accepted a slice of cake and tasted it, more for research than hunger. She congratulated herself; it was good. Hayse cornered his Uncle Luther, trying to get him to say more than two sentences in a row. And Millie was there with her beau, a tall young man with a sparse beard. Millie's little sister followed Lowell like a puppy, and Garnet couldn't tell if this pleased him or not. Adding to the noise and confusion, Henry and Violet raced around the yard, drinking cup after cup of lemonade.

On the porch Garnet greeted Miss Carter and Mrs. Lawrence who was holding a limp and sleeping Dessie. "Don't you just wish you could rest like a baby?"

Garnet shut her eyes for a second. "I think I could rest for hours. I can't believe all I've done the last two weeks."

"So is that husband of yours going to let you come back to work for me?"

"We haven't talked about it, but he knows how much I love the store."

Miss Carter cleared her throat. "This is a lovely wedding, Garnet. Your father would be so proud."

I'll not cry, Garnet thought, not on my wedding day. She managed another smile and said she hoped so and excused herself to get a cup of lemonade. The afternoon was hot and still, and her feet burned in the lovely new shoes. Oh, if she could only go barefooted! This amused her, and she was still smiling when she reached the table.

"I reckon the bride must be thinking about her wedding night to be smiling so big." It was Hayse with a naughty glint in his eyes.

"No, the bride is thinking how thirsty she is." Luther poured her a cup and she drained it.

Hayse grabbed her hand and pulled her into the center of the yard. David was near the garden talking to the Bledsoes, but he, as well as everybody else, looked up when Hayse started talking in a voice fit to carry to the next county.

"Here's the beautiful Mrs. David Foster, and it's a tradition for everyone to kiss the bride, so line up, everybody, and wish her well!"

There was general laughter, and Garnet plastered a big smile on her face even though she was mortified. Joking and chuckling, everybody obeyed him and formed a ragged line. Pure devilment danced in Hayse's eyes. He announced that the kissing must start with his Uncle Luther and end with David. If Hayse intended to embarrass his uncle, he was disappointed. Luther moved right up and bent to kiss her forehead. "Be happy, girl."

Mama came next, all smiles, and Garnet shut her eyes when her mother kissed her cheek, wishing Mama would always be this pleased with her. And then her siblings trooped up, and she bent low to embrace first Henry, who had a very sticky face, and then Violet. Lowell looked shy, and she said, "Don't you want to kiss your Nettie?"

He brushed his hair back from his forehead and stood on tiptoes to press his lips against her cheek. "It's just that I'm going to miss you."

She touched his silky hair. "You come see me any time, Lowell," she said, stooping to kiss his cheek in return.

Miss Carter and Mrs. Lawrence followed Lowell, along with Brother and Mrs. Bledsoe. Garnet went fire red when the preacher stood in front of her, but he lifted her gloved hand briefly to his lips and winked at her.

"No fair, no fair," cried Hayse, monitoring all this. "No one's kissing the bride like she deserves to be kissed. Come on," he said to Millie's fellow who was behind Garnet's friend in line. "Do the job right."

Millie's brows rose nearly to her hairline, but she gave Garnet's cheek a quick touch with her lips and stood aside to see what her young man would do. He shrugged apologetically at Garnet and aimed for her mouth, hitting about half mouth and half nose. Garnet couldn't believe David was enjoying this, but he stood behind everyone else and kept grinning. Millie's little sister was next, and then Hayse stood before her.

"I reckoned David would appreciate us getting you primed for the evening's activities, but this is a tame lot," he said.

Garnet's hand flew to her throat. She couldn't make a fuss with David standing right behind Hayse acting like he approved of this foolishness. Hayse was a tall man, nearly as tall as his Uncle Luther, and she felt as though he was swooping down on her like some bird of prey. With his hand under her chin, he lifted her face and pressed his lips right against hers. It went on longer than was proper, and she felt half-dizzy from tilting her head back. Just as he seemed to be finishing, his wicked tongue flicked against her closed mouth.

"There," he declared. "Now she's ready for her groom."

There was general laughter at this, and no one seemed to notice anything except that she was as red as a tomato. Then David was there and put his arms around her. With one hand she held onto her hat, unsettled by Hayse's antics, and David kissed her once, and then again with a huge smack that made everyone laugh. "I'm going to kill him," he said, one inch from her face, and this made her laugh as well.

And so it went, with people visiting and leaving as the afternoon lengthened. Garnet wondered what her family would do for supper and then remembered that it was no longer her concern. After what seemed like hours, she caught David's eye, indicating she was ready to leave. They said their good-byes and thanked Mama and Luther for the party. Everyone but Luther thought they were going home.

"Oh, David," she moaned, once she got in the cart. "I'm miserable."

He turned sharply. "What's wrong?"

"My feet. They're dying."

He chuckled. "Do you suppose Lorena'll care if you eat supper barefooted?"

"I hope not, but if I take these shoes off I may never get them on again."

Lorena had been listening for them and was holding the door open when David helped Garnet hobble toward the porch. "What's wrong with you, girl?"

"My shoes are pinching the ever-loving hell out of my feet."

Lorena laughed, but David dropped his jaw at Garnet's language. She limped up the steps, stopping when Lorena put a hand on her arm. "Let me see you." She gazed at Garnet, touching the dress and eyeing the hat. "Beautiful. You're an absolute picture."

Garnet knew she was disappointing them, but she'd smiled until her jawbones ached and chatted until her head hurt. And these discomforts didn't begin to rival her feet. "This picture," she announced as she went through the door, "is about to change."

She could sense the raised eyebrows behind her as she struggled into the front room. With a flourish she pulled out her hatpin and laid her hat on the lamp table. Then she pulled off the gloves sticking to her damp hands and placed them next to the hat. Lurching to the sofa, she reclined upon it and looked at David and Lorena hovering in the doorway. "Could I *possibly* have something to drink?"

Lorena grinned and hurried to the kitchen. With wide eyes, David stared at his bride, who was behaving like someone he'd never seen before. "The shoes, David."

Without speaking, he unbuttoned her shoes and pulled them off her swollen feet. She wiggled her toes, resting her feet on his knee. "You have no idea how good that feels."

"Maybe I do." Opening one eye she saw that he'd removed his tie and high, tight collar. Both of them had their eyes shut when Lorena returned with two cups of tea.

"Lord, I'm sure you all are anxious, but I didn't think you'd commence undressing in my front room."

Laughing, Garnet opened her eyes and thanked her. She blew on her tea and took a sip. "I feel better already." Then she grinned at both of them. "I just had to have one more go at being a princess."

They both laughed and Lorena admired Garnet's ring. Wonderful smells drifted from the kitchen and her stomach growled. "I'll feel just dandy after I've eaten."

"Didn't I see you eating some cake?"

"I had a few bites."

David took a healthy gulp from his cup. "That was the best cake. Garnet's mother is quite a cook."

It was lucky she didn't have tea in her mouth or else she would've spewed it all over her wedding dress. She glanced at Lorena, and they both started giggles that turned to belly laughs. Garnet laughed so hard the sofa shook.

David's face scrunched up. "What's so funny?"

"I baked the cake. Mama can't cook a lick."

"What kind was it?" Lorena asked.

"A Lady Baltimore Cake."

Lorena chuckled again. "Oh, that's even better."

"Poor Luther," Garnet said, shaking her head.

David looked confused again, but then it seemed to dawn on him. "So you done all the cooking, and now they're all going to suffer from your mother's."

Both women nodded. "You're the winner in this deal," Lorena said, "Garnet's a dab hand in the kitchen. Speaking of cooking, I need to finish a few things. Set still."

David grinned, glad to see her merry again. "I know I'm the winner in this deal."

He massaged her feet, and she groaned. The tensions of the day melted out of her, and, ignoring how his hands were creeping past her ankles, she was about a quarter of the way to falling asleep when Lorena called them for dinner.

Lorena sat in Grandpa's place at the huge table, and Garnet had a brief bittersweet memory of the times he'd overseen jolly family dinners. But Lorena was nearly as good; she laughed loud and long at the tales David and Garnet told about their preparations for the wedding and all the events of the day.

"And then that devilish friend of yours organized the kissing ceremony. Why didn't you stop him?" Garnet narrowed her eyes at David.

"What friend?" Lorena asked.

"Your nephew Hayse," Garnet replied.

David shrugged at Lorena, "I thought she *wanted* to kiss everybody!"

Regretting her bare feet, Garnet aimed a kick at David's leg. "I've never been more embarrassed in my life." She giggled at David's reaction to the kick. "I did like the way Brother Bledsoe handled it, though."

And Lorena had to hear about this. Garnet doubted that David had any idea quite how intimate his friend's kiss had been, but she certainly wasn't going to tell him. They ate the delicious food, which led to stories about Mama's cooking, and went on to observations about Luther looking like a proud father of the bride, and, Lorena brought in her famous jam cake. "Two wonderful cakes in one day," David said.

By the time they'd finished and drunk more tea, Garnet heard the old clock in the hall wheeze and then strike seven. David had fallen silent, and most of the talk was between Garnet and Lorena who made Garnet stand up so she could closely examine her dress. "We've made awful fun of Louise's cooking, but there's no better hand at dressmaking."

"I know," Garnet replied. "I'm awfully glad Mama came around, for several reasons, but I never could've done so well." She ran her hands down the smooth seams.

"How did you get her to change her mind?" David asked. He was gazing intently at the dress, but somehow Garnet didn't think he was admiring the stitches.

"Oh, I told her that you wanted me to move to Covington, but I wouldn't because I knew she needed me. It was always about her, David; it had little to do with her opinion of you or those plans of hers."

This seemed to please him. He asked, "She was plenty mad at Luther too, wasn't she? For supporting you?"

Garnet crinkled up her nose. "I got her to change her mind on that too."

"Oh, really?" Lorena's eyebrows shot up.

"I just told her she'd be in a pickle without him, and she'd better keep him happy," Garnet said with a quick toss of her head. They laughed, and then they were silent. David gave Garnet a meaningful look, and she nodded. Lorena caught on.

"Well, I promised that you all could leave as soon as you wanted, and it appears to me it's time. One thing, though: is there any food up at that house of yours, David?"

"Uh, not much, I reckon. Guess I wasn't thinking about that."

"Probably not." Lorena's mouth twitched at the corners. "I'm going to pack up a little box, and then you can be on your way."

She stacked their dessert plates and went into the kitchen. Garnet felt so full and relaxed that it was all she could do to walk back into the front room. She looked at her shoes, those instruments of torture that lay so innocently on the floor. She couldn't do it, she decided, and sat, reaching up under her skirt to grab a garter and roll one stocking down her leg. Just for a second, David got a glimpse of smooth, white leg, for he was watching; she could tell. He'll see more than this before the night's over, she thought, and this gave her a quick flash of panic.

Lorena bustled into the room with the wooden box Luther had used to bring food to the Grants. "This should keep you fed," she said, handing it to David. Then she gave what looked like a ball of white tissue paper to Garnet. "Don't unwrap this until you get home. It's Miss Caroline's cut glass compote."

"Oh, Lorena!"

The woman took a deep breath. "I know Deke would want you to have it."

David said he'd bring the cart to the door and left. Lorena kissed Garnet. "There. Since I wasn't present for all the kissing this afternoon, I'll get mine now."

"I wish you could've been."

"I think I done better to have just the two of you this evening." She tilted her head toward the door. "He's ready to eat you up, girl."

Garnet ducked her head.

"Maybe you're just as anxious," Lorena said with a chuckle. "I guess you know all about what's going to happen here afore long."

"Mama wanted to talk, but I wouldn't let her."

"Well, be patient with him 'cause it's for sure he won't have much patience himself at first." Then she repeated what her twin brother had said. "Be happy, girl."

So Maggie started her slow, steady gait, and Garnet, holding the precious compote in her lap, waved at Lorena as they drove down the lane. She felt nervous again and wished David would start his easy talking, but he remained silent too. "I think we're talked out."

He nodded, and she watched his hands on the reins. They looked heavy and strong, and for some foolish reason, she felt a little afraid of them. Silly, she thought, those were David's hands that had been nothing but good to her. As they passed the store, she said, "Oh,

Mrs. Lawrence asked if I'd be coming back to work, and I said I would. You don't mind do you?"

"I don't guess so," he replied. "But I reckon I can support us."

Uh, oh, she thought. "It's more for helping her out than anything, although getting a few free groceries never hurt a body, did it?"

"She does enjoy having a little help."

"Oh, yes. She suffers awfully with her feet."

He grinned sideways. "Then you'd better not wear your new shoes to work."

She laughed. This was better, although she couldn't get much more out of him and felt like she was chattering. They neared the little house, and she stretched to peer at it. "I want to see the porch."

"It's on there. You'll be able to see it better in a minute."

He drove the cart near the small outbuilding that housed both it and the horse. The grass felt cool under her sore feet as she rushed toward his project. "Oh, it's wonderful, David! Where did you get the chairs? Did you make them too?" She sat in one of the rocking chairs and gave it a push.

"No. They were broken, and Pa always said he'd put them back together. He never did, so I mended them."

"They're very comfortable. You've worked so hard."

He shrugged. "Well, go on in. I tried to get everything all cleaned up for you. I'll unhitch Maggie and then I'll be along."

The house did look tidy. There was a light blue coverlet on the bed; she supposed that Walter Foster had taken the quilt. Passing into the kitchen, she saw a new tablecloth. She peeled off layers of tissue paper to uncover the bright, glinting compote. It made little prisms on the kitchen walls. Removing the last bits of paper, she saw a white envelope folded into the bowl. Inside she found fifty dollars. My stars, that was a huge sum of money, and Lorena had already bought her so much. She placed the envelope in the compote to show David.

Back in the bedroom, now painted a light blue, she noticed another new item: a large mirror in an ornate frame. She took off her fancy hat and peered at herself. Her hair was flat on one side, looking lopsided, so she pulled out the pins and let it fall down her back. Glancing into the back bedroom, she saw her trunk and went to find her brush. She was struggling with the stubborn latch when she heard David's step behind her. "Can you unfasten this? I can't seem to get it open."

She felt his hands in her hair and straightened. "It'll wait. Take your dress off, Garnet. I don't want to ruin it."

"It's not even dark."

"I'm not waiting for dark." Eyes white hot, he threw his jacket on the bed and started unbuttoning his shirt. Her hands went to her neck where she unbuttoned the first of two dozen pearl buttons running down her dress. Her fingers were clumsy, and she broke off from his staring eyes to look down. How carefully she had sewn them on, she thought; she mustn't damage them. By the time she finished the long row and glanced up, David was naked, and the sight of him made her catch her breath. She'd never seen a grown man completely undressed and certainly never one in such a state. She shrugged out of her dress, being careful with it. "Hurry," he said.

He looked like he was in pain. Unfastening her petticoat, she let it drop in a puddle on the floor. She reached over to pick it up, but he didn't give her a chance. Grabbing her arm, he pulled her to him and kissed her, squeezing his mouth against hers and forcing it wide open with his tongue. He eased her onto the bed, and then he lay on her, thrusting his hips. She hardly knew what was happening and had no time to feel anything but weight and pressure. With one hand he fumbled with the top of her camisole and pulled one of her breasts free. Only then did he break away from her mouth to attack her breast with teeth and tongue and lips. She felt like whimpering. He seemed angry, his hands jerking at the waistband of her knickers and pulling at them until he yanked them down her hips. She felt him, hard and hot against her belly and couldn't imagine accepting that into her body. Sliding his hands under her rear end, he pushed and she realized she could. Once, twice, three times he heaved against her, tearing her, hurting her, and it was done. Breathing like a winded horse, he collapsed, and she put a trembling hand on his back, glazed with sweat. She moved a bit, and he popped out with a warm wetness that dribbled onto the bed. When she moved again, he seemed to come to his senses.

He lay with his arm over his face. "Oh Lord, Garnet, I'm sorry. That's not the way it ought to be, and I know I hurt you. I couldn't help myself."

She sat up. It had hurt, and she was still stinging. She looked down at her one exposed breast, red and chafed, and tucked it back into the camisole. "It's all right," she whispered. What was she supposed to do now? She'd imagined wearing her fancy, embroidered nightgown that Mama and she had stitched on for hours, climbing into bed in the dark, doing whatever this act was, and then falling into sweet dreams together. It couldn't be more than eight o'clock. Should she dress again?

David didn't look so threatening now. Curious, she noticed his powerful thighs, covered with light brown hair. They were strong, she thought, and had almost crushed her but his manly parts lay quiet now, against a nest of light brown hair. She rose from the bed, not quite sure what to do next, and he looked up, David again, instead of some frightening stranger. "Let me open that trunk for you," he said.

She felt absurd walking around with nothing on below the waist, but David had nothing on at all. He bent over to unlatch the trunk. "I'm sorry," he repeated "I've wanted you for so long."

Later, she sat on the front porch brushing her hair. He rocked gently in the other chair, and she remembered Lorena's words. Maybe it was this way for many new couples, she thought. Before it was completely dark, they walked, hand in hand, over to where she hoped to dig a garden. She said that she knew it was late in the summer, but she could still plant a few things, and he agreed to till a small plot for her. Fireflies flitted in the distance. She told him about the gift from Lorena, and he expressed surprise and gratitude, his eyes warm and affectionate.

But after a while there was nothing to do but go to bed. She took her time washing her face and finding the special nightgown but could only delay it so long. She comforted herself with the notion that he was satisfied now, that the fierce coupling wouldn't be repeated. When she asked if he liked her nightgown, that tormented expression returned to his face. "It's pretty, but you might as well take it off."

She was wrong; three more times in the night he took her until her thighs trembled and bruised. Each time he was tender and apologetic after he finished, and she told him all was well.

Garnet had no one to compare David to. He wasn't anything like Grandpa or Papa or her brothers, and Mama'd never said much about the nature of men. He confounded her to the point where she almost thought she was married to two different men. Most of the time he was still her dear David, sweating as he tilled her garden and greeting her when he came home from work. Every evening he complimented her cooking, and he even pretended to admire the curtains she stitched. Most of the time she liked being married and reveled in her independence from Mama.

She started working for Mrs. Lawrence on Thursdays and Fridays since David often worked only a half-day on Saturdays. One or two Saturdays they traveled to Ashton where they spent a little of Lorena's money, laughing like children at the fun of choosing some trinkets. They saved money for the winter when there would be fewer jobs for David, and she went to her mother's to help with the canning, bringing home some of the harvest for her own pantry. She felt they were making a good marriage.

Except for one part. She'd come to dread the nights or evenings or Saturday and Sunday afternoons when David wanted her, and it seemed like David always wanted her. She couldn't bring herself to discuss this with her mother or Lorena, and, besides, she had the impression that they *liked* that part of marriage. Garnet wondered if his demands were excessive, but when she built up enough nerve to voice this to David, he told her she should be glad he loved her so much. She couldn't help but question how much love had to do with it. She loved *him,* she assured herself, putting love into each shirt she ironed and pie she baked. She loved making him laugh, and she had loved it, once, when he'd held her or kissed her, but those tender kisses were rare, replaced with heated ones which resulted in another assault in the bedroom. He wasn't choosy, though, and sometimes took her in the workshop or the front room or on the grass behind the house. He joked that she ought to quit wearing knickers so she'd be more accessible, but she didn't think this was one bit funny.

One time, a few weeks after they married, he finished with her and sighed, saying he understood that virgins were shy and uncomfortable at first, but she should be over that by now. "Maybe if you took a little more time with me," she'd whispered, barely able to say it.

"Sure," he'd said, bobbing his head and grinning.

From then on the pattern rarely differed: he'd kiss her twice, once on the mouth and once on the neck, and then he'd rub at her right breast and attack her left with his mouth. This lasted about a minute; eventually she counted seconds, and then he would moisten his finger with spit and jam it into her, groan that he couldn't wait and enter her, lasting four or five strokes. She counted those too. He complained that her suggestion hadn't improved things at all.

One Saturday in late September David came home with a tall, dark bottle. She twisted around from the stove to give it a suspicious glance. "It's wine," he explained. "Not real liquor. Hayse said he didn't want it. I thought it might relax you so you would, you know, enjoy things a little more."

"I don't know that I want to be drinking even if it is just wine."

"Why even Jesus drank wine, Garnet. You might like it."

As the autumn evening closed in, he poured the blood red liquid into two cups and settled in the armchair. He urged her to try it, and she took a cautious sip. It was sour and fruity at the same time, but she didn't mind it too much. David drank his down and poured more, coaxing her to drink up. They talked about what they'd done that day, and, after several swallows, she did feel sort of queer and light and prone to giggle. He smiled at her, that heart-breaking smile of his, and she perched on the arm of his chair. He put his arm around her, and she liked this, and even when he started unbuttoning her dress she felt good, her nipples tingling when he brushed them.

"Come on, Garnet. Let's go to bed." His face had that hungry look.

"No." She fluttered her eyelashes. "I want to sit a while longer."

He closed his eyes in exasperation but gave in. Kissing his neck, she felt a warm lassitude that seemed to promise some kind of bliss. But David wouldn't be put off any longer and rose from the chair, nearly toppling her onto the floor and yanking her into the front bedroom. She'd been tipsy enough to giggle at this but quit laughing when he ripped her dress.

In October, shortly after she discovered she was pregnant and just before her birthday, he gave her a small gold watch on a chain to wear around her neck. He joked that he was tired of her always asking him what time it was. Happy about the coming baby and the gift, she resolved to do better; she'd fix whatever was wrong with her. But no matter what she tried, he didn't give her the opportunity for pleasure. Through the winter, when there were fewer jobs, David was home more and grew grumpy and restless. His father had used this time to do his fine carving and toy-making, but David had little patience with that kind of work. She cleaned and cooked around him and tried to be tolerant when he used her body as entertainment. Sometimes she wondered if the constant lovemaking was his way of marking territory like an animal. He started grumbling about her working for Mrs. Lawrence.

She glared at him. "Are you or the house suffering?"

"No, but I wonder if there are fellows coming in the store that you like talking to."

Incredulous, she pointed at her bulging belly. "I reckon anybody who comes in the store would know I have my own man."

"And don't you forget it," he growled.

As her body swelled, she expected him to find her less attractive. He seemed thrilled about the baby and was always asking if she felt healthy, but he continued to want her all the time. When she became too ungainly to accommodate him, he relented, but then he became edgier than ever, sighing mightily when they lay apart and sometimes insisting she use her hands or mouth on him. There must be, she thought for the hundredth time, something very wrong with her.

Her pregnancy was easy enough, and she was rarely uncomfortable until the last few weeks when her back hurt and it seemed like she needed to run to the outhouse every few minutes. She worried that when her time came there would be no way to fetch help, but Lorena made Lowell check on her every day after school.

Fortunately, her labor began in the afternoon. Since dinner she'd cramped low in her belly and shortly before Lowell arrived, she felt an unmistakable contraction. With big eyes, the boy flew down the hill in a steady rain to find Luther who fetched the midwife. David was working half-way to Ashton and arrived home to find his mother-in-law and the midwife in his house. They told Garnet later that he turned pale at her stifled cries and escaped to his workshop. He stayed there throughout the wet May evening until Mama told him he had a son.

They named him Ruben, and everyone came to see him, all of Garnet's family and what seemed like most of Bethel and Deer Creek as well. People argued over who he took after, and Mama made quite a show of staying for three days. David kept away as much as he could as long as she was there.

On Sunday, Luther came to take Mama home, and the three Fosters had the house to themselves. Garnet tucked little Ruben in the pretty cherrywood cradle his daddy had built for him and sat with them on the front porch. David mimicked the baby's twitches and frowns, making Garnet smile at the two of them. It was a soft, cool day, and the sky blurred with clouds. She exhaled as she wriggled her uncomfortable lower body against the rocking chair.

David chuckled. "You used to sigh like that every time we'd leave your mother."

She returned his smile. "Well, she's the one who left this time. I think it has more to do with her than the house."

"Are you cold?"

She shook her head. "I'm just glad to be outside."

He rose anyway and brought her shawl. "We need to write my pa and tell him he has a grandson."

By this David meant that she needed to write. He could read and write, but he left most of it to Garnet. "I'll do that in the morning when I write Franklin."

"We haven't heard from Pa since Christmas. He's not much better at writing letters than I am."

"Do you suppose he's married the woman in Covington?"

"He can't. He's still legally married to my mother, and we don't know if she's dead or alive."

"Can't he divorce her? I've heard of people doing that."

"He could if he wanted to marry again. I don't figure he has any interest in it."

She'd never asked him anything more about his mother, but he seemed soft now, ready to talk. "How old were you when she left?"

"Oh, about six or seven, in school anyway. When I come home that day, she was gone. We never heard from her again."

"So what did you do?"

"I went to my Aunt Martha's; she's my pa's sister and a finer woman you'll never meet and stayed with her until I was twelve. Then Pa came, said I'd had enough school, and it was time for me to help him."

"That's sad." Ever since Ruben's birth she'd cried easily, and the idea of David as a forsaken child made tears hover behind her eyes.

"Oh, it wasn't so bad. I had cousins to tussle with and some schooling, and Aunt Martha was as good a mother to me as she was to her own children. I reckon we ought to write her too."

"Sure, I'll write her."

A misty rain started, but it was too light to invade the porch. They had these sorts of conversations too seldom, and she was enjoying his company. Eyes lit with pride, David declared for about the seventeenth time, "Ruben's a fine baby, ain't he?"

"He is. Everybody says he looks healthy and stout, and," she blushed a little, "I'm able to feed him just fine."

David gazed out into the hazy distance again. His words came slowly. "I know things ain't been perfect between us, Garnet. Oh, you keep house just fine, and I don't know of nobody who cooks any better. You just don't seem to be the kind of woman who likes the bed part of marriage, and I guess there are some women like that."

Tears threatened again. "I'm sorry," she whispered.

He lifted his shoulders like he did when he was uncomfortable. "I'd be lying if I said I wasn't disappointed since you let on like you was going to enjoy that kind of thing before we was married." A touch of bitterness soured his voice but left as quickly as it came. "So I reckon I'll just have to accept things the way they are. We're making a home and have a son now, and that's what a marriage is about, at least partially."

She nodded, not trusting her voice. She felt every bit as shamed as when Papa used to scold her.

"I ain't saying I won't lay with you no more; a man has his needs and it's your duty to take care of them, but I'll quit hoping you'll ever welcome me." He kept his eyes, gray as the rain, on the horizon.

"I've never refused you." Her voice vibrated with tears.

"Damn it, don't cry." He stood. "No, you've never refused me, but you always look like a little cornered animal." He turned to face her, his mouth thin. "Oh, you ain't got nothing to be afraid of for a few weeks, that's for sure. That midwife about scared me to death saying I'd nigh on to kill you if I touched you for the next six weeks. "

Tears rolled down her cheeks, and it was all she could do not to sob. He shut his eyes for a long moment. "I'm just sick to death of feeling like I have to apologize every time I love on my wife."

She raised eyelashes heavy with tears. "I'll try, David. I really will."

"It ain't like it's something you can try at."

As the weeks passed she recovered from his words, much as she regained her strength after childbirth. Since she'd been pregnant at planting time, Lowell and David had sown a huge garden that she watched every day. Ruben grew as fast as the beans and tomatoes, and David had plenty of work. Things were going passably well. When the time came, she tried to keep her face serene and pleasant when David wanted her, even though she sometimes got bruises despite her efforts. He was often surly about her unresponsiveness, and the more frustrated he became, the rougher his lovemaking. She didn't know what to do. Since touching him, even in a friendly way, seemed to inflame him, she tended to avoid any contact with him, even though she ached to touch him. She slept on the very edge of the bed so there was less of a chance that he'd wake and want her in the night. He insisted that she keep Ruben's cradle in the back bedroom, so when she heard the baby and rose to feed him in the night, she often rested on the narrow bed in the smaller room and sometimes fell asleep there with the baby at her breast. David muttered that she was finding excuses to leave his bed.

She helped Mrs. Lawrence at least one day a week, laying Ruben in a large basket behind the counter. David still complained about her working at the store, but she begged patience from him, explaining that when Ruben started crawling she'd have to quit anyway. Occasionally she visited Lorena or her mother, but David never accompanied her. He lingered more and more in his workshop and sometimes went to the Simpson's to see Hayse. She wondered if he was visiting Flora as much as her brother but wouldn't let her mind travel down that road.

One steamy evening in August he told her that Albert Simpson had died the night before. "I reckon I should go up and pay my respects to their father," he said as he washed his face.

"Of course you must." She'd baked that day and wrapped up a loaf of bread.

"Here, take these too," she said, handing him a pint jar of pickles.

David ran a finger across her hair. "That's mighty thoughty of you, Garnet."

"It's just what people do."

After he left, she shook her head. It seemed like she'd traded Mama's unpredictability for David's. She could never tell which David she was going to get. Singing to Ruben, she cleared up the supper dishes and took him out to lie on a quilt in the yard, where at least there was a hot breeze, while she swept the front porch and picked black-eyed susans she'd started by the house. She loved the long summer evenings when it was light until bedtime. Ruben cried, and she put him to her breast and then to bed. It was nearly dark, and she was surprised that David hadn't returned.

Hours later, she was still sitting on the dark porch waiting for him. An owl hooted from the woods across the road, and crickets sang along with the creaking of her chair. After midnight she heard the crunch of David's step and saw his ghostly white shirt cross the yard. He was walking strangely, loose-jointed and slow. She called, "Are you all right?"

His grin flashed white in the dark as he stumbled onto the porch. "My little wife's waiting for me." His voice sounded odd.

She stood to help him, convinced he was coming down with something when she smelled the liquor on him. "Why, you've been drinking!"

"Just a little," he said, giving her a stupid grin. "Hayse had a jug and me and the boys helped him drink it."

"Seems like an odd thing to do when people are grieving," she murmured, but he paid no attention.

He clutched at her breast. "Pretty Garnet; pretty, pretty Garnet."

She could hardly stand the smell of him, but he seemed more foolish than frightening. He nuzzled her neck and started trying to unbutton her dress. Taking hold of his arm, she maneuvered him into the house before he embarrassed both of them.

"Was Flora drinking with you boys too?" she asked. His silly smile never wavered. She got him seated on the side of the bed, and he trapped her between his legs.

"Flora." Although he was running his hands up and down her body, he wasn't thinking about Garnet. "Pretty Flora. Warm, pretty Flora. Not cold like Garnet."

At that Garnet did turn cold despite the humid closeness of the house. She unbuttoned his shirt, and he leered at her. "Hmm, maybe Garnet's jealous of Flora. Maybe that's what'll make you hot."

He stood and swayed, clutching at her as he tried to get his pants off. Thinking he'd sleep immediately, she pulled back the coverlet so he could fall into bed, but he watched as she undressed, that absurd, drunken grin pasted to his face the whole time. Before she could crawl into bed, he scrunched up her nightgown in his fist. "Off," he demanded. She obeyed, appalled at the idea of him wanting her like this. Then he rolled heavily onto her and started claiming her as he always did, grabbing and groping, but this time he couldn't manage it.

Frantic, he jerked his hips against her and bit her shoulder. Endure, she told herself. He assaulted her breasts until milk leaked, pressing and biting and clawing until she wondered if the dribbles were milk or blood. She whimpered, but he paid her no mind, growing more frenzied and angry as he rammed against her. But his efforts were futile. He bellowed, "Move, bitch, move!"

Terrified, she moved, clasping his sweaty body in an imitation of an embrace. He attacked until her hipbones and thigh muscles screamed, and dozens of scrapes and bites stung from their sweat. He rose above her, angry and massive, and oily sweat from his face dripped upon her lips. Holding himself up with one arm, he punched her face with the other. If he'd been sober, the blow might've knocked out every tooth on that side of her head, but he hit her high on the cheekbone and into her eyebrow, making the world explode into red and white stars. "Look what you've done to me!"

And then he collapsed, rolling onto his side. Pulling on her dress, she listened for Ruben, but all she heard was her own ragged breathing. Clumsy as David, she staggered to the kitchen where she took a tea towel, dipped it in water, and patted her face to wipe off his spit and sweat. She made a pot of tea, and then, carrying the pot, cup, and towel to the porch, she sat until she heard Ruben, then returned to watch the dusky night until a pink stripe of light touched the horizon.

She glanced into the bedroom and disgust rolled over her in waves, like nausea. She had a sudden urge to hurt him while he slept, but she walked to the kitchen instead. Picking up the small mirror David used when he shaved, she looked at herself. Her left eye was swollen shut, and she nearly cried at the hideous swelling and discoloration. Pretty Garnet, she thought. Raising her dress, she looked at the rest of the damage. Blue fingerprints and livid bite marks littered her shoulders and breasts. One nipple was crusted with blood, and she reached for the wet towel. Ruben would need to eat soon, and he mustn't suffer from this.

She'd heard Grandpa say that a man felt hell running through his veins the day after a drunk, and she hoped it was true. In a flat voice she told David to wake up. He groaned but didn't move. She dreaded touching him but wanted him out of the house. After a few more unsuccessful attempts, Garnet pinched his foot until he jerked awake.

In the kitchen she poured tea and sliced bread. She heard him moving in the bedroom and steeled herself as she heard him approach. Standing at the stove with her back to him, she heard him sit heavily at the table. Side meat sizzled in the skillet. She turned, wanting to see his reaction to her face. At first he grasped his cup of tea like it would save him and drank. It had to be scalding his mouth, she thought, pleased at this. Then he saw her. His tanned face turned an odd yellowish color, and he opened his mouth as if to say something. Instead, he jumped out of the chair, hurrying toward the back step where she heard him retching and heaving.

Good, she thought. She lifted the fatty pork, letting the pungent grease drip back into the pan. He probably wouldn't eat any of it, she thought, but she set it on the table to torment him as much as anything. Keeping her back to him, she heard him return and pour more tea, rattling the spout against his cup. If he was that shaky, it might be right interesting to watch him shave.

Garnet heard Ruben making ironically cheerful morning noises. She changed him and took him to the front room to nurse, thankful she hadn't lost her milk. Opening her bodice wide to reveal her ravaged chest, she called David. Looking dreadful, he stood in the doorway, pale and puffy-eyed.

"You're still painting at the school, aren't you?"

He nodded once.

"I guess you'd better stop at the store and tell Mrs. Lawrence I won't be coming in today unless you want her and everybody else to see me like this." She smoothed Ruben's golden hair. "Just tell her whatever lie you want."

When she raised her head, David was gone.

Over the next few days she alternated between nursing her anger and praying no one would see her face. Sometimes she cried but never when David was home. And sometimes her anger melted into a puddle of remorse. She was a bad wife; she'd caused the problem and deserved to be hit. He never apologized, wouldn't even look at her, and she wished she knew whether this was from guilt or whether she was repulsive to him. She felt ugly, inside and out.

They talked when they had to, skirting around each other and giving Ruben all their conversation. In the evenings David carried the child out to pet Maggie or walk around the yard. Holding the baby against his shoulder he nuzzled Ruben's downy hair and whispered to him. She slept with him, awash with fear and guilt, but he never touched her.

On Saturday she wondered if he'd come home as usual by mid-afternoon or go up to the Simpson's. His comment about Flora haunted her. Maybe he should've married those hot, fringed eyes. Garnet spent most the day canning in the suffocating kitchen, and the tedious work fertilized her worst thoughts. Hearing a horse, she glanced down at her watch. It was early for David. She heard a quick tap at the back door, and Luther walked in. So much for nobody seeing her, she despaired, and turned her back to give herself a minute.

"Hello. Hope I didn't scare you," he said.

There was no way she could hide it, and he'd never believe some tale about falling. She turned. "No, you didn't scare me."

He stood dead still and stared at her, his eyes narrowing into an anger she'd never seen in Luther Colson. She'd never seen him with a full beard, either, black and gray mixed.

Her voice jittered. "Why, you have a beard now, Luther."

His gaze didn't waver. "Your mama's idea. Supposed to make me look distinguished, she said. Bunch of foolishness."

"Well." Her laugh was shrill. "If that's the only thing Mama's scheming right now, we're all lucky."

She turned back to the sink and poured boiling water over canning jars. "Talk to Ruben while I finish up. I won't be a minute."

Ruben looked up from the quilt on the floor and lifted his head. This was his latest trick, combined with a gummy smile. Luther lifted the boy.

"I brought some sweet corn. Ain't none of us seen you for a spell."

"Oh, that's wonderful! I do love corn." She wiped her hands on her apron. "We can sit in the front room where it's cooler. Do you want a drink? It's dreadfully hot out there."

He didn't move. Ruben was digging his fingers into the intriguing facial hair, and Luther gently pulled the little hand away. "Pack your things, Garnet. I'll take you home."

Her mouth flew open. "Oh, no, I could never go home. Mama would say she knew all along that I made a bad marriage. I can't do that."

"Well then, I'll take you to Lorena. She won't fuss."

"I can't do that either. I can't just leave."

"I don't know why not. A man who beats his wife is a sorry excuse of a husband."

"It was the whiskey. He never hit me before." She hadn't meant to mention it.

"Oh, so he's drinking now, turning into his Pa."

"No, no, I don't think so. He went up to see Hayse, and they were drinking. It's only the one time." She shook her head again. Sweat was running down between her breasts.

"Hayse?"

Garnet had forgotten that Luther was his uncle. She became even more agitated. "Oh, please don't say anything to Hayse or anybody. It won't happen again, I'm sure. Just promise me you won't say anything!"

He lowered Ruben to the quilt. "I won't say nothing, but I bet there's marks I ain't seeing and things you ain't telling. I promise, but you promise me this, girl: if you have any more trouble with him, if he even acts like he's going to hit you again, you tell me. Once they start up with the drinking, they ain't likely to stop."

She nodded. The idea of facing her mother sent pains to her gut. "I promise."

Chapter Fourteen

There were times when Garnet almost wished Luther would break his vow so she'd have someone to talk to, preferably Lorena. As it was, she had no one to confide in except Jesus. And, although Garnet talked to him all the time, he wasn't much of a conversationalist, leastwise in any language she understood. But the bruises faded and, along with them, some of the hurt and anger. Garnet resolved once again to be the very best wife she could possibly be. She'd always been successful at achieving whatever goal she set for herself. How much different could marriage be from long division or buttonholes? Never again would he have cause to complain about her or, even worse, consider Flora Simpson an alternative.

Once David didn't have to see the evidence of his violence, he actually looked at her again and they shared smiles over Ruben's antics or funny stories he brought home from work. But he still avoided touching her. As much as she disliked his lovemaking, this wouldn't do. For weeks he slept with his back to her, reminding her of some great, rocky boulder even though she suspected the barricade bothered him more than her. One night she rubbed his shoulder, not sure whether he'd respond. Then she pressed against his back and stretched to kiss the soft skin just below his curling hair. With a low moan, he turned to her, and they were back in business. It was no better than it'd ever been, but it was tolerable, and if acting a role saved her marriage, it was a small price.

October brought changeable weather, and David fretted about his work. Millie's parents had hired him to build a room onto their house, but on the day David was scheduled to start, rain poured in gray torrents from the sky.

"Well, that kills it," he said. "I can't work in this."

Ruben had been whining the last day or two. Mrs. Lawrence diagnosed it as teething, and he did seem to calm down when Garnet rubbed her finger against his lower gum. She raised the baby against her shoulder and rocked him. "It'll probably be fair tomorrow."

David peered out at the soggy yard. "We've had so much rain, I'll have mud for days." He turned and watched Ruben rub his face against Garnet's dress. "Are you sure he's just teething?"

He reached for the child and Garnet gave him up gladly. "That's what Mrs. Lawrence thinks."

David pressed the baby's little cheek to his own. "He don't seem feverish, but look how red his cheek is. He's got your skin, so fair and fine it shows everything."

Garnet didn't know whether this was a compliment to her complexion or a vague reference back to what she thought of as The Horrible Night. Freed of the baby she started taking everything out of old Walter's kitchen cabinet. "I thought I'd give this a good cleaning since I can't do anything outside today."

David nodded, uninterested. "I'm worried about how much work I'll have now that we're getting on toward winter."

"Oh, I expect there'll be a few more jobs. We'll be fine. We've saved, and I've done all this canning."

He smiled faintly at that. When the pantry overflowed with jars, he'd built shelves in the workshop to hold more. "No, I don't reckon we'll starve, but I get restless when I don't have work."

Ruben fell asleep against David's shoulder. "Should I put him to bed?"

"Just a minute." She tiptoed into the back bedroom to plump up a makeshift pallet on the floor.

David eased the baby down and said, "That's something I could do today."

"What?"

"I could work on that new bed for the baby."

"That's true. He's too big for his cradle."

David grinned, his old crinkling smile. "Growing like a weed, ain't he?"

She nodded, delighted to see a real smile. "Oh, and David, I was wondering if we might do some visiting on Sunday. We haven't gone anywhere in ages, and I'd like to see Lorena and my family."

"Sure."

"And it's my birthday. I thought visiting might be my treat." She gave him her best smile, warming her eyes and encouraging him to return it.

He did, at least a little, and gave her shoulder a squeeze on his way to the workshop. She tried not to flinch.

While they were eating their evening meal, the rain slowed to a drizzle, and he said he thought he might go up and see Hayse. They'd enjoyed the day, and she mustn't dwell on the past or act suspicious and tense. After all, he'd only drunk with Hayse that one time. She replied that sure, he should go.

But the muscles in her neck tightened when he left. Ruben was cranky. Usually he enjoyed being bathed, but tonight he fussed and twisted at the washcloth. He acted hungry but didn't want to nurse, and she was just about to give up and put him to bed to cry himself to sleep when David walked through the back door.

"Terrible mud, but the rain's stopped," he said. She watched him carefully, but he seemed to be all right. "What's wrong with this little squirt?" He hoisted the fussy baby onto his shoulder. "Can't get comfortable, little man?"

"He won't nurse, he won't settle down. I don't know what to do with him," she complained. David walked the baby, humming softly to him, and Garnet relaxed. All was well. Things were going to be fine.

In the night the rain stopped, giving way to clear, warm autumn. David worked on the room addition, putting in two more days before another patch of bad weather arrived. On Saturday he stared at the sodden landscape and said he was glad he had a roof over what he'd completed. "And," he said, "I'm glad I haven't cut into their house yet. I've got tarps to cover the doorway, but it still would be awfully damp. Seems like the temperature's dropping too."

Garnet agreed, feeling a chill in the house. David said he was nearly done with Ruben's bed and the rain would give him an opportunity to finish. Through the morning she swept and dusted, interrupted by Ruben's fussing, but she saw the white bud of his tooth and thought it might not be long before it erupted, giving the child some peace. She didn't have to call David for dinner. He clomped into the house saying he could smell the food all the way into the yard, and it was starving him to death.

She smiled. "Mrs. Lawrence gave me a little piece of fresh pork yesterday. I thought with you being home today, I'd fix it for the noon meal."

Fresh meat was a treat, available only when someone nearby butchered, but Mrs. Lawrence had given it to Garnet as a birthday present. She told David this, leaving out Mrs. Lawrence's additional comment that Garnet looked peaked and needed some meat. They savored it, and David reared back in his chair. "I'm full as a tick."

She smiled at him. "And there's some left to piece on at supper time."

He groaned. "Don't even talk about eating again." Lowering his chair, he said, "Do you have a minute? I want you to come see the baby's bed."

Throwing her shawl over Ruben to shield him from the rain, she slogged through the marshy grass to the workshop.

"I made it fairly tall so you wouldn't have to lean over too far as he gets heavier," David explained. "And I made sure the slats were close together so he couldn't get his head stuck."

"Oh, it's beautiful," she exclaimed, reaching out her hand to the gleaming wood.

"Don't touch! I just put a coat of shellac on it. It'll need another, but with this rain, it won't dry any time soon."

"You say you're not much of a hand at furniture making, but I don't believe it. This is as nice as anything I've seen."

He smiled and grabbed her fingers, pressing them to his lips for an instant. "Well, if it's turning cold, I don't want this boy sleeping on the floor."

They returned to the house. Ruben was fussy and before long he escalated to full-throated crying. Garnet reached for a small blue bottle Mrs. Lawrence had given her. She tipped it to get a drop on her finger and rubbed it against his fiery gum. David looked anxious. "Are you sure he's all right?"

"I remember Henry and Violet acting like this. They hurt so they won't nurse, and then they get hungry. This medicine will numb his gum for a little bit so he can eat. Come on, little fellow, get comfortable now." She opened her dress and he set to his job, whimpering as he nursed.

David watched her. "I thought they'd turn color, get darker with a baby."

At first she didn't know what he meant but then realized he was staring at her breasts. She blushed.

"Yours are just as pink and fair as when we got married."

Embarrassed, she shrugged. He prowled the front room, looking out both windows. "I reckon I'll go up the road to see Hayse. He's probably stuck in the house on account of this rain too."

She nodded but felt her spine tightening. "You know he's welcome to visit here too. You don't always have to go to him."

"Well, there's always lots of people up there, sitting around and talking; it's just more sociable than it is here."

She didn't reply, and the silence became awkward. "Anyways, I guess I'll be going." He seemed to be waiting for permission.

"Go on. If I can get this boy fed and happy, he might be willing to sleep a while, and I'll get my bath this afternoon instead of this evening. I'm looking forward to us going visiting tomorrow."

The temperature really was dropping. She lit the coal stove in the front room, and, sitting near the heat, brushed her damp hair and let it lay on her shoulders to dry. David liked it that way. Tomorrow she'd wear her pretty skirt and blouse to church, but there was no sense in asking David to accompany her; he hadn't gone since they married. She wondered if he'd give her a present. Probably not, although she'd given him a leather wallet for his birthday back in the winter. She didn't care; it would be treat enough for him to take her visiting.

The rain and blustery winds made evening come early. Ruben woke up in a better frame of mind, and, when she inspected his drooling little mouth, she saw that the tooth had worked its way through his gum.

The hours passed, and she couldn't help but worry. Even if he wasn't drinking, he might be messing around with Flora. It hadn't taken much prodding for Mattie Lawrence to reveal Flora's scandalous reputation. A girl like that wouldn't care if a man was married. Although suppertime came and went, Garnet wasn't hungry. They'd eaten such a large meal at dinner maybe David wasn't either, and if he didn't feel hungry perhaps he'd lost track of time.

By ten o'clock she'd fretted herself to death. For company, she kept Ruben up far past his bedtime but finally put the little fellow down, covering him with an extra blanket. She stared out the windows but could see nothing but black, wet night. The glass felt cold. David would catch his death in this weather, she thought. What if he walked home drunk, slipped in the mud, and lay there all night? Before long she was envisioning pneumonia and widowhood and had about driven herself crazy when there was a sharp rap at the door. Not waiting for her to open it, Hayse Simpson walked in, dripping rain.

"I seen the light and thought you might be waiting up for that husband of yours," he said. He dark eyes sized her up, pausing at her breasts and hips.

She could smell cold air and rain on him, and she caught a whiff of liquor, although he seemed sober. "What's wrong?"

He shut the door and shrugged. Cocky, Mrs. Lawrence would call him. "Oh, I don't know as anything's wrong. It's just that David's laying dead drunk up at my place, and I didn't want you worrying. Ain't no way he'll be coming home tonight."

Reaching up lazily, he removed his hat and shook it, scattering droplets on the floor. "I never knowed a man with such a thirst, except maybe his pa. 'Bout drank everything in the house, and that stuff's not cheap."

Suddenly furious, she whirled toward the kitchen, her hair flying out behind her and returned to thrust some coins at him.

"Oh, now, I wasn't asking for money. David'll pay me." Wrapping his cold hand around hers, he pushed it away, letting his fingers linger over hers. She dropped the coins into the armchair.

"It's illegal in this county," she spat. "It's a wonder you all don't get in trouble with the law."

Hayse chuckled. "They ain't no danger of that. The judge hisself joins us now and again." He slitted his eyes. "Of course, if David had a chance of having some fun at home, maybe he wouldn't be so fond of my whiskey."

She was too angry to speak. He stepped toward her, a wicked light in his eyes, and grasped a handful of her hair. "I'd always been told that red-headed gals liked it. They's supposed to be hot-blooded."

He tugged at her hair until she was forced to step closer to him. The smell of whiskey was stronger there, and he was tall enough she had to crane her neck to see his face.

"Let go of me."

He didn't. Taking his time, he ran his other hand through her hair, weighing it, testing it. "Says it's like bedding a corpse."

She couldn't look at him anymore. Lowering her eyes, she saw drops of rain dripping from his coat like blood oozing from a wound. Her guts were clenched together so tight she thought she might be sick any minute. "Let go of my hair," she said through gritted teeth.

He ignored her. "We're all sorry for him. Poor boy thought he was marrying him a little peach, and it ended up she really was the high and mighty schoolteacher's daughter. Too good for the likes of David and the rest of us."

"Stop it."

"Don't like hearing the truth? Yeah, we all sympathize with David."

He still had his fingers trapped in her hair.

"Flora feels sorry for him too. A natural woman has feelings," he drawled. His hand cupped her head. She tried to jerk away, but he tightened his grip.

"I just thought the schoolteacher's daughter might could use a few lessons about loving. You're a ripe little thing. Maybe you just need the right teacher." He stepped closer and she could hear his breathing change. His mouth came closer to hers, but she couldn't duck. "I might be a fair teacher myself about certain subjects."

Using both hands, she pushed and hit him, kicking at his shins. He dodged most of it. "Get away! What would David think about you going after his wife?"

Unperturbed, he released her hair and continued to smile as if her blows had been nothing but air. "I reckon he might be grateful if I could teach you a few tricks he'd enjoy. That's just being a good friend. Then maybe he wouldn't be drowning himself in whiskey. That's not good for a man. But then sticking it in a block of ice every night's not good for him either."

Her chest was heaving. Raising a trembling finger, she pointed at the door.

"Well, I was just being neighborly," he drawled as he beat his hat against his leg.

"Reckon he'll come home tomorrow; he's awfully fond of that boy of his."

He left and the room spun. When she heard the muffled sound of his horse on the road, she flew to the back door and vomited over the side of the stoop with the rain pouring onto her hair and face. When she tilted her head back, the chilly needles stung her cheeks. She dragged herself back inside and locked both doors, something she'd never done before.

She blew out the lamps, afraid someone could see her despite the shades and curtains. Sitting in the old armchair, she rested her head against her hand. She couldn't fight whiskey. Garnet remembered Walter Foster's venom that day in the store. Luther had said that once it started, it would happen again.

Tiptoeing into the back bedroom, she bent over to check Ruben and then stretched out on the single bed by the window. She picked over the things Hayse had said. She was no better than a corpse, she was cold.

Garnet moaned at this and reached down to pull a quilt over her body. She was cold, shivering with it, and wondered if she was getting sick. I'm a bad wife, she thought. Nothing I've tried has been any good because if it had, my husband wouldn't be drinking himself to death and seeing another woman. Her guts griped. Breathe, she told herself and rubbed her belly to ease the cramping.

Her mind wandered into an ugly daydream of what it must be like up at the Simpson's. She'd never been there and had no idea what the house looked like, but she imagined David, Hayse, and maybe two or three faceless men sitting around a crude kitchen table, all of them drinking. What would they be drinking from? She thought of teacups or tumblers. Maybe they used no cups at all and simply passed around a rough jug. Grandpa's whiskey had come in tall glass bottles. Maybe they slurped from those, wiping the lip of it with their sleeves as they passed it on. Garnet imagined Flora standing behind them, calling for a sip every now and then and draping her body around the back of David's chair, her black curls brushing his neck. It was agony but her mind flew on, imagining David roaring drunk, pulling Flora onto his lap, calling her his pretty, pretty Flora. He'd kiss on her and all of them would laugh at the tales David told about his wife, how silly and childish and cold she was. They'd laugh at her. Flora would laugh the loudest and say she didn't know why any woman didn't want him and dig her hands into him and he would groan, that groan Garnet knew so well. And then--- she sat up, refusing to invent any farther. If she couldn't sleep, she must at least stop this craziness. She opened her eyes and concentrated on what vegetables she'd plant next year. When she completed that list, she started counting, just to see how high she could get.

***

The sunrise was beautiful with a milky blue sky hanging over the rain-soaked grass. It hadn't frosted but the air was clear and crisp, scented with smoke and wet earth. Garnet followed her usual Sunday routine, dressing in what she'd planned the day before, although she dismissed the idea of church. She drank tea and ate a few bites of breakfast, thinking if she pretended nothing was wrong, it wouldn't be. But she lost heart. David was gone, and she had no idea when he'd return.

Nor did she have any idea what she'd say to him. At first she rehearsed hot, scathing insults, and then she planned a long apology, full of remorse. This stuck in her craw, though, because no matter how bad a wife she might be, he didn't have the right to air private matters in front of other people. That's what kept her temper flaring.

When it was noon, she went to the kitchen to see about dinner, but she had no appetite and there was no one to cook for. She fed Ruben and admired his new tooth, giving him extra kisses and hugs. But by two o'clock, he was napping, and she didn't even have him to divert her. What if David never came home? She sat on the chilly front porch and rocked, half-heartedly working on a shirt she was making for Ruben. There was enough breeze to dry a few fallen leaves and send them skittering like bits of colored paper.

When she heard a horse approaching her heart started pounding. David was on foot, but maybe Hayse loaned him his. Other people used the road; it could be anyone, but she sat tight and rigid, waiting to see if the horse stopped. It did, but from the wrong direction and was accompanied by a fashionable black buggy. It took her a minute, but then she recognized that the driver was Clifford Clark. "Hello," he called, touching the brim of his impeccable hat.

She stood and returned his greeting.

"Do you remember me?" he asked, holding out his hand for her to shake. It was covered in fine, black kid and felt warm. "Clifford Clark, from the bank in Ashton. I'd heard you married the Foster lad and moved up here. How are you?"

He was dressed up, probably for church, in a slim dark suit that made him look taller and thinner than ever. Immaculately groomed, his dark hair caught dark lights from the sun, and his snowy shirt gleamed. She asked him to sit, and he did, talking and smiling all the time. She was mystified.

"I'm delighted to see you again. I suppose I've told you how much the girls and I revered your father. Oh, I call them 'the girls,' but I should say my sisters, Gert and Fanny. Have you met them? They were at your father's funeral too. Thought the world of him. Anyway, Fanny played her fiddle at your church today, and of course Gert and I always come along with her, and I hoped I would see you and Mr. Foster; Mattie Lawrence said you usually attend, but you weren't there. Mattie wondered if you were ailing. Are you well? It's chilly out here." He just talked and talked, which made it easier since she felt frozen, from her insides out. She insisted she was warm enough.

"I was trying to kill two birds with one stone, because I wanted to see your husband about some renovations we're planning at the bank. Is he at home?"

Garnet was certain that David would be interested in any job this man could offer. "No, Mr. Clark, he's visiting." Now I'm lying for him, she thought.

"Well, that's what I'm doing too, but he's out paying calls without you? That seems a shame." And he smiled yet again, showing wonderfully white teeth for a man his age. He must be at least thirty. "I left my sisters at the Bledsoes. We had a grand Sunday dinner, but when the women started in on who's sick and dying and who's marrying whom, I confess I found it deadly boring. Since I needed to talk to Mr. Foster anyway, I found an excuse to leave. Will he be returning soon?"

He had one of those faces that moved up, down, and sideways the whole time he was talking. It amused her to look at him, and for a moment she was diverted from her own troubles. "I'm not sure."

He pondered this for a moment. "I suppose he could make a trip to Ashton to see me about it some time, couldn't he? We've heard about the quality of his work, amazing in a man so young, and we're anxious to get him. We're planning to do an overhaul of the offices above the bank, putting in new conveniences. Although we've contracted with other craftsmen, we need someone to do plastering and painting and carpentry. It's a huge job, undoubtedly lasting months."

My stars, this would absolutely thrill David. "Oh, yes, Mr. Clark, I'm sure he would be interested."

"Clifford, please. You make me feel like one of the graybeards outside Trosper's. Splendid. Is he in the middle of a job now?"

"Yes, he's been delayed by all the rain, but I think he needs only another week or two to finish," she replied, trying to sound business-like.

"Even better! It's a complicated process, and our tenants upstairs are dragging their feet, although I'm certain they'll be delighted with the end product. So, we probably wouldn't need your husband until, oh, well into November. There's a spare office with a cot, and he could live up there, free of charge. He'd need to get his meals somewhere, but that could be arranged. And boarding for his horse as well. We don't want this to cost him anything out of pocket."

"This is most generous of you, um, Clifford." It sounded dreadfully disrespectful. "I'm sure he'll come see you in the next day or two." She was terrified David would come staggering down the road any minute.

The man stood, looking down at her with a slight frown. "Would this be a terrible imposition for you, Garnet? Of course your husband could come home from time to time, but we want him to work steadily once he's started, and it may be necessary for him to work weekends. Will this inconvenience you?"

She didn't know why he'd care. "Oh, no. I'm fine here." Trying to think of something, anything to say, she blurted out, "I need to come get molasses from your sisters."

He smiled, putting on his hat. "Ah, how disloyal of you! Mattie says you work at her store, and I'm sure she has somebody's sorghum for sale."

Garnet wrinkled her nose. "She does, but it isn't as good as Miss Clark's."

"Gert will be delighted to hear that. Perhaps I can remember to bring some to the bank and your husband can get it when he sees me." He waved at his buggy. "Or maybe I'll stop by again."

"I wouldn't want to trouble you."

Pointing, he said, "My new buggy. Isn't it a beauty? And I make excuses to use it at every opportunity. Just a substitute while I wait, however."

His conversation skipped around like a rock on a pond. "Horseless carriages, Garnet. Automobiles. Although they're not common now, I'll have one someday. The new buggy is just to tide me over until progress catches up with my dreams."

She smiled uncertainly, not quite understanding what he was talking about. He was tipping his hat to her when he stopped and softened his voice. "Are you sure you're quite well? You have a pale, forlorn look about you."

She shook her head and forced a smile. "I'm well, really."

"But your husband will be along soon, right?" he asked, still holding his hat just above his head.

She nodded, embarrassed.

"Well, then," he said. "Good-bye." And with that he leaned down and planted a swift little kiss on her hand and hurried off to his buggy. Garnet's face burned. She could only imagine David's fury if he'd witnessed that. Then she wondered why she cared. This man was a friend of her father's, and David's best friend Hayse had behaved far worse.

Later in the afternoon, when she was changing Ruben's diaper, she heard David come through the front door. He stood in the doorway and reached for Ruben when she finished. She said nothing; all the speeches she'd rehearsed jumbled together in her head. David collapsed into the armchair with Ruben performing his best baby grins in what looked like an attempt to show off his new tooth. She didn't have much respect for a person who hid behind a baby but kept silent, gathered a pile of mending, and sat in the rocking chair. David looked dreadful, the stubble of his whiskers ashy against his pale face. Threading her needle, she waited him out.

David stared out the front window for a long time but then spoke, "I guess you was worrying about me, but I fell asleep up there and nobody woke me up."

She smoothed the gaping seam of one of his shirts, thinking that maybe she should send it to Flora for mending. "Asleep?"

"Yeah, I had a couple of drinks and got sleepy, and the next thing I know they're asking me if I'm going to sleep all day," he buried his face in Ruben's neck, causing joyous giggles.

"You slept all night and all day? You must've been mighty tired."

He kept playing with the baby, blowing on his tummy and bouncing him.

She tried to sound nonchalant. "Oh, I wasn't worried. Hayse came down here last night and said you were dead drunk."

"He come down to the house?"

She nodded, trying to pierce the fabric without shaking. "He had lots of things to say, your friend Hayse."

David narrowed his eyes. "What kinds of things?"

"Oh, he was talking about how you drink up all his whiskey. By the way, I hope you paid him for it; I offered, but he wouldn't take my money. Then he talked about how they all feel sorry for you because you have such a terrible wife. He said that Flora grieves for you especially." She was doing fairly well at keeping her voice low and even, but her trembling hands betrayed her. "Just how sorry does she feel for you, David?"

"You're lying!"

"No, you're lying. Ask Hayse."

David jerked his head away and stared at Ruben who smiled. Anytime anyone looked at Ruben, he smiled, but his father didn't seem to be paying much attention. "All right, I lied. I drank too much, passed out, and woke up puking my guts out, so I drank some more to settle them. Then I passed out again."

She felt icy, like she'd traveled to a cold, hard place where she was too frozen to feel the heat of anger. She thought she heard him mumble something about not thinking she'd want him to come home like that.

"So," she said, intent on her sewing, "what do you tell them about me? Have you told them about that mole on my backside or described how my nipples are still pink? Hayse seemed to know an awful lot about our private life. He hears that I'm a cold, unnatural woman. I wonder where he gets those ideas." In spite of her efforts, her voice rose with each statement, and she knew her eyes and face were blazing.

"You are a cold, unnatural woman!" Ruben jumped, startled by the noise, and David lowered his voice. "You have never once wanted me. You just suffer through it."

She couldn't make another stitch. "I don't see how you can say that. I wanted to marry you, God help me, and I never refuse you."

He squirmed, probably regretting that he had Ruben in his lap so he couldn't storm around and hit things, Garnet included.

"'I never refuse you,'" he mimicked in an ugly imitation of her voice. "No, you don't refuse me, but you don't want me neither. Damn it, a man can tell."

His face contorted into a furious mask, and she knew she was risking his fist. She lowered her voice. "All right, let's say you're right and I'm the worst wife on earth. I still can't believe you're telling people things that should be kept in this house. How would it make you feel if I told my people that you hit me?"

He shut his eyes. When he spoke again it was in a quiet, long-suffering tone. "You'll never let me forget that, will you? It's the drink. When I'm drinking I get angry and then I get saying things I shouldn't. It's just the liquor."

This was a lie too. Oh, he'd never punched her when he was sober, but there'd been some mighty rough grabbing. She folded his shirt and stood. "I don't like people knowing about us, David. It's humiliating. Our problems should be kept in this house. And if whiskey makes you act like that, you should give it up."

Suddenly he shifted Ruben to his shoulder and reached forward to grab her skirt. She flinched, sure he was going to hit her. Instead, he buried his face in the fabric and started crying, big hoarse sobs coming from his gut. "Help me, Garnet. I don't want it to be this way," he sobbed, rubbing his face against her good crepe skirt. She pulled it away. He'd never said a word about Flora.

She said, "I'll put on some water for a bath. You smell bad."

Later she made food for him and forced herself to be sympathetic in her choices. He looked a little better for his bath, and she put a bowl of potato soup in front of him and made toast. Although she knew the job offer from Clifford Clark would cheer him, she took pleasure in keeping it to herself. She sat down with her own bowl and said, "I had a visitor today."

"Oh?" His head was down, the damp curls waving into furrows.

"Clifford Clark."

This caught his attention, and she wondered if he'd react with his usual jealousy. She supposed she could use his friend's betrayal as ammunition, but more than likely even that would be turned against her. She couldn't figure out how David could think she was so cold and disdainful of anything pertaining to lovemaking and then accuse her of encouraging other men, but there was little logic in David.

"He came to see you."

He frowned. "What did you tell him?"

"That you were visiting. I lied. He thought it was strange that I was sitting here alone while you were visiting, but he didn't say much about it." She smiled at the memory. "He said plenty about other things, though. He's quite a talker."

She was prolonging it out of meanness. David asked what Clark wanted, and she told him, but with all sorts of interruptions to sip her soup or check on Ruben. Little by little she doled out the information, and gradually, from the news and the food, David's color came back along with his energy and optimism.

"I'll go see him in the morning," he announced. "Think of the money they'll pay, Garnet. And it's always hard to get jobs in the winter."

"What about the addition up at Millie's?"

"I'll leave real early for Ashton, and then I can get back there in the afternoon. Mr. Clark must've heard good reports of my work." He was a puppy again, squirming with pleasure.

She told him about the other details Clark had mentioned. "He said you'll be busy for weeks and may not be able to come home much."

He tried to look concerned about this. "Well, I'll hate that, but you and Ruben will get along, won't you?" She realized that he was delighted at the prospect of being away from her, and, to tell the truth, she wasn't too sorry herself.

He grabbed her hand. "This is a fresh start. This'll give us a chance to work things out. I won't be tempted to drink while I'm on a job like that, and when I come home, everything will be fine. We'll put these bad times behind us."

"Sure," she said. She removed her hand and took the dishes to the sink.

He moved toward the back door. "I'd better finish Ruben's bed this evening if I can. I may be working long and late to finish that addition, and I don't want to go off to Ashton without making sure everything's snug and safe here for the winter."

She nodded without turning around. Everything was just fine in his mind. Then she heard him ask, "What are you all dressed up for, Garnet? Didn't you change after church?"

Facing him slowly, she replied, "I didn't go to church, David, but I did think we were going visiting this afternoon. Remember? It's my birthday."

Chapter Fifteen

After David left, life was peaceful. But remembering how her mother used to mourn whenever Papa was away for even a night, Garnet concluded that David might be right: maybe she was an unnatural woman and a bad wife since she gloried in his absence.

For one thing, she enjoyed working with Mrs. Lawrence without returning home to interrogations about what men had come in the store. And she visited her family. It was fun to watch Dessie and Ruben, only about a year apart, discovering each other. When Violet begged to visit her, Garnet let her spend a Friday night. They ate popcorn, and Garnet washed Violet's hair, tying it full of ribbons.

She also went to see Lorena, and although the woman scrutinized Garnet closely, Luther had definitely kept her secret or Lorena would've been asking hard questions. Rummaging around at the farm, Garnet found enough fabric scraps to start a quilt. She'd never liked to crochet or embroider but figured quilting took perseverance more than skill if she wasn't too ambitious in her designs. So, during the long, chilly evenings, she cut and pieced. She remembered how at home she'd felt like the Grants were as crowded together as chicks in a nest and savored the solitude.

David didn't come home for two weeks but appeared the next Saturday afternoon. She hadn't known whether to expect him, so she was scurrying around the kitchen to find something to cook when he put a fat envelope on the table and announced proudly that these were his earnings so far. Cuddling Ruben, he talked about his progress and news from town. That night she opened her arms to David and tried her best to be welcoming. If he was right, that there were ways a man could tell if a woman really wanted him, he probably wasn't fooled. But he took his pleasure calmly enough, leaving the next morning after dropping her at church.

She didn't see him the next weekend, but on the following Saturday she made a cake, thinking surely he'd arrive that afternoon. It was a bright day for December but cold and windy, and she tied her shawl around her to gather the last of the turnips and watch for him. She bent over to scrabble in the cold dirt, unwilling to kneel since she wanted to keep her dress clean. It was her old dark blue one, now nearly worn out, and as she dug she considered making a new dress. She hadn't had a new one since her wedding. The wind made her eyes water, and, across the way, trees that looked as if they'd been sketched in ink swam against the hills.

The problem with a new dress would be getting the fabric. Mattie Lawrence only kept cheap flannels and calicos, and there was no easy way for Garnet to get to Ashton. David was gone, and Luther had taken the tobacco crop to Lexington. She'd left her hair down to please David, and wisps of it blew into her face, but her hands were too dirty to push them back. Even though Mama was the better seamstress, Lorena was more fun. Garnet pictured them making a dress in the sewing room, taking turns amusing Ruben.

So she was cheerfully windblown when she heard the sound of hooves on the road, and she straightened to greet David. The hooves were brisk, however, and she saw that it was Clifford Clark's jaunty buggy rather than David's wagon. She whisked the dirt from her hands while he stopped and turned to fetch something from the buggy floor.

"Hello, there!" he shouted through the gusts. "Are you about to blow away?"

He was balancing four pails, undoubtedly full of sorghum. "I'm finally getting around to delivering your molasses. Gert told me this morning that I'm ornery. As I recall, she used the word 'do-less' in reference to me, her beloved brother. Can you imagine? How are you? You're an absolute picture out here in the wind with your cheeks all pink."

She replied that she was fine and asked if he'd come in the house. Between her basket of turnips and his pails, they struggled through the door. Waving away her suggestion that they sit in the front room, he stayed in the kitchen and talked the whole time she made tea, considered, and then decided to cut him a slice of the applesauce cake she'd baked for David. There was plenty, and, after all, Clifford Clark was her husband's boss, a man to be treated with her best hospitality. Perhaps David would arrive any minute and they could have a pleasant visit. Clark smiled and said he hadn't expected such a treat. Garnet watched him as he talked. When he smiled, and he smiled nearly all the time, his cheeks fell into creases, not just single furrows like Luther's, but duplicate parentheses like ones she'd seen in algebra problems on her father's blackboard. .

"Thank you for bringing the sorghum, but it's terribly out of your way to come up here. You should've given it to David."

He ate as quickly as he talked and deposited the last bite of cake in his mouth. His strong, dark eyebrows were as mobile as the rest of his face. Raising these, he said, "That was my intention, not that

I don't find visiting you delightful. When Gert fussed at me this morning, I loaded up the pails and took off for town, hoping to find David. But the fellow who looks after his horse said he'd already left. He's not here?"

Garnet looked down at her plate. "No."
He'd been using his fork to mash cake crumbs against his plate but stopped, bewildered. "I'm certain I make better time in my buggy than he does in his cart. Surely I would've seen him along the road if his horse went lame."

She raised her head and tried to smile. "I don't know where he is."

He frowned. "We're tremendously pleased with his progress. He's right on schedule even though he's come home every weekend." It was a question.

Standing up, Garnet took their plates to the sink. Clark lowered his voice. "Garnet, how many times has he come home?"

She wouldn't lie for him. Not anymore. "Once."

He made a soft noise and poured more tea. "Sit down," he ordered, and she did, keeping her eyes down. "Look at me," he said more gently. She did, but with her chin raised. "Where's he going when he's supposed to be here?"

She didn't want to meet his kind, amber eyes. "I don't know for sure."

Clifford had been leaning toward her, his arms lying on the table like folded wings, but he straightened and when he spoke it was slower than his usual quick patter. "Look, I'm meddling, but I cannot tell you how important your father was to me. During the short time he worked with us he became my friend. The man was brilliant, could discuss science just as well as Shakespeare. I know I wearied him with long discussions, but there aren't many people around here who enjoy that kind of discourse. John understood. He grasped how the mind needs exercise."

He paused. "When your father said something, it behooved a man to listen. And one definitive thread running through his thoughts was how much he loved his children. You, especially. I cannot bear to see John Grant's daughter neglected."

If he hadn't mentioned Papa she might've been able to reply. He remained quiet too, waiting to see if she'd contradict him. She pushed her spoon around the table and unconsciously adopted his formal language. "I suppose, Mr. Clark, you could say that my husband finds our home unsatisfactory."

"Good Lord."

From the bedroom she heard Ruben, and, relieved to interrupt the awkward conversation, she excused herself to get the child, rosy from his nap. She sat with Ruben on her lap. He was too sleepy to smile but gazed intently at the strange man. "This is Ruben," she said.

She could tell he wasn't a man to warm to children just because they were children, but Clark said, "A handsome boy, a cozy home, and a lovely and intelligent wife. What more could the man want?"

"I'm proud Papa spoke so highly of me. I miss him something dreadful, and it seems like nothing has gone right since he passed away."

She knew she hadn't answered his question, but if she talked about David's drinking she might jeopardize his job, and she certainly couldn't discuss other, more private matters. Ruben was becoming more alert by the minute and started chattering nonsense and rooting around. He was probably hungry, but she couldn't feed him in front of this man.

"Is he seeing another woman?" The question was cautious.

Unwilling to answer him, she stood with the child resting on her hip and walked to the kitchen cabinet. Maybe she could hold Ruben off with some applesauce. She poured a small amount into a cup and sat again, using the tip of her spoon to feed him. "Not meaning to be rude, Mr. Clark, but I don't feel right about discussing these matters with you." She focused on Ruben's scrunched up face, contorted with the effort of trying an unfamiliar food.

As if she'd confirmed rather than avoided his suspicions, he murmured, "How could he, with an absolute dream of a woman waiting right here?"

She knew it was wrong, and if it'd been anybody but Clifford Clark who'd known her father and, by his own admission, talked too much, she would've risen on her dignity to discourage such a comment, but she drank in his words even as she pretended to ignore them. "There are problems, but we've said too much as it is."

He seemed to come to himself, giving her a rueful smile. "I invariably say too much, and I do apologize. Thank you for the delectable cake." He stood.

"What do I owe you for the sorghum?" He shook his head but she persisted. "No, I'll pay you for it. It's enough that you made the long cold drive to deliver it."

Insisting that it was a pleasure, he finally, however, relented, saying it was Gert's business, not his, and named a price. Then he frowned again, drawing his dark brows together. "Is David sending you money?"

Embarrassed, she gushed, "Oh, we're fine. He brought home all he'd made so far that weekend he was home." She tried for a merry smile. "I may try to get into town soon; with Christmas coming I need some things. I'll see him then."

As soon as she said it, she regretted it. His face lit up like a flare. "When are you planning to go to town? How will you get there? Surely you wouldn't dream of walking, would you? I'd be delighted to take you to town so you could shop and see your husband. I'm sure you need an excursion. Must be dull for you up here alone."

"Oh, no. No, thank you. Luther Colson's my step-father, you know. He'll take me some time."

They'd edged their way into the front room. Ruben was fussing, not at all satisfied by the applesauce. Clark looked tall and imposing in their little house, his head dangerously close to the ceiling. He shook it impatiently. "Colson's taken his crop to Lexington, hasn't he?"

"I can wait."

"But you shouldn't have to do so, and you need to see your husband. If he won't come to you, then you must go to him." The man had no idea how foolhardy it was to confront David.

"He'll probably come home next weekend."

"Perhaps, but that's uncertain, isn't it? Now, calm yourself; I promise not to chastise your husband for his unconscionable neglect. I have ventured into matters where I do not belong. However, I'm certainly able to be a good neighbor to my friend's daughter. Let's say Tuesday. I'll be here at nine o'clock," he announced.

"Oh, but I couldn't ask," she floundered. "I simply couldn't."

"You didn't ask."

"But your work! That would mean taking a whole day from your work."

He waved a dismissive hand. "I'm the bank manager; God knows, I hardly work on a good day. I insist and will be anticipating your charming company on Tuesday."

With this he adjusted his hat, smiled, and was out the door before she could say more. Defeated, she collapsed into the armchair and submitted to Ruben's frantic demands. Mortified by the man's generosity, she wondered what David would think about her riding in Clifford Clark's buggy and how annoyed he'd be when she confronted him. And then Clark's revelations came crashing down, and her mind turned to the fact that David wasn't in Ashton and he wasn't home. She closed her eyes and listened to Ruben's gusty sucking, deciding that she didn't care about David's reaction.

***

On Tuesday she rose early wishing for the hundredth time that she wasn't going to town. It was a cold morning, gray and sullen, and she wrapped Ruben in blankets before carrying him to the farm long before Clark was due to arrive. Lorena had agreed to keep the baby, assuring Garnet that Ruben wouldn't starve by being deprived of his mother for a few hours. But Lorena had looked at her quizzically, not understanding either the trip to town or the way she was getting there. Knowing that only a full confession would satisfy the woman, Garnet told Lorena she'd spend the night; they could sew and she'd tell her everything. The promise made Garnet as anxious as the trip did.

Looking jaunty and cheerful, Clifford arrived on time and solicitously wrapped a blanket around her before he took off at a speed that astounded Garnet. She'd never ridden in a buggy. Clifford entertained her with all sorts of conversation until she felt easy with the man. At one point she mentioned her mother, and he responded with a dramatic sigh, lifting one gloved hand to his heart.

"Ah, Louise King, my first true love!" he declared. My stars, she thought, Clark was certainly old, but he not old enough to have been one of her mother's beaus.

"Oh, I must have been all of seven or eight when she broke my heart. Back then Fanny and Gert paid calls from time to time, and they'd troop me along with them. Most times the only thing I enjoyed was the food, and even that wasn't always good, mind you, but one time we drove to Deke King's house, and there was his daughter, beautiful as a princess. She laid a soft white hand upon my cheek, calling me the sweetest little man, and I was besotted for life."

Garnet grinned. "I guess she had a way even with very young men."

"Absolutely. And when we left she reached down and kissed my cheek, lips like a cloud. I was distraught when Fanny wrote me at school that Louise King had married your father." He turned his head toward Garnet and gave her a wry smile. "I was about twelve at the time." More seriously he said, "You're very like her, you know. The coloring, the shape of your face, that lovely low voice. But your personality is more like your father's."

"How's that?" She tried to conceal how his compliments warmed her soul.

"I know you left school early, John regretted that, you know, but you have your father's intelligence. Louise was captivating, but no one ever accused her of being an intellect."

This made her uncomfortable all over again. She changed the topic. "You said you were at school. Did you go away?"

"Oh yes. I was sent to boarding school in Virginia when I was eleven and attended until I finished at eighteen. My father thought the girls were spoiling me, which was undoubtedly true. You knew that I killed my mother?"

Garnet's mouth flew open, and this seemed to please him. "My mother died giving birth to me. She was forty years old, and my sisters were already eighteen and sixteen. My father was devastated and, although he denied it, resented and blamed me for her death. I was a confounded nuisance to the entire household, and he was convinced my sisters had refused all suitors in order to mother me. I'm not so sure that was true; Gert and Fanny are independent souls and would've been that way regardless of their annoying little brother, but by the time I was eleven, he'd had enough and bundled me off to Virginia. The girls mourned my leaving, and I was abysmally homesick, but my father brooked no opposition. It was to no avail: my sisters were firmly placed on the matrimonial shelf by then."

It was pure pleasure just to listen to him talk, even if she didn't know half the words he used. She murmured, "How sad for you never to have known your mother."

"I had two mothers, thank you very much, and a person doesn't miss what he never had. Of course I'm sorry I caused her death." He paused for a quick breath. "I'm just amazed, however, how some women can pop out babies easy as pie, while others have so much trouble." Perhaps he felt this was inappropriate for he stopped abruptly and started over. "Easy as pie, now there's a curious expression. Is pie easy? Never having made one, I wouldn't know."

Catching his change of mood, she widened her eyes and made them sparkle. "Which kind: apple or three point one four?"

He laughed far louder than the feeble joke merited, but she joined in and almost felt like Garnet again. He patted her hand, which didn't seem forward or immodest at all. "Ah, a mathematician, John's daughter for sure. So, tell me, what color will your new frock be? The girls rarely wear anything but black or perhaps a somber gray, but surely you'll choose something livelier than that."

"I suppose it depends upon what they have," she replied. It was hard for her to imagine he'd have any interest in the color of her prospective dress. Changing the subject as arbitrarily as he did, she commented upon what long journeys he must've made going back and forth to school. He said they were long but exciting because he went by train.

"I've never ridden a train."

"But you must! It's so exhilarating to see the countryside rushing by and realize those miles of rail stretch all over the continent. I must take you on a train trip!"

She didn't reply. They were nearing Ashton. Despite the congenial buggy ride, the prospect of facing David clotted into dread. She hardly knew what to say to him. Clifford interpreted her silence as disapproval of his comment. "What a fool I am!" he declared. "You're a married woman, and I'm speaking inappropriately. Let me rephrase that. I hope," he emphasized, "that someday you'll take a journey by rail."

She nodded, not paying much attention to him. Tension crept through her limbs as he maneuvered the buggy through Ashton. Looking stricken, he whispered, "I'm sorry to have offended you."

"You haven't offended me." Surprised at her courage, she faced him. "David won't like this, Mr. Clark. As generous as you've been, you more or less forced me into coming to town. He'll think I'm checking up on him, and when finds out I know he's been lying about the weekends, he'll be angry." She shook her head. "It's not wise to corner an animal or a man."

Her spirit surprised him. Frowning, he said, "I'm hoping that when Foster realizes that you know, and, more importantly, that I know about his deceptions, he might change his ways."

She knew she was being impertinent in light of Clark's kindness, but this odd man didn't know everything. "And I might be setting myself up for real trouble. Some things don't get fixed that easy."

Startled, he stared at her. "He wouldn't hurt you, would he?"

She lifted the blanket from her lap. "He's upstairs, isn't he?"

Speechless, he nodded, and before he could get down to help her, she jumped from the buggy. Climbing the imposing staircase up to the offices, she smelled shellac and sawdust, odors she'd once pleasantly identified with her husband. Upstairs she followed the sound of sawing until she found him, standing in the middle of an empty room trimming a door that rested on two saw horses. It was chilly, and David wore a heavy flannel shirt.

He heard her step and looked up, eyes narrowing at the sight of her. Any hope she might've held evaporated. "What're you doing here?"

"And I'm glad to see you, too," she replied. "I came to shop and to warn you."

"Warn me about what?" He set down his saw and moved close to her, close enough for an embrace if he'd wanted one. She toyed with the idea of touching him but wasn't sure how he'd react.

She spoke quickly. "On Saturday Mr. Clark came up to the house with some sorghum. He brought it to the bank first, meaning to give it to you to bring home, but you'd already left. He came on out to the house and was surprised when you weren't home and made me tell him that you'd only been home one weekend since you've been on the job. He said you leave every weekend and wasn't pleased that you hadn't been coming home."

David shut his eyes and shook his head as if she were a great fool. He grabbed her arm. "Why didn't you say that I go visit my sick grandma or something?"

His thumb was pressing hard into the fleshy part of her forearm, separating the muscles and bones. "He took me by surprise, David. I couldn't think of anything to say but the truth. I'm not a natural liar and sneak."

"What else did you tell him?" He kept digging into her arm until she squirmed.

"Stop it. You're hurting me," she hissed. "I didn't say anything else; I just let him think whatever he wanted to think."

He let her wriggle against his grip for a moment or two more and released her. "What's it to him whether I go home on the weekends?"

"He was a friend of my father's. I guess he thinks he's looking out for me."

David made a disgusted noise. "Luther's gone to Lexington. Did your watchdog bring you into town to scold me? And where's Ruben?"

Rubbing the sore spot on her arm, she replied, "He's with Lorena. Yes, Mr. Clark insisted on bringing me into town. I mentioned I needed to buy some things, and I couldn't tell him no without being impolite. He *is* your boss, David."

David looked at the doorway as if Clark might appear any minute. She'd thought he'd at least have the grace to cook up an explanation, but he said nothing. "What *have* you been doing those weekends when you don't come home?"

"Not your business," he muttered.

"I reckon it is my business. Do you just drive past the house, not stopping to see Ruben or me, and go straight to your whiskey? Or do you run to your beloved Flora?"

He sighed mightily, out of patience. "Garnet, you know it probably is a good thing for us to have a little time apart."

"It's real strange how you never answer me when I ask about her. I reckon that's as good as an admission of guilt." She whirled around, scattering sawdust. "And you said this would be a new start for us, didn't you?"

"I'll be home Saturday," he said. And he started sawing again, his face red and puffy. She didn't even like the look of him anymore.

"We both have to try," she said softly. "Or we might as well give up on it."

He turned his back to her.

"I did love you, David," she whispered to his back. More than ever it looked like an insurmountable barrier. She waited but he said nothing. She turned toward the door, her footsteps hollow in the empty room.

Her heart felt nearly as bruised as her arm. Clark stood at the bottom of the steps, waiting for her. His well-intentioned meddling annoyed the spit out of her. She could've lived several more weeks in blissful ignorance except for this man. He seemed to be expecting some kind of report, so she said tersely, "He says he'll be home on Saturday. He wasn't exactly pleased to be caught out."

"I imagine not, but he'll have to stop his deception now."

She glared at him. "You don't understand at all, Mr. Clark. He's bold enough to go without lying to me. This isn't anything new." Fidgeting with her gloves, she reached for the door. He opened it for her. "I'm going to Trosper's now."

"And I'll join you. It will be great fun to choose fabric for your frock."

Thoroughly exasperated, she almost stopped right there in the street to give him a piece of her mind, but she reconsidered. As they walked, every second person spoke to Clark and gave her a curious glance. Insisting they must eat, Clifford bought thick sandwiches, then pored over bolts of dry goods, commenting upon which colors would favor her complexion or hair. She chose a rich rusty brown instead of the pale blue he preferred, telling him the light color was impractical. Quickly she bought the fabric, thread, and other items she couldn't get from Mrs. Lawrence.

By early afternoon they were in the buggy again. He talked again about Henry Ford's automobiles and how these would change the world. It was his dream, he said, to own one. "And what's your dream, Garnet?"

She felt past dreaming but said, "I've always wanted to own a store. Like Mrs. Lawrence. Since I was little."

"Why, that's a fine dream! I'd expect nothing less of you." He smiled.

She felt too tired and dispirited to say more than that. And her breasts were uncomfortably full. She squirmed, pushing her shoulders against the buggy seat.

"Is something wrong?"

"I'm fine."

He frowned. "Look, I realize I forced you into an unpleasant confrontation today, but I want ever so much to be your friend, just like your father was mine. You can be honest, and if you're very angry with me, I'll understand." He stared at her so directly she had to turn her eyes from the horse's gleaming hindquarters to meet his. She thought he had the most genuine eyes she'd ever seen, not that this lessened her annoyance with him.

"You want honesty from me?"

"Absolutely. And I promise you'll get the same from me."

"All right. Honest answer to your first question: I'm well, but my baby hasn't nursed since this morning, and I'm about to bust."

A sudden laugh bubbled up from his chest. "Fair enough. I'll try to get you home as soon as possible."

His laugh pleased her, but she refused to be distracted by his friendliness. "I don't reckon I'm exactly angry, but I don't understand what you're trying to do. What do you want from me? I have nothing to give you."

To be such a talker, he certainly kept his mouth shut for a while. This time she held her eyes on him. His reply came slowly. "I don't know that I can ask for anything but your friendship. I'm concerned about your welfare, and I'm not certain your husband is caring properly for you."

Garnet pleated the blanket covering her lap. "And I'm not certain that it's any of your business, friendship or not. He's already calling you my watchdog and with all those people in town seeing us together, it'll likely get worse. I know you mean well, but he's a jealous man. I've never given him any cause, but he is."

Clifford grimaced. "So I might make things worse."

The afternoon was dull, but there was enough light to play upon the planes of his cheeks, shadowing and highlighting the strong bones. It was some kind of strange pleasure to look at him. Forcing herself to look elsewhere, she replied, "Right now, he's your employee, but that won't last, and then you won't have any control over him."

"Oh, but I could."

"I don't doubt that. You could keep him from working anywhere in the county. But that would hurt me just as much as it does him."

"I'd never do it. But I'm not sure he realizes that."

"And if you start coming to see me, to check on me, and to take me places, people will talk and it'll get back to him. That could hurt me too." Her voice trailed off so low she wasn't sure he could hear her. More loudly she said, "It's not that I'm not grateful; I am, but I don't think it's smart for you to adopt me, to take my father's place. David will see it as something else."

He kept his eyes on the road, and all she heard were the horse's hooves. Then he said, "I understand." Reaching over, he gave her twisted up hands a quick squeeze. "I'll keep my distance, but that doesn't mean I'll quit thinking and worrying about you."

"I thank you."

Clifford frowned and shook his head as if her response bothered him. She didn't know what to make of him. Straightening his back, he asked, "So I'm allowed to be your friend as long as it's from a distance?"

Wary, she nodded.

"Then in honest friendship I have a few more questions, all in confidence." She didn't understand why on earth he was bothering with her. "Does he drink?"

She hesitated but then felt reckless. Clark knew too much already. "Not when he's working." Her half-answer raised his eyebrows.

"Is he visiting a woman on the weekends?"

She couldn't think of a polite way to avoid it. "I have no proof."

He cleared his throat, and she wondered if he was going to spit right into the road. "An intelligent woman can sense these things."

She hoped he was finished. She didn't know why she'd told him, a near stranger, what she couldn't confide to her family, and then she remembered that she'd promised the full story to Lorena. At least this strange man wouldn't be the only one to know her secrets. She felt both guilty and relieved.

Suddenly he pulled on the reins and stopped the horse right in the middle of the road. The weather was so gray and blurred, she felt like she was in a dream. He wrapped his long, thin hand over hers again and said, "Look at me."

She did, uncertain but unafraid.

"Does he hurt you? Has he ever hit you?" His eyes insisted on an answer. Pride and loyalty forbade a truthful answer, yet she wanted to tell him. Once, twice she nodded.

"Oh, dear heart," he sighed, and she lowered her head, blinking hard.

Returning both hands to the reins, he made a clicking noise and the horse started up again. Neither of them spoke. She glanced sidewise and saw that his jaw was grim and set, much like Luther's had been when he'd seen her damaged face. She wavered, appalled that she'd said so much. Swallowing to rid her throat of tears, she said, "It isn't all David's fault."

Clifford swiveled his head toward her. "How can you say that? What possible excuse could there be for hurting you?"

"I'm a bad wife."

He flapped a bony hand at the gray horizon. "What do you do? Burn his dinner? Scorch his shirts? Good Lord, Garnet, how could anything justify hitting you?"

She'd never been so embarrassed. Somehow she wanted to know if he, her father's friend, but a man after all, would think she was a bad wife too. David said so, and she had no one else's opinion about it. Her mouth went tense with the effort, but she whispered, "The bed part. I'm no good at that."

She thought he was going to stop the buggy again; instead, his loud roar startled the well-mannered horse into a sudden burst of speed. "Good Lord Almighty!" he bellowed, jerking on the reins. "And how much patience and effort did that boy put into his endeavors? No, I don't want to know. Did he treat you with love and tenderness? Don't answer that either. Look at you, the loveliest, most desirable girl I've ever seen, and he probably just used you as, as, a receptacle!"

She couldn't begin to say more. He kept mumbling and muttering, but she couldn't make sense of it, although it was gratifying to hear him say that David was as much to blame as she. Turning her head away, she saw that they were at the turning for the farm and was relieved that she needn't say more.

He drove up the lane and stopped the buggy. "I know you must hurry in to your child, but I implore you to listen to me for one more minute."

She was already lifting the blanket from her lap, ready to reach for her parcels.

"I promise that I'll keep all of what you've told me in strictest confidence, as friends do. We bankers keep many secrets," he added, coaxing a wavering smile out of her. "And I beg you not to be embarrassed by what you've confided to me. You've not told anybody else, have you?"

She shook her head.

"Tell your friend Lorena or your mother or someone. You may need their assistance. I wish I could help, but I cannot, and, as you say, it would be misinterpreted if I did. Nonetheless, if I can ever assist you, I beseech you to call upon me as your trusted friend. Will you promise me this?"

She felt as if she were making a vow in church. "Yes, I promise."

Then he smiled, jumping down to help her. Lorena was at the door, holding Ruben on her hip. Clifford walked as far as the porch, touched his hat, and handed Garnet her packages. "Make a lovely frock," he said and returned to his buggy.

Garnet wasn't sure he heard her thanks as she hurried into the warm house. She shrugged out of her coat and reached for Ruben. "Oh, I hope this child is hungry. I'm about to explode."

"I haven't let him starve, but he's missed you."

Garnet opened her dress for the baby, a great relief for both of them. Lorena was standing in the doorway staring at her. "All right," Garnet said with a sigh, "I've confessed to a near stranger; now I'd better tell you."

Chapter Sixteen

"Open the window a crack, will you? These lamps are making a terrible stink," Lorena mumbled with pins between her lips. It was long past sunset, but the sky still had a milky glow. Garnet wondered if it would snow. They were in the sewing room, where Lowell had been so sick, and the soft brown wool she'd bought lay stretched over the cutting table.

Lorena scrutinized Garnet's midsection. "Are you sure you want me to fit this to your old pattern? You're skinny as a rail these days."

"I guess we could take it in a little, but I might fill back out when I stop nursing."

"Hmm. Or you might start eating again. Course, I understand why now."

Garnet had talked. After the embarrassment of confessing to Mr. Clark, it was a blessed relief to pour out everything to Lorena, although she, unlike him, demanded every ugly detail. Garnet craved the woman's advice, but Lorena had listened through supper and the dishes and Ruben's bath without commenting except for a volley of cuss words aimed at David and her Simpson kinfolk.

Lorena finished pinning the pattern pieces and offered the scissors to Garnet who started cutting. It seemed silly how this once had made her nervous. Lorena settled into the rocking chair by the fire and watched Ruben roll around on his blanket. It was the same spot where the woman had done her own confessing about Grandpa.

Lorena stared at the fire. It was her nature to simmer ideas before she served them up, but Garnet was content to wait. For the first time in weeks she felt secure. She didn't know whether it was the room, lamp-lit and filled with the sounds of a happy baby and pleasant work, or the relief of confessing, but something inside her had melted.

"Why don't you stay up here until Saturday morning? You and Ruben can still go to Mattie's on Friday, we can take our time with this dress, and I can try to feed you up. I'd enjoy your company."

"I'd need to run up to the house to get a few things, but sure, I'd enjoy it."

Lorena nodded and rocked in the same tempo while Garnet cut steadily, laying pieces on top of each other. "When will Luther get home?"

"Another week." Lorena's blackberry eyes snapped with mischief. "I wonder how things are at your mother's."

Garnet rolled her eyes. "Sometimes I feel awfully sorry for Lowell."

"He's doing his time just like you did. I was plenty upset with my brother about marrying Louise, but it's probably been the best thing for the children. Luther don't say much, but I have a feeling he keeps Louise in line, at least on the important stuff. Have you seen his beard?"

Garnet chuckled and said that she had, but this turned her thoughts back to the day when he'd wanted her to leave David. Lorena's mind must've been traveling the same direction. "I can't believe that rascal didn't tell me nothing."

"He kept his word."

"Oh, Luther's honorable even if he does frustrate the living hell out of me."

There was silence again, companionable enough, but Lorena had to know that Garnet was waiting. The woman sighed. "I know you're wanting me to fix your troubles, but I can't. There've always been men like David, and all women can do is tolerate it or run off if they have somewhere to run to. I'll admit I'm worried. David's strong, and if he has the drink in him, he might hurt you past mending."

Garnet was appalled. "Oh, I don't think he'd kill me!"

"When they're drinking they don't know what they're doing." Lorena reached down to pat Ruben's silky head and when he lifted his arms, hoisted him onto her lap. "Now Louise'd tell you to use your body to control him, but I don't reckon Louise has ever come up against this kind of man. She'd be telling you to make fancy nightgowns and wear sweet-smelling powders and the like, saying a woman who can't keep her man at home ain't no kind of woman at all."

Garnet shook her head. "I told you what he's like. He'd rip a pretty nightgown into pieces. If I touch him, he goes at me, and there's no love in it. Maybe he loves Flora. But if he's the same with her, I don't see how she'd like it any better than I do."

Lorena rubbed Ruben's back with her knuckles. "We don't know what he's doing with Flora. Mind, I think there's something, but it could just be some kiss and tickle."

Garnet gave her a skeptical look, and Lorena shrugged. "But here's what I do know, and you may not like it: you and David both married too young and too quick."

Garnet started to protest, going so far as to set her scissors down, but Lorena held up her hand. "You wanted your own house. Folks marry for worse reasons. You meant to make a good marriage, and, God knows, you've tried and suffered. But I ain't at all sure you were ready." She shifted Ruben. "He's liable to go to sleep any minute. Should you nurse him?"

Garnet took the heavy baby and sat in the other chair.

"And David," Lorena went on, folding her hands over her middle, "married you because he wanted to win the prettiest girl in the county. Every time he makes love to you he's still claiming his prize. I reckon he's still afraid somebody's going to take you away from him. He thinks you're better than he is, and I ain't sure he's wrong. It's eating him up, and that's why he's so hard and jealous."

"But if he wants me so much, then why does he go off to Flora?" Garnet felt her back tightening.

Lorena flicked her hand toward the fire. "Flora's a tempting little piece even if she ain't much more than a whore. But she's no prize; she ain't Deke King's grand-daughter, nor the schoolteacher's daughter. With you he has to be the big man and show you who's boss. I wouldn't be surprised if he's easier, sweeter with Flora."

"If that's the way it is, I'll never win."

"Well, he could grow up a little, but I'm afraid he's going to hurt you so bad both in the body and the soul that you won't love him at all by the time that happens."

Lorena's words pained Garnet more than David's bruises.

"And we ain't even talking about the drinking. Maybe time and growing up might help the loving. I don't doubt you both could get better at that. Some men have a time keeping their pants buttoned when they're young, but they grow out of it. And maybe he'd get more sure of hisself and stop being cruel and jealous. You say he's sweet ever now and then, and maybe that part of him would come out more with time. But drinking, well, drinking is a lifelong problem; look at his father." Lorena said most of this to the fire, but when she shifted her eyes back toward Garnet, she saw the tears creeping down her cheeks. Garnet hadn't cried so much since Papa died.

"Oh, honey, I don't mean to upset you, but everything I've told you is just the honest truth. I don't see no easy way out."

Garnet pulled the sleeping baby away from her breast. Without speaking she extinguished all but one lamp, and put the baby to bed. "So there's nothing I can do," she said when she sat again.

"Well, you can keep trying. Love him as best you can and try to keep from hardening your heart." Lorena's rough voice was as soft as it ever got. "Or you could go back to your mother's; you know Luther'd do his best by you."

Garnet shook her head.

"You're welcome here, and you know it," Lorena went on. "But I'm not sure David would put up with it. Ruben's his son, and you're his wife. He has every right to expect you to be in his house."

"And I'd pay."

"That's what frets me. Anything you do might lead to another beating."

"I have no choices." She was a rabbit in a trap.

"There's divorce. I don't know much about it, but Deke used to beg me to divorce Tom. There was no sense in that because Tom was a good man in every way, and you have to prove someone's at fault." She gave a brief, bitter laugh. "In that case, Tom had reasons for divorcing me rather than the other way around. But it makes you air all your dirty laundry in the courtroom where anybody can hear it. The churches say it's a sin. They think a divorced woman's about the same as a whore, and I'm not sure you could stand that, girl."

"Even if the man's to blame?"

"Even if he is. Too many of these holier than thou biddies feel the same way your mama does: a good woman don't let her man stray. Or if he does, she ignores it because that part of marriage is sort of dirty anyways. It ain't one bit fair nor sensible, but everybody looks down on the woman when there's divorce. And then there's the problem of a woman, especially a woman with a child, trying to make it on her own. About the only way she can survive is to move back home in disgrace or find a man to marry her, and not too many of them want used merchandise."

It was ugly, too ugly to consider. How could beatings, drunkenness, and adultery have become part of her life? And the thought of divorce, all but a foreign word to her, was beyond her imagination.

"Did you think I'd have a magic solution?" Lorena's eyes glowed in the firelight.

"I told that man, Clifford Clark, more than I should have. Maybe I was stupid enough to think that he, and you would think of a way everything could turn out the way I dreamed."

Lorena's eyebrows raised a good half-inch. "You've told me about Clark getting into all this, but I don't understand."

"I don't either. Oh, he talks about how much he thought of my father, and I suppose he's trying to take Papa's place in some kind of strange way. He's an odd man, with a million interests, and I wonder if I'm just some little project he's working on right now." Garnet sighed. "I told him straight out that he'd be making it worse for me if he kept on meddling, and he said he wouldn't."

Lorena made a skeptical noise.

"What?"

"Oh, you'll be thinking I'm an evil-minded old woman, but I wonder if there ain't another reason why he's taken such an interest in you."

Garnet had her mouth open to protest but closed it. The loveliest, most desirable girl I've ever seen, he'd said. She hadn't told Lorena that part. "I don't think that's likely. He's old, Lorena. And I'm married. I just think he has this crazy notion he can help me."

"Not that old. Deke was better than twenty years older than me," Lorena said with a sharp laugh. "After Miss Caroline died, Clark's older sister, Fanny, as I recollect, set her cap for Deke. Can you imagine that big old thing with your Grandpa? Anyway, Clifford was a little boy then, so he'd be thirty, thirty-one now."

"I wonder why he never married."

Lorena crinkled up her nose. "I ain't never heard nothing bad about the Clarks, but they're queer, independent folk. I've got a notion his sisters probably wouldn't want him to marry a woman who'd take their place."

They heard the clock downstairs chime nine times, and Lorena yawned. "I'll be heading to bed now, but, no, Clifford Clark ain't too old to be interested in you and not in a fatherly way neither. You don't half-realize how pretty you are." She touched Garnet's cheek. "But he sounds like he's trying to be a friend, and that's good. I like what he said about you needing to let people know what's going on so's we can look out for you. But even if Clark's motives are pure as snow, he could make things rough."

Lorena patted her on the shoulder and left. Things were confusing. No, Garnet corrected herself, things were horrible and not likely to get any better. But tonight she was safe and comfortable, and maybe she'd learn to be happy with little crumbs of peace. She crept into bed beside Ruben's limp warmth and cuddled him to her. As much as he adored his son, David never wanted him in their bed so she savored this. And she savored what Clifford Clark had said

throughout that strange trip. For the moment they made the ugliness
fade.

***

David did come home on Saturday afternoon, and he stayed there.
When he strode through the door he sniffed appreciatively at the stew
simmering on the back of the stove but gave her a strange, suspicious
look. She'd feared reprisals from their confrontation in town, but, even
though her pulse was racing, she smiled and asked him what was
wrong.

"I seen Hayse in town this afternoon as I was leaving, and he
said there ain't been light here the last few nights. Where've you been?"

This was the pot calling the kettle black, she thought, but
replied cheerfully, "He's right. I've been at Lorena's making this dress
and a few things for our growing boy. Do you like it?" Doing a half-
whirl to show it off, she beamed at him, although she hated the idea of
Hayse Simpson watching their house. Apparently satisfied with her
answer, David nodded but still acted like his skin was too tight. She got
the impression he was behaving well only because he thought he had
to. As she moved about the house she touched him on the shoulder,
the hand. If Lorena was right, and she probably was, there was no
other alternative. At one point she brought up Christmas and asked if
he planned to make something for Ruben. He lit up at this, and they
had a few pleasant moments discussing a gift for the baby. Deciding
upon some simple blocks, he hurried off to his workshop to start
them, and Garnet sighed with relief. She must, indeed, start measuring
out happiness in teaspoons.

He came home the next weekend and Christmas Eve as well.
Garnet baked and cooked all day for Christmas, and the house smelled
festive with cinnamon and sage. On Christmas morning, Garnet woke
early to put a turkey in the oven and lay presents on the kitchen table.
For Ruben there were the blocks and for David two new shirts, one
flannel and one of softest blue cotton that she'd sewed for him while
she was with Lorena. Although he was gruff and impatient with
Garnet, especially in bed, there'd been no ugly words or bruises.
Things were all right.

When she heard Ruben stirring, she woke David and poured
his tea. Wishing him a merry Christmas, she pushed his gifts toward
him, but both of them were more interested in Ruben. They spread a
quilt on the kitchen floor and placed the blunt-cut, differently shaped

260

pieces of wood in front of him. Although he seemed to enjoy chewing them more than building, they both smiled at their baby.

"What's this?" David squeezed the soft packages in front of him.

"Open them and see." She stood by his elbow and laid her hand on his back.

He declared that the shirts were finely made, and raised his arm to encircle her waist. "But I didn't get you anything." It did seem to bother him.

"That doesn't matter. I have my new dress."

After dinner, Ruben napped while she washed up a mountain of dishes; she seemed to dirty every dish in the house when she made a big meal. David sat at the table and said it was a shame Ruben couldn't enjoy the meal. "By next Christmas, he'll be wanting his own drumstick," she replied, relentlessly cheerful.

"He'll be walking before long, won't he?"

"Well, he isn't quite crawling yet. It'll be a little while."

They heard a brisk tapping at the front door, and Garnet, up to her elbows in dishwater, glanced back at David. She had barely enough time to dry her hands when Clifford Clark walked into the kitchen holding a box and a toy bear, followed by a sour-looking David.

"Merry Christmas!" Clark declared.

"Merry Christmas." Garnet took the box. "Won't you sit down?"

"Oh, no. I'm out making deliveries for my sisters. That box contains Fanny's famous pecan cake, and she insisted that Mr. and Mrs. Foster should have one." He looked over his shoulder at David. "She's always hearing me talk about the amazing David Foster, master of all carpentry."

David's smile was weak.

"And this wooly creature was just too tempting. I thought your son might enjoy playing with a little bear, of the toy variety, mind you. Christmas is for children, you know." He beamed, swiveling his head back and forth between them. He was working hard at ignoring the awkwardness.

"Why that's very kind of you, Mr. Clark," she said. "Ruben's asleep right now, but I'm sure he'll enjoy his little bear." She pointed toward the front room where David and Ruben had scattered the new blocks. "David made these for him."

Clark hunkered down to examine them. "Aren't these beautifully crafted! I'm in awe of people who work with their hands.

Mine, alas, are useless." He looked at his long, bony hands with a dramatically sad face.

"Set a spell, Mr. Clark," David said stiffly. Probably the last thing he wanted was an extended visit from his interfering employer, but the man had been kind.

"Yes, please do," Garnet said. "I'll put the kettle on. I have jam cake as well."

"No, no. We eat our Christmas dinner at sunset, and I still have to stop at the Bledsoe's. Fanny will give me a scolding if I'm late to Christmas dinner." He laughed and bowed and was out the door before David and Garnet could do more than thank him.

She waited for David's reaction in order to gauge her own. She thought Clark had been generous and there was little about the visit that should upset him. Relieved, she saw that David grudgingly felt the same way. "Let me see that silly little bear," he said.

She nodded. "Do you want to try some of Fanny's cake?"

David rolled his eyes in mock pain. "Not after all that dinner you fed me."

He sat in the armchair, and she perched on the arm beside him, both of them examining the toy. "There's an awful lot of food in the house," she said. "Maybe you can take some of it back with you tomorrow."

"That would be good. I get mighty tired of the food in town."

"I wish you didn't have to go back tomorrow," she said. It wasn't true, but so far her efforts had been successful.

"Well, I do, and since I had this time off in the middle of the week I won't be back on the weekend. As a matter of fact, I probably won't be home until the job's completely done." He didn't seem unhappy about it.

She picked bear fuzz off her dress.

"Really, Garnet. I'll be in town working that whole time. Your watchdog will make sure of it."

"I told him I didn't want him meddling in our business."

"That don't mean that he won't. Whew," he exhaled, "this has been a good job, good pay, and steady work, but I don't know if it's been worth it."

She made no comment and sat with the bear on her lap until David left for his workshop, telling her to come get him when Ruben awoke. Idly she played with it, hoping the child wouldn't prefer the bear to his blocks. After finishing the dishes, she opened the box to see Fanny's cake. It was a dark, shiny loaf full of nuts and raisins.

Although it was appealing, she, too, was stuffed from dinner. Then she noticed a slip of paper tucked mostly under the cake. Going to the window she glanced out to make sure David was still in his workshop and then read it.

I'm keeping my word, but it's inordinately difficult. I hope you are well and safe and remembering your promises. Do not fail to contact me if you are in need of help. He hadn't signed it, as if that would've mattered. Lord, what if David had seen it? She burned the note in the stove.

That night she brought out her box of stationery and wrote Christmas letters to David's father and Aunt Martha. Then she wrote Franklin, trying to keep her message cheerful. Wherever he was, it must be hard being alone at Christmas. His last letter had said he'd made friends and his boss was hard but fair. Nonetheless, he must be missing home this time of the year. Then she pulled out another sheet of paper and wrote a short note of thanks to Mr. Clark. Before she addressed the envelope she waved the note at David and asked whether she should send it to the bank or the Clark's farm.

He scowled. "What are you writing him for?" Ruben was in his lap chewing on the bear.

"Don't let him put that in his mouth. It's all fuzzy," she said. "Just a thank you note. It's the polite thing to do. Here, do you want to read it?"

He took it and read the four sentences with narrowed eyes, but couldn't find anything wrong with them. "Just send it to the bank."

He left before daylight, his footsteps crunching on the thick frost in the yard. Wrapping Ruben in blankets, she carried the boy down the road to the store and deposited him in Mrs. Lawrence's welcoming arms before she crossed the road to mail her letters. Viola Williams ran the tiny Bethel post office from a little box of a room tacked onto the front of her house. She was a short, stooped woman with an unfortunately large mole on her cheek that used to make Franklin declare she was a witch. Actually, it was more her sly and sullen attitude that made her seem evil. The woman took her time handling Garnet's letters and then said, "You ain't checked your mail in a while."

Garnet said she supposed not. She'd received a letter from Franklin a month ago, and no one else corresponded with them much. Moving at a turtle's pace, Viola pulled two letters from a cubbyhole and said, "From Ashton and near two weeks old."

Puzzled, Garnet thanked her. The spiky, disconnected handwriting looked familiar, but she tore one of them open to make sure. Inside was a newspaper clipping of a recipe for sugar cream pie. Written in tiny letters along the margin were the words, "Is this as easy as pie?" There was nothing else, no letter or message. She smiled and tucked the clipping in her pocket, saving the other letter for later. When Mrs. Lawrence asked what she was smiling about, Garnet said it was Christmas, and shouldn't they all be merry?

The notes kept coming at a rate of about two per week. Although Garnet couldn't imagine how Viola Williams would know who the sender was, she always looked sly and knowing when she gave them to her. Of course Viola looked sly most of the time anyway. Clifford's intent, Garnet supposed, was to send a smile her way now and then, and he succeeded. They were usually clippings from newspapers or magazines with a short comment scratched across them. One showed a new automobile, and he'd written, "I *will* have one of these!" Another was a photograph of a small child with a bear with the words, "Ruben and his teddy!" scrawled below it. There were pictures of groceries and funny little stories. He also sent tracts published by the Women's Christian Temperance Union telling of their crusade against alcohol and support for women's suffrage. With these he included a note saying his sisters were members. Garnet read the pamphlets, noting how the WCTU blamed alcohol for most incidents of wife beating.

Even though the newsy, clever clippings brightened her days, twice he actually sent letters, and she memorized these before burning them. One read: *Dear Heart, I know I should not have come on Christmas Day, but I could not endure one more hour without assuring myself that you are well. I bought Ruben's bear a week ago and could have sent it with your husband, but I selfishly treasured the idea of delivering it myself. I worry, you see. I pray that you did not see my visit as a violation of my vow.*

I received your short note of thanks, and you know that Ruben is more than welcome to his little gift. If in the future you wish to write me, it would be more discreet if you sent letters to the farm.

He never signed them, and this amused her because if he thought that made the correspondence anonymous, he was fooling himself. After receiving his response to her thank you note, she silently called herself "dear heart" for a week even though she struggled with the discrepancy between the tone of the letter and his self-avowed fatherly role. Halfway through January she received another one. It read: *Dear Heart, I have told myself numerous times that you are being prudent rather than annoyed with my silly letters, and that is why you have not written. There's so little I can do. Your husband nears the end of his task here, and I fear his presence at home will renew your problems. Please, just one sentence to let me know you are well!*

Garnet gave in and wrote a brief reply and was relieved that for several weeks his envelopes contained only innocuous clippings. Once

David came home, keeping any kind of secret would become more difficult. She kept telling herself the notes were innocent but took guilty pleasure in being cunning with them. Perhaps one clipping out of four she casually left on the kitchen table where David could read it. These were mostly recipes or articles about the Wright brothers, who fascinated Clifford. She burned the others. Making things even more difficult was the fact that Ruben was crawling by the end of January, and she quit working at Mattie's store. It'd been easy to pick up the mail when she went there every week, but once David was home and unemployed, she feared he might visit the post office out of boredom.

Since she no longer could work at the store, when the weather was decent enough she went to her mother's house once a week. Mama welcomed the help, although Mama gave her appraising looks sometimes. She never asked about her marriage or whether Garnet was happy. Garnet would've lied anyway. As usual, Mama was more interested in her own concerns, but she did fuss at Garnet for being too thin and working too hard. "A nursing mother needs to take care of herself or the baby suffers," she pontificated from the sofa while Garnet dusted the front room.

Garnet pointed to chubby little Ruben chasing after Dessie on his hands and knees. "Does he look puny?"

"Well, no. First babies are often the healthiest. You were. Just take care with your next one."

"As long as I'm nursing I don't reckon there'll be another any time soon."

Mama raised an elegant eyebrow. "Many women have been surprised by the failure of that old belief."

Garnet stopped with the dust rag in mid-air. "Really?"

"I was still nursing Violet when Henry was conceived. You want more children, of course." This was not a question.

Garnet resumed her dusting, thinking she might nurse Ruben until he was five if it was any protection at all. "Oh yes, but not right away."

Mama nodded in her usual serene way. "Back in the fall I thought I might be expecting again, but it wasn't meant to be."

"Oh, but Mama, the midwife said you're too old to have any more children."

Louise gave her a withering look. "I'm perfectly healthy. Why else would I have married again if I hadn't wanted more children?"

To feed the ones you have, Garnet thought but didn't say anything.

At first David seemed happy to be home. He enjoyed Ruben but soon tired of long days with a small child. For a few days he cleaned his workshop, discovering a few unfinished projects that occupied him. But then there was nothing for him to do, and he prowled the house like a caged animal, with Garnet as his keeper.

Every day she expected David to announce that he was going up to visit Hayse and dare her to protest it. If only he had some work, this good spell might last. She had to admit it wasn't wonderfully good. He was grouchy and short with her, but he wasn't drinking or hitting, and his lovemaking had been surprisingly infrequent. What few times he took her, he still grumbled about her being cold and would spit into his hand and rub her roughly, saying she was as dry as an old maid. His only real pleasure seemed to be her cooking, and he gained weight.

His nineteenth birthday was in early February, and she planned to make a special meal. That day he was more restless than ever, shouting at Ruben, which was a rare thing, and then announcing he'd go up to visit Hayse to see if anyone knew of any work. He didn't meet her eyes, but she commented only that he should be home for his birthday supper. With a curt nod, he jammed a cap over his brow.

That time he was only a little late, his eyes glittering with drink and his talk silly, but he was happy in his liquor. But on the weekend he left on Saturday afternoon and didn't come home until Sunday morning, still drunk but walking, and he smacked her when she said she'd worried about him. And so it started again. Often he returned from the Simpson's angry and spouting about how Clifford Clark was keeping him from getting any work. When Garnet protested the logic of this, he called Clifford her lover and insisted they were plotting against him. Before long he was drinking two or three nights a week, sometimes coming home and sometimes not. When he didn't she worried that he might be freezing on the road, but when he did, she feared his fist or sexual demands. These were the worst because if she tried to refuse him, and it had come to that, then he would batter her with ugly words or force her. But if she submitted, he was often too drunk to perform, and then he'd hit her.

She debated whether to write Clifford but didn't see what he could do about it. Idled by winter weather, Luther paid an occasional visit, sizing her up when David was there and bluntly asking how things were when he wasn't. She knew Luther could see through her lies, but he couldn't solve her problems either.

The only solution she could think of was work. Never had she yearned more fervently for spring if it meant work for David. Every day she scanned the hills for the green mist that meant spring, but God wasn't going to change nature for the likes of Garnet Foster. They had a couple of days in February when an early thaw cheered David. He went out one afternoon to talk to people about jobs, and she asked him to pick up cornmeal from the store. By late afternoon heavy clouds and wind replaced the sunshine, and she shivered as she added more coal to the stove. As the day crawled toward dark, she gave way to despair once again, wondering how many times her expectations could rise up and then plummet before she lost the capacity for hope.

Well past suppertime, Garnet ate some soup and left the rest on the stove. Sleet started up and sounded like someone pitching gravel at the windows. Surely he would stay up at the Simpson's in this weather. She'd just made up her mind to go to bed when she heard a loud thud on the front porch. When she opened the door, she saw David lying face-down on the ice-glazed floor. He didn't budge when she shook him.

More than likely he'd slipped on the ice, she thought, probably banging his head and knocking himself out. At first she struggled to turn him onto his back, but she couldn't get any purchase on the slick porch. She braced herself against the house and with a mighty heave managed to turn him. Dark blood oozed from a gash on his forehead. She stopped for a moment to catch her breath and think about how she could get him over the threshold. His clothes were sodden with ice and water, and he'd die of cold in no time if she left him there.

Garnet grabbed his jacket and tugged until the top half of his lifeless body was lined up with the doorjamb. Then she considered how she could get him over the threshold without further injuring his head. Shivering, she ran into the house to get a towel to place under his head. It seemed to take forever, but after dozens of tiny pulls and pushes, she maneuvered him into the front room far enough to close the door.

Blood from the cut at his hairline dripped into his dusty brown curls, and there was an angry graze high on his cheek. He'd literally fallen on his face. Sitting on the floor, she dabbed at his wounds with a damp cloth. Whiskey fumes rose every time he exhaled.

She continued to blot the cut, gently diluting the blood with warm water, and it struck her that this was one of the few times she'd been able to touch him with tenderness. Wringing out the cloth, she used the clean end to wipe his entire face: the tiny wrinkles by his eyes, the narrow mouth that had smiled so easily. Slow tears fell from her face to his. What had happened to that boy and girl? She patted his face dry and let her fingers plow his springy hair. Regardless of what Lorena thought, she'd loved David. This drunken bully wasn't that boy.

The bleeding slowed, but she had more work to do. He'd catch pneumonia if she didn't get his soaked clothes off. It was much harder work to undress David than Ruben. First she removed his shoes and managed to work water-logged socks over his heels. Then she attacked his jacket, stiff with icy water. She wrestled one arm out and rolled him back and forth to free up the other. As she lifted the jacket away from his body, a piece of crumpled paper fell from his pocket. It was an envelope, addressed to Mrs. David Foster in Clifford's hand. David had gone to the post office. She dove into his pocket and pulled out another envelope and two clippings. One was a drawing of Carrie Nation with a face that resembled the hatchet she wielded, and upon it Clifford had written, "A strong resemblance to Gert, don't you think?" The other was a newspaper column on cacti with brackets around the paragraph about night-blooming cereus plants which she'd described on their trip to Ashton. There was no comment, and she was relieved these hadn't contained personal notes headed by "Dear Heart."

It didn't matter. David would still see these as confirmation that she was hiding things because the clippings she showed him had come at infrequent intervals, not two in less than a week. And there was no telling what Viola Williams might've revealed. Although it irked her that he'd opened her mail, she was more afraid than angry for she knew the messages meant more to her than they should. David would too.

The heavy coat had kept David's shirt dry, so after removing his ice-soaked pants, she threw a quilt over him and worked a pillow under his limp head. He was warm and dry, and that was the best she could do. In the morning there'd be hell to pay over those notes, and the wicked part of her wondered why she'd worked so hard to keep him safe. She would've done the same for a stray dog, but that didn't say much.

As she expected, David never thanked her for lugging him into the house probably because he had no memory of it, but he lit into her about the letters, accusing her of plotting behind his back, of carrying on with the "rich old jackass." And she got a slap or two, one of which loosened a tooth. She was grateful there were no visible bruises.

For the next few weeks they slogged through the mire of their marriage, as muddy and dismal as the yard outside. Sometimes he'd stare out the front window, his eyes hollow and yearning, and she wondered which he wanted: whiskey or Flora, although since his fall, he'd drunk little. He was so despondent that occasionally she felt a sudden urge to comfort him. He seemed to want no part of her, not even in bed. She was grateful for that small mercy but wondered where this would lead. She'd seen him angry and frustrated but never so completely dispirited.

March came, bringing a few teases of spring but still no work for David. One sunny day she decided to wash bedding even though it was still chilly and hanging the wet sheets on the clothesline hurt her chapped hands. The laundering steamed up the kitchen, and she felt nearly as limp as the sheets. She and Ruben had terrible colds, her nose as red and raw as her hands. Passing the mirror in the bedroom, she shook her head at her reflection: thin, pale cheeks accentuated her ruddy nose and wisps and twigs of hair escaped her hairpins. Her dress was old and faded with the sleeves roughly rolled so she could scrub clothes. She looked like a gaunt, hard-set country woman now, not pretty Garnet, and certainly not the loveliest, most desirable girl. There'd been no messages from that quarter, and she didn't expect any. A day or two after David's fall, she wrote Clifford a terse note asking him not to send any more letters. She hadn't explained, nor did she think she needed to. She told herself that she was nothing but a pastime for him, but he'd provided daydreams that comforted her, and now she had no comfort at all.

She was having a terrible time keeping Ruben out of the wash tub. He could pull himself up to the tub now and wanted to float bits of wood or splash in the water. As a result, his clothes were wet and dark puddles pooled on the kitchen floor. She wished David would come home and amuse the child, but, as usual, she had no idea where her husband was. He'd said he was going to stores to sell picture frames he'd made, but he could be anywhere.

He puzzled her. Recently he'd go up the road several times a week and spend an hour or two but then come home sober or nearly so. This should've pleased her, but the other scent he brought home, that of sharp, flowery perfume, was just as devastating.

She'd just thrown another armful of clothes in the tub when she heard a knock at the front door. Wiping her hands on her apron, she hurried out of the kitchen with Ruben crawling after her and opened the door to Clifford Clark.

"Garnet!" he exclaimed. "How are you? And Ruben, mobile at last!"

The child used his mother's skirts to pull himself up. Then he plopped back down on his chubby bottom, grinning cheerily despite his dirty nose. Garnet reached in her pocket for a damp handkerchief and bent over to wipe it.

"Hello, Clifford," she murmured, trying to hide the quick joy she felt.

"Bless you, you've finally quit calling me Mr. Clark! Is David here?"

"Not just now."

Released from his mother's attentions, Ruben crawled toward the kitchen, and flashing Clifford an apologetic look, she went after him. "He's fascinated with the wash tub today."

Clifford followed her with long, slow strides. The kitchen is upside down, and I look a sight, she thought. But the man continued to beam as she pulled a protesting Ruben away from the tub. "We can go in the front room."

"No, no. This is fine. And the boy can play in the water if you're here to watch him, can't he?"

She nodded and deposited Ruben on the floor where he gripped the side of the tub and swirled his stubby fingers in the gray water.

"So you're here to see David?" she asked, sniffing. It would be so embarrassing to blow her nose in front of this impeccable man.

"I have a work opportunity for him, if you think it'll improve things." His face creased with concern. "It's bad, isn't it?"

"Yes." They sat, and she stretched her arm along the table. It wasn't quite an invitation for him to touch her hand, and she wasn't really sure she wanted him to anyway, with it all rough and reddened from the wash.

"He might come in any minute. Or he might not come home until tomorrow. He's never stayed away more than one night, but I never know. He picked up a couple of the letters and was furious."

"I'm sorry. I thought that might be why you wrote me." He did touch her hand, and she felt unreasonably happy. "Did you suffer for it?"

Her hand twitched under his. "I suffer for just about anything he decides is my fault. He thinks you and I are plotting against him and blames us for him not getting work. If he comes back while you're here, and especially if he's been drinking, there's no telling what he'll say or do."

"But I came to tell him that a man on the farm next to ours wants him to construct some outbuildings. Why would he think I'd sabotage him?"

She shrugged, loving the warmth of his hand over hers. When, exactly, had it come to this? She was silly to think this important, distinguished man cared about her as anything more than an obligation to her father. Ruben was leaning too far over the water, and she used her other hand to steady him. She had to know. "He calls you my beau." She'd be mortified if this man realized that she'd turned their friendship into some moony-eyed schoolgirl crush. And yet, she had to know.

He chuckled, and she took this as confirmation that he thought the idea absurd. It wasn't what she wanted, but it was for the best. She was a fool.

"Beau? I think I'm a little long in the tooth to be called that." He lowered his voice. "But suitor, admirer, lover? What I wouldn't give to be those things to you."

Ruben was humming along with his splashing noises, and she must've been breathing, but all she could see were Clifford's eyes. She was drowning in them like she might drown in a barrel of warm, sweet molasses the very same color. Unable to think of anything coherent to say, she simply whispered, "We can't."

His eyes flared. "Don't you think I know that? Don't you realize I've thought of nothing but you these last months? Worrying, fretting, yearning." His voice became a caress. "It torments me like the fires of hell that you live with a drunken, philandering bully when all I can think about is cherishing you."

Oh my, she thought. His affirmation thrilled her but also horrified her. For weeks she'd been afraid to hope for such words, and now she was afraid of their consequences. Lorena had warned her. "I'm no good for any man," she said, trying to pull back her hand, but he wouldn't let go, reversing it so the white underside of her arm lay gleaming against the table. "I should've stayed at home to help my mother or been like your sisters and never married."

"How can you believe that? He never gave you a chance, dear heart."

He'd uttered them, those two words she'd recited in her head so many times they'd become an amulet. He glanced down at her arm and murmured so softly she could barely hear him. "See those tender blue veins? I would kiss them, follow them up your lovely arm, and there, that little hollow below your jawbone, I would taste, knowing it would be sweet as spring. I would worship every part of you, and then we'd see if you're a bad wife, no good for any man." He held her eyes, and she felt as if she could see straight into his soul. "That is, if you could care for me as I do for you."

Her breaths were coming in little bursts. He'd not touched her except for holding her hand, but she felt as if he were making love to her in a way she'd never experienced. Afraid of what she was feeling, she simply looked at him. Then she gave him the tiniest of nods. His face broke into a dazzling smile. From what seemed like a great distance she heard Ruben splashing and humming like a mosquito.

Giving her hand another squeeze and releasing it, his face tightened. "Even though I rejoice that you return my affection, I'm more grieved than ever, for both of us. As things stand, the best I can do is be your friend, and it seems as though even my friendship causes you pain."

She still couldn't speak, but he stood and looked down at her. "Tell your husband to see Mac Oliver at the farm this side of ours."

There was a loud crash as David came in the back door, slamming it hard behind him. He came within a foot of Clifford and stood with his arms and fists tight. "Get away from my wife, Clark."

Clifford looked mildly at Garnet. She had both arms in her lap. "I don't think I'm anywhere near your wife, Mr. Foster."

"Too near for my liking," David spat. "What brings you up here anyway?"

"I came to tell you that Mac Oliver, who lives on the farm this side of ours, needs some building done. Go talk to him if you're interested; I gave you a good reference."

Garnet thought this would take the heat out of David's argument, but he didn't relent. "I guess you think if you have me working every day then you can come up here and mess with my woman."

"David!"

"Shut up, Garnet. The letters I saw weren't the only ones, were they? I bet there were all kinds of juicy ones I never read. You two have been carrying on for months now." His face was a dull red, but she didn't think he was drunk.

"Let me assure you all my correspondence with your wife has been innocuous and meant only in the spirit of friendship." Garnet wanted him to leave but knew he wouldn't as long as he thought David might hurt her.

"Don't you be using those big words with me. You're no better than I am, and neither is she." He pointed his finger at Garnet, jabbing it toward her as if he regretted the table standing between them. By this time Ruben was crying.

"You're scaring him."

"He'd be more scared if he realized what a whore his mother is."

"I really do think this is uncalled for," Clifford said, acting as though David's tirade was hardly worth his time, but Clifford's hands were as tightly clenched as David's, the bony knuckles white. "I sent your wife a few bits of news and information from the papers I receive, and she asked me to quit doing so. It is I, not Garnet, who is to blame for any perceived indiscretion."

Short of calling him out into the yard for a cold, muddy fistfight, there wasn't much else David could do. Or so she thought. But he smiled then, a malicious, slow grin that chilled her heart. "Well, I don't guess it matters none, Mr. Clark, because you ain't going to have a chance to be sniffing around Garnet any more. I wrote my Pa and told him we'd be moving up to Covington when the weather gets better. I just rented this house to someone, and we'll be moving come May."

Garnet felt her heart hammering against Ruben's shoulder. She glanced wildly at the two men, their eyes locked. David's grin continued, evil and triumphant; Clifford's face was passive. "Well, then, I congratulate you on your news. I assume I should tell Oliver you aren't interested?"

"Oh, I could do that job over the next five or six weeks, weather permitting. I'll go see the man. You just stay away, Clark. You have no business here, and she won't be around much longer as it is."

Clifford gave a curt nod and without saying another word, left the house. David strode behind him, watching through the front window to see him leave. When Ruben struggled to get down, she let him.

"He's gone. I knew I'd catch you eventually."

"Catch me doing what?" Garnet asked. She felt too tired to move, but she'd rather scrub laundry than talk to David. Bending over, she resumed her work, the soapy water stinging her hands.

He didn't answer but stood fidgeting and twisting. It astonished her to see him this angry when he was sober. Perhaps she couldn't blame his temper entirely on whiskey. David sat, and Ruben crawled toward him, pulling at his father's pant leg until he stood. David stretched his hands, popping his knuckles.

"Look, Garnet, we've got a real chance this time. I know I ain't been behaving so good. I've been drinking and getting angry way too much. And you ain't been much of a wife either, all friendly with that high-falutin' jackass. There's nothing good for neither one of us in this county. But moving to a new place will change things. I'll have steady work, and Pa's lady owns a two family home. I got a letter from him and he says the other side's just come open, and it's real pretty with stained glass in one of the windows. You'll have a good time fixing it up the way you want." It had been a long time since she'd heard David use this engaging, boyish tone. "If we get away from here, we'll get along just fine."

She swished the sheets, squeezing and wringing and dipping them. The water was cold. Looking up, she saw genuine pleading on his face. "Why do you even want us to get along when you think I'm a whore?" She'd never uttered that word before and said it in a whisper.

"Oh, Garnet, that man makes me crazy whenever he's around you. You haven't been with him, have you?" He actually had doubts; his face was twisted with them.

"How can you even ask?" There was more despair than heat in her reply.

"See, I'm going to believe you. I know you don't like that kind of thing anyway. Maybe he just had a little crush on you, but I reckon I chased him away. Up north we won't have to worry about him."

As if he hadn't spoken, she murmured in a dead voice, "How can you ask me about that when you come home smelling of her?" She rose with a rough bundle of wash dripping from her hands and stared at him.

"And I'll quit drinking. With steady work up there and nobody tempting me, I won't drink no more. I promise." These words came out rapidly, a plea.

Garnet dumped those sheets in the sink and fished out the rest, wringing and letting them drip. At first her head had spun with his vicious accusations and startling news, but her thinking became crystalline, turning to that efficient place where she'd once solved algebra problems for Papa. She said, "Empty that tub for me, will you?"

He jumped up. Why he wanted her approval or permission she didn't know; he could make her go. In the meantime, however, she'd let him wonder and worry. When he returned with the empty tub, she started filling it with warm water from the kettle. He waited, looking like her brothers did when they desperately wanted something.

"Ruben's growing like a little weed," she said. David nodded impatiently, trying to stay in her good graces.

"And I won't have a sewing machine in Covington. Maybe I'd better take what fabric I have up to Lorena's tomorrow and make him some bigger clothes. Warm weather will be here before we know it."

He grinned, that eye-crinkling, heart-breakingly sweet grin that used to move her very soul. It had no power now, but he didn't realize it. He bobbed his head. "That makes good sense."

She agitated the wash. "Are you going to see that man?"

"Might as well. I could get most of it done, depending upon what he wants. That would give us a little nest egg to move on. Maybe I could buy you a sewing machine. Would you like that?"

Oh, he was happy now. Steeling herself, she raised her head to give him a stingy smile. "That would be nice."

"Come on, boy." He scooped Ruben up. "Let's get out of your mama's hair."

Outside in the raw, bright air she pegged the wash to the clothesline. There were no leaves on the trees yet, but tender buds were popping from the ground and emerging from withered branches. This was her place; oh, not necessarily this house, but the county with its hills and creeks and farms. In Covington she'd shrivel like an oak tree in the desert. And when David started drinking again or found another Flora, and he would, where could she look for comfort? Walter Foster? His lady friend? She jammed clothespins onto the line. He might chase Clifford away, and he might be right to do it. But David couldn't force her away from her people, from her family and Lorena and Luther. She'd die before she went north with him. This was a vow.

Chapter Eighteen

A week later Garnet sat tense as a wind-up toy in Luther's wagon, bouncing along the road to Ashton. So far her plans had fit together like a well-pieced quilt. She'd told David that she needed fabric and notions from town, and, satisfied that he'd outsmarted her, he'd been willing to go along with anything she said. But most of the time he didn't seem particularly happy with his victory. Quiet, often morose, he lingered in his workshop, telling her he was organizing things for the move. It helped that he never touched her these days. And it also helped that he worked every day at Oliver's farm, coming home late. He hadn't been to the Simpson's for more than a week.

The day after he announced their move, she walked to the farm and told an indignant Lorena about his plans. At dinner Luther joined them, and she repeated her story, outlining her scheme for staying in the county and asking if he'd take her to town. Luther agreed and when he told her he'd heard that Flora Simpson was marrying, she understood David's eagerness to leave the county. And she understood David's recent bout of moodiness. Even with the news about Flora, both Lorena and Luther were skeptical about Garnet's plan, but she had no choice.

As usual, Luther said little as the wagon inched toward town. "So, I'll see Mr. Pierce first and then Clifford, and afterwards, I'll buy fabric at Trosper's like I told David I was intending to do," she said.

Luther nodded but tried again to dissuade her. "I'd just pack up and move to the farm if I was you. No sense trying to convince him to stay."

"And I'll do that if I have to, Luther, like I told you. But I want to show my good faith in making the marriage work, and I'm offering him an interesting proposition."

He absorbed this for a quarter of a mile. "Lorena's right, though. Even if you get him to stay, it'll all start up again."

"It's all going to start up again anyway, and at least here I have some place to run."

He didn't have an answer, and, despite her determination and the tiny, nearly depleted vein of hope in her heart, she knew her plan was weak. David had all the power. Maybe, though, she could convince him.

When they reached Ashton, she hopped out of the wagon, telling Luther she didn't know how long her business would take. He said he'd be at the courthouse, just to see what was going on. Knowing what he was referring to, she grinned. As she strode toward the bank building, she straightened her new hat. Well, it wasn't new. Lorena had stretched dark brown velvet over an old one, and the two of them had trimmed it with ribbon and a bit of veil. While they worked, they'd giggled over Louise, who thought she was pregnant again. Lorena'd snorted and said the woman was starting The Change and didn't even realize it. For two minutes, Garnet had forgotten her troubles.

She entered the building and started up the steps, smelling a faint echo of paint and turpentine from David's work. Upstairs the doors looked different, shinier, with brass plates proclaiming who occupied each office. She entered the lawyer's office, and Mrs. Pierce greeted her in her tiny, surprised voice.

"Well, it's Garnet!" she said. "Garnet Foster now, isn't it? Look at how fancy that husband of yours made our old office! What can I do for you?"

She explained, and Mrs. Pierce, again reminding Garnet of a squirrel with her keen little face and protruding teeth, apologized, saying her husband had somebody with him. Despite the new paint and doors, the furnishings were much as Garnet remembered. She sat on the same slippery leather sofa, but her feet reached the floor now. Through the interior door she heard Mr. Pierce's loud, booming voice and wondered if he'd still remind her of a lion. She waited for quite a while, but this gave her a chance to rehearse what she'd say, first to the lawyer and then to Clifford.

A man she didn't know came out, and there were handshakes and remarks before Mrs. Pierce said he had someone waiting. He did still look like a lion, although the lion's mane was thinning. Mr. Pierce exclaimed about how grown up she was, David's work, his sorrow at her father's passing, and escorted her into his office. She felt ill at ease facing him across his big desk but managed to tell him her business. "It's my understanding that my grandpa, Deke King, left each of us grandchildren a hundred dollars we can collect when we're eighteen. I turned eighteen last October and was wondering if I could get my money."

It ended up being an easy process with a signature or two and a paper to take downstairs to the bank. She feared he might question her about what she was going to do with the money, but he didn't.

Handing her the papers, he said, "Just give this to Clifford Clark. He'll get your money for you."

He'd be expecting her. She'd written him a few days before, and sure enough, as soon as she entered the bank, Clifford spotted her. She couldn't help the joy that leapt up in her heart.

"I thought you might want some privacy," he said as he guided her to a small office behind his desk, closing the door behind them.

The room was small and gloomy with a single window facing the alley behind the building. Clifford sat next to her rather than behind the desk and started talking as if only moments had passed since he'd been in her kitchen. "Dear heart, I was so afraid to leave you last week. But I thought staying might exacerbate the situation. Oh Lord, those hideous things he said! So help me God, I wanted to smash his face and whisk you away!" More agitated than she'd ever seen him, he spoke in quick, jerky bursts. Then he softened his voice, reaching for her hand. "You're all I think of, Garnet."

Clutching the lawyer's papers, she kept her hands firmly in her lap. "I need your help, Clifford. You've always said you're my friend," she started. This was harder than she'd expected. Over the past week she'd labored at dousing her feelings for him, but it was a slow, stubborn fire. He seemed puzzled that she wouldn't let him touch her.

"Anything, you know that." His eyes swallowed her. Had anyone ever looked at her like that? David's eyes had once showed pleasure, but for months they'd reflected dislike or, worse, disdain. But this slow, steady light was the most beautiful illumination she'd ever known.

She pulled her lower lip back with her teeth and began. "I have to try to make it work, Clifford. I have no other choice. And I have to stay here in the county. If he moves me up north, I'll die. I know that sounds silly, but it's the truth. Living in the city with no family or friends will kill me."

He nodded. "I was so appalled by his accusations that I hardly took notice of his talk about moving. Was he serious? Really? No, you mustn't go away with him. No. You'd have no sanctuary whatsoever." Agitated, he squirmed and once again he reached to touch her hands, but caught himself and gripped the chair's arms until his knuckles whitened.

"He's convinced that moving will improve everything, the drinking, the anger, everything."

Clifford couldn't sit any longer. He paced around the room in long, loping strides, twisting his hands behind his back. "You can't believe that. The patterns of behavior . . . from what I've read in my sisters' literature about drinking . . . the wounds he's already inflicted . . the suspicion. Even if he believes this, it will never work." He paused by her chair until she looked up at him, tilting her head so far back that her hat slipped. "You break my heart," he whispered.

"I know." She inhaled deeply, gathering her good intentions like armor.

Sighing gustily, he sat, and she tried again. "I need you to do something for me." She told him about her inheritance. "This is my money from Grandpa. Is there a way to make sure that only I can get it?"

"Certainly. Shall I do that now?"

She nodded and he left with the papers, giving her a moment to collect herself. There would be more things to sign, she imagined, so she pulled off her gloves and aligned them with the edge of the dusty desk. This was the easy part.

After the signatures, she said, "Now, I want you to do something else for me." She could hear a faint tremor in her voice. "I want you to see if there are any properties close to Ashton that David and I could buy. We don't need much land, maybe enough for a garden, a workshop, and a small house. About what we already have, I'd say."

He looked bewildered.

"So many people are saying nice things about David's work that I think he'd get plenty of business if we lived closer to town where there's building going on. If he could get enough work he might be willing to stay here. And I think it'd make him proud to have his own place rather than renting from his father."

Clifford listened, his brows drawn close. She sensed that, like Lorena and Luther, he doubted her plan was bait enough to keep David from leaving.

"And, there's something else," she added. "The woman, the one he's been seeing, is getting married today and won't be around anymore. I think this is mostly why David wants to move, that and trying to keep me under his thumb. But with her gone, he might stay home."

Clifford raised an eyebrow.

"It's Flora Simpson. She's marrying that traveling photographer who's been in the county recently. From what Luther hears, she'll go with him when he moves on."

"So, that problem's removed, and this money could go toward the purchase of a house," Clifford thought aloud. "Not a bad scheme, Garnet. If he'll buy it, or should I say, if you can buy him."

She looked at her lap. "I have almost thirty dollars hidden away at home. With Grandpa's money that would go a ways on buying something, wouldn't it? Lorena says we could probably get a bank loan for the rest."

"Oh, certainly. That wouldn't be a problem. You know, I'm thinking of a place right now. The house is in poor condition, but that shouldn't present any difficulties for a carpenter. I'll check into it." He kept gazing blankly at an old map of Kentucky on the wall behind the desk. "But I don't think it'll work."

"I have to try."

"And I'll help you," he said. "If I can't have you, I can at least make sure you're where you can get help."

"The information mustn't come from you," she warned.

Waving his hand, Clifford dismissed her concerns. "Oh, I'll pass it along through Mac Oliver or Luther." Then he hunched forward, his face too close to hers. "Isn't it ironic?" he murmured. "He's the philanderer, but he suspects us."

It would have been wiser to move away. She gazed at his lips, bracketed by lines when he smiled but now serious and quiet. Far different from David's, Clifford's lower lip looked plump, like a pillow, and she imagined kissing it, wondering how that fullness would feel. She turned her eyes to the papers in her lap. "But he isn't wrong, is he? I mean, except for the doing, aren't we guilty? What you said in my kitchen, and . . . ." Her voice trailed off as her gaze moved to his eyes. Despite the stark evidence in them, she still doubted his fondness for her.

"Very much excluding the doing, dear heart. But, yes, I suppose your husband is justified in his accusations. It's almost like he encouraged our affection by suspecting it."

"And that brings me to the last favor." They were trespassing where they shouldn't go, and she must end it. Realizing she'd been leaning toward him, she stiffened her back.

"Clifford, we must never see each other again. If you see me in town, you mustn't speak to me. You mustn't send letters or Christmas cakes or toys for Ruben. You must pretend I don't exist." She all but counted the points on her fingers. Then in a softer voice she added, "David can't have any reason to doubt me, and, if I see you or hear from you, there'll be reasons."

As she spoke, Clifford's mobile face registered hurt, disagreement, and anger. He slammed his fist on the arm of the chair and started pacing like a tiger. "This is madness! Obviously we care for each other even if we're afraid to say the words, and yet we're stifling this, this genuine joy, for a brute who abuses you! Are you trying for some kind of martyrdom here, Garnet? Do you enjoy suffering? That's not my particular pleasure, nor do I relish the thought of what he does and will continue to do to you. Must you pay the rest of your life for a bad decision and make me suffer for it too?"

He paused by the little window, staring out at the bleak alley, and she compared his anger to David's. She felt a painful stab of delight at Clifford's; he wanted her, he cared about her. David's fury held nothing but malice and distrust.

"What other choice do we have?"

Still with his back to her, he said, "There's divorce."

"No. It's a sin. The whole county would condemn me for it."

"It's permissible when there's adultery." He didn't move.

"I can't prove there's adultery. He comes in stinking of her perfume, but I don't know what they've done. And now she's gone." She knew she was asking a lot of him, but she was asking the same of herself. "I have a son. I must try."

Clifford faced her. "And if your plan doesn't work?"

"I'll move to the farm and live with my son. But I'll still be a married woman."

He dropped his head, and she took it as a concession. Picking up her gloves and papers, she walked to where he stood. He looked as though he'd been beaten. As light as a moth on a bloom, she raised her hand to his face, feeling the line of his jawbone under her fingers, the warmth of his cheek. For a second she touched her thumb to his mouth, to the lower lip that tantalized her. He only had time to graze her hand with his before she stepped away. She met his eyes, dark and turbulent, and whispered, "Something to dream on." And she left.

***

Outside Trosper's she met Luther who reported that the wedding had occurred in the judge's chambers, the traveling photographer wearing what Luther called a suit fit for the circus. He'd watched them leave in a big, bright wagon right after the ceremony. Garnet was too numb to care. She made her purchases, buying a few things to make an especially nice meal, and soon after, Luther headed the mules down the road. He asked no questions, but she told him that Clifford might be passing information to him about properties. Luther shook his head. "David ain't going to let you win."

Watching the robins in the road scatter in front of them, she supposed he was right. Nobody thought it would work. But she had to follow her conscience, just like they told her in church. Clifford thought she was wrong to deny the two of them happiness, but the road to any happiness was paved with shame.

After a quick stop at the farm to retrieve Ruben, Luther took her home. He hesitated before leaving. "Are you planning on telling David your plans this evening?"

"I intend to."

Luther rubbed at his nose. "Then how about me sending Lowell up in case there's trouble."

Garnet said, "That would make David suspicious."

"I don't like it."

"He hasn't been drinking in a while, and it's never as bad when he's sober. Even if he doesn't like the idea, he may not get too upset." Loaded down with a cranky baby and packages, Garnet tried to shrug. She was worn out with it all. "I'll do the best I can. Thank you, Luther."

Weak sunshine seeped into the kitchen. Garnet alternated between cooking David's favorite foods and pacifying Ruben, tired and fussy from his day with Lorena. She'd put him to bed right after supper; it would be best not to have any interruptions when she talked to David. But time dragged for both her and the baby.

Well after dark she heard Maggie and saw David light the lamp in the horse's shed. It seemed like he was taking an awfully long time, but she was nerved up and anxious. She could stand it no longer, and the food was cooling, so she called from the stoop, "David, I've got supper ready."

She could see him move to his cart. "Be right there," he replied.

Standing at the stove to slice the meat, she heard him wash his hands behind her and sit heavily in his chair. "Tiring day?" she asked, trying to sound sympathetic. She must try. She must keep trying.

He grunted and started spooning food onto his plate. He looked drawn and pale, and his eyes were red-rimmed and watery. Chattering away, she told him what she'd bought and who she'd seen, leaving out Clifford of course. David wasn't eating much. Neither was she, and she regretted the effort she'd expended on the meal.

"And I can't tell you how many people commented on the work you did at the bank. Everyone's praising you."

A wan smile flitted across his face, but he looked ill. Head down, he kept chewing and chewing the same mouthful of food. Although she'd planned to talk to him after dinner, his silence unnerved her and she jumped ahead. "I have something important to tell you, David, an idea I think you might like. "

He nodded, but she wondered if he'd heard her. He hadn't spoken one word since he'd come in the house. Ruben was whining on her lap, and his were the only replies she was getting. She asked, "Are you coming down with something? You look peaked."

Abruptly he scraped his chair back and mumbled, "I need to go outside."

He'd eaten little, hadn't even drunk his tea. Maybe he had some kind of griping in his belly. Idly Garnet mashed a piece of canned peach with her fork, giving Ruben a taste of the sweet pulp. Lorena had said today that he was nearly ready to be weaned; maybe she should start giving him real food. At first the baby crinkled his nose; then he opened his mouth for more.

David didn't return. She heated water and started the dishes. As she scrubbed, she looked through the window and saw that he'd lit a lamp in his workshop. He certainly was behaving oddly. When the kitchen was tidy, she got Ruben ready for bed. It was early, but he seemed so delighted to snuggle into his bed that Garnet yawned in sympathy. She was tired too. Maybe she shouldn't present her plan tonight, especially if David was feeling poorly.

She'd just gone back into the kitchen to wash out diapers when David came in and sat at the table again. Without turning from the sink, she asked, "Are you all right? I set food on the back of the stove in case you wanted more."

"No," he replied, his voice dead and slow. "What did you want to tell me?"

She was surprised that he remembered. Rinsing the diapers in a bucket of clean water, she squeezed them into a ball. Beginning brightly, she said, "Well, I told you how everybody is praising your work."

He grunted.

She still had her back to him. It was easier to start this without facing him. "And I'd forgotten all about my inheritance from Grandpa that I came into when I turned eighteen. Anyway, it's a hundred dollars, and I was thinking we could use that money to buy a house close to Ashton. There's so much building going on in town, I bet you'd stay ever so busy. I know you've rented out this house, but we could ask around and maybe there'd be some place we could buy, and it would be ours, our very own house."

Summoning up her courage, she turned to face him with her widest, most encouraging smile. His face was still pallid and eyes red-rimmed, but they had that glassy look she recognized. He was drunk. As shivers crawled over her scalp, a realization stabbed her brain: he knew that Flora had married today. Of course he'd known. And he'd been grieving into a whiskey bottle over it.

She babbled on, trying to sound cheerful and encouraging despite her sinking feeling. Why hadn't she noticed before she started? He'd never drunk at home, but he must've, maybe out in his workshop. She jabbered, "It frustrates you no end when you don't have plenty to do; you're a hard worker, David, and I thought a house closer to town would make it easier for people to give you work."

"What the hell are you talking about? We're moving to Covington."

She twisted her fingers in her skirt. "But David, I really don't want to move," she faltered. "My family, friends. . . ." Her voice trailed off.

"We're going. Don't you buck me on this." His hands folded into fists.

She knew she should just shut up, but she'd gone too far to turn back. "But it's a good plan. We'd have our own place, not be dependent upon anybody. And we know people here; you've built a good working reputation." She pressed so hard against the sink that it dug into her back.

"You're the one dependent on people. Up north we'd be free of your family and friends." He said the last words in a cruel mockery of her voice. "Who thought this up, your old man? I reckon you saw him today, didn't you? Did he give you that hundred dollars? You don't come cheap, do you?" He didn't move, but she saw violence rising in him.

"No, this is my idea. I did see Mr. Clark today but only to get my money. It was strictly business." She tried to keep her voice steady, crooning to him like she would a crazed and dangerous animal.

He slammed his fist on the table. "I knew it!" His words were slurred now. "Can't even let you go to town without you sneaking off to see that son of a bitch. And you wonder why I want to move us up north? You're a sneak and a whore. Reckon you learned it from your beloved Lorena." He mumbled something about her being no better than his whoring mother.

She fought to control her voice. "No, David. I saw him on business and told him I never wanted to receive another letter or visit or anything from him, that he was making trouble and should leave me alone." Tears were coming up in her eyes, and she hated them, dashing them away with her fist.

"And then you two snuck off somewheres, didn't you? You don't want it from me, but you'll open up for him, won't you? So, that's what gets you hot, huh? Rich old jackasses with big words? Or is it the money he gives you? He ain't man enough to give you nothing else," he sneered, his eyes evil slits. His venom flew all over her, escalating her hurt feelings to boiling, seething rage. She hated him, truly hated him.

"How can you call me a whore when you've been running to Flora for months? I guess we might as well move," she retorted, her anger matching his in scorching waves. "Nothing left for you around here with your easy woman married off, is there? Guess you'll have to find you a slut in Covington, won't you? Because I'll not go with you. Did you hear me? I'm not going."

As soon as she said it she knew she'd made a deadly mistake. Her hand rose to her lips as if she could snatch her words and stuff them back, but it was too late. With a roar he was out of the chair. "Please, David," she begged. "Please don't hurt me."

She tried to move toward the front room but had only advanced a step or two before he grabbed her and clenched his hands around her neck, squeezing with his thumbs and shaking her, gripping and jerking until her brains felt scrambled. "Oh yes, you will. You ain't deserting me like my mother done my pa." His fingers dug into her throat, deeper and deeper. She tried to cough, to get more air, but she couldn't.

"And don't you dare talk bad about Flora! Worst mistake I ever made was marrying you instead of her. And now she's gone, you bitch, she's gone!" He kept throttling her, cutting off most of her air. His face was red, contorted with fury, but despite the incessant shaking, she could see tears running down his cheeks, distorting his already thick voice.

She struggled, kicking at him and tugging at his arms to free herself, digging into his iron arms with her fingernails. So little air was going down her windpipe that her screams were mere gurgles. Trying to twist away caused even more pressure on her neck. He continued to sob and yell abuse at her, calling her names she'd never heard, but the sounds faded in her efforts to free herself. His face faded too, turning dark around the edges as she struggled to breathe. She was going to die. Lorena was right; David was going to kill her. With effort she jammed both her hands up under his forearms and succeeded in breaking his hold. Gasping for air, she turned dizzily to run for the next room, setting off in a burst, but he caught hold of her left wrist and jerked her back toward him. Garnet almost heard it snap; she certainly felt it. The wrenching tumbled her to her knees, and excruciating pain sent waves of nausea and faintness through her. The room turned gray, and still he screamed that she wasn't hurt, that she'd do what he said, that she wasn't going to desert him. Again and again he said, "Damn you, Garnet. Damn you," sobbing as he cursed her.

He dropped her arm, and it flopped against her side, flashing fresh currents of agony. She couldn't breathe for the pain. Maybe he was done now, she thought. Maybe he'd leave and she could run. Maybe he'd kill her. He'd quit shouting; all she heard were his ragged sobs. She didn't move, couldn't move, from her knees in front of him. Then with a last roar, he kicked her in the back, and her head connected with the warm black iron of the stove. White lights exploded in her head, and the fire in her arm bubbled over as her body crumpled on top of it.

***

She had no idea how long she was unconscious, but when she came to herself, she had enough sense to see that she was alone in the kitchen. Cautiously she used her right arm to raise herself until she could lean against the stove. She glanced down at her watch, her vision blurred and dancing. It was only eight thirty so she must not have fainted for long. She heard nothing but a roaring cadence that kept time with the throbbing pains in her neck, head, and arm. Raising her hand to touch the wound on her forehead, she found a hard, pulsing lump dripping blood that caught at her eyebrow. Swallowing hurt like the dickens, and she was sure her arm was broken. He'd done quite a job this time.

Outside she heard something, maybe a shifting sound from Maggie or the wind kicking up, but it panicked her. She must get out of the house. Gripping the stove, she lifted herself, whimpering as she did it. She reached for the sink and leaned against it, using one of the clean, wet diapers to wipe the blood dripping into her eye. Squinting to clear her vision, she looked toward the workshop. It was dark. Could he have passed out in bed or run off to Hayse? He obviously had liquor here, and there was no Flora up there to comfort him. More than likely he'd stay home. She inched along, using walls and furniture to support her. Her left arm dangled at her side, shooting out explosions of pain. She crept into the front room, her breathing noisy. She managed to get to the bedroom doorway and peered into the dark room. There he was, lying on the bed fully clothed with his back to her. Was he asleep or waiting to attack her again? She moved as quietly as she could. If she could somehow gather up Ruben and get out the door, she'd go to Lorena.

David didn't move, but she feared every creak in the floor. Slowly, slowly she staggered toward the baby's room. She wasn't sure she could lift him with one arm. It was chilly outside and damp, but she was afraid to get her coat. Moving to the baby's bed she steeled herself against the noise he'd make when she disturbed him. Clumsily she reached over the railing and tried to lift him with her good arm. Limp with sleep, he was dead weight, but on her first try she turned him onto his stomach and wrapped his blankets around him. Her left arm was throbbing and screaming, but suddenly she had a coherent thought. With her right hand she unbuttoned two or three buttons above the waist of her dress and tucked her left arm between the dress and her underclothes. Her waistband supported it and eased the pain a little. Then she listened, holding her breath. All was quiet.

Maneuvering her right hand under Ruben's soft tummy she hoisted him like a sack of flour. He only grunted a little as she held him close and tiptoed toward the light in the front room. She skittered clumsily to the back door. He would be less likely to hear her if she went out the back. She was having trouble seeing;; some things were doubled and others were sickeningly blurry. It made it hard to walk straight, but she managed to open the door and step onto the back stoop.

The cold air revived her for a moment. For a second she worried about leaving lamps burning but ignored them. It would serve her drunken husband right if the house burned down around him. She shifted Ruben onto her shoulder as best she could and, shivering, staggered down the road. The sky was gray with night clouds, offering her little light. She hobbled, out of breath and whimpering. At one point pain darkened everything again, and she feared she might have to drop down in the road. Doubting whether she could ever get up again, she gritted her teeth.

Garnet hadn't gone far when she heard a noise. Whether it was her own sluggish feet dislodging pebbles, an animal moving through the bushes, or David following her, she didn't know, but she sped up a step or two and stumbled, causing Ruben's leg to bang against her broken arm. Again the sickening waves came, threatening to drop her, and she vomited, barely able to bow her head. Sickness splashed onto her dress, but she started moving again, a step at a time. By the time she reached the store, Ruben was whining, awake now and not happy about it. Garnet considered stopping there; Mattie had a light on, but she pushed on, weaving toward the safety of the farm. "Hush, baby," she murmured to Ruben. She tried to shift him to her hip, but then his leg rested on her tucked left arm. There was no comfort.

The only warmth came from Ruben. Shivering from cold and pain, she clenched her teeth to keep them from chattering. She counted her steps, each one so halting and agonizing that she wondered if it would take her all night to get to Lorena. In shifting Ruben around, his blanket had loosened and flapped free. He'd be cold too.

She passed the darkened school and thought how many times she'd walked this direction thinking nothing of the distance, an easy stroll. When she and David were courting, it was much too short. Tonight it seemed insurmountable. From her hairline, blood trickled again, catching briefly in her eyebrow and then oozing into her eye. Although this was nothing compared to her other aches and pains, it annoyed her that she couldn't wipe the blood away. Her right arm ached with the strain of holding Ruben who thrashed around and whimpered. She lifted him higher on her shoulder where he couldn't kick her arm, and he calmed down, grasping her coiled braids.

Twice more she was certain she heard something, and once she even stepped off the road to hide behind some pine trees, but the effort exhausted her, and she surrendered to the thought that if he murdered her in the road, that was what was meant to be. She prayed. At first she asked Jesus to save her, to forgive her for having impure thoughts about Clifford and get her to safety for the baby's sake. But her mind wandered, and she whispered to Ruben that Grandpa would take care of them if she could just get to him. Grandpa had a gun. And so she repeated this every few agonized, faltering steps: Grandpa's got a gun, Grandpa's got a gun. At last she turned up the lane to the farm.

Ruben was crying again, but she couldn't do anything but put one unreliable foot in front of the other. Behind his sobs, she heard a harsh rasping sound and recognized it as her own breathing. She saw the house. She'd closed her left eye to keep blood from dripping into it, but with the other she saw blessed lamplight pouring golden from the windows. Another few steps and she'd make it. She climbed one and then another. There were three of them, she remembered. She had no way to knock. Raising her foot she kicked at the door but needn't have made the effort. Ruben was screaming by then.

Garnet saw the door fly open, but it wasn't Grandpa. Standing in the warm pool of light were Lorena, and strangely enough, Lowell. The woman's mouth and eyes shot open and she exclaimed, "Jesus God, get the baby, Lowell!" Garnet crumpled then, folding up on the front porch and murmuring that Grandpa should get his gun.

Chapter Nineteen

They poured her onto the front room sofa, and she vaguely heard Lorena tell Lowell to fetch Luther and tell Mama what had happened. At the same time the woman crooned to Ruben, she used a warm cloth to wipe blood from Garnet's face. Then it was quiet, and there was a quilt around her even though she protested, mumbling that she'd been sick on her dress. At some point Lorena held a cup of sweet tea to her lips and begged her to sip. It hurt to swallow, and she nearly spilled it when she heard a noise.

"It's only Luther and Lowell, honey," Lorena soothed. "You're safe now."

She had trouble finding her voice, buried deep in her damaged throat. "He'll come after me. He means to kill me."

She didn't hear Lorena's reply, but Luther knelt beside her, taking her cold right hand in his. "I'm going to pick you up, Garnet, and get you upstairs. Can you put your good arm around my neck?"

And so she floated up the stairs, or at least it felt like floating. Luther tried not to jostle her arm as he set her upon the bed in the sewing room. Everything was dim and foggy. She heard Lowell saying, "Let me. I'll go fetch the doctor so you can keep David out. I'll go." But they must not have let him because from the fog she heard Lorena ask him to fix Ruben a bed and Luther tell his sister to get Garnet out of her dress or the doctor would have to cut off the sleeve. She felt Lorena unbuttoning her dress and easing her left arm to the side. Although the woman worked as gently as she could, Garnet screamed and her eyes overflowed with tears.

"Lord, I'm sorry to cause you any more pain, but I have to get you out of this dress," Lorena fretted. "Can you stand for a minute so I can slip it over your hips? Lowell, let the fire wait a minute and come hold your sister up."

Her little brother was as tall as she now. He stood on her right side, holding her arm and shoulder, and Lorena moved swiftly and carefully to pull the dress into a puddle at her feet. "My Lord," Lowell breathed.

They were both staring at her, and she had to pull against Lowell's support to sit on the bed. She shivered. "Get my shawl, Lowell. It's on the chair in my bedroom," Lorena said.

Garnet looked up at Lorena's eyes, dark with glittering anger. "He like to killed you, honey. Your throat's a ring of bruises. That son of a bitch should be in jail."

Lowell ran in with the shawl and wrapped it around Garnet's shoulders. "Lay back," he told her. "It'll be a while before Luther gets the doctor."

She shook her head just the tiniest bit, and even that intensified the throbbing. "Prop some pillows," she whispered. They did and spread a quilt over her. This was better. For a moment she relaxed, listening to Lowell coaxing the fire. Then she tensed. "Where's my baby?"

"He's fine. I put him in the middle of Lorena's bed with pillows on either side so he won't fall out. He went right to sleep," Lowell assured her.

This eased her for a while, but then she raised her head off the pillow again and croaked, "Where's Lorena?"

"Right here," said the woman, coming through the door. "I brought your tea, thought maybe you could get another sip down. Lowell, you'd best be heading home."

Garnet saw him shake his head, standing straight and reminding her of Papa. "I'll not leave until Luther gets back."

Lorena placed something dark on the cutting table and brought the cup to Garnet who managed a painful sip. "Luther knew, didn't he?" Lorena asked Lowell. "Thank God he told you to come over here. And I was about to send you home."

Garnet didn't understand. "What?"

"Oh, Luther was afraid you'd have trouble, wanted to sit outside your house and watch, but I said that might really rile David. So he reckoned you'd come to the farm if you needed help and sent Lowell over here to fetch him just in case. Louise don't know nothing about all this," Lorena explained.

"She will now."

Lowell said, "I told her you were bad hurt, and Luther had to get the doctor."

Garnet shut her eyes. The bump on her head was pounding again, worse than ever, and it made her eyes hurt. "What's on the table?"

"It's the little derringer Deke give me when we married. I don't think for a minute I'll need it, but it's there in case I do. That wicked husband of yours is probably sleeping it off, damn him. I reckon he was drunk?"

Garnet managed a tiny nod and rested until loud noises shocked her out of a half-sleep, her heart pounding in panic all over again. But Lorena was on one side of the bed, and Lowell stood by the other. "It's Luther and the doctor, Garnet. Hush, now," Lorena murmured.

As Garnet remembered from when he'd tended Lowell, Dr. Thomas did nothing quietly. He filled the room, brushing everyone aside. "Who did this to her?"

"Her husband," Luther replied.

The doctor made a disgusted noise. "I hope you tell the sheriff. This is attempted murder and I'll testify to it."

He examined her head, making her wince, and then addressed her neck and throat, shaking his head in disbelief. "Are there any other injuries besides your arm?"

She whispered, "He kicked me in the back, but it doesn't hurt."

"Hmm," he sniffed. "Everything else hurts too much for you to notice, I'll wager. When I come back tomorrow I'll look at that. As for now, you have a concussion from the blow on the head. Is your vision blurred?"

"It was at first. Not now." Every hoarse, garbled word hurt.

"Cold cloths for that, Mrs. King. And I'll tell you how to make poultices for her neck. No solid food until that throat heals; it's grossly inflamed. Don't talk unless you have to, hear me?"

She nodded. Then he took a deep breath. "Now we have to set this broken bone. I'll need her flat with you at her shoulder, Mr. Colson, and you at her elbow, Mrs. King. Young man, it would be charitable if you let her squeeze your hand. This will hurt."

She screamed, and it hurt to scream and shamed her, but she couldn't help it. Afterwards he poured syrupy liquid down her throat and told Luther he'd be back the next day. "Oh, and get that wedding ring off," he said to Lorena. "She's going to swell, and if you don't remove it, we'll have to cut it off."

"Gladly," Lorena growled.

Once the agony of setting her arm receded, it hardly hurt at all. They'd splinted it to some thin boards, padded with batting and tied all around with long muslin strips. At first she noticed all the details, but then a warm, foreign fuzziness seized her and at last she felt comfortable enough to stop noticing anything.

At one point her mind rose out of the muffled blur, and she awoke. The room was dark except for the low light of the fire. Blinking, she saw Lorena in the rocking chair by the fire with the gun glinting in her lap. Garnet's arm was hurting again, a different kind of pain this time, and she croaked, "Lorena." The woman jumped up and set the pistol on the table. "Feels tight," Garnet croaked.

"Oh, you're swelling bad now. Let me loosen them bandages." Lorena set to work, and there was immediate relief.

"Thirsty."

Lorena gave her water and made her drink more of the medicine that was both bitter and sweet. "There," she murmured. "You'll soon be off to sleep again, and that's the best thing for you. It's still an hour or two before daylight."

With her good hand, Garnet pulled at the quilt. "What will I do now?"

"Right now we'll get you healed up. We won't think about nothing beyond that."

Lorena put a fresh cloth on her forehead and gently brushed her hair back from her face. The medicine warmed Garnet's stomach and brought waves of drowsiness. Just as she was falling asleep, though, she murmured to Lorena, "He said he should've married Flora." But she was asleep before she heard the woman's reply.

The next time she awoke it was daylight but dim with rain splattering against the window. At first she wasn't sure what had awakened her; everything ached, but if she didn't move, nothing hurt too badly. The medicine made her thoughts fuzzy, but all at once she jerked alert. From downstairs she heard David's voice.

"Hello, little rascal," he said. "Papa's come to take you home."

Lorena said something, but Garnet couldn't hear it. Was Luther here? David would flick Lorena away like a mosquito if she didn't have the gun. Panicked, she tried to raise herself but felt weak as a newborn.

David's voice, hearty and concerned, carried up the stairwell. "Well, she did take a fall, but she wouldn't let me help her. I don't know why she came down here."

This time Garnet could hear Lorena. "That weren't no fall and you know it. You beat her half to death and broke her arm. She ain't going nowhere."

Then Garnet heard Luther's slow drawl and exhaled. Would she ever feel safe again? She heard Ruben whining, probably wanting to be nursed, and she tried again to sit up. Her petticoat was twisted up beneath her, but she managed to raise her hips enough to prop against the headboard. Lorena's light footsteps flew up the stairs followed by the louder clumping of the two men. Lorena deposited Ruben by Garnet's right side and stood by the cutting table.

"I'm sorry to bother you, Garnet, but I wanted your husband to see his handiwork," Luther said. David came in, his cap and jacket drenched with rain, and glanced at Lorena whose right hand rested not two inches from the gun. Then he gazed at Luther who held up his hand to halt him just inside the doorway. "You don't need to get no closer."

David's eyes settled on Garnet. She took wicked pleasure in seeing his shock. Since he was already the color of buttermilk, he didn't turn pale, but his eyes widened and he stuffed his hands in his pockets. He stammered, "I told them you fell but wouldn't let me help you."

Her head throbbed, but she turned it toward the window so he could get a better view of the bruises wreathing her neck. Luther said, "So you're not only a bully and a drunk, you're a liar."

"Tell them, Garnet," David pleaded. "You fell, didn't you?"

Ignoring him, she cradled Ruben. He was pawing at her breast, and she started to leak through her camisole.

"Doctor Thomas said it looked like attempted murder to him," Luther said.

David stood rooted to the floor, but he pulled his hands out of his pockets and rubbed them down the sides of his pants. His face was shiny and sickly. "I reckon you better stay here and heal up."

"I reckon so," said Luther. "And she'd better be able to do it in peace."

Lorena spat, "She needs hers and Ruben's things. She was so hurt and scared she didn't even wear a coat when she ran away. Somebody'll be up to get them directly."

David backed up as Luther walked toward him, and in a flash he rushed down the steps and was out the door with Luther standing in the upstairs hall watching him. Lorena helped Garnet to hold Ruben so he could nurse. Weak tears dripped onto her bare chest.

"You're safe, honey. Don't fret. Just relax and feed that boy, and I'll bring you some breakfast here in a minute. We ain't going to let him hurt you ever again."

By mid-morning Luther brought her trunk with everything he'd been able to find. He'd even folded up the quilt she was piecing and searched in the kitchen cabinet for her grandmother's compote. In the sewing room Lorena emptied drawers and shook out dresses as Garnet spooned dabs of boiled custard down her raw throat. "Just as soon as I get this stuff put away, we'll wash you up, put you in a fresh nightgown, and brush out your hair. You do look a sight, but I'm glad that sorry husband of yours saw you like this. He just breezed in and informed us that he was here to take you and the baby home."

It worked best to let the custard slide down without even attempting to swallow it. She wasn't hungry at all, but Lorena had made the custard as well as cooking dinner for Luther and two laborers, watching Ruben, and running upstairs to check on Garnet every little bit. The least she could do was eat it. "I'm trouble for you," she whispered.

"Hush, you're not supposed to talk." Lorena unfolded a nightgown and threw it across the end of the bed. "Most times it's too quiet here; I like having work to do." She dipped into the trunk again and came up with a stack of diapers. "I'm happy to have these," she declared. "I've been pinning tea towels around that son of yours, and they don't work too good. Thank God Luther notices things. He even brought me the wet ones balled up in the sink."

"One's bloody."

"I noticed, honey. I'll get the blood out. Now, have you finished? Good. I've got some chicken broth simmering, and you can have some of that once we get you cleaned up. You'll feel better after you wash."

Late in the afternoon Garnet felt feverish, but when Dr. Thomas came, he said they shouldn't worry about it. He insisted upon looking at the place on her back where David kicked her and pronounced that it wasn't serious. All in all, he said, she was a lucky girl. She wanted to smile at the man, but her lips wouldn't do much more than twitch. As he was packing his bag, Lorena came into the room with a fussy Ruben on her hip. "This little boy is hungry," she announced.

Dr. Thomas frowned. "Do you have a cow, Mrs. King?"

"Yes, sir. I put top milk in this girl's custard."

"How old is the baby?"

Garnet whispered, "Ten months."

"Don't talk," he thundered. "Wean him. You're feverish and debilitated from your injuries, and that baby's stronger than you are. Wean him. Come downstairs with me, Mrs. King, and I'll tell you what you can start him on."

Lorena held Ruben like she didn't know what to do with him. "Not right this minute, Lorena," Garnet murmured, reaching for him.

"Don't talk!" The doctor left the room with Lorena following him meekly.

But she had to talk thirty minutes later when the Sheriff came and asked her what happened. Standing in the doorway, he peered at her neck, arm, and head. Luther stood by her bed and said that he thought it made sense to let the law know what David had done. She didn't see how it would matter. David would just leave town.

Dr. Thomas had left more of the medicine, laudanum, he called it, but she quit taking it during the day because it muddied her thoughts and made her feel stupid. Lorena told her not to think, just to concentrate on getting well, but she couldn't stop the images that swirled through her head. She supposed she'd live at the farm for the time being, and David would go on up north. The doctor had said it would be six to eight weeks before her arm healed, so he'd have to leave without her if it was going to take that long.

Late the next afternoon Lowell stuck his dark head through the door and brought her two books and a bunch of buttercups. "I know you're not much of a reader," he said. "But you can't sew or garden or cook so I thought you might want something to do."

"Thoughtful," she murmured. Her voice seemed stronger. "Flowers?"

Lowell shrugged. "They're from Mama. Even though I told her Lorena said she could come visit, she's not about to, and she knows better than to cook you something." Garnet managed a smile. "Luther told her what happened, and she like to had a fit." He mimicked his mother perfectly: "'I told that girl she shouldn't marry common trash, but would she listen to me?' Anyway, she picked some of the buttercups you planted and had me bring them."

After he left, she sat, feverish and a little weepy about how kind people were, even Mama. She could make a life here with Ruben, if David would let her. After she healed she'd ask Mattie Lawrence if she could work for her again; Lorena loved having Ruben around and would watch him. Along with her hundred dollars, this would help to pay her way. She hated to be beholden to people, but she doubted that David would send her money, even for Ruben.

The lowering sun slanted through the window. Soon Luther would come up to say good-bye before he left for home, and Lorena would bring her supper. Garnet felt awful that the woman had to trudge upstairs with trays, but Dr. Thomas had decreed that Garnet must stay in bed for at least a week. She amused herself by trying to figure out what Lorena was doing by listening to the sounds floating up the steps. Right now she was banging pots and chattering to Ruben, but then Garnet heard a horse and tensed. Had David come back?

Whoever it was came to the back door, and she could hear both Luther and Lorena talking to him. It was definitely a man's voice. She fretted until Lorena appeared.

"Clifford Clark's down there and wants to see you. He come by to tell Luther about a house near Ashton that's up for sale, but we said them plans of yours are out the window now. He got real upset when Luther told him what David done and begged me to let him visit. Do you want to see him?"

Garnet nodded, not attempting to hide her eagerness. "The shawl," she whispered, and Lorena draped it around her shoulders to hide her nightgown. Garnet pulled the quilt up to her waist.

"Mr. Clark," Lorena called as she went downstairs, "she can see you, but she's not supposed to talk and I'll have her supper ready soon."

She heard his steps, different from those of the other men. He stopped in the doorway and shut his eyes, whispering, "Good Lord, Garnet, I was so afraid of this."

He stood awkwardly, his big hands twitching. She gestured at the straight chair by the sewing machine, and he whisked it next to the bed. The chair was too small for him. Shaking his head, he took his time looking at her arm and the wound on her forehead. When she shifted the shawl away from her throat, his eyes glistened. "Why, he nearly choked you to death."

She could tell he wanted her hand, but the left one was bound up and it was too far for him to reach across for the right one, so he fidgeted, touching the edge of the bed and the buttercups on the table. "I know I'm breaking my promise to you, but I had no idea you were here. I came to tell Luther about a house that's for sale."

She waved her right hand. "So much for my plan," she whispered.

"Oh, your throat, your poor throat. Lorena said that you mustn't talk. I'll talk for you. Think how handicapped I'd be if a doctor said I wasn't allowed to speak." He smiled nervously. "But you're safe here. Perhaps he'll leave the county right away. Luther said he threatened to bring charges against him. You should, you know. Oh," he paused, seeing her expression, "I know you're in no condition to endure that right now, but truly your husband should be locked up." His mouth looked hard.

"If he'll just leave."

"Of course, of course. But he'll continue to behave like this, to another woman if not you. He's a menace, a brute. I... I... ." He broke off and shifted, clenching his hands into a bony knot. "I've never wanted to kill someone before, but I swear before God it's a temptation."

She didn't reply, not so much because of the doctor's decree but because she didn't know what to say. Bringing her right hand across her body, she stretched it out to him, fingers splayed, and he clutched it like a drowning man grabbing a rope. "Oh, dear heart, what can I do for you? Do you need anything, anything at all? I must be able to help in some way. Shall I stay here and make sure he doesn't bother you? Please let me do something," he begged. David would've scoffed and called Clifford a sissy for the tears swimming in his eyes. But David had cried too, hadn't he?

"He said he should have married Flora," she murmured. "While he was choking me he was crying."

Clifford rubbed at his eyes and didn't seem one bit embarrassed. From downstairs there was the sharp sound of the front door opening so hard it banged against the wall and then feet pounding up the steps. Lorena was hollering, but the person rushing up the steps paid her no heed. "I knowed it! I've said it all along. And there's his buggy sitting in front of the house to prove it." David burst into the room, red-faced but with satisfaction lighting his eyes.

Garnet withdrew her hand and gasped, drawing her body up tight. Clifford stood, shielding her from her husband so she could barely see him. David noticed and moved to the end of the bed; he wanted her to see him. "You've been caught now, you sneaking little whore!" he hissed. "This is one more proof to add to the list."

What list? She was safe; she knew she was safe, but would she ever get over this dreadful clutching in her belly when she saw him? Lorena's quick, light steps flew up the stairs followed closely by Luther's heavier ones. The woman held Ruben who, unlike everyone else, seemed happy to see his father and held out his little hands. "The last thing Garnet needs right now is more abuse, Foster," Clifford said. "Why are you here?"

David had their attention and was enjoying it. Taking his time, he peered at everyone crowded into the small room and then focused on Garnet. "Oh, we're all worried about little Garnet, aren't we? She's got you all fooled, except for Clark here who knows she's not the pure little miss she pretends to be. Can't you do no better, Clark? What makes you think she's not giving it to a whole mess of other men?"

David wants Clifford to punch him, Garnet thought. Clifford looked like he might do it except that Luther stepped between them. "This is stupid talk, Foster. What do you want with Garnet?"

"What I wanted from Garnet I never got." An ugly smile stretched his narrow lips. "And I'm surprised you did, Clark. Reckon the little bitch only gives it to rich men, like her mama wanted her to."

"Damn you to hell, David," Lorena swore.

"Spoken by the biggest whore in the county," he retorted.

A sob escaped from Garnet's ravaged throat and made the men step closer to David. Unfazed, he drawled, "Well, I came to let Garnet know that I've filed for divorce on grounds of adultery. It's all on this here paper. The judge can hear the case in three weeks, and then we'll see what the county thinks about perfect little Garnet." He pulled a paper from his pocket and flung it on the bed.

"But I never!"

"Guess you'll be the only one who'll have her then, Clark. Are you sure you want a woman who'd betray her husband?"

Both Luther and Clifford inched closer to him, but David held up his hand. "Don't get no ideas. I'm the injured party here." He stepped toward the doorway where Lorena stood with the baby. She moved aside so he wouldn't brush against her. "Oh, and one more thing," David said over his shoulder. "I'm asking for custody of my boy. Don't want him raised by a whore. He bared his teeth in a malignant smile as he left.

She cried. It seemed like she cried for weeks. Luther contacted Mr. Pierce and when he came to hear her story, she cried. She cried when Lorena made her two simple blouses that she could wear over her splint. Clifford stopped by a time or two bringing expensive fruit from town, but Garnet wouldn't see him, crying that she'd ruined his life too. Mostly she cried over Ruben, baptizing his soft curls with tears at the thought of losing him. She knew Lorena despaired that she'd ever be herself again. Tirelessly the woman cooked special treats for her, gave her little tasks she could do with one hand, and alternately comforted and scolded her in an attempt to stem all those tears.

On the day of the divorce proceedings, Lorena stuffed half a dozen handkerchiefs in the bindings around her broken arm and told her to be strong. The previous day both she and Luther had warned that despite their best efforts, things would probably go David's way. Luther had discovered that Hayse Simpson spent most of his time bootlegging from area stills and trips to wet counties. And the judge for their case, Merrill Stephens, was the money behind Hayse's operation as well as a regular patron at the Simpson farm. They were all in cahoots, Luther said.

It went the way they predicted. Although Mr. Pierce argued that David had abused Garnet and was given to drunkenness, David's citified lawyer listed damning evidence against her. There was an affidavit from Viola Williams about the vast quantity of letters Garnet received from Clifford. When Garnet protested that they were innocent and described the clippings, Judge Stephens asked her to produce them and cleared his throat when she said she'd burned them. Mr. Pierce objected that the so-called evidence from the postmistress was inadmissible and even illegal, but the judge ignored him. There was a sworn statement from Hayse Simpson saying there were nights when the Foster house remained unlit while David was working in Ashton. Garnet declared she was at the farm, but the judge waved his hand like she was a pesky fly. Then David testified that he'd caught Garnet with Clark several times and stated that she was hiding money from him, supposedly from an inheritance. It was all trumped up nonsense but sounded much more compelling than Garnet's clear and simple denials. She tried not to think of the people sitting behind her in the courtroom; Luther was there, but others were relishing the drama, savoring the scandal.

The judge concluded it quickly, saying that Mrs. Garnet Foster had filed a complaint with the sheriff about physical injuries caused by her husband and that he had no doubt Mr. David Foster was guilty of these abuses. However, he went on, in light of Mrs. Foster's behavior, he could certainly understand her husband's motives. He declared the marriage dissolved and gave custody of the infant child to his father. When the judge asked if David had made provisions for the baby, Garnet felt a small measure of relief at learning Ruben would be living with David's Aunt Martha. And the judge told David firmly that he was to cause no more injury to his divorced wife and would be better off leaving the county.

She held up fairly well until the end when, once again, she cried, pulling out the handkerchiefs. When David walked over to her, he did, at least, have the grace to look sober rather than triumphant. "I'll come after Ruben in a week. Aunt Martha's looking forward to having him, and I'll stay a while to get him settled."

Head down, she nodded, unable to look at him. He hesitated, his bulky shadow lingering across the scarred table like he wanted to say something else, but Luther murmured, "You'd best go."

Garnet, however, whispered that he should wait and dipped into her pocket, pulling out her wedding ring and shoving it across the table. It glinted there, shiny and barely worn, until David picked it up.

Certainly she cried that day, but even worse was the day when David collected Ruben. Only the week before, the baby had taken his first steps, and he wobbled across the front room to greet his father. From the sofa Garnet watched David exclaim over his son's feat and then lift him up into a hug. Lorena and Luther sat faithfully on either side of her, but there was nothing they could do. Her face was shiny with tears when she handed David an envelope. "This is what he's been eating, what he likes. He always wants a cover at night even if it's warm. Thunder scares him. I thought you might give it to your aunt." Although her voice had healed, her words were as choked as when she was injured.

From the high perch of his father's arms, Ruben crowed joyfully. David took the envelope and handed the baby to her one last time. With one arm she clutched the child to her chest and laid her cheek on his head. Giving way to sobs, she struggled to speak in a breathless, contorted voice. "I don't know why you hate me so much; I tried my best to be a good wife, and I swear on Papa's grave I never committed adultery. But I beg you, David, if you ever cared about me at all, don't let this child grow up thinking his mother doesn't love him. Please don't make him hate me."

David took Ruben from her. "I promise," he said. His eyes were the open clear gray she remembered from when she thought he loved her. Blinded by her tears, she wasn't sure, but she thought she saw a flicker of remorse in them. Or maybe it was pity. They left, and she watched from the window, clutching Lorena's lace curtain until it crimped. She sobbed until she thought her stomach would rise up in her throat, but after that day, like flooded land swept by a strong, icy wind, the tears dried up, leaving her seared and barren.

PART THREE

Chapter One

June 1909

Two months later, Garnet sat on the front porch at the farm smelling the lilies blooming below her. She wore her gray skirt and thin, lovely blouse that her mother had intended for such purposes. It struck her as odd that she sat waiting for a gentleman caller just as her mother had done on this same porch more than twenty years ago.

It'd taken all of Lorena's cajoling and fussing to make this happen. After David took Ruben, Garnet turned solemn and solitary, trying not to cause trouble and doing her best to help around the farm once Dr. Thomas decreed her arm was healed. More hands were working, so she helped Lorena prepare mountains of food for their midday meal. She spent hours in the garden trying to save Lorena work but also seeking solace in the dirt.

Worst were the days when her grief for Ruben nearly paralyzed her. She'd sent countless letters to David's Aunt Martha, hoping the woman would tell her how Ruben fared. It'd become part of Lowell's routine to stop at the post office since Garnet couldn't abide looking Viola Williams' ugly face, but so far there'd been no letters.

Then there was Mama. She was appalled by the scandal but peevish that Garnet hadn't moved back home. Luther'd said that Garnet needed to talk to her mother. It hadn't gone well. Mama was alternately horrified that her daughter had been branded an adulteress and incensed because "that common boy" made off with their child. And living with Lorena, Mama had declared, wasn't doing much to polish Garnet's tarnished reputation. Nothing Garnet said changed her mind.

The first Sunday after the splint came off, Garnet had gone to church. She'd been naïve enough to think everything would be the same, but no one spoke to her. Mrs. Bledsoe looked at her lap, and Mattie Lawrence did no more than flicker the tiniest of smiles. Even though no one came near her, Garnet had held her head high, sung the hymns, and dropped a bit of change in the plate, knowing that everyone was watching her. She'd stayed in the church until everyone left, not wanting to be snubbed again during the socializing in the churchyard. After the congregation had dispersed, Brother Bledsoe had come back in and told her that some had wanted to shun her, but he'd refused to support it. Fiddling with his Bible, he'd mumbled that it might be best if she didn't come back. Maybe she could attend church down in Deer Creek.

That same week she'd visited Mrs. Lawrence to ask if she might work in the store again. Mrs. Lawrence had said that even though she believed Garnet was innocent, especially considering David's ungodly father and the stories she'd heard about the Simpson farm, her presence in the store would be bad for business. A new grocery was going in down the road, and she feared Bethel folks would trade there if Garnet worked for her. The woman's eyes had darted around the store, looking everywhere but at Garnet.

So Garnet had resigned herself to a new way of life. She and Lorena worked hard through the lengthening days and sat quietly in the evenings, sewing on their quilts. Sometimes Garnet read aloud to Lorena who loved Mark Twain, and sometimes there was a blistering letter from Franklin still expressing disgust about David Foster.

"It's just as well Franklin wasn't in the county while all that was going on, or he'd have gone to jail for sure," Garnet commented after the most recent one.

"Lord save us, he would've murdered David and caused more trouble for all of us," Lorena agreed. She knotted her thread and stitched on one of Luther's shirts while Garnet pieced. A steady rain pattered against the house, making her drowsy. "This rain'll be good for the garden," she murmured, stifling a yawn.

The only reply she got was the popping of Lorena's needle. Then in her usual brusque fashion the woman said, "So how long do you plan on making him wait?"

Garnet jerked up her head. "Who are you talking about?"

"You know who I mean. No one's begrudged you time to heal, and I don't mean your arm, girl, but Clifford Clark's waiting to hear whether he has a chance." Lorena bit off the end of her thread. "You're not even nineteen and sitting around every evening quilting with an old woman. Is this the way you plan to spend the rest of your life?"

Garnet was flustered. "I like it here, Lorena, but I'll go home if you want me to."

"You know that ain't what I mean," the woman said, her black eyes flashing. "I purely enjoy having you, and you know it. But what kind of a man are you going to meet here? One of the hands? Willie Martin's been sweet on you for years, and I reckon you could marry him and live in his little cabin down in the holler." She made a disgusted noise. "You're too young to give up and live like an old maid."

Garnet pulled at the fabric. "I'm not much concerned with marrying right now."

"And I don't blame you for that, but here's a man interested in you, and you was partial to him too, if I'm any kind of judge, and you're letting him hang. It ain't right."

"I'm just trouble for him. He tried to help me and got blamed for things he didn't do. People are probably talking about him and shaming him like they're doing to me."

Lorena laughed humorlessly. "I doubt it. Men don't suffer these things like we do. Nobody scorned Deke King. Why, they all said he was quite the man for carrying on with me, and then they'd curse and call me every name in the book for the same thing. Clifford Clark ain't suffered much." She paused and softened her tone. "But I allow he's suffering in other ways. Don't you think he feels just as guilty about the part he played as you do for involving him? Just think: if he'd never got mixed up in your business, David could never have accused you of adultery. I bet it's eating him up."

Garnet hadn't thought of it that way.

"You know he cares about you."

"He was my father's friend," Garnet said. "He felt a responsibility for me."

Lorena snorted. "That's a crock of shit, as Deke used to say. It might've started that way; it probably did. But the man's totally and completely pixilated with you, and I ain't sure but you're feeling the same. Are you aiming to punish yourself?"

The words sounded familiar, and she remembered that day at the bank when Clifford lost his temper, when she'd touched his face. She anchored her needle and set the quilt aside. "If we started seeing each other, the county will say David was right."

"And what do you care what the county thinks? God knows the truth of it. None of them so-called Christians is showing you any charity as it is; can it get any worse? I been there, girl, and let me tell you, you have to find your own happiness and to hell with what everybody else thinks." Lorena took her hand. "Look, maybe you don't care for the man no more, but he stood by you. When you was hurt, he brought you that fruit even though you wouldn't see him. The day after the trial he come up here and talked to Luther, said he didn't want to bother you, but he'd heard how the trial went and wanted to know how you was. Luther told him what went on in the courtroom and said Clifford stood in the barn and cried right in front of him. It only made sense for him to keep his distance while there was still a chance you might defend your name, and it was a kindness for him to let you alone until David took Ruben. But even if you don't want nothing to do with Clifford Clark, you need to tell him."

Garnet took a deep breath. "You're right; he deserves that much. I'll write him."

The problem, Garnet thought, as she sat on the porch that Sunday afternoon, was that she didn't know what to say to him. He'd answered her letter quickly, writing that he'd come on Sunday, after dinner, but that didn't mean either of them was eager to pursue a romance. It was so tangled and complicated. She wasn't sure that Clifford hadn't been merely an escape, a shelter during troubled times, much as she'd once viewed David.

She heard his buggy rattling up the lane and straightened her skirt. When he jumped out he seemed uncomfortable too, climbing the porch steps hesitantly with a basket in his hand. "Everybody welcomes the man who brings strawberries," he declared with a smile that didn't reach his eyes.

"I love strawberries." She called out to Lorena who took the basket with great approval, promising they'd have a treat later.

They both rocked with several feet of porch between them. The great talker didn't have much to say, and the creaking of their rocking chairs grew louder. He then cleared his throat and gestured toward her arm. "You're healed now, I take it."

"Oh, yes. It was a little weak at first, but now it's fine."

He squirmed, putting a finger between his collar and neck. She knew she wasn't making things easy for him but didn't know how to remedy it. Then they spoke at the same time.

"I've been so worried about you."

"I'm sorry I didn't write sooner."

Both laughed nervously. "I knew you were going through such a terrible time, and I thought I might make it worse if I came to see you. Seems like all I ever did for you was make things worse," he murmured.

"That's not true. Things were already bad; you know that."

"But I complicated the situation. So much of it was my fault. At first I was just looking out for you like your father might've done, but then . . . well, then it turned into something else, and I . . ."

"Hush," she said, but he misinterpreted this and looked miserable.

"I understand," he said. "You don't want to be reminded that my feelings changed into something more than friendship. I'm the reason you lost your son."

She shook her head. "No, I said hush about all this blaming. Luther chastises himself because he didn't do something when he first saw that David was beating me. Even worse, he blames himself for the divorce because he backed David into a corner by bringing the sheriff in. Lorena says she should've seen David for what he was and warned me, even though I don't know how she could've known. I've gone to bed every night for months blaming myself and thinking about what I might've done different, but I can't find any answers. Don't you start taking the blame too."

He sat stone still, absorbing her heated reply as if she were scolding him. She'd hurt him again, she supposed, and sighed. "Look, Clifford, I'm not saying all this hasn't been painful. I've lost my son, and I guess the whole county thinks I'm a . . . a . . . bad woman. My church doesn't want me to darken its doors, and Mrs. Lawrence says having me work for her would be bad for business. My mother is ashamed of me. But you aren't to blame. You were an easy way for David to escape trouble and get what he wanted, which was to be shed of me. He used you, and I'm awfully afraid I used you too. There wasn't much happiness in my life right then, and you were a comfort."

His eyes lit up. "I'm so glad."

She unbent a little. "Those clippings made me smile."

The lines around his mouth creased into a grin. "I hoped they would."

He was too eager, and she wasn't ready for it. Abruptly she suggested, "Let's walk. I want to see how our peaches are coming along." She called to Lorena through the door and told her they were going to visit the orchard. When she turned back she saw Clifford staring at her. He shifted his eyes, but she wasn't sure how this made her feel. "It's hot," she said, fanning herself with her hand to cover her blushes. "Why don't you leave your suit coat here?"

He obliged and she started walking, hurrying a bit to keep up with his long stride. Luther claimed to be six feet tall, but Clifford was even taller. They stopped at the garden, which he praised.

"We made it bigger this spring. Lorena hasn't been able to do much gardening since Luther married Mama, but I have plenty of time to work in it." She sighed. "It's the only way I can pay my way since Mrs. Lawrence won't let me work. Lorena paid for the doctor and the lawyer, and I don't like being beholden."

He started to reach inside his pocket, forgetting his jacket was on the porch. "Do you need money?"

She stepped away. "No, I intend to pay her out of Grandpa's money, but I haven't been able to face going to town since the trial. I reckon I'll need to do that soon." She gave him a wry smile. "Lorena says I need clothes."

He said, "Why, I'd love to take you to town. You could shop and then we could have a little picnic somewhere and . . ."

She stopped him. "Oh, Luther will need to go to town sometime. But thanks." It wasn't that she was ungrateful, but the thought of parading around Ashton with the man accused of being her lover sent shivers down her spine.

Having his suggestions squashed twice seemed to take some spirit out of him, but he was moving too quickly. Her mind cast around for something to talk about and settled on automobiles. She asked if he was any closer to owning one. Thankfully this ignited him, and he chatted away, moving to local events and his sisters.

"I guess they disapprove of you visiting me," Garnet murmured. They were in the orchard, and she reached up to examine one of the peach trees.

"Not at all. They're passionate about the Women's Christian Temperance Union, believing that most of society's ills can be placed at the feet of Demon Rum. They did have some harsh words about me exacerbating the situation, but when I told them about the divorce and your son, they were ready to lynch Foster."

She moved on to the peach trees. "We'll be picking soon, and there'll be cobblers and pies. Can't wait." She smiled at him.

Clifford couldn't take his eyes off her hair, which was probably glowing like a burning bush in the sun. She sensed his need for reassurance and wished she felt able to give it to him. "I reckon we could turn around now," she said.

But he wanted to walk farther, and they wandered until they were far behind Mama's house, near Franklin's walnut trees that cast dappled sunlight on the ground. Without realizing it, she sighed.

"What is it?" he asked, his hand aiming toward hers but stopping.

She clasped her hands behind her back. "There are so many things I wish for, mostly, of course, to have Ruben back, but other than that, what I want most is to see my brother Franklin."

"Lexington's not such a great distance. How long's he been gone?"

"Two years. I don't think he makes much money tending horses, nor does he get much time off. Not that he cares; he's always preferred horses to humans." She picked off a sliver of walnut bark. "I get a letter now and then, and I think he misses us, but he'll never forgive Mama." He followed as she turned back toward the house. "Both of them would deny it, but Mama and Franklin are an awful lot alike in the way they hold grudges. And yet they've never got along. Ironic? Is that the word?"

He replied that it was and asked her about the Colsons and the Kings. Although he knew most of the story, she told him the rest. When she'd related the tale to David, she'd felt uneasy about airing such private matters, but Clifford hardly seemed like a stranger. By the time she finished, the house was in sight.

Lorena served them strawberry shortcake, and afterward, although there were still hours until dark, Clifford announced that he should get on the road. He took his time getting back into his coat and seemed to be waiting for her to say something. Actually, Garnet thought, he'd been waiting for her to say something all afternoon.

"I'm glad you came to see me," she offered, knowing this wasn't enough.

He beamed, and she thought again how fine and handsome he was. She loved the way the skin stretched over the bones of his face, making planes and hollows and ridges.

"I'm delighted that you invited me."

She lowered her head. "I don't know what to say to you. I swear I'm not being coy, but I can't say any more than that I'm happy to see you."

"'Had we but world enough and time, this coyness, mistress, would be no crime,'" he quoted, smiling down at her.

She raised an eyebrow.

"Andrew Marvell's 'To His Coy Mistress,' one of your father's favorite poems. He said it was a lusty version of a perfect exercise in logic."

"My father said that?"

"Yes. And we do have time, Garnet. I'll not rush you. But if you're happy to see me, may I visit you next Sunday?"

"Yes. I'd like that."

"Good. Until then."

When Garnet entered the kitchen, Lorena was expecting a report. "He's coming next Sunday." Garnet tied an apron over her skirt. "I reckon we'd better go to town tomorrow if we can manage it. I can't wear the same thing every Sunday."

Lorena grinned until the gaps in her teeth showed.

Although Garnet had dreaded the trip to town, especially when Luther said he was too busy to go, there were no uncomfortable incidents. Oh, a few people stared, and some turned their heads to avoid her. But more than likely Lorena was right; in a town the size of Ashton new scandals erupted every week, and Garnet was old news. Lorena insisted on buying fabric for blouses, a suit, a summer dress, new underwear and nightgowns. When Garnet complained that it looked like she was being outfitted for a wedding all over again, Lorena glared at her. She did need clothes. Most had been mended many times, and even though she'd only used her wedding dress once, she couldn't abide the thought of wearing it. Lorena had the bright idea of taking it apart, discarding the bodice, and making it into a skirt. With an ivory blouse, she said, maybe it wouldn't remind her of past times. And Lorena insisted on treats as well. She bought lemons for Sunday lemonade and urged Garnet to choose some face powder and rouge. "Sounds like you're putting me up for auction," Garnet complained, but Lorena just laughed at her. The only thing Garnet stubbed up about was Lorena's suggestion that she visit Clifford at the bank. "Unless you're going to let me withdraw some money to pay for all this, I'm not going," Garnet declared.

They rushed to finish the dress first, in time for Sunday. Made of dimity, it was summery yellow with tiny pink rosebuds scattered across the fabric. Clifford told her she looked a perfect picture sitting on the porch in her flowery frock. They walked again, inspecting the tobacco fields and barns and visiting the pond to see the ducks. He brought amusing stories about his sisters, and she told him again her dream about owning a store someday. When they returned to the porch Lorena brought out lemonade and chocolate cake, and Garnet felt more comfortable than the previous week. And so it went through June and July. One Sunday Garnet presented him with a fancy tea that included little sandwiches and pie. He declared it heavenly, and she finally let him hold her hand.

"You're blossoming," Lorena announced as she measured Garnet. They were in the sewing room finishing the last of the garments, a dark green skirt and jacket trimmed with black braid and coppery buttons. "We need to cut this a little fuller."

"Am I getting fat?"

"No, look at the pattern. You're just now back to where you were before you married. It's about time."

"You know," Garnet said. "I'm almost happy. I've quit running those terrible scenes through my head, I'm enjoying living with you, and I finally heard about Ruben."

Aunt Martha's letter had stated that the child was fine, running all over the place and healthy as a horse, and she'd come just short of taking Garnet's side about the divorce. In the last line she'd promised to send occasional news about Ruben and hinted that Garnet could visit her baby. Although it was unlikely that she'd travel north of Lexington to where Ruben was living, Garnet was relieved that the woman held no grudge.

"And, of course, they ain't no other reason why you should feel happy, is there?"

The woman had her trapped, encircled with a measuring tape, and the best Garnet could do was duck her head. "I do enjoy seeing him."

"Uh huh." Lorena replied, taking away the tape. "I think I'll fry chicken this Sunday and make up a picnic for you two to take to the orchard. It's a pretty spot, and you all have walked this entire farm over."

"Well, he always asks if I want to go for a ride, but it's so hot and tiring for his horse." Garnet giggled. "I guess I'm like Franklin, always thinking about the horse."

"Let's think about the man instead."

The room was hot and bright with evening sun, and Garnet hated to put her housedress back on. "What about him?" she asked with the dress over her head.

"How long are you going to let him dangle on your chain?"

What a curious expression, Garnet thought. "Is that what I'm doing?"

"He comes every Sunday. Why, it's been two months now, and have you given him any encouragement? You know he wants to marry you."

Garnet smoothed the pattern over the dark green fabric and reached for the pincushion. "I make no secret of the fact that I enjoy his visits." It sounded prissy.

Lorena straightened up and stared until Garnet was forced to meet her eyes. "Last I heard there's no way to regain virginity, Garnet. It ain't like you're some shy, blushing miss. You had a rough time with David, but you know the facts of life. It seems a little silly that you don't even give the man a kiss ever now and then. And I'll bet the farm you haven't, have you?"

Garnet's eyes dropped to the table. "No." Then she looked up at Lorena. "God knows, I might as well be a virgin. That's where it all started going wrong for David and me." This was the closest she'd come to crying in months. She whispered, "I don't know how to do that sort of thing, and I won't encourage Clifford if I can't be a good wife in every way."

Lorena's face softened. "Oh, honey, this man adores you. He'd do anything for you. I don't know what that sorry David's problem was: marrying too young, pride, jealousy, pure damned meanness, but Clifford loves you. And," she added with a quirk of one crow-feather brow, "he's older, probably had a little experience. He's been gentling you like a skittish filly for weeks now; I think he can bring you joy."

Neither of them said any more, but every night that week while lying in bed hoping to catch a wisp of breeze, Garnet thought about it. She knew she loved him and that she often gazed at his hands, wondering how they'd feel on her skin. Maybe she was ready to see if things could be better, but she wasn't going to marry him until she was certain of it, no matter how much she cared for him.

***

On Sunday she wore the silk skirt. Clifford arrived without suit coat or vest, with his collar unbuttoned and his sleeves rolled up. The sun was merciless and what little puffs of breeze there were felt like they'd escaped an oven. He apologized for his informal attire and Garnet fluttered her hand at him. "We're going to have a picnic anyway. I hope you didn't eat much dinner."

He'd been arriving earlier and staying later every Sunday, and she doubted if he'd eaten at all. Lorena had packed a basket, including a flask of cold sassafras tea, and Clifford carried this while Garnet clutched an old quilt. They were sweating before they passed the garden, and she was glad she'd left off her face powder; it probably would've turned to paste.

When they reached the orchard, she spread the quilt in the shade and immediately asked for the tea. "It's too hot to move," she

312

said. Sweat tickled her back, and tiny tendrils of hair around her face were kinking into corkscrews.

He pulled out a giant handkerchief and wiped his face. "It's been dreadful all week," he said. "You'd think the bank would be cool, but there's no cross-ventilation and we nearly smother."

She unpacked the basket. There was a pie pan full of crisp fried chicken and a packet of Lorena's incredible biscuits. Garnet laid these out along with plates, napkins, and utensils. "She packed tomatoes too and some peach pie. I wish I were hungry."

He stretched his lean body along the edge of the quilt. Patches of sweat darkened his white shirt. "It's a lovely meal, but it's simply too hot to eat. Pass me that tea, would you?" He sat up and Garnet watched his long neck as he swallowed.

"You'd be cooler with your sleeves rolled up," he said. "Do you need help?"

She nodded, and he moved across the quilt to sit in front of her with his legs crossed. His head was bowed as he unbuttoned her cuffs. Business-like, his elegant fingers folded up the narrow sleeves to just below her elbows, touching her only as he needed to. A faint lemony scent came from his skin. Some kind of shaving soap, she thought, or maybe it was something like Grandpa's bay rum. Before he could move back across the quilt, she touched his arm, just above the wrist, with the tips of her fingers. He looked up abruptly, his amber eyes questioning her. Leaning toward him just the tiniest bit, she gave him her face, and he kissed her. Finally she knew how those lips felt: warm, soft, and tender. When he pulled away he took both her hands. "I've been dreaming about that for so long."

Feeling slightly dizzy, she smiled at him.

"Please?" He lifted his hand to her face.

She didn't know what he wanted but she trusted him. His fingers traced her cheek, her jawbone, and lingered on her lips. "You are absolutely exquisite," he breathed. This made her smile again. Sweat was trickling between her breasts and down her back, and she felt about as far from exquisite as could be.

Then he picked up her arm, stroking it. "Those adorable freckles," he whispered. She cringed. Mama'd always said freckles were common. "Look," he said. "They're the color of fresh peaches. I wonder if they're as sweet." His eyes had gone dark. Since he seemed to be asking permission again, she dipped her head, and he lifted her forearm to his lips, first biting it gently and then touching it with his tongue. Despite the scorching sun, shivers ran through her body. "Very sweet. And salty." He smiled.

Then he turned her arm over, exposing the white underside, patterned with blue veins, and she remembered what he'd said months ago at her kitchen table. He did as he'd promised, kissing the veins and tracing them with his tongue until her breath came in little gusts and her eyes shut to block out everything but his touch. "Beautiful," he announced, and he sounded a little breathless too.

She raised her other hand, trembling a bit, toward his neck. The dark hair curled there from his sweat, and it tempted her. She hesitated, her fingers mere inches from his skin, and he noticed. "Oh, touch, dear heart. I won't ravish you if you do."

How had he known? She'd just been thinking that by now David would've had her impaled on the ground. She ran her finger against the damp, silky skin on the back of his neck. Twining a curling tail of his hair around her finger, she rubbed it with her thumb and for a moment ignored what he was doing to her arm. But when he took her little finger into his mouth, licking it, sucking it, she felt sensations she'd nearly forgotten. Too soon he kissed her knuckles with a humorous smack to indicate he was done, and immediately she returned both hands to the quilt in front of her. She knew her eyes must be glazed, intoxicated.

Clifford couldn't quit smiling at her. He handed her the jug of tea, which she upended, a drop dribbling down her chin. He wiped it with his finger. "We should try to eat Lorena's food, shouldn't we?" He tore off a piece of crisp chicken and held it to her lips. She took it, enjoying the touch of his fingers more than the food.

"It can be like this?"

He was chewing and smiling at the same time. "This and even better and there's wonderful joy in the learning."

Feeling naughty, they threw most of the picnic over a hill for the raccoons and sat under the apple trees until the sun encroached on their space. It was early yet, but the heat shimmered and roasted them until they walked back to the house for shade. Clifford asked for water, and after gulping it, said he was going home. At first she was disappointed; he never left this early. Then he bent down and kissed her, and she understood. It was enough, plenty for one day. He ran his fingers down her sweat-damp cheek and whispered, "I adore you, Garnet."

She nodded, still dazed and flushed and wondering if she was suffering from heatstroke or some other dire consequence of the weather. "Next Sunday?" she asked.

He sprang up into the buggy. "Absolutely." He grinned, and laying his hand against his chest, declaimed, "'Parting is such sweet sorrow that I shall say good-night till it be morrow.'"

Giggling at him, she stood in the sun, watching him drive away. Feeling foolish but doing it anyway, she pressed her mouth to the cup where his lips had touched. She was a goner, she decided. Done for. Feeling like she was gliding rather than walking, she picked up the basket. Lorena sat fanning herself in the kitchen with her shoes off. "Did Clifford leave already?"

"Yes." Garnet pulled the dirty dishes from the basket.

"Oh, leave them until evening when it's cooler. You two have a fight or something?"

"No." There was a stone crock by the sink, and Garnet dipped out more tea into Clifford's cup and drank. Lorena was about to explode, but Garnet teased her, not saying anything more until she'd sat and unbuttoned her own shoes. Freeing her feet and peeling down the sweaty stockings felt like heaven.

"Damnation, girl, you'd try the patience of Jesus Himself. Did you kiss him?"

"Yes." Garnet smiled dreamily.

Lorena's eyebrows flew up farther than Garnet thought possible. "And what else? You're grinning like the cat that got the canary; there must be something else."

Garnet drank again. "Well, I guess you could say he made love to my arm."

Lorena shook her head and muttered, but Garnet paid no attention. She was too busy feeling adored: peculiar, but adored.

***

The next week brought no relief from the heat. Once or twice thunderstorms roared through Bethel, but, as Luther said, they were all talk and no action. Garnet felt all but feverish. Lorena swore that Clifford would propose the following Sunday, and Garnet reckoned the woman was right. He'd thawed the fear in her, and she knew she wanted him. Still, she was jumpy: certain he'd propose, afraid he wouldn't, and totally discombobulated by the whole situation. Lorena said she was nervous as a hen on a hot rock and then laughed, saying it was part of being in love.

At the first of the week she went to her mother's and canned tomatoes for two days in a row. She hinted to Mama that Clifford might be getting serious about marriage, but her mother was stingy with her encouragement. How would Garnet like sharing a house with those two peculiar sisters? Maybe they were peculiar enough to accept a girl with a reputation like Garnet's. She ignored her.

Then she picked blackberries and made jam with Lorena. When there was nothing left to put up, she washed curtains and tablecloths and bedding, ironing until after dark. Lorena said she'd make herself sick, but Garnet couldn't sit still nor sleep. Several nights she crept downstairs and sat alone on the porch in the blood-warm dark, listening to night birds and thinking about Clifford.

On Saturday, Lowell sauntered up the lane with Henry trying hard to keep up. It was good to see them. Luther had been keeping them away on Sundays by taking them fishing. Just helping with the courting, Lorena said. "Got a letter for you, Nettie," Lowell hollered.

She identified Clifford's writing, and her heart sank. What if he wasn't coming? Tearing open the envelope, she scanned his brief note telling her he was obliged to attend a church function until up in the afternoon on Sunday, but he'd come after that. He asked if he could share supper with her and Lorena and signed it with all his love. Relieved, she thanked Lowell, hugged Henry in spite of his dusty clothes, and ran to ask Lorena what they could cook.

It was nearly five o'clock before Clifford arrived. Every detail about him fascinated her now, and she watched as he put his hat on a chair and ran his hands through his hair. Garnet rearranged things on the table, moving the vase of chicory blooms to the other side of the salt cellar and aligning the plates once again.

Clifford explained that his delay was due to a church picnic, followed by a meeting about purchasing an organ for the Ashton Baptist Church. "I don't know that I had much to contribute, but Fanny's keen on the church getting an organ and said I had to be there. Still, I wasn't going to let it interfere with my plans." He beamed.

What plans? Usual Sunday plans or plans for today in particular? Garnet could hardly swallow, and she couldn't think of a thing to say. Of course, nobody ever had to talk much when Clifford was around. Lorena looked pointedly at her a few times, and she tried to make some kind of intelligent remark. You're acting like an idiot, she scolded herself. When she jumped up to serve the cobbler, Garnet delighted in the fact that Clifford's dark eyes followed her. With trembling hands she put a slice in front of him and glowed when he said thanks. By this time Lorena was so amused she could hardly keep from laughing. As soon as they'd finished, she shooed them out of the kitchen, giving Garnet a wink when Clifford wasn't looking.

Garnet asked, "Do you want to sit or walk?"

"Oh, walk, I suppose. I've been sitting all afternoon."

So they walked, revisiting paths they'd covered again and again over the last weeks. He breezed along, unaware of her turmoil. And he hadn't so much as touched her hand. "So what have you been doing this week?" he asked.

"Canning, mostly. I worked up at Mama's the first of the week, and then Lorena and I put up a lot of jam."

"Hot work. Fanny's been doing that too."

"Any news from town?" She didn't really care. What she craved were sweet words about love and adoration, things she'd been imagining all week.

"Not really. Everybody's busy on their farms this time of year."

And so it went. They walked until she was exhausted, more from nervousness than exercise. When they returned to the porch, Garnet brought lemonade, and they rocked without saying much. It was nearly as awkward as the first time he'd come. He's decided he doesn't want me, she mourned. The light faded, turning the sky a rich blue above the riotous oranges and reds of the sunset. Watching the sky, Clifford didn't seem to realize he was annoying the ever-loving spit out of her.

Then he nodded as if he'd received some mysterious portent from the heavens. Reaching for her hand, he said, "Come with me, dear heart."

She felt twitchy as a witch. It was nearly dark, and he was probably fixing to leave. Was he ending it? Dear Lord, she wasn't sure she could endure that after opening her heart to him. He led her into the yard, gently pulling her against him. It was bliss to feel his body so close.

He pointed to the sky. "Do you see that?"

"Sure, that's the evening star, the wishing star."

She glanced up and saw his gentle smile. "Star light, star bright, first star I see tonight."

"Wish I may, wish I might, have the wish I wish tonight." She shut her eyes like a child.

"It's a good thing to make wishes," he murmured. "But it's really not a star, you know. It's a planet, Venus. And it's named after the goddess of love."

Garnet nodded like a schoolgirl. "I knew that."

"Of course John Grant's daughter would know that." He smiled. "Do you realize that I've never seen you in the dark?"

She heard insects start their evening songs and off in the distance a cow moaned. Clifford moved his hand from her shoulder to her neck. "I've never seen your skin shimmering in the dusk, nor your glorious hair turned dark in the night."

She couldn't breathe. Keeping her eyes upon the star or planet or whatever it was, she waited while he ran his finger from her jaw down her neck until she could feel her pulse against it.

"Now I've seen the evening star with you."

She encircled his waist with her arm and turned to watch his face. He was looking at her, not Venus.

"It's a wondrous thing," he said, gathering her even more closely. She laid her head against his chest, and it felt like home, a shelter.

"But that very same planet, when it goes through its cycles is also the morning star. Did you know that?" His voice was so quiet that she felt it in his chest as much as heard it. She shook her head against him.

"Well, it is, and the very most wondrous thing in the world would be to share the morning star with you before the dawn breaks." He shifted until he could hold her shoulders in his hands. His eyes were dark and deep, and she was completely lost.

"The only way I could ever have the wish I may, wish I might that I wish the most and see the morning star with you is if you'd marry me, dearest, dearest heart." He took her hands, pressed them against his chest, and kissed them. "Would you make my wish come true?"

First she nodded, and then she said, "I love you, Clifford. I do love you."

He smiled hugely, his teeth glowing in the twilight, and folded her into his arms, one hand fluttering to her hair, her back, her neck. Once again struck by his height, she flattened her face against his chest and kissed his shirt and then raised her face for a better one. He touched his lips to her nose, her eyes, her cheeks, and then lingered at her lips, and tasted them with his tongue. If it hadn't been for his arms, she might have just sagged down to the sunburned grass.

Clifford broke away. "Shall we tell Lorena? I think she's been anticipating this."

Garnet giggled. "Actually, she laid odds on it being today."

His laugh rang out. "She ought to take her money to the track."

Side by side they climbed the porch steps, but then he stopped her. "One thing, dear heart, and it's terribly selfish, but I do so want it."

Lorena had lit a lamp in the front room, and its light turned his eyes golden.

"Would you mind if I plan our wedding? I know that's your prerogative, but I have so many ideas." He looked like a boy pleading for a favor.

She didn't care and said so; after all, she'd planned one wedding and if it meant so much to him, she didn't mind.

"Oh, good!" he exclaimed. "I promise you everything will be perfect."

They entered the house and he called out, "Lorena! I'm going to marry this glorious girl!"

Coming from the kitchen, Lorena grinned. "And soon, I hope. She's so lovesick she's not worth a nickel."

They all laughed, and he said he must go. Garnet walked with him, sorry she'd doubted him for a minute. He kissed her again and cupped her face in his long, bony hands. "Something to dream on," he whispered and left.

Chapter Two

Parting the lace curtains to peek at Main Street, she drank in the exotic novelty of Lexington. She hadn't seen much of the town on the trip from the train station to the hotel. Garnet grinned and glimpsed a faint reflection of her happiness in the glass. Trains, hotels: this was heady stuff for a country girl from Evans County who was getting married in a little over an hour. Tightening the sash of her new silk dressing gown, she supposed she should start dressing, but never in her life had it taken her longer than a half-hour.

He was just full of ideas, and she smiled at the prospect of a lifetime of his whims. The week after he proposed he'd sat in the kitchen at the farm, insisting that Lorena join them, and placed a Sears Roebuck catalog and an envelope of cash on the table. Choose whatever you want or use it to get ideas, he'd said. Then he'd tapped the envelope and declared that if they needed more, he'd supply it.

Since he'd once promised Garnet a train trip, he said they'd marry in Lexington and travel there by rail. It would be easier, he remarked, than working through the complexities of marrying in Evans County and suffering prejudices against Garnet's past.

For several weeks she prepared for the wedding even though there was little for her to do. She and Lorena made another wedding dress, this one of smoky blue wool crepe, and pored over the catalog ordering tantalizing little things: fancy garters, a cunning handbag, shoes, and scandalously sheer silk stockings. One Sunday Clifford brought a trunk saying she needed one for the trip and another to pack things that needed to go to his house.

The only cloud on the horizon was their life after the wedding. Garnet smiled at the memory of Clifford's performance with Mama. He'd charmed her shamelessly, calling her his first true love and complimenting her beauty. Luther gave Garnet a quick wink that said this man knew how to handle Louise. Garnet didn't think she'd done as well with his sisters. They'd evidently concluded that their brother would never marry, and they could continue their odd but workable living arrangement forever. Fanny had said little, but Gert had fired questions at Garnet about farming. Although Garnet had answered some of these easily enough, her lack of experience with animal husbandry and corn had made Gert sniff. Clifford had enthusiastically brought up Garnet's cooking abilities, her sewing expertise, and the books she'd read, but the two formidable sisters merely nodded. Garnet had felt as though she'd failed a test.

She sat on the bench in front of the dressing table and looked at her bits and pieces arranged on its marble top. Worrying about Fanny and Gert was work for another day. Today was her wedding day, and she was going to enjoy it, she resolved, as she smoothed a dab of rouge on her cheekbones. She was marrying the kindest, most wonderful man in the world. He'd already given her so much. Although Luther had muttered that for all the distance they'd traveled to catch a train, they could've been halfway to Lexington by wagon, that morning she'd sat, eager as a child, as countryside flew by the window.

And the hotel he'd chosen, so imposing and elaborate, thrilled her too. With a flourish, Clifford signed them in as Mr. and Mrs. Clifford Clark, although she'd touched his sleeve, whispering that this wasn't exactly true. The hotel clerk smirked, but Clifford declared that it would be absolutely true in only a few hours, and it was perfectly correct to sign them in as married. Weeks before, Clifford had booked the most elegant room in the hotel, one with its own bathroom.

Dusting powder on her face, Garnet gazed around the huge room reflected in the mirror. A table, two chairs, a wardrobe, and this adorable little dressing table, complete with a folding mirror. She felt quite sophisticated perching there and seeing three views of her face. And behind her was the bed, a tall four-poster covered with a heavy, dark green coverlet. The bed did cause her a little tingle of apprehension. These past few weeks Clifford had, in Lorena's words, gentled her, but she still worried that when it came time for the actual *doing* she would panic.

Glancing down at her old watch, she started unpinning her hair. The watch reminded her of David, and she remembered how nervous she'd felt before their wedding. It seemed like decades ago. She wondered if he'd found any happiness. Her own was so overwhelming that, today anyway, she felt no animosity toward him except for the loss of Ruben. A week ago, Clifford had asked if she wanted to visit her child since it was only a short trip beyond Lexington. But she'd declined. This was their wedding, their trip, and she didn't want sadness to cloud it.

She brushed until her hair was a rippling stream of copper. She did plan to see Franklin in a few days. Again, Clifford had suggested that she write her brother and arrange a meeting. He'd be coming at dinnertime on Saturday, and she could hardly wait. Twisting and puffing her hair just so, she managed to make it look like drawings in the Sears Roebuck catalog. Securing one or two more hairpins, just in case, she rose and shrugged out of the dressing gown. She was corseted, dressed, and primped by the time Clifford knocked on the door and entered.

Standing against the door as if he feared coming any closer, he breathed, "You are gorgeous, Garnet."

She picked up her hat and sat again in front of the mirror to pin it. "I'm just me, a country mouse in city clothes."

He looked handsome himself. She'd never seen his suit or the dark blue tie and guessed these were new. From the look of his hair and the spicy smell floating across the room, she figured he'd been to the barber. Shortly after they arrived at the hotel, he'd left her, telling her to rest and dress; he'd amuse himself down in the saloon. Seeing her horrified face, he hurried to tell her the newspapers were kept there. It was considerate of him to give her time, but it almost seemed as if he was avoiding her.

"I'd never compare you to a mouse," he said. She preened a bit as she secured her hat and picked up her gloves. She knew she looked good; Lorena had demanded that she put on the whole ensemble the previous night, although Garnet refused to risk the fragile stockings. Strangely enough, it was Clifford who seemed uncomfortable now.

Tilting her head, she said, "Are we going to be late to our own wedding?"

"No, no," he said, lighting on one of the chairs. "I've ordered a buggy for twenty minutes from now." He pulled a small paper bag from his pocket and handed it to her. "I brought you something."

"I swear, you're embarrassing me, Clifford. The train, the hotel, these clothes, the lovely dressing gown, and now this." She set down her gloves and pulled out a tiny glass vial. "Perfume?" She'd never owned perfume.

He nodded happily and watched while she lifted the little stopper and dotted a little behind each ear. "Lovely. Sniff," she commanded, bending close to his face.

Stiffly he obeyed and said, "Very nice."

She'd expected a quick kiss at least, but there was none of that, nor had there been all through this long and exciting day. He'd held her hand on the train and touched her shoulder at the station, but he hadn't so much as come close to her for hours. Narrowing her eyes, she asked, "What's wrong, Clifford? You act like you don't want anything to do with me."

"I'm afraid I'll muss your dress."

She shook her head, and he looked sheepish. Fluttering a bony hand in the general direction of the bed, he blushed. Garnet had never seen him blush. "I am so determined," he declared, "not to *pounce*. You're so breathtakingly beautiful. And we're alone in a hotel room, and I will not be compared with Foster. I'm exercising self-control." This last was said so pompously she had to laugh.

"You are not, nor will you ever be anything like David, whose name we won't mention or make any comparisons with ever again," she said, trying to be serious despite his comic rigidity. Then she gave him an impish grin. "Besides, there's hardly time to pounce now. Let's get married."

And they did. Naturally he had it all planned. Through a flurry of letters, he secured the services of a minister and brought in a long-time banking associate and his wife as witnesses. Everything was in order as they quietly married in a downtown Lexington church. Although Clifford had worried that she might miss her family and friends, she didn't mind their absence at all. It was better this way, she assured him, because she felt no anxiety about being a divorced woman. Whether the minister knew or not didn't matter for she supposed she'd never see him or the witnesses ever again. This time she paid attention to the ring placed on her finger and was dazzled by diamonds sparkling in the early evening sun. She wasn't sure but she thought she might've married a rich man without ever intending to.

After brief congratulations at the church, they rode back to the hotel, not an hour since they'd left it. In the buggy, Clifford gripped her hand until the new ring dug into her next finger. "I've never been so happy in my entire life," he declared. "Not Christmas or coming home from school or my first horse or anything can compare."

Smiling at the comparison to a horse, she touched his face, tracing the creases of his smile. "I'm crazy with happiness too," she said, and then her stomach growled loudly enough for him to hear it and laugh.

"You ate hardly any lunch."

"Too nervous. But now I'm *famished*." She loved using his big words. "Can't you shoot a rabbit to feed your starving wife?" She touched her wrist to her forehead to complete the melodrama. Their laughter filled the buggy, causing people on the street to stare, but they didn't care.

Of course he'd even prepared for their wedding supper. Cajoling, bribing, or using whatever method necessary, he'd secured a table in a small alcove of the hotel dining room. It seemed impossibly elegant to Garnet: the candles, white tablecloth, even a few bedraggled asters.

"You're having all sorts of adventures, aren't you?"

She nodded and looked around, awed by her surroundings: the richly flocked wallpaper, the swirling flowers on the carpet. The hotel even had electricity. But her awe soon dissolved into more practical matters when food arrived and she began eating with abandon.

"This steak is really good, Clifford. Don't you like yours?" She popped another piece in her mouth. Clifford ate more slowly, watching her with amusement.

"It's very nice."

She swallowed and suddenly blurted out, "Are you rich, Clifford?"

He chuckled and set down his fork. "It would be more accurate to ask if *we're* rich, Garnet. We're a family now, you know."

She smiled. "Isn't that lovely?" Another bite disappeared into her mouth.

"Lovely, indeed." He sipped water before he answered. "I've always held that wealth is a relative thing. We're richer than some but poorer than others. I suppose you could say we're comfortable, able to afford a few luxuries now and again. Why?"

She was chewing again and smiled apologetically until she swallowed. "Oh, it's just the ring, the gifts, this trip. I can't imagine what it's cost."

He shrugged it off. "This is what I wanted. I told you I've been dreaming a while and saving for it too. And as to the expenses, well, not all of them are as extravagant as you might imagine. Your ring, for example, was my mother's."

She held up her left hand, wiggling it so the diamonds glittered. "Shouldn't your sisters have it?"

"My father intended it to go to my wife. Fanny owns my mother's pearls, and Gert has her ruby ring squirreled away somewhere, not that she'd ever wear something like that. All I needed to do was have it cleaned and made to fit you." He ate another bite. Garnet began to be embarrassed by her appetite, but she felt jumpy and kept shoveling in forkful after forkful.

"So, what are we doing tomorrow?"

"I've hired a buggy again and thought we'd see the sights."

"And the next day?"

"There's shopping to do." He saw doubt on her face. "The girls gave me quite a list. I'll try to curb my urges to buy more gifts for you."

"Could I get some more water? Well, if we're sort of rich, could I buy a gift for someone?"

Clifford summoned the waiter. "Certainly. Shall we buy gifts for your brothers and sisters?"

"No, that's too much, but I'd really love to get something for Lorena. She's been so good to me."

"An excellent idea."

She continued to eat and chatter until he asked, "Are you whistling in the graveyard, Garnet?"

Her head jerked up. "I don't know what you mean."

"It's an expression that means you're trying to keep fear at bay, like someone who attempts to be brave in a frightening place."

Realizing she was far too full of dinner, she set down her fork. "I guess I am."

The waiter refilled their glasses and disappeared. "Dear heart, we don't have to do anything upstairs if you're uncomfortable or frightened."

She looked at her dirty plate and realized she felt nearly sick from stuffing herself. "We have to eventually so we might as well get it over with."

Clifford grimaced. Wonderful, she told herself miserably. That didn't sound at all romantic. "That's not what I mean. It's just that it's something I need to get past. It's a . . . a . . . ." She couldn't think of the right word.

"A hurdle, I suppose," Clifford supplied. "I understand. But it's been a long day; we left Lorena's at dawn. We can wait."

The waiter appeared again so she kept quiet while he took away their dishes. Most of Clifford's food was still on his plate, and she wondered what they did with the leftovers. Clifford was supplying her with an excuse, but then it dawned on her that he might actually be providing one for himself. When the waiter left she asked, "Do you want to wait?"

"Good Lord, no."

Anxious as she was, she had to smile. "Then we won't. What's this?" The waiter was returning with a small silver tray. With a flourish, he placed it at the center of their table. "Our compliments and best wishes," he announced.

Circled with flowers was the most cunning little wedding cake, frosted with swirls of white icing and topped by a single pink rosebud. "Oh, Clifford!" she exclaimed. The waiter brought out two small plates.

"I didn't have anything to do with this," he explained and looked up at the waiter. "Thank you very much, sir. This is an unexpected pleasure."

They both ate tiny pieces, and then there was nothing else to delay their trip upstairs. It was too dark for a stroll, and Clifford said he'd consumed all of the hotel's reading materials that afternoon. Once in the room, Clifford switched on one of the lamps and started fussing around. Complaining that the room was stuffy, he opened the window and then pulled the heavy drapes across it, blocking the breezes he'd hoped for. Then he stared at the window and opened the drapes halfway. Garnet put her hat and gloves away and found her nightgown, which she kneaded uncertainly until Clifford suggested she undress in the bathroom.

Her hands trembled as she unbuttoned her dress. You're not some green little virgin, she told herself; quit acting like you've never done this before. She eased off her precious stockings and then everything else. She'd responded to all of Clifford's loving so far, she thought. Slipping the beautiful, gauzy gown over her head, she shivered although the room wasn't cold. Maybe the gown was a little too transparent, she worried, looking down and seeing her nipples poking through the thin fabric. She wished she'd brought her dressing gown into the bathroom.

With only one lamp burning, the room was dim and shadowy, the gleaming furniture and heavy wallpaper making it strange and exotic. My stars, she thought, what was she doing in such a place? She put her clothes away and then sat at the dressing table. Clifford's luminous eyes never left her. She started plucking out hairpins and suddenly he was behind her. "Let me," he murmured.

She watched him in the mirror. He'd removed his coat, vest, collar, and tie, and his shirt was startlingly white in the dim light. Deftly he picked out the hairpins, releasing the heavy waterfall of sassafras hair. Tall as he was, he had to stoop to brush it. Gradually she relaxed; she'd always loved to have her hair brushed. At one point he gathered a handful of the golden red silk and rubbed it against his cheek.

"That's lovely embroidery," he said, pointing at the yoke of her gown covered with pink and blue flowers. "But what's that?"

"It's supposed to be a bee, but I didn't quite get it right. Henry was at the farm while I was stitching this, and he said I needed a bee if I was going to have flowers."

Clifford chuckled. "Will it sting if I touch it?" His finger grazed the yellowish blob right under her collarbone.

"No," she whispered.

He set down the brush, and lightly grazed his hands across her nipples. She was hardly breathing. Turning down the coverlet along with the quilt and sheet beneath it, he said, "Come to bed, dear heart."

She lay on her back, reaching at first to pull up the sheet and then reconsidering. It crossed her mind that she probably looked like a skimpily clad corpse. Clifford stood by the bed, undressing. "I'll warn you," he said, "I have skinny legs and knobby knees."

She giggled. He turned his back to her, considerately, she supposed, as he slipped out of the rest of his clothes, and his back stretched long and smooth on either side of his spine. Evidently there'd be no pretense of a nightshirt, she gathered as she gazed at his pale rear end, firm as melons. In one swift motion he reclined on the bed, and she saw with a little wave of panic that he was ready for her.

He lay on his side, head propped on his forearm and said, "Look at me."

Obediently she turned, and he bent to kiss her. It was quick but continued down her neck and to her ear, his lips coming back to hers where they lingered until she opened her mouth to him. They'd done this a few times; everything was all right so far. But then he shifted her until she was again lying flat and continued to kiss her while his right hand skimmed over her breast. This they had not done. Totally different from David's harsh twisting and pulling, Clifford's fingers were butterfly wings, and Garnet felt a powerful pulling deep in her belly.

He sat up. "That's a splendid gown, but I wish you'd allow me to remove it."

She sat up and wriggled the fabric up until he pulled it over her head. "The light," she whispered.

"Must I turn it out? I so want to see you."

She shut her eyes and gave him the tiniest nod while trying not to squirm under his examination. "Exquisite," he breathed. "Your skin's the most glorious satin." He traced the veins of her breasts with his lips and then with his tongue.

With trembling fingers she ran her hand down his back. Satin here, too, she thought, flattening her palm against his smooth shoulders and running it along his bumpy spine. She'd never figured him to be a well-muscled man, especially compared to David's bulk and breadth, but Clifford was lean and firm. Then her hand traveled into his hair, combing it, and letting the silky stuff caress the valleys between her fingers.

Slowly, slowly he made love to her, moving his hand from her breast to her belly, covering it and easing down the slope of it. Rising a bit, he looked down, whispering, "The same glorious copper." And then he kissed her until some inner need compelled her to press against the hand that fluttered, ever so lightly on down, down, until she had no choice but to open her legs to him. I'm losing my mind, she thought as her hips rocked against the sensations between her legs.

And then the melting was replaced by a swift surge of urgency. Her hips jerked and her hands tightened on his firm flesh. Clifford rose above her, his eyes intoxicated, glazed. In a choked voice he asked, "May I?"

"Yes." She'd never felt like this. Carefully, gently, he entered her. She heard him breathe her name like it was holy, and the joy of this made her pull him down so she could feel the length of him.

He moved cautiously, but her hips were impatient, greedy. She felt him shake his head, and then he cried out, a strangled noise muffled by the pillow. Her hips had no sense; they kept churning until her rational mind told them to stop. He was done. With a grunt, he raised up and looked at her.

"I'm so sorry, my dearest heart. I promise I'll do better next time." His hair was tousled, making him look like a forlorn boy.

She touched his lips. "That was lovely, Clifford." From her experience their lovemaking had been a delight, and she couldn't understand his concern. Then her mind sharpened. Was he apologizing to cover his displeasure with her? He was the kind of man who'd do that. "Did I disappoint you?"

"Good Lord," he exploded, shaking his head. His arms trembled from holding his body above her. "No, Garnet. I'm disappointed in myself."

He collapsed beside her. "They say hunger makes the best sauce, but sometimes the sauce is too good," he mumbled, rubbing long fingers over his face.

"Hush," Garnet said, rolling over to snuggle against him, laying her head in the hollow between his shoulder and chest that seemed fashioned just for her. She shivered. Without his warm body over hers, she was cold. He reached down to pull up the covers.

"The light?" she murmured, feeling limp and sleepy.

"Right." He rose, and she watched him turn out the light, noticing that he did have knobby knees. He slid in beside her, gathering her to his chest again and whispering into her hair. "Goodnight, Garnet. I adore you."

"This is the happiest day of my life," she whispered back.

During the night she dreamed about a flower garden. Rain fell lightly, and the flowers welcomed it. She could hear drops beating upon the earth and feel the damp breeze blowing against her face. Then she felt the bed shift and woke up just enough to realize that it was, in truth, raining, and Clifford was shutting the window. It must be a cold rain. When he returned to bed she snuggled against his warmth and slid back into her dream. There were petals everywhere, creamy soft peonies and feathery daisies. In the absurd nature of dreams she was walking naked in the garden, sensing the delicate petals on her breasts and belly. She felt the light skimming of rose blooms and long-necked lilies, caressing her even between her legs. She opened herself to them, yearning for them to touch her again and again.

At some point she realized that Clifford was moving gently and steadily into her, but she kept the images in her head, this time seeing the dramatic night-blooming cereus trembling wider with each second. She could have sworn she smelled its sweet, strong scent. Her body urged the bloom to unfurl, to expand. Panting, she pushed against him, seeking some unknown treasure. It was tantalizingly close, just as the saucer-sized blossom was nearly open. Little noises came from her throat as something approached. And then the petals uncoiled, fully opened and growing more magnificent with each thrust Clifford gave her, and she uttered a thin cry of delight.

Garnet lay still, too spent to move. A hot flush began at her neck and flooded over her cheeks and chest, and she was barely able to lift her hand to his face hovering over hers. "Oh," she said. "My."

He chuckled and rolled onto his pillow, grabbing her hand and bringing it to his lips. Gradually she came to herself and knew, despite the dark, that he was grinning at her in a curiously self-satisfied manner. This was the secret prize, she realized, what David knew was absent and Clifford was sure he could provide. Garnet stretched. "So that's what I was missing?"

The room was so dark she could barely see his nod.

"And I can have it again?"

Clifford's teeth flashed white in the gloom. "Well, not just now perhaps, but yes, any time you want it. Gladly."

“Hmm.” She raised up to peer around in the dark.

“What do you need, dear heart?”

“My nightgown. I’m cold now.”

He found it, and she yawned and stretched beside him. Just as she was going off to sleep she remembered to thank him.

"Wake up, Garnet, and put on your dressing gown." Gray light filtered through the window, but she didn't hear rain. "I've asked them to bring coal; it's turned cold."

With a giant yawn she emerged from the warm bed just long enough to wrap the silken gown around her and dive back into her cocoon, feeling deliciously rested and content. "Hand me my brush, would you?"

Clifford brought it, and she wiggled up to lean against the headboard and coax tangles out of her hair. It made more sense to braid it before bed, but if her husband liked her hair flowing over the pillows and snarling into knots, she'd manage.

A boy arrived with a small hod of coal, which he arranged in the fireplace. She'd love to have a marble-faced fireplace like that. Candles in crystal holders sat in front of an ornate mirror, and she thought that maybe tonight they could make love by candlelight rather than electric lamps, modern as they were. Wicked woman, she smiled to herself; not even out of bed yet and thinking of getting into it again. The boy ignited the coal, and Clifford tipped him, another thing she'd never seen before.

Clifford took the brush. "There are some almighty tangles here."

"Hmm." She winced as he attacked one. "And I wonder whose fault that is?"

"Guilty as charged, ma'am."

"What time is it?"

"Just after seven."

"When are we leaving for our tour of Lexington?"

"Whenever we want. Did you bring a coat?"

Sticking out a leg, she tested the room temperature. It was tolerable. "No, but what I wore on the train has a jacket. You'll think I don't have any clothes."

Mischief lit his eyes. "You have lovely clothes, Garnet, but I like you better without them." He went over to the fire and poked at it. "I think women primarily dress for each other. All that fabric simply forces men to use our imaginations."

Of course she blushed. Would she ever outgrow her blushes? But she chose to ignore his remark. "I wonder if a body could get breakfast around here."

"You can't be hungry after that dinner last night."

"Oh yes, I can."

He laughed. "I'm ready for breakfast too. Dress warmly, and we'll eat and start our adventure."

Although it bore no resemblance to David's clumsy groping, Clifford couldn't quite keep his hands off her. He touched her back as he helped her into the buggy and tucked the lap robe around her hips more thoroughly than was necessary. "Where are we going first?" she asked.

"I thought we'd go out into the countryside, see some of the big farms. But we'd better be back in town before dinnertime when you're famished again."

She stuck the tip of her tongue out at him. "You're to blame for that too, you know. I'm only hungry like this when I'm happy. And you're the one tempting me with all these lovely things: steak last night and French toast this morning. I need to figure out how to make French toast."

Under a pewter sky they drove out of town toward Henry Clay's mansion and beyond. Light breezes tossed the gaudy goldenrod by the side of the road, and a few trees sported equally brilliant swatches of color. Occasionally a skiff of fallen leaves blew across the road scattering gold, red, orange, and brown in their path. Dry stone walls rolled and dipped around their fields.

The cool air invigorated Garnet, making her feel keen and alert. She exclaimed when they caught sight of a grand house rising behind trees just beginning to turn. "Beautiful," she murmured.

He squeezed her hand. "You're rather an autumnal girl yourself."

"What do you mean?"

"Well, your coloring, I suppose. That magnificent hair of yours matches the fall landscape, and in this breeze your cheeks have gone all rosy like autumn apples, unless you dipped too heavily into the rouge pot this morning," he teased.

She punched him playfully in the shoulder. "No rouge at all this morning, sir," she replied. "I never thought about having a favorite season, but I love the changes from one to the next: warm when you've been longing for it and cool when you're worn out with the heat." And then she thought for a moment. "I suppose I should like fall best since that's when I was born."

"Which day?"

"October twelfth, a week from Monday," she replied. "I'll be nineteen."

He shook his head. "Such an advanced age! We must celebrate it early."

She glared at him. "Don't you dare spend another penny on me."

"Getting bossy now that you're an old married woman of, what, sixteen hours?"

She grinned. "When's your birthday?"

"I reached the advanced age of thirty-one in May. On the twentieth."

Suddenly earnest, she said, "I don't mind, Clifford. That you're older, I mean. Unless it bothers you that you've married a silly young girl."

"I sometimes worry that I'm too old for you, but you're never silly, Garnet."

She shook her head. The sun burned through the clouds, thinning the gray to white and then a faded blue. Garnet folded up the lap robe as they re-entered the city. They'd circled around and were approaching downtown from the south, near the tobacco warehouses. She wondered which of these Luther used and noticed saloons and seedy-looking rooming houses nearby. He probably stayed in one of those when he brought the tobacco to market. She marveled at the tallest building in the city, a bank, where Clifford's friend and the witness at their wedding was vice-president, and Garnet's eyes opened wide at the sight of the new public library, a grand building with columns and steps. She couldn't imagine that many books in one place. There were elaborate houses, a huge stone courthouse, and countless shops. "We'll visit those tomorrow," Clifford said.

"So many," she murmured. "Why there's a butcher shop! A whole store just for meat! And back there we passed one just for jewelry and a photographer's store. No, what was it called?"

"Studio. Whoa," Clifford called out suddenly to the horse. "I've just had the most brilliant idea." His entire face glowed. "Let's have a photograph made. A wedding photograph."

"Sure," she said. "But I'd want to wear my wedding dress and look nice." She wiggled her fingers at her windblown hair.

He told her to wait, leaped out to enter the studio, and returned in minutes. "It's all set. We'll come back this afternoon, and he'll have it ready for us on Saturday. Will that give you enough time to primp?"

So they had their picture taken, posing soberly for the intriguing process, and ate another lovely dinner served by their waiter. His name was William, and he soon knew that Mrs. Clark loved a pot of tea, and Mr. Clark had coffee with his dessert. William told them about a show at the Opera House that promised barber shop quartets, a harpist, and magicians. Garnet clapped her hands, and Clifford said they must go.

On Friday morning they shopped. Fanny had sent a long list of items ranging from rosin to books. Garnet was careful not to exhibit too much enthusiasm over anything because Clifford wanted to buy everything she admired. In one store she found just what she wanted for Lorena: a silk-lined sewing basket which she outfitted with fine needles, thimbles, and thread.

Clifford said they must go into the jewelry store, an elegant and, to Garnet, intimidating little shop because Gert wanted him to buy her a new pocket watch. "A man's?" Garnet asked when he lingered at the case full of men's watches.

"Oh, yes. You haven't been around Gert much, have you? She wears men's shirts and shoes and would probably wear trousers except it would scandalize Fanny." He waved her away. "Look at all the treasures while I'm choosing this."

There were plenty of beautiful things to see. In one case she looked at rings: diamonds, rubies, pearls, and the most amazing little coral ring cut to look like a flower. A young man asked if she required assistance, and she mumbled that she was waiting for her husband to choose a watch. The salesman hovered, however, and she wondered if he was required to watch over such valuable merchandise. In one case there were brooches with all kinds of stones, some set in silver and some in gold. One caught her eye: it was shaped in an oval with golden swirls and swoops, sometimes narrow and sometimes wider, twined like an artistic vine. Not quite in the center was a purple stone with two tiny pearls below it, looking like dew dripping off a lovely purple flower. "Oh," she breathed and turned to make sure Clifford hadn't heard her.

She whispered to the young man, "What is that stone?"

"Amethyst, ma'am, with seed pearls and set in ten carat gold. Very new and fashionable right now. Would you like to see it?" He started to open the case, but she shook her head.

"No, thank you. I was just curious." She joined Clifford.

"Did you see marvelous things?" he asked.

"Many marvelous things. Not that I need any of them."

He shook his head as if she confounded him, and they moved on to the next shop. By afternoon her feet were tired and when they arrived back at the hotel she asked if she could have some tea. Clifford said certainly, and a boy appeared at their room with a huge tray holding a full pot of tea and a plate of dainty cookies. It was magic, she thought, expensive magic perhaps, but terribly exciting. How strange it would be next week to go back to regular, ordinary life. But it wouldn't be ordinary; she'd be living in a different house with two eccentric women who didn't seem to like her much. Brushing her concerns away like a cobweb, she thought stoutly that, after all, she'd be living with Clifford, dearest Clifford, and she'd manage.

After enjoying the show at the Opera House on Friday evening, they spent most of Saturday morning in their room, which she'd come to think of as home. When she remembered they were leaving the next day, she sighed.

He lowered his newspaper. "What's making you sad, dear heart?"

She was playing with Lorena's sewing basket, placing the little items in it just so even though they'd probably get scrambled on the trip home. "I'm not sad, Clifford, not at all. It's just that everything has been so perfect that I hate for it to end."

He smiled and folded up the paper. "I know. But it needn't be over, Garnet. Why, I'm looking forward to next week when I can come home every evening knowing you're waiting for me." Reaching for her hand, he continued, "We'll have my room, and it's the largest, sort of a rat's nest right now with things stuck every which way, but you can make it yours, change things about if you want. We'll put two chairs in there and sit in the evenings and watch the evening star. It'll be our haven."

"You give me so much," she murmured. "And I've brought you nothing."

"You've brought me your sweet self, and that's more precious than anything. Now, why don't you have one last bath in your beloved bathtub and get ready to meet your brother. He's coming at noon, isn't he?"

He was, and a little before noon Clifford and Garnet situated themselves in the lobby so they could see Franklin as soon as he came through the door. She was concerned that he might be intimidated by the hotel's elegance, but she needn't have worried. Right on time Franklin swaggered through the door as if he owned the place, wearing a cheap, gaudy suit and a sprouting moustache. She ran to him and, disregarding the hotel's pretensions, hugged him with abandon, adding a quick kiss on his cheek. "Franklin!" she exclaimed. "You look so grown up and distinguished."

Well, it wasn't quite true. The scraggly moustache might've added a year or two to his age, but he looked like what he was: a farmboy trying for sophistication. And his feigned refinement evaporated when he grabbed Garnet's arms and hollered, "Lord Almighty, Sis, you grew up pretty!"

She grinned and reached for Clifford's hand. "This is my terrible, wonderful brother Franklin, and this is Clifford. He won't like it if you call him Mr. Clark."

Franklin shook hands with his new brother-in-law who smoothly guided them into the dining room and just as smoothly had Franklin talking about horses in no time. Franklin was just as much a victim of Clifford's charm as anybody else. But when the food came, her brother turned somber. "You should've told me about your troubles, Garnet. I'd have come home and kicked Foster's ass into the next state."

She didn't want to talk about David but knew it couldn't be avoided. "Lorena said that if you'd been in the county, you would've probably ended up in jail." She liked how his eyes lit up when she mentioned Lorena. "And it wouldn't have done any good. Everything just came back on me."

Franklin scowled and narrowed his eyes at Clifford, as if he should've done more to protect Garnet. "It's true," Clifford said. "If thrashing Foster would've benefited your sister, I'd have happily done it. I *yearned* to smash that bully's face." His vehemence startled Garnet but certainly earned points with Franklin. "But enough of that; it's over, thank God, and we're living proof that happy endings, extraordinarily happy endings, do exist. How often do you get into town? Can you believe all the building that's going on in Lexington?"

"Folks say they wonder where all the people are coming from," Franklin replied.

Clifford nodded. "Now there's coal money coming into town along with the tobacco and horses. The city's only going to get bigger and bigger when the automobile becomes more common."

Rolling her eyes, Garnet turned to Franklin. "Now he's on his favorite subject. I can't believe he married me instead of an automobile."

"I seen one once," Franklin said, "but they ain't never going to replace the horse. The owner of the farm where I work has a friend who drives one: dirty, noisy things."

"Sort of like a horse, wouldn't you say?" Clifford joked. Franklin didn't laugh. "No, like you, I appreciate good horseflesh, and I think horses will remain popular for sport and pleasure. Nonetheless, automobiles will change the way we travel. And the way we live, for that matter." He passed the rolls to Garnet who was intent on watching the two of them. "For example, I see you, Franklin, as the wave of the future."

Franklin took a swig of milk and nearly used the back of his hand to wipe his mouth. "How's that?" he asked, choosing his napkin instead.

"Well, it's good news for the towns but indicates tough times ahead for our rural counties. Young, ambitious men like you will be flocking to cities for the opportunities offered there. When more factories are built, it'll become even more prevalent. What could Evans County offer you compared to Lexington?" Clifford was in his element, espousing theories like a country store professor.

"Not much, I reckon. I wanted to work with horses, really good horses."

"But that's not the only reason you left," Garnet protested.

"No, Sis, not right then, but you know I would've gone eventually. I reckon maybe I'd have saved up a little more before I came, but working on Grandpa's farm wasn't what I wanted." This was a long speech, nearly a confession, for Franklin.

She placed her hand on his arm, momentarily stopping his attack on the mashed potatoes. "Is this what you really want? Living away from all your kin?"

He reddened. "Aw, Garnet, you know I miss you and Lorena and the little ones, but yeah, this is what I really want. They're pleased with me and keep giving me more responsibilities all the time. Maybe I'll save up enough to settle around here, have a wife and family. Not that I'm anywhere near that now," he mumbled.

Garnet shook her head. "Oh, I know a man has to go where there's work, but there's always a way to manage, and I can't imagine going so far from family."

"Women always want to keep you to home," Franklin said to Clifford.

Clifford nodded. "And thank God for them. Sometimes we men let our ambitions become the priority, and, when all's said and done, it's family that's important. But if you'll pardon me for bringing it up again, the automobile will change that too."

Garnet and Franklin shared a sideways grin.

"When people can return easily for Christmas or a visit, they won't be so hesitant to move away from the homeplace. They'll keep old roots and establish new ones at the same time. You two don't believe me, but it's coming. And as young men move to the cities, the rural areas will become more and more backward and distressed."

This wasn't very pleasant talk for a reunion, and Garnet frowned at Clifford. He winced and switched topics. "So will you have many horses racing this fall, Franklin?"

Her brother attacked this subject as eagerly as his dinner, and they chatted on until Clifford told them he had a few errands. "Oh, yes," Garnet said, "you need to pick up our photograph, don't you?"

"Yes, ma'am. Enjoy yourselves. I'll probably be back around three."

The table suddenly seemed very quiet. "Quite a talker, ain't he?"

"He's that, all right."

"Seems like he's crazy about you."

"I feel the same way. He's been so good to me, through all the troubles and since then too." She couldn't help but glow.

"Good. It's high time you had something nice after all you been through, and I ain't just talking about Foster. I hated leaving you with all of it, but I couldn't stay after what she done." Garnet knew what he was talking about.

"You know, it really turned out better than you'd expect. Now that I've been through some real troubles, I can't believe I let Mama's marriage bother me so much. Oh, it hurt Lorena dreadfully, but otherwise Luther's been a blessing for all of us." Garnet asked for tea. Franklin said he wouldn't mind a cup of coffee.

"I can't stay much longer myself," he said, peering at his watch. "Have to meet my ride in Cheapside around two."

"Such a short visit," she murmured.

"Well, it appears that your husband has plenty of bucks so maybe you two will come up here ever now and then."

She nodded. Franklin doctored his coffee, adding sugar and a lot of milk. "So how can you say that her marrying Luther turned out when Papa was hardly in the ground?"

"Papa was gone, and I know he would've wanted us to be cared for. We barely had enough to eat and wouldn't have had that if you and Luther hadn't helped."

"She just used him."

"Sure she did. But he did it willingly. Lorena said Luther had a terrible crush on Mama when they were young. I think he jumped at the chance to marry her even if she was doing it to keep food on the table."

"She wanted a man in her bed too," he said, reddening.

"That too, I reckon. But they get along, and he's better than Papa at keeping down her scheming. Lorena seems to have gotten over it even though Mama still won't have anything to do with her. Luther manages both of those women pretty well. And he's wonderful with the little ones."

Franklin brightened. "Tell me what they're like now."

"Well, I wrote you that they skipped Lowell ahead two years at school, didn't I? He's so smart, just like Papa, and now he says he wants to be a doctor. The new schoolteacher says he'll do what he can to make sure Lowell gets the schooling he needs. Wouldn't that be something?"

"And Violet," she went on, "is Mama made over. Everybody tells me I look like Mama, but she's the one who acts like her. The world is hers and nobody else matters. She's a terrible flirt; she was all over David when we were courting."

"Bad taste in men."

"Yes, well, I was guilty of that too."

"Why'd you marry him, Sis?"

"He was so sweet while we were courting. And home was wretched."

"What about the baby?"

She dropped her head. "I told you David's aunt took him, but even if she takes good care of him, I miss Ruben like part of my soul's gone."

"Aw, Sis," he murmured. "Maybe you can have another baby."

She wanted to touch his cheek. "I don't think having another replaces the one that's gone, but I reckon it might help. It's early to be thinking about that."

He set his half-full cup down and looked at his watch again. "Got to go. I'll write to you at your new address." She lifted an eyebrow. "Well, I'll write ever now and then, and you be sure to share the letters with Lorena."

"I will, and I'll tell her you sent your love."

She hugged him, not caring if it embarrassed him, and he thumped her back. He hesitated. "You've got a good man this time."

"I thank God for him."

There was still tea in the pot, so she lingered in the nearly empty dining room and thought about her brother, her family, Clifford. All that talk about leaving kin and establishing new families made her think about her own situation. There'd be no quick trips to help Mama like when she was married to David and lived close by, and the farm was nearly as far away. She and Clifford were a family now, and he was her home. For the hundredth time, she wished she could find a way to show her gratitude. He'd empty his wallet if she asked, but that was no proper gift. No object could begin to express how much she appreciated him.

All of a sudden she wanted him fiercely. Glancing at the clock in the lobby, she saw that it wasn't even two thirty yet. He'd said he'd be back about three. Her skin felt unnaturally sensitive, vibrating with every touch of her clothing. My stars, she thought.

As she unlocked the door it struck her that this was the gift she'd give him: seducing him, in broad daylight for heaven's sake, would show how he'd healed her. Her fingers scrabbled through her hair, throwing hairpins haphazardly onto the table. Then she rushed to unbutton and unfasten. Tossing her clothes on one of the armchairs, she slipped into her dressing gown, the silk slithering over her skin. She tied it loosely and went to the bed, arranging first the pillows and then herself. This was foreign territory for her. Women like Mama were practiced at it, but she could only hope her instincts and imagination were enough.

The window was open; it was a balmy day and the drapes billowed in the breeze. She relished the draughts through the robe's thin silk. Envisioning herself, she extended her leg to the breeze, and at the top, she pulled the fabric so one breast peeked out. Now, she told herself, pretend you're asleep and wait for him. It wasn't easy. She feared being truly asleep when he arrived. What if she drooled or flopped over with her naked fanny greeting him when he came in? She tried to arrange her face into the serene expression of a sweet afternoon nap but felt stiff. Come on, Clifford, she urged, I can't stay like this forever.

After waiting for what seemed like hours, she heard long, slow steps and shut her eyes at the sound of his key. He entered the room quietly, perhaps suspecting she might be resting, and breathed, "Charming!"

Behind her she heard him deposit packages on the table and start undressing in as much of a hurry as she'd been. At one point he said, "Damn," under his breath, and it was all she could do not to giggle. Then the jangling of change announced that his pants were off. Good, she thought, and allowed those insistent sensations in her belly to wash over her. He padded to the other side of the bed, and, leaning over, claimed that one nipple with his mouth. What was smoldering caught fire.

In one swift motion, she pushed his shoulders onto the bed and hooked her thumb to loosen the knot of her sash. When she straddled him the gown fell open to become a tent, and she hissed, "Be still!"

Clifford's eyes flew open, but he nodded. First she attended to his mouth. Take your time, she told herself. She spent delicious minutes on his face and neck, and then nibbled at his shoulder. When he tried to wrap his arms around her or rock his hips, she stopped and frowned until he quit. Then she brushed her breasts up and down his chest, his hair tickling her and making her breath come in ragged little bursts. A fine sheen of sweat covered his upper lip, and she licked it.

She shifted but didn't allow him what he desperately wanted. He cried, "Dear Lord, Garnet, please!" Then she allowed him home, and his arms crushed her hips into him until they both found what they were seeking, and she collapsed on him.

He lifted a slow, heavy hand to her head and smoothed her hair away from his face. Feeling wanton and proud of herself, Garnet stretched a bit and pulled his hand to her mouth to kiss it. "Do you," he asked in a deliberate, ironic voice, "still maintain that you're no good at the 'bed part' of marriage?"

She chuckled. "I reckon I just needed the right teacher."

"You reckon?" With a great effort, he scooted up to rest against the headboard.

"That was a present to thank you for loving me."

"The loveliest present of all. "It's almost frightening how much I adore you."

"Sometimes I'm afraid it's a dream."

"Maybe because it seemed impossible for so long."

"But it's real, Clifford, isn't it? Even though tomorrow we have to leave our hotel and go back to living normal lives?"

"It's real, dear heart, forever and ever." He smiled at her, those creases in his face breaking one after another like ripples in a pool. "Oh, our photograph is on the table. See what you think."

She scrambled from the bed, and, ripping off the brown paper, she uncovered the picture. "We look so serious!" she exclaimed. "You sitting there in that fancy chair like a judge. And I, oh Clifford, I look absolutely dumpy!"

"You do not." He sat on the edge of the bed and peered at the photograph. "You're deliciously curvaceous and absolutely perfect, Mrs. Clark."

She scrunched up her nose. "What's the other box?"

Instead of replying, he started dressing. It had to be another gift for her. When he'd put on his pants and shirt, he handed the small black box to her. "Since Evans County cannot begin to offer the amenities of Lexington, I decided to proclaim today as your birthday, even if it is a few days early."

"Clifford!" She tried to put censure into her voice but couldn't hide her pleasure. Inside was the exquisite amethyst brooch. "How did you know I admired this?"

"Spies. I suspect you'll have to get dressed to wear it."

"I love it." She ignored his remark. "I love you."

"Ah, dear heart, I'm delighting in that more every day," he said.

Chapter Four

The trouble started as soon as they'd returned from Lexington. Garnet sat in one of the armchairs facing the window over the Clarks' front porch and absorbed the mellow evening sunshine. It did little to relieve the gloominess of what remained, despite her efforts, Clifford's room remained his, not theirs. From the porch the sound of Fanny's fiddle floated up on the soft spring breeze. Garnet corrected herself; actually, the first night hadn't been bad. With all their honeymoon purchases from Lexington, it'd felt like Christmas. But trouble had reared its head early the next morning and gained intensity for seven long months until tonight, when Garnet finally quit trying to be agreeable.

The first day set the tone. She'd risen before Clifford, eager to fit into the household and make this room their haven, as he'd called it. Dressing quickly, she'd kissed him awake and promised she'd have his breakfast ready by the time he came downstairs, but when she'd gone into the kitchen, she found Fanny standing at the stove frying bacon. Garnet had asked, "Is that for Clifford?"

Fanny said, "I always feed Clifford his breakfast."

Two places were set at the kitchen table, but Garnet wasn't sure one of them was for her. She'd replied, "Sure, but I'd like to do that for him now. And I'd be happy to fix breakfast for you and Gert too."

Still staring at the skillet, Fanny had shaken her head. "Can't. Gert eats early. Keeps farmer's hours."

"Do you make a separate breakfast for her?"

The big dark head had nodded.

"Well, then, I can save you from having to cook two breakfasts. Do you eat with Gert or Clifford?" Garnet had kept her voice cheery. From the looks of Fanny's well-upholstered backside, she probably ate with both of them.

Fanny had shot her a sharp look. With lips pursed she'd said, "I reckon I could have my breakfast with Gert."

Remembering the scene, Garnet rubbed her hand up and down the worn plush of the armchair. She counted that as one of her small victories, but even though Fanny didn't eat with them, she never left them alone in the kitchen.

Garnet recalled that throughout that day, Fanny had blocked every attempt Garnet had made to change things in Clifford's room.

The linens stored in the big chest absolutely could not be moved even though Garnet needed the space. There were no spare armchairs for their room. Plenty of pictures adorned the walls of Clifford's room; there was no need to hang the wedding photograph. Garnet remembered stacking folded clothes on the bed next to the photograph and hoping Clifford would help when he came home. Eager to see him, she'd changed into the cheerful yellow dress, the one he liked so much, dabbed a bit of perfume behind her ears, and gone into the kitchen to ask if she could help with supper. They'd acted annoyed, Gert sprawling at the kitchen table and Fanny waving a raw-knuckled hand and telling Garnet she'd just be in the way. So, hurt and guilty, she'd waited in the front room until she'd heard Clifford's step and rushed into the hall. His amber eyes lit up, and he'd crushed her into a hug, whispering that he hadn't been able to concentrate all day. His big hands crept down her back to rest against her hips, pressing her against his body.

They hadn't realized that Fanny was standing in the doorway. "That's not decent, Clifford," she'd said.

He'd grinned at his sister. "I don't much care, Fan. She's my wife, you know."

Fanny had sniffed, and they'd giggled up the stairs where he'd nonchalantly claimed an armchair from the spare bedroom, emptied the linens onto Fanny's bed, and gone after a hammer and nail to hang their photograph. He'd said, "They've had things their way for years. They'll adjust."

But they hadn't, and he'd done little after that first day to insist that they should. With time, the situation had deteriorated into a quiet battle. In fairness, she conceded, most of the skirmishes happened during the day when Clifford wasn't there to observe them. According to Fanny, Garnet couldn't possibly iron Clifford's shirts properly, nor could she cook to suit him; only Fanny knew how he liked his food. So Garnet was either idle or relegated to peeling potatoes or setting the table, and even the way she performed those tasks displeased the woman. In some ways she didn't blame Fanny for her obstinate behavior; it'd been her house for years, but she did blame Clifford for not taking his wife's side. Since his sisters seemed to think he was the sole provider of the moon hanging above their farm, a tactful word or two from him might have eased the situation. But he never seemed to hear Fanny sniping at her during dinner or sighing that she supposed she could trust Garnet to do the dishes without breaking anything.

And he always caved to Gert who reminded Garnet of an overgrown
baby.

Garnet paced around the room, listening to Fanny's fiddle
singing out a mournful rendition of "Rock of Ages." The two
armchairs sat there, inviting intimacy and coziness, but after the first
week, they were seldom used. When Garnet was grudgingly allowed to
wash dishes, Clifford always went to the front room to read his papers
and magazines. The first week or so, he'd read until she finished and
then they'd gone upstairs. She'd lit the lamp and done some sewing,
and he'd shared interesting bits from the paper with her. This had been
the highlight of her days, a treasure after suffering a day of Fanny's
unfriendly silence or curt rebuffs. One evening, however, before they'd
even been married two weeks, Gert complained about this routine.
"You never sit with us of an evening anymore," she'd said. "Fan's got
her sewing, but you know I don't like that foolishness."

They'd been halfway to the steps.

"Why, I haven't had a game of checkers in ages," she whined.

Clifford had shrugged an apology to Garnet. In seconds,
checkers clattered onto the board and she grabbed her unfinished quilt.
It was bedtime before the games ended, and that had been the nightly
pattern ever since. By midwinter she'd finished the quilt, but this was
little compensation for losing her husband's company. Of course they
still had their nights, filled with love and delight, but she longed to
have him to herself other than in bed, and even there the sisters
intervened.

Mama'd always said that eavesdropping was rude, but Gert and
Fanny rarely bothered to lower their voices, and she sometimes
wondered if they intended for her to hear. One day Fanny had allowed
her to polish the dining room table and from the kitchen she'd heard
Gert remark that Clifford looked tired. Fanny had said it was no
wonder, considering the ruckus he and "that girl" made in the bed
every night. Gert, who slept downstairs, made a disgusted noise, and
afterwards Garnet had felt shy when they made love.

Fanny was playing a wistful, pretty song. The sky turned violet,
and Garnet lit the lamp, noticing that her fingers trembled. Maybe
she'd gone too far. The prevailing attitude of the house was that
Clifford shouldn't be inconvenienced, and Garnet knew she supported
this as much as his sisters. Back in the fall she'd hoped each Sunday
that Clifford would take her riding, and occasionally they did manage a
lovely afternoon traveling around the county or visiting her family or
Lorena. But when Clifford had come down with a slight cold, Fanny'd

blamed it on the outings and then managed to invite either the preacher or some acquaintance for dinner nearly every Sunday, saying it was better for Clifford to rest at home. These afternoons were deadly tedious, and even her talkative husband ran out of things to say before the guests left. One Saturday afternoon, Garnet had asked if he would take her to Lorena's. It'd been late January, but the weather was clear and crisp. Fanny had asked how long Clifford would be gone, that he'd probably miss supper. Before Garnet could reply that it would be a short visit, he said it wouldn't hurt him to miss a meal, and Lorena always had food. Both sisters had a conniption. He needed a good, healthy meal, and Garnet could wait. Hadn't she just visited Lorena before Christmas? Clifford had promised to take her soon. She hadn't complained.

Fanny really did play well, Garnet admitted, collapsing in her chair. Often when Fanny played, Garnet would join them and sing along, hymns mostly, because those were the only songs she knew, and it surprised her when Gert sang with her in a high, clear soprano. But tonight she was in no mood for music. She fretted about what her actions might cause. Probably nothing. Every little detail of her idle, restless life would stay the same, according to the Clark sisters' rules. Once she'd mentioned to Clifford that she'd love to have a house of their own. Maybe someday she could show him what a fine cook she was. Clifford had smiled and nodded.

He just might notice something tonight. After finishing the dishes, Garnet had come upstairs rather than going to the porch. Any minute now Clifford would be folding up his newspaper, joining his sisters, and wondering where she was.

From the porch, Garnet heard Gert say, "Where's Garnet? She's finished washing up." Fanny kept playing.

"Maybe she's resting. I thought she looked sort of puny at supper." Gert paused. "She wouldn't be in there disturbing Clifford while he's reading, would she?" Her voice expressed near horror at this.

Fanny continued to play without responding, but Gert was persistent. "You don't suppose she might be breeding, do you? It seems like she should be breeding by now." Garnet's cheeks burned.

"Course we know she's fertile, but do you reckon Clifford's up to snuff?"

Miserable as she was, Garnet had to stifle a giggle at this, wondering what the man himself would make of his sister's comment.

The fiddle screeched to a halt. "There's nothing wrong with Clifford," Fanny said.

Fanny played a few more bars and finished her song. "Pouting," she said succinctly. "Little Miss Garnet is pouting."

About this time Garnet heard Clifford's step on the porch floor. "Who's pouting?" he asked. Sometimes she wondered if his cheerfulness wasn't a method of avoiding realities.

Fanny snapped, "Garnet's pouting."

"Now why would Garnet be pouting? I've never known her to pout."

Fanny resumed her playing, but Garnet heard a soft hmph.

"You two get into it again today, Fan?" Gert asked.

Wispy strains from the fiddle traveled out into the darkening sky as Fanny kept playing, refusing to answer.

"Get into it?" Clifford asked. "Again? Have you been fussing with Garnet, Fanny?" He sounded disturbed. About time, thought Garnet.

Fanny stubbornly sawed away at her fiddle until Clifford said in an unfamiliar voice, "Fanny, answer me."

His older sister broke off in the middle of a phrase and stated flatly that Garnet had asked to use the sewing machine and she'd refused. She went on to say that the girl had stormed out of the house, walking for most of the afternoon. Did he realize how much of his wife's time was spent walking around the farm instead of doing something useful? As if she'd let me, Garnet retorted in her head.

"Why won't you let her use the sewing machine?" There was an edge to it.

Fanny's voice rose, loud enough for Garnet to hear every note of spite. "Because it's mine, and I'm tired of sharing everything in this house with her. She's always pestering me about something and getting in my way." She sputtered to a stop and then spat, "She's always *here.* I'm sick to death of her being in our house."

Dear God, Garnet whispered into the hand she'd clutched to her mouth. She hadn't realized the woman resented her that deeply. What did she want Clifford to do? Send her away? It was deadly quiet on the dark porch. Then he spoke, as if he were talking to an angry child. "Of course she's always here; this is where Garnet lives now. She's my wife, part of the family."

Fanny didn't reply, but Gert made a clumsy attempt to break the silence. "I don't suppose she'd hurt that sewing machine, Fan."

Fanny started playing again. Garnet heard Clifford come inside, and she flew to close the window, not wanting the sisters to hear what he might say. She rushed to her chair and waited with that squirmy feeling she'd had when a scolding was forthcoming. With heavy steps he walked into their room, shutting the door and looking weary. It was all she could do not to bubble over with apologies and excuses, but she kept her mouth shut as tight as Fanny's. He sat. "I get the impression that there are troubles in this house."

She nodded.

"Do you and Fanny quarrel often?"

She shrugged; it wasn't exactly quarreling, but then she nodded again.

"Am I correct in assuming this has been going on all along?"

"Yes." The self-righteous anger she'd stoked all afternoon was smothering in guilt. This was the first he'd ever shown anything but delight in her.

The muffled sound of the fiddle stopped. "Why didn't you say something?"

Her words came out in a tumble. "I didn't want to upset you. I didn't want to be carrying tales or making you choose sides. And I guess I thought it might get better. You said they'd adjust."

"And what do you all fuss about? What's important enough to disturb the peace of this house?"

She told him, and relating all the little spats fired her indignation all over again. He might view them as petty, but she lived with them on a daily basis. "I swear I'm trying to be sweet and cheerful and helpful, but they won't let me help, find fault with anything they do let me do, and then complain that I'm idle. They resent me."

"Resent? That's a strong word."

She lifted her chin. By God, she hadn't escaped from one bully to suffer the same from two old women. "What else would you call it? Haven't you noticed how Fanny picks at me all the time? How she and Gert won't let you spend any time alone with me? They want you and their house to themselves. Maybe they'd like it better if you kept me in a shed on the back of the farm or something."

He shook his head. "I don't see why you women can't get along."

Sliding out of her chair, she knelt by his long legs and touched his knee. "Please, Clifford, can't we have our own house? I know I'm young, but they make me feel like a child. I want to make a home for us."

He wasn't moved. "That would cut them to the quick. They've cared for me since I was born. I can't just buy a house down the road and wave good-bye."

Why not? Despairing that this was a war she'd never win, she tried to rise with dignity and went back to her chair. She wouldn't beg again. Although he acted more perplexed than angry there was an uncomfortable edge to his voice when he repeated, "I don't understand why you didn't tell me about this."

"And I don't understand why you didn't notice."

This silenced him momentarily. "So what do you want me to do?"

Thoroughly angry now, she hardly trusted her voice. She'd told him what she wanted, and he wouldn't do it. "I want you to take me to Lorena's on Sunday. I have sewing to do."

"Oh, I'll make sure you can use Fanny's machine," he replied grimly.

Just as grimly she fired back, "I'll not touch her sewing machine. I've been bullied before, Clifford, and I won't let it happen again."

"Things will change. I'll see to it."

"Then they'll resent me even more."

He lifted his hands helplessly. "Then what do you want me to do?"

"Take me to Lorena's. Or if Fanny has company coming, I'll walk. I'll stay for a week, maybe help my mother a day or two, do my sewing." She wouldn't look at him.

"Are you punishing me?"

"Maybe."

"All right, I'll take you, and while you're gone I'll talk to the girls."

It was no victory. She felt heartsore and miserable but was determined to hold her ground. There was no reason they couldn't have their own house. Either Clifford respected his sisters more than her or he was half-afraid of them.

***

An armed truce ruled the house until Sunday. Not wanting to be accused of pouting, Garnet was polite, but steered clear of the Clark sisters. Fanny was no friendlier than she'd ever been, but the picking and sniping stopped. Gert didn't seem to get it. Every evening as usual, she begged her brother to play checkers and made no secret of her disappointment when he refused.

Their time alone was awkward as well. She supposed she should be glad he hadn't dismissed her comments as a fit of moodiness and gone back to life as usual. But she hated the uneasiness, and he was unusually quiet, even on their drive to the farm. Half a dozen times Garnet nearly relented and asked him to turn the buggy around, but she reckoned she'd never escape the misery if she capitulated.

When Lorena came to the door, her dark eyebrows took wing. Garnet told her she'd come to do some sewing and hoped it was no trouble. Lorena shook her head, but her eyes narrowed. Before Clifford's buggy had reached the end of the lane, she was asking questions. "Could we have tea?" Garnet asked wearily. After listening for a while, Lorena shook her head. "Why on earth did you need a sewing machine so bad that you had to leave your husband?"

"I want to make him a shirt for his birthday, but that isn't the point."

"She made you mad, and you wanted Clifford to take up for you. He didn't so you had a little fit to get even with the old bitch. She's probably tickled to have you gone for a week. That weren't too smart, girl."

Garnet snapped, "They treat me like an orphan! They resent that Clifford brought me into their house, and, make no mistake about it; they consider it theirs." Lorena let her rant again about the slights and hurts, but when Garnet ran through all her complaints, the woman was silent, one finger drawing patterns on the oilcloth.

"What?" Garnet asked. "I know you have something to say."

Lorena nodded, moving her concentration to the sugar bowl. "First off, ain't this a terrible situation compared to where you was a year ago? Beaten half to death, sued for divorce, shamed, and forced to give up your baby? You've come to a sorry pass."

This certainly wasn't what Garnet had expected.

"And the other thing is that you ain't mad at those big old women near as much as you're put out with your husband. It's Clifford you're mad at, and it's Clifford you're trying to punish by coming up here." Lorena leaned back in her chair and squinted at Garnet. "And he knows it. He ain't a stupid man."

Garnet burst out, "It seems awful stupid for him not to notice what it's like for me to live with those sisters of his. How could he be so sweet and sensitive while we were courting and not see how unhappy I am now?"

Lorena chuckled. "Well, you're won, wed, and bedded now. He don't have to worry about pleasing you like he did last summer. And, truth be told, he's got the perfect situation: Gert's running the farm and making more money than he does, I'd say. Fanny's keeping the house all smooth and comfortable, and pretty Garnet's there willing to warm his bed. What more could a man want? What were those stories you children used to read about over in Arabia where the king, or whatever he was called, had lots of wives, making him feel like he ruled the world? I reckon Clifford's got it made."

Frustrated as she was, Garnet had to smile at a mental picture of Clifford as a sultan, but she soon sobered. She didn't like hearing it, but Lorena was right. "And now I've disrupted it."

Lorena went to the kitchen cabinet. "Do you want some cake with your tea?"

Garnet shook her head. "Do you think I've made a terrible mistake?"

"Oh, I reckon it'll all come right. He loves you dearly, but you've upset his peace. Didn't Louise teach you none of her little ways? You might've done better working on him with that pretty face instead of getting all riled up and stubborn."

"I never had much respect for Mama's scheming."

"Depends on the purpose. I wasn't above sweet-talking Deke ever now and then if it was something important."

"I'm a fool."

"Naw. Just young. When's he supposed to come back for you?"

"Next Sunday, I guess. I said a week."

"Hmm. He'll be back before that, and he'll have some kind of solution. This'll be another puzzle for him, and Clifford Clark's a great one for puzzles. And Garnet," Lorena said, more softly now, "you're right too. Oh, you ain't done such a good job handling it, but there's no way you can keep living in that house. Them old gals've had things their way too long to make room for their brother's wife. They was going to bully any woman who came between them and their baby brother."

"He'll come up with something, won't he?"

"No doubt about it. Now, let's get started on that sewing. I don't think he'll last past the middle of the week."

Even with the painstaking handwork that Garnet used to make tiny tucks and perfect edges, they were well on their way to finishing Clifford's shirt by Monday evening. Garnet's anxiety disappeared in the face of Lorena's gruff cheerfulness, but at night she worried, missing Clifford and wondering what he was thinking. As penance, she went to her mother's house on Tuesday and spent the day in a whirlwind of cleaning and cooking, enjoying the pull of hard work deep in her muscles.

Mama never questioned why Garnet appeared so mysteriously, but she did ask about why there was no baby yet. This was a sore point. Since shortly after the wedding, Garnet had mourned each monthly show of blood. Although she'd assumed she would conceive as quickly with Clifford as she had with David, her belly remained flat. Ruben would be two years old by the end of the month, and even though infrequent letters from David's Aunt Martha indicated the child was thriving, pieces of paper were a poor substitute. Another baby would help, at least a little.

On Wednesday evening, as Garnet was washing dishes, she heard a buggy. Lorena grinned. "Told you he wouldn't last the week. Run upstairs and tidy your hair."

When she came downstairs, Clifford stood in the front hall looking uneasy, but his eyes glowed when he saw her. "I know it's only Wednesday, but I thought I'd take a chance that you'd finished your sewing," he said.

"I did. Last night, actually," she replied and held out her arms to him. Relieved, his face broke into a huge grin, and he hugged her close, murmuring that he couldn't stand to be away from her one minute longer.

Ignoring their embrace, Lorena swooped in and asked if he had eaten.

"Well, no," he said. "I left the bank, stopped to tell the girls I was coming over here, and didn't even think about it."

Lorena shook her head at him, and they followed her into the kitchen, Clifford grasping Garnet's hand as if she might try to escape. "Actually I want to talk to you too, Lorena. I have this plan," he said, acting unnaturally shy, "and I wanted your opinion."

"That's fine, but you'll do better with food in your stomach. Quit mooning at your husband, Garnet, and slice up some bacon. It'll just be breakfast for supper, Clifford, but maybe it'll hold body and soul together."

In no time they had him seated at the kitchen table with a full plate of bacon and eggs. Lorena and she sat patiently, replying to his questions about how they'd spent the last few days. Evidently he didn't want to talk about his plan until he finished, and even after they cleared the table and refilled his cup, he seemed in no hurry to start. Garnet had never witnessed such awkwardness in him.

He cleared his throat and looked straight at her. "First, I apologize to you, Garnet, for being so naïve as to think we could set up housekeeping in a house that's already been kept by two women for decades. I never looked past the joy of our wedding. And, even more earnestly, I beg your pardon for ignoring signals of your discomfort." The speech sounded rehearsed but no less sincere for it.

"I shouldn't have waited to get angry before saying something."

He shrugged. "You took it better than most women would, but I wish you'd knocked me in the head earlier and made me see how untenable the situation was."

Garnet wished she could wriggle into his arms and enjoy the reconciliation, but she knew his apology was merely the beginning and she was a little leery of what he might propose. He spoke less formally now. "And you were right about my sisters. They truly don't want you there. It's made them spiteful, and I'm ashamed of them especially since they're mistreating you out of some kind of distorted loyalty to me. I've lived with them too long." He drank some coffee. "Why, Sunday night, when I came back from bringing you over here, Gert sat down in front of the checker board, and said, 'This is the way it should be. Let's have a game.' I was already missing you sorely, and for her to take joy in your absence floored me. And Fanny, well, the next night at supper she said, 'What a treat, just the three of us again.'

"I couldn't eat; I swear it, Garnet, and I asked her why she couldn't accept that you're part of the family. She wouldn't reply, so I told her we'd have to move out if she wouldn't treat you properly. She said I'd never leave. I was so upset that I just left the table and walked for an hour."

About time, Garnet thought. "What do they want you to do with me?"

"I don't know."

Clearing her throat, Lorena rose, poured more coffee and drained the last of the tea into Garnet's cup. "They can't have you and not your wife."

"No, they can't," Clifford agreed. "But, and I'm desperately sorry if this hurts you, Garnet, I cannot in good conscience ignore their feelings either. Since I waited so long to marry, they thought things would never change. I considered alternatives: buying a house in Ashton, building a house on the back of the farm. But they'd be insulted by either option and expect me to be up at the house all the time anyway. It would be nearly the same as it is now."

Garnet's heart sank. Moments before, she'd been exulting in her victory, but now she wondered how she'd fare in this tangle of loyalties. Out of the corner of her eye she saw Lorena flash her a cautious look, but whether it was concern for her feelings or a warning, Garnet couldn't tell. Clifford's fingers, all knobs and knuckles, twitched against the table. "So I started thinking. Haven't been worth a nickel these past three days. And I came to an uncomfortable conclusion about myself: I get bored easily. It's not a noble trait, doesn't show much character or discipline, but it's a fact. Part of it's because my work bores me. For a while there, courting and marrying you distracted me, but the fact is that I'm tired to death of the bank."

Lorena and Garnet watched him, not sure where he was going. He continued with a self-deprecating laugh, "Over the years I've tried to amuse myself with different interests. Sent off for courses, tried painting pictures, read about serious horse breeding. The girls have despaired of me for years, especially since what they want me to do is run the farm."

Garnet wished he'd get to the point. She fidgeted, restless as Clifford's fingers. Lorena rose to light a lamp. He kept talking about the same things until Garnet couldn't tell if he was being hesitant or dramatic. She felt like kicking him. Lorena cleared her throat and was about to say something when he said something new.

"So I wondered if a complete change of work, even a change of scene might not be the best thing. New work for me, a home of our own, a real beginning of our life together. Since Gert and Fanny know how tired I am of my job, they could probably swallow this more easily than a move within the county. You see, it would more of a case of Clifford moving on rather than Clifford moving out."

She narrowed her eyes. "I wish you'd tell me what you're getting at."

He wriggled all over. "You see, dear heart, I know how much you hated the thought of leaving this area when, um, Foster proposed it. I'm not sure how you'll feel when I suggest the same thing. Unfortunately," he paused. "I cannot see any other way out of this muddle without hurting my sisters or making you miserable."

"Maybe you'd better tell me."

He inhaled noisily. "I thought we'd move to Lexington. You liked Lexington, didn't you? Sam Wallace, that's the man who stood up with us at our wedding, has been pestering me for years to work at his bank. I, uh, sent him a telegram today asking if the offer was still good."

She frowned. "But you'd still be working in a bank."

He grabbed her hand, his voice rising. "Yes, but it would be a different bank in a different city, and that's not all. I thought we could build a store, just like what you've always dreamed of, with a house behind it. I'd have to work at the bank until the store was established, but then we could run it together and make a lovely home. I know you'd miss your family and Lorena, but Franklin lives nearby, and I wouldn't be a bit surprised if Lowell won't be in school there before long."

He said most of this in one breath and then was silent, his eyes pleading, hoping he'd pleased her. After waiting so long for him to get to the gist of his idea, she was bewildered. "Well, I. . . I just don't know."

"It'd be a hell of a lot of work for you, girl," Lorena said, ignoring Clifford.

He spoke quickly. "Oh, I know that, and I've told Wallace I could only work short hours so I'd be available mornings and evenings."

"I've never been afraid of work."

"Be different with babies," Lorena said.

Clifford reddened. "Maybe I'd only have to work at the bank for a year or so to pay off the debt."

"Debt?"

"Well, yes, there would be debt. I don't have the money to build a store, stock it, buy furniture for a house. Certainly I have a bit saved, but . . ."

At the same time, Garnet and Lorena said, "I have a little money."

He smiled at Lorena. "And I appreciate that, but I'd rather owe a bank than a friend. And I know you have your hundred dollars, dear heart, but that's yours. I'd need to talk about financing with Wallace, but I'm sure we could work it out."

His eyes were begging for her acceptance, but she hesitated. "But what about Mama and the little ones? I can't just go off and leave them."

"Why not?" Lorena's voice was blunt "It ain't your job to take care of your mother's children. Now I ain't saying you have to swallow this idea whole." She looked darkly at Clifford who sobered. "But you shouldn't dismiss it on your mother's account."

Garnet shook her head, trying on the idea like a pair of stiff shoes. "I'd hate to be so far from you, Lorena."

"I'd miss you too, girl, but you need your own place."

Clifford chimed in, "Well, and if there's money enough, I still yearn to buy an automobile. Why the trip down here would be nothing!"

Garnet smiled at him. "Except that we can't close a store to come visiting and hope to pay off debts."

He soaked up her smile. "We'd manage." Saying nothing more, he watched her. Her mind swept from one idea to the next, considering, weighing. It was a good plan. Although moving scared the daylights out of her, she remembered his ease in Lexington. She didn't have to do this alone.

She nodded, meeting his eyes across the table. "You're my home, Clifford, and all I've ever wanted is for me to be your home too. We'll build a store."

His grin lit up the kitchen. Garnet was sent to fetch paper and pen, and the women pulled their chairs on either side of him to offer ideas as he sketched a plan for the store and the house behind it. Lorena said there must be a plot for a garden; her girl wouldn't be happy without one even if there was little time to tend it. And Garnet said there must be room for dry goods and a place to measure and cut them, and they chattered on, ideas and dreams flying faster than Clifford's fingers could draw. It could work, could even be the happy refuge she'd always dreamed of. He was trying to please her, not entirely his sisters, she thought, watching him sketch the chicken coop she'd requested, his long arm brushing her own as he drew. She felt the heat of him through his snowy shirt and shifted so the next time his arm brushed it was against her breast. And then she realized he was keenly aware of her too, his breath coming a bit faster and color staining his neck. Lorena glanced up at Garnet and then eyed Clifford. One eyebrow raised.

"It's nearly nine o'clock," she announced. "You all ain't planning to go home at this hour are you?"

He cleared his throat. "Well, much as I don't want to, I have to go to work in the morning." Clifford's hip pressed against hers. "And I imagine my sisters expect us back this evening."

Lorena rolled her eyes. "They know where you're at. Go to bed; I'll wake you all early enough to get you to Ashton on time. Bed your horse down, Clifford."

He glanced at Garnet, his eyes warm as fresh sorghum. "Suit you?"

He left for the barn while she gathered the scribbled papers. Lorena said good-night with a quirky little smile, and Garnet ran up to the sewing room to turn down the bed. He rushed up the steps, and she swayed against him with eager, fluttery hands. "You realize we probably wouldn't have made it to the end of the lane," he said, unbuttoning his shirt recklessly.

"This is better than lying in a ditch."

"Won't scare the horse either." He crushed her against him and kissed her like he was about to die. They grappled as much as they made love, each of them punishing the other for the loneliness and frustration of the last days.

When they came to their senses, Clifford settled her onto his shoulder. "I suppose you can tell how much I've missed you."

She chuckled. "It's not been that long."

"Felt like forever, dear heart, especially since you chose to leave me."

"I'd never leave you." She made circles on his chest with her finger. "But it seemed like you'd never notice. It probably wasn't the best way to handle it."

He kissed the top of her head. "Oh, I don't know; it was pretty effective."

"And I did have sewing to do."

"So did you make a new frock?"

"Oh, wait," she said clambered out of bed. She handed him his shirt, wrapped in tissue. "No, I made you a birthday present."

He unfolded the dress shirt. "So the sewing was for me?"

She nodded.

"What a fool I am!" He reached for her, crushing the shirt between them. Garnet started to protest but supposed she could always iron it again. She snuggled against him, home again, but stayed awake for a long time vacillating between anxiety and joy.

Chapter Five

Well before daylight Garnet stumbled into the kitchen, yawning cheerfully, to see Lorena at the stove flipping pancakes. Garnet fetched plates and the molasses pitcher, fitting right into Lorena's pattern. They'd always worked well together, and Garnet felt a prickle of sadness at the thought of moving away from the woman who'd been more of a mother than her own.

"You seem frisky this morning. Slept well, did you?"

Garnet grinned.

"Thought I'd better offer you all a bed before you embarrassed yourselves."

They could hear Clifford's heavy steps above them, and Lorena, suddenly serious, grabbed Garnet's arm. "He come through for you, girl, and I'll allow it's a good plan. But ain't none of them heroes all the time. Remember that."

Garnet halted.

"Not to say we don't let them down too; I'm sure we do. But don't go expecting any man to be everything for you. They ain't one of them can do it."

Garnet only had time enough to nod soberly before Clifford came into the kitchen, rubbing the dark stubble along his jaw. "Good morning, Lorena. I hate to disgrace your table with an unshaved face."

She flipped another pancake onto a platter. "They's probably an old razor of Deke's around here somewhere, but I doubt it'd be much count. You'd probably cut yourself so bad people'd think you slept with a wildcat last night."

Ducking his head and blushing fiercely under the stubble, Clifford made quite a process out of seating himself, and Garnet, recalling the pink marks she'd left on her husband's back, had to bite her cheeks to keep from laughing.

The sky was still gray when they left. She leaned against him, a hand against his leg as he drove the buggy. "It would be best," he said, "if you didn't mention anything to Fan or Gert. I'll handle that tonight."

"Oh, I wouldn't. Besides you might have a telegram from Mr. Wallace today."

"Yes, and I'd feel better about talking to the girls once there's a solid offer."

"I wonder what they'll say."

"I hope they'll be kind to you. I'm the one who's changing things." He squeezed her hand. "It'll be intriguing to see which matters more to them: keeping things the way they've always been or keeping me. I suspect routine will win."

Garnet was dubious. "I think they want both."

He turned his head to smile at her, looking disreputable with his whiskers. "They can't have both. I'm yours now."

She ran a finger along his jaw. "Have you ever thought about growing a beard?"

His laugh rang out along the road. "Now that would be a change indeed! I had a moustache for several years and shaved it off. Why? Do you want me to grow one? I suppose I'm half-way there right now."

She wrinkled her nose. "No. But Mama made Luther grow one, said it made him look distinguished."

He chuckled. "So, do you think I need facial hair to make me distinguished?"

She kissed him high on his cheek, the soft part above the hairline. "You're perfectly distinguished the way you are."

Knowing what was coming made the day long, and she tried her best to stay out of Fanny's way. However at noon, when Gert complained about the weeds in the garden, Garnet offered to work on them, and the woman said she could. The sun warmed Garnet's back and loosened her muscles, and, as always, tending a garden calmed her soul. One tenacious tree root had grown to the edge of the beds, and she tugged, first with her right hand, and then with both to force it from the ground. She enjoyed the strain on her arm muscles and thought back to when her arm was broken. After Dr. Thomas removed the splint she'd been cautious about using it, but he'd said that when a broken bone healed it was often stronger than ever. She wondered if that was true with marriages. She dusted the dirt from her hands. Be strong, Clifford, she pleaded silently. For both of us.

Like the night before, he waited until supper was over before he started talking. Garnet yearned to escape to the kitchen, to start the dishes or do anything but witness the confrontation, but a pointed look from Clifford told her to stay put. Fanny kept all the leaves in the polished walnut table in case there was company for Sunday dinner, and Garnet's place had always been at the far end, facing her husband but a mile away from him. She'd always felt like Clifford was in another county.

He talked calmly, bringing out the expected telegram from Mr. Wallace and explaining how he wanted to explore this opportunity. Gert protested first, waving her huge, calloused hands in the air as she talked.

He countered her arguments, one by one, and reached for the woman's arm. "Gert," he murmured. "I had to grow up eventually, and I've taken a good long time to do it. Let me be a man."

She turned her head aside, and Garnet realized that gruff old Gert was weeping. Fanny sat silent as a stone. She glared once at Garnet, making her want to slide under the table, but said nothing, just cocking her head at her brother and appraising him with glittering eyes. She pursed those familiarly full lips and said, "Hush, Gert. He's made up his mind, and you'll not change it."

When Clifford turned to his older sister, Garnet's heart beat faster; what Fanny said counted for more than her sister's tears. The stern-faced woman clasped her hands and began. "When Father was ill, he asked Gert and me to keep this farm in trust for you. You never showed any interest in it, but we tried our best to preserve it for you."

He started to say something, but Fanny stopped him with a shake of her head that set her jowls quivering. "We've been patient with all your foolishness, the wild schemes you cooked up and all these years at the bank, which you didn't seem to like. We allowed you to do whatever you wanted while we kept the farm, even though you never had the slightest sense of duty or discipline about it."

Garnet felt her insides shrinking in sympathy, but Clifford continued to look at Fanny warmly, nodding in agreement with her. Fanny worked her mouth, not to stem tears, Garnet guessed, but from restraint. "All the while we thought you'd settle down, abide by Father's wishes, and run the farm as he meant for you to do. We made a sacred promise, but apparently that means nothing to you, nor does the land. It grieves me that you're tossing away this farm to be a shopkeeper."

The last word was uttered with such distaste that Garnet felt a quick wave of sickness. Spit gathered in her mouth, and she had to swallow again and again to fight the sensation. Keeping a store was her dream, not Clifford's, and an agony of guilt coursed alongside the nausea. She almost spoke.

Big tears snaked down Gert's face, but years of deferring to her older sister prevented her from saying anything. Fanny had the pulpit and no one was about to challenge her ownership. "You had to up and marry, and I suppose that's the natural way of things." She stopped but didn't even glance at Garnet. "And we thought, now he'll settle down and run the farm. But, no, you just trotted off to your fancy bank and then came home to play with your pretty new toy."

She turned her eyes, dark with spite, on Garnet. "I don't relish having a stranger in my house. You're not kin even if you do bear our name. You're just another one of Clifford's hare-brained schemes, and I'll be glad to be shed of the both of you."

With this she stood, gathering her self-righteous dignity around her like a cloak. Outside the open window Garnet heard a mourning dove calling, but there were no other sounds; even Gert had quit sniffling. At the doorway Fanny paused, filling it with her bulk, and said, "I suppose you've completely squandered your inheritance from Father and you'll want help from us."

Such harsh words would have dissolved Garnet into a puddle of shame. Maybe years of facing Fanny had enabled Clifford to handle irate bank customers and face David in such a dignified and powerful way. Still, Garnet inched down in her chair. "No, I still have savings, Fanny: some left from Father and some I've invested over the years from my salary. You and Gert were always generous in allowing me to keep my earnings." Once again he patted Gert and smiled sweetly at her. "I was asking for blessings rather than money, girls, and I'm deeply sorry that I've disappointed you. I've made serious errors in judgment over the years, but as you said, Fanny," and with this he stood and faced his older sister, "it's time for me to go."

As soon as she heard his chair move, Garnet fled to the kitchen. She slopped hot water into the dishpan, adding soap and dirty dishes. At first she sped through them, but then she made herself slow down; she was in no hurry to face anyone, including Clifford. Her demands had brought this ugliness upon him.

She wiped and polished every surface, dried every dish, emptied and rinsed the dishpan. She swept the floor, laid out dishes for breakfast, and spread towels to dry. When she could delay no longer, she crept through the shadowy dining room to the front hall where she heard the sisters' chairs creaking outside on the porch. Peeking into the front room, she saw no sign of her husband. Perhaps he was so utterly destroyed by Fanny's words that he'd hidden himself upstairs.

Even in the gloom she could tell their room was empty. Without lighting a lamp, she stood at the window, arms clasped around her waist. Maybe he was walking or tending his horse; there were dozens of places he could be. He'd come to her eventually, but wherever Clifford was, however he was reacting to Fanny's scolding, it was her fault. When she started all of this with that silly little spat over the sewing machine, she'd never dreamed he'd pay such a price.

She heard him step onto the front porch, speak quietly to his sisters, and come upstairs. He entered the room, but she didn't move. "Why are you standing in the dark?" She heard the scrape of a match as he lit lamps.

She hugged herself more tightly but said nothing. When he came up behind her and touched her shoulder, he saw the silvery tracks on her cheeks. "Oh, dear heart, you're crying!"

She choked out, "I'm crying for the things she said to you. And it's all my fault."

"No, no, it's not your fault. This is our decision," he whispered. "And it's not the first time I've felt the edge of Fanny's tongue. I'm fine, sweet girl."

Although he wound his arm around her, inviting her to lean against him, she wouldn't unbend. "After all she said, how can you be? I just don't understand," she said, gulping a big breath. "I was brought up to think that kin was what you were supposed to value more than anything. You do for your people, you care for your people, and you stick to your people. And yet, it seems to me that kinfolk treat strangers better than they do each other. They expect this or they expect that, and if you don't do what they want, they lash out at you." The more she spoke the angrier she became. "My mother hurt me, hurt Grandpa, hurt people all the time because they didn't do what she wanted them to do. Is that being kin, Clifford? If it is, I'd just as soon be an orphan."

"Families do seem to have this uncommon urge to control each other," he agreed. His lips moved against her hair. "Garnet, can you really see me as a farmer? And after all this time, can you see Gert and Fanny doing anything but laughing at me when I made farming decisions?"

She couldn't help but smile. He was cradling her, rocking her with his arms. Moving her over to his chair, he sat and folded her onto his lap. "I can't deny a thing Fanny said about me. It's all true. I've been spoiled and foolish, and I knew they expected me to take my place and run the farm. I simply didn't want to." She squirmed.

"But they are, regardless of everything, kin. What makes you go back to your mother's house to help out even when she's ugly to you? That's the pull of kinship. We have to ignore what they say and love them in spite of themselves."

He seemed so wise and calm, as if Fanny's criticisms hadn't bothered him a bit, and she wanted to slow her jumpy body to the steady pace of his heartbeat, regular and soothing under her ear. "People should be better to each other," she murmured.

"I wouldn't argue with you there." He smoothed her skirt. "You know, much of this old argument is moot anyway. I'm sure Fanny's telling the truth when she said my father's last wish was for them to keep the farm for me, but I also suspect that she adds her own interpretation to the story. My father was forty six years old when I was born; he never knew me as an adult and always seemed like a very old man who never wanted much to do with me especially since my birth caused his beloved wife's death. I think he was telling the girls to take care of me more than issuing some kind of deathbed edict declaring that I *must* be master of the farm when I came of age." He laid his arm down her hip, gathering her closer. "Of course that's the way I want to see it," he admitted. She could sense that he was smiling.

His neck smelled familiarly lemony, the result, she'd discovered, of a shaving lotion specially ordered from New York. She loved his scent more than the perfume he'd given her although she'd never tell him so. "For all these years, then, your sisters have believed that they've run this farm for your sake?" Skepticism raised her voice.

He chuckled. "I should've known you'd see through the façade. They love the independence, and they're welcome to it. Truth be told, Joe Hardy and his boys do most of the farming. You've met them, haven't you?" She nodded against his chest. "They've lived on the back of the farm in a tenant house for nearly twelve years, and as Joe's sons got older, they've taken on more of the labor. That's where I went after supper: to tell Joe my plans. I don't know if he's been waiting for me to be his boss, but he needs to know I never will be." Clifford paused. "Now, I'm not implying the girls don't work hard. They do, but they love it, and wouldn't want to give it up, even to me."

She wriggled a little to see his face and then fidgeted more, clenching her shoulder up to her neck and down again. Every muscle in her body felt taut. "I wish we could just go to Lexington tomorrow."

She could tell by his voice that he was smiling. "Well, we'll have to go soon, maybe the middle of next week. There are innumerable things to do. We must choose a site for the store and spend hours with Sam Wallace ironing out the financial details. Then we must see a builder and contract with him to start construction. It won't be a pleasure trip this time."

"Yes, it will." Her dress irritated her, all bunched up beneath her, and she wriggled to free it.

He was amused. "You needn't sit on my lap if it's uncomfortable."

"No, no. I'm just jumpy."

"I noticed." He continued to stroke her, coaxing her to relax. He was still talking about Lexington. "And I'll have to make additional trips myself to check on things and consult with Wallace. I'm not sure when he intends me to start or even what he wants me to do. I may have to begin work long before our house is finished."

This startled her. "You'd leave me here?"

"I'll probably stay at a rooming house or the Wallace's, and that wouldn't be much fun for you. And it'll be cheaper if I go alone; we'll need to be thrifty." He was patting and rubbing her hip and arm, noticing, she was sure, that she was more anxious than ever now. "I don't enjoy being separated from you, but it wouldn't be for long."

"I can't imagine living here even a few days without you." Her voice wobbled.

"Shh," he murmured to her. "Don't be afraid of them. I told Fanny to focus her displeasure where it belongs, on me, rather than you. It won't be so bad. She's had her say and will calm down once she's resigned to us leaving."

Outside in the hallway, she heard his older sister's step as she went to her room, and instant panic grabbed Garnet. She sat up so suddenly that Clifford winced. "Oh, I've hurt you. I'm too heavy."

He poured her from his lap until she stood in front of him. "No, no. My leg just went numb from sitting so long." He kissed her forehead. "I need to fetch something. Get your nightgown on, and I'll be back in a minute."

How could she explain to him that living with his sisters bore a shadowy resemblance to her time with David? She'd never know where the next blow, albeit verbal rather than physical, was coming from. Hearing Fanny's ponderous steps from the next room didn't help. She felt spied upon, and it was a nasty feeling. Certainly she'd been taught that wishing away time was a sin; every minute was a gift from God, but how she wished the store in Lexington was built and ready to move into.

She was turning back the coverlet when he returned, holding a dark green bottle and two tiny glasses. Her eyes widened, and she saw that he'd expected her reaction.

"I know what you're thinking, but this is Fanny's blackberry cordial, for medicinal purposes only. Surely the Temperance Union sisters couldn't make anything too sinful. It'll soothe you so you can sleep." He set thimble-sized glasses on the dresser and poured a bit in each of them. The cordial looked dark and dangerous.

Handing her one, he said, "It won't make either one of us drunk, sweet girl. You'd get sick from the sugar before you'd become inebriated. I ought to know."

She held the glass as if it were some kind of noxious poison and sat down on the bed. With light behind it, the color was richly purple, actually rather pretty.

"Sit back, drink it, and calm yourself. You're jumpy as a yearling." He began to undress, leaving his portion on the table beside the bed.

Cautiously she raised the glass to her lips, smelling fermented fruit. It reminded her of the wine David once made her taste. She took a tiny sip and felt sweet, syrupy warmth slide down her throat. "How do you know a body would get sick on it before he'd get drunk?"

He chuckled as he hung up his suit. "One time I stole a bottle and tried very hard to get drunk. It goes down easily at first, but after a while all that sweetness turns your stomach. I gagged and retched for hours. Thought I was going to bring up my liver."

She smiled at him and took another sip. It was a pleasure just to watch him, she thought, as he wiggled into his nightshirt. She wondered what he'd been like when he was a boy. "And was sneaking your sister's cordial the only bad thing you did?"

He sat and drained the contents of his glass in one swallow. "Oh, heavens no. I progressed to some very bad quality whiskey a time or two and did a bit of gambling, convinced I'd be a millionaire by midnight. Would've lost my shirt if I'd had nerve enough to wager it."

Stretching out on the bed, he gathered her into the crook of his arm. "And I never did take to whiskey, if that reassures you, Mrs. Clark. Now I'll admit I've had wine from time to time, and I enjoy it, never to excess, mind you."

She let the last dribbles of cordial trickle onto her tongue and stretched, peering at her bare toes that peeked out from the hem of her gown. His toes were much farther down on the bed and weren't at all pretty: bony and knobby and sprinkled with dark hairs. But she loved them anyway, just like she loved his homely knees. Maybe it was his patience or maybe it was the cordial, but she was feeling calmer. "I've had wine before."

"And what did you think?"

She wrinkled her nose. "It was sort of sour, but it didn't taste too bad after the first couple of sips."

He laughed. "That's the way with spirits, the road to perdition, my sisters would say. And how did it make you feel?"

Garnet blushed and handed him her glass. He immediately refilled it. She supposed another drop wouldn't hurt. "I was sort of giggly and happy at first."

"Mm hmm. And then?"

She sipped, searching for the right word. It tickled him when she tried to improve her vocabulary. "Then I was, um, is amorous the right word?"

He laughed. "Probably. So it loosened your inhibitions? And to think of all the trouble I took to accomplish that very thing. I should've just brought countless bottles of wine out to Lorena's."

She punched his chest. "I don't think that would've worked at all, Clifford." Then more seriously she added, "That time with the wine, David tore my dress."

He took her hand. "That first husband of yours hangs over us like a menace, but you shouldn't be afraid to taste wine again. Don't ever be afraid, Garnet, not of my sisters, not of spirits, not of anything. I'm no knight on a noble steed, but I'll try to keep you safe."

She nodded, feeling warm and safe for the moment. Finishing her cordial, she waited while he extinguished the lamp and then scooted down to rest her head against his shoulder. It always surprised her how a room could seem cave-dark after lamps were put out, and then, in just a minute, her eyes would adjust enough to see squares of gray at each window. She murmured, "About being bad, was it all drinking and gambling? Weren't there any women?"

He stiffened, and she was glad the dark concealed the wicked grin on her face. He sputtered, "Well, of course there were. I mean, well, after all, you really didn't imagine that I was pure as snow for thirty-one years, did you?"

Making an ambiguous noise, she left him dangling.

"Why, I never meant to imply, I never led you to believe that. I . . . . Garnet, you don't really want to know about other women, do you?"

"No, I really don't," she said, reaching up to kiss him. His lips were sweet with cordial, and she smiled against them.

Chapter Six

Garnet was trying to appear alert and interested while Mr. Wallace droned on about banking business. On her wedding day she'd hardly noticed the little man, but now she had ample opportunity to observe him. Short and rather portly, he had a round, pink face that should've been jolly but wasn't. Wispy white hair fringed his bald head and continued down his face into a full white beard and moustache. She wondered why men with little hair on their heads seemed bent on compensating for it with hairy faces.

At first the men discussed Clifford's new position, something about serving commercial interests, loans, business expansion. It was a foreign language to Garnet, but Clifford absorbed all of it. She tuned most of it out, but when the banker suggested that some private entertaining, perhaps dinner parties in their home, would go along with the job, Garnet's eyes flew to Clifford. Not missing a beat, he replied that he didn't see why that would be necessary. Wasn't that what luncheons at hotels were for? Wallace shrugged and agreed.

In fairness to the man, there'd been little time or opportunity to communicate their desires, but it seemed to her that Wallace saw their goals as something different than she and Clifford did. Or at least she hoped so. Wallace acted as if Clifford was embarking on an ambitious career at the bank, but, as of this morning, Clifford had regarded the position as strictly temporary until they paid their debts and the store was a going concern. She wondered if a small store would be enough for her husband.

Focusing again on their conversation, she realized they were discussing the store's financing. She remembered some of the terms from arithmetic problems worked with her father at the kitchen table: principal, compound interest. Then Wallace said, "I have a young man, Archie Morris, who's done some preliminary research into available sites for your store. He's going to show you some properties after we finish here, but competition's stiff. We already have several successful grocers. I'm not sure why you want to venture into these waters at the same time as pursuing a banking career, and I do question your plan to live behind your store."

Wallace's face showed more fatherly concern than disapproval, but Garnet clenched her hands. Clifford, his long legs stretched out in front of his chair, replied, "I do apologize, Sam, for springing this on you so suddenly and expecting you to read our minds, but, you see,

Mrs. Clark and I are more intent upon building a home and family than a fortune. Now, I'd never say that the position you're offering me is just a means to an end because it's interesting work, and I'm enthusiastic about it. Nonetheless, having a store is our true dream, and my work at the bank will be financing the store until it's successful. During that time my wife will need to manage our home and business in one place, and if that means we'll be starting small, so be it."

Wallace fussed with his immaculate cuffs. "So you're telling me that working here will be temporary."

"It's hard to say, Sam, and if this doesn't suit you, I understand. You're privy to our finances. Even a modest store will be expensive to build and equip. It won't be profitable for quite some time. And we cannot predict what might happen; hiring employees, having a family . . . ." His voice trailed off, leaving Garnet a bit flushed. As much as she yearned for a baby, one would complicate things right now.

A whisper of a smile crossed Wallace's solemn face. "I don't suppose I can be choosy. I've wanted you to work with me for a long time, and if I can only have you for a short time, so be it."

Clifford acknowledged the compliment with a brilliant smile. "I'll give you my best for as long as I can, Sam."

Wallace rose. "I'll have someone fetch Archie. He'll take you around, give you a meal, and if you have any luck, we can meet back here to iron out the details."

He called to someone in the outside office and continued. "As I mentioned, Morris has been mostly focusing on downtown properties, but I think he also was looking at sites in some of the more affluent suburbs."

Garnet hadn't said a word since their initial greetings and introductions, but she couldn't keep still any longer. Mustering her courage, she told herself to imitate Papa's wisdom and Mama's voice. "Mr. Wallace," she said softly. "I'm not sure that's what we had in mind. Those people will have housekeepers or cooks to do their shopping or they'll pay to have groceries delivered. We envisioned a neighborhood store for regular folks, where the housewife steps down to the store to get what she needs to fix supper or lunches for the next day. Poor people have to eat too."

Wallace seemed startled to hear her speak. Clifford hovered behind her, but, for once, didn't open his mouth. Wallace furrowed his bushy, white eyebrows. "So you're planning a small country store in town. You'll get small profits from a small endeavor."

"We'll also have less invested in our inventory and property," she replied. "And a community can soon become dependent upon a neighborhood store. Convenience can become tangible."

Where had that come from? Clifford must be rubbing off on her. Nearly hidden by all those white whiskers, Wallace's mouth twitched. He glanced up at Clifford who topped him by half a foot. "Clifford, at your wedding I saw that you were marrying a beautiful girl, but I had no idea you'd chosen a budding entrepreneur."

Clifford laughed and squeezed her shoulder. "She's a wonder, all right."

A young man came to the doorway and was introduced as Archie Morris. He was very handsome with soft, light brown hair and clear pale skin that blushed as he shook their hands. He looked very young, not much older than Garnet herself, and his large blue eyes widened when he nodded at her. Wallace explained that he'd misinterpreted the Clarks' needs and Archie would need to reconsider the sites they'd visit. Morris seemed to grasp things quickly, and soon the three of them were seated in a large, handsome buggy with Garnet between the two men. Once or twice, Archie's arm brushed against hers, and he blushed painfully each time. Feeling sympathy for someone who reddened as easily as she did, Garnet tried to put him at ease by asking countless questions about Lexington. She glanced at Clifford to see his reaction to what David would've considered flirting, but Clifford seemed amused.

Although Archie scratched his plans to show them downtown storefronts, he did drive east on Main Street to let them see the newly constructed suburbs Mr. Wallace mentioned. They drove for quite a while, craning their necks to get a feel for different neighborhoods, but he agreed that they hadn't found what they were looking for. "You do realize, don't you, that if you live behind the store, you'll be living in a, well, working class neighborhood," he said, turning back toward town.

"We're not snobs, Archie," Clifford replied, softening the words with a genial smile. "We're still country folks, despite my new position."

"It's just that most of the men in similar positions at the bank . . ." Archie seemed too uncomfortable to continue.

Clifford said, "I've visited Sam's house, and I imagine most of the bankers live equally well. But Mrs. Clark and I have other plans."

Archie nodded and noted that it was nearly noon. They'd stop to eat, he said, and he'd ponder some other areas that might suit their needs. They ate at a different hotel from the one where they were staying, and Garnet imagined Clifford bringing important Lexington businessmen into the cavernous dining room to discuss finances over elegant meals. Several tables of soberly dressed men seemed to be doing just that, and she noted their suits and ties, realizing quickly that her husband's wardrobe needed improvement. Even if their home and store were "working class," as Archie called it, Clifford must look like what he was: a respectable and distinguished banker.

While they were eating dessert, the young man snapped his fingers. "I have it!" he exclaimed. "I think I may know just the place for you."

Clifford smiled at Archie's eagerness. "You have a knack for this."

Blushing yet again, Archie grinned. "Oh, I love matching people up with properties. It's profitable for me, certainly, but it also makes people happy. Homes are emotional."

He drove them up the Broadway hill until they saw long, low tobacco warehouses on both sides of the road. Clifford exclaimed over the few automobiles they encountered, and the two men talked machines across Garnet. "Yes, sir," Archie declared. "As soon as I get enough money saved, I'm going to buy me one. My father swears the price will come down in a few years."

"I agree," Clifford said. "I've been following Ford's progress now for several years, and he has the common man in mind. The more luxurious models are enticing, but I support Ford."

Archie's head bobbed. "It'll change everything. I keep telling my father he should get into the paving business. Twenty years from now nearly every street in Lexington will be paved."

With this he turned onto a decidedly unpaved lane. On the left a brick tobacco warehouse, blank and windowless, stretched to the end of the short street. Most of the right side of the street looked like rough pasture, level and covered with weeds, but three or four new, white frame cottages dotted its length with what looked like another two or three under construction. Archie stopped the buggy.

"Fred Catlett's been in the tobacco business all his life, managing warehouses, growing, selling, you name it. My father's known him for years and thinks he's a straight shooter. Anyway, Catlett's wife, Hazel, grew up on a farm right here; the town didn't stretch this far back then. When her people passed on, she inherited the land, and Fred built his warehouse on part of it." Archie gestured to the left. "It's been open about two years and from what I hear, he's doing very well. But Fred's selling the rest of the land in parcels for houses. He's building on some himself to rent to tobacco workers; it's a special deal between him and his employees— they work for him and he gives them a nice new house for low rent. Interesting concept. But he's selling some for private dwellings. As I recall, this street is named after his son, Jasper Avenue."

Driving on, Archie turned right down a short alley that led to another street. "There are several private houses on this one, Catlett Avenue, and then if we go on through," he said, doing so, "we run into Hazel Avenue: three parallel streets with small but respectable houses on them. Obviously most people who'd build or rent here work tobacco, but it's not far from the railroad station. Lexington's going to come this way, and they plan to extend the streetcar lines out this direction."

Garnet sat forward, scanning both sides of the street. The few existing frame houses were nearly identical: white with a shingled roof that slanted down and dipped over a tiny porch, a door in the middle, and a window on each side. They reminded her of cleaner, newer versions of the house where she'd grown up. Clifford said, "I assume these little ones are owned by Catlett."

Archie nodded. "He's sprinkling them around the neighborhood, hoping private owners will build between them. The lots are small, though, and that's a detriment."

He continued to drive to the end of Hazel Avenue, and Garnet shuddered at how close together the houses were. She'd never been able to see another house from where she lived, and it gave her the willies to think of living cheek to jowl.

At the end of Hazel Avenue, Archie paused. "This is a private home. See how they have a second story and a larger porch." The house he pointed to was painted gray and seemed too large for its tiny lot. "Now over here," and he gestured to the house across the street, "the people bought two lots and built a bigger house. You all would probably need at least two lots to accommodate a store with a house behind it."

She leaned against Clifford to get a better look. The larger house was white, like the little cottages, but it was good-sized and had some young shrubs around the porch. A maple tree shaded one corner of the yard, making it more homey and pleasant. "It looks like they've left a few trees," she murmured.

"A few," Archie agreed. "This was pasture, so there wouldn't be many. Is this more what you all are looking for?"

Clifford glanced at Garnet whose eyes were jumping from side to side. She nodded distractedly, and he told Archie to turn so they could travel the length of the middle street. "I don't think either of us would relish looking out onto the warehouse on that first street."

Garnet agreed. When Archie turned up Catlett Avenue, she noticed that the first house was again, obviously, privately owned. A white picket fence enclosed its yard, and the front door was situated to the right rather than in the center. Across from it were two rental houses and then undeveloped lots until a full two-storied house, painted a distinctive dark green, caught her attention. "Oh, that one's nice."

Archie stopped. "I believe the man who built it is a druggist downtown. They've used two lots and put some money into it, haven't they?"

The green paint should've made the house gloomy, but instead it looked cozy compared with all the white ones. The occupants must love plants, Garnet thought. Peony bushes bordered the porch and a mimosa tree decorated the front yard. She turned to see what was across the street. Nothing but vacant lots. "This is it," she declared. "If I have to look at another house, I'd like it to be this one."

"Let's check it out," Clifford said, helping her out of the buggy. "Do you know where the property lines are, Archie?"

They explored and walked off the dimensions. Garnet was delighted to see a mulberry tree on one of the lots. She couldn't imagine not having any trees at all. "What do you think?" she whispered to Clifford.

He grasped her hand. "I think it's exactly what we're looking for, but we'll have to buy two lots at least, especially if you want a bit of garden."

"Will that be dreadfully expensive?"

Archie heard her. "No, ma'am. These go fairly cheap, and I wouldn't be surprised if Catlett gives you an even better price if he knows you're building a store. That's a nice thing for a neighborhood and might improve his chances of selling the remaining lots as well as renting his houses."

Clifford gestured at the lots. "Can you make a note of what we want here, Morris? I think we need to see Mr. Catlett."

Forty-eight hours later, aided by Archie, Sam Wallace, and an army of clerks, messenger boys, and various bank and courthouse employees, the deal was done. Garnet and Clifford sat in a tiny, crowded restaurant close to the courthouse, eating their noon meal.

Dazed by the flurry of important and expensive decisions, she declared, "My stars, I can't believe what all we've done in three days."

Clifford was tucking into a plate of turkey and dressing with great enthusiasm, but she could hardly eat. He wiped his mouth. "What amazes me is that the builder says he'll break ground in three to four weeks. Makes me wonder why he's not busier, but Sam says he's good."

Garnet sipped her lemonade. "It's probably another example of Sam's magic."

Clifford chuckled. "Magic is right. He opened every door for us. Is your chicken all right? You're not eating much."

"It's fine. I'm more thirsty than hungry. After that huge meal at the Wallace's last night, I don't think I'll be hungry for a week."

Sam Wallace had insisted that they dine with him and his wife, and, although their grand house intimidated Garnet, she found the evening pleasant, mostly because of Adele Wallace's graciousness. Faced with a daunting array of silver, crystal, and unidentifiable dishes, Garnet simply followed Clifford's lead and ended up enjoying herself. "I'm still not exactly clear on how you got to know them: their son, right?" she asked, picking at her chicken salad.

"Yes, their son, Andrew, was with me at boarding school. After we discovered we were the only Kentuckians at the place, we arranged to ride the train together when we left or came home. I'd usually stay a night at either end here in Lexington."

"I never hear you talk about Andrew, though."

"Strangely enough, I became closer to Sam than his son. I suppose Sam's the reason I went into banking, and whenever the Evans County Bank needs to do business in Lexington, I go through Sam. He became a sort of father to me, and Adele, well; she's just a sweetheart, isn't she? More than likely I'll stay with them when I come up here."

Garnet hadn't quite made her peace with this. "So when will you come back?"

"Oh, I suppose in about six or seven weeks. The builder said he'll have the framing started by then, and Sam wants me to meet with some developers. I'll probably stay three or four days, like this time." He raised his eyes from his plate. "I know you want to come with me, but you wouldn't have a thing to occupy your time. I'll be busy with Sam, and I have to honor his requests. As it is, he's being generous about letting me start work as late as September."

Although the builder said he'd put a rush on the job, he estimated that the store couldn't possibly be completed until October, and then it would need weeks of outfitting. She would have to endure nearly three months of living with those female dragons. But they had much to celebrate, so she tried to ignore her concerns. "I reckon there was some of Sam's magic influencing negotiations with Mr. Catlett too."

Stretching back from the table, Clifford laughed. "I think that magic came from your beau Archie. He was extremely persuasive in convincing Catlett that our store would be a boon to the neighborhood. Do you realize we bought three lots for the price of two? We'll have room for your garden as well as a nice shed which can become a garage for my automobile someday."

Disregarding the comment about Archie, she added, "When we can afford it."

"Oh, sure, when we can afford it." He was happy and replete, and she could've kicked herself for being unenthusiastic. She *was* happy but couldn't ignore her nagging doubts about money any more than she could dismiss those weeks without Clifford.

"It's so much money."

"Dear heart, you must stop worrying about everything and enjoy this. Yes, we've spent some money, although actually I had enough to pay for the land and give a generous deposit to the builder without touching the line of credit Wallace established. Buying fixtures for the store as well as inventory and furnishings will be expensive, but Sam's paying me well. It'll all work out."

She gave him a tentative smile. "I do borrow trouble, don't I?"

"You're more in debt than I am." She sensed that if they'd been alone, he would've kissed her. Mischief lit his eyes. "Did you enjoy the morning with your admirer?"

He'd teased her about Archie Morris since the young man first blushed at meeting her. She retorted, "You know he's not my admirer!"

He flashed a wicked grin. "To the contrary, I'm positive young Mr. Morris admires you greatly, but he's far too much of a gentleman to act upon it. Did he escort you to several of the local groceries?" That morning, while Clifford met with the builder, Garnet and Archie had, in the young man's words, "done research."

"Yes, he did." She fished around in her handbag and pulled out a tiny notebook. "I felt like a spy, but I learned all sorts of useful things. We'll have to buy an icebox, Clifford, no matter how expensive it is. And these stores use the most cunning slicing machines." She chattered on, ignoring her food as well as the indulgent half-smile on her husband's face. All right, Garnet admitted, she was excited about the store, and Archie's compliments and perfectly circumspect admiration hadn't hurt either. If she could forget about Clifford's sisters and the mountain of debt, she'd be in bliss.

She wound down and slurped the last of her lemonade. "What now?"

"I was going to ask you the same thing. We have this afternoon and evening free, so your wish is my desire, pretty lady."

Running her finger around her beloved amethyst brooch, she pondered for a moment, smiled, and shook her head. "You'll think I'm silly."

"I doubt it. Do you want to find Franklin and kidnap him?"

"No, I'd love to see him, but we'll have plenty of time when we've moved."

"Then what?"

In a rush, she said, "I'd like to go back to Catlett Avenue and see where our home will be. Is it too much trouble? Can we hire a horse?"

Clifford grinned. "It's no trouble at all. Let's go."

They turned down Catlett Avenue, *their* street, Garnet thought, and she patted Clifford's arm. "Go slowly, please."

He obliged, and Garnet twisted her head from left to right. The block was short, and in no time they approached the green house. Of course everything looked much as it had two days previously. As they came closer, she saw a woman, young and heavily pregnant, sitting on the porch. Tentatively, Garnet waved, and the girl returned the greeting with a quick smile.

They strolled around their land, truly theirs now, Garnet realized. It felt like a solemn occasion. Even the cloudy, windy afternoon seemed momentous. "It's the most wonderful thing," she breathed.

"What's that?"

"Owning land. Maybe now I understand why Grandpa and your sisters are so proud of their farms. I always thought, oh, it's just land; what's so important about dirt? But it's a piece of the earth, Clifford, and it belongs to us, to use, to keep, to pass on. I don't guess my papa ever owned a piece of land."

"I always took it for granted," he admitted. "Most times I felt like the farm was an albatross. But it's different when it's your work that's paid for it and your dreams that are going to be built upon it."

In the distance, she heard hammering and a rooster crowing. Some of her neighbors must have a chicken or two, and she wondered if she should keep some to sell eggs. She asked where the house would sit and where they might plant the garden, and they walked until she had her fill.

In the west, clouds thickened, and Clifford remarked that they'd better head back to town if they didn't want to get soaked. But as she climbed into the buggy, that same odd sensation of anxiety corroded the day's joys. Before thinking about it, she asked, "Am I your partner?"

The question surprised him. "Why, of course you are. My helpmeet, my wife, my lifelong companion."

"Yes, yes. I know all that, but am I truly your partner in what we're doing here?"

"Yes. As of now we are business partners in addition to all those things."

She turned to look at him full-on. "You're not just doing this to pacify me? To give your pretty toy another gift?"

He frowned. "Oh, that's what's brought this on. No, you are not, in Fanny's words, 'my pretty toy,' Garnet. You are a capable, intelligent woman, and I want to share dreams and successes and yes, even failures with you. Full on. I trust your judgment and rely on your insights. Look at how you impressed Wallace. Fanny said that in spite, and there's not a bit of truth to it."

She nodded, satisfied for the most part, although his sister's words still stung. She figured that Fanny and Gert would always think their brother was making all the changes to give his wife a hobby. It would take a while for that not to bother her.

Suddenly rain dumped in torrents upon them, and Garnet fumbled for the buggy's lap robe to cover their shoulders as much as it would.

"I'm so sorry, dear heart," Clifford said, barely audible above the roar of the rain. "We're going to look like bedraggled cats."

She grinned. "It doesn't matter. I'd rather not look like a pretty toy."

Chapter Seven

"Garnet."

Clawing her way out of the cobwebs of sleep, she came to a half-conscious awareness. For the third night in a row, she'd slept poorly, missing Clifford beside her.

"Garnet!" This was an urgent bark, and she jumped out of bed, thinking fire, sickness, death. Once she reached the hall Garnet saw a thin line of light under Fanny's closed door. Without bothering to knock, she burst into the room to find the woman sitting up in bed, her nightgown incongruously trimmed with frilly lace and a flirtatious pink bow. A thick, gray pigtail draped over her shoulder.

"I've taken a spell," the woman said without any preface. "Something bad's wrong with my foot."

Barefooted and self-conscious, Garnet struggled to become alert and raised the bedcovers. Fanny's big toe and most of her right foot were so inflamed that the skin glistened like rose-colored satin. "Oh my. Did you step on something or fall?"

"No," Fanny said. Her voice was sharp and unpleasant but Garnet reckoned this might be from pain.

"It must hurt something awful," she murmured.

With a grimace, the big woman shifted. "It does pain me."

Not quite sure what Fanny wanted, Garnet suggested fetching Dr. Thomas, and the woman nodded. "I've been awake for hours studying what we need to do. Gert will be up and wanting her breakfast, and there's the doctor to send for, dinner to make, and pole beans to work up. And the front room rug needs to be beaten." Fanny's voice rose higher and higher as she spoke, her fingers clutching the covers.

Garnet tried to soothe her. "You just rest easy. Let me throw on some clothes, and I'll get Gert's breakfast, and then we'll manage all this."

"Gert has her work to do. What'll we do if I'm down with this foot?"

Garnet paused at the door. "We'll let Garnet do something useful for a change," she said, making her tone light rather than snide. "I'm perfectly capable of it."

She had the stove going and coffee percolating before Gert arrived in the kitchen. "Fanny's having trouble with her foot," Garnet announced, "and wants somebody to fetch Dr. Thomas."

Immediately alarmed, Gert started for the steps, but Garnet stopped her. "Wait until the coffee's done, and you can take a cup up to her."

Gert stood in the doorway, rubbing her hands down the sides of her usual black skirt. "Is she bad?"

"I don't know. Her foot's all puffed up and red. Must be hurting miserably."

"I've got haying to finish," Gert mused. "And I was planning on doing some work in the cane. You'll have to go after the doctor, I reckon. And there'll be four hands to feed at dinner."

Garnet poured steaming coffee into a cup and added several spoonsful of sugar, the way Fanny liked it. "I'll feed the hands as well as doing other things Fanny can't do, but you should go after the doctor, Gert. I'm not much good with horses. You could do it and be back before I'd be able to get a harness on."

She handed Gert the coffee. "Give this to your sister, comfort her a minute or two, and I'll have your breakfast on the table. You'll want to catch Dr. Thomas before he leaves for his calls."

Gert blinked a time or two, but, accustomed to following Fanny's orders, she complied, trudging up the steps. Garnet set a skillet on the stove and added a dollop of bacon grease. In short order she broke eggs, sliced bread, and set out butter and jam. "Fanny wondered if you could poach her an egg," Gert said, when she sat.

"Sure." It would've been easier to fry another egg or two; the skillet was hot, but she set a pan of water to boil and thought about her mother.

Upstairs Fanny was fretting, her face nearly as red as her poor foot. She couldn't possibly see the doctor while wearing her nightgown, she said. And she was worried about Sunday. The Clark sisters had agreed to play and sing with three other musicians at a special service to raise money for the organ at Ashton Baptist church. The others were coming to the house to rehearse day after tomorrow. Fanny had planned to bake.

"Don't worry," Garnet reassured her. "You may be just fine by then, and, if not, I can bake something. You can practice your fiddle sitting down, can't you?"

Fanny agreed but fussed, not at all pleased that Garnet was searching in her chifferobe for underwear and clothes. She insisted that

Garnet leave while she dressed, not that Garnet minded this at all, and bemoaned the fact that the doctor would see her uncovered leg. "Would some cool cloths soothe your foot?" Garnet asked, ignoring her crankiness Suddenly quiet, Fanny replied that yes, cool cloths might feel good, and when Garnet returned, she thanked her meekly.

Throughout the hectic morning, Garnet moved from one task to another, pausing every half-hour or so to run upstairs and lay a fresh cloth on Fanny's foot. On one of Garnet's trips upstairs, Fanny asked, "What are you fixing for dinner?"

Garnet wrung out a cloth and laid it gently over the immense foot. "I'm heating up your good canned pork and making gravy. Sliced tomatoes, of course. I thought I'd stew some dried apples, make cornbread. Should I mash the potatoes or boil them?"

"You have enough to do; just boil them. I was going to fry up that big head of cabbage. Will you have time for that?"

"Sure," Garnet replied. "I wish I could get some more air in here for you. It's mighty hot today." She fiddled with the heavy curtains at the windows, trying to open them as widely as possible. This was only the second time she'd ever been inside Fanny's bedroom, and she was appalled at all the dark, heavy furniture crowded into the room. It looked like a tomb.

Fanny shrugged like the heat didn't matter. "Now, Gert expects three heavy meals a day, but Clifford's not here, so you just make the evening meal a light one. You have enough to do."

Surprised, Garnet smiled at the woman. "I don't mind," she said. "But I don't think we need all that food in this heat."

Fanny reminded Garnet of some royal personage ensconced upon her bed with her swollen foot lying on a cushion. However, the woman snorted and rolled her eyes in a most unregal manner. "Tell that to Gert. She lives to eat rather than eating to live."

Garnet was able to exit the room before her grin escaped. It'd be difficult to say which of the two sisters weighed more. Insisting that Clifford deserved a full meal every evening and adding a hefty farmer's dinner at noon, the amount of food the two of them packed away during the course of a day was phenomenal.

She was up to her elbows in pole beans when she heard Dr. Thomas's buggy. Wiping her hands, she went to greet him and was surprised to see Lowell with the doctor. "Well, I'm glad you're hale, Garnet," the big man declared in his usual booming tones. "How's that arm?"

"Just fine, sir." She turned to her brother. "What're you doing here?"

Before the boy could speak, Dr. Thomas said, "He's been my assistant the last couple of weeks. I'll be losing him when he goes back to school, but in the meantime, he's a great help."

The doctor bounded up the steps, but Lowell lingered in the hall. "Hi, Nettie," he said, his voice cracking. Lord, she thought, he was thirteen now, almost a man.

"When Miss Gert came this morning, I was scared you were sick, but she said it was Miss Fanny's foot. Then I was glad because it gave me a chance to see you."

She hugged him. "Come in the kitchen while I snap these beans, and tell me what you're doing with Dr. Thomas."

He sat and picked up a handful of beans to break. "About a month ago, Luther called the doctor to see Mama. She keeps swearing she's in the family way, and then nothing happens. Truly, Garnet, I think she's a little touched now," he said, trying to balance his new professional persona against embarrassment at speaking so intimately about his mother. Garnet handed him a cup of water and he gulped it down. "Or, as Dr. Thomas would say, she has a 'nervous ailment'."

When had Mama not been just a little odd? "But she's not pregnant, is she?"

"No. Dr. Thomas says she's just going through what comes naturally for women. He didn't explain, maybe because it's my mother. Most times he explains more than I want to hear." Lowell grinned. "Anyway, while Dr. Thomas was there, Luther told him that I was hankering to be a doctor someday, and that I was really good in school and could maybe do it if I got the right training. Well, you know how Dr. Thomas is: he said, was that a fact, and asked Luther if I could come stay with him and Mrs. Thomas for a month to see if I had any aptitude for medicine. I was surprised when Luther said yes. Mama didn't like it since she usually has me gardening and looking after Dessie."

Garnet refilled his glass. "Mama never liked it when I worked for Mrs. Lawrence either, although I was mostly minding you then."

Lowell raised an eyebrow at the totally absurd notion of himself as a little boy. "So I've lived with them a month, and it's awfully interesting, and Mrs. Thomas bakes wonderful pies. I make up medicine for him and go on calls, help out when he needs someone to hand him things."

"And he's pleased with you?"

"Appears to be. I don't really want to go back home, although school's starting soon, and I really like this teacher. He says I'll be finished with my graduation requirements and can go off for medical training by the time I'm sixteen. If there's money for it." His eyes roamed the kitchen, and she remembered how hungry Franklin always was at this age. Rinsing her hands, she cut him a thick slice of bread and slathered it with butter.

"Say, that's nice," he said, taking a huge bite.

"We'll just have to make sure there's money. What does Luther say?"

"The same thing." Pointing at the ceiling, he whispered, "Is Miss Fanny bad?"

"I don't think so; her foot's all swollen and red."

"Did she injure it?"

"She says not."

Lowell shrugged. "It's probably gout, then. Dr. Thomas says people who are too stout are prone to it. Stout gout," he said with a giggle that cracked.

"Your voice is changing."

"Well, yes."

"Lowell!" Dr. Thomas's voice thundered down the stairs.

"Yes, sir."

"Bring up a pitcher of water, a cup, and some dry linen if Mrs. Clark has it."

They scurried to obey, and Garnet set the beans aside. There'd be time to finish them this afternoon. She was peeling potatoes when Lowell reappeared in the kitchen. "Gout," he announced smugly.

"Is that very bad?"

"Naw. He has good medicine for it, but she'll need to eat a light diet. Won't like that much, will she?" Mischief danced in his eyes. "And the medicine sometimes gives them nausea or diarrhea. You won't like that."

Garnet rolled her eyes, and they chuckled together. Suddenly he was serious. "You're going to come home before you leave, aren't you?"

The wistful note in his voice touched her. He looked so grown-up, taller than she and speaking, occasionally, in his new deep voice. "Of course. I'm going to Lorena's two weeks before I leave for Lexington, and I'll be over several times. I may get Lorena to come to Lexington with me to help buy furniture and get the store opened."

"Won't you get lonely so far away from everybody?"

"I'll probably be too busy to get lonely, but you know I'll miss all of you. It'll be nice to see Franklin every now and then, though." She wiped a hand on her apron and squeezed Lowell's shoulder. At this age Franklin had hated to be touched, and she felt regret at not knowing whether Lowell felt the same way. He patted her hand.

"Lowell!" Dr. Thomas shouted as he came down the stairs.

"Yes sir?"

"We need to be on our way." He rattled off orders. "Her medicine's on the table upstairs with instructions. It may upset her stomach, although I didn't tell her that. Folks are awfully suggestible sometimes. Oh, and she must eat plain food. Nothing rich or greasy. I'd say no spirits, but I know how the Clark sisters feel about alcohol."

"Gout?" Garnet asked.

He looked surprised. "Yes, gout. You suspected it?"

"No. That's what my little brother diagnosed."

The doctor laughed as loudly as he spoke. "He's an amazing fellow. Soaks up knowledge like a sponge. There's no doubt he'll make a first-rate physician." He moved toward the door, Lowell swaggering behind with a cocky grin. "As long as the foot is swollen she should keep still, elevate it, and the cool cloths won't hurt. I'll be back, oh, let's say day after tomorrow to check on her. It should be better by then."

By sundown when Garnet lowered herself into a chair on the front porch, she was worn out. It must not take long to lose the knack of working hard, she reckoned, and told herself she'd better get used to it with long hours in the store facing her soon. It hadn't been the cooking that had tired her out so much as the many trips up and down the stairs. Dr. Thomas had prescribed lots of fluids for the invalid, and since Fanny was immobile, emptying chamber pots became a frequent task. Garnet chuckled to herself. Mama always referred to them as chamber pots, but Fanny bluntly called them 'slop jars.'

A velvet dusk floated over the hills, and she listened to the soothing hum of crickets as she rocked, the creaking of the chair itself resembling some huge, slow insect. Thank goodness Gert was spending the evening upstairs with her sister because Garnet had done about all she could for one day. Throughout the day Fanny had kept mentioning something about beating the carpet in the front room. Tomorrow's work, Garnet thought with a yawn. She'd been so busy that she'd hardly thought of Clifford. Today was to have been his first day of work at the bank, and she wondered how it'd gone for him. She missed him something fierce, but there hadn't been a spare minute for moping about it.

And that was the case for the next couple of days as well. Fanny protested her diet, but Garnet wouldn't budge. "You want to wear shoes when you play your fiddle on Sunday, don't you?" Garnet asked her, and this took the wind out of Fanny's wide sails.

When Dr. Thomas called, he pronounced Fanny "on the mend" but uttered dire warnings about her being on her feet too much. Fanny fretted and fussed. They were rehearsing that night, and the musicians would expect refreshments. Garnet tried to calm her. "It's only two o'clock. I have all afternoon to bake, especially if we eat a light supper. When are they coming?"

"Seven. But can you bake? You've been doing well with the regular cooking, but I wanted to make something nice."

For about the thousandth time, Garnet swallowed a tart retort. "Yes, I can bake. I'm actually pretty good at it. Why don't you rest, and I'll get busy."

Fanny looked doubtful but had little choice. All afternoon Garnet expected to hear her descending the steps to supervise, but she must've fallen asleep or decided to give over. After a plain, cold supper, Garnet set the refreshments on a lace cloth spread over the dining room table. Hobbling downstairs, Fanny assessed the preparations. On a big platter, Garnet had arranged her good, flaky biscuits, made with Gert's best triple leaf lard, with thin slices of pink ham between the halves. The prettiest of the sisters' cut-glass bowls held Fanny's homemade pickles, and on a large glass plate sat Garnet's applesauce cake: dark, moist, and inviting. She'd stacked small plates, forks, and napkins near the cake. "Does this suit you?" Garnet asked.

Garnet thought that just maybe Fanny was pleasantly surprised, but the woman merely nodded, reserving judgment, Garnet supposed, until everything was sampled. Garnet heard the musicians arrive and was listening to the caterwauling of stringed instruments being tuned when a louder noise, Fanny's voice, called her.

Now what? She'd planned to listen but assumed that her duties, except for cleaning up, were over for the evening. Stepping outside, she nodded to two men leaning against the porch posts. She thought there'd be another woman, the guitar player's wife, but there was no one else. Fanny came right to the point. Nodding at the guitarist, a man about Clifford's age with a drooping black moustache, she said, "George's wife's mother broke her hip, and she's had to go help out. That leaves us without an alto, but I told them you could do it. You sing harmony just fine."

Garnet shook her head in alarm. "Why, I'm no musician. I can't get up in front of people and sing."

"We're going to be singing tunes you know. Give it a try."

The mandolin player, a wiry older man, added, "Sounds awful thin without the alto in there, and Fanny can't play and sing at the same time."

Fanny was sitting with her foot resting on a stool. She nodded at Garnet. "Do what you can. Just sing down a third if you can't come up with anything more interesting. Let's start with "I Love to Tell the Story." You know that one."

Despite the muggy air, Garnet's hands turned to ice. She had no idea what Fanny meant by singing down a third, but there was no time for explanation. The three instrumentalists nodded at each other and started the song. She'd have to open her mouth any minute, and the next thing she knew, Gert was singing, with the men's voices harmonizing, and Garnet had to jump in. She was tentative at first, and then her brain shifted into place; she'd always sung harmony on this song, knew it in her soul, and suddenly the task didn't seem too hard. The older man sang tenor, a high, reedy whine that sounded pleasantly mournful, and she sang just above him, slipping her voice into the chord like a penny in a slot. The music took her, and she found herself swaying with the tempo. When they finished the last chorus, Garnet lowered her eyes, wondering if they'd decided she was just too poor an excuse.

At first no one spoke, but then the mandolin player remarked, "No offense, George, but she's ever bit as good as Alene. Where you been hiding her, Fanny?"

Garnet looked up to see a broad grin on Fanny's face. The woman rested her fiddle on her thick lap and actually winked at Garnet. "She'll do."

They were kind, letting her choose songs she knew. Gert grabbed her hand and gave it a friendly, painful squeeze, and George, a low, thunderous bass, suggested a couple of things she could do with "Near the Cross." By the time the musicians crowded into the dining room and gobbled up her cake and biscuits, Garnet glowed, although she was already battling tremors of stage fright when she thought about Sunday.

She was stacking plates when the sisters announced they were going upstairs. She told them goodnight, but they lingered at the bottom of the steps. Gert smiled, and after all these months, Garnet realized she had a particularly sweet smile, much like her brother's. "I thank you for helping us, Garnet."

Garnet ducked her head, feeling shy in the face of this unusual graciousness. Fanny said, "I misjudged you, girl. I reckon Clifford has more sense than I gave him credit for." And then she turned and made her slow and painful way up the steps.

***

Everything changed after that week. Gert and Fanny continued to be bossy and acerbic; they were, when all was said and done, firmly set in their ways. But Garnet, as long as she stayed flexible part of the time and stubborn when she thought it was worth the battle, rubbed along with them pretty well. The weather changed, and, as usual, cooler air invigorated her. Gert allowed her to help with the sorghum, and Garnet was busier and happier than she'd been in a while. Still, though, missing Clifford felt like a constant toothache. He'd been gone for nearly three months now. Although letters came regularly, she wasn't sure whether this helped or made her miss him more. She sat on the floor packing her mammoth trunk. Luther would come tomorrow to take her to the farm where she'd visit Lorena and her family before joining Clifford.

It was a chilly evening. She considered lighting a fire but decided against it. Fanny thought fires in bedrooms were wasteful unless a body was sick, and Garnet didn't want to ruffle any feathers on her last night. From downstairs she heard the sisters squabbling. Clifford had asked them to sort out his books and ship them to Lexington, and evidently Fanny and Gert were having trouble deciding what to pack.

Garnet was trying to be sensible, placing things she wouldn't need for the next two weeks at the bottom of the trunk. Her quilt was already stuffed in the bottom, along with her grandmother's compote, wrapped in towels she'd stitched for her new home. She picked up Clifford's letters. They wouldn't be necessary either, but she often reread them. Searching until she found the first one, written the day after he arrived in Lexington, she traced her finger over his handwriting. He'd written about living with the Wallace's and enclosed Adele's recipe for corn pudding which she'd requested. And he'd expressed displeasure at how little progress was being made on Catlett Avenue. She'd predicted that their separation would last longer than

385

the eight weeks Clifford estimated, and delays on the construction
proved her right. Clifford called her clairvoyant, and she'd had to pore
through Fanny's huge dictionary in the front room to find out what he
meant.

Garnet heard serious clattering and thumping from downstairs.
Surely they must be nearly finished. They'd been at it since supper, but
she had no room to criticize since she'd made little headway herself.
She put the next several letters, full of his new job and dealings with
the delinquent builder, in order behind the first but, even though she
scolded herself for wasting time, opened one she'd nearly memorized.

Dear, dear heart,

*It's a rainy evening in Lexington, and, although I am warm and well-nourished
from Sam and Adele's hospitality, I must confess to low spirits. Your letters have
been so brave and cheerful, and I am delighted that you and my sisters have worked
out your differences. It seems you have been both a Florence as well as a singing
Nightingale. Bravo! If Fanny says you acquitted yourself well, you surely did. She
has no patience with false praise, especially regarding music.*

*So I should endeavor to reply in kind, to be hearty and cheery as well, but I cannot
seem to effect those emotions tonight. Perhaps it is unwise for me to write while in
such a mood, but this is the closest I can come to talking to you, let alone touching
you.*

*I recall your concern when I blithely announced that our separation was certainly
unfortunate but of no great import, seen in the larger sense. I dismissed your sweet
sadness like an unfeeling cad, and now I, alas, suffer for it. You have shouldered
the burden masterfully, but, although they are kindness themselves, I weary of polite
chatter with the Wallace family and yet dread going to my lonely bed each night. I
yearn for you, my sweet girl, and dream of you in ways you perhaps can imagine,
but I am too circumspect to put on paper. Suffice it to say, that I may, oh, yes, I
may pounce when next I see you! My fingers itch with needing to touch your hair,
your face, and, oh, I could succumb to temptation and explicitly list every caress I
desire, but it would serve no purpose except to cause me even more distress.
Moreover! What if Fanny and Gert were to read my long and lascivious list? Even
the remarkable cordial might not be enough to revive them!*

*There, I have finally regained some humor. I seldom resort to despair, but being
apart from you brings out the worst in me, as being in your presence culminates in
producing what little good I am capable of. I am incomplete without you.*

*That said, I should end this pathetic missive and hope that, if I do indeed mail it,
you will receive it with a sad smile, because, of course, you, oh, wise one, knew how
difficult the separation would be. Surely it will not be for much longer.*

With all my deepest love,

She kissed his signature. If she saved no others, she would never part with this one. Two more weeks, she told herself again. Then she reached for the letter she'd received today. Just one more, she begged her sterner self.

My dear heart,

Although I intend to continue writing you over this last portion (Thank God!) of our penance, I will send subsequent letters in care of Lorena. I pray this arrives before you leave for Bethel.

I hope you are faring well as I, aside from a noisome but fortunately brief bout of the sniffles, am doing. Undoubtedly you are looking forward to your stay with the remarkable Lorena as well as satisfying visits with your family.

As to business, I have requested that Fanny and Gert pack my books, with specific instructions about which ones I want. Fanny generously replied that she and Gert wish to ship my father's desk to me. You say that you will have only your trunk and a few boxes, which should be no problem for you, Lorena, and Luther (bless the man!) to accommodate. I will meet you and Lorena at the station. As I told you, Sam's son bought my horse and buggy but insists that I use them during our settling in.

I cannot wait for you to see our house. There remain a few details to be completed, but I foresee that we may move in as soon as you and Lorena purchase furniture for us. However, between choosing the fixtures, finishing the shelving, and stocking, I fear the store will not be in business until early January.

I'm like a child waiting for Christmas, which will occur this year during the first week of December rather than the last! Give my best regards to Lorena and your family and know that I am perishing until I see you.

All my love,
Clifford

He did sound like a boy, she thought, tying up the letters and placing them in the trunk. Bouncing up, she started folding her summer clothes. They should go in the trunk next, she determined with a shiver, because she certainly wouldn't need them for a while. From the subdued conversation downstairs, it sounded as if Fanny and Gert had settled their differences. She was reaching for her hatbox when she heard steps outside the door. Gert stood in the doorway holding a shiny pail of sorghum.

"I know we're shipping a case of molasses for the store, but I thought you might want some for your table," she said. "It'll be a while before all these boxes arrive."

Garnet managed to fit the pail into her trunk. "That's mighty thoughty of you, Gert. I'm sure Clifford's been missing your good sorghum."

"It should be safe in the trunk. I pounded that lid on as hard as I could."

Which was powerfully hard, Garnet thought. She'd seen few men with the strength of Gert Clark .The woman gazed around the room, looking at stacks yet to be packed and the clothes Garnet meant to wear the next day, stretched across the armchair. She seemed to want to say something but was having a hard time doing it.

"You'll make sure he visits us now and again, won't you?" Gert asked.

"I will. After all, I have people down here too."

With a jerky motion, Gert pulled a small box from her pocket. "You're a pretty little thing and seem to like trinkets. This was Mama's ring. I don't wear it, never have, and it's a waste to keep it in a box." She thrust the box at Garnet, who opened it to find an ornate ruby ring, blood-red and winking in the lamplight.

"Oh, but Gert, I already have your mother's wedding ring. You should keep it."

Gert rubbed her nose. "No point in having it if I never wear it. You're family now, and maybe you'll get some use out of it."

Bowing her head in acceptance, Garnet slipped the box into her trunk. "Well, then I thank you, and I'll think of you when I wear it."

At this Garnet thought Gert colored a bit, although it was hard to tell with her weather-reddened skin. "I'll ask one thing."

Garnet waited.

"If you and Clifford have a daughter, I want her to have it." Garnet nodded, but Gert went on. "Do you think you all will ever have any young'uns? Someday maybe?"

"I imagine we will, Gert. Someday."

Her broad face softened. "I'd love to see some young'uns."

"The first daughter," Garnet promised.

The house settled in for the night, although muffled sounds still came from downstairs. Fanny was probably going through the drawers of her father's desk. Joe Hardy and his sons were coming tomorrow to cart off the items being shipped.

The only unpacked stacks were her underclothes and nightgowns. She separated out a gown and was stuffing the others in the trunk when she heard Fanny's step in the hall. Like Gert, she paused in the open doorway.

"The books are packed and the desk is emptied," she announced. She held a bulky flour sack in her hands.

"That's good."

"You don't have much room left in that trunk."

"No, but I have a small satchel too. I'll get everything packed."

Handing the sack to Garnet, Fanny said, "I wanted you to have some of the cordial. After all, you helped me bottle it this fall. It's nice to have on hand in case somebody suffers a shock."

"Why, thank you, Fanny. I appreciate it." Garnet peered inside the sack. All she could see were bulky white lumps.

"There are three bottles, should last you a while unless opening this store causes you terrible strain," the woman explained with a ghost of a smile. This was a major joke for Fanny. Garnet grinned appreciatively.

"I wrapped them in pillowcases I embroidered for you and Clifford. Sort of a housewarming gift, I reckon."

This was more generous than the blackberry cordial. Fanny waved off Garnet's thanks, but, like Gert, she lingered.

"When's Colson coming tomorrow?" Garnet had told her the details days ago; nonetheless, she repeated, mid-morning.

Fanny fiddled with her collar. "You'll make sure Clifford writes us, won't you? He didn't always write when he was away at school."

"Why, certainly I will. I was telling Gert that we'd come visit now and then, especially when he buys his automobile." Garnet winked at the woman, but Fanny remained serious.

"You'll have to watch him, you know. He gets notions. Sometimes he doesn't act much older than a boy. Charming with it, you know, you just want to let him do as he pleases. But sometimes he doesn't have much sense."

"I love him, Fanny. I'll do my best."

This seemed to satisfy her. As she walked down the hall, she said a curt good-night, and Garnet closed her bedroom door. Although her soul was jumping ahead two weeks with joy and anticipation, she felt a twinge of sympathy for the two old women. They were, in essence, losing a child more than a brother. She understood from losing Ruben, although they'd enjoyed Clifford for years, unlike having a baby literally torn from her arms. She had something she wanted to discuss with Lorena. Perhaps, after they put the new house to rights, she could visit David's Aunt Martha and see Ruben. She thought it might be easier to go with Lorena than Clifford. As far as Garnet knew, David was in Covington, but she dreaded what David might say if he wasn't. Ruben wouldn't recognize her, of course, wouldn't know she was his mother, but just the thought of holding him, smelling him, kissing him, filled her with longing. She'd see what Lorena thought. She wedged Fanny's lumpy bag into the trunk.

Two weeks later, Garnet stood at her new stove, laughing and shaking her head. "So Lorena gives him that look, like when she's ready to light into somebody, and says, 'That ain't good enough, sir!' and then she actually stomped her foot!"

Clifford was paying more attention to his empty plate than her antics but murmured, "Lord, you can mimic her." He stretched his long legs under the table. "So I suppose that worked. It's incredible that you two managed to get all this furniture bought yesterday and delivered today."

She turned the pork chops. "The salesman didn't pay her any mind at all, just stubbed up and glared at her. He's a short fellow, looks like a little pig with one of those turned-up noses, you know, like he'd drown if it came a big rain. Is the butter on the table? I declare I can't find anything."

"It's here," he replied, sounding weary. "So how did you two convince Mr. Pig?"

She scrunched up her face against the heat as she stooped to take baked potatoes from the oven. "Well, I told him to consider that we're opening a store and will be coming into contact with dozens of people. Some of those people might be needing furniture, and wasn't word of mouth the best kind of advertising?" She faced Clifford with her hands on her hips.

"And it worked." He didn't seem nearly as tickled as she was, but the man was probably starving to death. "Do you care if I fill your plate from the stove? I haven't unpacked the serving dishes yet."

"Of course not."

She set a full plate in front of him, touching his shoulder and beaming with pleasure. "Oh, I do love my new dishes. Lorena was so kind to buy them for us."

He was already cutting into the meat. "How did she know you wanted these particular ones?"

"We spent hours going through the Sears Roebuck catalog when I visited. I said these were the prettiest ones I'd ever seen, and then, sneaky old thing, she got Lowell to help her make the order." They both attacked their food; it had been a long, wonderful, exhausting day. Garnet went on. "She's been so good to us, Clifford:

buying things, coming up here to help with the furniture, and staying to get us settled."

A glimmer of a smile crossed Clifford's face. "She's a wonder, all right. I nearly fell over laughing this afternoon when she was talking about her precious bathtub."

On the previous day, Garnet and Lorena had shopped "like we was rich women," Lorena had declared, and today boxes of linens, kitchen goods, and furniture came through the door like a parade. One of these contained the dishes from Sears, and another box held a handsome clock, a gift from Adele and Sam Wallace. Clifford had immediately set the time and placed it on the bedroom mantel, and when Lorena had heard the clock strike four, she'd straightened up from tucking new sheets on their bed, and announced, "It's time for me to go now."

Clifford and Garnet had protested. After two nights in the hotel, wasn't she ready to sleep in a friendly place? No, she'd declared, they should have their first night in their new house to themselves. Then she'd grinned. "Anyway, I plan on having me a big, fancy meal in the restaurant, and then I'm going to soak in that bathtub for at least an hour. I'll be back early in the morning and stay the rest of the time with you."

They were nearly done eating when Garnet remarked, "Do you realize this is the first time I've ever cooked a meal we've eaten by ourselves?" He hadn't said much through supper, but she'd chattered enough for both of them.

"And a fine one it was, too."

She waved off his compliment. "Lorena and I picked up enough to get us by. It seems strange to need a store when there's one just off my kitchen, but I must get some food in. You're going to the bank tomorrow, so I'm not sure how I'll manage that."

She laid her hand on his and then stood, stacking their plates and carrying them to the sink. It seemed like she couldn't get enough touching.

"Food is no problem. Tell me what you need, and I'll drop off a list in town tomorrow and have the groceries delivered."

"Oh, I didn't think of that. Everything's so new and strange! Where's some paper? I could give you a list while I'm doing the dishes."

Despite the warm stove and the lamplight glowing off Clifford's burnished hair, the kitchen hardly seemed cozy yet. Its two windows were dark, gaping squares that allowed the winter night to creep into the room. It bothered her to think people could see into her house. She thought aloud, "I could start on curtains tonight."

"Not tonight. I'll rig up something in our bedroom. Anything more for this list?"

She shook her head and reached for the tea towel. Things were an awful muddle; she hardly knew where anything was, but it was an exciting, wonderful muddle. She just wished Clifford would act more like his usual enthusiastic self. A full stomach hadn't improved his temper. Finishing the dishes, she went out the back door to dump the dishwater and called him.

"What? You'll freeze out here."

"Look, Clifford. The evening star," she murmured, reaching for him. Two nights in the hotel hadn't been enough to erase months of longing, and, bless her, Lorena's determination to give them the night alone seemed as precious a gift as the dishes.

He squeezed her hand. "Indeed, the evening star."

"Seems like that hot night you proposed to me was a million years ago."

"Does it?" He turned toward the door. "Seems like no time at all to me. Now, come in the house before we both catch our deaths."

Maybe he was just tired. When she and Lorena arrived on Sunday, he'd glowed every time he looked at her. They'd made love nearly all night, and then he'd risen early to go to the bank and work longer hours than usual to make up for being off today, which had been hectic from sunrise on. No wonder he was subdued. Garnet heard him hammering in the bedroom, probably covering the windows as he'd said he'd do. Ignoring her disheveled kitchen, she opened the door into the store.

It was cold and shadowy in the big room, lamplight from the kitchen casting eerie flickers on empty shelves. Smelling strongly of paint, the store seemed hollow and expectant. Some things were already in place. The long counter, covered by a slab of white marble, was waiting, and the new icebox stood ready but empty. Across from the counter was a long showcase, wood and shimmering glass, which would hold candy and dry goods. "It's so elegant," she whispered, running her hand down the wooden rim.

"Garnet?" Clifford called from the kitchen.

"I'm in here."

He came to the doorway, blocking most of the light. She ran her palm against the smooth marble. "I don't know what possessed you to get a marble top for the counter, but I like it."

He watched as she made her way from one spot to another, touching, admiring. "Well, marble will last forever. Remember how pitted Mattie Lawrence's counter was?"

Garnet nodded, holding her hands behind her back so she wouldn't touch the freshly painted shelves behind the counter. "Did I tell you I went to see her?"

"No."

"Luther won't trade with her any more after she wouldn't let me work there, but I reckoned that was holding a grudge too long and told him so. She looked surprised when I came in, and then she got teary when I told her we were opening a store. She's closing hers come spring and moving in with her daughter."

He asked abruptly, "Are you done in here? We'll never get the house warm with this door open."

Obediently she joined him and stood on tiptoes to kiss his cheek, warm despite the icy store, but she couldn't seem to get his insides to thaw. "Thank you for this beautiful store, Clifford. I can't wait to see it full of merchandise."

That squeezed a smile out of him, but he made no reply. She couldn't think of anything she'd done to upset him. He'd seemed delighted that Lorena had come up to help; surely it couldn't be some kind of strange jealousy of their shopping and camaraderie. She didn't know what was ailing the man.

She peeked into the bedroom and saw that Clifford had already lit a lamp and made a crackling fire. This room looked the most finished even with sheets tacked over the windows. He walked past her into the front room, which was almost as long as the store but not as wide. She and Lorena had bought a sofa, two chairs, a fancy lamp, and a table to place it on, but there was room for much more. They'd grouped these pieces near the fireplace, but half the room stood dark and empty. "It's so spacious," she exclaimed, in a voice she hoped would express admiration rather than complaint. "We thought we'd bought enough to fill it but didn't come close. It can wait, but I believe this room needs a carpet, don't you?"

"Yes. Maybe you and Lorena can look for one."

"Oh, I didn't mean right away."

"Well, it needs *something* and we'll want to start using the room. We can't just live in the kitchen and bedroom." A testy note crept into his voice.

She thought she probably could. Returning to the bedroom, she warmed her backside in front of the fire. "This is my favorite room. And I love my dressing table."

Early yesterday morning, when Clifford was acting like himself, he'd made Lorena promise that she'd have Garnet choose nice furniture and plenty of it. There should be pieces that were useful, he'd said, but also ones that were pretty or pleasing. Lorena had insisted that Garnet buy the dressing table, all elegant with its folding mirrors and intriguing little drawers for gloves and jewelry. It reminded her of the one from their honeymoon, and it hadn't taken much persuasion from Lorena to make her buy it. She perched on the perfect little stool and began taking pins from her hair.

"I swear, I'm nearly befuddled from spending so much yesterday," she declared, watching Clifford's reflection. Then she put a wicked glint in her eyes. "But it was so much fun! I've never had such a day."

He smiled faintly. If she needed to put on a show to jolly him, she supposed she could do it. The fire had warmed the room, and she stretched like a cat. There was so much to do, but she refused to worry about it tonight. The big trunk stood open, clothes thrown haphazardly around it, but Lorena would be there in the morning, and it would be amazing how much they'd accomplish.

Clifford sat on the side of the bed and stared into the fire. She couldn't remember him ever being this quiet. Rooting around in her trunk, she found her brush and nightgown, the pretty one with the flowers and the funny bee, and started undressing. Normally he would've watched or even helped, his fingers eagerly unbuttoning and touching, but he didn't so much as notice.

Garnet tossed her dress onto the jumbled trunk. "I think you'd better tell me what's wrong," she said, holding up a hank of hair and running the brush through it.

The flames flickered against his somber face. "Oh, my back's hurting some."

"Well, you *would* insist on helping those men carry everything in. You made more trips than they did, and they were being paid. Where does it hurt?" She didn't believe him, but it was a starting point.

"Across my shoulder blades."

Setting down her brush, she again went to her trunk, digging in it and lifting a few things onto the floor. "It's nice and warm in here now; take your shirt off and I'll rub your shoulders for you."

She heard him stand and remove his suspenders and shirt. She found the bottle and pulled out a small vial of orange and glycerin lotion. Fanny made the stuff, not as sweet smelling as ones made with rosewater, so perhaps it wouldn't offend his masculine sensibilities. He sat back down on the bed, and she tried to figure how she could get enough leverage. "That won't work. Lay down."

Still silent, he lay on his stomach, his naked back porcelain against her vivid quilt. She knelt beside him on the bed and poured lotion on her hands, rubbing them together to warm it. The sharp, bright scent of oranges filled the room

She began to run her hands over his shoulders, making his skin glisten, moving her palms in steady circles. His muscles were taut, but that could be from tension as much as activity. Try as she might, she couldn't get enough purchase on his back unless she dug in with her fingers, and that wouldn't do. She hitched up her gown and straddled his bottom, resting on her knees above his backside, and reached forward. There, she could apply some pressure this way.

She worked, adding a dab more lotion occasionally, until she felt his shoulders loosening. "Now," she murmured, "are you going to tell me what's bothering you?"

With his head buried in a fluffy, new pillow it was difficult for him to sound too indignant, but he managed to insert some self-righteous annoyance into his voice. "You obviously don't think me worthy of consideration when you make important plans."

All right, she thought, she'd done something wrong but wasn't quite sure what. She continued smoothing her hands over his skin; Lord, it was like silk, and assumed he'd tell her all about her transgression now the gates were open.

He did. "How could you have planned this trip to see the baby without consulting me? I would've taken you; why, I've offered to take you several times, but you're going with Lorena, not me. You're even planning to go on a Sunday when I'm off work, but I'm not allowed to go. I don't like it, Garnet. I don't like it one bit."

His shoulders tightened again beneath her fingers, but she kept at it, not breaking the rhythm of circles. She should've figured it out. Although she'd been making plans to see Ruben for weeks, she and Lorena had only mentioned it in front of him today when they ate their hurried noon meal. "Why, we'll be fine, Clifford. Lorena manages a horse as well as anyone, you said so yourself."

"I'm sure she does, but I'm not so certain she can manage Foster."

"Oh, he won't be there. His Aunt Martha assured me that he wasn't coming home until Christmas Eve. There's nothing to worry about."

Hampered by the pillow, he tried to shake his head. "You never know. She wrote over a week ago. He could've changed his plans. What if he's there when you arrive?"

"Well, then I suppose I'll ignore him and spend my time with Ruben. He'd never dare drink or act up at his Aunt Martha's, and she invited me." She couldn't tell Clifford her reasons for excluding him. He was, in many ways, what David had accused him of being: educated, odd, and definitely wealthy compared to the Fosters, who were, from what she gathered from Aunt Martha's letters, well, common. Clifford's ways would be like a spark on coal oil, but she couldn't tell him this.

"You don't seem to comprehend that it could get ugly."

This irritated her, but she continued. His skin had turned to warm butter. "Well, just suppose he's there, not that I think he will be. If I go with Lorena, we'll talk babies with Aunt Martha, stay out of his way, and if he says anything nasty, we'll ignore him and come home. But if you were to come, you two would be glaring at each other the whole time, and I'd be hard-pressed to keep you all from wrestling in the front yard. Which do you think is the better plan?" She tried to keep her voice light, but her imagination was much darker. They'd likely turn the visit into a cockfight, and that would ruin her chance to enjoy her baby as well as prevent any future visits.

The room was very warm now, and Clifford's back glowed in the lamplight. She rocked on her knees as she pushed up against his shoulders and then down his spine. With each movement up his back, her thighs brushed against the coarse wool of his pants, and she wished she'd asked him to remove those too.

Indignation dripped from his voice when he spoke again. "You act as though you're terrified by little things like my sisters or debt, but then you put yourself in true danger by foolishly exposing yourself to that despicable bully. How can I protect you as I've sworn to do if you make this damned trip without me?"

Hmm, he wasn't getting any calmer. Leaning far up to address the thin muscles of his neck, she kept her voice as soothing as her hands. "Fair enough. You're right; it does seem like I'm contradicting myself, and as to foolish, well, I've never been foolish before, have I?" She laughed lightly and was rewarded by a slight noise. Stopping to put another dollop of lotion in her hand, she turned her eyes to the ceiling, thinking, Mama, let me have a little of your skill right now. She consciously used Louise's low voice." Of course you're right. Here I've been acting timid about everything and now I go and set out on something that, as you say, might be dangerous. But Clifford, I don't think it will be; David won't be there. And maybe I've found some courage. Why I spent all that money yesterday like it was nothing, and I told you how well everything turned out with your sisters."

She had the most overpowering urge to lick his knobby spine, all hot, glistening, and fragrant. Shifting her knees, she moved so her rocking back and forth insured contact with the scratchy wool covering his buttocks. His muscles seemed loose and fluid now, and certainly she felt as if she were ready to melt.

He murmured, "All right, I concede. I have to let you find your own way even if I don't like it." She moved her hands down from his shoulders to his waist, dipping her fingertips below the waistband of his trousers. "What bothered me most was that you kept it a secret."

She wasn't sure, but it felt like his hips were rocking, matching the motion she was using to lean up to his shoulders and back again. Every now and then she felt a small squirming motion in his thighs, but she had him penned and wasn't going to let him up just yet. "I'm sorry," she said, surprised at the breathlessness in her voice. "I should've told you, and I think I would've if there hadn't been so many other things going on. I swear it slipped my mind."

Again he made a low noise. Up, she leaned, and this time she didn't resist temptation; pressing her lips to his shoulder blade, she scattered kisses down his moist, fragrant skin. Her breasts brushed his back, and the warmth of it made her nipples tighten.

"Garnet," he said.

"Hmm?"

"If you don't let me turn over and get these pants off, I'm going to die."

"Really?" She raised her leg, moved to his side, and smiled when she saw how quickly he moved, sore back forgotten. She pulled down the quilts, and then he clasped her to him. "How's your back?" she asked, pulling off her gown amid his hands and legs.

"Fine, fine," he mumbled into her hair. Just before she succumbed to his loving, she opened her eyes, looked at the ceiling, and mouthed silently, "Thank you, Mama."

Chapter Nine

The next day Lorena arrived late along with a truck, two grunting deliverymen, and a shiny new sewing machine. Garnet stuttered with gratitude, but Lorena brushed it off. "An old woman like me's got to spend her money on something." Lorena also unpacked bolts of muslin, shiny chintz, and heavy, pale green linen for the front room drapes but wouldn't allow Garnet to do anything more than touch the fabric. "We need to get everything to rights first, girl. Then we'll sew, even if we have to do it by lamplight. I don't know how you made a meal in that jumbled-up kitchen last night." She all but giggled. "I seen you touching this material the other day, so I snuck around and measured windows yesterday while you were busy."

A couple of busy days later, Luther, having just arrived with the tobacco crop, knocked on the door and asked if he could join them for dinner. He refused to stay with them, saying the boarding house was close to the warehouses, but he declared that the food was a fair sight better at Garnet's and ate with them every evening. By Saturday, she and Lorena had finished curtains for the bedroom and kitchen as well as the luxurious linen drapes for the front room. Those, however, needed heavy curtain rods, and Luther promised to come on Sunday to help Clifford hang them. But when Luther heard that Lorena and Garnet wouldn't be there and where they were going, he turned stormy and protested as strongly as Clifford. Garnet was surprised when her husband didn't renew his attack upon her trip, now that he had an ally, but he told Luther that, although he didn't like it either, there was no stopping the women.

"It's nine wonders they didn't open their mouths in front of Franklin, and then we really would've had trouble," Lorena declared on Sunday morning, her steamy breath billowing as she talked. She drove one of Luther's mules, hitched to a small cart, a rough ride on such a cold day. Garnet shivered, tucking the blanket more tightly under her hips.

"Franklin would've raised a complete ruckus," she agreed. Late Saturday afternoon, her brother had arrived, all smiles and frost-reddened cheeks to share their dinner. She delighted in the fact that she could see him occasionally now. Time did do wonders for healing resentments. Franklin had greeted Luther as he would've before the man married their mother, and he'd absolutely glowed when Lorena hugged him. It was a fine reunion.

"It's not like we're two frail flowers," Garnet said. "They forget I lived with David Foster for over a year and a half."

"Oh, they just want to protect you, I reckon. And that's noble and good, as far as it goes. But sometimes their protecting gets bullheaded." Lorena's hands, elegant in their kid gloves, looked incongruous against the weathered reins.

Garnet sat quietly while the cart rumbled over frozen ruts. The sky was a chilly, milky white. Lorena glanced sideways. You excited or scared?"

"A little of both. I'm sure Ruben won't know me, but I'm afraid he won't make up to me. That'll hurt, even though the child can't help it. He probably doesn't see many strangers out here."

"This is God's Knob, that's for sure."

"And it's bound to be awkward. Martha Allen has been friendly in her letters, but who knows what David told her or what they think I've done. I think she realizes her nephew took Ruben away from me rather than me giving him up. At least I hope so." Garnet's fingers were so tightly twined they hurt. She stretched them.

"You've got the toy?"

"It's in the back. I hope he likes it."

"No doubt in my mind he'll like it. These is poor folks, ain't they? He won't have many playthings."

"Oh, Walter might make him some toys; he's a dab hand at carving." Her nose wrinkled up at the man's name. "But maybe the one I bought is too fancy. I don't want them to think I'm trying to buy my son."

"It's Christmas, or nearly so. I reckon a mama can buy her baby a toy for Christmas."

From what Garnet could gather from Martha Allen's brief letters, they lived on a small dairy farm, so she'd bought Ruben a tin wagon with two horses that might resemble the vehicle that took their milk to market.

"We've gone near ten miles from town. Ain't we supposed to turn off somewheres along here? "Lorena asked.

"Yes, to the right. And then she said we'd go for another five miles. But I don't see anything yet."

They bounced along in silence until Garnet spotted a lane. "That must be it. She said it ran between two pastures."

Lorena maneuvered the mule onto an even more primitive track. "Lord, this is rougher than Evans County. It reminds me of Deer Creek."

"I get the idea they don't have much."

"Seems like old Walter could send a little money his sister's way."

"I hope David's giving her money for Ruben, but I get the impression she's a proud woman. And she never says much about her husband. Maybe he's the same way."

"Not that we'd know anything about proud, cantankerous men, would we?" Lorena asked with a sideways grin. "Useless as tits on a boar when they got their dander up," she declared, exhaling a huge cloud of steam.

They were both thoroughly chilled and jostled by the time they arrived at the Allen farm. It was dead winter, but the view was bleak and dismal. The only impressive sight was an imposing new barn. They hadn't passed another house or sign of civilization for at least three miles, and the little unpainted house looked desolate and depressing. "Hmm," Lorena said, slowing the mule. "I'm getting a case of nerves now myself. If there wasn't smoke rising from the chimney, I'd say this place was deserted. You sure that sorry David ain't going to be here?"

"I'm sure." Garnet reached for Ruben's package.

"Well, I'd like to get this mule out of the cold, but nobody seems to be around."

There was no porch, only a large flat rock serving as a doorstep. Before Lorena could knock, the door opened and a squat, square woman with gray hair scraped into a knot at her neck opened the door. She twisted her hands in her apron.

"Well, hello, Mrs. Allen. I'm Lorena King, and this here's Garnet Clark, Ruben's mother. Pleased to meet you." Lorena's smile was big and nervous.

Martha Allen stared at Garnet as if she'd like to bury her in the barn.

"We was wondering if we could shelter the mule for a bit. It's mighty chilly out here," Lorena continued. Garnet smiled, bobbing her head like an idiot in order to coax some kind of friendliness out of the woman. Her letters hadn't seemed so cold.

Then Garnet realized why Martha Allen was upset. Coming to the door behind his aunt was David. Her heart sank, and that old clenching seized her gut. "I'll tend to your mule," he said to Lorena, giving the tiniest of nods to Garnet as he passed. Lorena stared after him, her brows flying up like crows.

Aunt Martha relaxed enough to ask them into the house, and they went directly into a large kitchen, with stove, table, and a cupboard to the left. On the right were three cane-bottomed rocking chairs, each with a well-worn cushion smashed against its back. Martha's husband George sat in one of them; he looked frail and much older than his wife. The other two were empty. "Set a spell," Martha said, gesturing at the chairs. "Dinner's going to be a mite longer. We just come home from church, and Lissy and I have more cooking to do."

A girl, perhaps a little younger than Garnet, stood glaring at her from the stove. This was evidently Lissy, Martha's youngest daughter. Entwined in Lissy's skirts stood a small boy, peeping around at the newcomers with shy, curious eyes. Garnet thought her heart was going to stop. All thoughts of David disappeared, and she counted any discomfort he might cause a small price to pay. The child was beautiful. Strong, bright, and beautiful. "Come here now, Ruben. These ladies has come to see you, you little rascal. See, I told you your mama was going to visit." Martha stood next to her daughter, talking in that bright voice people use to get children to do their bidding and trying to disengage his chubby hands from Lissy's skirt. He relented and, with one hand at his mouth, agreed to walk toward them.

From her chair, Garnet smiled, hoping she didn't seem too eager. Step by step he came toward them but stopped at George's knee, laying his dimpled hand upon it. George set a ropy hand on the child's head. Ruben's hair had darkened but was still fair and curly. "Ain't he the prettiest boy!" Lorena whispered.

"Hello, Ruben," Garnet murmured. "I've been wanting to see you for a long time."

He hesitated and almost turned back but kept gazing solemnly at Garnet. His eyes were wide, a bright, liquid blue like her own. "You have a fine barn, Ruben," Garnet said, leaning down to get closer to his level. "What's inside the barn?"

Muffled by his hand, his reply was garbled. "Cows."

"I bet you do have cows. Are there any other animals in the barn?" Her fingers tingled with the need to touch him.

Ruben inched a little closer to Lorena. "Kitties," he said, putting down his hand and speaking clearly.

"Kitties!" Lorena exclaimed. "I bet you like to play with them, don't you?"

He nodded, agreeing but never taking his enormous eyes off Garnet. Lord, please let David stay in that barn for a while. The child seemed to be building up his nerve, coming another step toward her and then saying, "And the kitties go meow, meow."

She and Lorena chuckled, and Ruben gave them a satisfied smile, pleased with his performance. Finally with one or two more tentative steps, he came to Garnet's side and put his hand on her leg. Holding back, she patted his soft hand and asked, "And how do the cows go?"

He whispered dramatically, "Moo, moo!"

Again she laughed. From the kitchen she heard Lissy and Martha Allen clattering plates, and she smelled the warm scents of food and wood smoke, but all she could see were those eyes, cheeks, curls. He rubbed his little hand against her skirt, patting and smoothing it. "Pretty," he murmured.

"Thank you." She hardly dared breathe.

He came closer still, leaning against her leg, and her arms ached to pick him up, but it would kill her if he cried or resisted. Then he lifted one arm and reached toward her face, running his dimpled fingers down her cheek. Oh, don't let me cry. "Pretty," he said again and reached up with his other arm. Then he was in her lap, a warm bundle of baby flesh close to her heart, and she nuzzled his neck to make him giggle. They chatted about important things: cows and buttons and kitties and toes, and she thanked God dinner was late and David stayed in the barn.

It couldn't last forever, though. Aunt Martha sent Lissy to fetch David and told them to come to the table. Ruben scrambled down from Garnet's lap to claim his chair, a tall one that allowed him to eat at the table. It looked like David's handiwork. The boy pushed his chair close to the table and said to Aunt Martha, "By my mama!"

Garnet's heart sang, higher and more sweetly than her voice had ever done. "Well, for certain, child. You can set by your mama."

They were all seated when Lissy and David came in, bringing the cold with them. Garnet was glad that he was down the table from her so she could avoid meeting his eyes. Ruben clutched his spoon and raised it in a solemn greeting. "Papa!" he crowed.

"Ruben," David replied in the same tone and rubbed his hands together. "It's dropped ten degrees since we come from church." Garnet remembered those hands.

After a lengthy blessing, the only words George said throughout the meal, there was a general confusion of passing dishes and exclamations over the food. Garnet suspected that the Allens had done their best. There was a large roasted chicken and mashed potatoes with gravy, and additional bowls of baked squash, turnips, sweet pickles, and bread. Martha was trying to tell her that her child wouldn't go hungry.

Too keyed up to eat, Garnet took tiny servings although she praised the food. To her right, Lorena chattered away to Martha, asking about their cows, how their garden had done the previous summer, and essentially providing cover so Garnet could focus on Ruben. It was a tremendous performance considering that Lissy and David said little, and George might as well have been mute.

Ruben showed off for her, dabbling with his mashed potatoes and making funny noises. At one point he got too loud and Garnet started to discipline him but couldn't bring herself to do it. He was, after all, glorying in her attention.

"Ruben," David said evenly, but with an unmistakable tone of censure. The boy popped a spoonful of squash in his mouth, looking up at Garnet with a comical expression, completely unfazed by his father's disapproval. Ruben knew he was the most important person at the table.

When there were unanimous groans about being too full to move, Lissy rose, silent as her father, and started stacking plates. "Pie, pie, pie!" Ruben announced, banging his spoon against the table, and Garnet reached for his hand to stop the noise.

She smiled at him. "I reckon you like pie?" He nodded. "What kind do you like best?" She could feel David's eyes on her.

"Apple."

"And apple it is, young Ruben, but you got to finish your meal first," Aunt Martha said. The woman threw quick glances between David and Garnet.

Ruben clouded up, lower lip protruding, and looked at Garnet to see if she agreed. She made her face mournful. "Aunt Martha's right, Ruben. Finish your dinner."

Scowling, he tried his father, who lifted his eyebrows, and the little fellow sighed mightily and set his spoon to work. By the time Lissy set a piece of pie in front of everyone else, most of Ruben's dinner was gone, and he looked expectantly at her. When she gave him a piece, he removed the top crust to uncover the filling and went after it, his face expressing bliss. "You don't like the crust?" Garnet asked. Either Lorena was chewing or she'd run out of steam. The room was silent.

Ruben ignored her, scraping his spoon against the bottom crust until every bit of apple was in his stomach. Then, just as eagerly, he started in on the crust. "Oh," she said, figuring it out. "You like them both, but separately." This amused her, but when she looked up, Lissy and David were staring at her. Don't let them buffalo you, she told herself, but what little she'd eaten twisted inside her stomach, and she felt a tightness crawl across her shoulders.

Garnet and Lorena offered to help with the dishes, but Martha insisted they should visit with the baby. Garnet wiped his face, removing a dollop of squash from his nose, and then he hopped down and took her hand, leading her to one of the bedrooms. Lorena grabbed a towel and stayed in the kitchen.

Two rooms led off the kitchen. The first one obviously belonged to Martha and George, but Ruben guided her to a more spacious bedroom, a good thing since it contained three iron beds lined up and sitting no more than a foot apart, as well as a chest and chifferobe. This had been the Allen children's room, Garnet figured, and more than likely another bed or two had been stuffed into it when they were small, especially while David lived there.

The little boy made a beeline for a wooden box at the end of his bed. Looking pointedly at her, he indicated that he wanted her to sit on his bed. It was the smallest one, very low and wedged against the wall. With great ceremony, he handed her his toys, one by one. First he offered her a little boat that looked like Walter Foster's work. She exclaimed over it, but Ruben was more intent upon getting everything out than hearing her opinions. Next he handed her some undoubtedly important rocks, and then he gave her two feathers and a bag made from a flour sack containing the blocks David had made him for Christmas two years ago.

"Papa made these for you, didn't he?"

He didn't reply. Several more mysterious playthings came from the box: a candle stub, a dilapidated man's hat, and then he murmured, "Brownie, see, it's Brownie." He held up the ragged remains of Clifford's bear. Tears threatened again as she remembered that Christmas.

"Brownie's your friend, hmm?" she asked, her voice catching.

"Uh, huh," he replied, stuffing the bear into her lap.

"He's a very nice bear."

Ruben nodded. Then he ignored her, littering the bed with blocks and pretending to be very busy with his building. Without a firm surface he wasn't having much luck, but she supposed that construction wasn't truly his purpose. This seemed as good a time as any to give him his gift. They were alone, and there was no one to disapprove, at least immediately. "Stay here, Ruben," she said. "I'll be right back."

He had his lower lip behind his teeth, such tiny white teeth, like the sweetest kernels of corn. She hurried toward the chair where she'd tucked the package when they first arrived. Martha, Lissy, and Lorena were still busy in the kitchen, and George dozed in his chair. David, however, noticed her step and followed her with his eyes. He slumped in the other rocker with his legs outstretched. She'd have to walk over them to pick up the package. "Excuse me," she murmured, but he didn't move. Stepping over him, her skirt caught on his legs, causing her a shiver of revulsion.

She noticed how much colder it was in the bedroom, but Ruben didn't seem to mind. Despite having carpenters in the family, the house was poorly built; the single, small window allowed a persistent draught into the dark room and the floorboards had wider cracks than the ones at Mama's house. She felt shivery all over, and the tautness between her shoulders was growing sharper. She hoped she wasn't coming down with something she might pass on to the baby. "Look, Ruben," she said as she sat on his bed. "Mama brought you something."

This caught his attention in a hurry, and he set to ripping the tissue paper. Oh, it was worth seeing scowling old David just to witness her son's joy. When the child uncovered the wagon, he set to rolling it on the bed. "What is it?" she asked him.

"Wagon and horses," Ruben replied, as if she were an idiot. He made clip-clop noises in the back of his throat.

She despised herself for doing it, but there was so little time. "Can you thank Mama for giving it to you?" she asked, her voice tremulous.

"Thank you," he said, intent on his toy.

"Maybe a little hug?"

He was reluctant to quit playing, but he reached for her across the wagon's path and put soft arms around her neck. Shutting her eyes, she grasped him tight for a second and then let go. "Pretty," he said, but she didn't know if he meant the wagon or her. The wagon's route curved along her hip, up over the pillow, and then back to the end of the bed, and he produced all the sounds necessary for the trip.

When Garnet heard a different sound, she looked up to see David filling the small space between the two beds. She had to resist the urge to scoot toward the wall.

"Look, Papa!"

"I see," David replied, but he stared at Garnet rather than the toy.

"Just a Christmas present," she faltered.

He said nothing, but the path of his eyes was just as discernable as the one Ruben's wagon followed. First he gazed at her face, then his eyes lowered to her breasts. They lingered and then dropped to her lap. She'd seen Grandpa and Franklin look at horses this way, noting every turn of muscle. It was all she could do not to scramble across the next bed to escape.

David was no more than two feet from her, and she imagined she could smell him, that sawdust and turpentine scent he always carried, except when whiskey seeped from his pores. There was no whiskey today. There was a grimy smudge on his shirt, and his cuffs were frayed. He was staring at her wedding ring, Clifford's diamond, and his mouth turned down into a thin curve. But when he spoke, it was with a smile, even though his eyes were cold. "You still look good," he said. "Damned good." And he lightly ran his hand down the front of his pants.

Oh, dear Lord, she thought, her heart thumping against her chest. The tightness in her back became a string threatening to break. She bowed her head, pretending his comment was a compliment.

"I hear you're going to get your store, just like you always wanted."

Ruben, bless him, was fully occupied with his wagon, but she wished he'd crawl onto her lap or divert his father's attention. From the kitchen she heard Lorena talking about pole beans. You're all right, she reassured herself. You don't need rescuing.

"So everything's all fine and dandy with your rich old man, I reckon. Diamonds on your fingers and a nice little store for you to play in." His voice was a sneer. "I'm wondering if he ever thawed you out."

Her eyes fluttered up to see that his face was contorted into its familiar mask of meanness, and as she slid her eyes back down, she noticed his pants. Horrified, she began to shake: her hands, her legs, there was no part of her that didn't tremble. Gripping her hands together, she met his eyes. "We're happy," she said as calmly as she could. She'd be damned if she let him know he was bothering her.

But he knew, and he was enjoying it. "Maybe so," he replied. "Can't get a baby on you though, can he?"

She'd have to; she'd have to climb across the next bed. Otherwise she'd scream right here in front of the baby. She turned toward Ruben. "Where's the wagon going?" Her voice shook.

"To town," the child replied.

David didn't relent. "I don't much like you coming in here with expensive presents." A wave of nausea joined the steel binding her shoulder blades.

"Christmas. . ."

He acted as though he hadn't heard her. "As a matter of fact, I don't much like you coming here at all. I ain't having you turning this into a contest."

From the other room she heard Lorena declare, "Lord, we'd better get on the road, Mrs. Allen."

David went on, "But I reckon Ruben's the only baby you'll ever have."

Lorena stepped into the room and assessed the situation in a heartbeat. Her voice was too loud. "It's started snowing, Garnet. We need to leave."

Garnet wasn't sure if she could stand up without brushing against David, and she abhorred the idea of touching him. She reached out her hand to the child. "Ruben, honey, Mama's got to leave now. You stay sweet, you hear?" Her voice was trembling so broadly that the boy looked up with a puzzled expression. Then she glanced at David, who was studying her again, his eyes slitted.

"I kept my promise. I ain't never said nothing bad about you to the boy."

She nodded. Her taut back burned now, pain binding it like a cutting wire.

"David, will you fetch our cart?" Lorena was behind him, loaded for bear.

After giving Garnet another hard glance, David left the room, and Lorena grabbed Garnet's hand. "Did he touch you?"

Garnet shook her head and turned back to Ruben. "Honey, can Mama kiss you good-bye?" Her voice still wavered, and an agonizing pain shrieked across her back when she reached for him. He suffered her kiss and mumbled good-bye. When she rose, she gasped, reaching a blind hand to Lorena.

"Good Lord, Garnet, what's wrong?"

"Nothing. Just my back. Let's get out of here." Touching Ruben's velvet cheek one more time, she followed Lorena. They thanked Martha Allen and Lissy for the meal, but the two women stayed by the stove and simply nodded, ready to end the visit.

Garnet felt the cold take her despite her coat and gloves, and the shaking that started when David confronted her turned into shivering. "Good Jesus," Lorena swore. "It's cold as a witch's tit."

David was bringing their mule and cart. "I'm afraid to ask them for more blankets. They probably don't have none to spare," Lorena whispered.

The snow wasn't sticking yet, just swirling around and stinging their faces. David stood by the mule, not making any attempt to help either woman into the cart. Lorena climbed up briskly, tucking the blanket around her lap, but Garnet was slow and clumsy. The pain in her back seemed to cut off her air. If David noticed her discomfort, he gave no sign of it; he simply removed his hand from the mule's harness and they left.

They hadn't traveled ten yards before Lorena started. "Damnation but those are the queerest people I ever seen! That poor old house, seems like Walter and his ornery son could at least slap a coat of paint on the walls. And that old man, did you ever? Just sat there without opening his damned mouth all afternoon. Jesus God, it's cold, and if it's snowing in Lexington the men are going to be worrying their heads off." She paused for breath, exhaled a white cloud of steam, and shivered.

"Now Martha's all right. She wasn't so much unfriendly as fretting herself to death about David being there. She said he just come in yesterday evening, so she wasn't lying when she wrote that he was still up north. She's a good woman, but that daughter! Sourest old puss I ever seen, and it's 'my cousin David' this and 'my cousin David' that! Good Lord, if they hadn't told me she's marrying in the spring, I'd swear she was sweet on the son of a bitch. Whispering and giggling to him. I believe in sticking to your kin, but sometimes you've got to realize when they's sorry, useless trash. And she was just plain rude. She wouldn't speak to me at all at first, but then . . ."

"Lorena," Garnet interrupted. "Stop the cart." Her voice was as insubstantial as the snowflakes swirling around them.

Lorena jerked on the reins and turned to stare at Garnet. It was agony to shift even a tiny bit but she did, and gripping the edge of the cart, Garnet lost what little dinner she'd eaten onto the road.

"Good Lord, are you sickening with something? Are you sure that ornery devil didn't hurt you?" Lorena yanked off a glove and touched her forehead.

Garnet wiped her mouth with a handkerchief. "No, my back hurts something dreadful."

Lorena ran her hand lightly down Garnet's spine. "Hmm, across here? Your back's as hard as a rock and you're trembling all over. Here," she said, lifting the blanket from her lap and wrapping it around Garnet's shoulders, tucking and fussing.

"You'll freeze," Garnet protested.

"So I'll be cold." She clucked to the mule, and they started down the rutted lane. Garnet's back snarled at every bounce, but there was no remedy for it. She tried to breathe deeply, but it didn't help. The pain was so intense it frightened her.

"Do you reckon I'm going to be crippled?"

Lorena was urging the mule go as fast as its nature would allow, but the road wouldn't accommodate much speed. "Naw, Deke had something like this once, pain so terrible it like to scared him to death. Dr. Thomas said the nerves had seized up. He told him to lay flat and keep it warm. We can't do much about warmth, but do you want to lay in the back of the cart?" She looked dubiously at the cart bed.

"I'm not sure I could get down in there. But Grandpa got better?"

"Yep. Next morning he was a little sore, but the pain was gone. You'll be all right." Garnet felt tears running down her cold cheeks. Lorena glanced at her, and her face crumpled. "Oh, honey, don't cry! I'll get you home. Are you sure he didn't hit you?"

Garnet shook her head as much as the pain would allow. "I'm all right. What caused Grandpa's back to seize up?"

Lorena shivered and snorted at the same time. "Tossing bales of hay around. Maybe some of the work we been doing caused it."

"It started when I saw David."

"That don't surprise me none. He's a pain in the back as well as the ass. What was he saying to you? If I'd knowed he was in there, I would've come."

Garnet took a shuddery breath. If she could just quit shivering, her back might not hurt so much, but the wind cut through the blankets, and she couldn't feel her feet. Lorena must be chilled to the bone. "He told me not to give fancy presents to Ruben."

"Huh! I reckon a mother can give her son presents any time she wants to," Lorena retorted. She turned the mule onto the main road.

"He said I shouldn't turn it into a contest."

Snowflakes peppered down from the leaden sky. So far they were more of an annoyance than a hazard, but Lorena was right. Luther and Clifford would be fretting.

"Well, it wouldn't be no contest at all if that child was allowed to see you on a regular basis. Did he allow that you could come visit?" Lorena's teeth were chattering, and they still had miles to travel.

Garnet blinked away a snowflake. "He said he didn't like it."

"Too bad! Course, I don't know how often I'd want to make this trip, but in good weather, it might not be so bad. And after that homely Lissy gets married in the spring, she wouldn't be around to sour things. I don't know if David could stop you unless he tells his aunt you can't come."

Garnet's entire body was as coiled as her back. Little by little she tried to relax it; her toes, her fingers, her legs, but then she had to tense up again to brace herself against the jouncing of the cart. She hoped she wouldn't vomit again; that had left her shaking worse than ever. Riding the waves of pain and nausea reminded her of childbirth. But there'd been a prize at the end of that trial, a dear and wonderful prize.

"Wasn't he sweet?"

"Oh, yes," Lorena answered, her face thawing into a broad smile. "He's a fine boy, healthy-looking too. He favors you."

"Do you think so?" Garnet's voice was eager. She didn't know why it mattered to find traces of herself in her son, but it did.

"Lord, yes. He's got your eyes, all bright and blue, and your mouth, thank God. David's mouth is pinched up and thin, always was, but Ruben's got a sweet mouth, full and pretty. He's mighty fetching and bright too; you can tell."

For a moment she forgot the cold, miserable afternoon, the harsh pain racking her back, the ugliness of David's words, and lost herself in recollecting Ruben's hugs and that particularly wonderful soft spot just beneath his blurry jawbone. She thought she could still smell him, fresh and milky, reminding her of hay, pastures, and cows. Already she was yearning to touch him again, imagining the child sleeping upstairs in their new house, prowling around the grocery, playing in the back, but this was foolishness.

"David spooked me," Lorena announced suddenly. "He kept staring like he was going to take a bite out of you, but he wasn't drinking, was he?"

"No."

The clomping of the mule and rattling of the cart were the only sounds. On the trip to the farm they'd met other wagons; now the road was deserted. Garnet spoke again, her voice strained. "He said Ruben's the only baby I'm likely to have."

"Son of a bitch."

"Maybe it's true. The part about Clifford being too old."

Lorena wiped snow from her face. "Clifford ain't that old. Plenty of men father children way up into their fifties, even sixties. Your Papa was way older than Clifford when Violet, Henry, and Dessie was born. Bunch of hogwash." Lorena snorted. "You all ain't been married much more than a year, and you was apart three months. Just cause that jackass got you pregnant in a month don't mean he's more of a man."

Lorena made sense, she always did, but David's words had opened a pit of shadowy fears. What if Ruben, kept away from her, seen only in glimpses, was her only child? Not only would she mourn her childlessness, she could see years of David, still and always, exerting power over her through Ruben. Thinking of him hovering over her in that chilly bedroom sent a deeper shiver through her body, causing her back to issue a thin scream of pain.

"Worse, honey? Lord, it's taking forever to get home."

Garnet gulped the damp air, fending off nausea. "I'm all right. I just never want to see his face again. Never."

Lorena frowned. "What else did he say? They's something you ain't telling me."

Garnet clutched the blanket. She should give it back to Lorena who was visibly shivering. "He didn't say much else. Oh, that I looked good, but he didn't mean anything nice by it."

The mule plodded along, each step bringing them closer to warmth and shelter, but they could've been nearing town or miles away, as far as Garnet could tell. Stubbled fields stretched dull and sullen on either side of the road, and what dwellings they passed seemed deserted. The world was nothing but snow flying into her eyes, wind swirling up her skirt, and this hot, bright pain cutting into her spine. Lorena waited.

"He just stood there, too close, like something waiting to swoop. And he said those ugly things, but that's David; I didn't expect anything else. But the whole time he was talking, right there next to the baby, he was, umm, well, he was . . . aroused." She had trouble saying it.

A deep growl of disgust came from Lorena's throat. "You don't mean it!" she exclaimed. "Did he act like he was going to take you right there in the baby's room?"

"No." Distaste became a metallic tang in her mouth. "He, well, he touched himself. He wanted to make sure I knew."

"Good Lord!" Lorena swore. "God knows you're pretty enough to make a man want you but . . . "

"It wasn't like that," Garnet interrupted. "It was a threat. Like he wanted me to know he could still own me."

"Jesus," Lorena muttered. "No wonder your back seized up." She drove on, and Garnet swallowed, her mouth suddenly full of spit. Lorena was humming; Garnet thought it was "Shall We Gather at the River," but her voice quavered with the cold, distorting the melody. The woman broke off in the middle of the chorus. "I don't believe I'd tell Clifford none of this."

"I won't."

"He don't need to know that Foster was faulting his manhood or that he got hard just from talking to you." Despite the cold, Garnet's face warmed with embarrassment. "That's more than any man should have to tolerate. Or any woman, for that matter." Although Lorena's cheeks were reddened by the wind, the rest of her face was pale and pinched.

"Take this blanket, Lorena. You're chilled through."

"Set still. See that barn up yonder? I remember it; we're at the edge of town."

She was right; Lorena was always right. Lorena would get her home; she could always count on Lorena. Hugging her arms to her chest, Garnet settled into a last effort at endurance. When they reached Lexington, the streets were deserted; people with any sense were staying by their stoves. There'd been more snow in town. As they neared the warehouses, Garnet smelled the pungent scent of tobacco, and papery fronds of it littered the whitened streets. She wondered how Luther would do with his crop. That morning he'd said he'd be in town another week. She'd have Lorena a while longer, and in the evenings, Luther, with his quiet, warm smile, would sit down to supper with them. Home, she thought, she wanted home and all that went with it: warmth, comfort, and Clifford.

Garnet wasn't sure she could move. She tried to unwind the blanket from her shoulders and lift her hips enough to loosen the one covering her lap, but the pain cut off her breath. Lorena grunted when she climbed down. "Come on, honey, we're home," she coaxed.

"I don't think I can," Garnet whispered, trying to shift her legs. Her back rippled in agony.

"Where are those damned men?" Lorena demanded, glaring at the house and waving. The front room windows showed a faint gleam of lamplight. "I ain't sure I can lift you out of there, Garnet. Hold on. I'll fetch Luther and Clifford."

Behind her, Garnet heard feet thud against the frozen ground. "What's wrong? Is she hurt? Was that bastard there?" My, how Clifford's language had deteriorated since he'd left his sisters, she thought, almost smiling. His voice sounded like heaven.

"Yes, he was there, and no, he didn't touch her. Her back's seized up, and she can't get out of the cart," Lorena said, impatient with having to explain.

Suddenly Clifford was beside her, his shirtsleeves spotted with snow. "Can you move, dear heart? Shall I carry you?"

"Get Lorena in the house," she murmured. "She's frozen."

"Don't mind me, girl, but this poor mule needs tending; he's served us well." Lorena struggled to spread a blanket over the animal.

Suddenly there was a terrific pain, so intense that she growled with it, startling herself, but then she was in Clifford's arms, weightless as the snow falling on her face. She heard Luther's low voice. "I'll see to the mule."

Then she felt and saw warmth: the fireplace leapt with red and yellow flames and lamps burned golden in the front room. Clifford eased her onto the sofa and knelt, unbuttoning her coat and peeling off her gloves. "Jesus God," Lorena announced. "I ain't never been this cold." She stood by the fire, but to the side so she wouldn't block its warmth from Garnet. "My hands is so numb I don't think I can get my coat off."

Clifford opened Garnet's coat and gently pulled it out from under her. Even his careful movements jarred the pain. He said, "Wait a minute, Lorena, and I'll unbutton you. Are you frostbitten? If I'd dreamed the temperature would plummet so drastically, I'd never have let you two start out."

Remarkably, Lorena waited until Clifford came to help her, unbuttoning her coat and lifting it off her shoulders. "It weren't so bad on the way up," she said, "but it started dropping soon after we arrived. When the snow came, I reckoned you and Luther would be worrying." Lorena's color was coming back, but her voice still trembled.

"We were." The door shut, and Luther came into the room. "I put the mule in your shed, Clifford."

"Good. Now sit, Lorena, and I'll get you all some blankets."

Soon both women were tucked up with quilts, holding steaming cups of sweet tea that Luther made. The men sat in the armchairs watching them, faintly accusatory. Lorena scrunched up her nose. "Well, I don't know what else we could've done. It was fair enough when we left, and I wasn't going to beg a bed from those people, that's for damned sure."

A wisp of a smile tugged at Garnet's mouth. "Lord, where would they have put us, the barn?"

"It was a foolish idea to begin with," Luther replied, pursing his mouth.

"What was foolish about it?" Lorena retorted. "We was invited. We just didn't know the roads would be so rough nor the cold so bad."

"He was there?" Clifford's voice was very low.

Garnet nodded, sipping her tea.

"Was he hateful to you?" Fire flickered in Clifford's eyes.

She started to shrug but winced. "He was David."

Clifford rose and paced the room. "You said he wouldn't be there. Did that woman lie to you? Why didn't you come straight home?" His voice edged toward anger, and since, thank God, David wasn't available, Garnet supposed she'd get the brunt of it.

"No. He came home unexpected, just yesterday evening. His aunt was as upset as anyone." She glanced beseechingly at Lorena.

"There weren't nothing done on purpose, Clifford. The woman give us a good dinner, Garnet got to see her baby, and we left. It weren't pleasant seeing that son of a bitch, and he's still the ornery cuss he always was, but we survived. It would've been all right except it turned so cold and Garnet's back went bad." Lorena set down her cup and wrinkled her nose. "Do I smell cigars?"

At this there was a general uproar of excuses and explanations. Well, yes, the men had decided to test the quality of the newly delivered tobacco order, and they thought they'd aired the house well enough, but, yes, they'd shared cigars that afternoon. Relieved that the conversation had turned, Garnet frowned at Clifford, more in surprise than disapproval. "I didn't know you smoked cigars."

"Well, every now and then when the girls weren't watching. Luther and I wanted to celebrate our work: how do you like the drapes?" he asked, pointing at the windows.

Not to be distracted and unable at that point to turn enough to view their endeavors anyway, Garnet said, "And Luther, I didn't realize you smoked either."

The quiet man reddened. "Just on occasion, Garnet, and your mama won't let me do it in the house." He added, "Lorena smokes cigars too."

Garnet turned her head, and the pain, temporarily eased by the warmth, reared up again, red-hot and powerful. She heard Lorena chuckle. "Well, I do like a good cheroot, but what I'd like now is food. Seems like I smell something besides cigars."

Both men jumped up. "Luther started a pot of soup beans right after you all left, and he's going to make cornbread," Clifford announced as Luther left the room.

Garnet, drowning in pain again, whispered, "Not for me, thanks."

Clifford stopped at the door, turning a worried face toward Lorena.

"She's in a bad way. It ain't just the cold. The pain's so bad she lost her dinner on the trip home. I don't think she'll be eating no beans, although they sound fine to me," Lorena explained. "Besides, I'm plumb mystified by the idea of my brother making cornbread, although, with him being married to Louise it don't surprise me none."

Within seconds, Clifford was kneeling at Garnet's knee, rubbing her hands to warm them. It was cozy in the room, but the fire hadn't penetrated to her bones. "What can I get for you then, Garnet? You need to eat something. Maybe some toast? I can manage that." She nodded, doubting he could manage much more.

Clifford laid his hand on Garnet's hair. "Should we fetch a doctor? I could go to Sam's; I'm sure he and Adele use somebody. What can I do, Garnet?"

She shook her head as much as the pain would allow. "No, Lorena says it'll ease once I get warm and relax." She tried to smile. "Toast and more tea would be nice."

When they'd finished eating, Luther declared he needed to get the mule in a stable and himself back to the rooming house before the weather worsened, and left, praise for his cornbread following him into the night. Lorena went to the windows to tweak the folds of linen, nodding her head in approval. Then she yawned mightily. "I'm ready for the bed. Just leave them dishes until morning, Clifford. You and Luther were mighty good to have supper for us." She touched Garnet's cheek, warm now, and pink from wind, and looked up at Clifford. "You'll see to her, won't you?"

Clifford nodded and turned to Garnet. "Shall we?"

"I guess you'll have to make up the bed again," she said, gesturing at the pile of quilts she and Lorena had discarded.

"Of course I can make up the bed. Boarding school, you know." He grinned and gathered up the bedding.

She tested herself, shifting her hips to the edge of the sofa and trying to stand. It was better, but the pain still burned a swathe across her shoulders. She didn't relish the idea of lying down. It was early yet, not but eight o'clock. Maybe if she stayed in front of the fire the pain would fade even more.

Clifford came back into the room with her nightgown and a shawl trailing across his arm. "All right," he said. "Let's see if we can do this without hurting you."

That was impossible, but he was gentle, clucking over her like a hen with a chick. But when she was in her gown with the fluffy shawl wrapped around her, Garnet surprised him by sitting back down. "Shouldn't you go on to bed?" he asked.

"It feels so good in front of the fire, and I dread trying to get comfortable enough to sleep. Can't we stay here a little longer?"

"Certainly." He went back into the bedroom and returned with a pillow, toasting it in front of the fire and squeezing it between her back and the sofa. It felt heavenly. "Shall I get you more tea?"

Crinkling her eyes, she said, "I wonder if a drop of Fanny's cordial might help."

He chuckled. "You know, it really might. I'll fetch some."

When he left, she shut her eyes and took a deep breath. This was good. Being loved, being warm, being safe. She'd always miss Ruben, but those people loved him; even his nasty father loved him. It wasn't good enough, not by a long shot, but she could rest easy about her son.

"I couldn't find cordial glasses." Clifford held teacups, which looked absurd holding a few teaspoons of the potent liquid.

"I never thought to buy any of those funny little glasses," she replied. "Thank you." She sipped, remembering how she'd helped Fanny with the cordial back in the fall. Certainly she and the sisters had made their peace, but oh, she was glad to have her own house and Clifford to herself. Breathing deeply, she felt another welcome touch of loosening in her back. "It's starting to ease up a little now."

"Good." He sat beside her and reached over to pluck her hairpins.

"You know, I've been thinking," she started.

"Always a good thing."

"Even though living with David was pure hell, if it hadn't been for him , we'd never have met."

"What a price!"

She touched his cheek, running her finger down one of the creases. "What a prize."

His smile was warm as the fire. "That's all of them. Shall I brush your hair?"

She shook her head cautiously. The cordial was spreading warmth into her stomach. "Well, think about it," she continued. "You never would've come out to Bethel looking for a sixteen year old girl, even if you did have fond memories of my father." She finished the cordial. "I reckon we should be grateful for old David."

"I have a difficult time harboring any gratitude for that villain, but I suppose you're right. When you came to get your father's money, I remember noticing how lovely you were, but I doubt I ever would've pursued you."

"It would've been so easy for us to have missed each other. It's frightening to think about." She raised her fingers to his head, running them through his dark, thick hair, feeling the solid warmth of his skull. "I do love you, Clifford. I love you for this," she said, cupping his head. Then she smiled, a glint in her eye, and lightly touched his pants. "And I love you for this," she said, adding, "but not tonight please." He grinned. "But most of all I love you for this." She placed her hand against his chest.

"You don't say it often."

"People who say it all the time sound like they're trying to convince themselves."

Clifford chuckled. "My wise Garnet." He kissed her. "Believe me, I don't have to convince myself that I love you."

"I know." She paused, shaking her head. "You show your love every day."

"You are my dearest, dearest heart."

"And you," she replied. She shifted. "I think I can rest now."

He helped her to stand. "Are you sure you don't need me to rub your back with Fanny's lotion?" His eyes were mischievous.

"And rub everything else too?"

"Well, a good husband wants to provide every comfort, doesn't he?" His merry mood was infectious, and she laughed cautiously. With his help, she inched toward the bedroom, afraid the pain would clutch her again, but it didn't. She was sore, but the spasm was over.

And by morning she was even better, miraculously so, although Clifford said it was bound to be if Lorena'd said so. The rest of the week he went to the bank, leaving the women to their many chores. They sewed, finishing up curtains for the house and aprons for Garnet to wear in the store. One afternoon deliverymen brought Clifford's father's desk, placing it in the empty end of the front room. That evening Garnet sat at the desk making lists of goods so Clifford could contact the wholesalers, and the merchandise started pouring in.

On Friday afternoon, Lorena emerged from the candy counter and declared, "It's starting to look like a real store now."

"It is, isn't it?"

"Did you check the jam cake? Is it cool enough to ice?" They'd baked a blackberry jam cake that morning, and its sweet, spicy smell joined the scents of licorice, lemon, and peppermint from the candy case.

"Not quite. By the time we finish unpacking the candy it'll be cool enough." Garnet thought about the cake: waxy, moist, and studded with black walnuts. She'd always considered it a Christmas cake, but it was only a week until Christmas, and this was their last night before Luther and Lorena went home.

"I left most of these candy trays closer to the back; no sense in you having to crawl all the way to the front to get things." Lorena opened a box of lemon drops and dumped them into a glass tray.

"It's plain to see you aren't a storekeeper, Lorena. We want to push them to the front to tempt the children who aren't tall enough to see all the way to the back, even if it is harder for me." Garnet filled little bags with candy and tied bows around them.

"Hmm, tricky. Well, it's nothing for me to push them forward. What're you making?" Lorena pointed at the sacks.

"Oh, these are for the little ones. Luther said he'd give them to Dessie, Henry, and Violet. What do you think? Should I send Lowell candy or pencils?"

Lorena emptied a box of Kis-Me gum into its tall glass canister. "Lord, but that boy loved candy when he was little, didn't he? I don't reckon he's changed even if he is thirteen and thinking he's a doctor already. Maybe you could give him both. You're sending ribbons to Violet, and you made that little cape for the doll Luther bought Dessie. All you'd have to do is think up some other trinket for Henry, and they'd each have two gifts from their big sister."

"Good idea." Garnet finished the candy bags and prowled around the store. She hadn't ordered toys since they wouldn't open until after Christmas. She'd gathered a nice box of notions for her mother and new suspenders for Luther. What little thing could she find for Henry? Grabbing Lowell's pencils, she peered into the showcase that held sundries, dry goods, and notions. Nothing. Crossing the store, she went behind the marble counter and touched the shiny brass cash register decorated with ornate fleur-de-lys. Clifford had insisted they buy it although she thought it was a terrible expense. On this side, the shelves were mostly empty, but on the other side of the cash register was the tobacco case with plugs and pouches and packets of cigarettes. She smiled at the memory of catching the men smoking. Then she had an inspiration. Stacked beneath the tobacco case were empty wooden cigar boxes. With a little airing out, the tobacco smell would fade. "I know! I'll give Henry a treasure box."

"He'll like that," Lorena replied. "But we may have to find me a box too for packing all the loot I've bought since I've come to town."

All week Garnet had been trying to ignore Lorena's inevitable departure, but it loomed now and she didn't like it. "I wish you could stay forever," she mourned.

"Now that would be a sorry situation." Lorena's head popped out of the candy counter again. "Hand me them peppermint sticks."

"Why?"

"Well, first of all, the farm would probably go to rack and ruin. God knows what my kitchen looks like after weeks of Willie Martin living there. He's a good boy, honest to boot, and I'm sure he's milking the cows and seeing to the farm. But there's no telling what kind of a mess he's made. Should these go here or over to the side?" Lorena asked, bobbing in and out of the case.

"Over there."

"And besides, it's about time you and that man of yours had a little peace and quiet. Do you realize you've always had an old woman or two butting in on your marriage?" She cackled. "Not to say that I resemble the Clark sisters in no way, shape, or form, but you all could use some time to get used to living by yourselves before the store opens. Besides, you're in real good shape; you don't need me."

"I don't want you because I need you," Garnet handed her a box of bullseyes.

"Never did like these things." Lorena dumped the candy into a tray. "I know that, girl, and I'll miss you too. But you'll have Franklin close."

"If we see him. He's made a life for himself out on that horse farm, and I'm glad for him. But I don't think he'll visit often. I asked him to come for Christmas dinner. We'll see if he does."

"Otherwise it's going to be a lonely Christmas, ain't it?"

Garnet started stacking empty boxes. "Clifford says Mr. and Mrs. Wallace want us to come over on Christmas Eve. I reckon we should go."

"I reckon so! Family ain't the only thing in life. You need friends too. Well, that's a job done." She straightened. "I hear a horse. Are we expecting anybody?"

"I don't think so." Garnet moved to peer out the window. "Oh, it's Archie."

She flew to let the young man in. Blushing from either the sharp air or Garnet's presence, he stepped in, took off his hat, was introduced to Lorena, and thrust the bulky bundle he was carrying into Garnet's hands. "This is a housewarming present. Or a Christmas present. Or maybe a store-opening present. Anyway, I remember you saying how much you like plants." Flustered, he smiled at Garnet.

"How kind of you!" She peeled away the tissue paper to reveal an African violet. "Oh, I do love these. Look, Lorena."

"Just a minute," he said, rushing back toward the door. "There's another; I couldn't carry both."

"Who on earth?" Lorena asked.

"He works with Clifford," Garnet explained. "And he helped us buy this place. You know, you've heard Clifford tease me about him."

Lorena grinned. "Oh, the one who's sweet on you, ain't he?"

Archie returned, holding another carefully wrapped plant. "I hope they didn't freeze. A family friend has a greenhouse, and he said they'd be safe if I came straight over. I kept them under a blanket."

This plant had leaves resembling flat lozenges with bright pink blooms attached. "I've never seen one of these," she declared.

Archie beamed at her. "He called it a Christmas cactus and wrote down instructions for both of them." He produced a slip of paper.

"I'm glad to have them, the instructions and the plants. Won't you come into the house and look around or have a hot drink?"

He colored even more. "Oh, no. I have to see Mr. Catlett. You'll be glad to hear he's sold more than half his lots now. They'll be building up a storm come spring."

"Good," Garnet replied. "We need to feed those folks."

Tapping his hat against his leg, Archie glanced first at Lorena, then at Garnet. She felt sorry for him. "Look, I have the perfect place for your plants." She walked past the tobacco case where there was a little ledge built under the front window.

"Well, I'd been wondering what that was for," Lorena said.

"Plants. Just like the little table in Mattie Lawrence's store. It's a southern exposure, and the plants will like it just fine."

The silence grew awkward, but then Archie asked, "Will you and Mr. Clark be going to the Wallace's on Christmas Eve?"

"Oh, I expect so. Will you be there?"

He nodded happily.

"Well, good. I only know the Wallaces, and I get sort of shy around strangers. At least I'll recognize you."

This seemed to thrill him. "Oh, yes, you'll know me."

Lorena was about to burst out laughing. Quickly Garnet said, "You said you have a friend with a greenhouse?" He bobbed his head. "Well, there's a plant called a night-blooming cereus I'd love to have. Have you ever heard of it?"

"No, I don't believe I have."

"I wonder if your friend might have one."

He lit up. "Say, I'd be happy to check for you. Would you write down the name for me?" He searched in his pocket and pulled out a slip of paper.

She wrote it down. "I hope he has one."

He glowed at her and mumbled, "Oh, me too! Well, I'd better go. Merry Christmas, Garnet, Mrs. King."

Garnet grabbed his hand and squeezed it. "I cannot thank you enough for the plants, Archie. They make me feel like I'm home now."

Turning nearly the color of the cactus blooms, the young man nodded, smiled, nearly bowed, and walked out the door. It was barely shut when Lorena began to hoot. "Oh, he's got a bad case, don't he? Lord, I'm glad your husband ain't the jealous sort."

"Hush, Lorena. He's just a very sweet young man, and he thinks the world of Clifford." Garnet was coloring a bit herself at Lorena's talk.

"Uh huh. And I bet he'd turn that shade of red if Clifford touched his hand too, wouldn't he?"

"Come on." Garnet couldn't help but smile. "We've got a jam cake to ice."

It was a very fine cake, and the four of them lingered after the meal, none of them wanting the evening to end. But finally Luther loaded up most of Lorena's "truck," as she called it, and drove off only to return before dawn to fetch his sister. Lorena assured Garnet that she'd probably come with Luther next year when he brought the tobacco, if Willie Martin hadn't ruined her house. But a year sounded like an eternity to Garnet as she said good-bye in the frosty, starlit dawn.

Suddenly Clifford told them to wait, and he ran back into the store, coming out with a hastily wrapped package. He handed it to Lorena, grinned, and kissed her on the cheek. Flustered, she asked, "What on earth?"

"Cigars." Clifford grinned.

Chapter Eleven

Over the next few days deliverymen brought in cases and cases of canned goods and boxed items, but Clifford couldn't persuade the wholesalers to do much of anything between Christmas and New Year's, so they'd have to wait for meat, dairy, and produce. Clark's Grocery was set to open on January 3, 1911.

The day before Christmas Eve, she arranged the last few items, checked her ledger, and moved a few things. But essentially she was done. Waiting made her restless. She visited her plant shelf and touched a Christmas cactus bloom. It felt like weeks since she'd been outside, not that there was much to see out there. Leaden clouds crowded the colorless sky, and a skimpy fall of wet snow dotted the trees and grass. It might be just as cloudy back home, but there she could see trees and hills and fields. She stretched until her spine popped. That piddly snow was probably melting into puddles on the porch. She snatched her broom and shawl.

Outside the air smelled damp and fresh, exactly what her lungs had been craving. She swept away the melting snow, trying to sweep away her anxiety at the same time, but she admitted to herself, she was more than restless. She was, in fact, some flavor of lonesome. Moving into the house and opening the store were about the most exciting things she'd ever experienced, but after Lorena left Garnet felt like a refugee. Certainly Clifford shared her enthusiasm, both of them bubbling over with news about his job, the store, their plans. And, true, she'd always been a girl who needed some time to herself, but she'd never realized how dependent she'd been on knowing her family or Lorena were just down the road.

It's just Christmas, she fussed at herself. She'd been awfully disappointed when Franklin's scrawled note said he wouldn't be coming on Christmas Day. There was a girl, he hinted, and he'd be joining her family for dinner. The door of the big house across the street bore a lush evergreen wreath with a crooked red bow, festive as a cardinal on a branch. Then, just as she was looking away, Garnet saw the door open and a young woman wrapped in a light blue shawl coming out with her hands full. She murmured to someone in the doorway, and the door shut behind her. "Hello!" she called to Garnet who returned the greeting.

Blonde hair, fine and wispy as a child's, escaped from a haphazard bun on top of her head. "I'm Agnes Byer," she said, picking her way across the wet street. "I've been wanting and wanting to meet you, but everything seemed so busy over here, and, well, I just didn't get it done. My husband Jacob says I'm not very efficient." She laughed, an infectious tinkling sound, and handed a tray to Garnet. "Merry Christmas," she declared, her pale blue eyes lit up like candles.

"Why, thank you. I'm Garnet Clark." Lifting the tea towel, she saw a loaf of sweet bread surrounded by pale yellow cookies, stamped with quaint patterns.

"It's stollen, just baked this morning, and the little bits are springerle. German, you know. I'm German, or at least my grandparents are, although they settled in Cincinnati. That's where we're from, Jacob and me. Are you from Lexington?"

"No, we've just moved up here from Evans County. Thank you for the treats; it's mighty kind of you to think of us."

"Well, I intend to be friendly, but sometimes it takes me a while to get things done." She sighed loudly. "Edith woke at dawn this morning so I told Margaret, that's my sister who's visiting, that we might as well get started on the stollen. If we wait much longer, I said, we'll miss Christmas altogether." And she laughed again, filling the quiet street.

"Can you come in? Would you like a cup of coffee or tea?" Garnet liked her. She was as invigorating as a tonic.

Agnes glanced back at her house. "I'd like that. Edith's sleeping, and I suppose Margaret will come get me if she needs me. Why do babies get up so early, do you suppose? Are they afraid they'll miss something? She's taken to waking at five o'clock every morning. Jacob says she's excited about Christmas. As if an infant knows it's Christmas! Willie does, though. He's four, and that's all we hear from him. I think he'll explode before it gets here." Pointing at Clifford's neatly lettered sign on the door, she read, "'*Clark's Grocery. Open 7:00 a.m until 6:00 p.m on January 3.*' The whole neighborhood's excited about having a store."

Once they walked into the grocery, Agnes exclaimed over everything. "Ooh, look!" she breathed. "A nice, big store too. And so close by! This will be grand."

Garnet smiled down at the woman who was, unbelievably, even shorter than she. Plump and round-hipped, Agnes peered in the candy case, scanned the shelves. She reminded Garnet of powder box pictures of pretty, delicately colored women. "Come back to the kitchen," Garnet urged. "I'll make us a hot drink."

In the kitchen, Agnes was examining and exclaiming again. "And isn't this nice! All neat and clean. I can't keep anything tidy, just not my nature. My mother says, 'Agnes, you'd have a gorgeous bouquet of flowers and a lace cloth on the table, but nobody'd be able to see them for all the dirty dishes.'" She laughed again, nodding at the new stove and touching the kitchen cabinet. Then she stopped and looked distressed. "Oh, you'll be worried about the food I made, won't you? I swear I'm very careful when I cook. I'm just not very tidy."

Garnet put the kettle on. "I'm not worried."

Agnes chattered, "Garnet, what a pretty name! Not like Agnes. Lamb of God, my eye! I suppose it's very reverent, but who'd want a name like Agnes, I ask you? Anyway," she sighed, "it's what they gave me so I have to live with it."

Not quite understanding, Garnet simply said thanks and asked if she preferred coffee or tea.

"It doesn't matter." Agnes scrutinized the room like a detective searching for clues. "No babies?"

"No," Garnet murmured, a bit taken aback.

Suddenly Agnes's face fell. "I'm sorry. Jacob says I talk without thinking, but I don't mean anything by it."

She was sincere, and Garnet felt her reserves crumble. "Well," she said slowly, "we've only been married a little over a year, but I do want a baby desperately."

Throwing both hands in the air, Agnes dismissed her concerns. "Oh, only a year! Now my older sister, Catherine not Margaret, she can see her husband's trousers hanging on the clothesline and get pregnant. She already has four children, but it took me nearly three years to have Willie."

Garnet grinned. "So, looking at britches helps?"

Agnes threw back her head and laughed, deep from her rounded belly. "Maybe! Couldn't hurt!" She said, "Oh, it'll be so nice to have a neighbor. Betty Keller is all right; she lives on Hazel Avenue behind us, but she's at least forty. I bet we're about the same age. I'm twenty-six. We can have so much fun!"

"I'm twenty," Garnet replied, setting out cups, saucers, and spoons.

"And that dreamy tall man who comes in and out, he's your husband?" Then she slapped her hand to her mouth. "I'm just a terrible snoop; it's a character flaw," she declared, shaking her head in despair.

Garnet giggled. "I think he's handsome too. Yes, that's Clifford. He works at the bank downtown."

"So you'll be running the store by yourself? My, you're brave. It's a good thing there aren't any children yet; you'd never get a thing done if you were chasing after little ones all day. My Jacob is a druggist, has a shop downtown, and he's not tall and handsome," she said, feigning wistfulness. Then she grinned, "But I like him fine even if he is short and stout like me." She ran her hands over her full bosom and wide hips. "He says he likes me the way I am too, but I sometimes wonder if he wouldn't prefer a willowy girl. But he says he likes a plump woman, that I'm cozy in the winter and make more shade in the summer."

Again, the tinkling laugh rang out and Garnet joined her. Agnes was irrepressible. They chatted, or at least Agnes did, as they drank their tea. She wanted to know if the trim dark woman was Garnet's mother and how many brothers and sisters she had. "Three brothers and two sisters, all younger," she replied. "And the woman is Lorena King. She's, well, it's sort of complicated, but she's my grandfather's second wife and my good friend."

"Ooh," Agnes exclaimed. "I love complicated family stories. We'll save that one for next time, won't we? I have a couple of good stories too."

Delighted that Agnes was promising a next time, Garnet learned that she was one of five children, next to the oldest and that her sister Margaret was here for a prolonged visit to get over a "sad affair of the heart." They discovered how much they both loved plants, and Agnes promised Garnet cuttings of anything she wanted.

When Garnet was able to get in a word or two, Agnes nodded and sipped, swinging her foot like a little girl. Then she slurped down the last of her tea and begged, "Could I look at the rest of your house? I saw so many lovely things being delivered that I'm just dying to see them."

Agnes admired everything, especially Garnet's dressing table, which she swore she absolutely *coveted,* even though that was a terrible sin, wasn't it? Moving into the front room, she admired the draperies, the furniture, their wedding picture, and then she paused, a small frown creasing her pretty face. "But there's no Christmas anywhere. Don't you celebrate Christmas?"

"There's been no time, with moving in and all the deliveries. We sort of celebrated with Lorena last week, but nobody's coming. I didn't see any point."

"But your husband, he'll expect Christmas, won't he? Men do. We Germans nearly kill ourselves over it, baking and decorating and all that. Still, you could do a little something, couldn't you?" She squinted at the mantel.

"I reckon."

"I know!" Agnes crowed, clapping her hands together. "There's a scraggly old pine tree down the street on one of the vacant lots. Do you have something we could use to cut branches?"

Swept up by Agnes's enthusiasm, Garnet strode into the store. She grinned. "I have this," she said, brandishing a wicked cleaver from the butcher's block.

Agnes burst out laughing. "A little vicious for that poor old tree, don't you think? And we'll get resin, sap, whatever, all over it."

"It'll wash."

They trooped down the street, Agnes chattering away and Garnet giggling more than she had in years, and cut branches. Bits of snow rained down on them as they worked, and they gasped as ice fell down the necks of their dresses. Back at the store, Garnet laid the greenery on the counter and asked, "Now what?"

Agnes' cheeks glowed. "You'll see. Surely you have ribbon. Red ribbon?"

"Oh, yes."

Agnes started bunching together the boughs and tying ribbon around them. When she was satisfied, she ceremoniously carried the trailing bundle into the front room, saturating the house with the sharp, festive scent of pine. She placed her creation on the mantel, tweaking a bough here and a ribbon there.

That's lovely!" Garnet exclaimed. "It makes the whole room feel like Christmas."

"It's nothing, but we need something for your table." She gazed into space. "Do you have candles?"

"Just plain white ones in the store."

"They'll do. Give me the scissors, find a candle, and I'll be right back." She disappeared outside. Garnet found a candle and waited until Agnes returned, bearing several sprigs of holly.

"Now," she announced, "let's get a saucer and more of that red ribbon." In no time she'd fashioned a centerpiece for the kitchen table and stood back to admire it. "It's sort of small, but it makes your table cheerful, doesn't it? You can light the candle while you're eating, and your Clifford will be very pleased."

Garnet remembered how Clifford had seemed wistful when she told him that, other than their visit to the Wallace's house on Christmas Eve, she hadn't planned to do anything special for Christmas. But she also remembered that Fanny had trimmed a tree last year and made a huge wreath for the door.

She'd reminded him that she didn't need any gifts; Lord, she was overwhelmed with the riches of the past few weeks. And even though she'd insisted that he have a fine new suit, specially tailored for him, she'd said this wasn't a Christmas present. He hadn't seemed happy about it. Maybe Agnes was right.

"This is wonderful!" Garnet squeezed her new friend's hand. "The decorations, the cookies and, what did you call it, stollen?"

Agnes squeezed back. "Just little things," she said. "I must fly. I'm sure Edith is awake by now, and Margaret is probably looking for me. Come over and see us. We'll be at mass on Christmas Eve but won't be doing anything on Christmas Day except suffering from indigestion and trying to stay awake. Besides, you must meet Edith and Willie and Jacob, and I," she winked, "must meet that gorgeous husband of yours."

"We will," Garnet promised, surprising herself. "Thank you again, Agnes. I can't wait to try the stollen."

"Well, if you ever need anything, we're neighbors now." She laughed again, the sound of it echoing into the street. "I started to say that if you ever need to borrow a cup of sugar, you should just come over. But you'll have a whole store full of sugar!"

Fluttering her hand, she was gone, like a sudden breeze leaving echoes of cinnamon, anise, and pine. Garnet hugged herself. Today she'd make Christmas. She'd bake, and when Clifford came home the house would smell and look festive.

Suddenly she was very busy: mixing, pouring, and watching her oven. By late afternoon she'd recklessly emptied candy and cigars out of their glass containers, washed and scalded them, and filled them with chunks of gingerbread, walnut cookies, and molasses toffee. Lining these up on the kitchen cabinet, she adorned them with red ribbon. Bows everywhere, she decreed. There was a scandalous abundance of food in the kitchen, but it was Christmas. She decided to make a box of goodies to take across the street on Christmas as well as fixing up a nice one for Sam and Adele Wallace.

Rushing again around the kitchen, she started supper, pausing to make a fire in the front room and light the lamps. She wanted everything cozy when Clifford came in. He'd probably be late since he was picking up his suit, and he'd have an awkward time on the streetcar with the large suit box. He had a hefty walk from the end of the line at the railway station to their house too. Although he hadn't complained, she knew he disliked riding the streetcar. It'd surprised her that he'd sold the horse and buggy, but he'd declared it an unnecessary expense both to shelter and maintain them.

She stirred the potatoes. Other men at his level at the bank lived in far grander houses and kept their own horses. A few of them even owned automobiles. Clifford still declared that he'd buy one of those eventually, when they could afford it, but they were years from being able to do that. Bills from the wholesalers were stacking up at an alarming rate, and Clifford's salary couldn't begin to keep up. He was forever reassuring her that their credit at the bank was solid, but she hated owing money and was fearful it would be months, maybe even years, before the store showed a profit. Until their neighborhood grew, the store wouldn't do much business.

At least they'd never go hungry, she thought as she opened a can of green beans from the store. But every time she considered smaller orders or cheaper items, Clifford overruled her. To be successful, the store must stock what the shoppers want, he declared. So the totals rose as the shelves filled, and she tried not to fret, at least aloud.

Then she heard him, scraping his feet and fumbling with the front door, and ran to open it for him. "Here, give me the box," she said.

"It's not a bit heavy, but, my goodness, it's bulky. Did you have a good day?"

"I had the most wonderful and glorious of days." Opening the box, she admired his new suit. "Oh, it's lovely, Clifford."

She draped it over the sofa, smoothing it. "I'll make sure all the creases are out for tomorrow. You'll want to wear it to the Wallace's, won't you?"

He nodded. "With that elegant shirt my wife made for my birthday." Pausing before he sat, he kissed her with cold lips and said, "Say, what's this finery I see upon the mantel? Has the Spirit of Christmas Present been visiting?"

Her laugh rang out like Christmas bells. "She certainly has! Wait until you see what I've been up to today. Don't get too comfortable; I have your supper ready."

He followed her to the kitchen. "And I'm ready for it. It's a slow, creeping cold out there, and, of course, the streetcar was late and crowded with people shopping."

She lit the candle on the kitchen table and turned with a flourish. He noted the candle, the baked goods, the bows. "Heavens, Garnet, you did decide to celebrate Christmas, didn't you? What brought this on?"

"Agnes. I have to tell you about Agnes."

Later, after she chattered all through dinner about her new friend, she told him to enjoy the fire in the front room and read his paper. She cleaned up the kitchen and then placed a plate filled with treats on the table beside him. "Would you look at all this," he said, choosing one of her cookies.

"This is the best Christmas ever," she announced with her mouth full of stollen.

"It is indeed, dear heart. The first one in our new house," he agreed, touching her hand. "But I'm sorry your brother isn't coming on Christmas Day."

"I am too. But we'll have a huge dinner. I have plans," she announced mysteriously. "And then we'll go across the street and you can meet Agnes."

He grinned, selecting a piece of gingerbread. "She sounds like a marvel."

Garnet lifted one eyebrow. "She thinks you're dreamy."

"Oh, really? I like her already."

"You two will probably get along just fine. She's like you: loquacious." She made her face quite serious.

He burst out laughing, almost choking on gingerbread. "Now that's a fine word. Are you endeavoring to improve your vocabulary?"

"No. It's the company I keep."

"I see."

"And then we have the party tomorrow night. What should I wear? Will it be dreadfully elegant?"

"Maybe a little bit elegant. Oh, everything you have looks glorious on you, Garnet. It doesn't matter."

"It most certainly does. If dreamy Mr. Clark is going to be wearing his fine new suit, I wouldn't want to shame him by looking less than splendid." She wrinkled her brow. "I thought about the taffeta skirt and cream shirtwaist, but those seem summery. And I wore the green suit when I went there for dinner."

"Well, it's a little late to make something unless you want to wrap the new drapes around you and go as a Roman matron."

"Matron!" she exclaimed in horror. She thought for a moment, mentally cataloging her wardrobe. "What about my wedding dress? The Wallaces were at our wedding, but do you think they'd remember?"

"Would it matter if they did?" he asked. "I think that's a lovely choice. And your amethyst pin would set it off nicely."

"It would, wouldn't it?"

"What are these?" He pointed to the cookies from Agnes.

"I forget what she called them, something German. Try one." Garnet pinched off a morsel of gingerbread.

"Ah," he said. "Anise."

"I thought they were licorice."

"Nearly the same thing." He sat back, resting his hand against her neck. "You'll look lovely. As usual, you'll do me proud."

"Well, it's not just that," she replied, dusting gingerbread crumbs off her hands. "When he brought the plants, Archie asked especially if I'd be there, and I want to look my very best."

Clifford arched one brow impossibly high. "Oh, really."

She glanced at him and looked away.

"I love it when you play the coquette."

She frowned. "Play the what?"

"Coquette. Flirt, dear heart, if you want to continue with vocabulary enhancement. Those bright eyes of yours simply sparkle, and your luscious mouth sits half-open, just begging to be kissed." He did just that, his lips warm now and sweet. "Poor Archie, if he weren't such a dear soul, I'd find it vexing that he's so besotted with my wife. But as it is, I just feel sympathy for him."

"I'm glad he'll be there. At least I'll know someone besides the Wallaces."

"True. I thought you were feeling a little apprehensive."

"I was." She tossed her head. "Until Archie said he'd be there."

Clifford let out a quick bark of laughter. "You stay away from that puppy. I 'm too out of practice with swords to fight a duel."

She kissed him. "Do you really know how to fight with a sword?"

"Oh, I learned a little at school. Rapiers, actually."

He was so worldly, and she knew so little. But her mind came back to the issue at hand. "So how are we going to get to the party? Will the streetcar run that late?"

His face turned blank. "Maybe. Perhaps your devoted Archie can bring us home."

Snuggling closer, she rested her head on his shoulder, the scratchy wool warm under her cheek.

"Mm, you smell of cinnamon, ginger, and all the spices of Araby," he murmured, burying his nose in her hair.

"I don't doubt it."

Her mind raced from one thought to another and landed suddenly on something that had perplexed her all afternoon. "Agnes mentioned something about her name: 'Lamb of God,' she said. That didn't make sense to me."

"Agnes comes from 'agnus' in Latin," Clifford replied. "It means 'lamb,' and in the Latin mass there's a part about the Lamb of God. It's a common enough name."

She closed her eyes to enjoy the movement of his hands over her body. "So Catholics give their children religious names?"

"No more than Protestants do. People choose names for all kinds of reasons."

"Mm." The conversation was becoming less and less important.

"Our families, for example, tend to use family names, don't they? You said your brothers have names from your father's family, and I have my mother's maiden name."

He sounded like a teacher, but at that point she really didn't care much about names, about Agnes, about anything except the delicious warmth creeping through her body. "And then there are names like Violet, Desdemona, and Garnet," she murmured.

"Yes," he whispered. "Flowers, Shakespeare, and jewels." His narrow hand found her bottom and pressed it closer. "I think, my jewel, it's time to go to bed."

She lingered, reluctant to move. "Not a very fine jewel. Not like diamonds or emeralds." She began to unbutton his shirt. Might as well be helpful.

He waited until she'd undone three or four and gently pushed her off so they could stand. "And how would you like being named Diamond?"

"Not much. But I'm not sure I like being called a coquette either. It makes me think of salmon or chicken."

Chapter Twelve

Garnet woke reluctantly, determined to doze again, but even though the bed was warm and tempting, her mind nudged her awake with two realizations: it was Christmas Eve and Clifford was already up. She threw on her dressing gown, thinking and planning as she went. She'd fix breakfast, tidy the house, and then she'd have a bath and wash her hair. It took hours for it to dry. And then she'd sponge and press their clothes for the party and make up a box of sweets to take to Adele.

"I'm sorry. I didn't realize you'd be up so early today."

He was shaved, dressed, and drinking coffee. "There's nothing to apologize for. I'm glad I didn't wake you."

"Why are you up so early?" She started heating a skillet.

"I'm going into town. There's some business I want to see to."

"But I thought the bank was closed today."

"It is, but some of the employees will be there, at least in the morning. It's of no consequence." He sounded pleasant enough, but it was obvious he didn't want to answer any more questions. She broke eggs into the skillet.

Rising to pour himself another cup of coffee, he raised the hair off her neck to kiss it. She hadn't taken time to braid it, and the tangled mass flowed down her back. "Glorious hair," he murmured, grabbing a handful of it. "You look like you've just come from your lover's bed."

She blushed. "I reckon I have."

"I probably won't be back until afternoon," he said when he left, running his finger along her cheek but not meeting her eyes.

More puzzled than ever, she nodded. Then an idea struck her and she warned, "Remember, we agreed you wouldn't buy me a Christmas present. I don't need a thing."

"I remember."

Her day passed in a flurry, and by by mid-afternoon, she was packing baked goods and wondering what on earth was keeping Clifford. The day had stayed sunny but cold, so she couldn't imagine any problems with the streetcars. She'd just finished wrapping the boxes in tissue paper and was tying scarlet ribbon around them when she heard a gusty, sputtering noise from the street. It sounded like an automobile, and when she heard it pull into their side yard, she guessed that someone had given Clifford a ride home.

Her hair was still damp and loose, and she hoped no one was coming to visit. When she heard the door open, she peeked to see if anyone was with Clifford. He stood alone at the door, nearly jiggling with excitement. "I have a surprise for you," he said. She hadn't seen the creases in his cheeks folded so deeply since their wedding day. She grabbed her shawl.

"Look!" he exclaimed, pointing into the yard. Isn't it a beauty?" It was, of course, an automobile, a Model T, and she realized that she should've known what he was up to. He was talking a mile a minute, running his hand over the shiny black metal and explaining the function of every little part. She didn't know what to say.

"We'll ride to that party in style tonight, won't we? Why, I can leave for work later and get home earlier to help you in the store. And we can drive out to see Franklin or go down home, once the weather is warmer. Won't this make our lives wonderful?" She'd thought their lives were fairly wonderful already. He was so full of unadulterated happiness that she was half-jealous of the hunk of metal.

"Get in, get in. See what you think," Clifford urged, ushering her around to the passenger side.

Still speechless, a dozen thoughts flashed through her head. Lord, she'd been worried that he was buying a small present for her: how on earth could they afford this? The sneaky, conniving rascal hadn't told her anything about planning to buy it. But he was so happy. She'd achieved her dream of owning a store; shouldn't he have his dream as well? But where were they going to put it? And how much had it cost?

He hopped into the driver's seat and grinned. "You surely do look fine sitting in this motorcar, Mrs. Clark."

"You bought it? You just went out today and bought it?"

A little of the light dimmed. "I did. One of the vice-presidents at the bank bought it six months ago, liked it, but decided to buy a larger one. He's been talking about selling this one for the last week or two, and I just couldn't pass it up. He's already added all the fancy stuff, the top, the headlights."

Notions, Fanny'd said. He gets notions. Garnet spoke slowly. "You knew you were going to buy it today, but you didn't tell me?"

His face fell. "No, I didn't, and I should have, but I knew you'd worry. We always said we'd buy one, and this was too good to ignore. Why, do you realize he took over a hundred dollars off the price of a new one, and this model is only six months old?"

Ain't none of them heroes all the time, Lorena'd said. Here she was, trying to pinch every penny, worrying about their quagmire of debt, and he went out and bought an automobile. Behind her back. That was what nagged at her worse than anything. He'd acted like a little boy sneaking around to get what he wanted.

"We'll be all right, Garnet. I promise. Archie says they'll be building like mad come spring, and the store will do marvelously. Wallace has promised me a pay raise in March, and we have everything we need. Don't worry," he pleaded.

There was no point in fussing about it now. The deed was done, and she'd have to accept it. But her chest felt tight. "Where are you going to put it?"

"Well, I thought we'd use the shed as a garage, temporarily. I know you want that for storing chicken feed and garden tools, so I'll have someone come out in the spring and build you another shed. We have to build the chicken coop then anyway. It'll work out." His voice rose with returning enthusiasm. He had it all planned out, but his schemes would take more money, wouldn't they?

His eyes implored her to approve, and part of her wanted to relieve him; an uglier one wanted him dangling in guilt. "I can't take it in. You never said a word."

He looked down, as abashed as Lowell after a rare scolding. "I know. I suppose I just figured it would be easier to ask forgiveness than permission."

She hadn't liked that sentiment when Grandpa said it years ago, and she didn't like it any better now. "It's about trust, Clifford. You didn't trust me enough to tell me."

He was a picture of guilt, his eyes solemn and dark. She was cold, inside and out, and wanted to go in the house. Moving slowly, she extricated herself from the automobile. "What's done is done," she said. "And I'm sure we'll enjoy having it. It does sound as though you bought it for a fair price, not that you've told me how much you spent." Her voice was hard, but she couldn't do any better.

"I'm sorry, dear heart, believe me. I just wanted it so much." His hands gripped the steering wheel. "It was just over two hundred dollars."

Her heart thudded. The store and its stock, the house and its furniture, his suit, his car: she'd have to sell a hell of a lot of groceries, she thought, her mind using language she wouldn't have said aloud. Hugging the shawl around her, she said, "Well, come on in the house.

Can it sit outside? There are things that need to be cleared out of the shed."

Bobbing his head in agreement to everything, he jumped out. "I'll take care of that, but it can sit outside."

"I'll start your bath. It's nearly suppertime, you know." This was meant as another complaint, and she relished his quick wince.

Meekly, he nodded, and by the time she brought the washtub into the kitchen, he had already gathered up everything he needed. "I'll do it," he said as she started to lift the heavy kettle, his contrition as thick as the steam from its spout. He peeled down to his underwear and stood at the sink to wash his hair over an old dishpan while she stirred the soup that had been simmering all afternoon. All she needed to do was add cabbage and make cornbread. Clifford had warned her that Adele would have mountains of food so they wouldn't need much supper. Bringing out her sharpest knife, she stood at the table shredding cabbage while he shed his underwear and lowered himself into the tub. Her knife bit into the fat globe, and the thud of it hitting the table satisfied her somehow. She glanced at him, naked and comically scrunched into the tub, soaping a piece of himself at a time. His sharp knees stuck up high above the tub, and his private parts floated, dusky and shriveled in the hot water. She turned back to her ferocious chopping.

In a mild voice Clifford said, "It's really rather unnerving for you to peer so maliciously at my testicles while you're wielding that knife, Garnet."

She cleared her throat to hide the giggle that threatened but was unwilling to let one joke melt her indignation. The only sounds in the kitchen were his splashing and her chopping. Gathering up the shreds of cabbage, she tossed them into the soup pot, keeping her back to him.

"You know, I wouldn't have been so secretive if you didn't worry so dreadfully about money. I knew you'd have an absolute fit if I brought it up." It might be true, but it certainly sounded like a self-righteous excuse to her.

"So, it's better if I have a fit afterwards, when I can't do anything about it, than to have some sense beforehand and keep you from getting what you wanted?" She stirred the soup, trying to drown the little snippets of cabbage.

He sighed. "See? I feared you'd behave this way. Garnet, I've been in the banking business for years, and we're fine. Even Sam agrees that we're not in over our heads."

He's decided he's done enough apologizing, she thought. It was time to get exasperated with her now. "Of course Sam thinks it's fine," she retorted. If he wanted a fight, she'd give him one. "As long as we're in debt, he gets to keep you at the bank." She lifted her iron muffin pan and began putting bacon grease in each fluted indention. "That suits me. I'm happy to run this store by myself, but I thought you wanted to get out of the bank as soon as possible."

Water splashed as he shifted in the tub. "This won't change our plans one iota," he thundered. "Lord, you're unreasonable when it comes to money."

She turned to face him as he was standing up and drying himself. His body was flushed with hot water, but anger had caused the two red spots high on his cheeks. "Someone around here has to think about being thrifty. You've never been poor, have you, Clifford Clark? You've always had just what you wanted, when you wanted it. I've never cared about having mountains of money, but I don't like not being able to pay my bills. You wouldn't have any idea of what that's like, would you?" She knew her voice was shrewish, sounding like her mother when she was lighting into someone.

Clifford raised his eyes to the ceiling but said nothing. This was probably no different from countless reproaches he'd endured from his sisters, and Garnet minded that comparison more than the one with her mother. Oh, just shut up, she told herself. It wasn't worth it. She stirred the cornbread batter.

They didn't say another word until supper, but he didn't allow her to get away with silence for long and was, she had to admit, behaving very well. He emptied the washtub, admired the boxes she'd packed, and made witty comments about the people from the bank who were sure to attend the party. After supper, he insisted on helping her tidy the kitchen, saying he wanted her to have plenty of time to dress, and her temper ebbed with every passing minute. Let it go, she told herself; you're trying to control everything like Mama. By the time she'd drawn on her wonderfully sheer stockings, smoothed the dress over her breasts, and attached the amethyst brooch, she felt better.

Maybe I'll just flirt with all the men, she thought, dabbing rouge on her cheeks. They were already pink with agitation, but she recklessly added a little more. Not that Clifford would care if she did. Powdering her face, she looked at her reflection and saw a strange woman. Her eyes were huge, glittering in the lamplight, and the rouge and powder made her look older. She'd arranged her hair high and puffy, and the woman in the mirror somehow seemed citified, sophisticated, and maybe a little dangerous. Daringly, she touched her finger to the rouge pot again and dabbed some on her lips. There, a painted woman, she said to herself. And she liked what she saw.

Clifford did too. He stopped dead in the doorway. "Lord, you look beautiful, Garnet," he whispered, almost reverently. She reached for the tiny vial of perfume. Flattery wasn't going to get him any farther than humor.

"I don't mean that as an everyday compliment," he said, almost stuttering. "You look absolutely stunning. I've never seen you so, so... " And Clifford Clark, garrulous, loquacious, talkative Clifford Clark couldn't find the right word.

"I'll do you proud?" Her eyes glinted with unquenched anger. He nodded mutely.

"I wonder what that automobile is going to do to my hair."

"I'll drive very, very slowly."

He did. She had to admit it was exhilarating to travel so freely down the streets. They were at the Wallace's in no time, and it was exciting to park on the street near their house and attract the attention of others going inside. There were several high-spirited calls of congratulations directed at them, and she found her smile.

Once inside it was even easier to smile. Adele hugged her and thanked her for the box of treats. Sam Wallace acted like the Santa Claus he resembled, and Archie simply glowed when he rushed over to her. She was thankful for him since Clifford disappeared soon after they arrived. Several of the men were anxious to see his automobile, and he was more than willing to escort them outside to have a closer look. She asked Archie to fetch her some punch, and he trotted off to the dining room. The Wallaces had a Christmas tree, sparkling with dozens of candles and making the rich mahogany, the shimmering crystal, and the glowing silver twinkle like a thief's cave. The women were nearly as decorative as the furnishings. Wearing deeply tinted velvets and silks, they moved about gracefully, their jewelry flashing in the candlelight. Garnet decided her dress was plain, but acceptable.

Archie returned with her punch. A bit nerved up, she drank it right down and asked if he'd had the opportunity to speak to his friend who owned the greenhouse. For an instant, his eyes popped wide, and she wondered what she'd said or done. Then he cleared his throat and admitted that he hadn't but would soon. They admired the tree, and he introduced her to a very old man who sat by the fire. Evidently this irascible old codger was a great personage, and Garnet did her best to be gracious to him in spite of his brusque manners. After complaining about the food, the noise, and the temperature of the room, the old rascal grasped her hand with his gnarled, arthritic paws and pulled her down to whisper to her. "You're the prettiest filly here," he declared, laughing in her ear and sharing his foul breath.

"Why, thank you, sir," she replied and tried to straighten up. He was having none of it. Keeping a firm hold on her hands, he lifted his whiskery face and kissed her. Only then did he release her, flustered and a bit damp around the lips.

He winked. "I can get away with it. I'm president of the bank and the oldest son of a bitch in the house." Then he cackled with laughter.

Clifford was still outside showing off his new toy, so she headed toward the dining room where Adele's table, as promised, creaked under trays and bowls of food, all of which looked festive and tempting. But Garnet wanted to eat with Clifford, so she asked Archie to refill her cup, wondering why he once again widened his eyes.

She drank deeply. It was delicious stuff, sweet and sharp at the same time. In the dining room, the convivial chatter was even louder than in the front room. Parlor, Garnet corrected herself. Adele called it that, and Garnet must learn to be ever so proper, mustn't she? This brought on a series of giggles, and Archie raised his eyebrows in alarm. "What?"

"Uh, Mrs. Clark . . ."

"Garnet."

"Uh, Garnet, do you realize you're drinking a fairly strong brandy punch?"

"Really?" Come to think of it, she did sense a slight fizziness behind her eyes. She was surprised at how light-hearted she felt after the afternoon's turmoil. Poor Clifford, she thought, married to a worrying old shrew who had evil thoughts about gelding him with a cabbage knife. Hmm, she thought, that would be cutting off my nose to spite my face or something like that. The thought made her burst out laughing, raising Archie's eyebrows even more alarmingly. "Then I suppose I'd better slow down," she said, setting aside her punch cup and giving him her best smile.

The automobile enthusiasts returned, clamoring for punch or the decanters on the sideboard. Whiskey, she supposed, and that made her think of David. Thank God she didn't have to worry about living with a drunk any more. Of course she was the one traveling down the road to perdition now, she thought, and giggled once again at the thought of Clifford's sisters. Archie gave her a troubled glance, and she patted his arm, setting off violent blushes. Across the room, she saw Clifford, dark and charming, speaking to this person and that and glancing over at her from time to time. He was forgiven, whether he realized it or not, but that didn't mean she didn't have a few things to say to him. She glanced up at Archie from under her lashes and found him all but staring at her. Good Lord, she thought, you know I'm married, and, God help me, I'm only flirting with you to irritate my husband. But she continued to do so, only a little ashamed of herself, and asked if he'd take her to that greenhouse some time. Coloring again and again in vivid waves of rosiness, he replied that he'd be delighted and succumbed to a fit of stuttering when she grasped his hand.

Across the room, Clifford was talking to Sam Wallace and pretending not to notice, but she saw his lips twitching. He knew exactly what she was doing. He was so handsome, his hair thick and dark against his snowy shirt. Taller than most men in the room and graceful with it, there were plenty of women smiling and chattering to him as well. She'd better go claim him.

They ate and made the rounds of all the various clumps of people, and she listened to Clifford make witty and pleasant small talk, and then they left. Many of the guests had already exited into the frosty night, shouting "Merry Christmas!" and declaring they had other rounds to make. She and Clifford had only their quiet little house, but that suited Garnet fine.

"Old Stillwell was bragging that he kissed you," Clifford said.

"Oh, and he did! Just grabbed my hand, pulled me down, and planted a big, hairy kiss." She chuckled at the memory. "He's a terrible old man, isn't he?"

"A terribly powerful old man. I'll probably get a promotion because you let him kiss you."

He opened the car door for her. "I didn't let him. He just grabbed me and did it. Ugh." She stretched. "That was fun. I can't believe I was worried about it." She realized what she'd said, but Clifford let it pass.

They drove slowly through the frosty, star-studded night. It was Christmas, magical, wonderful Christmas, and she wondered if the little ones back home were excited. She also thought of Lorena, alone on Christmas Eve.

Clifford interrupted her bittersweet thoughts. "Garnet, I am profoundly sorry I didn't tell you about buying the automobile. You're absolutely right when you say I was thinking only of myself and not trusting you. We're not only married, we're business partners, and there must be absolute trust between us. There's no excuse for my behavior."

He drove carefully, and she wondered if he'd just learned that afternoon. This helped, but it wasn't everything. "I've been studying how to tell you what I feel."

His eyes were steady on the road.

She licked her lips; my, but that punch had made her thirsty. "I think marriage is like a big old tree, maybe one of those huge oaks that've been around a hundred years. They're strong and solid, but then someone comes along and cuts off a branch, maybe just a little branch. Sometimes that makes the tree stronger, and sometimes it weakens it. When I raised such a fuss about living with your sisters, I cut off a branch, but I think maybe that made the tree grow even better, sort of like a good pruning."

He nodded. The streets were silent.

"Then somebody saws off another branch. Is it going to kill the tree? Maybe not, but it's a risk because you never know when a big storm might come along, not anybody's doing, just an act of nature, and the tree might have to withstand that kind of damage too. You're taking a chance when you test the strength of that tree," she continued. "And we need to keep the tree healthy so it can survive when outside forces threaten it." She paused. "Do you understand me?"

He turned onto Catlett Avenue and drove even more slowly. "I do."

"I believe the old tree is all right for now," she said, granting him absolution. "But we need to have a care for it."

He drove into the side yard and eased the car into the dark shed. It smelled of damp, hot metal, and gasoline. Shutting off the engine, he turned to her. "I need you, Garnet, your conscience, your wisdom."

She smiled. "Even if I consider butchering you in the bath?"

He chuckled. "Even then."

They sat, holding hands and ignoring the cold. It was late, but tomorrow was Christmas. His declaration was a fine gift. She murmured, "Clifford, I have a question."

"What, dear heart?"

Oh, those words still touched her. She remembered when they were one of the few joys in her life. But even now, when every day was joyful, they continued to pull at her heart. "I just wondered if women ever drive these machines."

His laugh echoed out of the tiny shed, probably carrying over to Agnes' house. "Yes, Garnet, women drive. Do you want to learn?"

"I do," she said. Then she kissed him. "Merry Christmas."

Chapter Thirteen

Long before dawn, she awoke with a start and crept out of bed to keep from disturbing Clifford. She wasn't sure what time it was but knew it was earlier than they needed to rise even on this exceptional day. In the kitchen, she lit a lamp and got the stove going. Then she walked into the store to light its stove, the floor icy under her bare feet. The grocery breathed an air of expectation. The shelves were stocked. Bushel baskets of sweet potatoes, Irish potatoes, and onions exhaled a solid, earthy fragrance. On the counter the cash register gleamed in readiness. She stood in the middle of the store, taking it all in. Their dreams were attached to this day like balloons tied to a string, and she could only hope the balloons would soar. She remembered telling Papa, Grandpa, and anyone who'd listen that someday she'd own a store. As of this cold January morning, it was real.

She heard the teakettle in the kitchen and roused herself to make tea and coffee. They had planned how they'd do it: her dressing, making breakfast and then opening the store while Clifford dressed. He promised her nearly an hour to straighten the house while he tended the store before leaving for work. Then in the afternoon he'd mind it again while she cooked their supper. It seemed like a logical plan.

The last few days she'd made the last of her many surveillance trips to other groceries and she'd added a penny to some prices, subtracted from others. Clifford had set goals of what sales they needed to break even and warned that until there were more potential customers, they probably wouldn't achieve any kind of profit. They must take the long view and consider things annually rather than weekly or even monthly. It made sense, but her chilly fingers shook as she measured coffee. Although he'd repeatedly told her not to place too much importance on the first few days, she couldn't help but consider today a test. The last of the deliveries had come yesterday, and they were the most expensive and perishable: the butcher, the dairy, the baker. What if no one came to buy?

The clock struck six. She woke Clifford, dressed, and made breakfast. Outside the morning was still young, the sky frigid black. At seven she unlocked the door with jittery fingers and slipped a crisp white apron over her dress. All right, she told her neighbors, you can come in now, but even after Clifford, annoyingly calm about it all, relieved her, and after she sped through the dishes and bedmaking, there had yet to be one customer. He kissed her before he left, whispering that she should keep faith, but as the morning ticked away, despair engulfed her.

The dairyman came, and she mourned that she hadn't sold any of what he'd brought the day before. She started plotting how she could use the extra milk. Most houses in the neighborhood had milk delivery and would rarely need more. What had she been thinking?

Then at nine-thirty, Betty Keller, a spare, wrinkled woman who looked as if she'd spent her life working hard, walked into the store. This was the woman Agnes had mentioned, and she did seem glad to have a grocery near to hand. She bought flour and exclaimed over the sweet potatoes. She left with a full basket. A few minutes later, Agnes burst through the door, twittering about the great day finally arriving.

"But you're in deep trouble, my friend," she said, shaking her head.

"Why?"

"Well, ever since you two came over on Christmas Day and Jacob rode in that vehicle of yours, that's all I've heard. He keeps saying it would be so nice to have an automobile. I told him we can't afford one, but he just thinks up reasons why we must."

"We couldn't afford one either, Agnes, but I don't think that stops them."

"Even Willie! Now he turns everything in the house into a Model T and makes vroom, vroom noises in his sleep!" Shaking her head until her hair started to tumble, Agnes urged, "But you must come again soon. It was such fun except for my sister moaning about her lost love."

"Especially when people were noticing," Garnet observed.

"Exactly!" Then she placed her hand on her rounded chest and fluttered her eyelashes at the ceiling. "And your Clifford! What a charming man."

"Oh, he's charming all right."

"Well, all I know is that Jacob likes him, and Jacob doesn't like just everybody. So you must come over, maybe Sunday? We'll talk about it."

Agnes peered around the store, her eyes lighting on several items. "Now, let me see what you have here, Garnet. I'm out of simply everything. Do you have any beef? I'm hankering for a stew. And these potatoes look nice." Agnes bought and bought and needed to make two trips to carry all her groceries. It made for a lovely total, but

Garnet knew her friend couldn't be the sole support of the store. No one else came in for a long time, and Garnet started feeling grim again.

But in the early afternoon, several women stopped in, and the little bell on the door chimed frequently. Some bought only a few items, more curious than in need of groceries, but a few purchased full orders. Garnet hoped the meat was as good as the butcher claimed. Two or three asked for milk and cream, and Garnet began to change her plans for making gallons of custard. And not long after this flurry, children coming home from school opened the door and immediately gravitated to the candy case. The girl in a faded and mended dress holding her little brother's hand reminded her of young Garnet and Lowell. It seemed an eternity ago.

When Clifford blew in with a faint scent of gasoline, she was slicing bacon for a woman who lived behind them on Jasper Avenue. A week earlier, Clifford had distributed flyers in the neighborhood, and it must've worked. After she rang up the woman's order, he took off his suit coat and handed her a stack of letters, telling her to sit; she looked exhausted.

Glad for the respite, she closed the door between the kitchen and the store and started a pot of tea. Clifford called tea her panacea, and she agreed once he told her what the word meant. Wearily she sat and pushed her back against the chair to relieve its aching. Through the door she heard the bell and hoped Clifford could handle it. About the only thing he didn't feel confident about was slicing, and she'd promised him a lesson. Then the bell tinkled again, raising her hopes. She hadn't allowed herself to count the drawer.

That's all the steeping you get, she told the teapot, and poured out the amber liquid. Sugar, she decided. Lots of sugar. As she stirred, she sifted through the letters. One was from Mama. That was unusual. She opened it, and a little slip of paper fell out. In big uneven letters, Henry had written: "Thank you for my box and candy. Love Henry." She smiled, glad her mother was teaching the little ones manners. Garnet worried sometimes that Mama had simply quit trying at all after Papa died. Her letter thanked her for the gifts, wished her well with the store, and complained that Luther had stayed too long in Lexington. Typical, Garnet thought, sipping tea. The bell was ringing every few minutes, and a sudden rush of hope warmed her as much as the tea.

The next envelope was from Violet who undoubtedly had demanded to send one by herself. Garnet shook her head at her sister's self-importance but envied it as well. If she had possessed that sort of confidence, perhaps she'd have avoided some heartaches along the way. Violet's letter thanked her for the candy and ribbons and wondered if she had any more ribbon in a "true violet color."

Then there was a letter from Lowell, again expressing thanks. He wrote that Garnet should send letters to Lorena when she could. He'd be happy to read them to her but planned to convince Lorena that she could, even at her advanced age, learn to read. And he intended to teach her. Garnet chuckled, wondering which of the two would prove more stubborn.

The final letter was from Martha Allen who hadn't written since that fateful visit, and Garnet hesitated before opening it. She yearned for news about Ruben but feared the woman would tell her not to come any more or that David had taken Ruben up north. It wouldn't be long until closing time, and she needed to fix supper, but she stared at the letter for another minute before she could bring herself to open it.

The first lines apologized for the misunderstanding about David's presence when she visited. The woman said she understood how unpleasant it must've been for Garnet. Then Martha went on to say that David had left the day after Christmas. He had a big job starting in January and wouldn't be back for months. She was writing to tell Garnet that she was still welcome to visit. Ruben, the woman wrote, was still talking about his pretty mama and playing with his wagon. Lissy would be marrying in March and moving away, so the baby would enjoy having company. She added that Ruben was healthy and not wetting the bed any more.

There was nothing to cry about, but tears welled up in her eyes anyway. She could visit him again: touch his soft skin and burrow her nose in his neck to smell his sweetness. When the weather warmed up and Lissy left the house, Clifford and she could drive up and see her boy.

During one of the afternoon lulls, she'd set a chicken to baking, along with some sweet potatoes. It was simple, and a bit expensive when it came to the chicken, but she figured they deserved an easy meal tonight. And, besides, she got the chicken wholesale. As she took the food from the oven, she heard the clock chime six and went into the store to tell Clifford that supper was ready.

"Good." Clifford locked the door while she extinguished all but one lamp. He rubbed her neck, and she leaned against him. "I know, sweet girl. We've been up and working hard for an eternity."

"I'm give out."

"Let me empty the cash drawer and see how we've done."

She shook her head. "It's on the table. Can't we do that after we eat?"

"Certainly. I just thought you'd be anxious."

"I am, but I'm more anxious to sit down."

She felt eighty years old, but the food smelled good and eating it cheered both of them. She shared her letters, and he laughed at the thought of Lowell teaching Lorena to read. "I wonder what she'll teach him in return," he said, opening his steaming sweet potato and mashing butter into it. "All kinds of new words, I'd bet."

"And there was a letter from Martha Allen too."

When she told him what the woman had written, he said, "So she's willing for you to visit again."

"Yes." She sliced some bread, made yesterday. "Do you think the bad roads would ruin our Ford?"

"Absolutely not. It's perfectly capable of withstanding rough terrain."

While they ate, she amused him with stories about her various customers. "Agnes bought two big baskets of food."

"She can't do that every day," Clifford commented.

"I know, but I think she wanted to make sure we had a good opening. For a while I was afraid that she'd be our only sale, but things picked up this afternoon." Garnet pushed her plate away and rested her elbows on the table, something Mama had always said was common. "I think I could sleep right here."

"Poor girl." He touched her cheek.

"I hardly slept last night, and, of course, I worried and fretted myself to death all day," she replied, shaking her head. "I wish I could figure out a way to stop my worrying. Do you suppose it's a habit like biting your nails?"

He stood up and took her hand. "You're improving marvelously. Come on; let's count the drawer. We'll do the cleaning up later."

The store was dim and cold after the warmth of the kitchen. Garnet noticed mud and a sprinkling of dried leaves by the front door. She needed to sweep, but maybe that could wait until morning. Today there'd been little business until mid-morning, and if that were the case tomorrow, she'd have plenty of time for tidying.

He emptied the cash bag, coins tinkling on the table as he stacked and counted. "Are you sure you're operating the register correctly?"

"I think so. Why? Do the figures look wrong?" He didn't reply. More than likely the receipts were so low he thought she'd made mistakes. Once or twice he muttered to himself, and, as long as it was taking, he surely must've counted everything at least twice. Just as she was about to pop, he scraped back his chair. "Well, I'll be damned."

"Clifford."

"Oh, sorry. This is truly amazing."

"What?"

"The drawer matches the receipts. Obviously you're working the register perfectly. And our take for today is what I set as our goal for the entire week," he announced, his voice more incredulous than excited.

"Well, Agnes. And maybe it was just curiosity today." She paused to let it sink in. "You really mean we took in as much today as you expected for six whole days?"

"I really do. Now, I think you're right. We may not match this daily total again for a while, but for the next five days, anything we take in is over and above what we expected." He stood next to her, showing her the receipt.

"Oh my, Clifford." She looked up at him, the information sinking in. He met her eyes and simultaneously they started laughing like fools. "It's going to work," she said, throwing her arms around his waist. "It's really going to work!"

He danced her around the kitchen until she was breathless. "Now, I'm not saying we'll be rich in a month," he warned. "I'm not saying we'll ever be rich. These were modest goals. But Garnet!" He kissed her.

She followed him into the store so he could stash the money bag and turn out the lamp. "What's this?" She pointed to a bundle on the plant ledge.

"Oh Lord, I forgot. Everything was so busy when I came in. Archie's friend found your plant, and he brought it to the bank today."

"Truly? He found a night-blooming cereus?" Her voice rose with excitement. She removed the paper from around the plant and touched a leaf. "Oh, I can't tell you how happy I am! I've wanted one of these forever."

Clifford peered over her shoulder. "It's ugly, Garnet, all gangly and reptilian."

She smiled, not at all discouraged. "I always thought it looked snakey too. But, oh, Clifford, when it blooms!" She shivered at the memory.

Clifford smiled. "It must be exceptional for you to look so rapturous about it."

"Incredibly beautiful, and it smells, oh, indescribably wonderful. Mrs. Lawrence said it smelled like heaven." Garnet kept petting the plant. "But it only blooms for one night. The bud keeps getting bigger and bigger, and then one night it blooms. And by the next day it wilts."

"How often does it bloom?" He lifted a long, trailing leaf.

"I'm not sure. Mrs. Lawrence's hadn't bloomed in over two years when it finally decided to bud."

"But until then we have to look at this homely, scraggly plant. I guess it teaches a person patience."

She smiled up at him and placed her hand against his cheek. It had been a lifetime since dawn, and another one would come in no time. It didn't matter. She could manage another day and another and another. "Maybe," she said. "But I think it makes us hope."

ACKNOWLEDGMENTS

I was the youngest child of the youngest child in my mother's family, so by the time I felt curiosity about the inevitable mysteries and stories in my family, there was no one to ask. My dear friend since high school, Susan Johnson, was deeply into genealogy at that time and said she'd help me research county records and whatever we could find to solve the mysteries. So we took off one golden fall day to visit the courthouse in the tiny county seat of a tiny county in Kentucky and started my quest.

I had a few names and vague dates and managed to be successful in going back a couple of generations, piecing together what little I'd heard with what was in the records. Most of it fell into place, into a story that fascinated and surprised me. Susan said that we'd need to dig elsewhere to trace more of the family history, but I said, this is enough. I had no desire to follow my ancestors back to a boat. I did have a story and I wanted to tell it.

Certainly names and dates don't tell the whole tale, but imagination is a wonderful thing, and mine kicked into turbo speed to fill in the blanks that afternoon when we drove home. And NIGHTBLOOMING is the result. Many thanks to Susan Johnson who provided the impetus for the whole project.

I also want to thank Cheryl Eschenbach, Joyce Hurst, and Connie Anggelis for their early encouragement. And family is a part of it:: I so appreciate the comments and cheerleading from Linda Cooper, Jane Cooper, and Kim Mackey. I owe a great deal to the unstinting faith and gentle nudges from my dear Number One Fan, Barb Burlew. As always, I am grateful for the support and love from my husband and son, Jim and Matthew Cooper.

And to my mentors from the Appalachian writers community: Lee Smith, Gwyn Hyman Rubio, Mark Powell, Maurice Manning, and Silas House, I offer my heartfelt thanks for their guidance in writing about the heritage that fills theirs and my soul.